SIMON & SCHUSTER CHILDREN'S PUBLISHING
ADVANCE READER'S COPY

TITLE: Misfit Mansion

AUTHOR: Kay Davault

IMPRINT: Atheneum Books for Young Readers

ON-SALE DATE: 7/18/23

ISBN: 978-1-6659-0307-3 (pbk); 978-1-6659-0308-0 (hc)

FORMAT: simultaneous paperback and hardcover

PRICE: $14.99/$18.99 Can. (pbk); $21.99/$29.99 Can.

AGES: 8 up

PAGES: 304

Please send any review or mention of this book to
ChildrensPublicity@simonandschuster.com.

Aladdin • Atheneum Books for Young Readers
Beach Lane Books • Beyond Words • Boynton Bookworks
Caitlyn Dlouhy Books • Denene Millner Books
Libros para niños • Little Simon • Margaret K. McElderry Books
MTV Books • Paula Wiseman Books • Salaam Reads
Simon & Schuster Books for Young Readers
Simon Pulse • Simon Spotlight

ATHENEUM BOOKS FOR YOUNG READERS • An imprint of Simon & Schuster Children's Publishing Division • 1230 Avenue of the Americas, New York, New York 10020 © 2023 by Kay Davault • Book design by Karyn Lee © 2023 by Simon & Schuster, Inc. • All rights reserved, including the right of reproduction in whole or in part in any form. • ATHENEUM BOOKS FOR YOUNG READERS is a registered trademark of Simon & Schuster, Inc. Atheneum logo is a trademark of Simon & Schuster, Inc. • For information about special discounts for bulk purchases, please contact Simon & Schuster Special Sales at 1-866-506-1949 or business@simonandschuster.com. • The Simon & Schuster Speakers Bureau can bring authors to your live event. • For more information or to book an event, contact the Simon & Schuster Speakers Bureau at 1-866-248-3049 or visit our website at www.simonspeakers.com. • The text for this book was set in Frog-prince. • The illustrations for this book were rendered digitally. • Manufactured in China • 0323 SCP • First Edition • 2 4 6 8 10 9 7 5 3 1 • CIP data for this book is available from the Library of Congress. • ISBN 978-1-6659-0307-3 (paperback)• ISBN 978-1-6659-0308-0 (hardcover) • ISBN 978-1-6659-0309-7 (ebook)

For my mom

MISFIT
MANSION

KAY DAVAULT

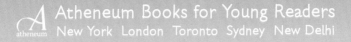

Atheneum Books for Young Readers
New York London Toronto Sydney New Delhi

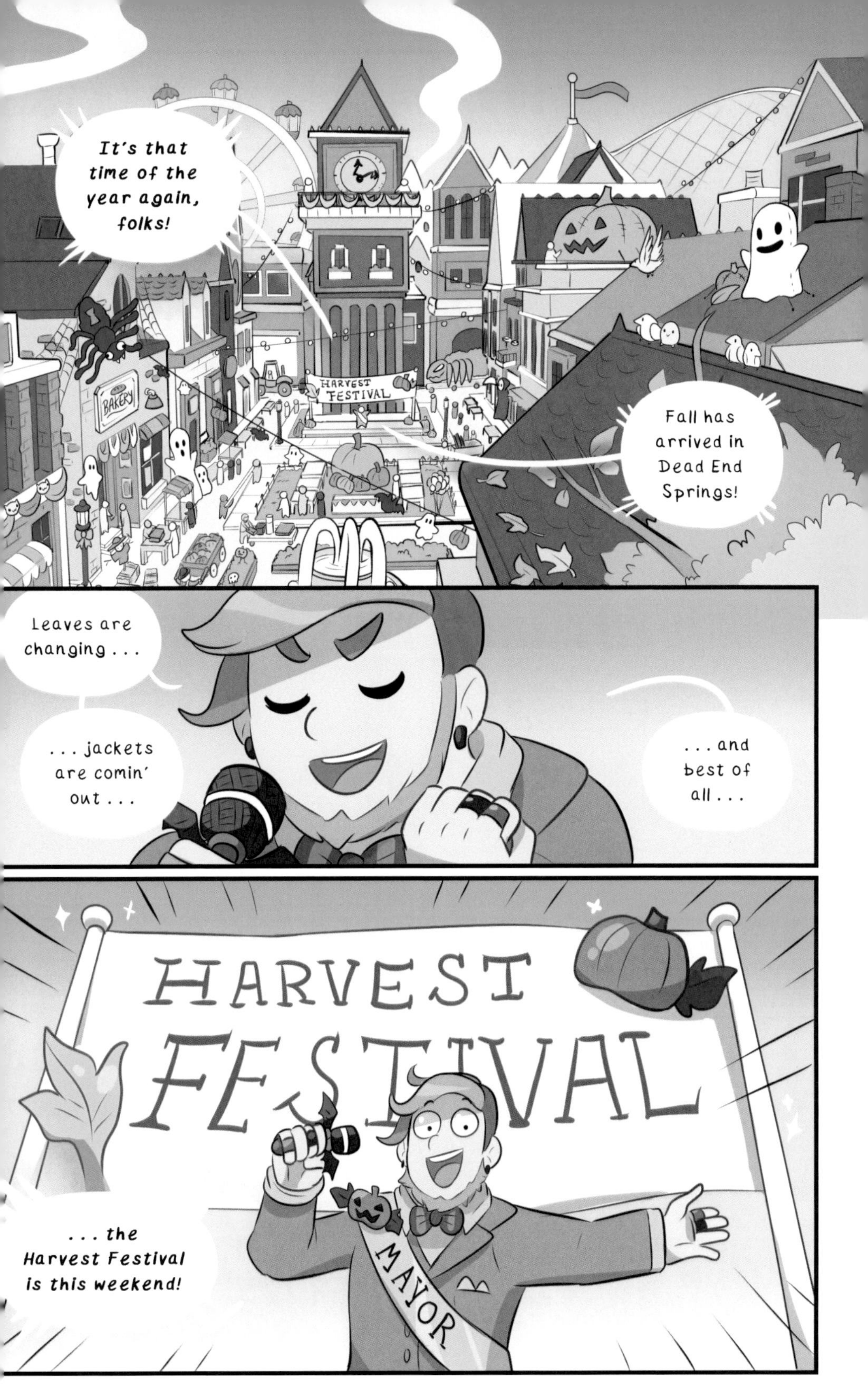

It's that time of the year again, folks!
HARVEST FESTIVAL
BAKERY
Fall has arrived in Dead End Springs!
Leaves are changing . . .
. . . jackets are comin' out . . .
. . . and best of all . . .
HARVEST FESTIVAL
MAYOR
. . . the Harvest Festival is this weekend!

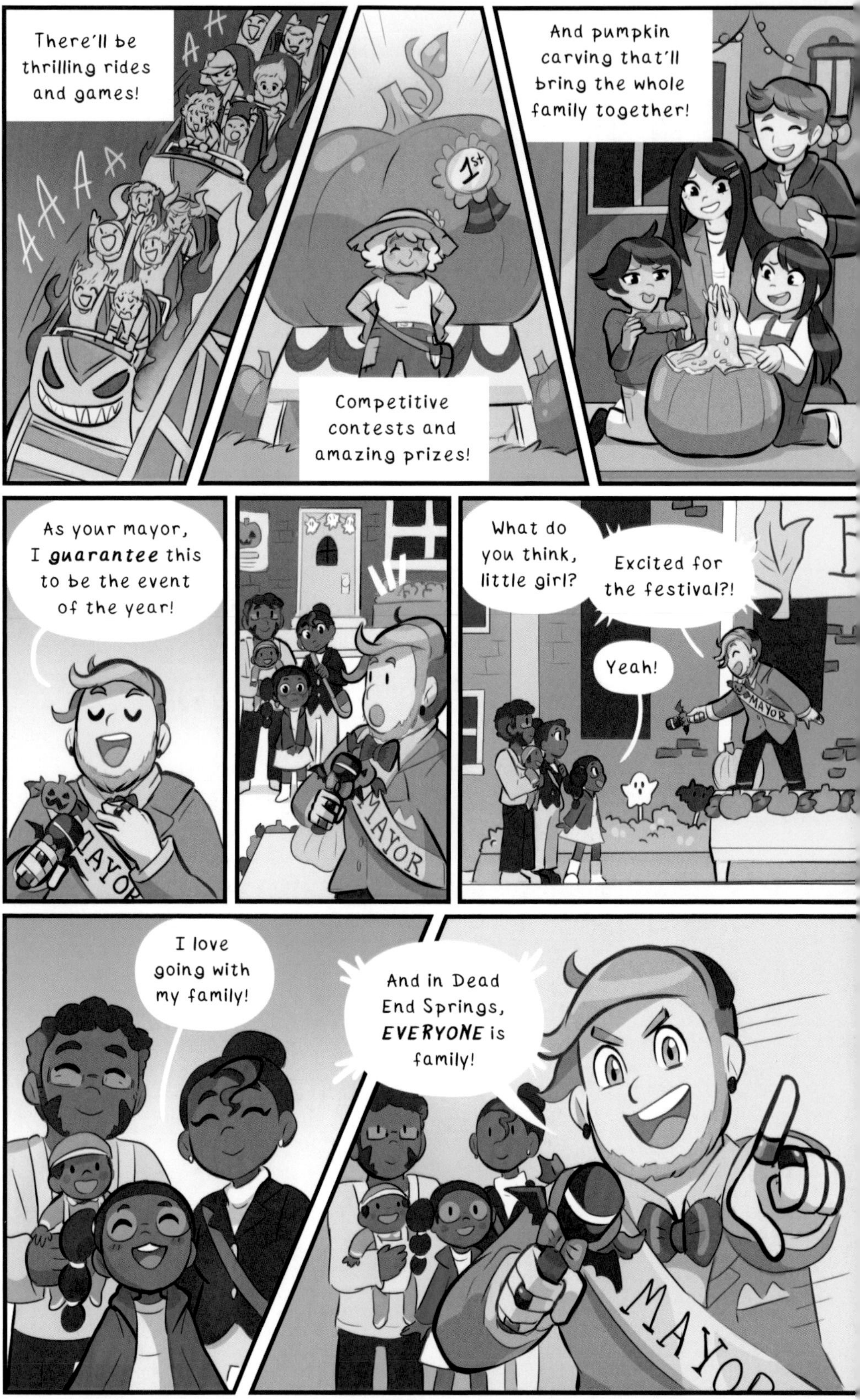
There'll be thrilling rides and games!
AAAA
AAAA
Competitive contests and amazing prizes!
1st
And pumpkin carving that'll bring the whole family together!
As your mayor, I ***guarantee*** this to be the event of the year!
MAYOR
MAYOR
What do you think, little girl?
Excited for the festival?!
Yeah!
MAYOR
I love going with my family!
And in Dead End Springs, ***EVERYONE*** is family!
MAYOR

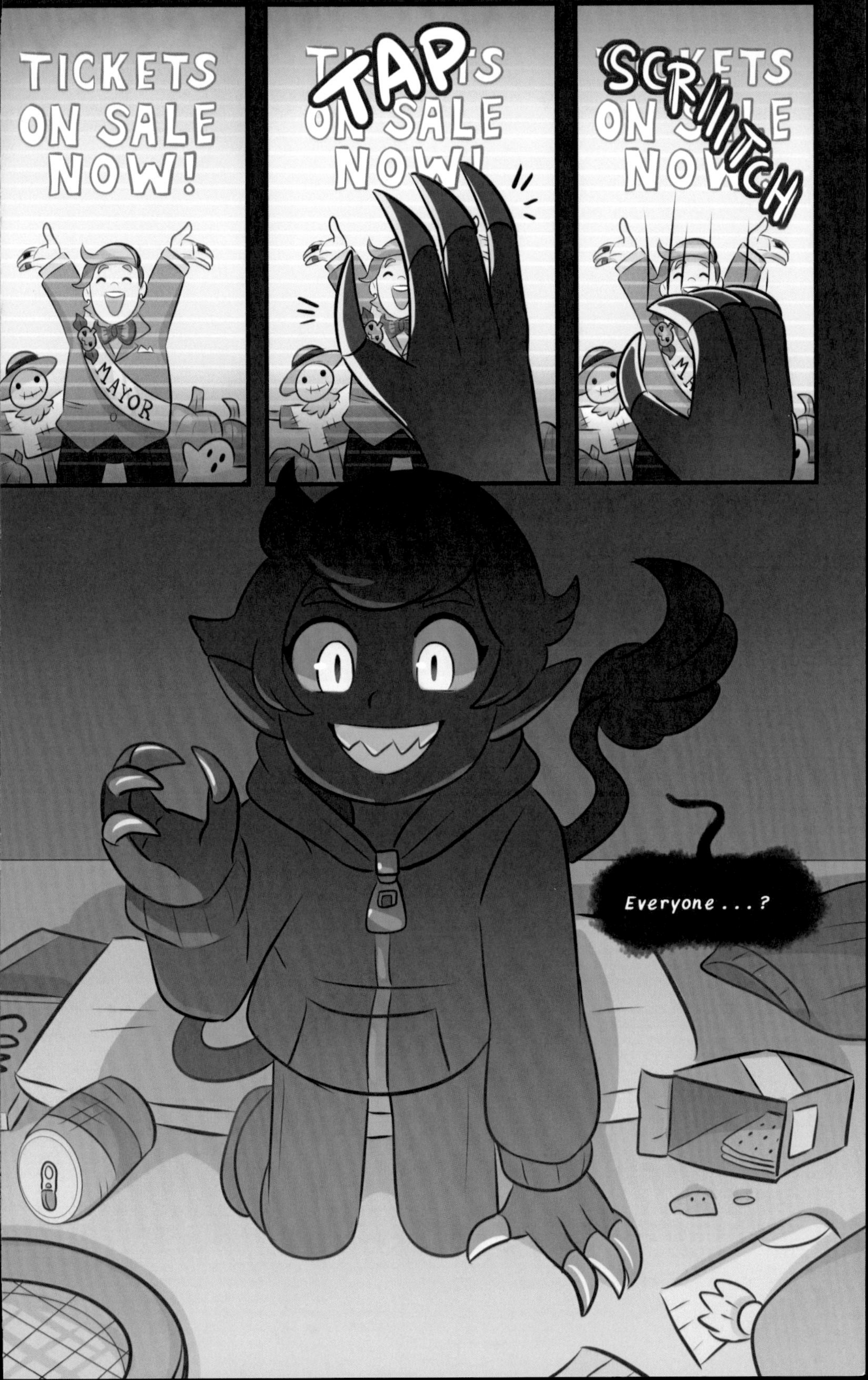
TICKETS ON SALE NOW!
MAYOR
TAP
SCRIITCH
Everyone . . . ?

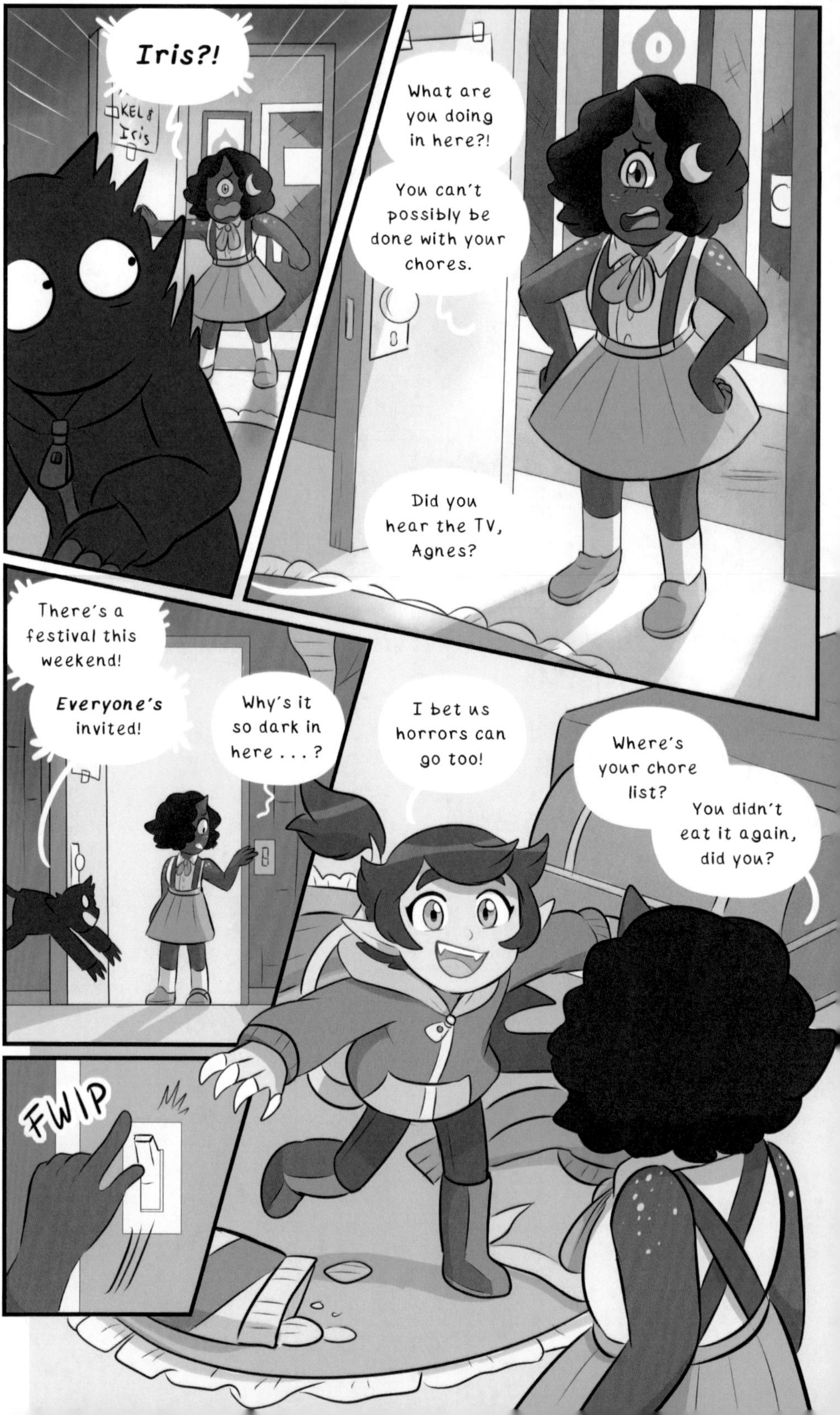

Iris?!
KEL &
Iris
What are you doing in here?!
You can't possibly be done with your chores.
Did you hear the TV, Agnes?
There's a festival this weekend!
Everyone's invited!
Why's it so dark in here . . . ?
I bet us horrors can go too!
Where's your chore list?
You didn't eat it again, did you?
FWIP

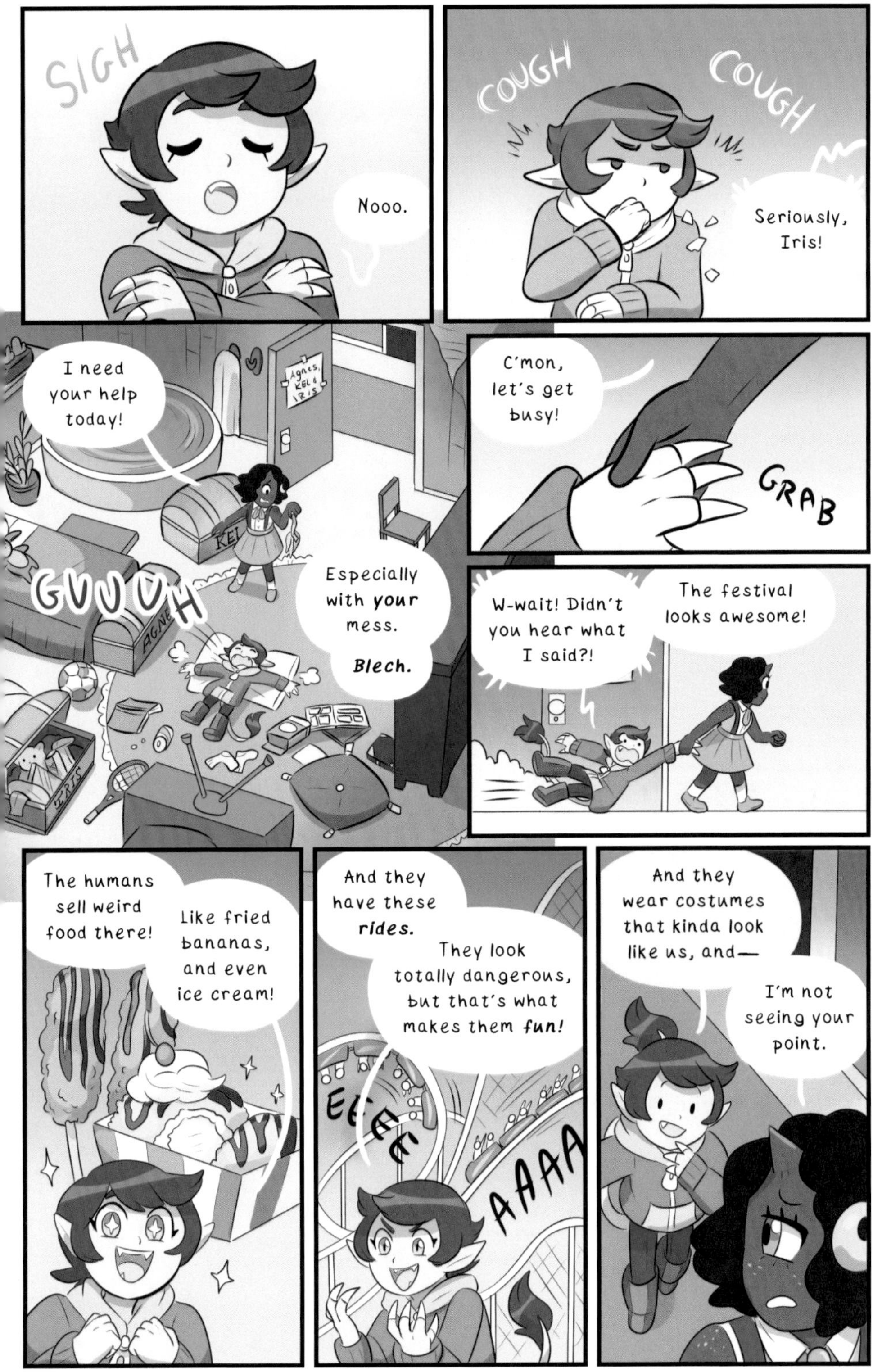
SIGH
Nooo.
COUGH
COUGH
Seriously, Iris!
I need your help today!
AGNES, KEL & IRIS
KEL
GUUUH
AGNES
IRIS
Especially with **your** mess.
Blech.
C'mon, let's get busy!
GRAB
W-wait! Didn't you hear what I said?!
The festival looks awesome!
The humans sell weird food there!
Like fried bananas, and even ice cream!
And they have these ***rides.***
They look totally dangerous, but that's what makes them ***fun!***
EEEE
AAAA
And they wear costumes that kinda look like us, and—
I'm not seeing your point.

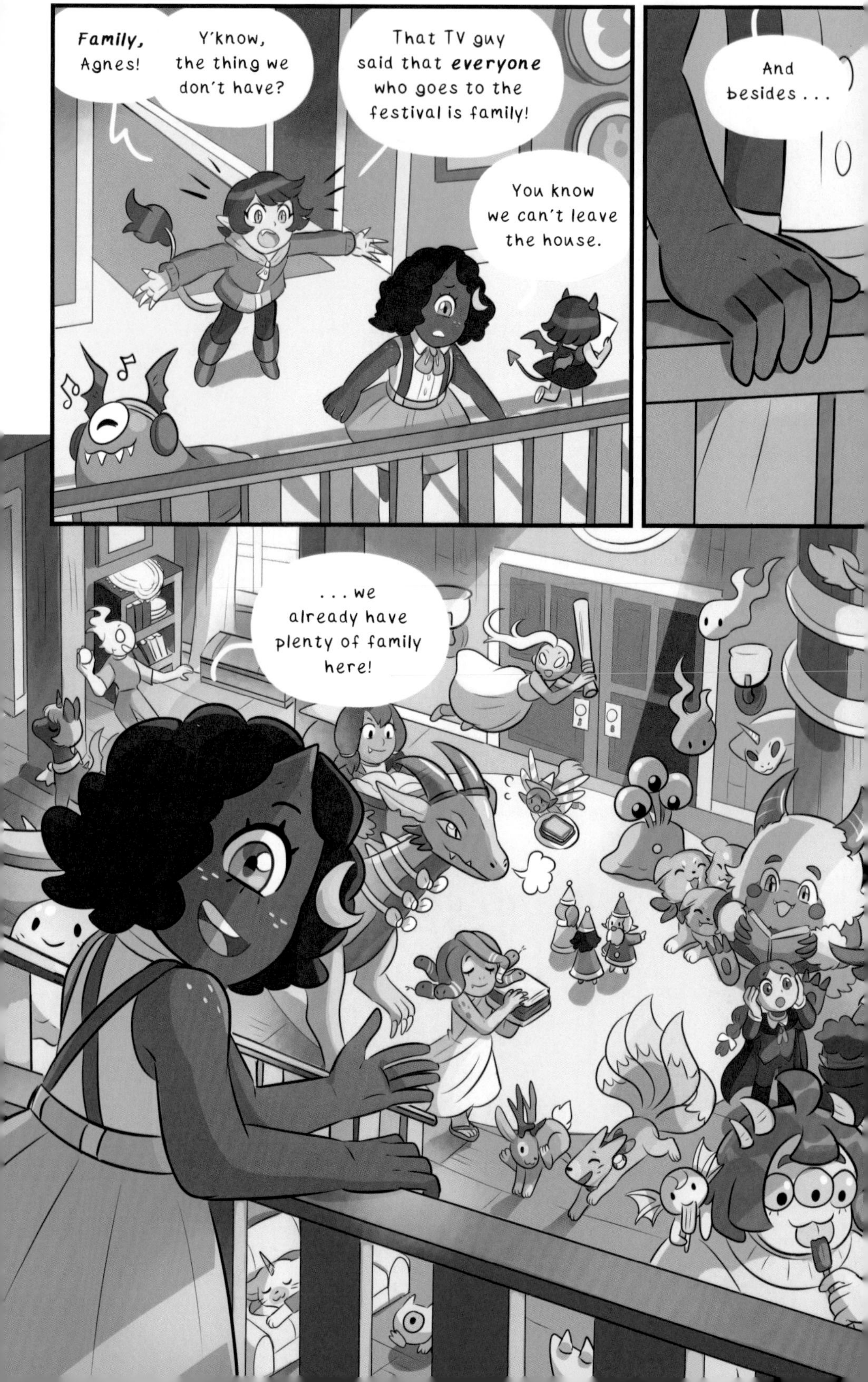
Family, Agnes!
Y'know, the thing we don't have?
That TV guy said that ***everyone*** who goes to the festival is family!
You know we can't leave the house.
And besides . . .
. . . we already have plenty of family here!

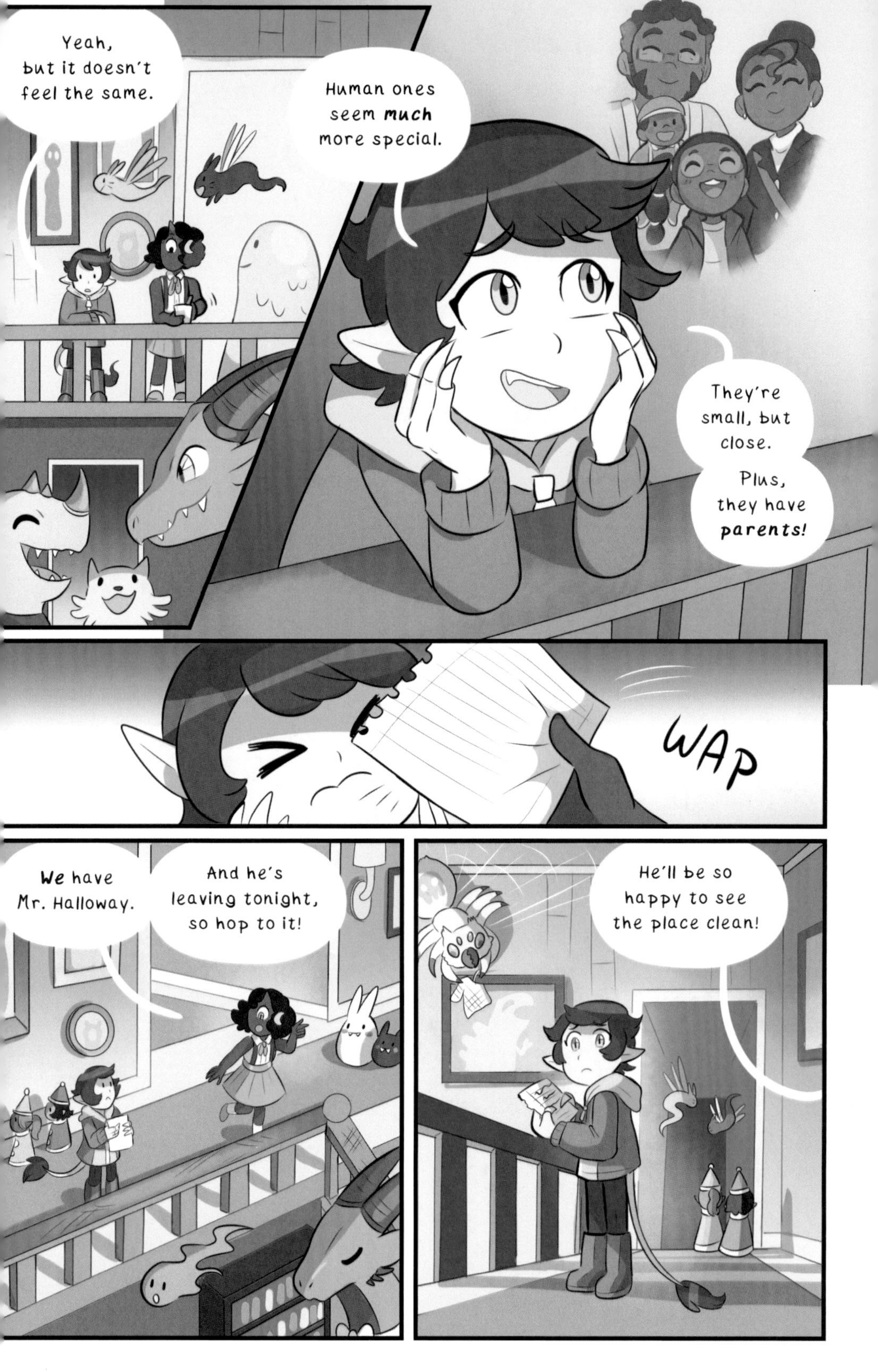

Yeah, but it doesn't feel the same.
Human ones seem **much** more special.
They're small, but close.
Plus, they have **parents!**
WAP
We have Mr. Halloway.
And he's leaving tonight, so hop to it!
He'll be so happy to see the place clean!

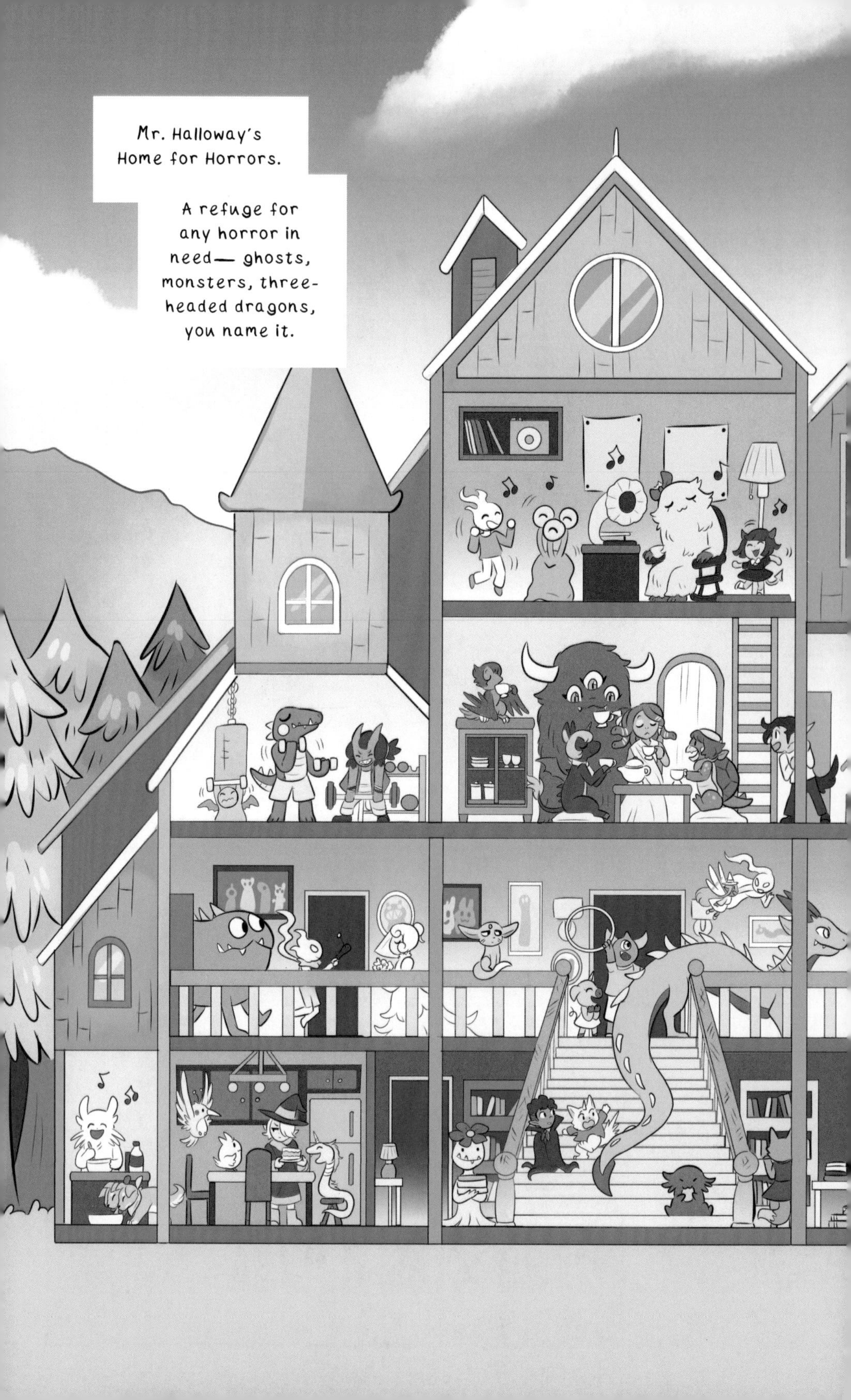
Mr. Halloway's
Home for Horrors.
A refuge for any horror in need— ghosts, monsters, three-headed dragons, you name it.

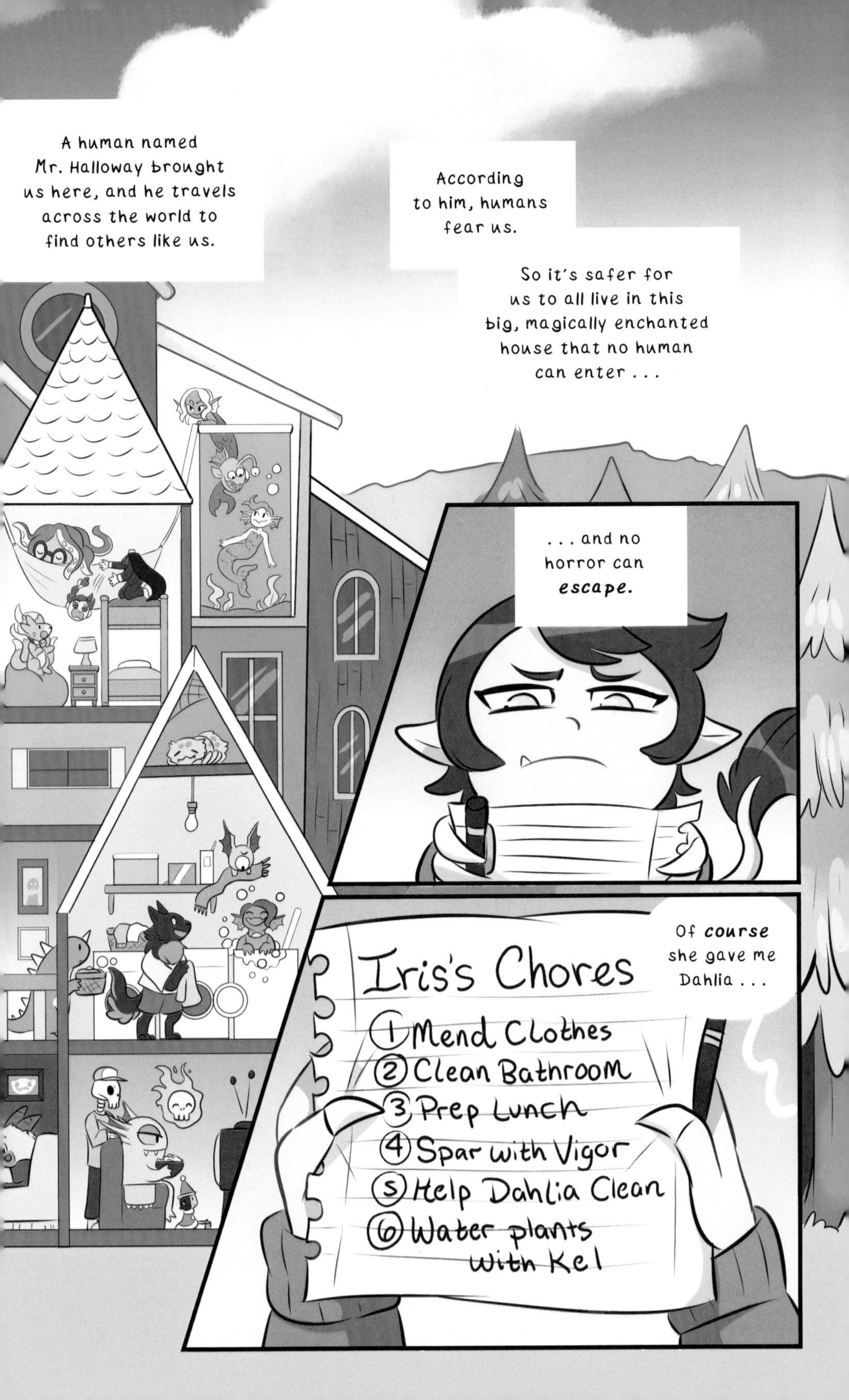
A human named Mr. Halloway brought us here, and he travels across the world to find others like us.
According to him, humans fear us.
So it's safer for us to all live in this big, magically enchanted house that no human can enter . . .
. . . and no horror can *escape.*
Of **course** she gave me Dahlia . . .
Iris's Chores
1 Mend Clothes
2 Clean Bathroom
3 Prep Lunch
4 Spar with Vigor
5 Help Dahlia Clean
6 Water plants with Kel

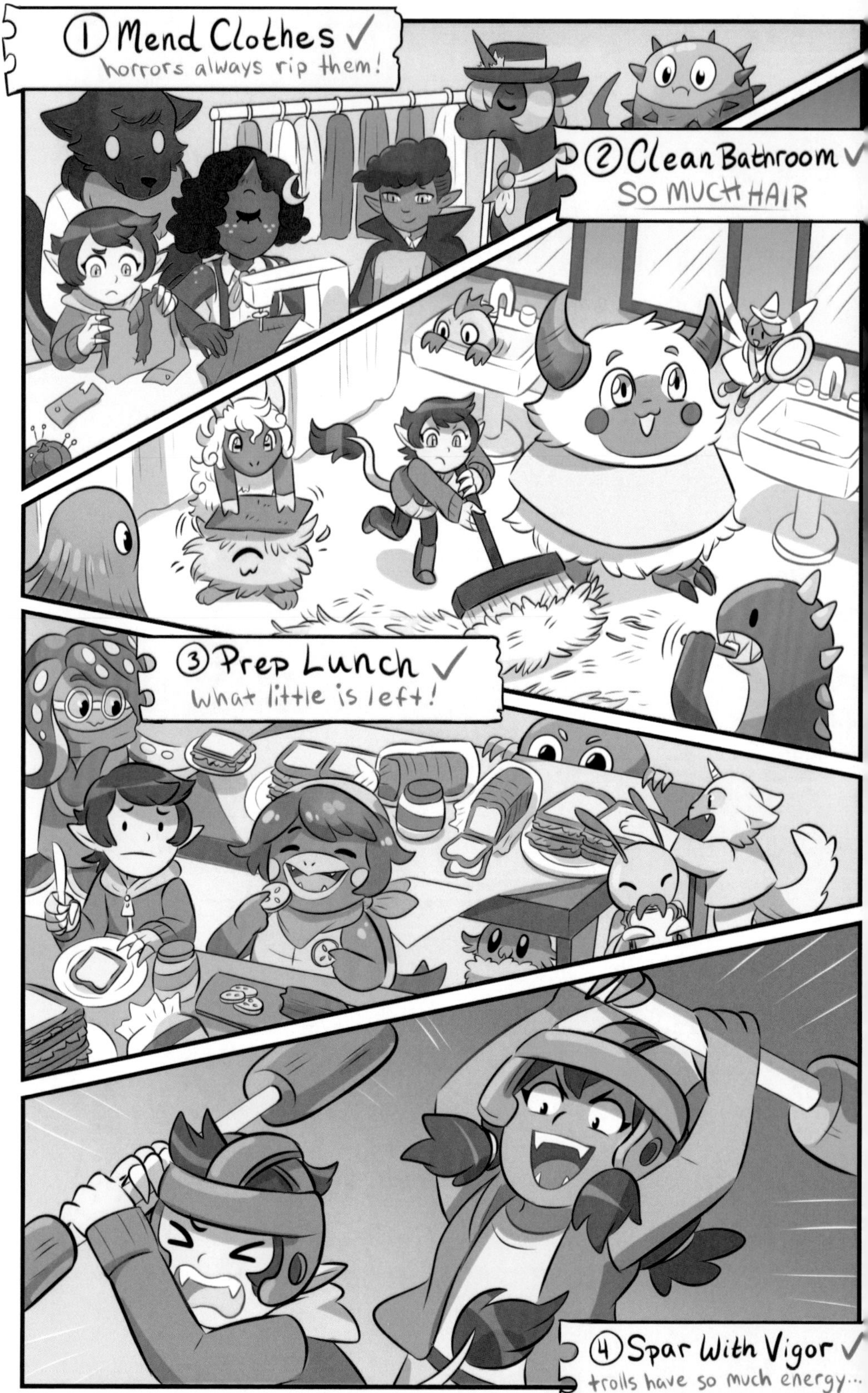

① Mend Clothes ✓
horrors always rip them!
② Clean Bathroom ✓
SO MUCH HAIR
③ Prep Lunch ✓
What little is left!
④ Spar With Vigor ✓
trolls have so much energy...

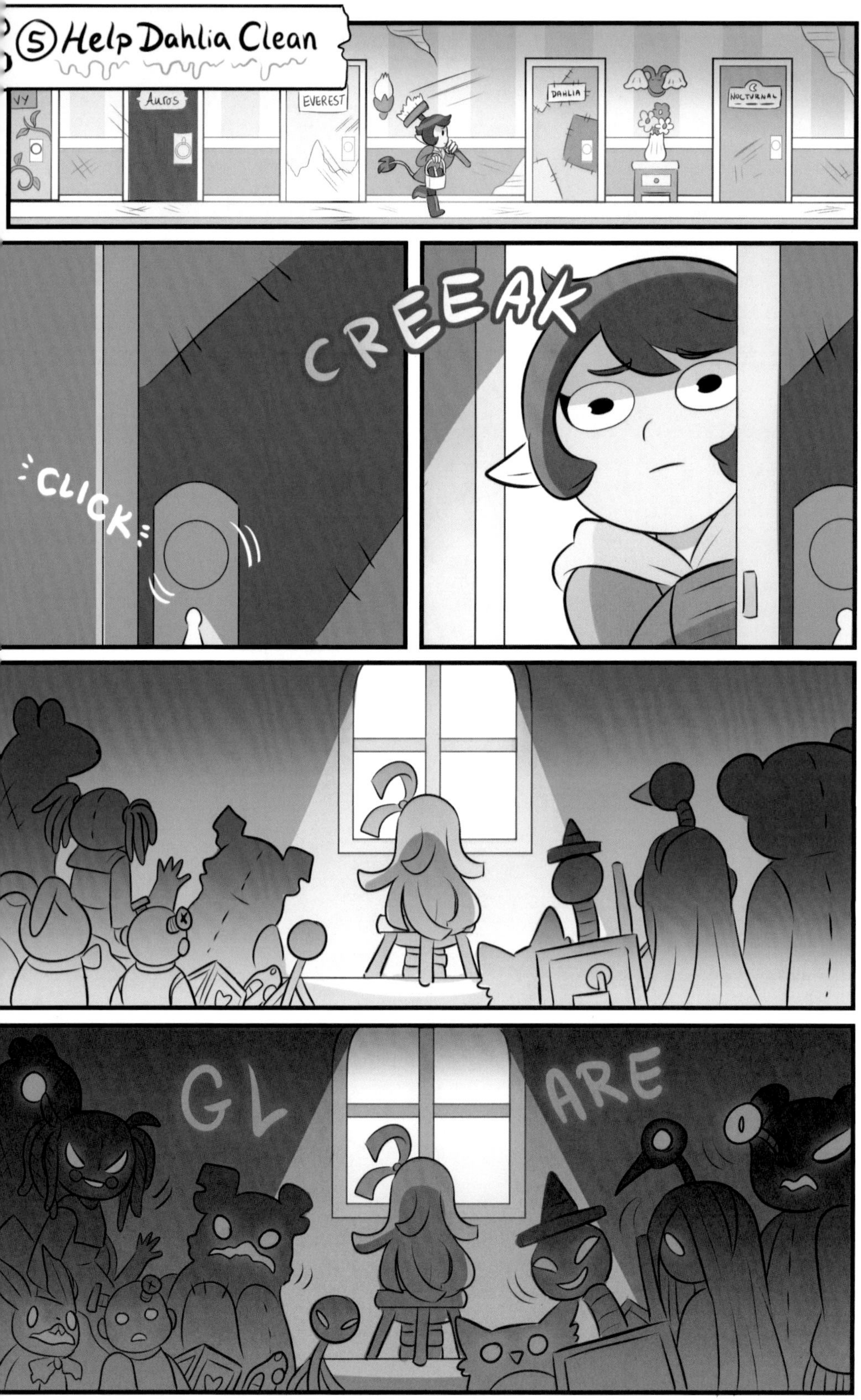
5 Help Dahlia Clean
Auros
EVEREST
DAHLIA
NOCTURNAL
CLICK
CREEAK
GL
ARE

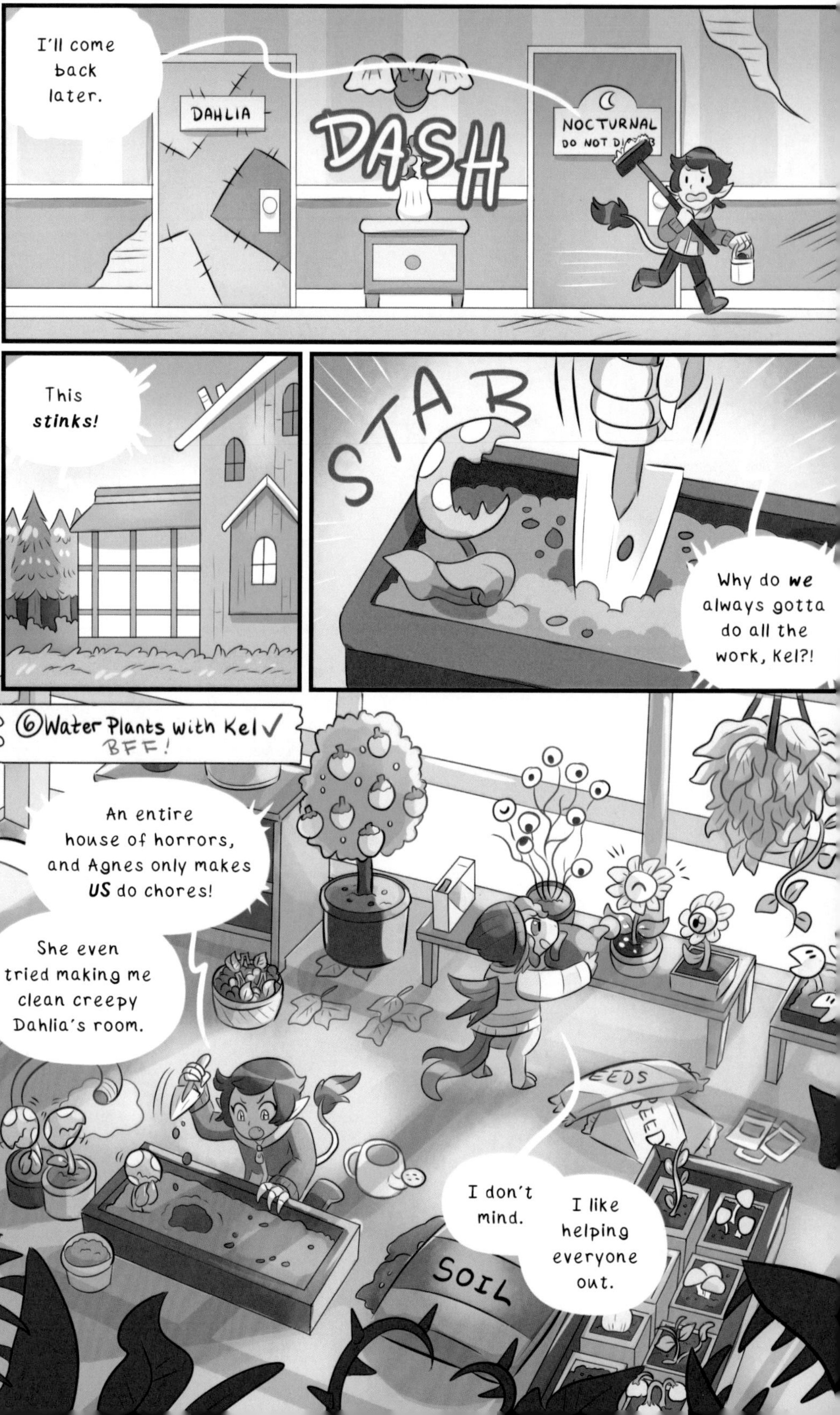
I'll come back later.
DAHLIA
DASH
NOCTURNAL
DO NOT DI
This *stinks!*
STAB
Why do *we* always gotta do all the work, Kel?!
⑥ Water Plants with Kel ✓
BFF!
An entire house of horrors, and Agnes only makes *US* do chores!
She even tried making me clean creepy Dahlia's room.
EEDS
I don't mind.
I like helping everyone out.
SOIL

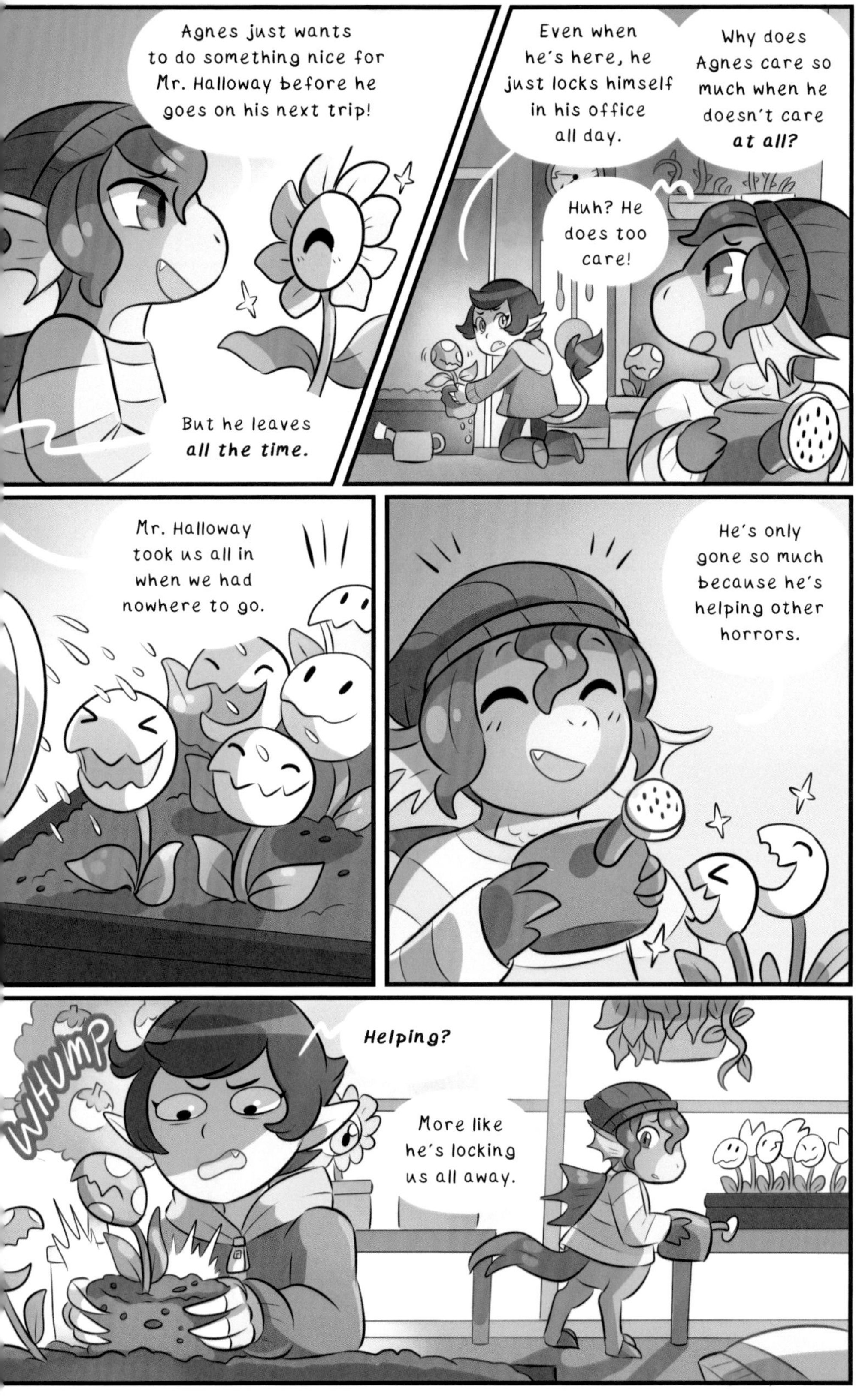
Agnes just wants to do something nice for Mr. Halloway before he goes on his next trip!
But he leaves *all the time.*
Even when he's here, he just locks himself in his office all day.
Why does Agnes care so much when he doesn't care ***at all?***
Huh? He does too care!
Mr. Halloway took us all in when we had nowhere to go.
He's only gone so much because he's helping other horrors.
WHUMP
Helping?
More like he's locking us all away.

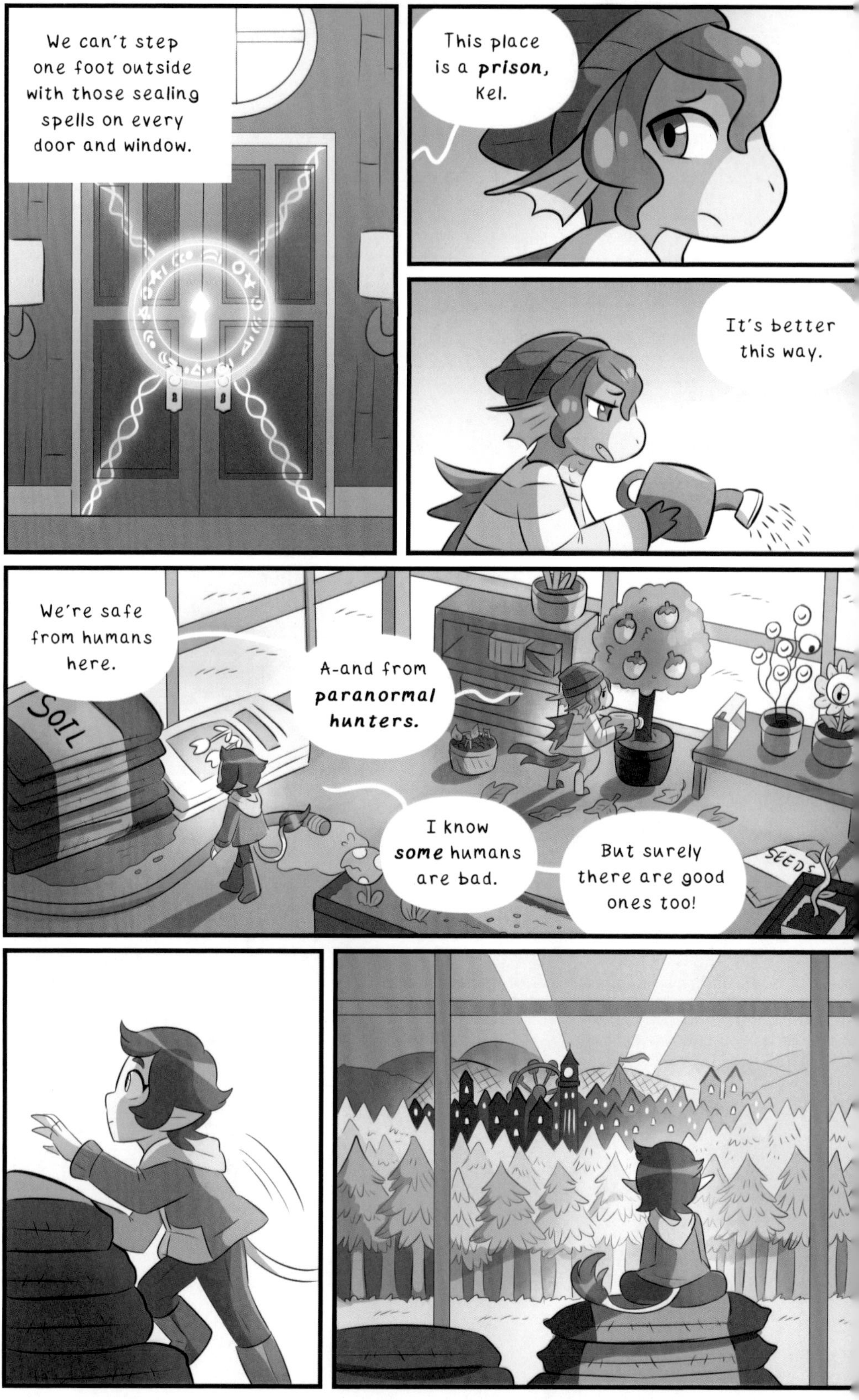
We can't step one foot outside with those sealing spells on every door and window.
This place is a **prison,** Kel.
It's better this way.
We're safe from humans here.
A-and from **paranormal hunters.**
I know **some** humans are bad.
But surely there are good ones too!
SOIL
SEEDS

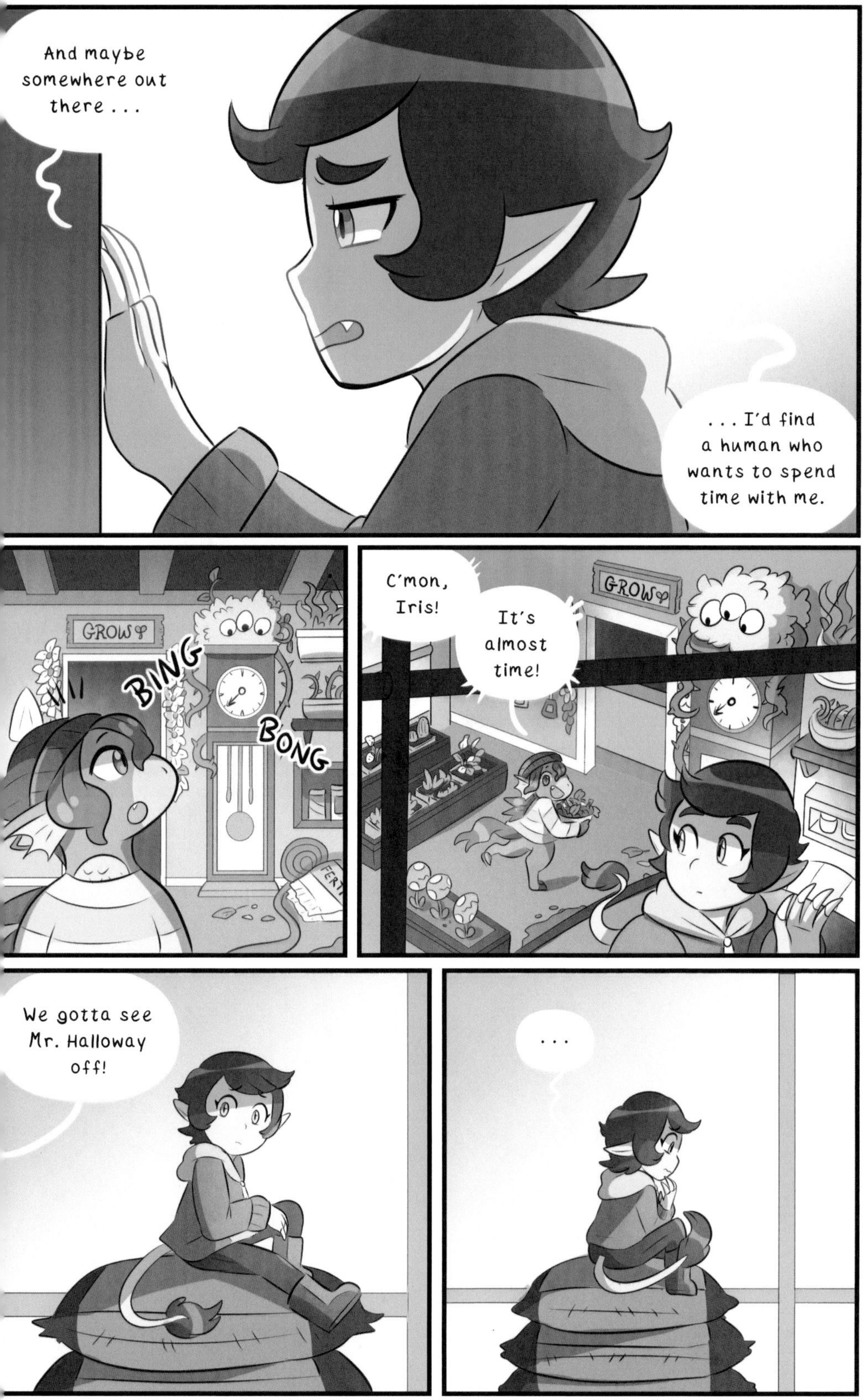
And maybe somewhere out there . . .
. . . I'd find a human who wants to spend time with me.
BING
BONG
GROW
C'mon, Iris!
It's almost time!
We gotta see Mr. Halloway off!
. . .

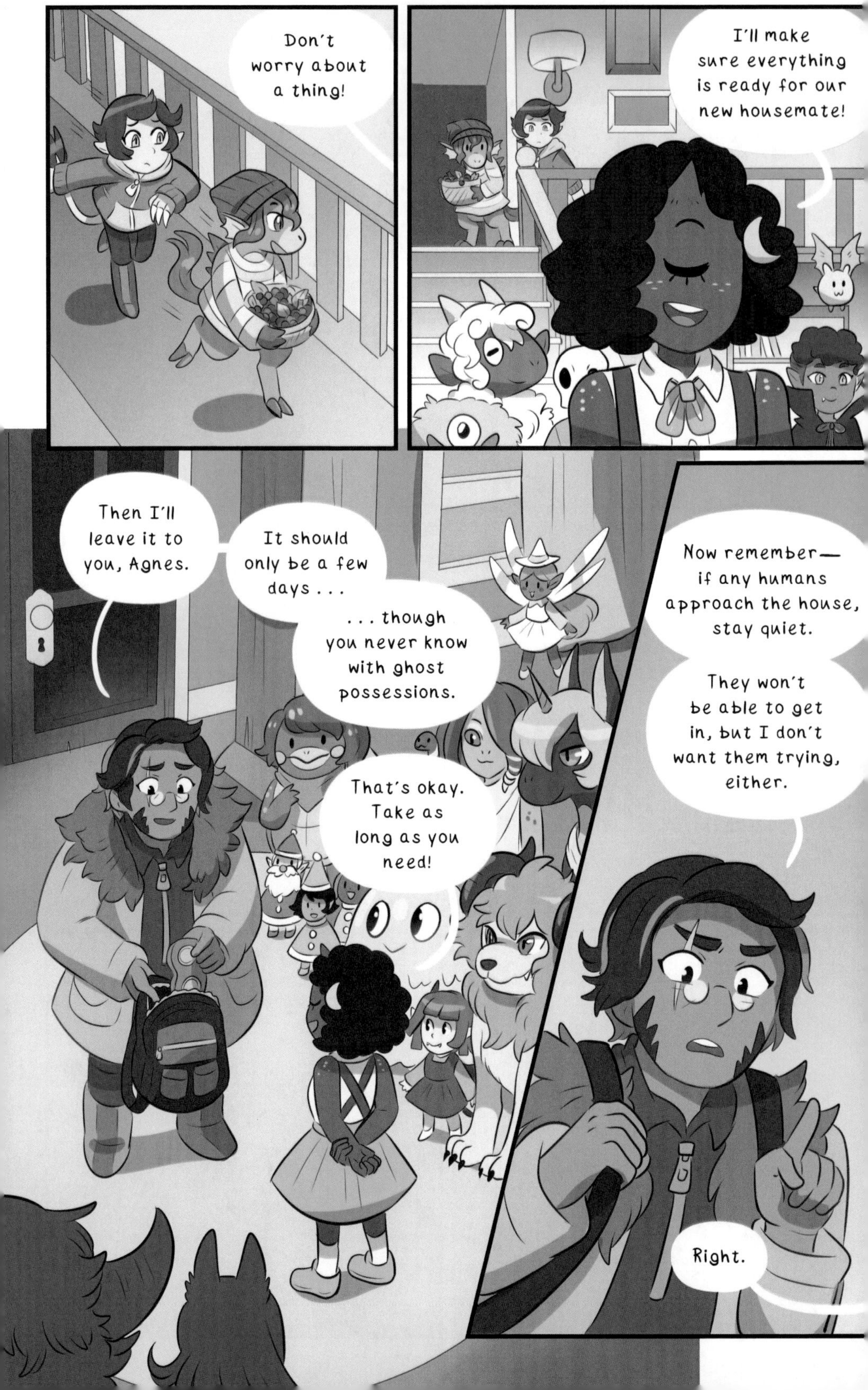
Don't worry about a thing!
I'll make sure everything is ready for our new housemate!
Then I'll leave it to you, Agnes.
It should only be a few days . . .
. . . though you never know with ghost possessions.
That's okay. Take as long as you need!
Now remember—if any humans approach the house, stay quiet.
They won't be able to get in, but I don't want them trying, either.
Right.

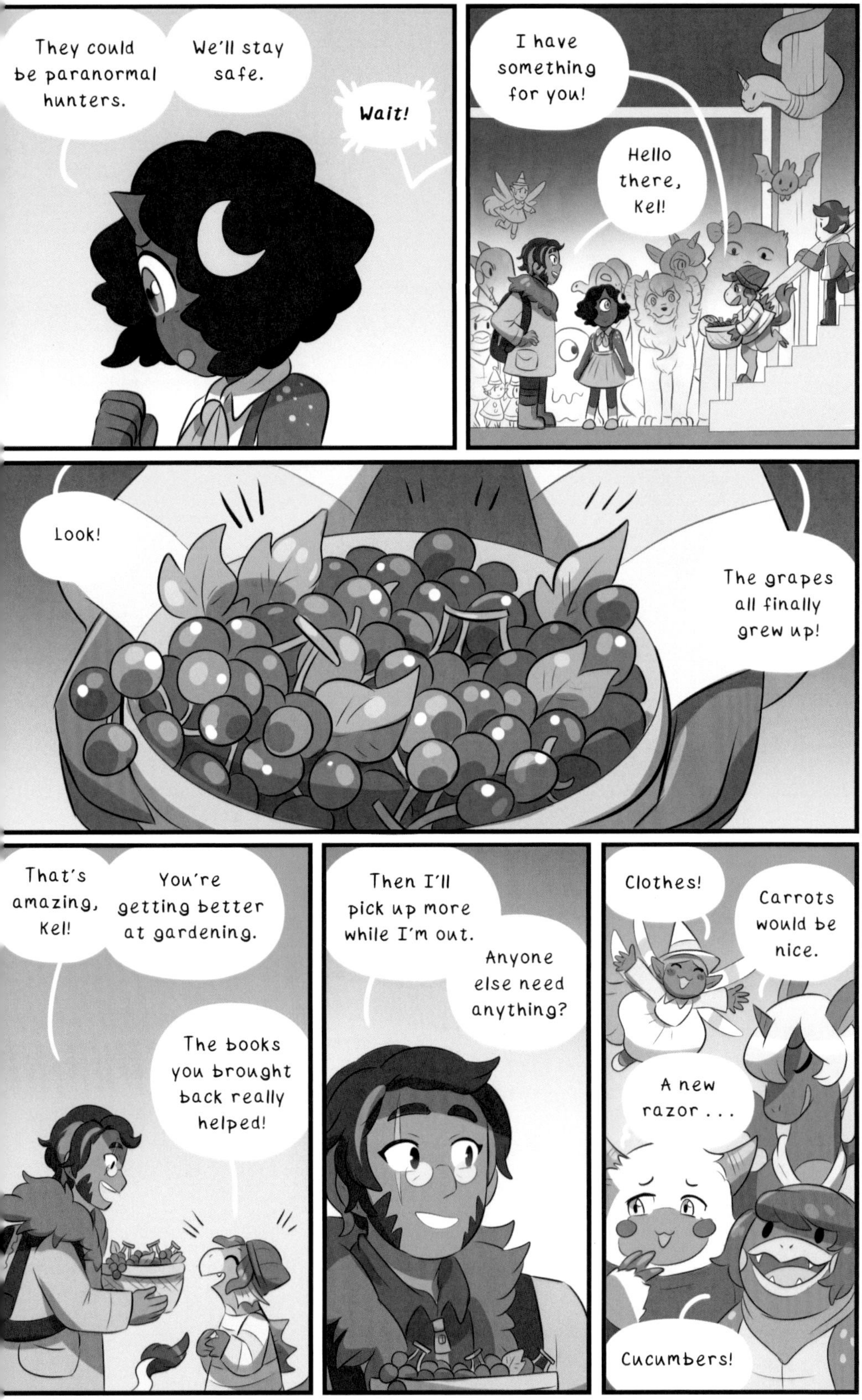
They could be paranormal hunters.
We'll stay safe.
Wait!
I have something for you!
Hello there, Kel!
Look!
The grapes all finally grew up!
That's amazing, Kel!
You're getting better at gardening.
The books you brought back really helped!
Then I'll pick up more while I'm out.
Anyone else need anything?
Clothes!
Carrots would be nice.
A new razor . . .
Cucumbers!

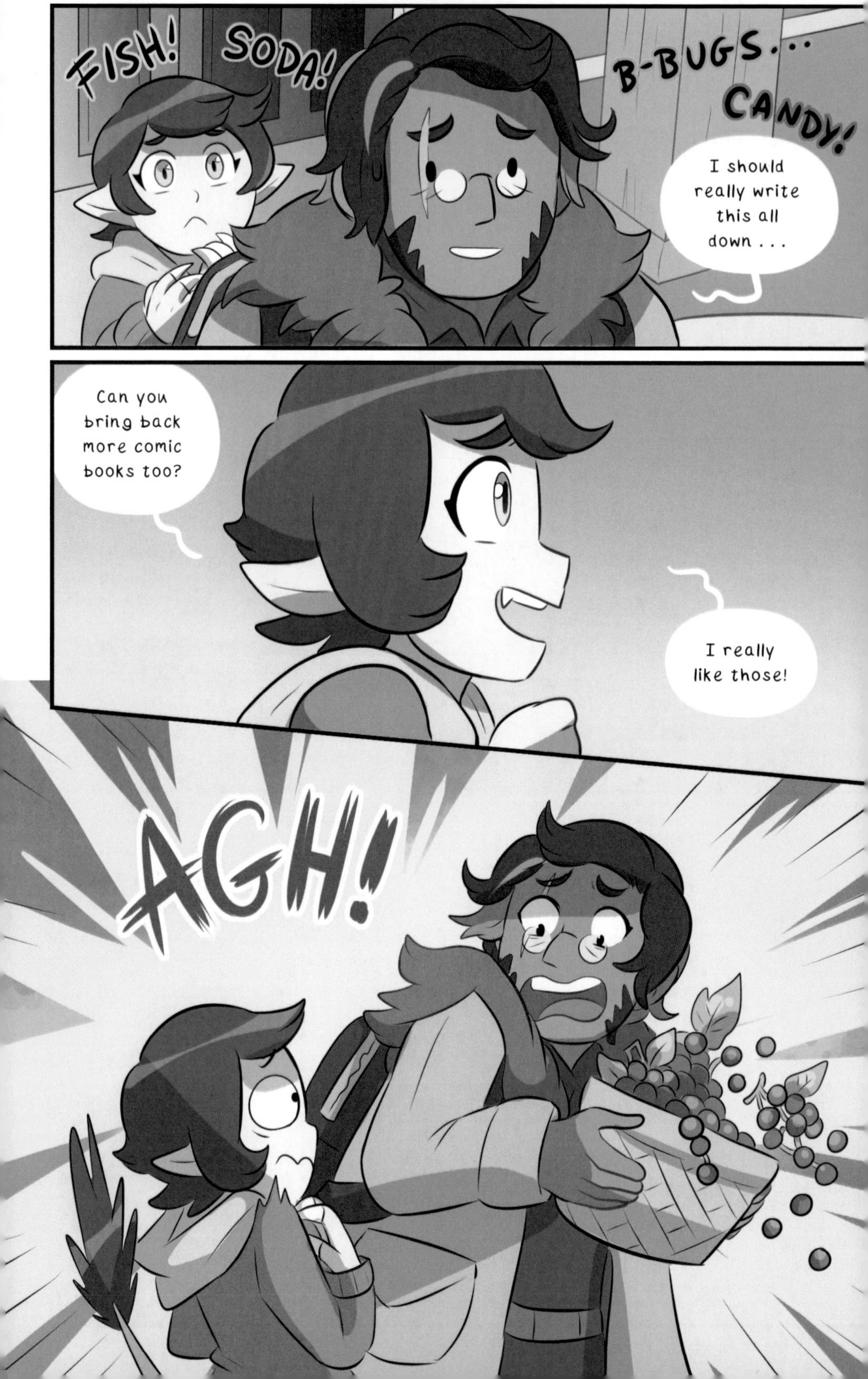
FISH!
SODA!
B-BUGS...
CANDY!
I should really write this all down . . .
Can you bring back more comic books too?
I really like those!
AGH!

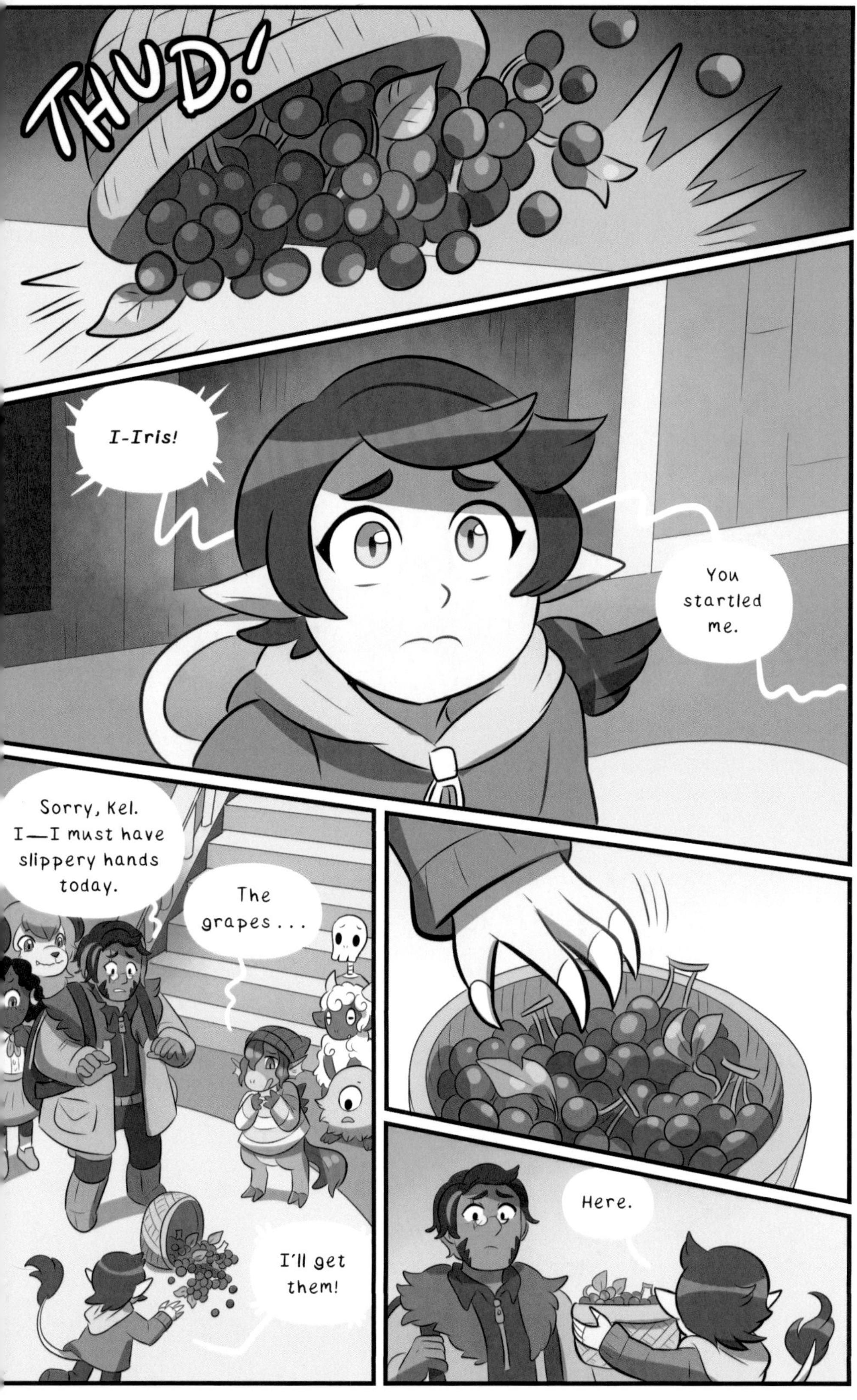
THUD!
I-Iris!
You startled me.
Sorry, Kel.
I—I must have slippery hands today.
The grapes . . .
I'll get them!
Here.

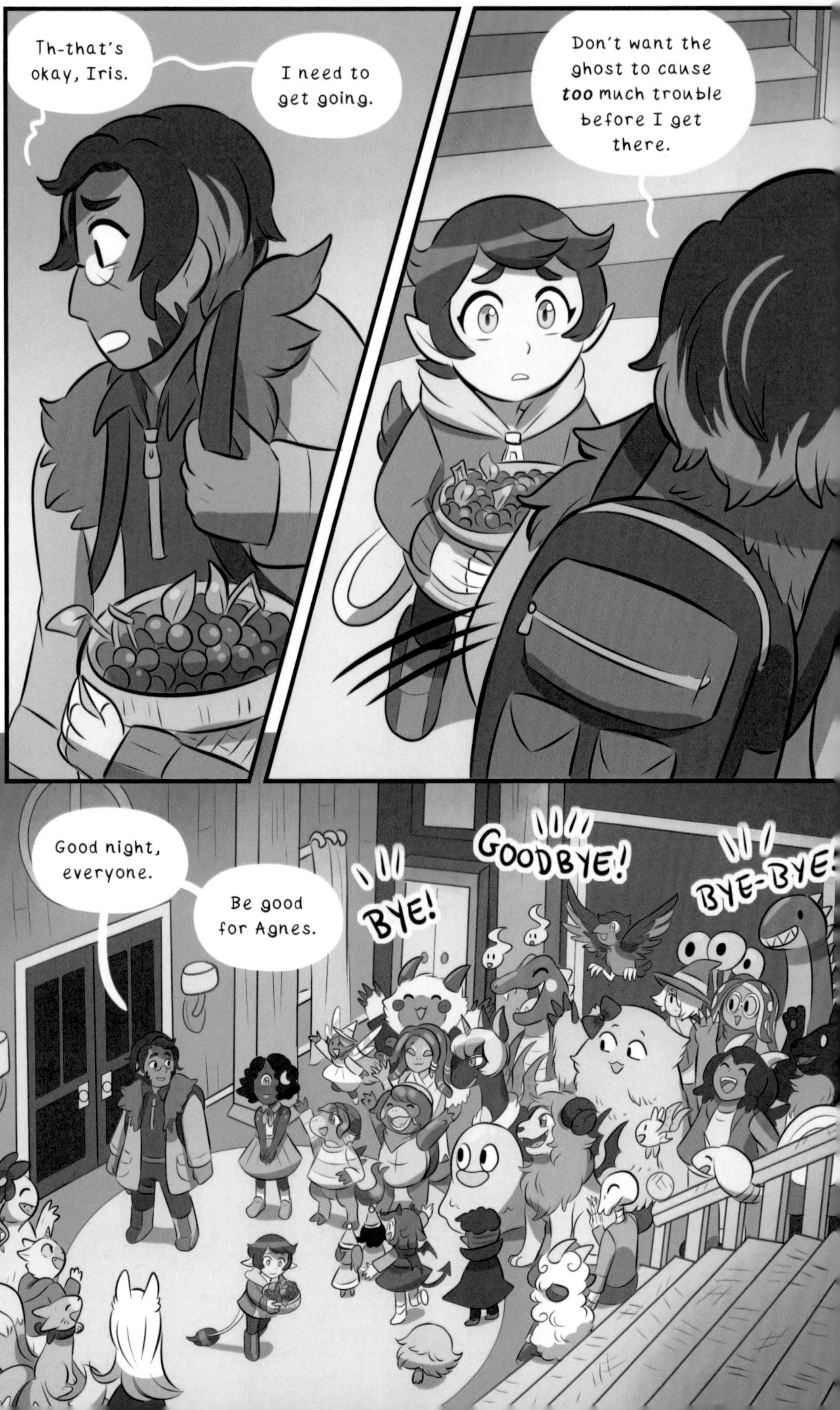

Th-that's okay, Iris.
I need to get going.
Don't want the ghost to cause too much trouble before I get there.
Good night, everyone.
Be good for Agnes.
BYE!
GOODBYE!
BYE-BYE!

SHINE
FADE...
Take care!
CREEAK
SHUT

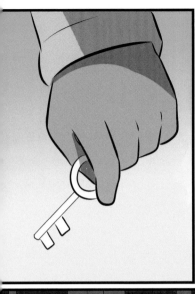

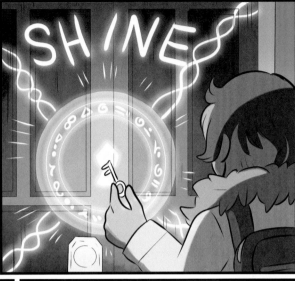

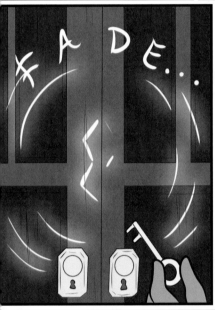

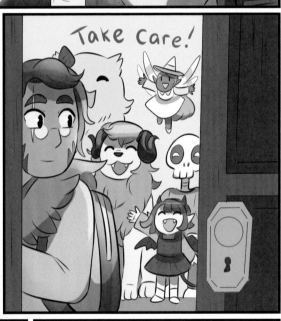

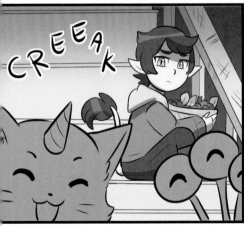

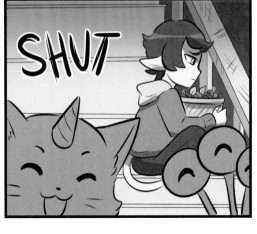

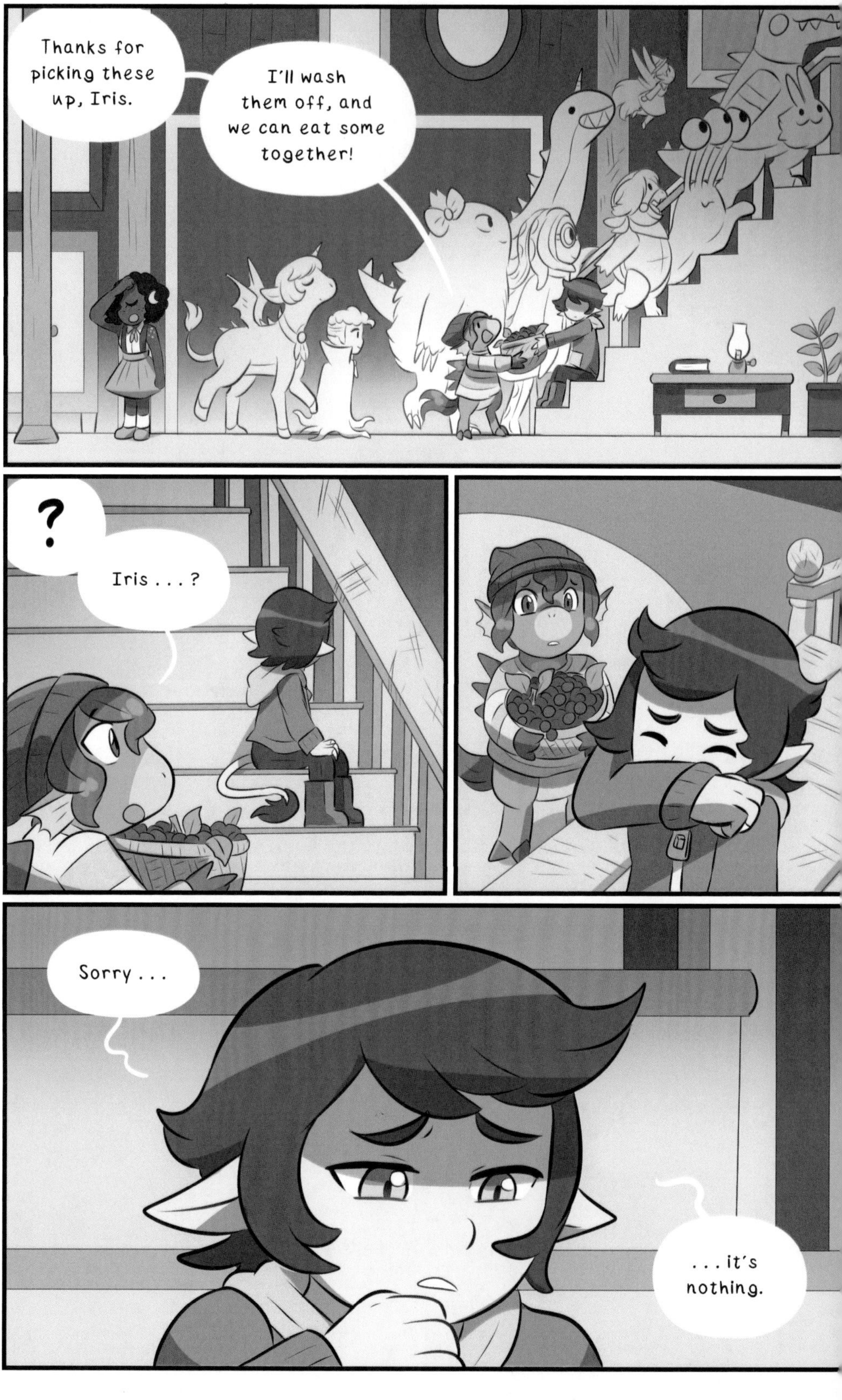

Thanks for picking these up, Iris.
I'll wash them off, and we can eat some together!
?
Iris . . . ?
Sorry . . .
. . . it's nothing.

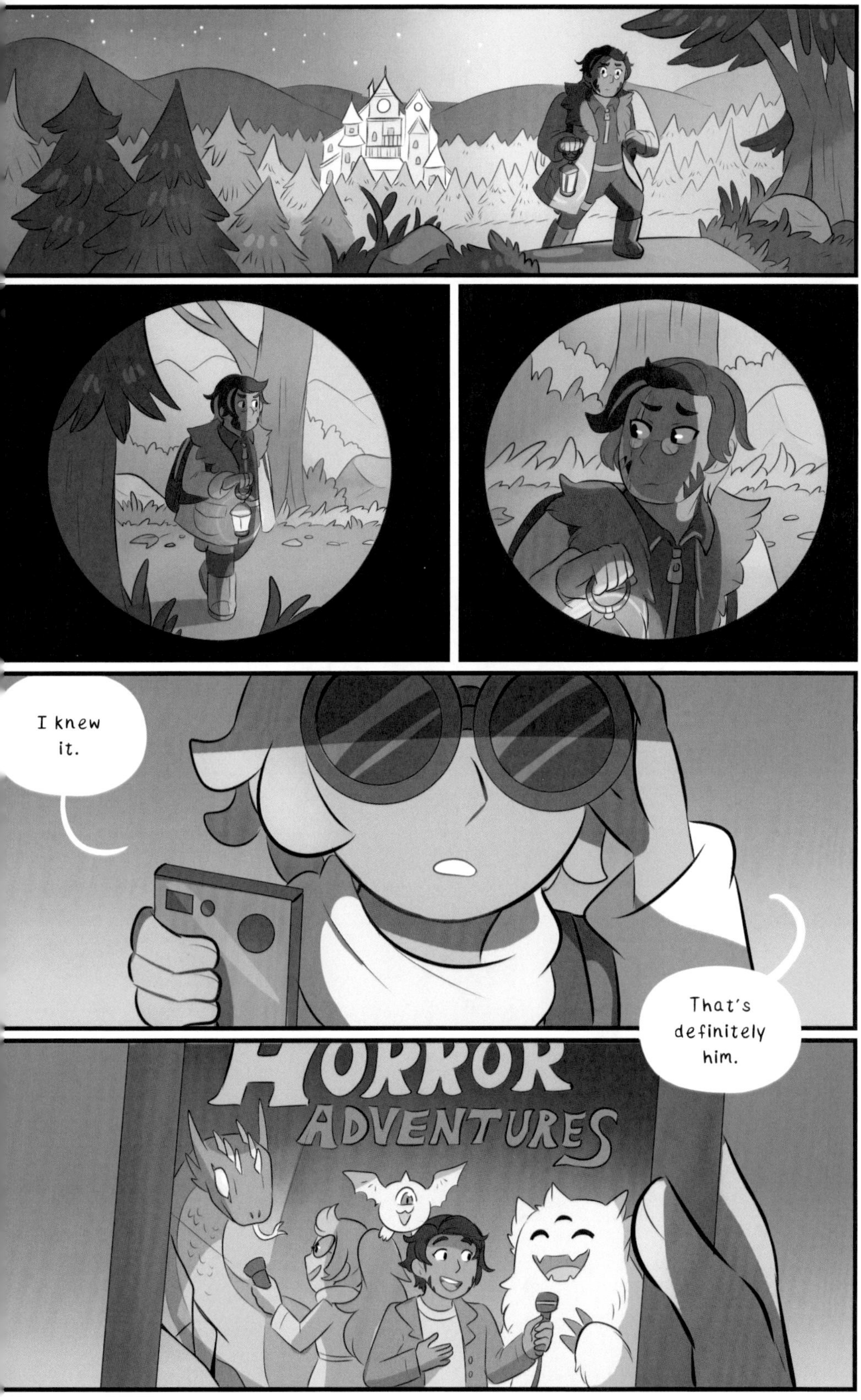
I knew it.
That's definitely him.
HORROR ADVENTURES

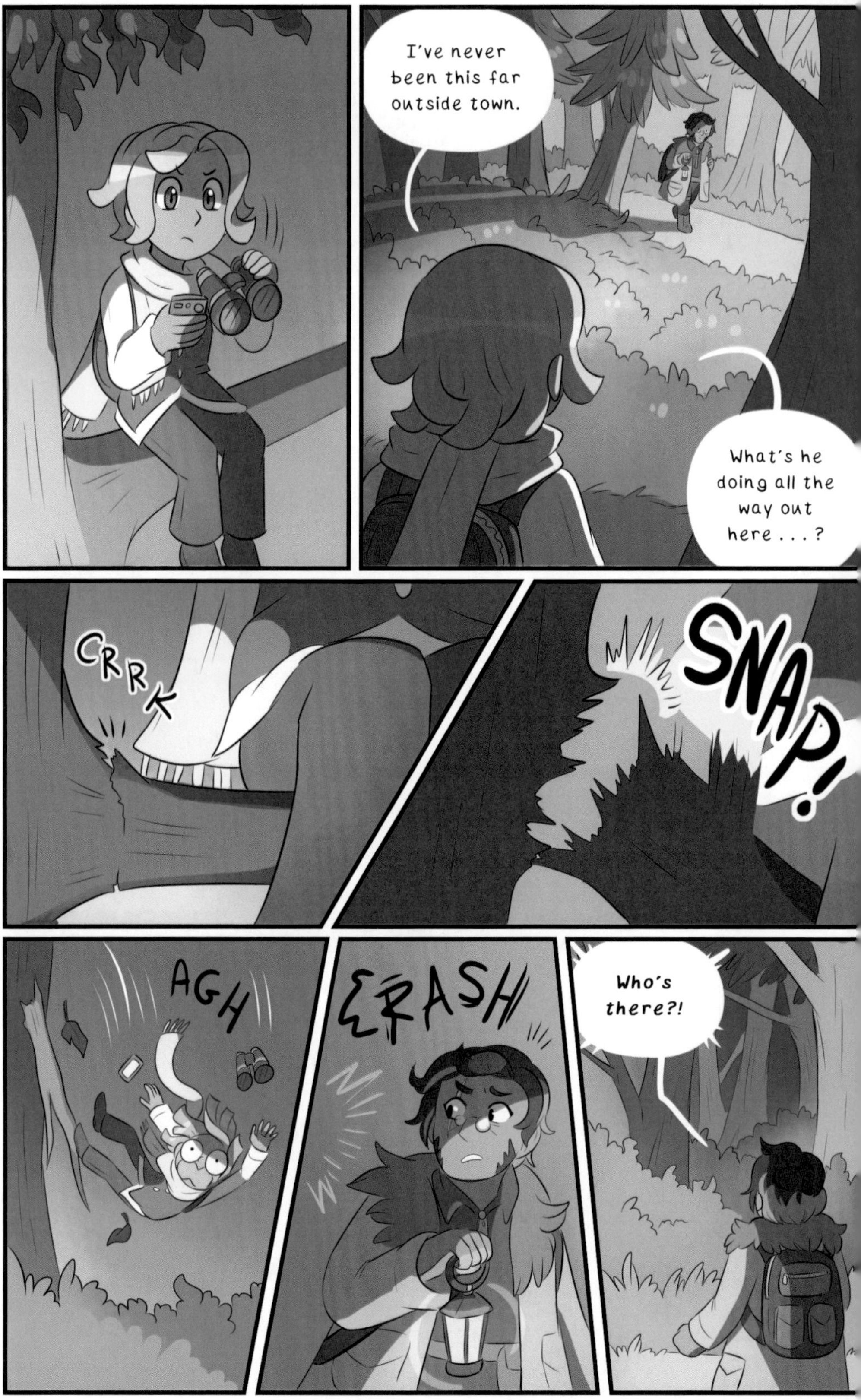
I've never been this far outside town.
What's he doing all the way out here . . . ?
CRRK
SNAP!
AGH
CRASH
Who's there?!

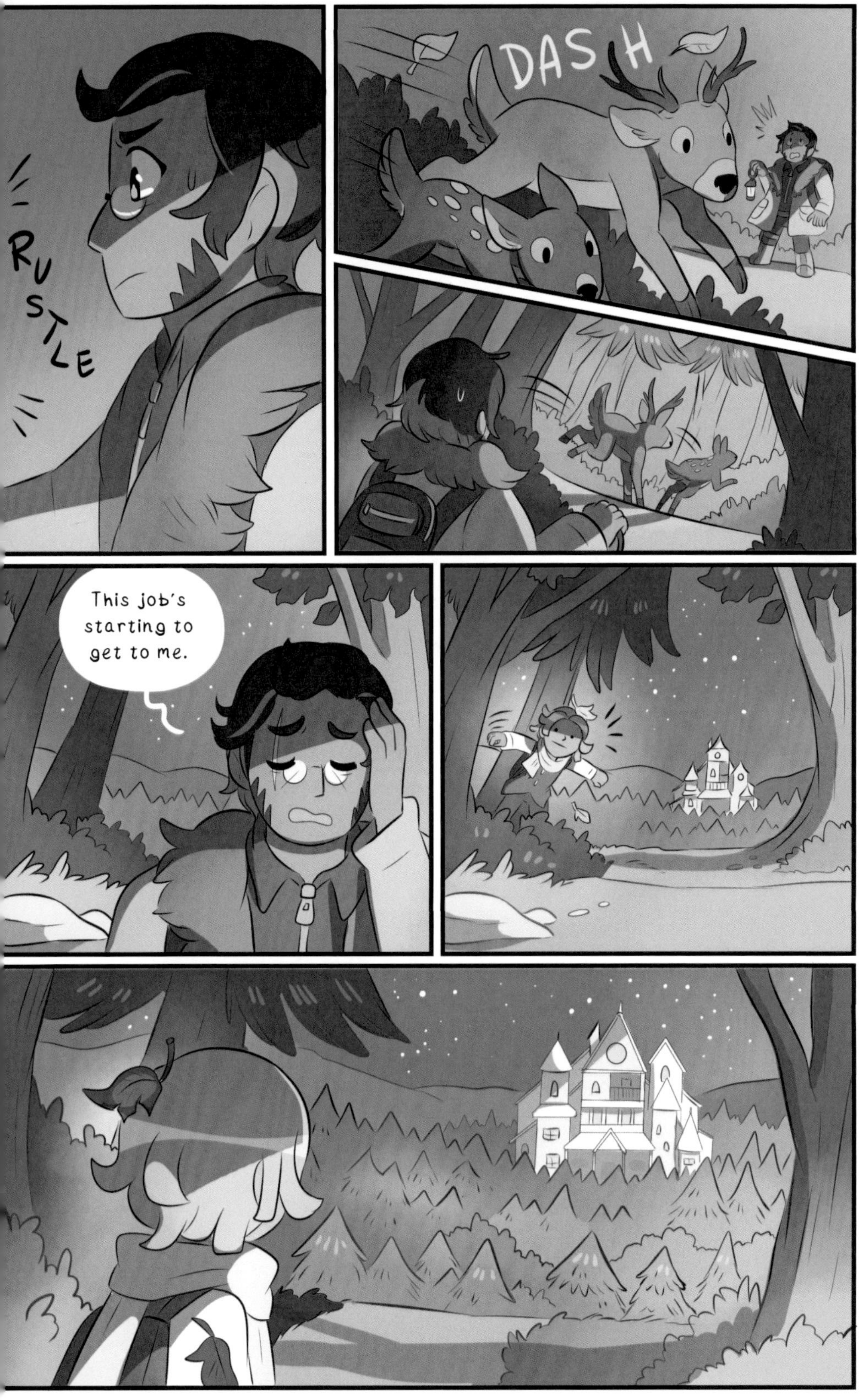
RUSTLE
DASH
This job's starting to get to me.

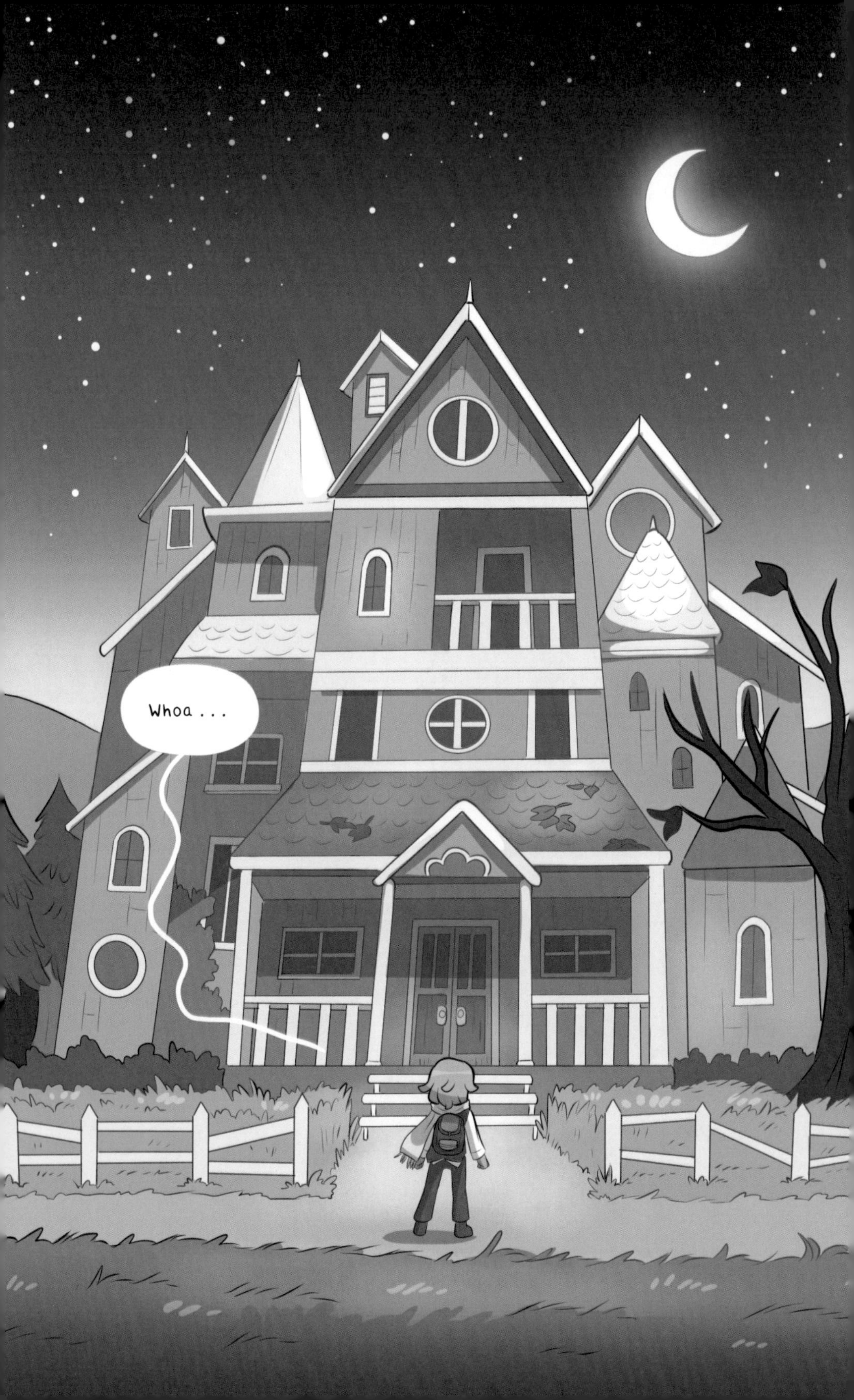
Whoa . . .

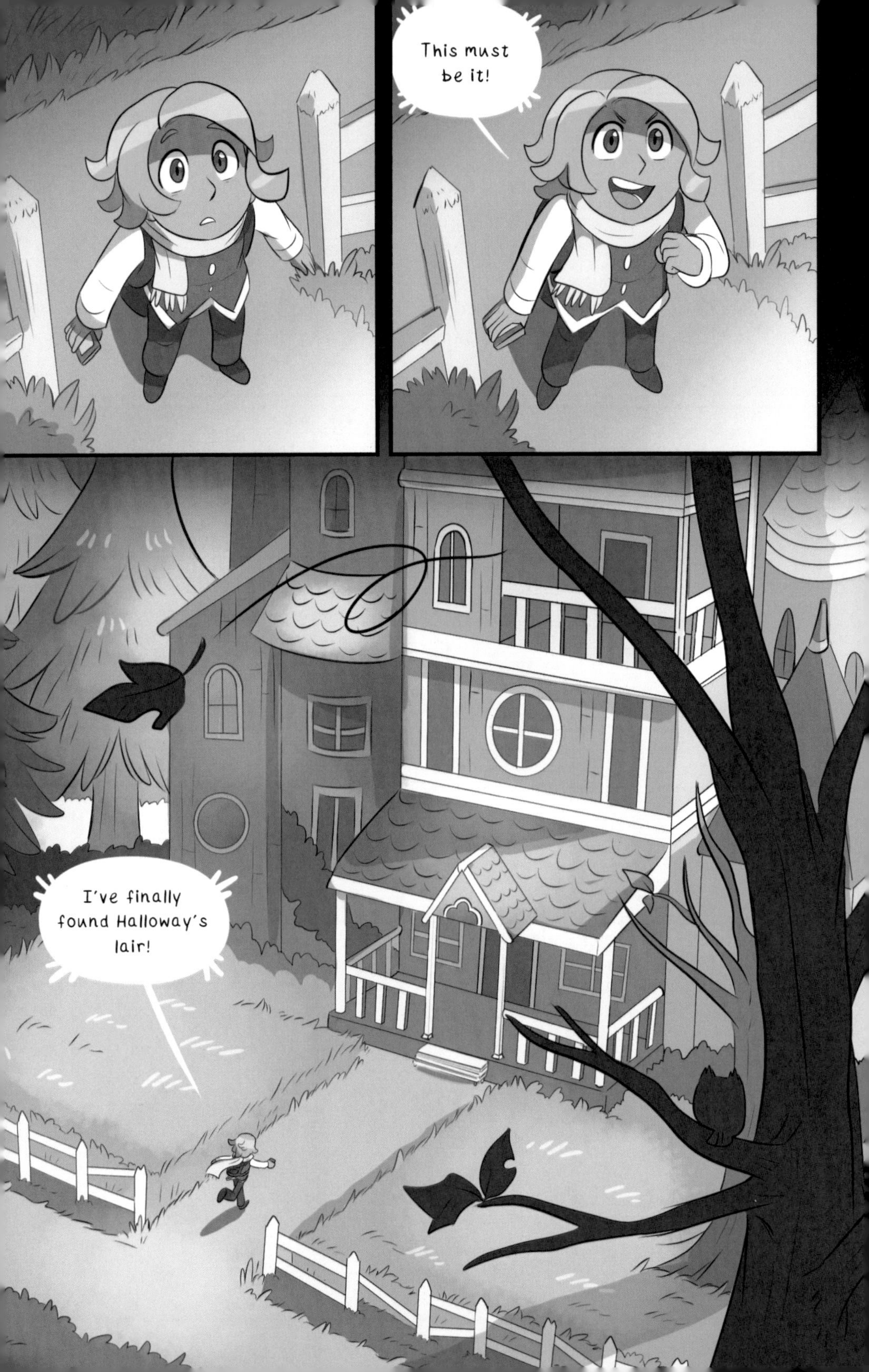
This must be it!
I've finally found Halloway's lair!

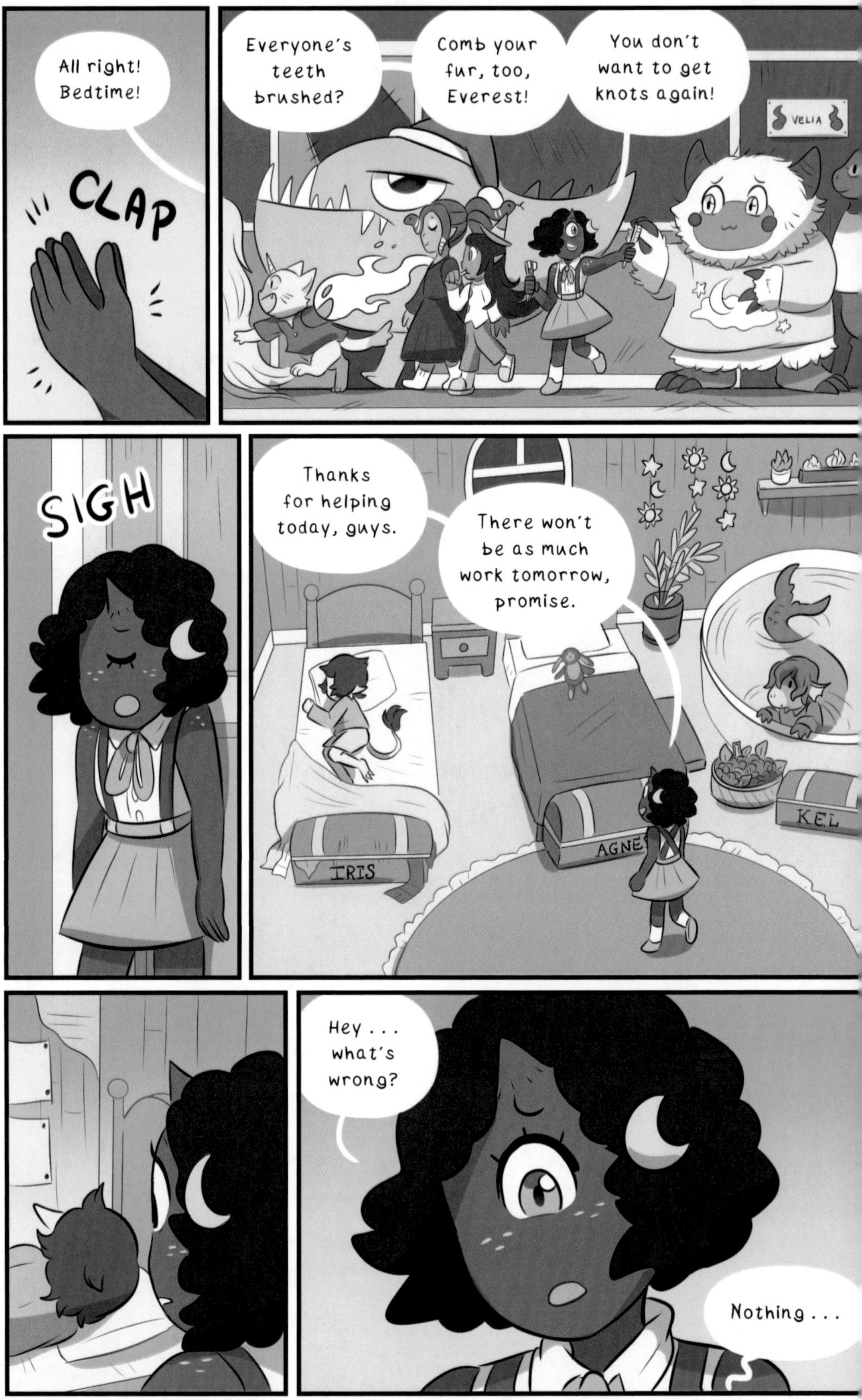

All right! Bedtime!
CLAP
Everyone's teeth brushed?
Comb your fur, too, Everest!
You don't want to get knots again!
VELIA
SIGH
Thanks for helping today, guys.
There won't be as much work tomorrow, promise.
IRIS
KEL
Hey . . . what's wrong?
Nothing . . .

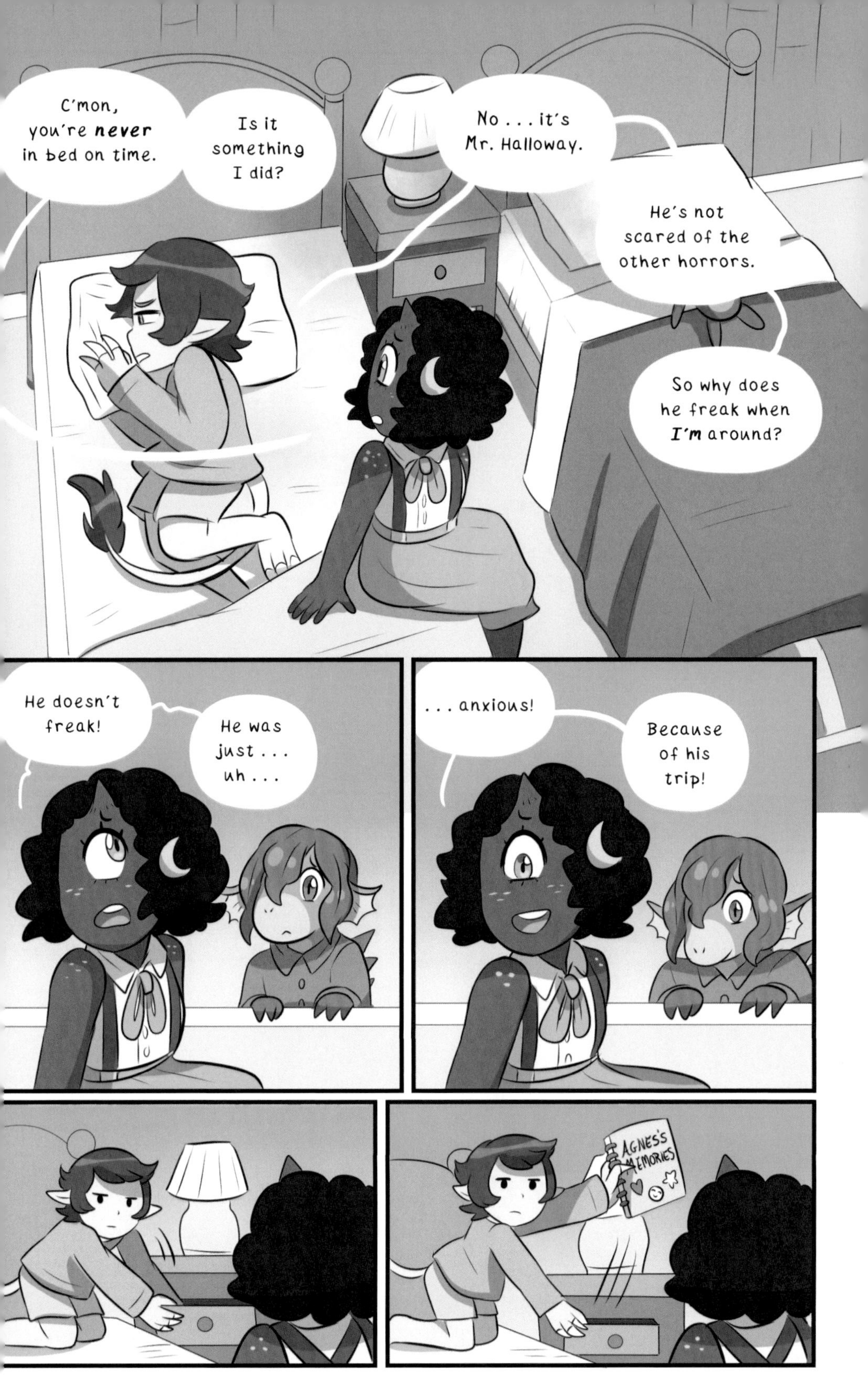
C'mon, you're **never** in bed on time.
Is it something I did?
No . . . it's Mr. Halloway.
He's not scared of the other horrors.
So why does he freak when ***I'm*** around?
He doesn't freak!
He was just . . . uh . . .
. . . anxious!
Because of his trip!
AGNES'S MEMORIES

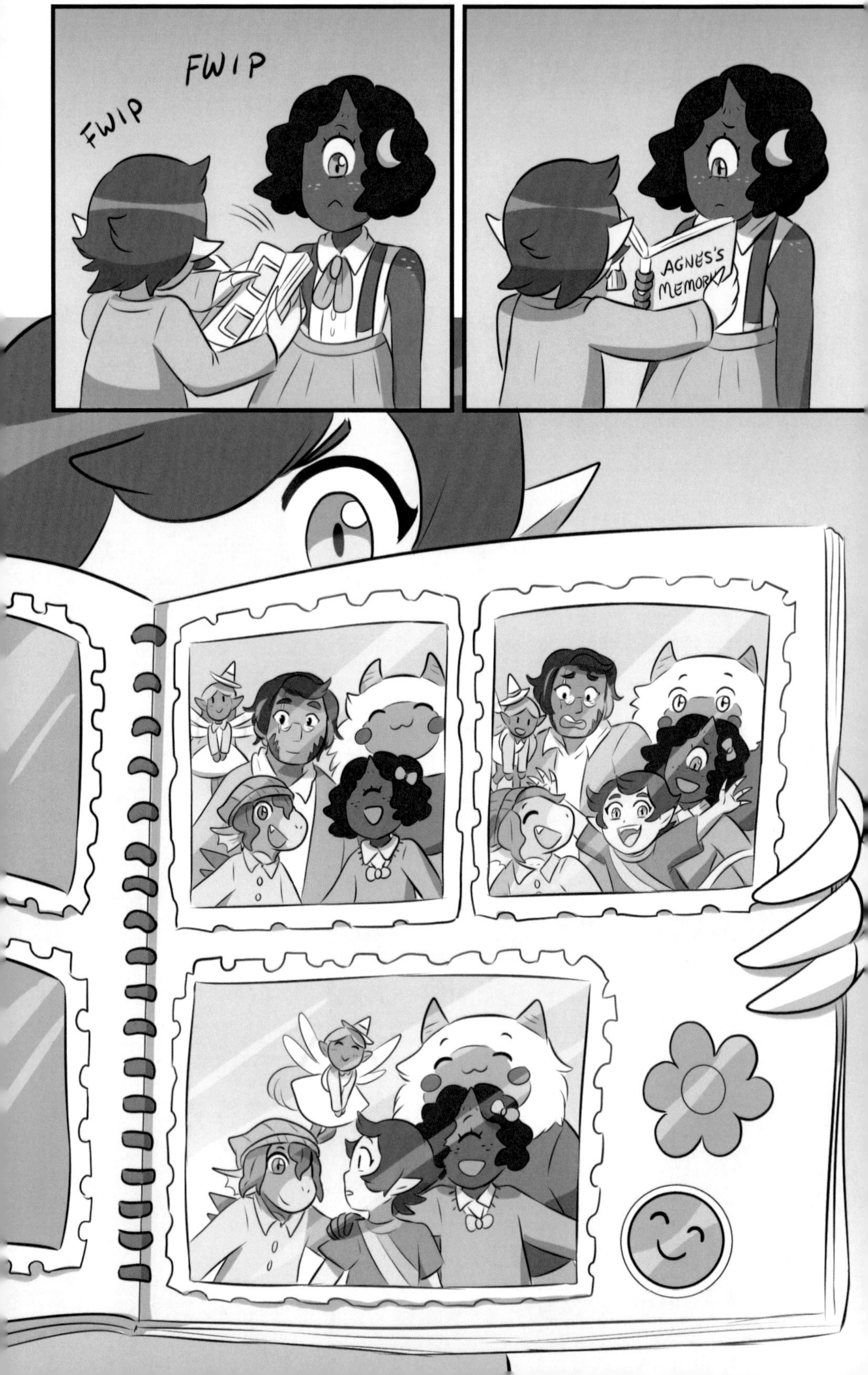
FWIP
FWIP
AGNES'S MEMORY

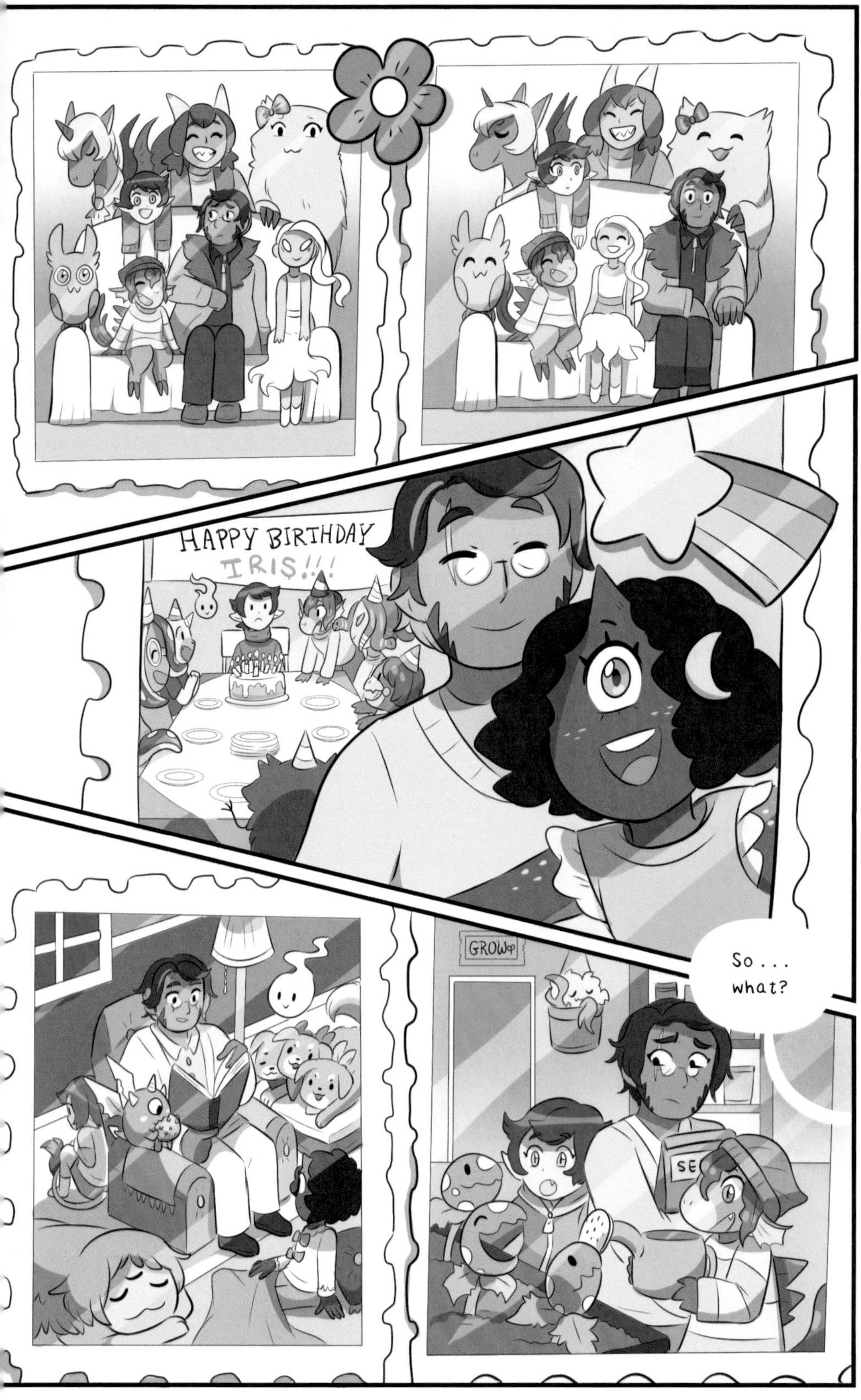
HAPPY BIRTHDAY
IRIS!!!
GROW
So . . . what?

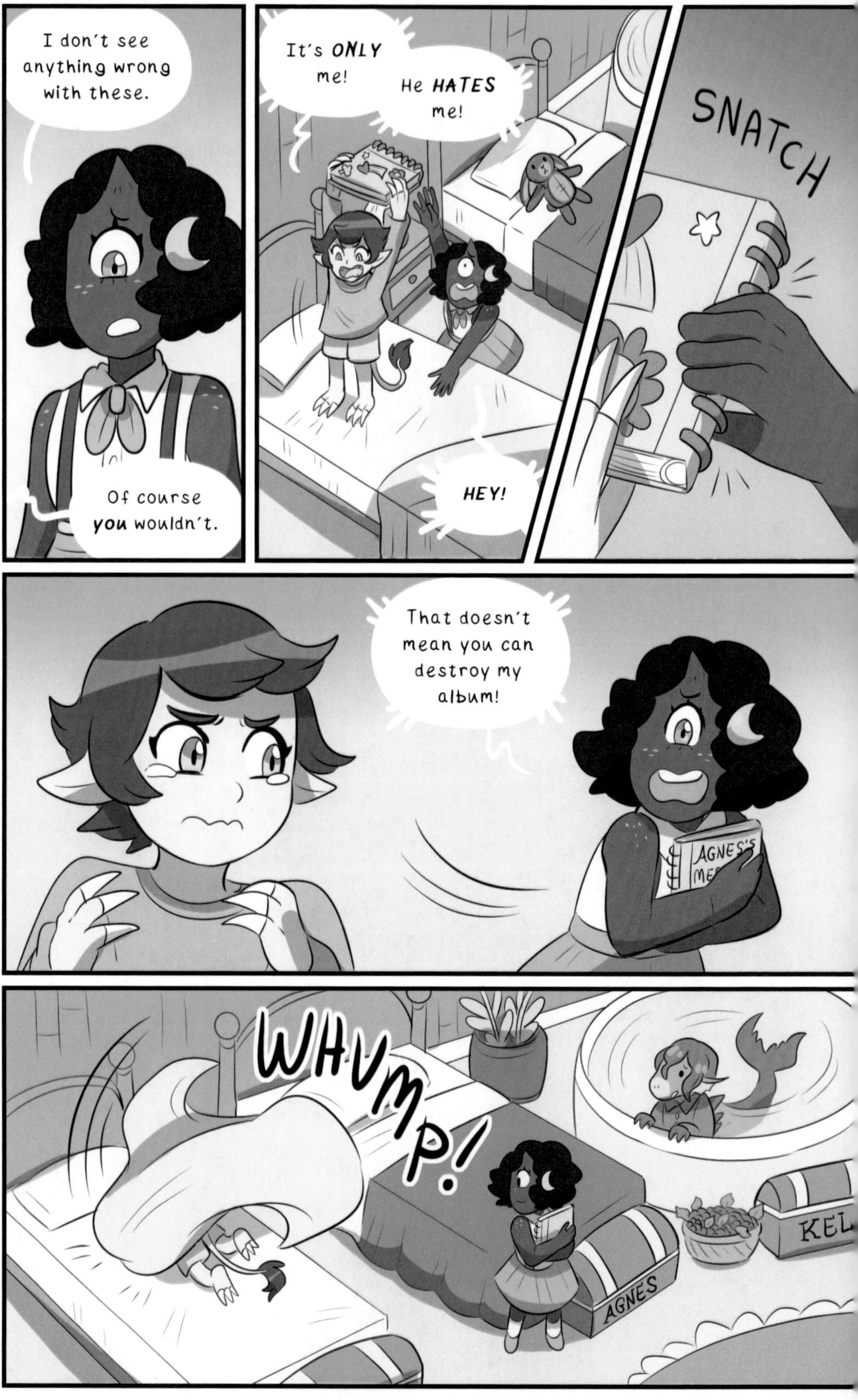
I don't see anything wrong with these.
Of course **you** wouldn't.
It's **ONLY** me!
He **HATES** me!
HEY!
SNATCH
That doesn't mean you can destroy my album!
WHUMP!
AGNES

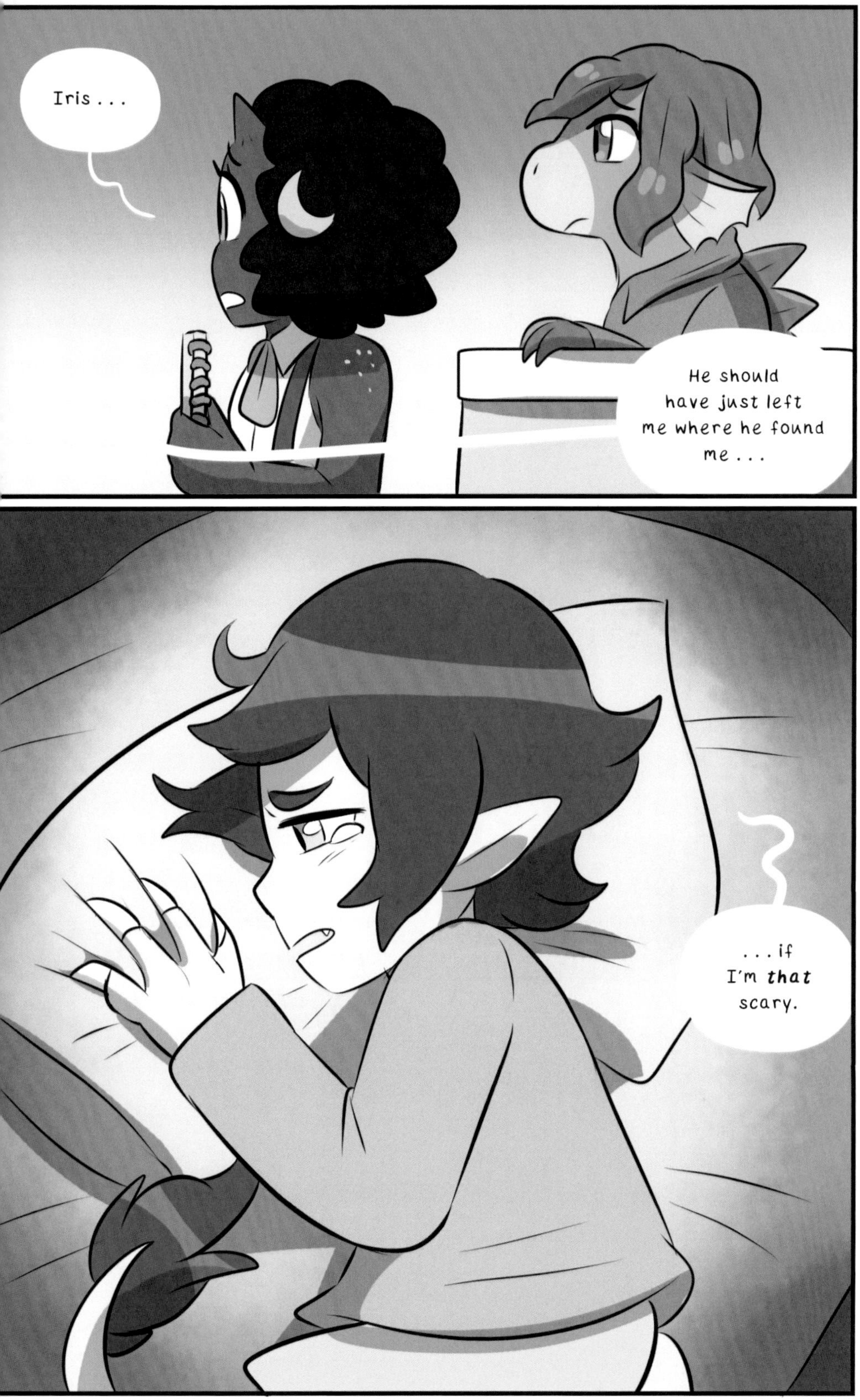
Iris . . .
He should have just left me where he found me . . .
. . . if I'm ***that*** scary.

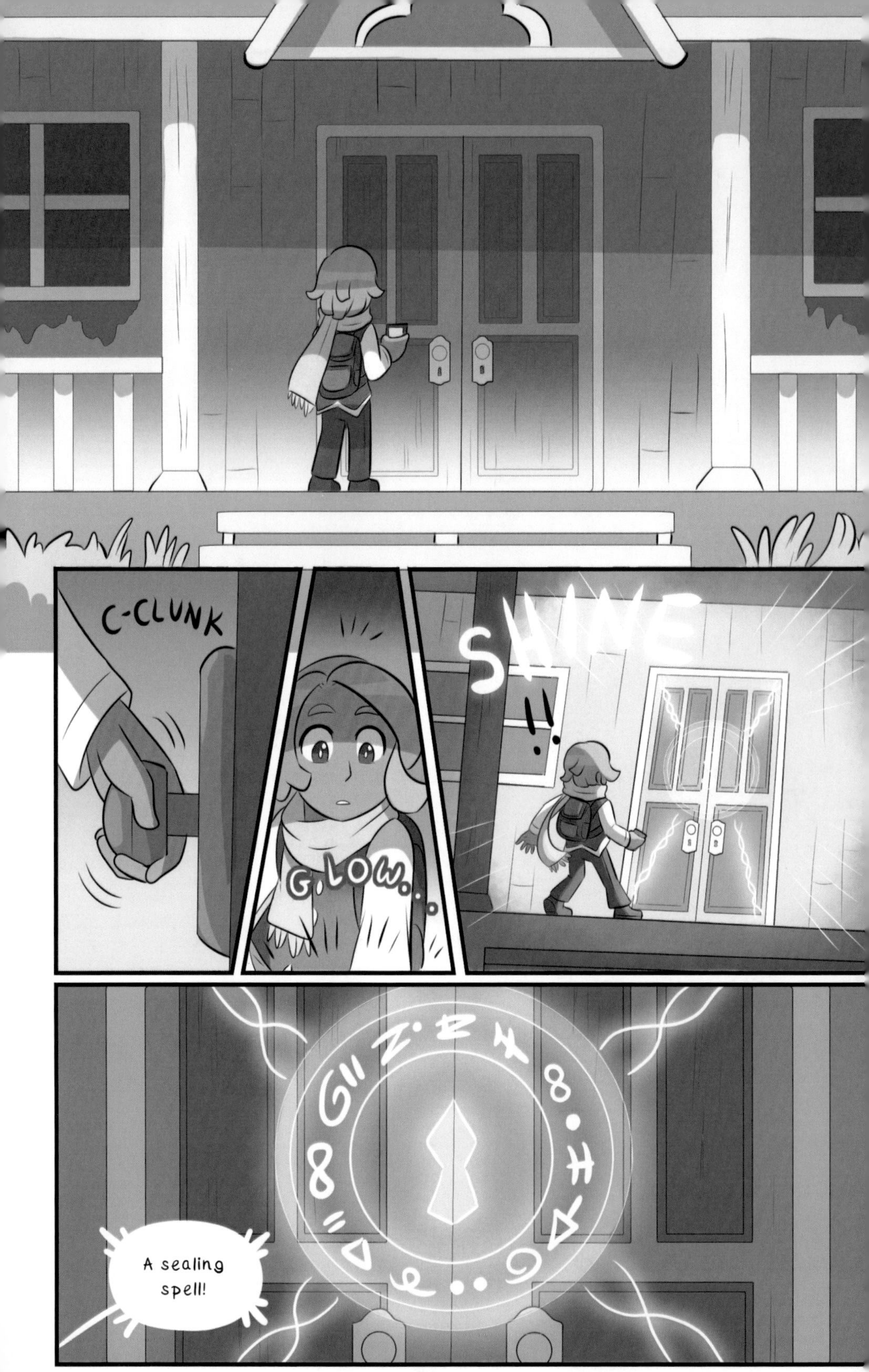
C-CLUNK
GLOW...
SHINE
!!
A sealing spell!

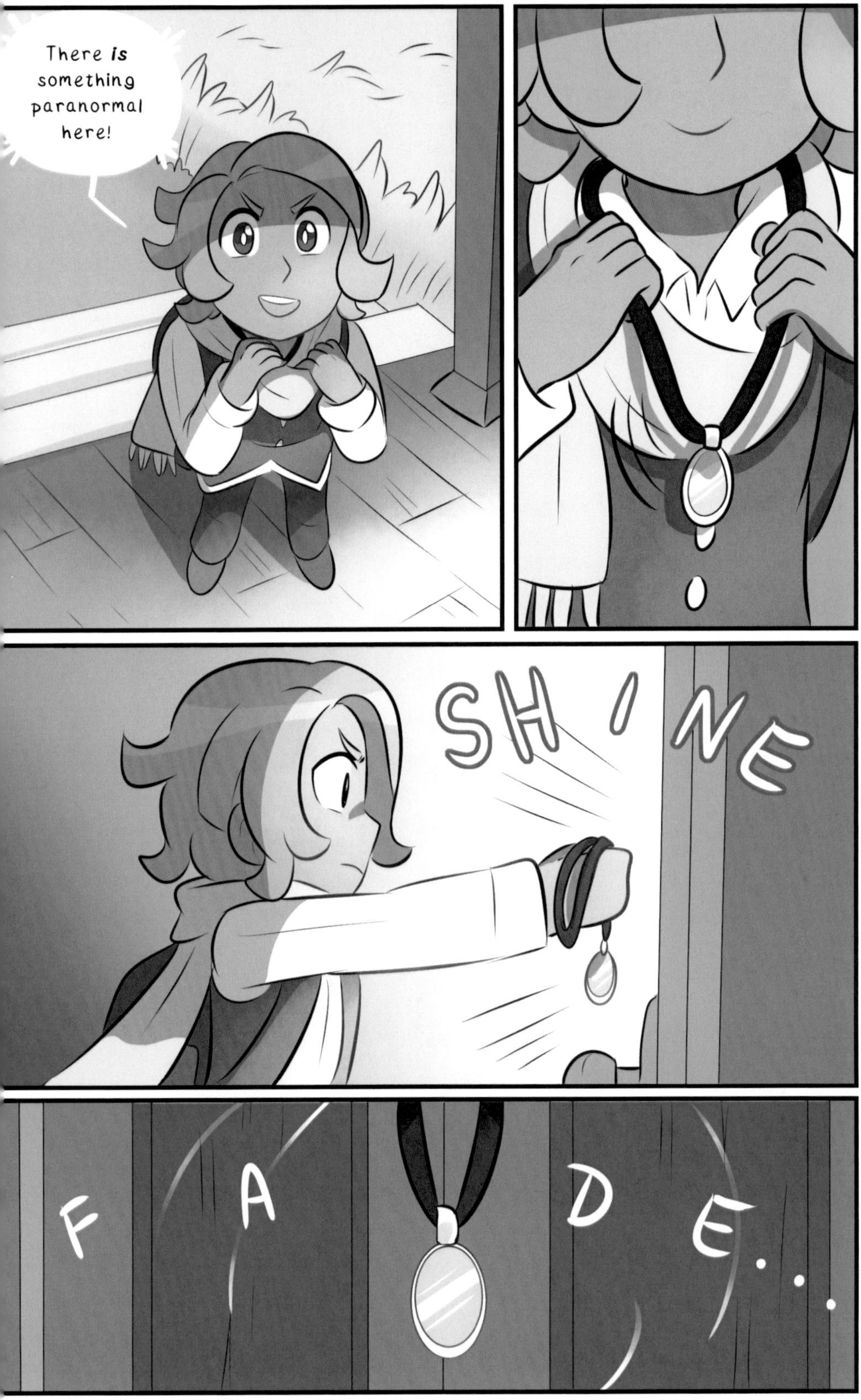
There **is** something paranormal here!
SHINE
FADE...

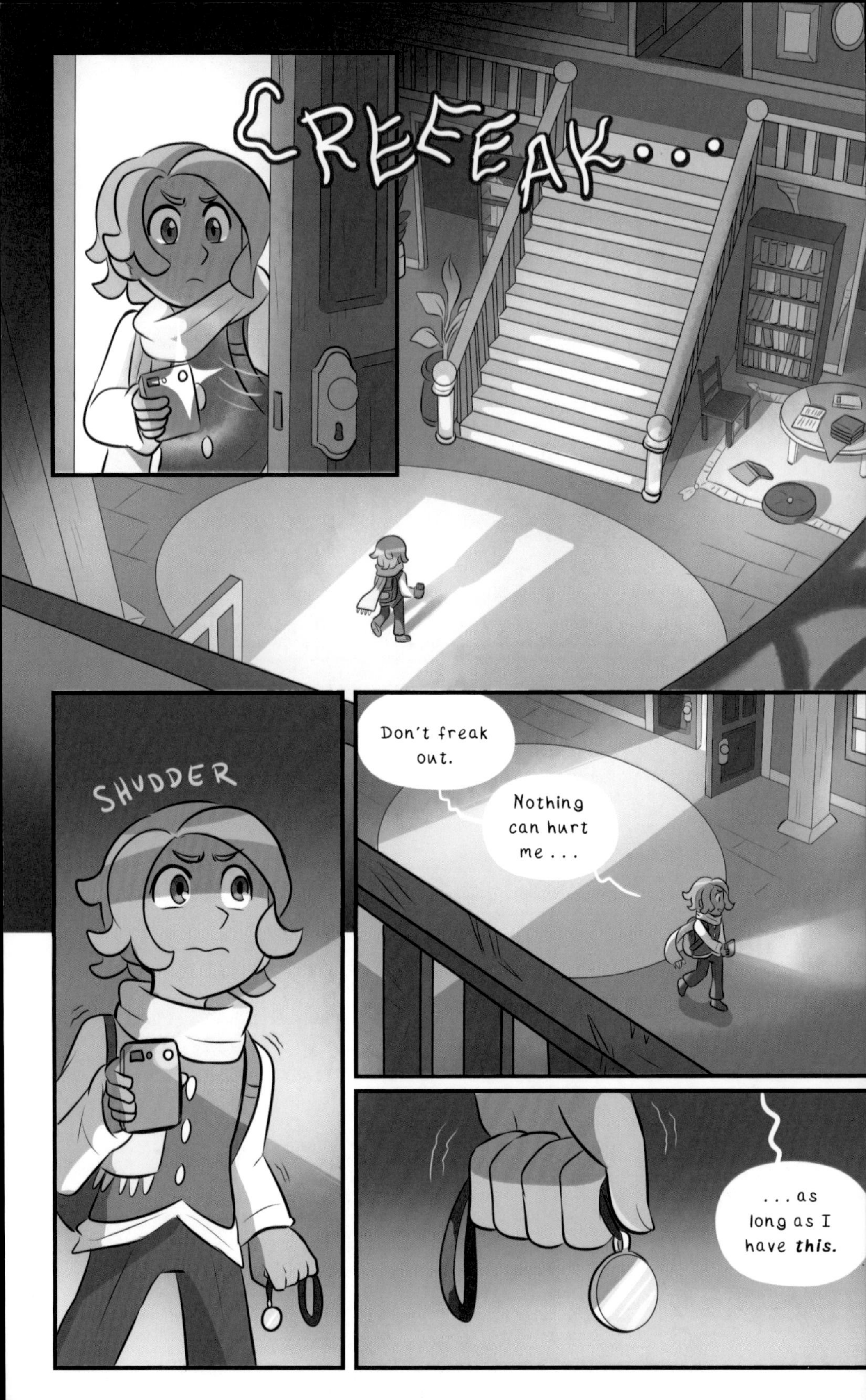
CREEEAK...
SHUDDER
Don't freak out.
Nothing can hurt me...
...as long as I have **this.**

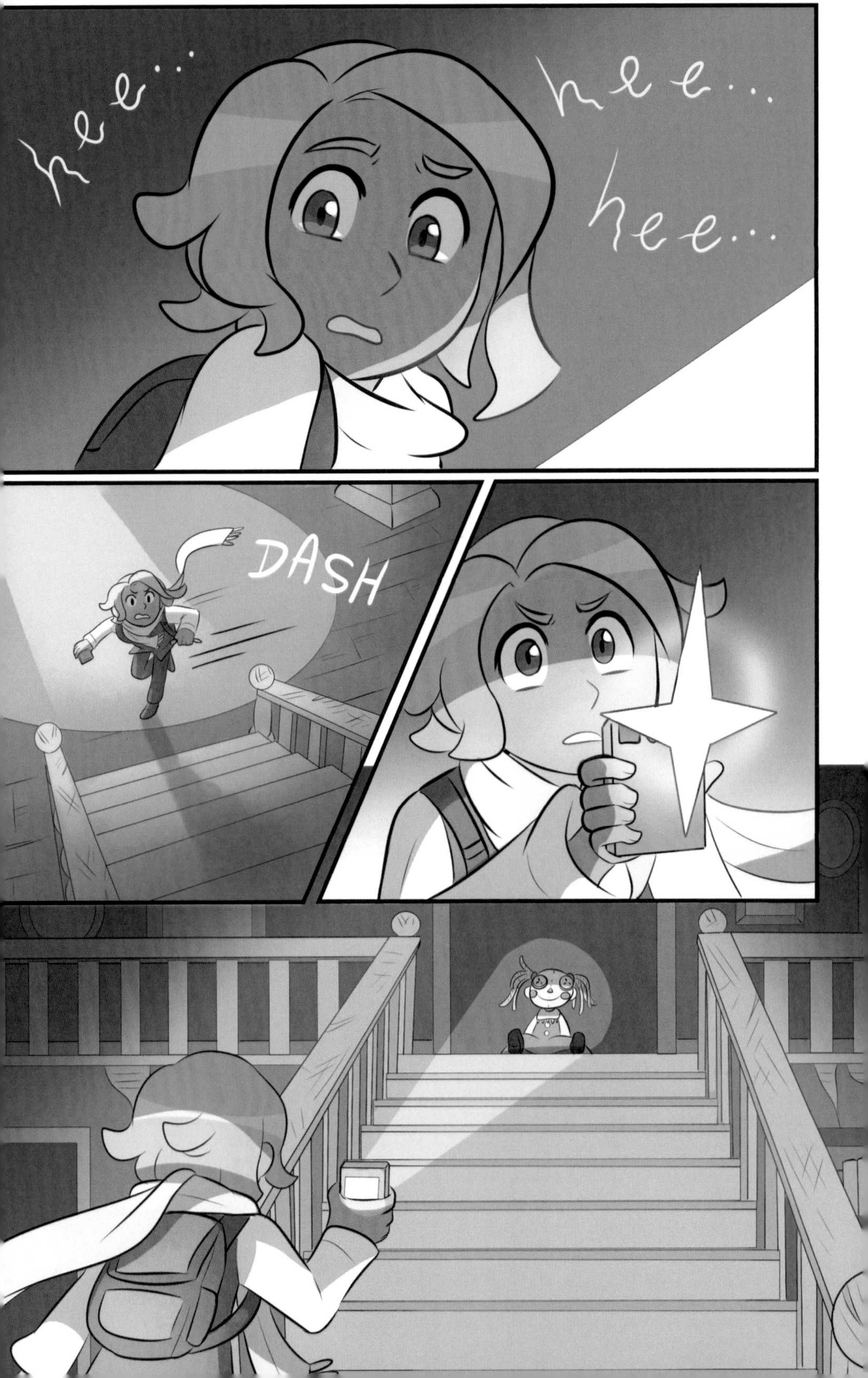
hee...
hee...
hee...
DASH

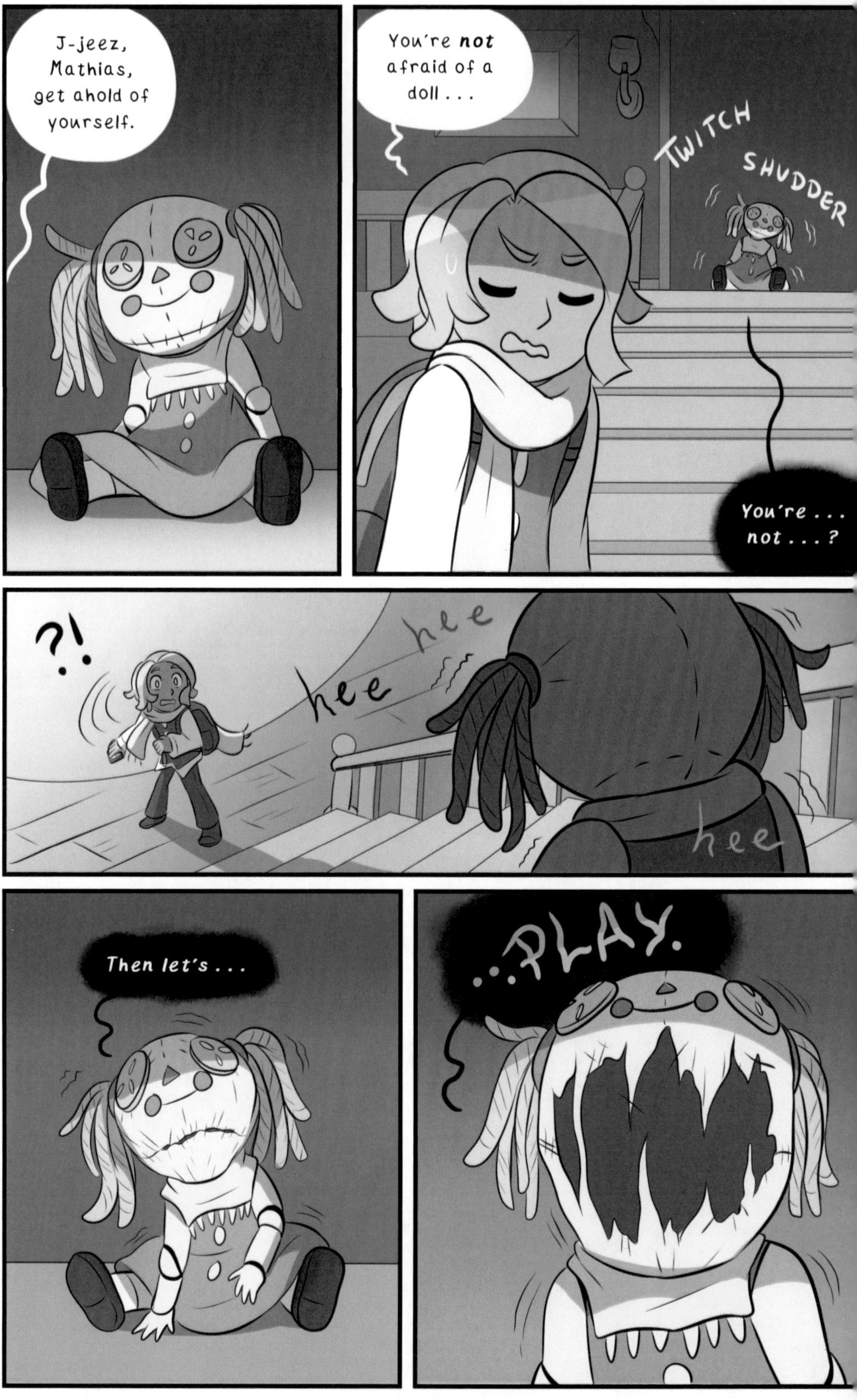
J-jeez, Mathias, get ahold of yourself.
You're **not** afraid of a doll . . .
TWITCH
SHUDDER
You're . . . not . . . ?
?!
hee
hee
hee
Then let's . . .
. . . PLAY.

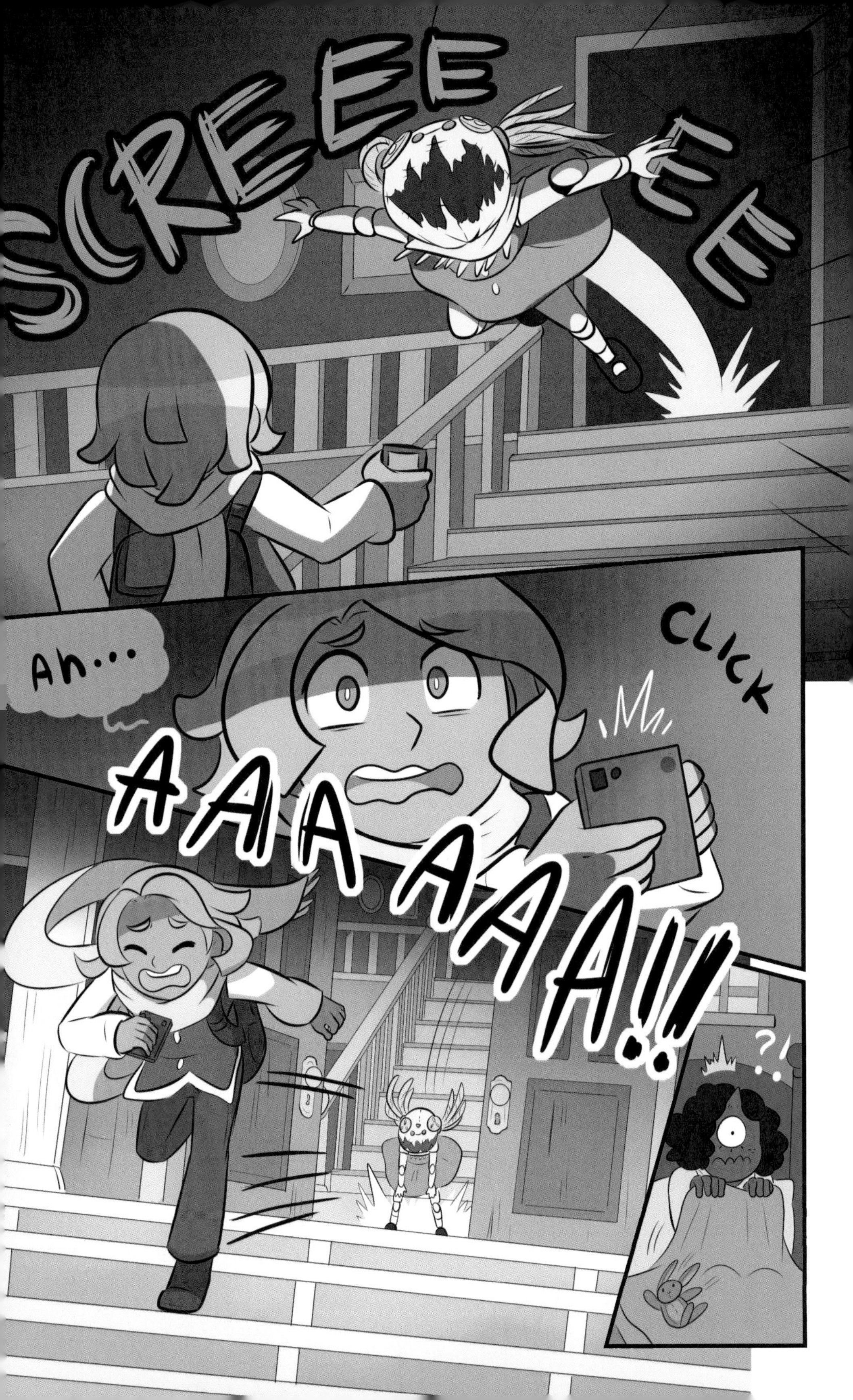
SCREEEEE
Ah...
CLICK
AAAAAAA!!
?!

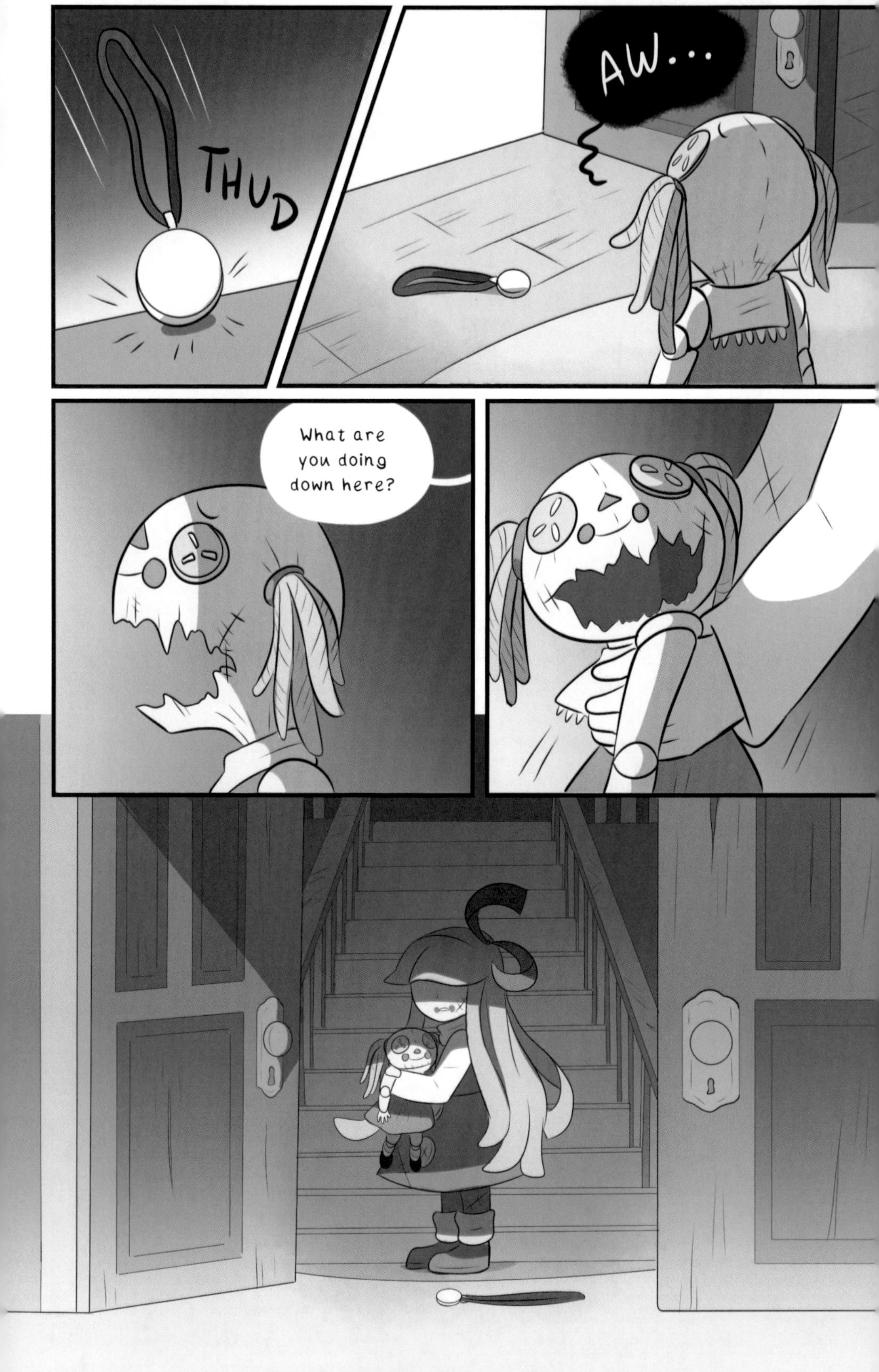
THUD
AW...
What are you doing down here?

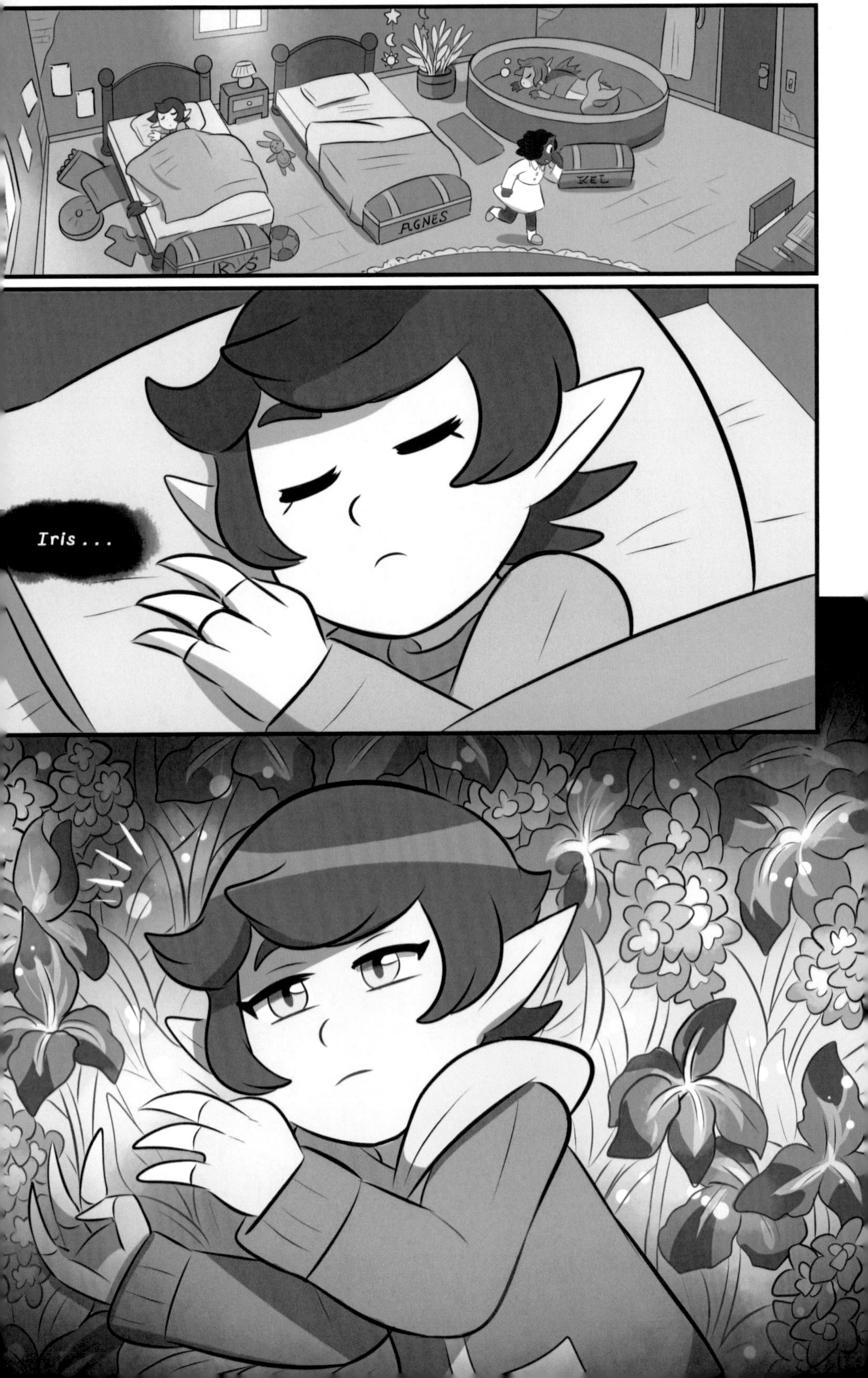

IRIS
AGNES
KEL
Iris . . .

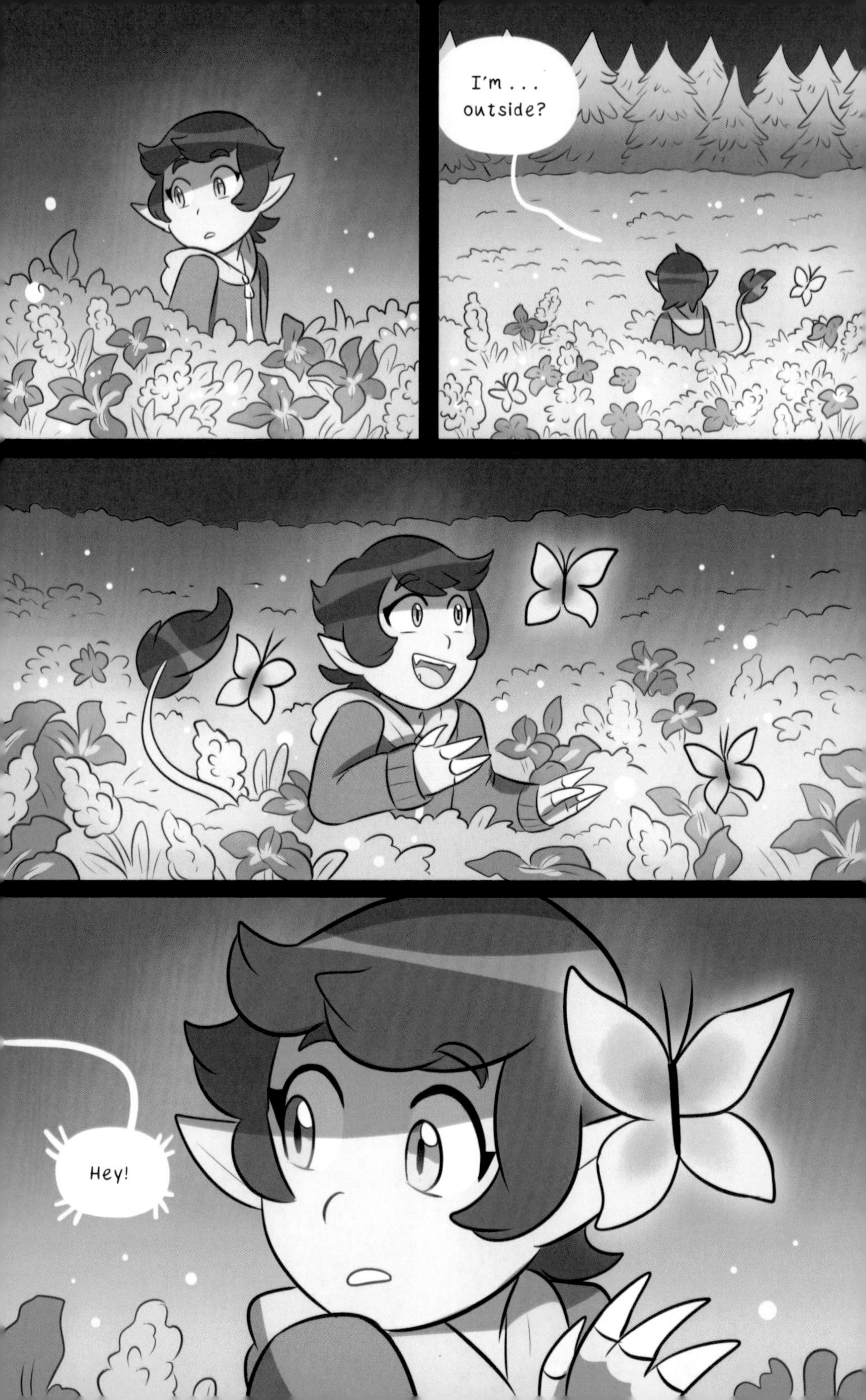
I'm . . . outside?
Hey!

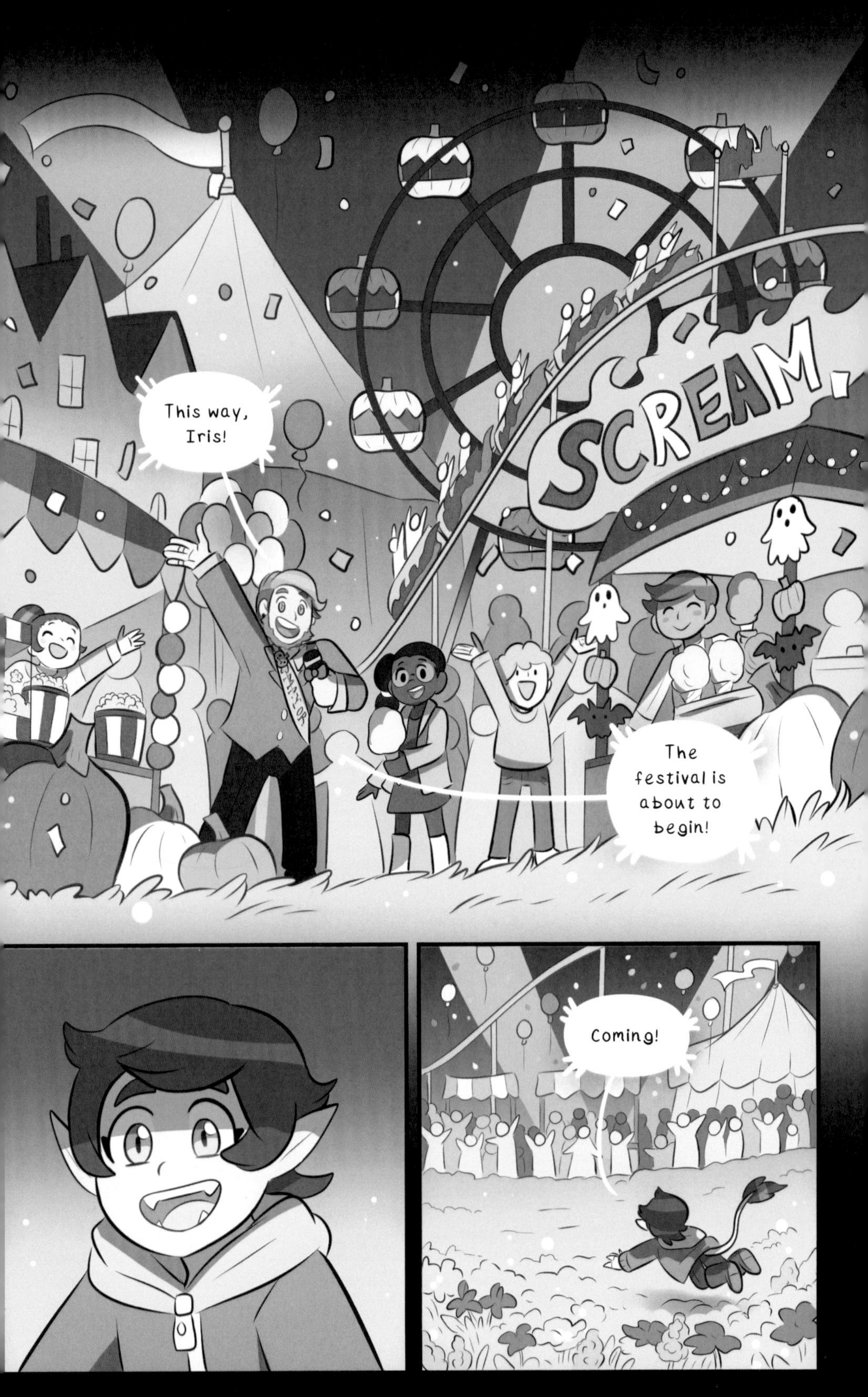
SCREAM
This way, Iris!
The festival is about to begin!
Coming!

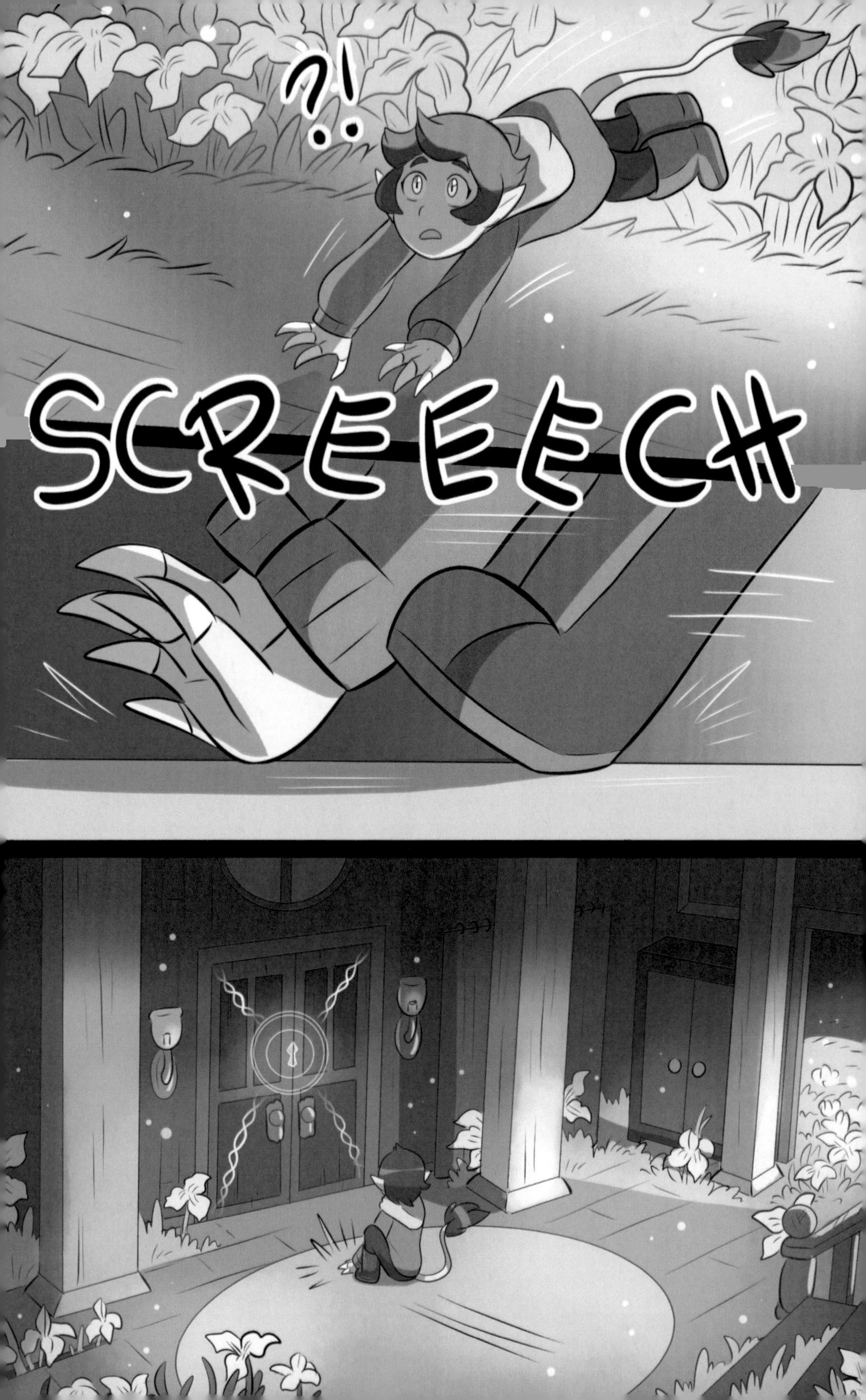
?!
SCREEECH

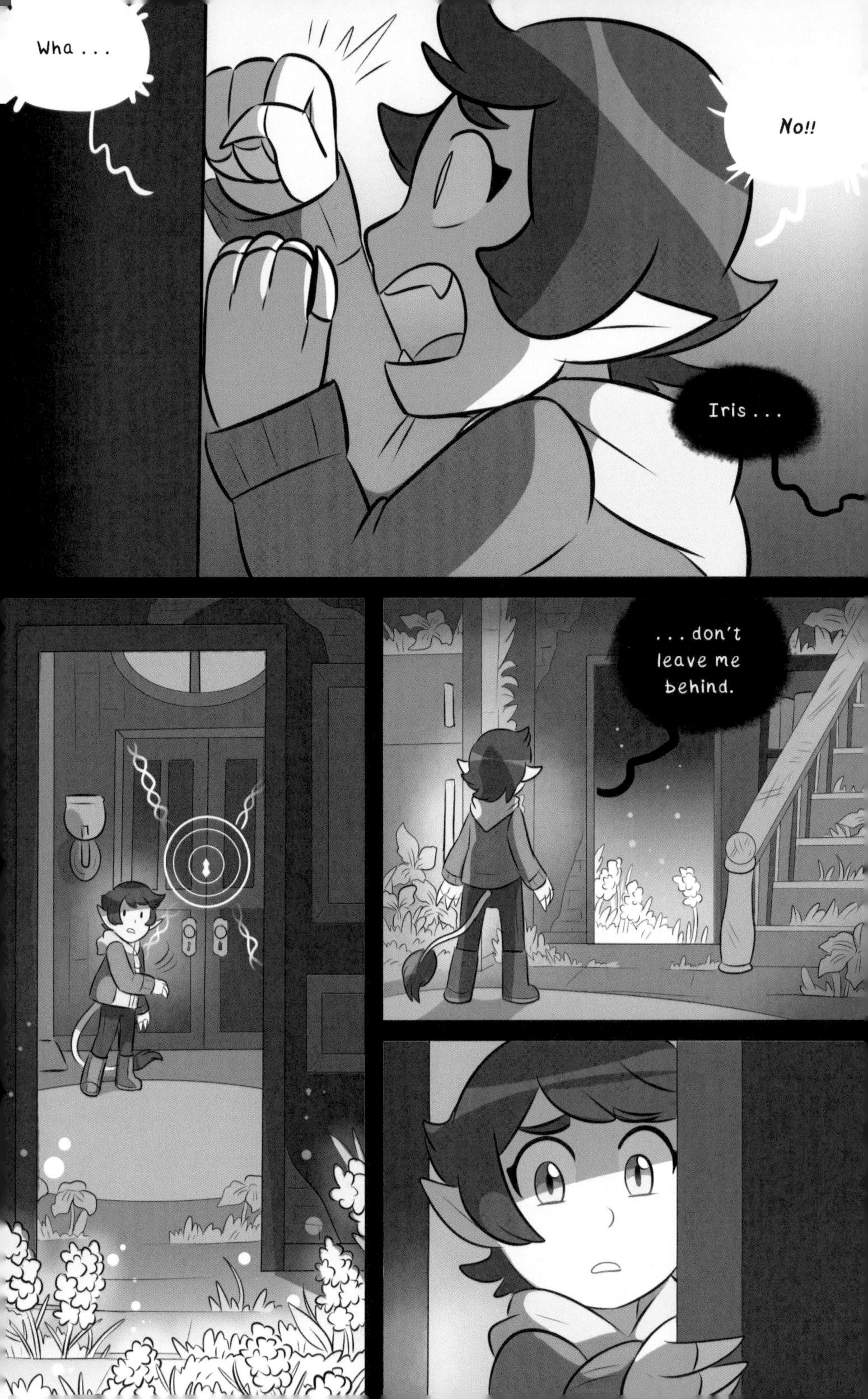
Wha . . .
No!!
Iris . . .
. . . don't leave me behind.

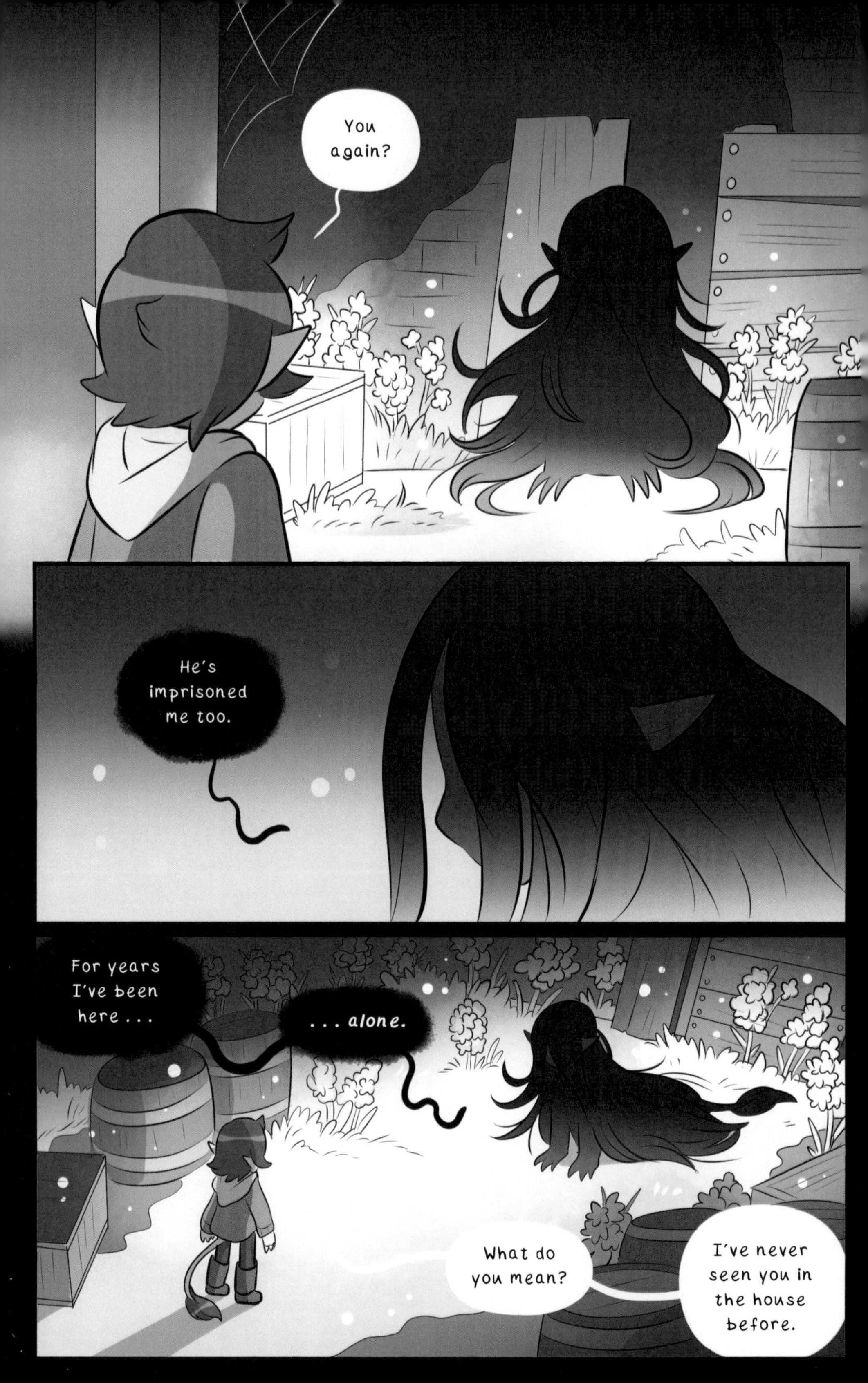
You again?
He's imprisoned me too.
For years I've been here . . .
. . . alone.
What do you mean?
I've never seen you in the house before.

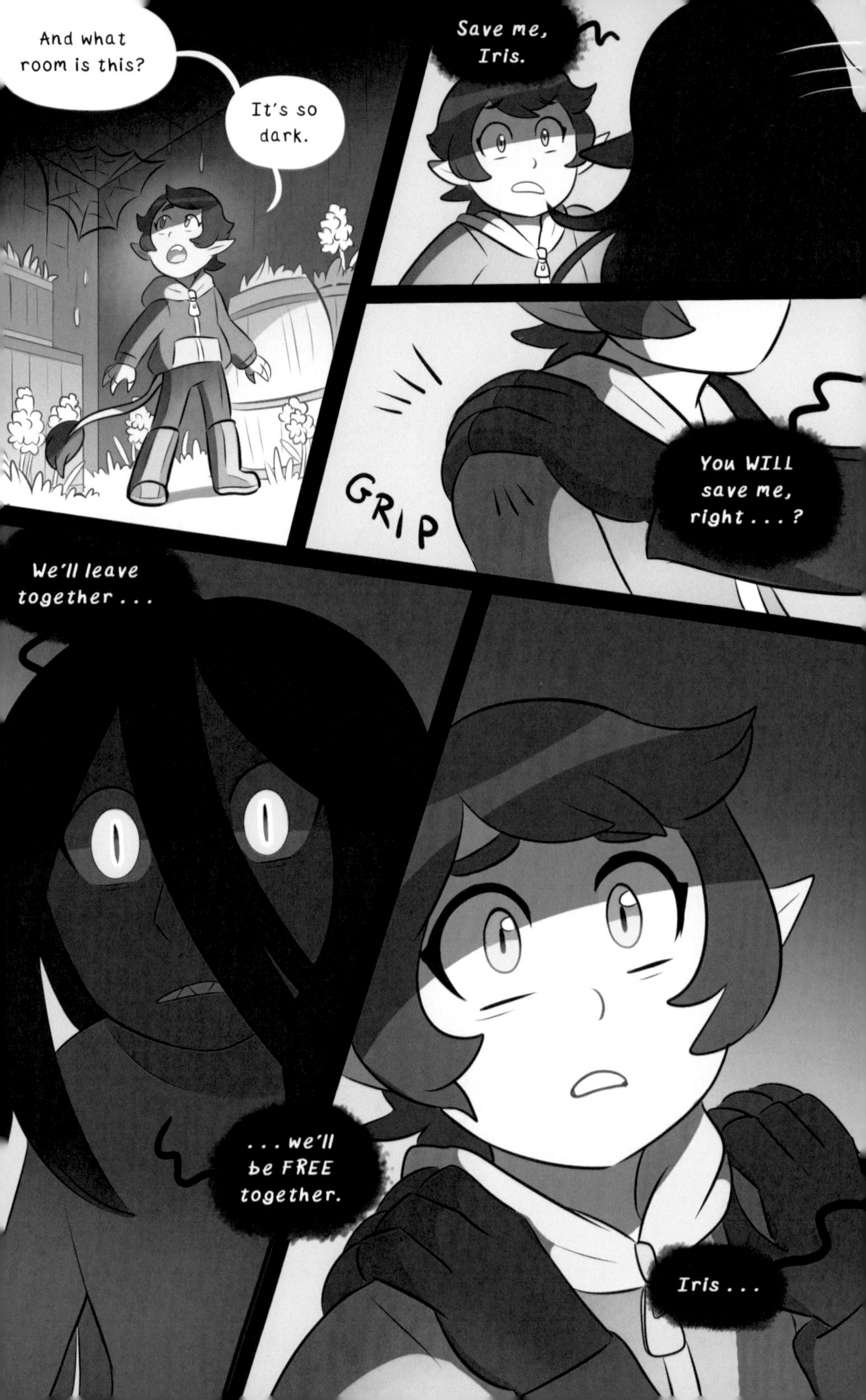
And what room is this?
It's so dark.
Save me, Iris.
GRIP
You WILL save me, right . . . ?
We'll leave together . . .
. . . we'll be FREE together.
Iris . . .

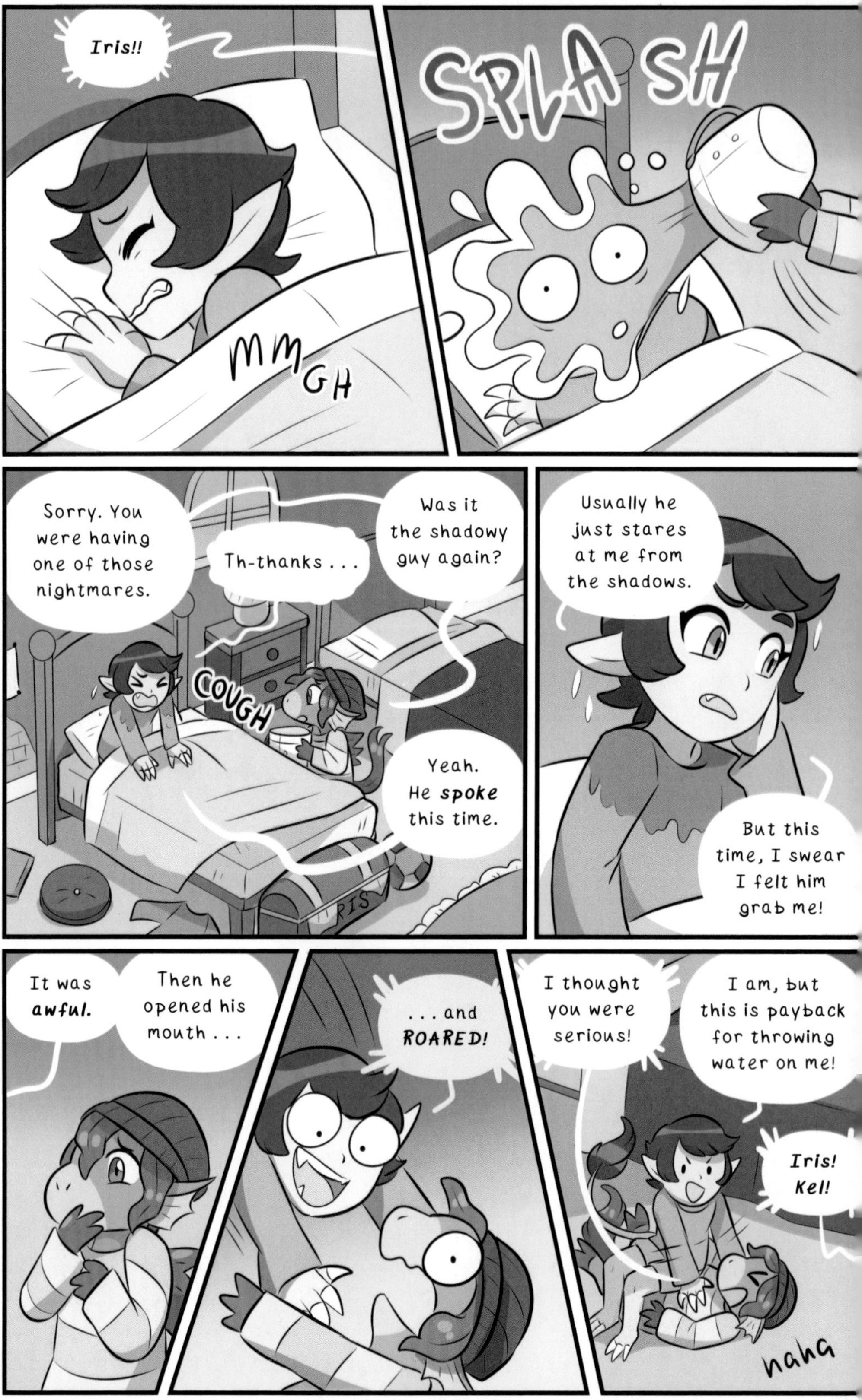
Iris!!
MMGH
SPLASH
Sorry. You were having one of those nightmares.
Th-thanks . . .
COUGH
Was it the shadowy guy again?
Yeah. He *spoke* this time.
Usually he just stares at me from the shadows.
But this time, I swear I felt him grab me!
It was *awful.*
Then he opened his mouth . . .
. . . and *ROARED!*
I thought you were serious!
I am, but this is payback for throwing water on me!
Iris! Kel!
haha

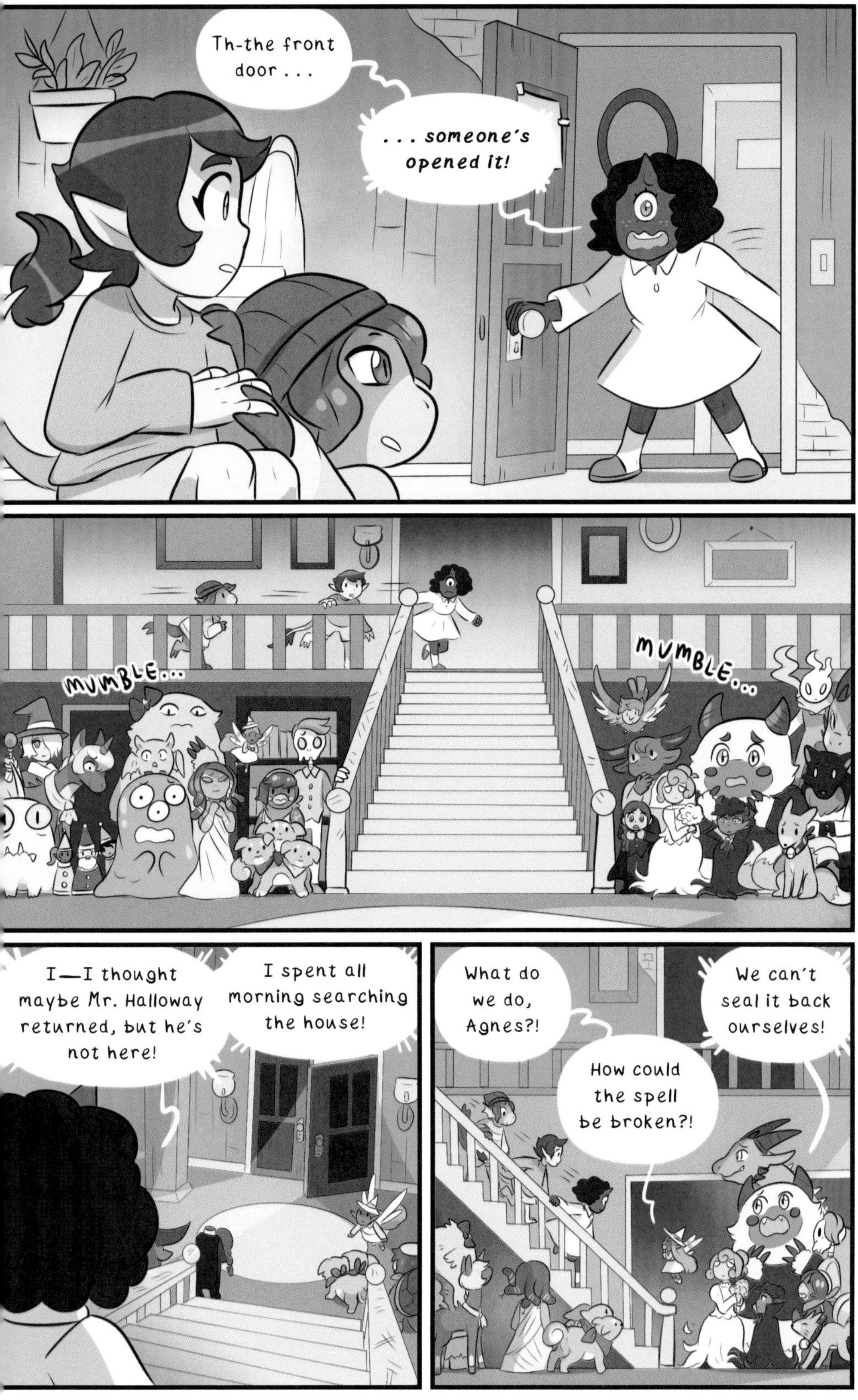

Th-the front door . . .
. . . someone's opened it!
MUMBLE...
MUMBLE...
I—I thought maybe Mr. Halloway returned, but he's not here!
I spent all morning searching the house!
What do we do, Agnes?!
How could the spell be broken?!
We can't seal it back ourselves!

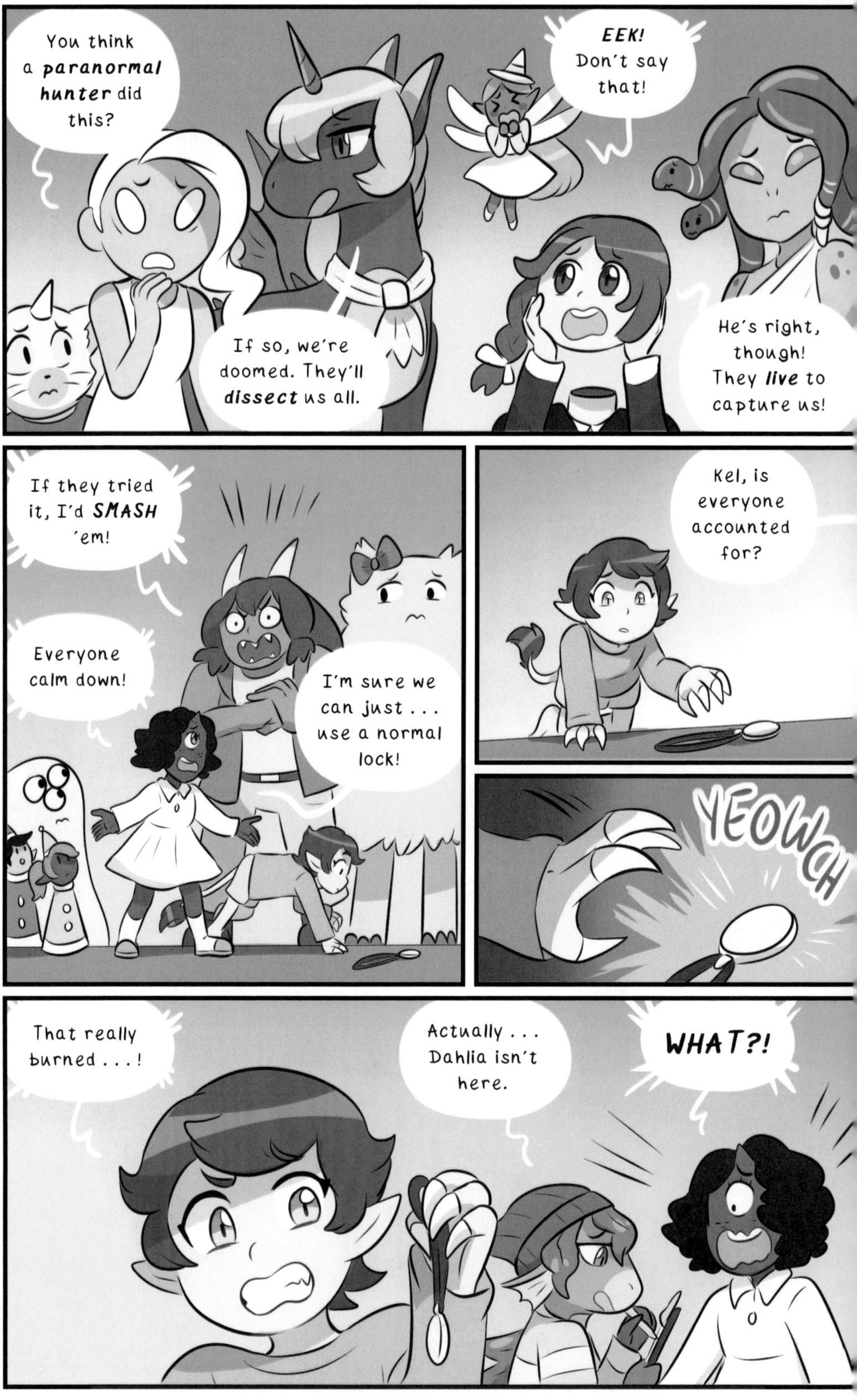

You think a **paranormal hunter** did this?
EEK! Don't say that!
If so, we're doomed. They'll ***dissect*** us all.
He's right, though! They ***live*** to capture us!
If they tried it, I'd ***SMASH*** 'em!
Everyone calm down!
I'm sure we can just . . . use a normal lock!
Kel, is everyone accounted for?
YEOWCH
That really burned . . . !
Actually . . . Dahlia isn't here.
WHAT?!

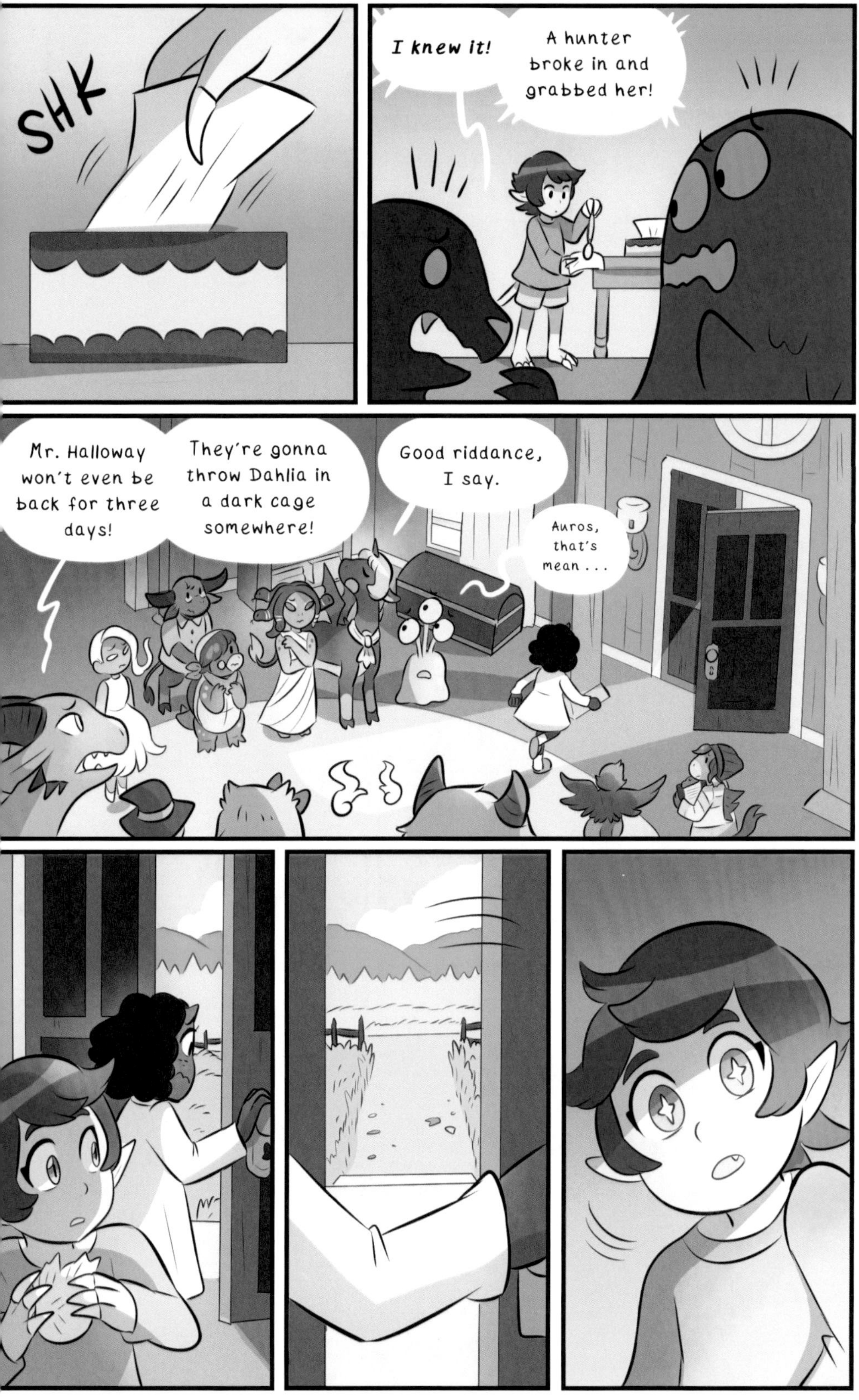
SHK
I knew it!
A hunter broke in and grabbed her!
Mr. Halloway won't even be back for three days!
They're gonna throw Dahlia in a dark cage somewhere!
Good riddance, I say.
Auros, that's mean . . .

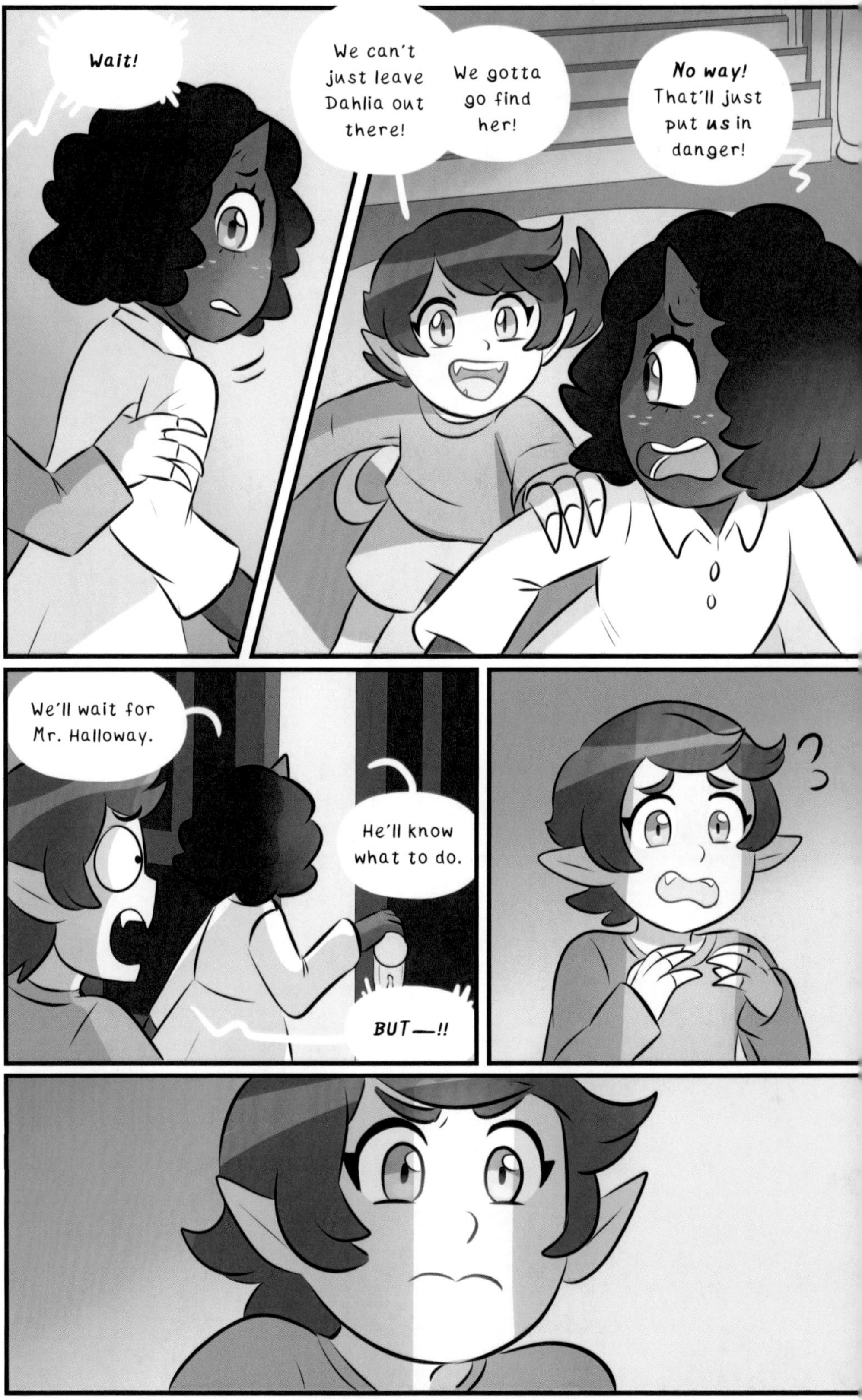
Wait!
We can't just leave Dahlia out there!
We gotta go find her!
No way! That'll just put us in danger!
We'll wait for Mr. Halloway.
He'll know what to do.
BUT—!!

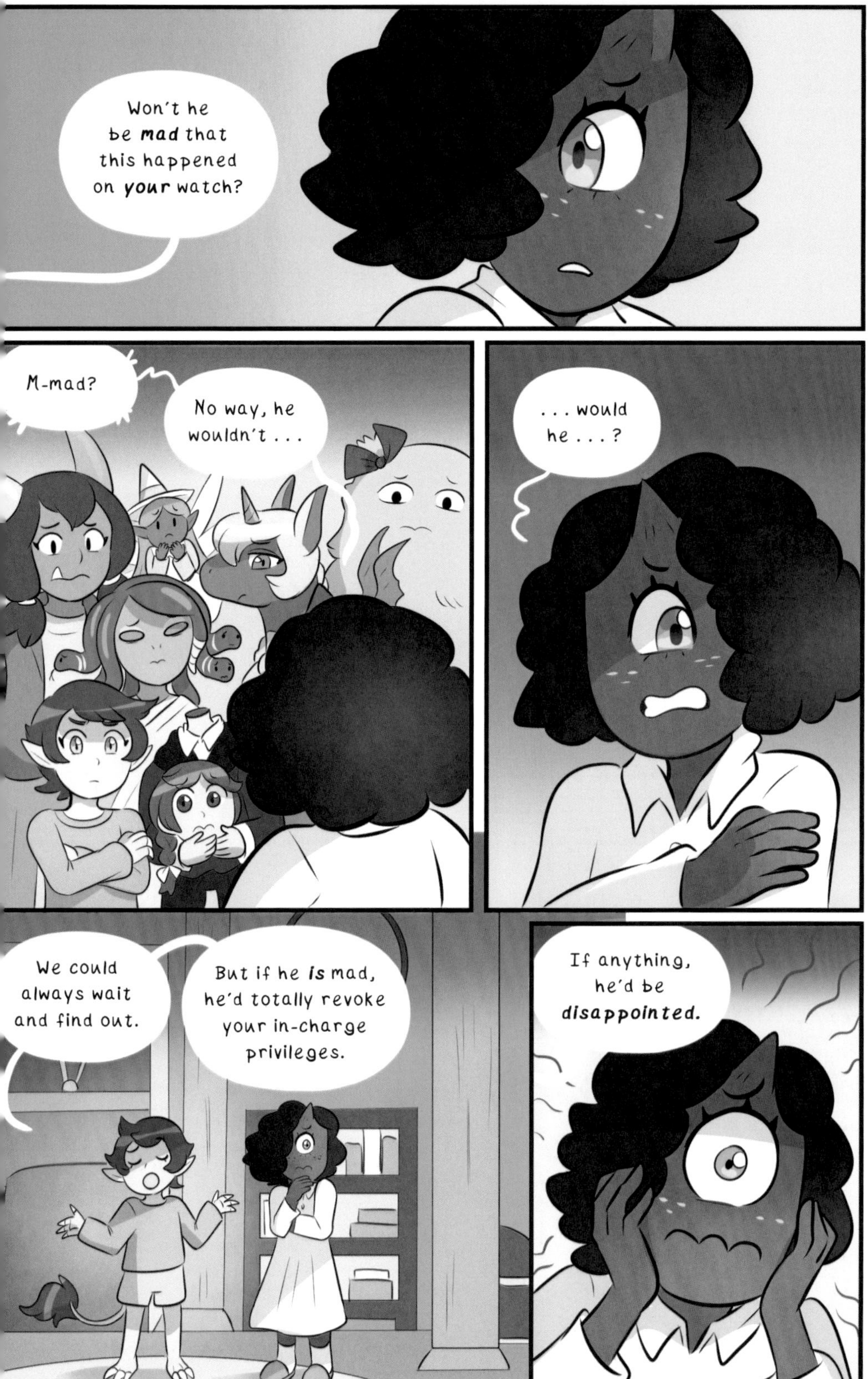
Won't he be **mad** that this happened on **your** watch?
M-mad?
No way, he wouldn't . . .
. . . would he . . . ?
We could always wait and find out.
But if he **is** mad, he'd totally revoke your in-charge privileges.
If anything, he'd be ***disappointed.***

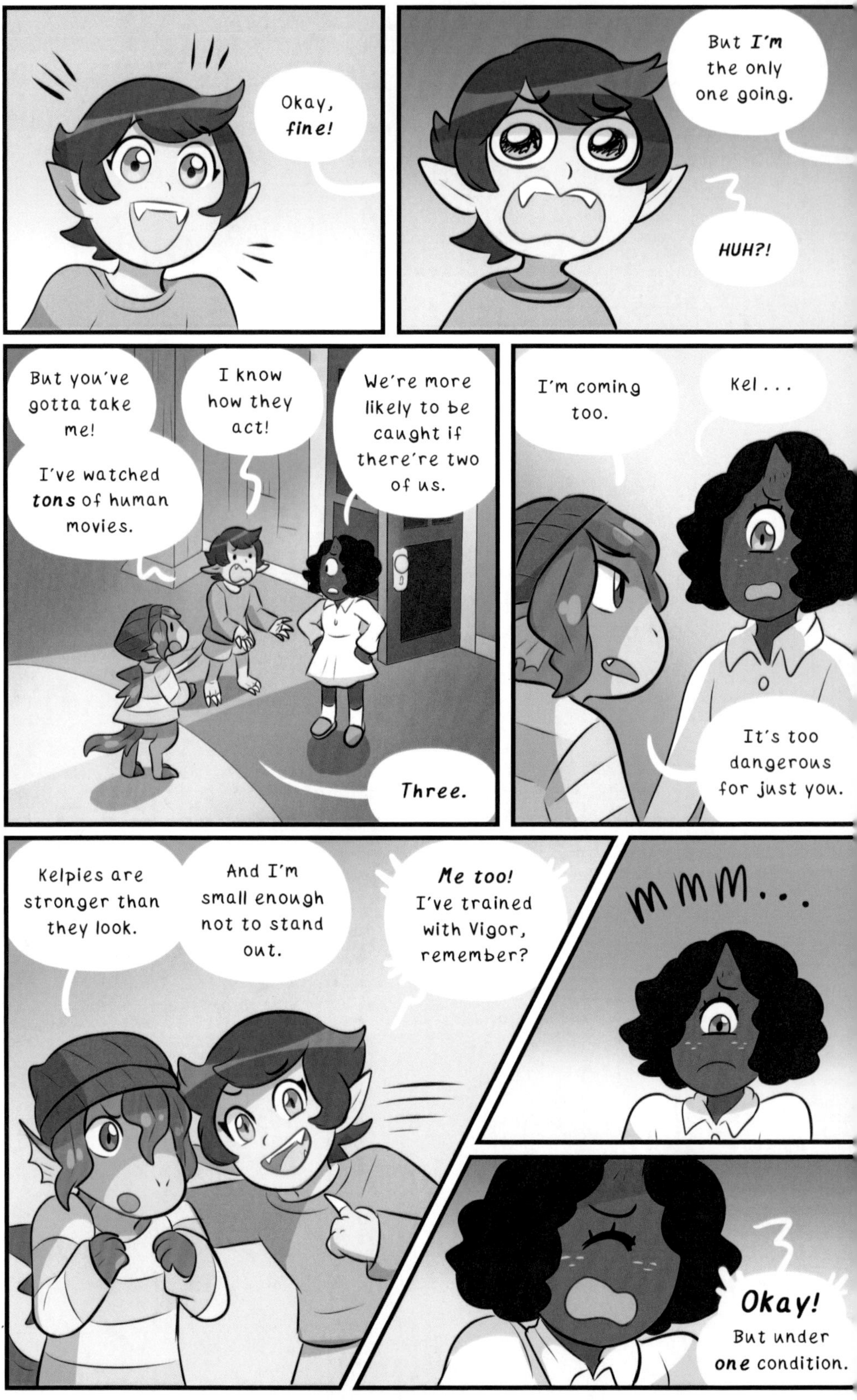
Okay, *fine!*
But *I'm* the only one going.
HUH?!
But you've gotta take me!
I've watched *tons* of human movies.
I know how they act!
We're more likely to be caught if there're two of us.
Three.
I'm coming too.
Kel . . .
It's too dangerous for just you.
Kelpies are stronger than they look.
And I'm small enough not to stand out.
Me too! I've trained with Vigor, remember?
MMM . . .
Okay! But under *one* condition.

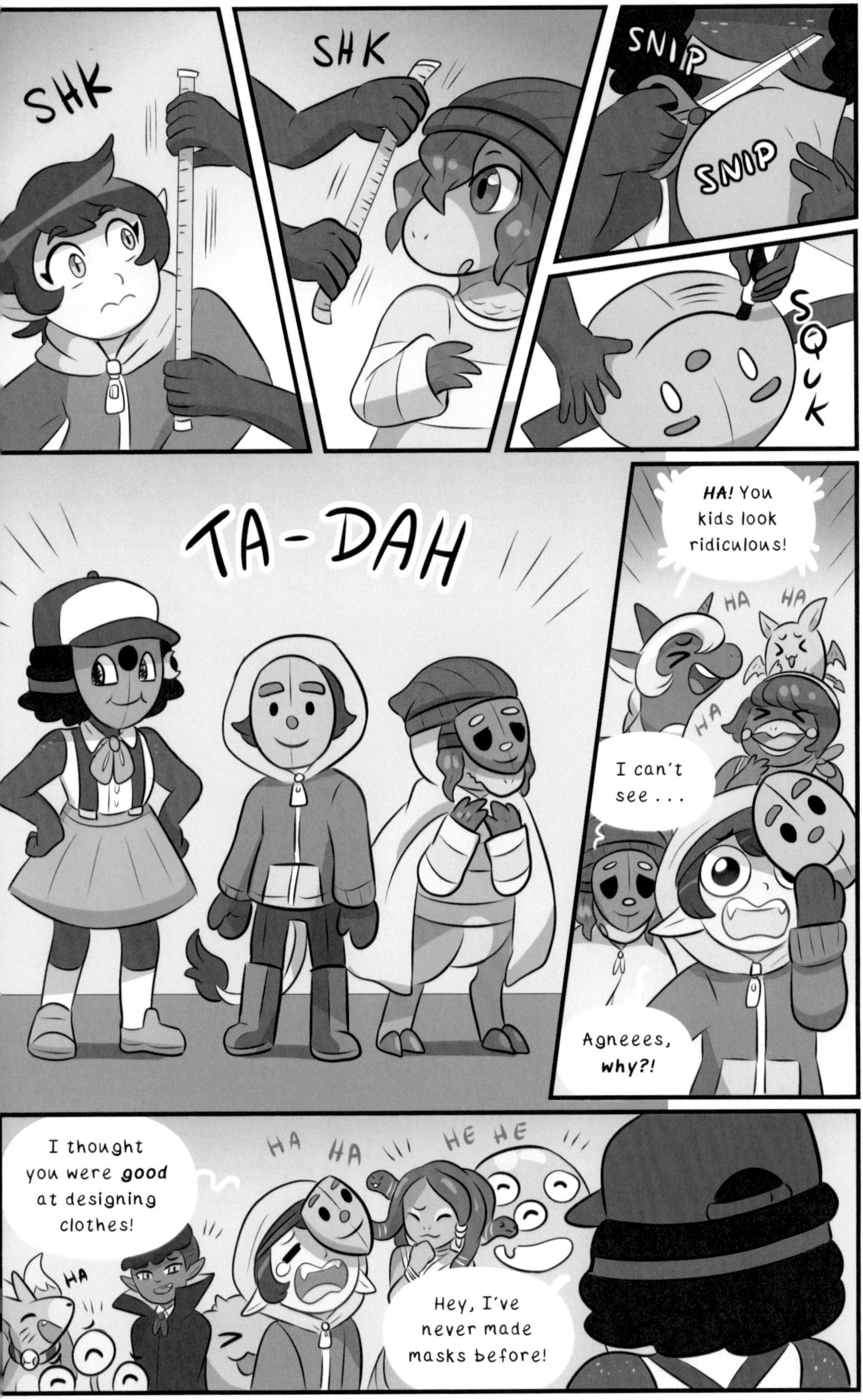
SHK
SHK
SNIP
SNIP
SQUK
TA-DAH
HA! You kids look ridiculous!
HA
HA
HA
I can't see . . .
Agneees, why?!
I thought you were good at designing clothes!
HA
HA
HE HE
HA
Hey, I've never made masks before!

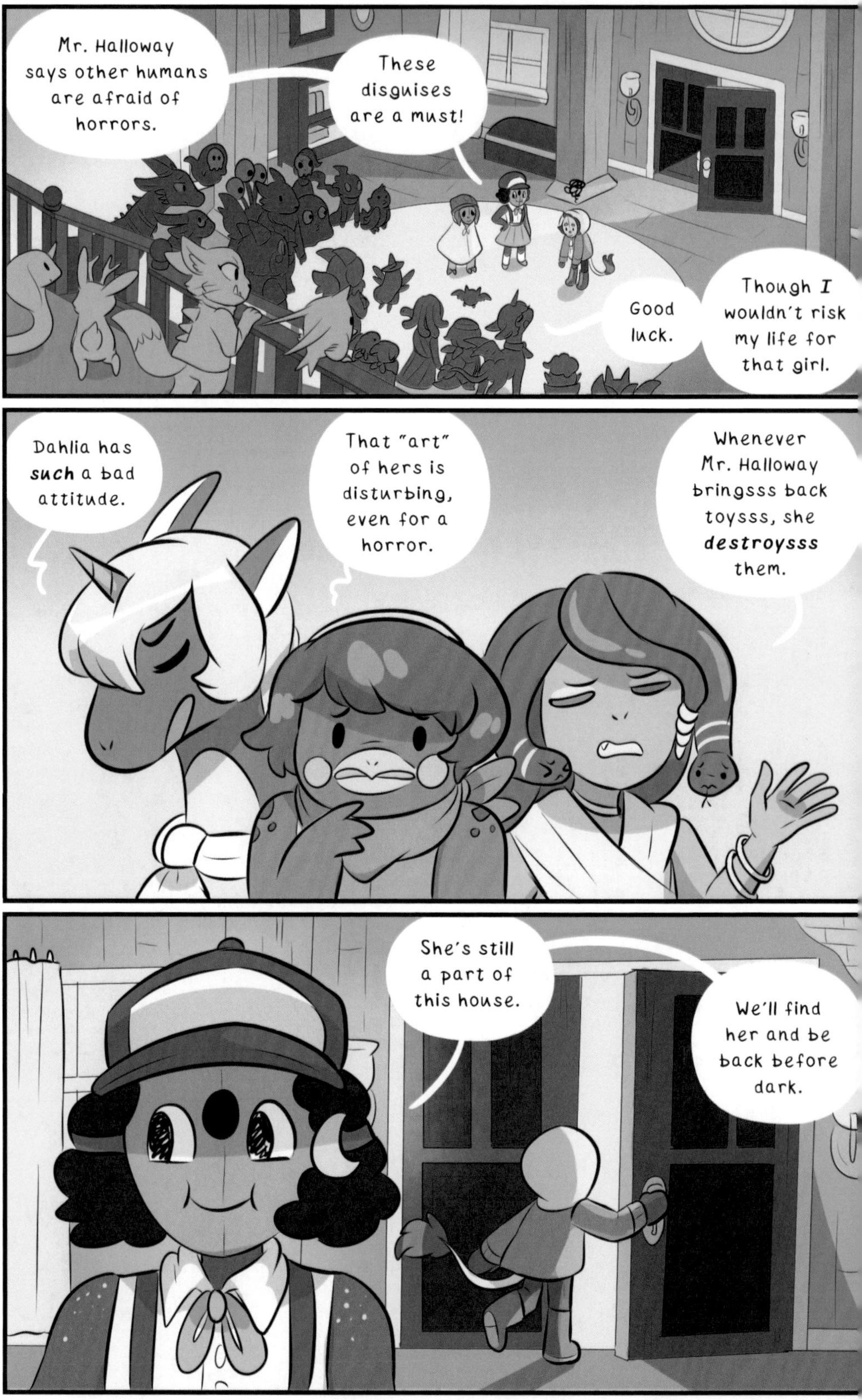
Mr. Halloway says other humans are afraid of horrors.
These disguises are a must!
Good luck.
Though *I* wouldn't risk my life for that girl.
Dahlia has **such** a bad attitude.
That "art" of hers is disturbing, even for a horror.
Whenever Mr. Halloway bringsss back toysss, she ***destroysss*** them.
She's still a part of this house.
We'll find her and be back before dark.

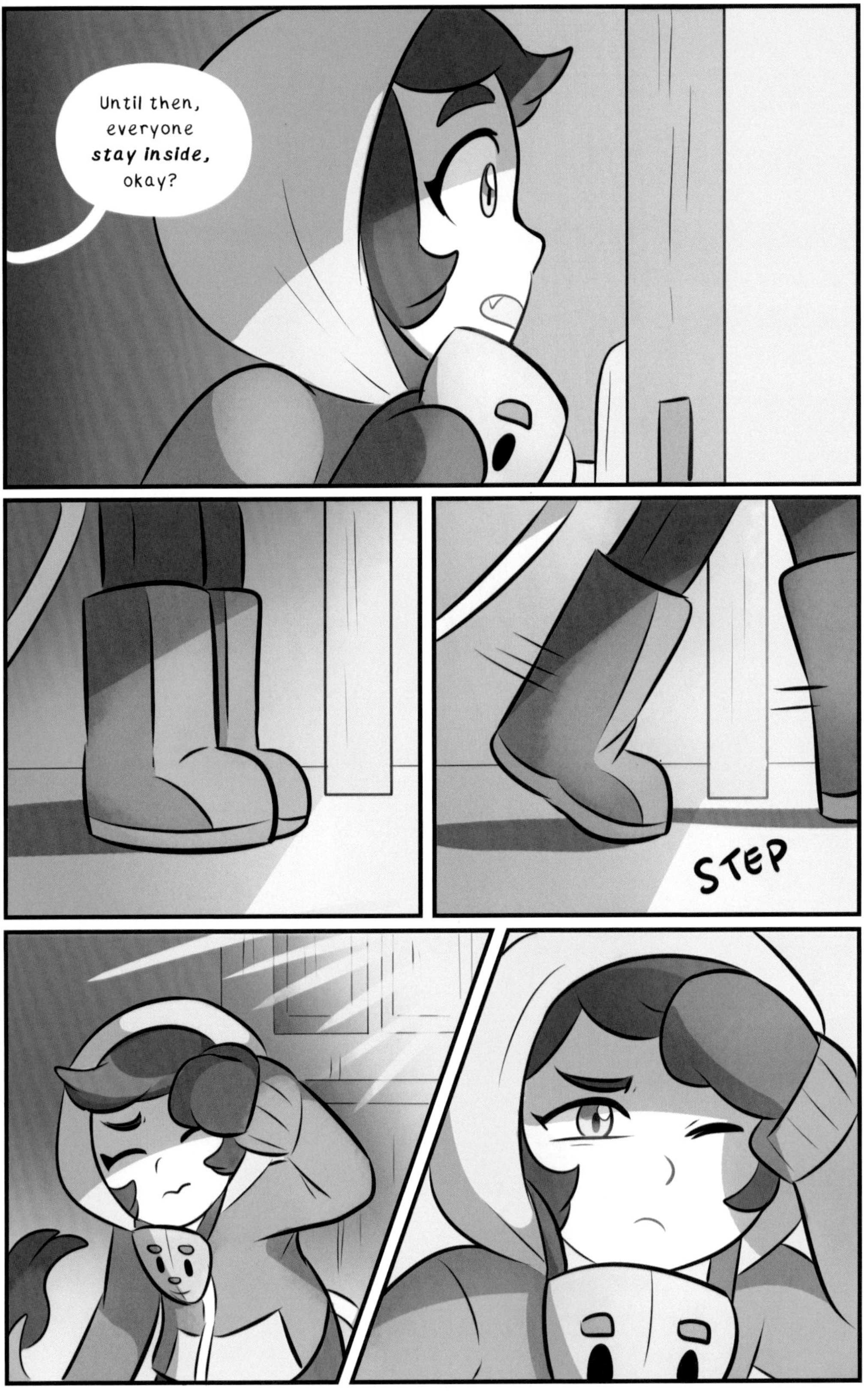
Until then, everyone **stay inside,** okay?
STEP

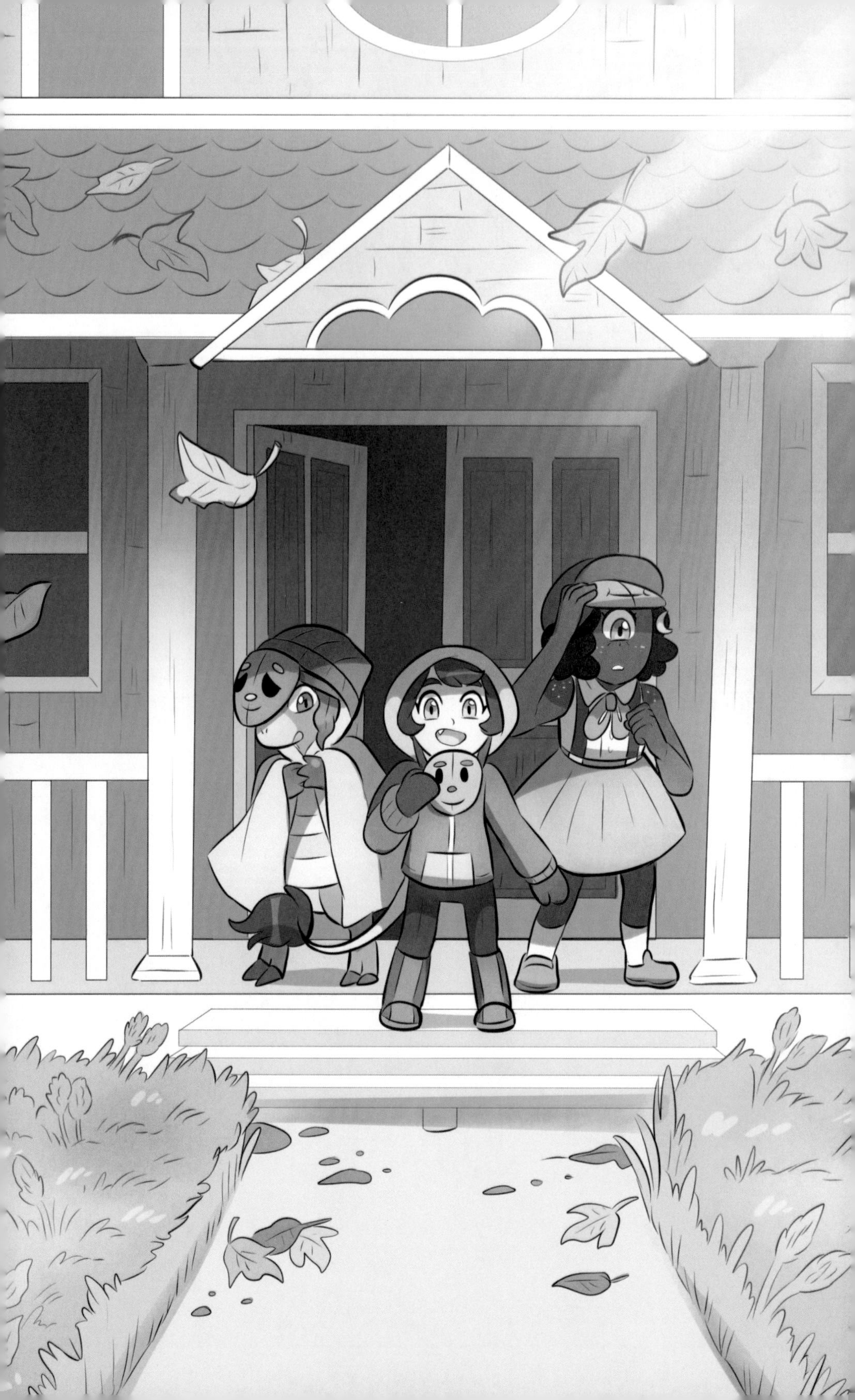

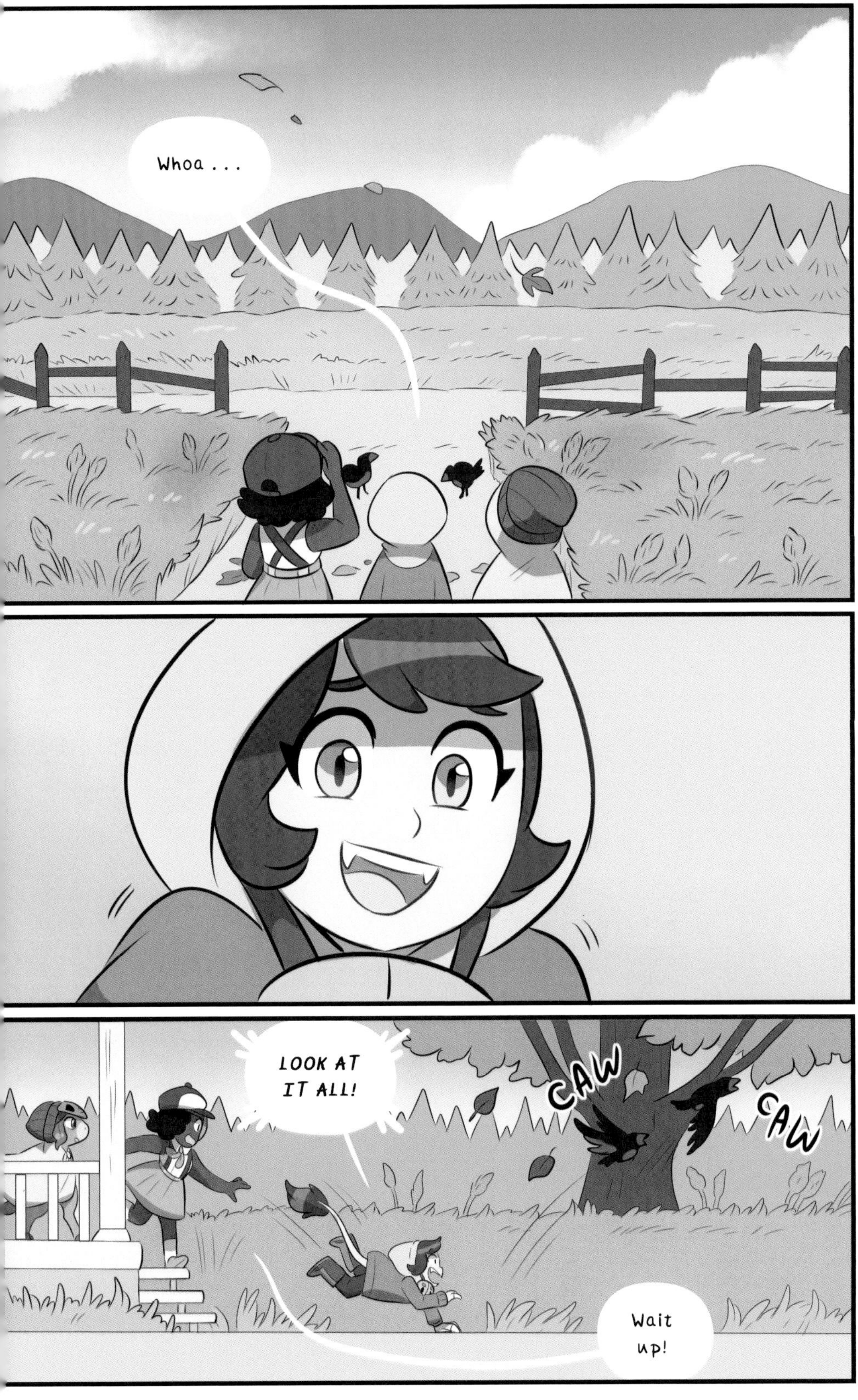

Whoa . . .
LOOK AT IT ALL!
CAW
CAW
Wait up!

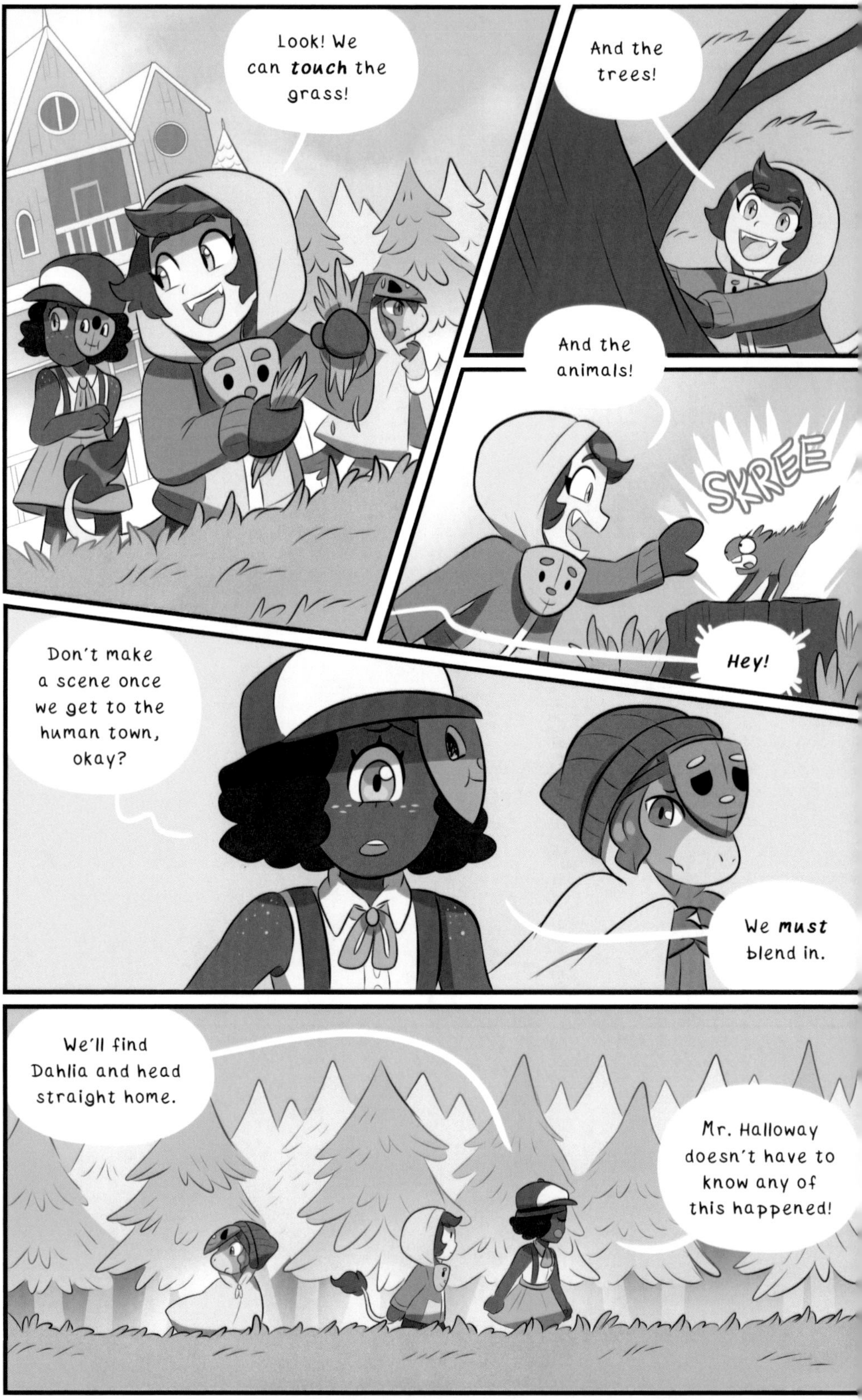
Look! We can **touch** the grass!
And the trees!
And the animals!
SKREE
Hey!
Don't make a scene once we get to the human town, okay?
We **must** blend in.
We'll find Dahlia and head straight home.
Mr. Halloway doesn't have to know any of this happened!

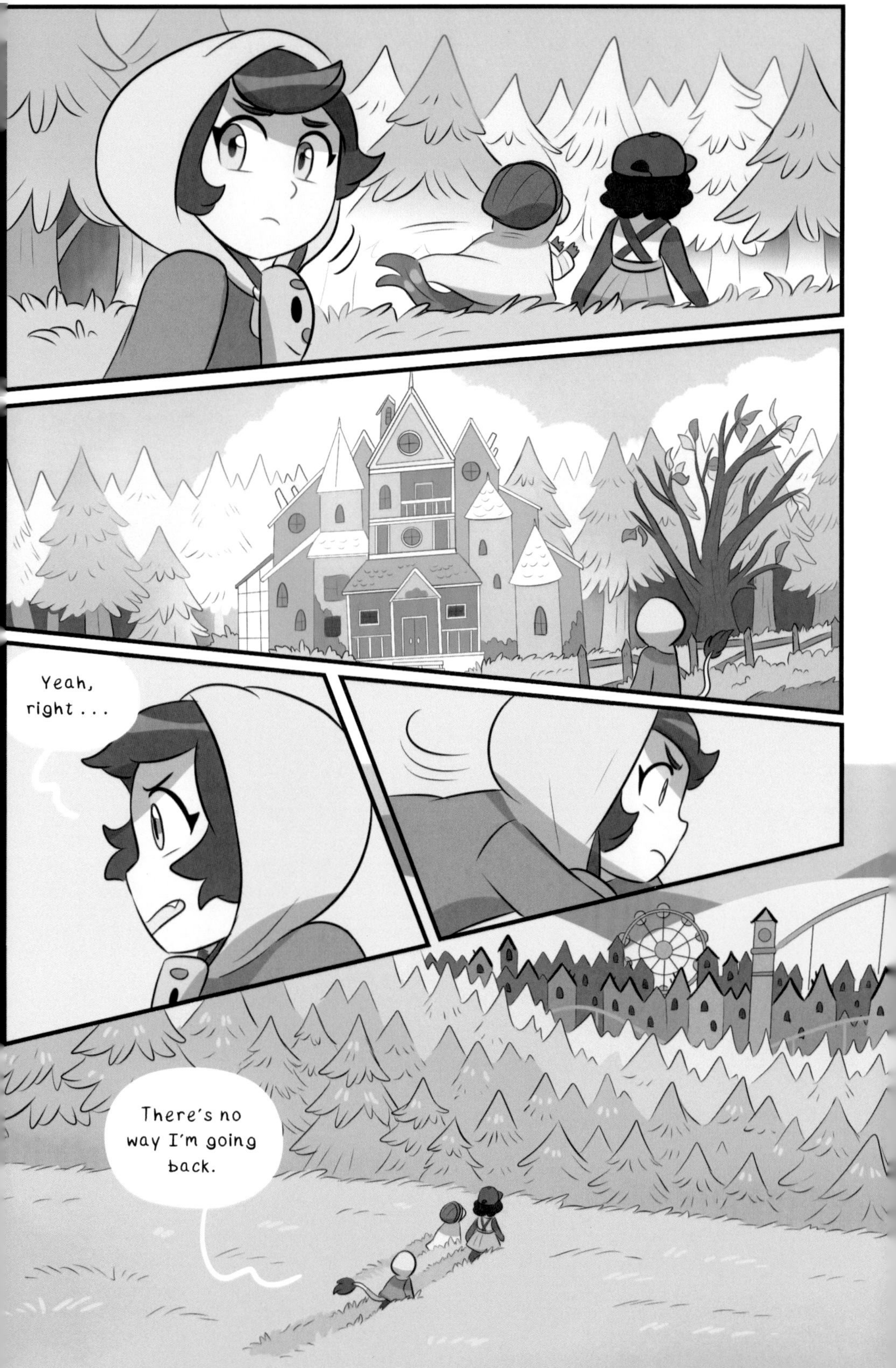
Yeah, right . . .
There's no way I'm going back.

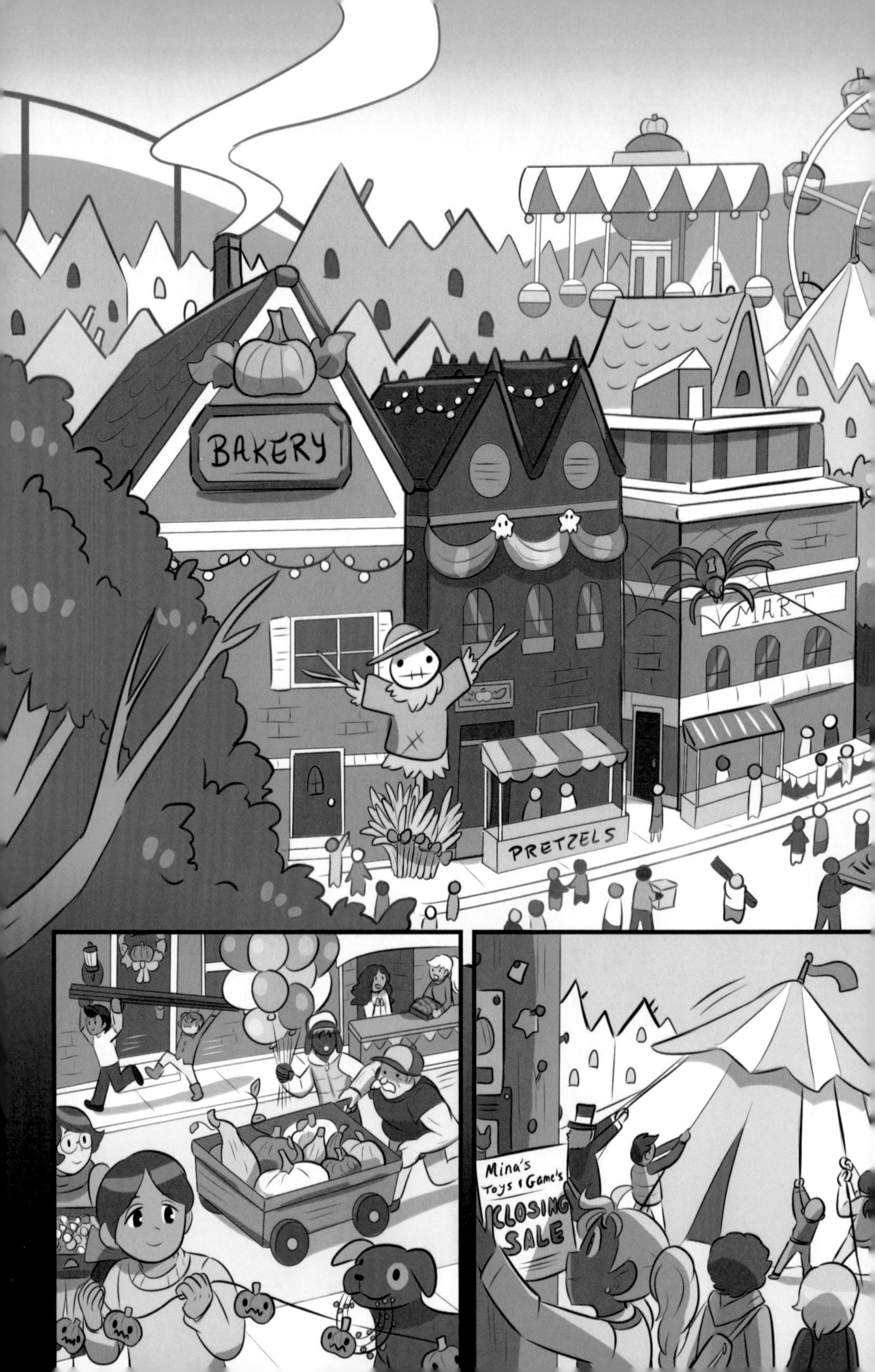
BAKERY
MART
PRETZELS
Mina's Toys & Game's
CLOSING SALE

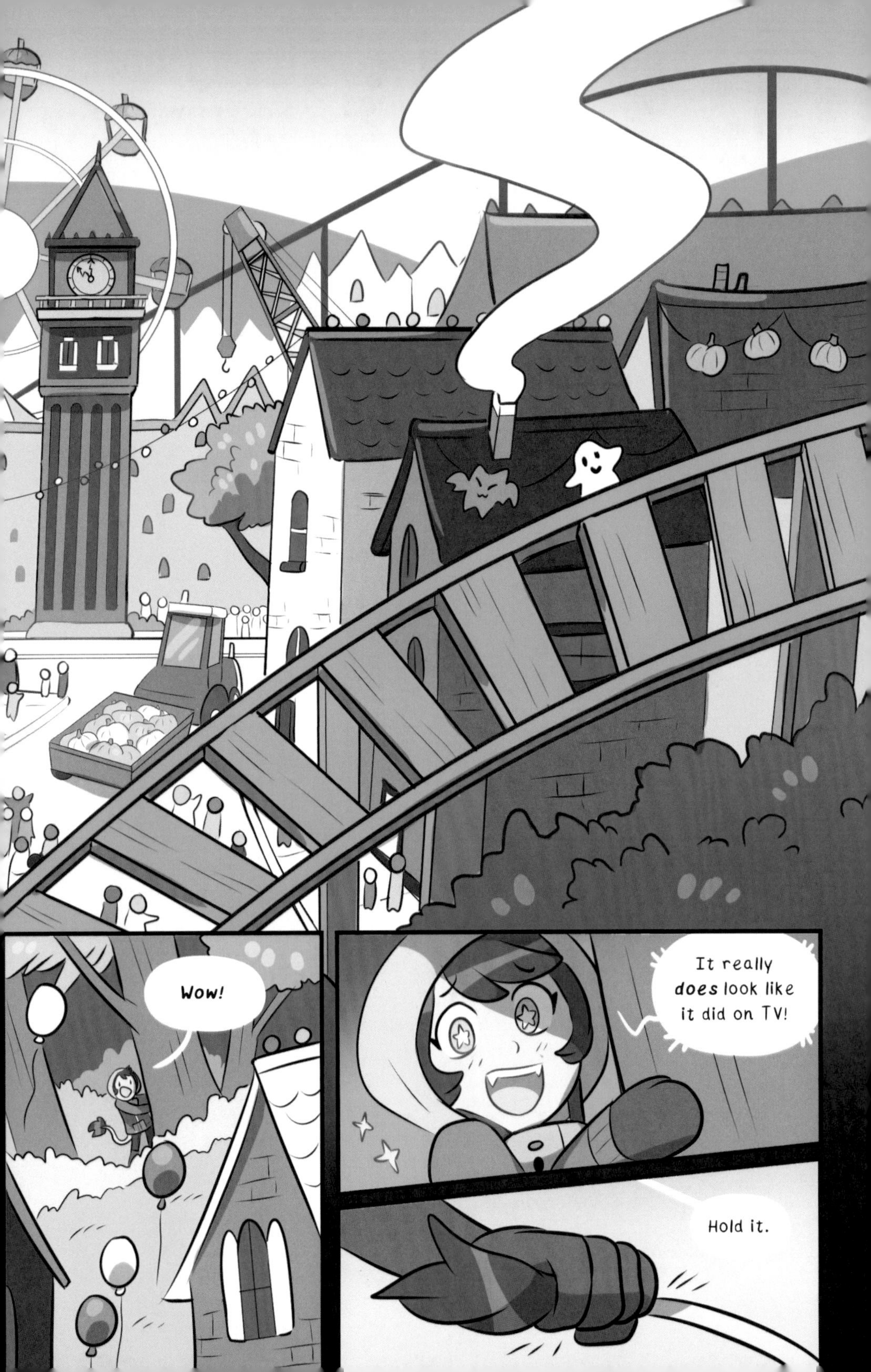
Wow!
It really does look like it did on TV!
Hold it.

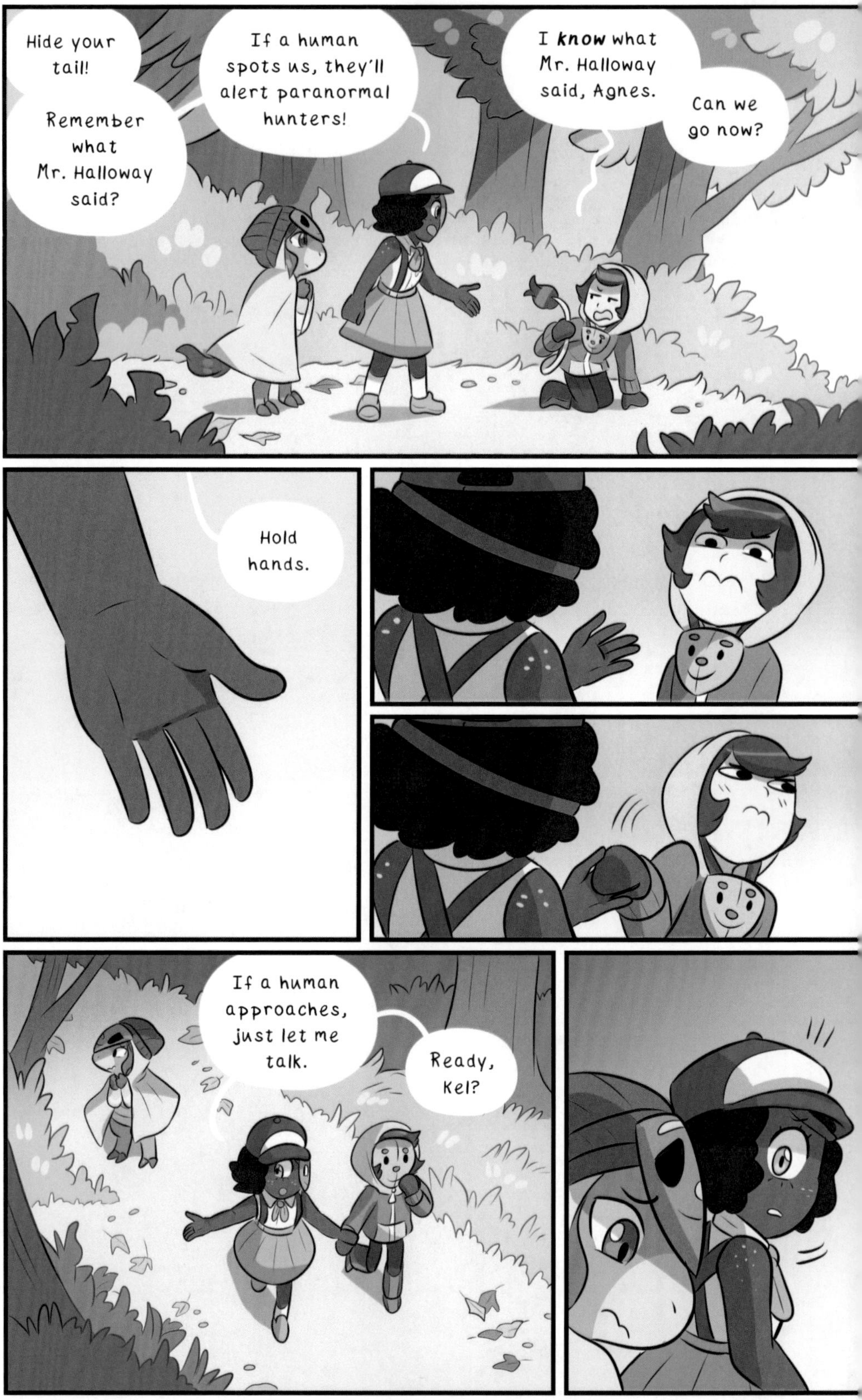
Hide your tail!
Remember what Mr. Halloway said?
If a human spots us, they'll alert paranormal hunters!
I **know** what Mr. Halloway said, Agnes.
Can we go now?
Hold hands.
If a human approaches, just let me talk.
Ready, Kel?

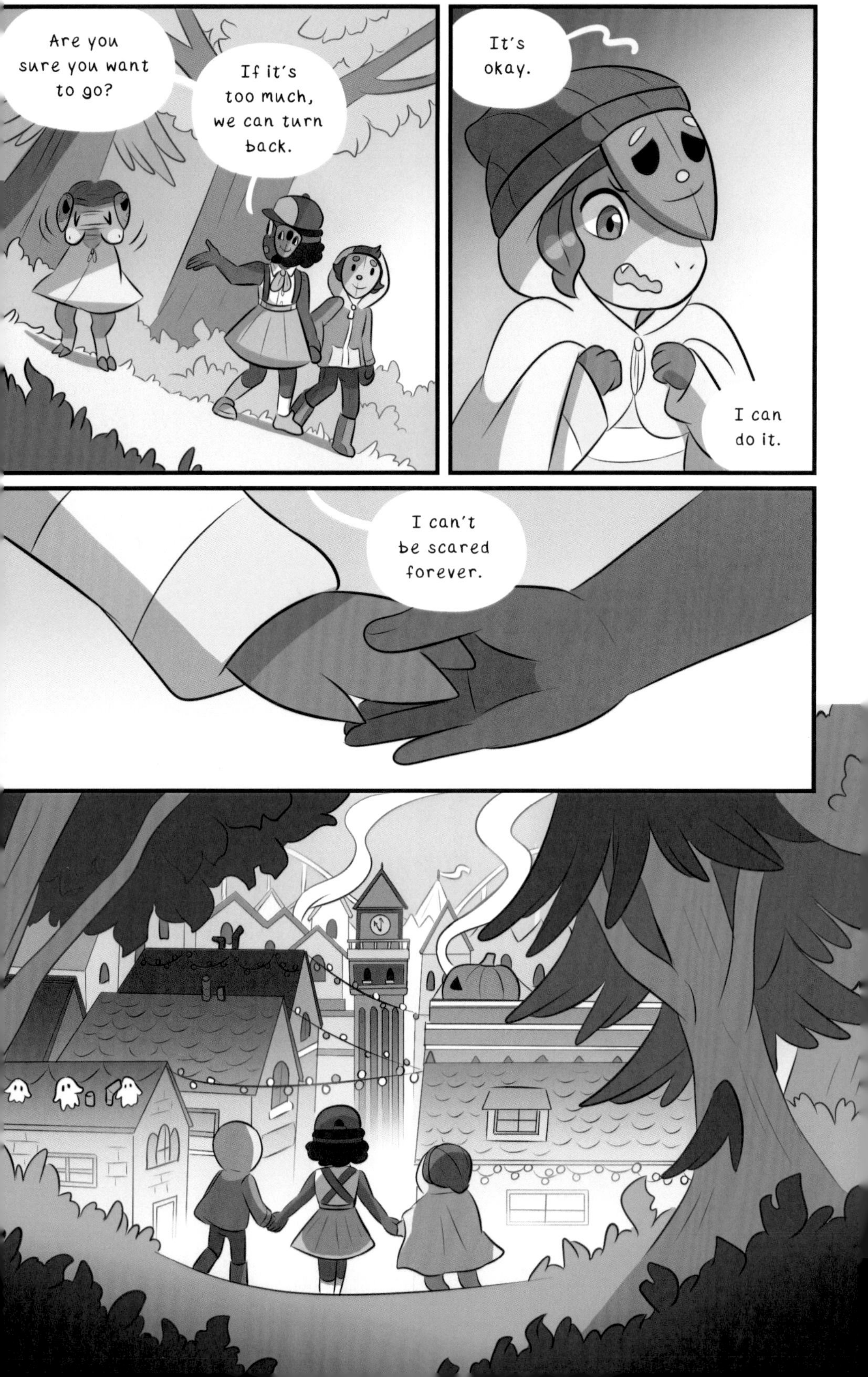
Are you sure you want to go?
If it's too much, we can turn back.
It's okay.
I can do it.
I can't be scared forever.

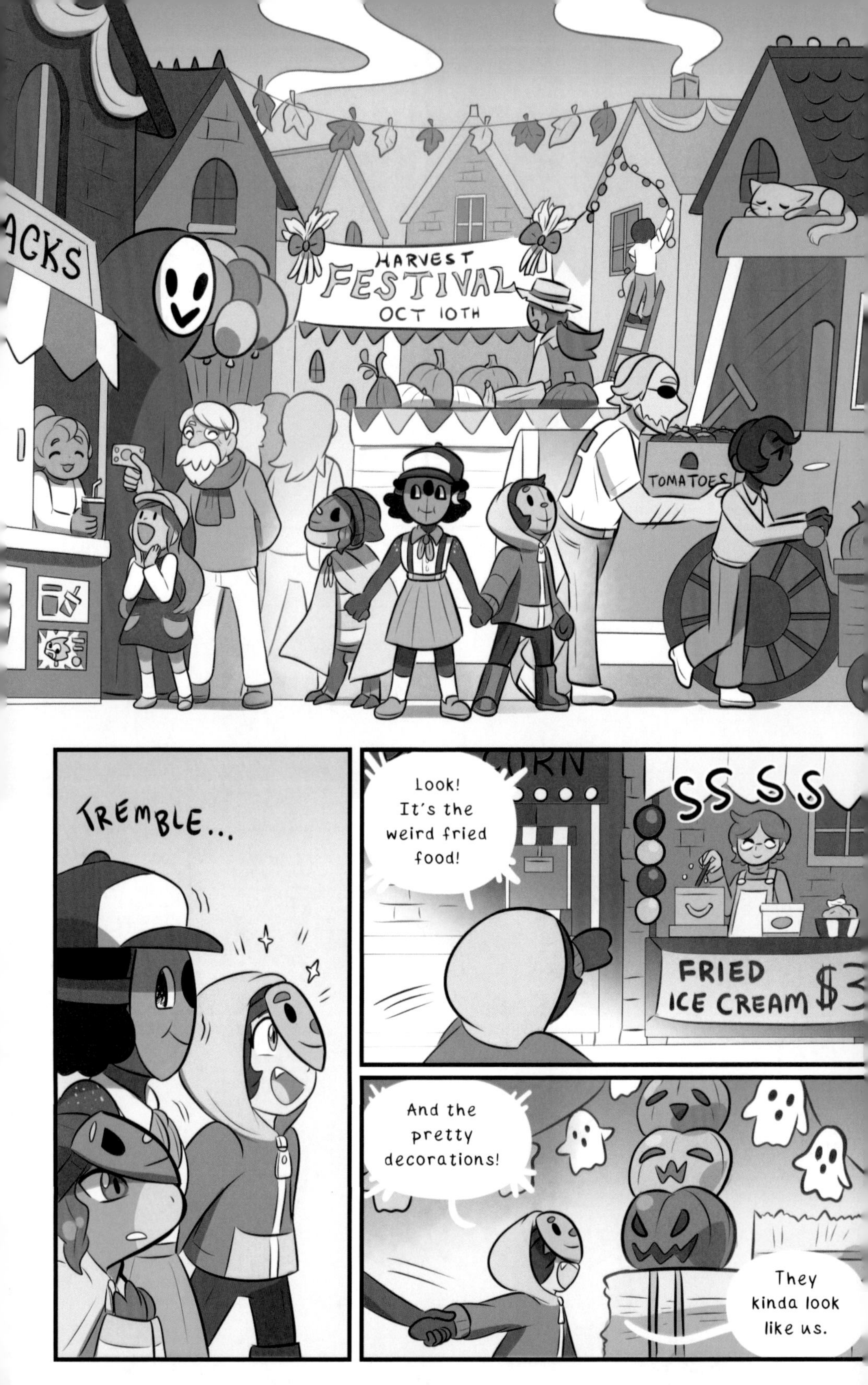
HARVEST
FESTIVAL
OCT 10TH
TOMATOES
TREMBLE...
Look! It's the weird fried food!
SSSS
FRIED ICE CREAM
And the pretty decorations!
They kinda look like us.

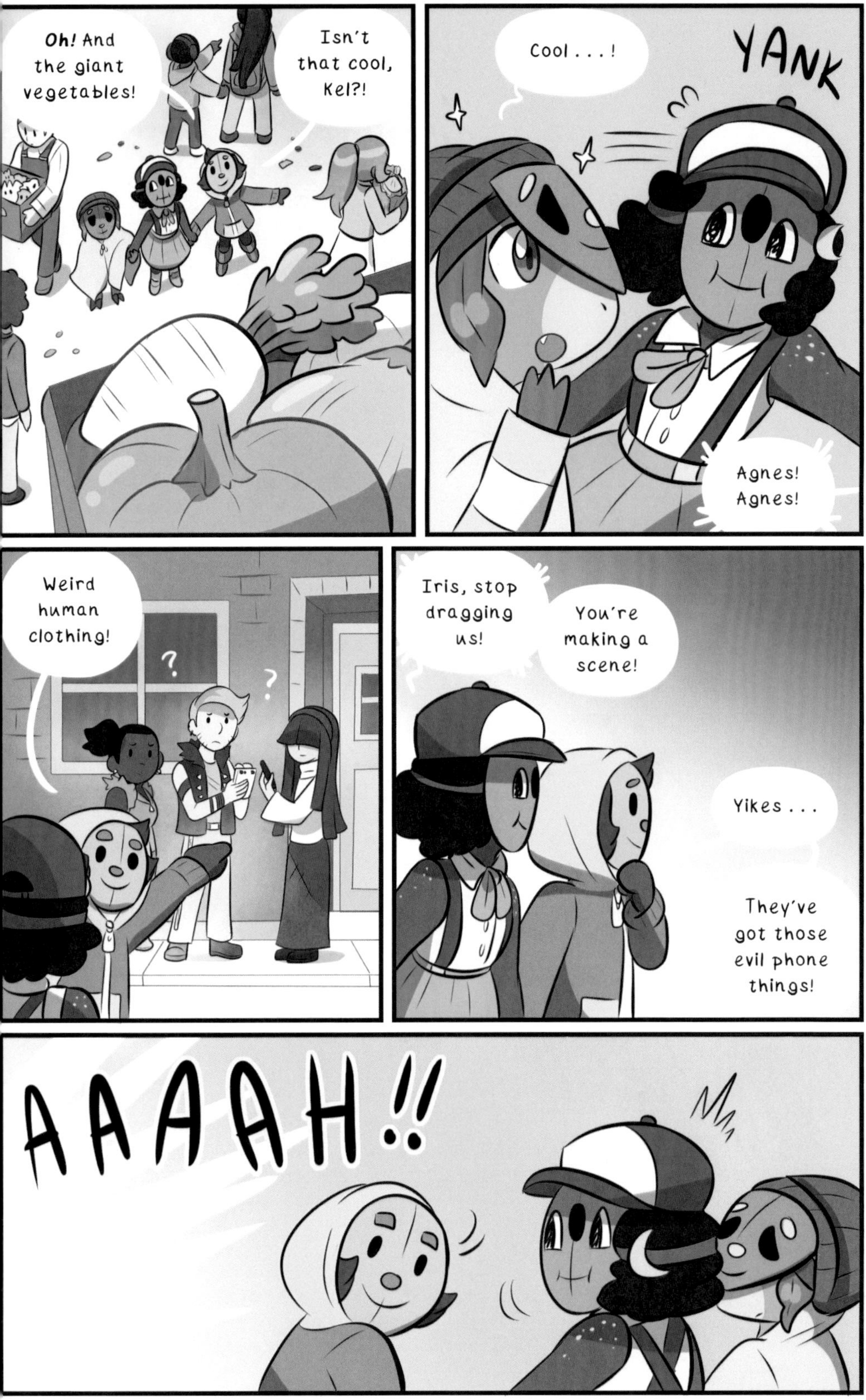

Oh! And the giant vegetables!
Isn't that cool, Kel?!
Cool . . . !
YANK
Agnes! Agnes!
Weird human clothing!
Iris, stop dragging us!
You're making a scene!
Yikes . . .
They've got those evil phone things!
AAAAH!!

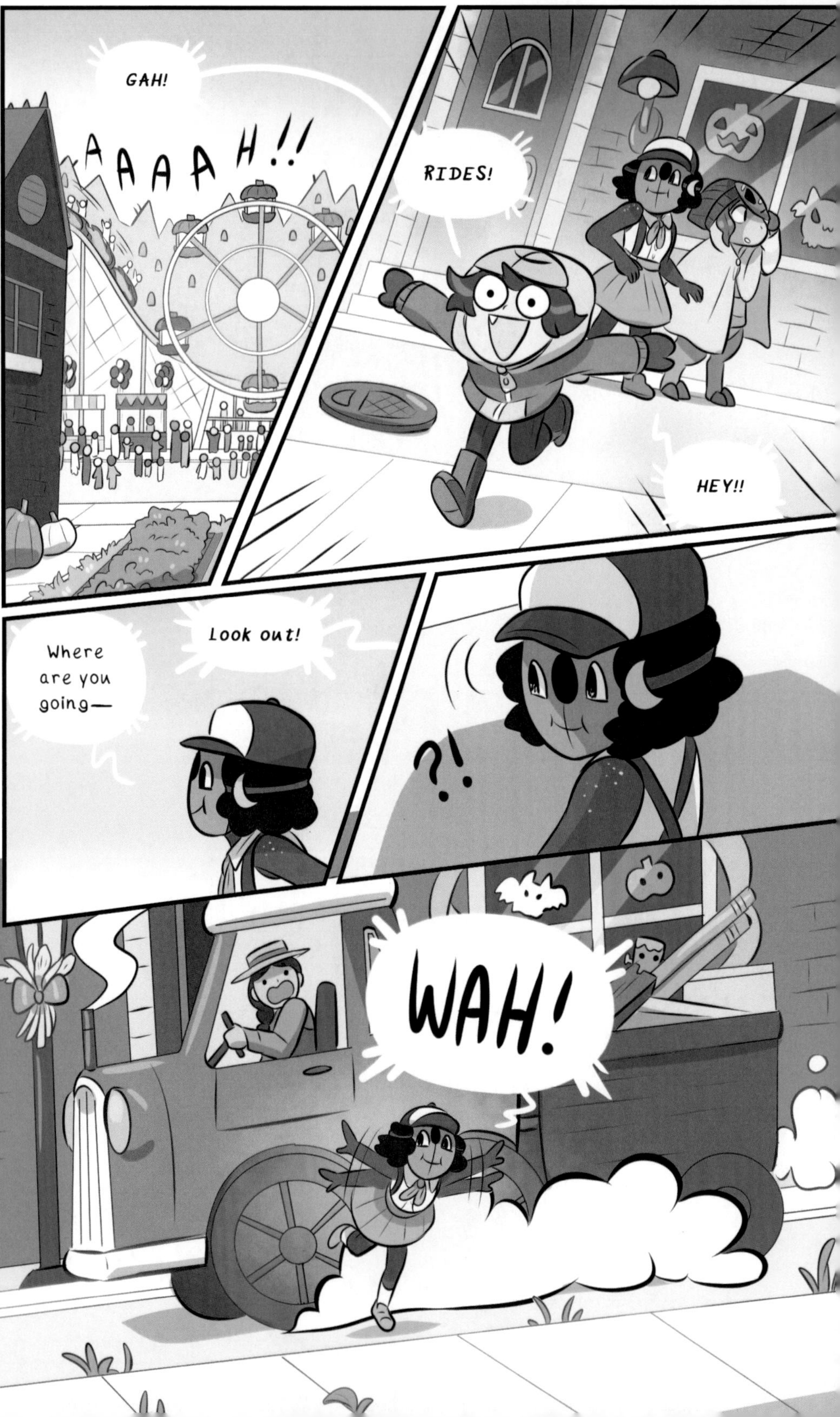
GAH!
AAAAH!!
RIDES!
HEY!!
Where are you going—
Look out!
?!
WAH!

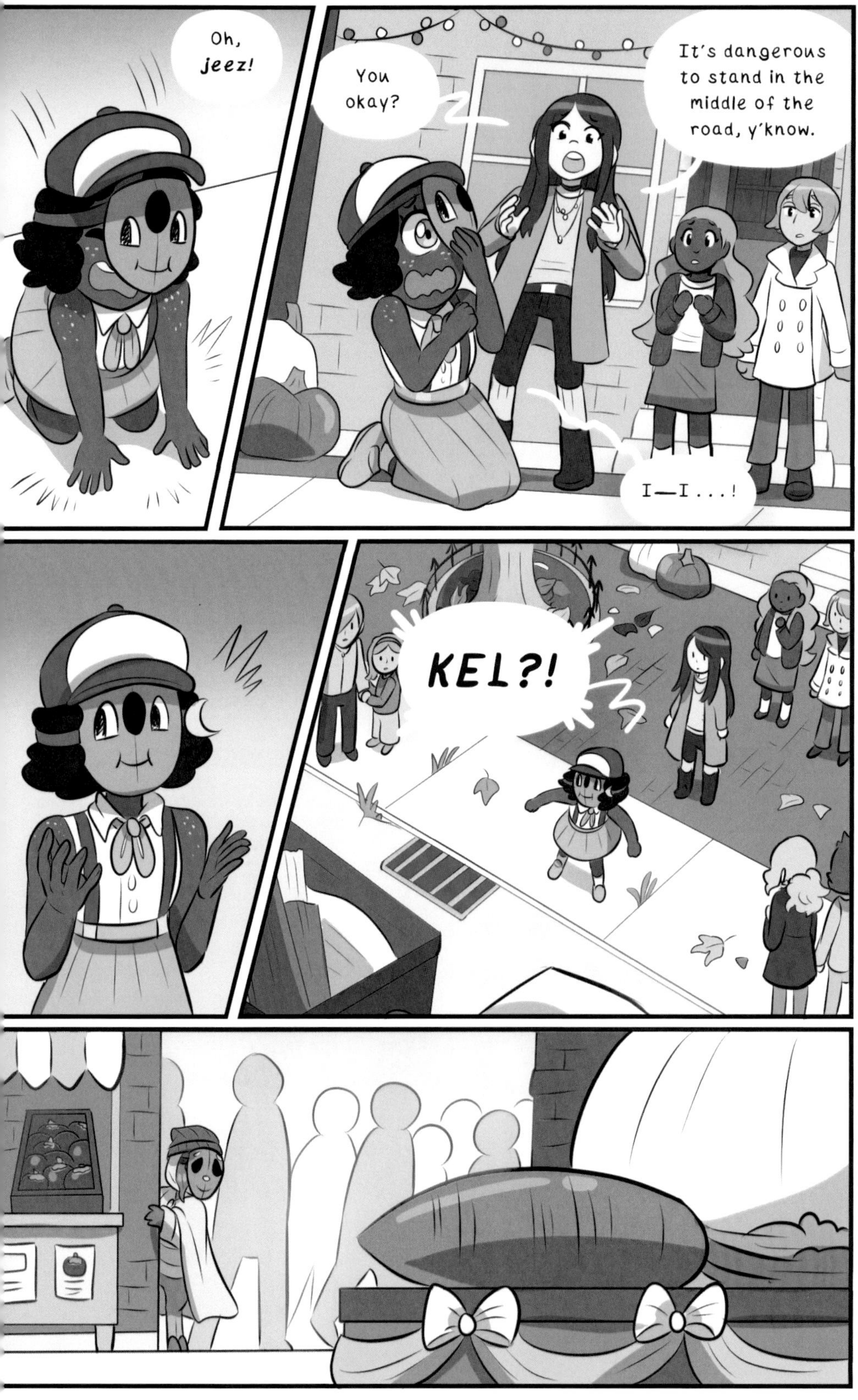
Oh, jeez!
You okay?
It's dangerous to stand in the middle of the road, y'know.
I—I . . . !
KEL?!

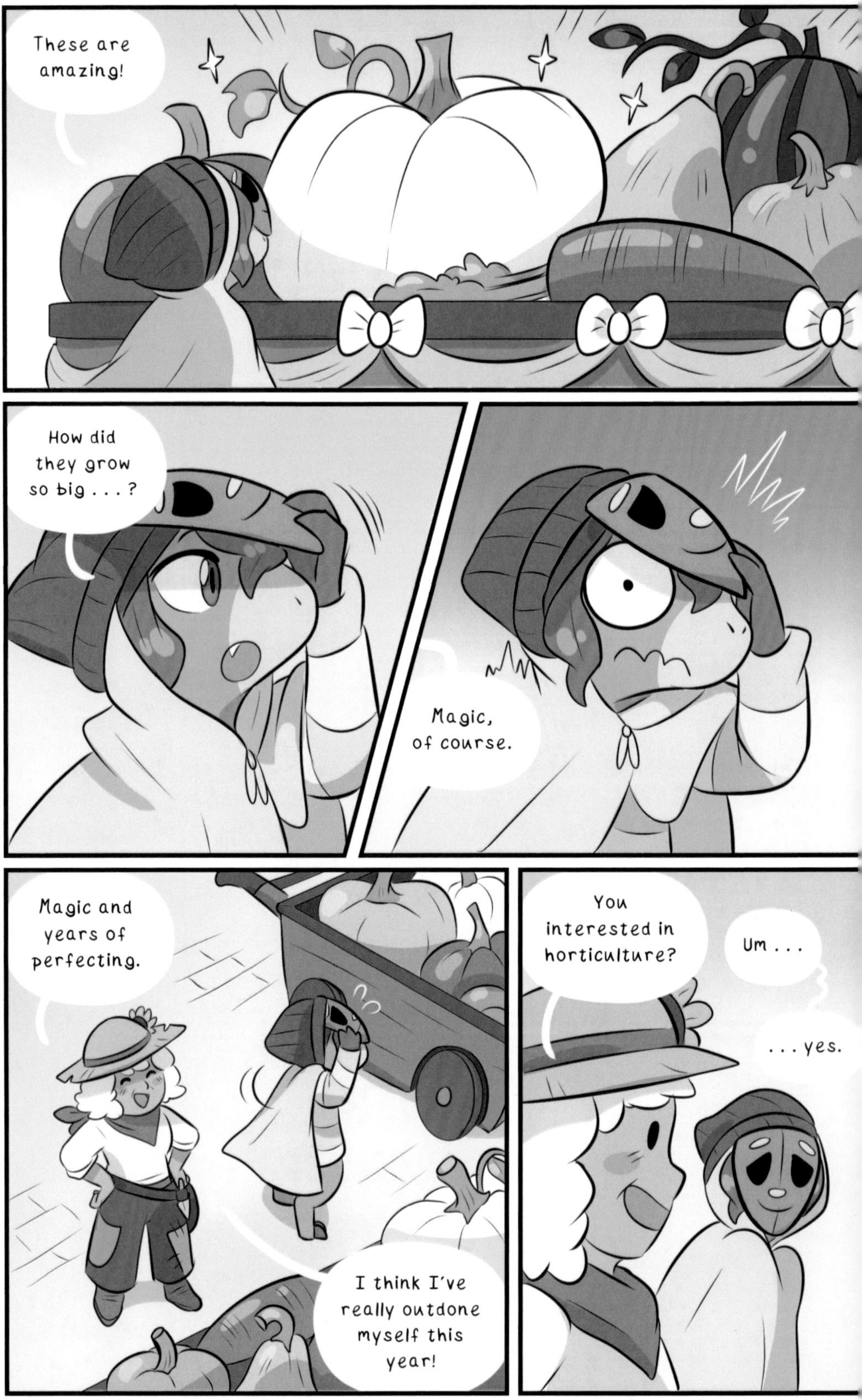
These are amazing!
How did they grow so big . . . ?
Magic, of course.
Magic and years of perfecting.
I think I've really outdone myself this year!
You interested in horticulture?
Um . . .
. . . yes.

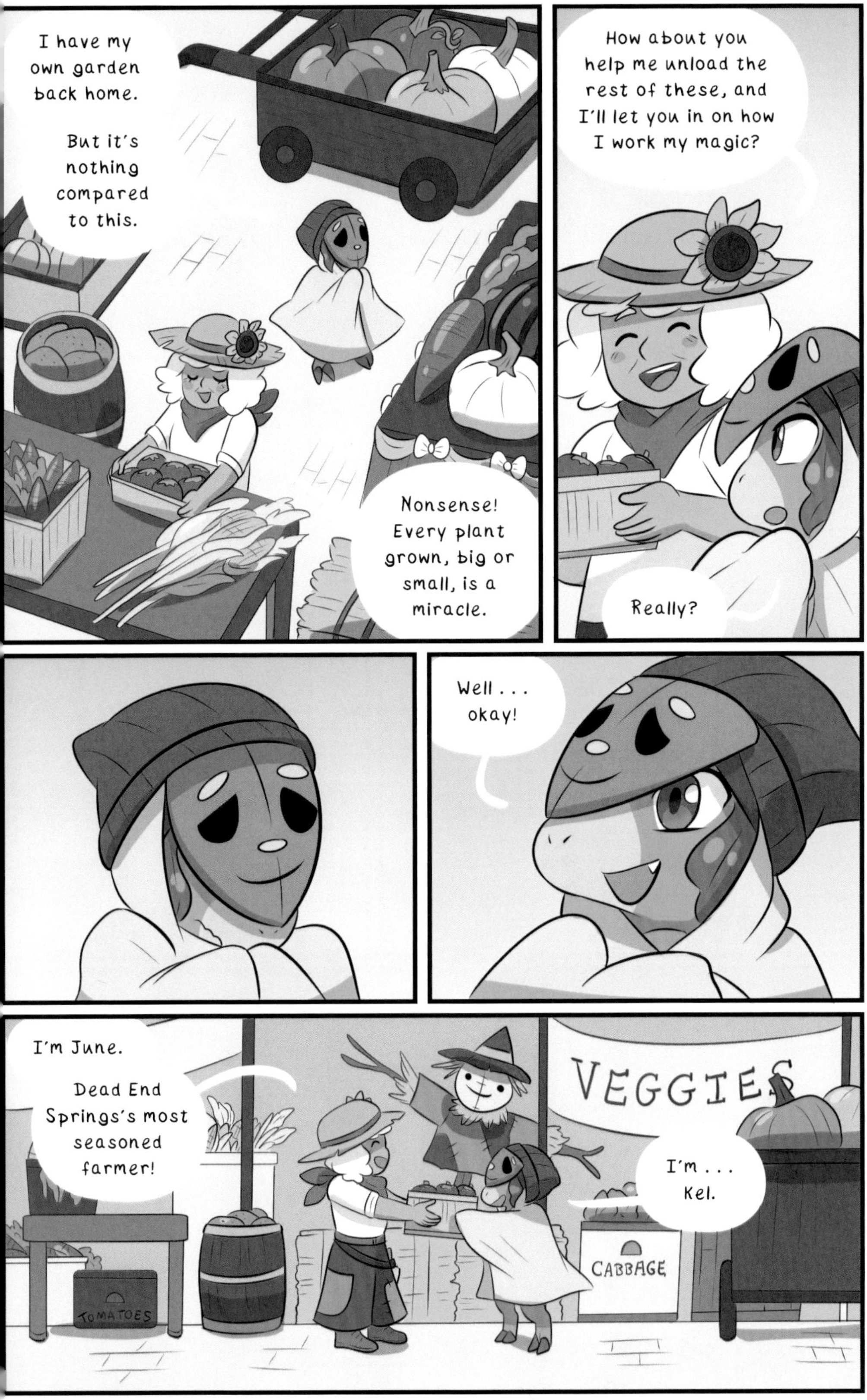
I have my own garden back home.
But it's nothing compared to this.
Nonsense! Every plant grown, big or small, is a miracle.
How about you help me unload the rest of these, and I'll let you in on how I work my magic?
Really?
Well . . . okay!
I'm June.
Dead End Springs's most seasoned farmer!
VEGGIES
I'm . . . Kel.
CABBAGE
TOMATOES

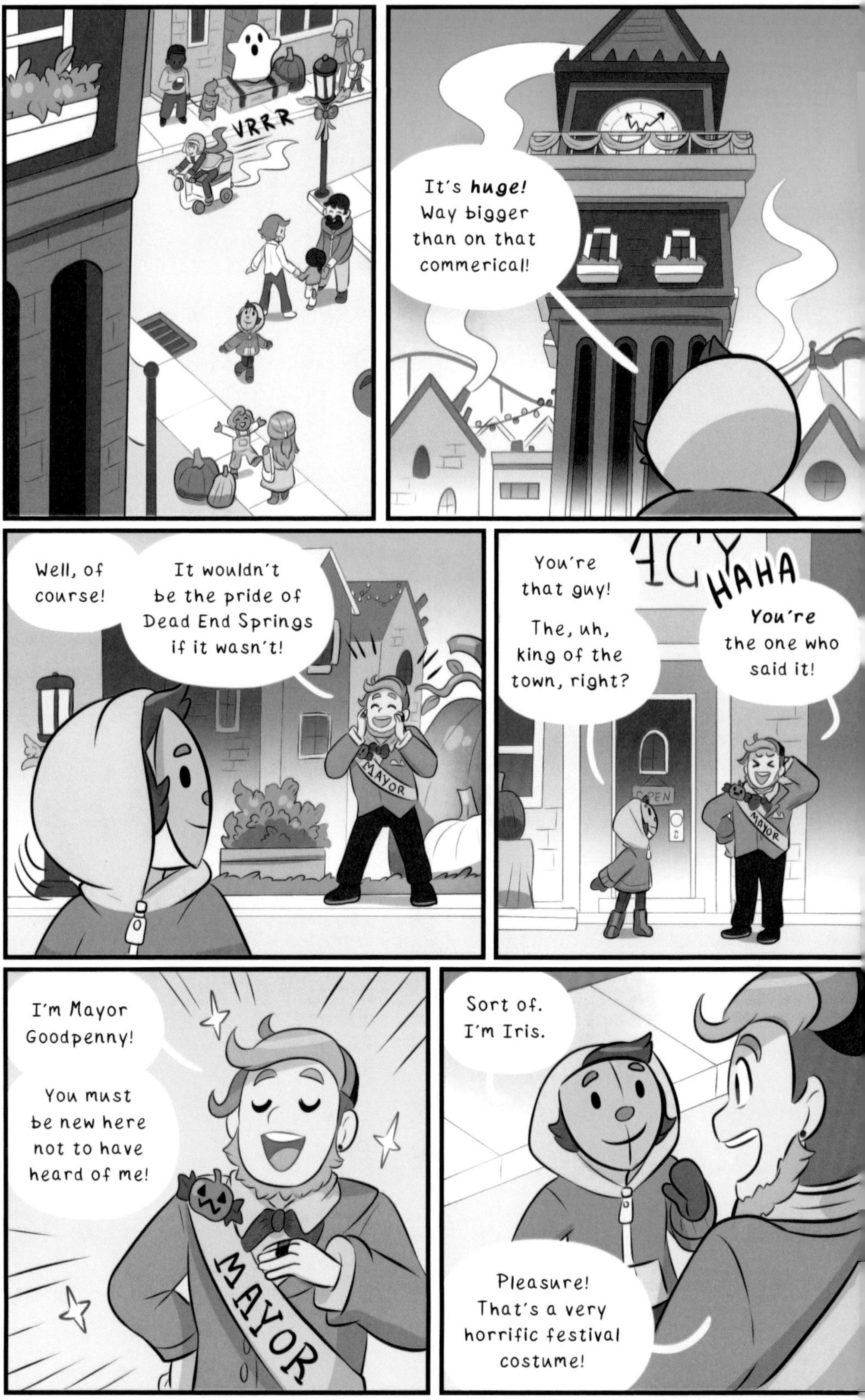
VRRR
It's **huge!** Way bigger than on that commerical!
Well, of course!
It wouldn't be the pride of Dead End Springs if it wasn't!
MAYOR
You're that guy!
The, uh, king of the town, right?
HAHA
You're the one who said it!
OPEN
MAYOR
I'm Mayor Goodpenny!
You must be new here not to have heard of me!
MAYOR
Sort of. I'm Iris.
Pleasure! That's a very horrific festival costume!

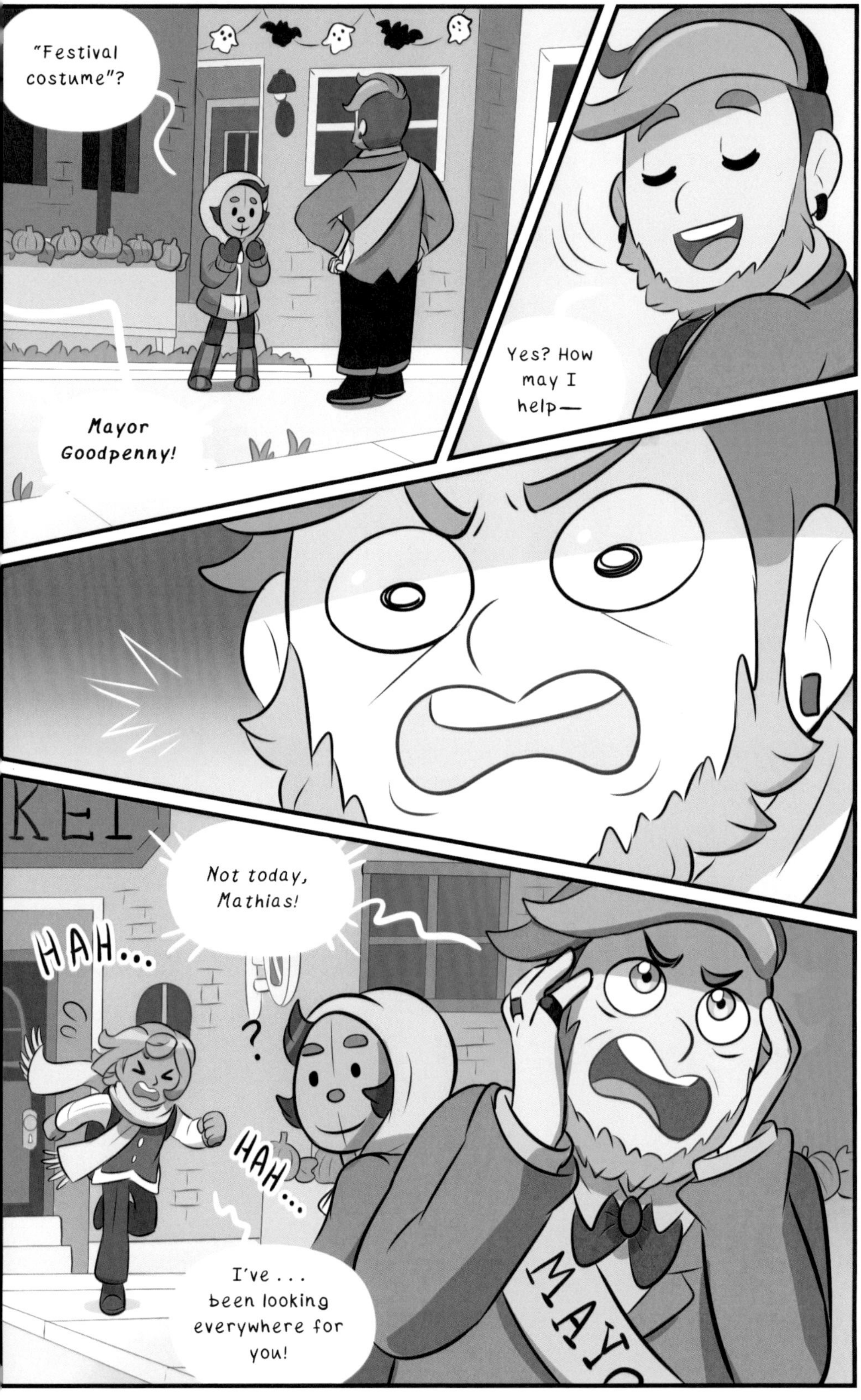
"Festival costume"?
Mayor Goodpenny!
Yes? How may I help—
KE
Not today, Mathias!
HAH...
HAH...
I've . . . been looking everywhere for you!
MAYO

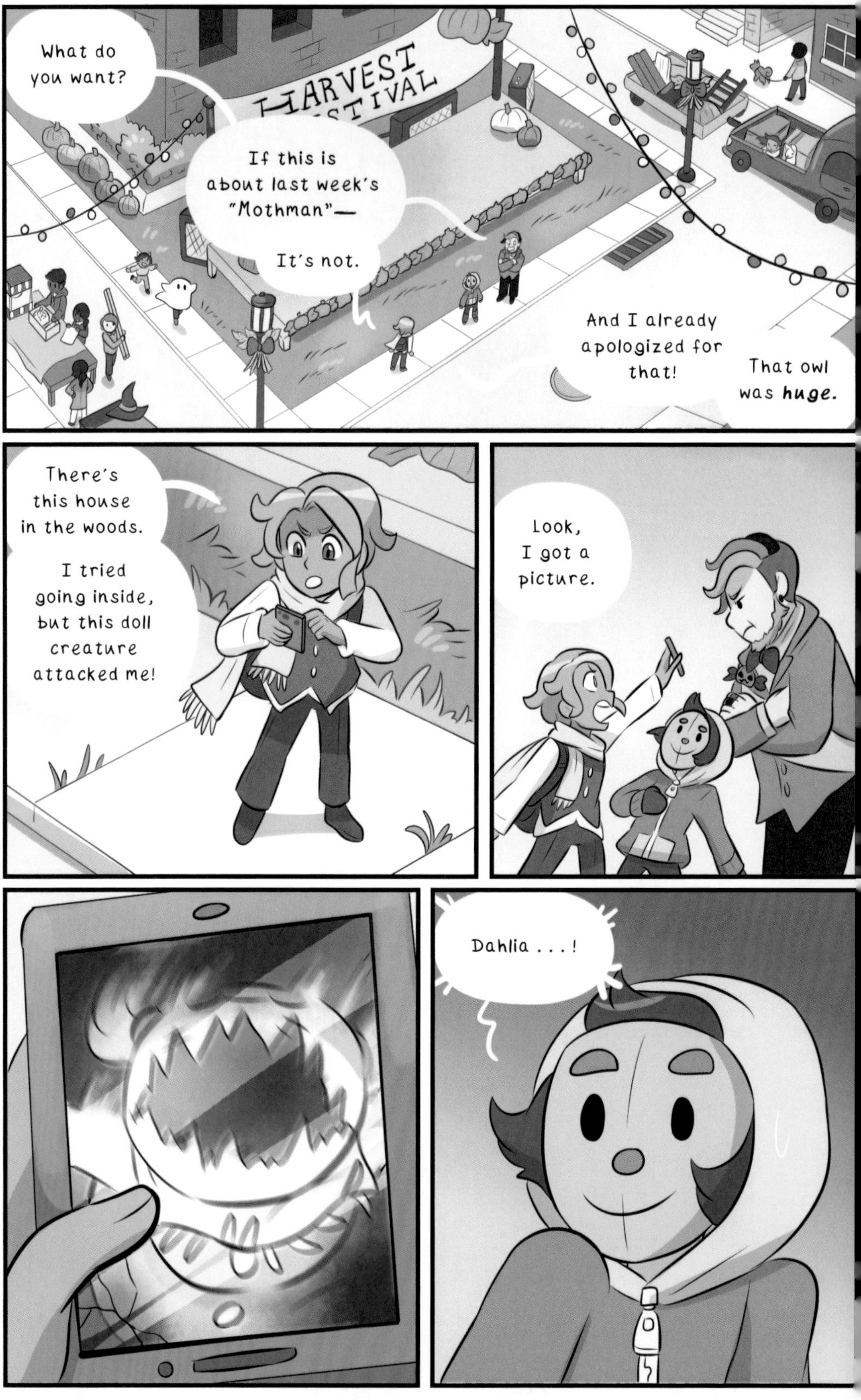
HARVEST FESTIVAL
What do you want?
If this is about last week's "Mothman"—
It's not.
And I already apologized for that!
That owl was **huge.**
There's this house in the woods.
I tried going inside, but this doll creature attacked me!
Look, I got a picture.
Dahlia . . . !

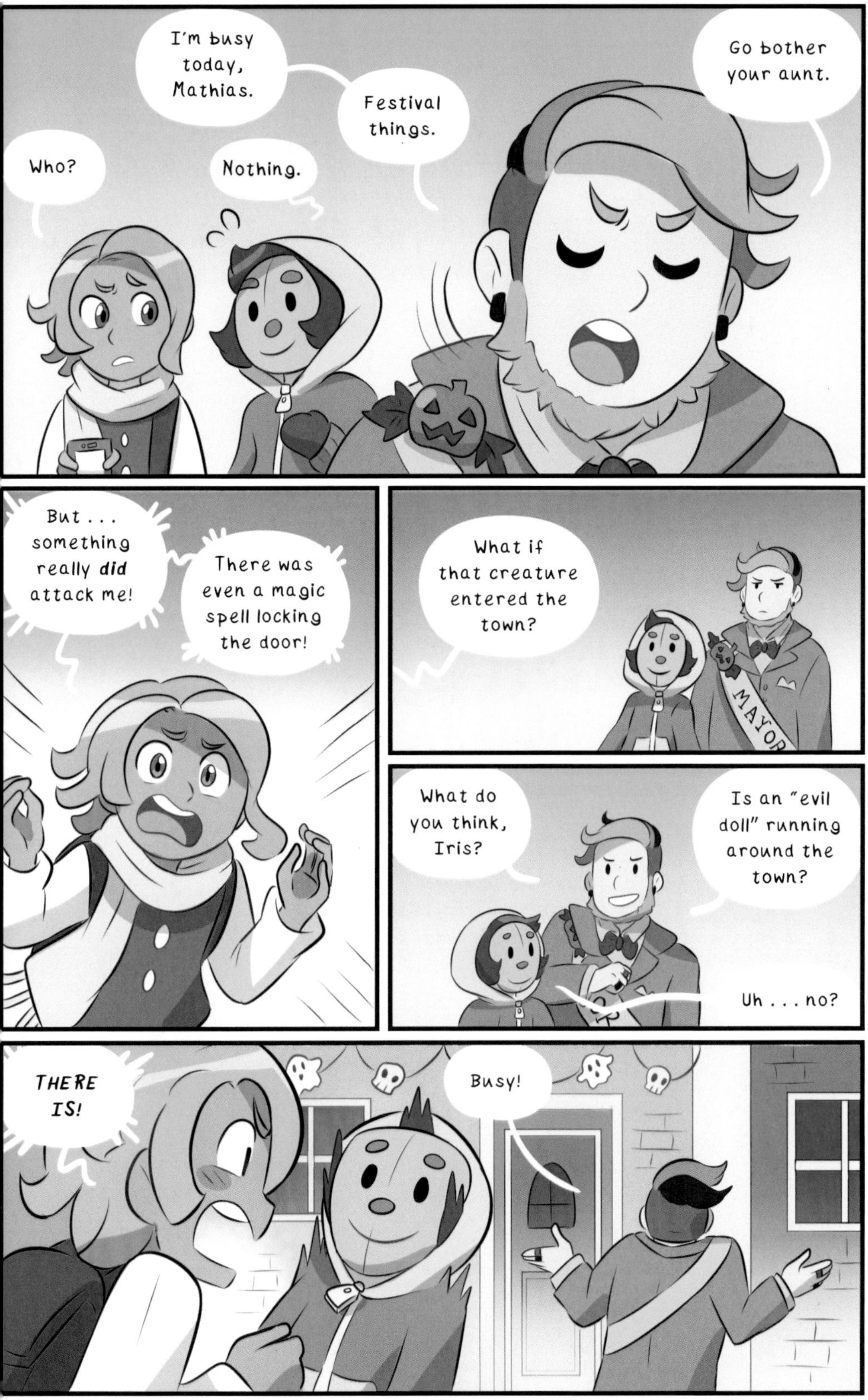
I'm busy today, Mathias.
Festival things.
Go bother your aunt.
Who?
Nothing.
But . . . something really **did** attack me!
There was even a magic spell locking the door!
What if that creature entered the town?
MAYOR
What do you think, Iris?
Is an "evil doll" running around the town?
Uh . . . no?
THERE IS!
Busy!

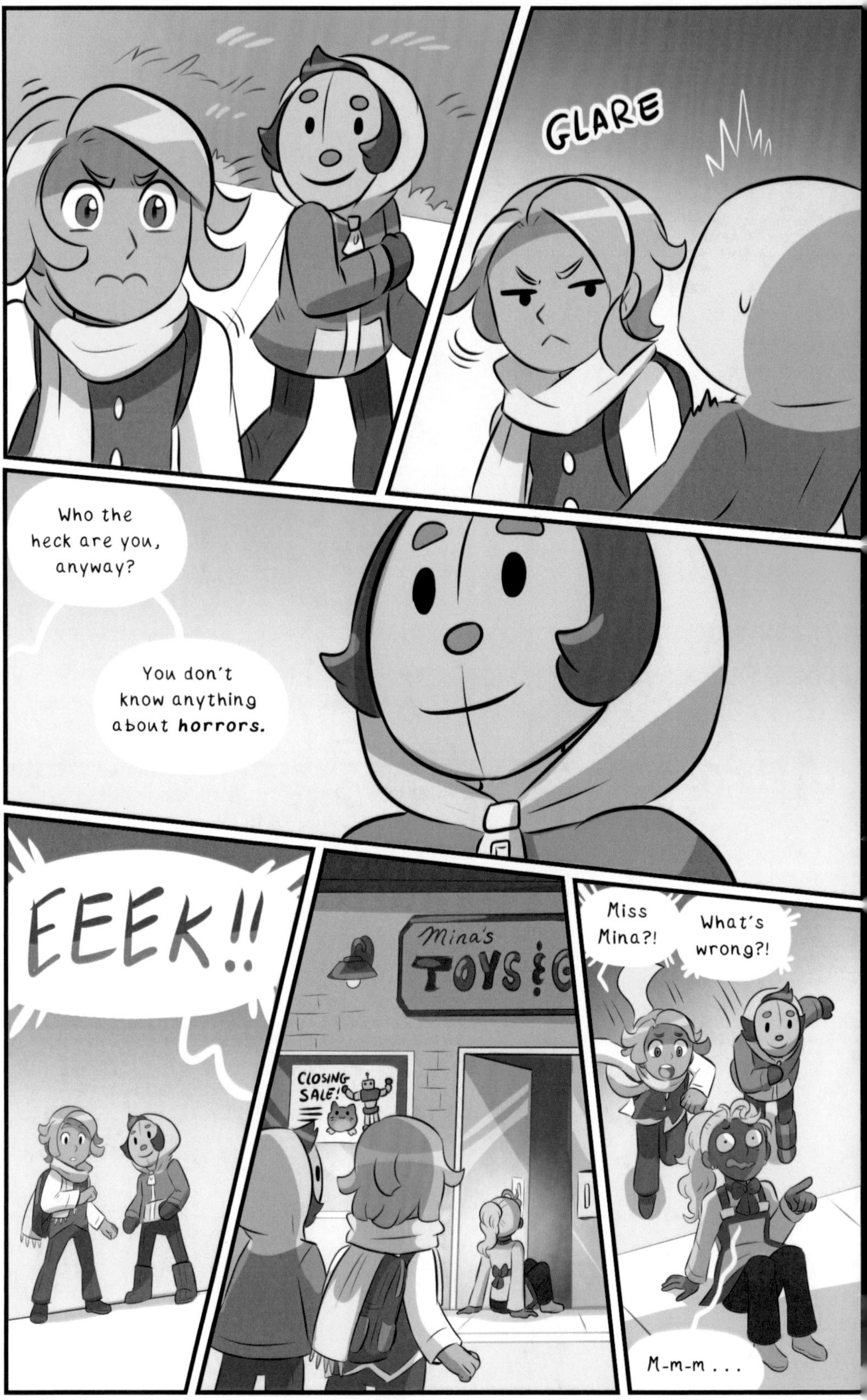
GLARE
Who the heck are you, anyway?
You don't know anything about **horrors.**
EEEK!!
Mina's TOYS & G
CLOSING SALE!
Miss Mina?!
What's wrong?!
M-m-m . . .

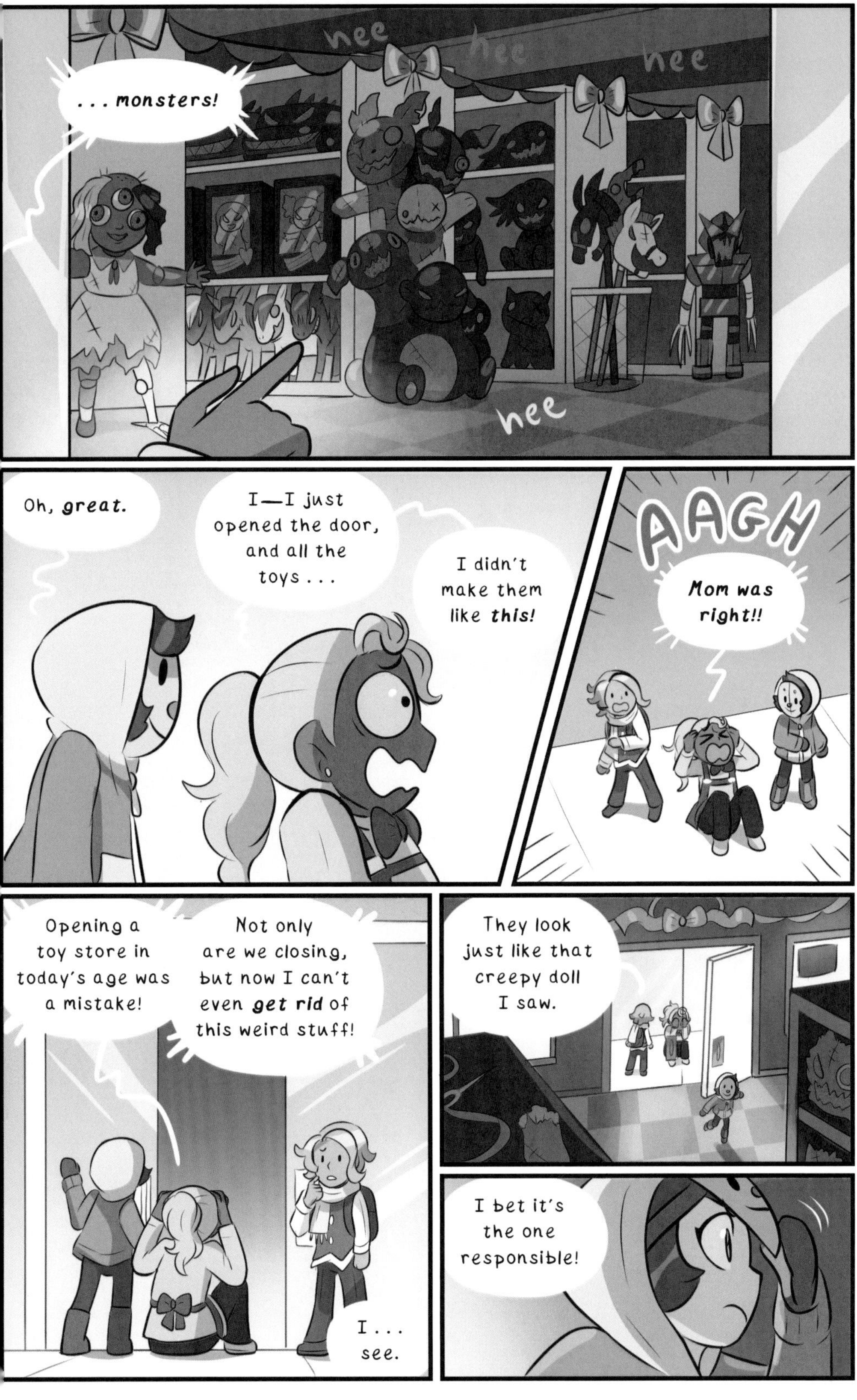
hee
hee
hee
. . . monsters!
hee
Oh, great.
I—I just opened the door, and all the toys . . .
I didn't make them like this!
AAGH
Mom was right!!
Opening a toy store in today's age was a mistake!
Not only are we closing, but now I can't even get rid of this weird stuff!
I . . . see.
They look just like that creepy doll I saw.
I bet it's the one responsible!

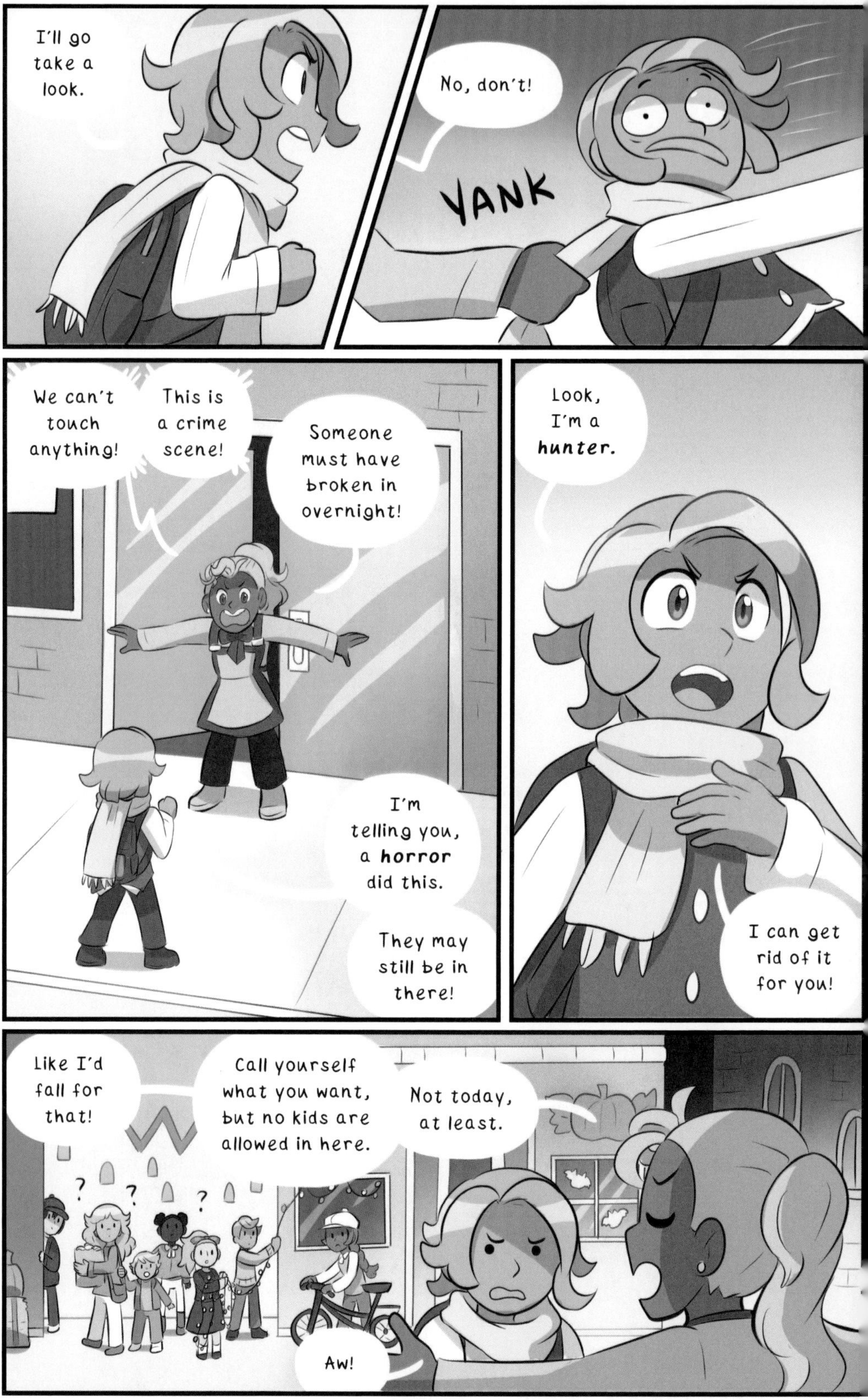
I'll go take a look.
No, don't!
YANK
We can't touch anything!
This is a crime scene!
Someone must have broken in overnight!
I'm telling you, a **horror** did this.
They may still be in there!
Look, I'm a **hunter.**
I can get rid of it for you!
Like I'd fall for that!
Call yourself what you want, but no kids are allowed in here.
Not today, at least.
Aw!

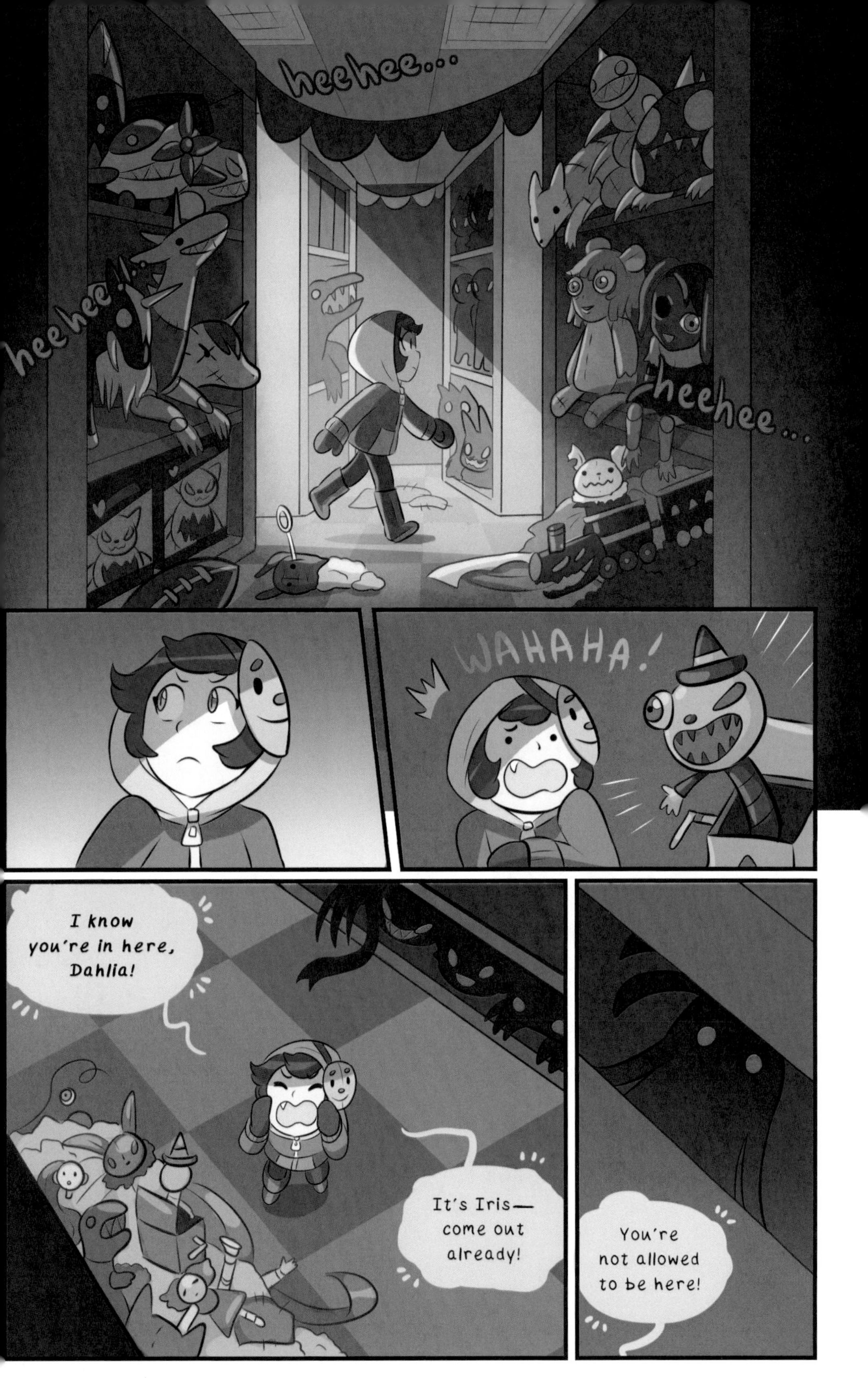
heehee...
heehee
heehee...
WAHAHA!
I know you're in here, Dahlia!
It's Iris—come out already!
You're not allowed to be here!

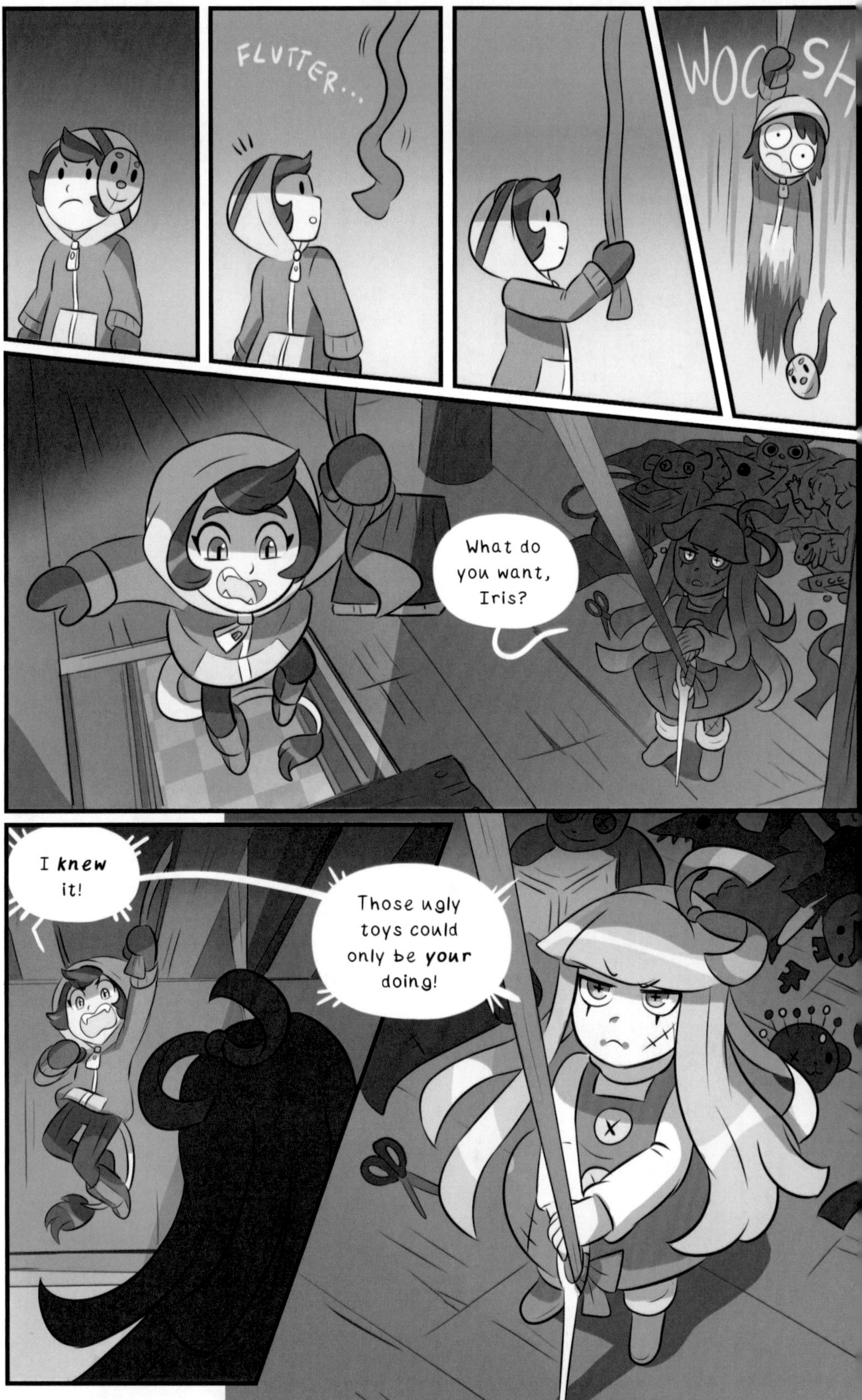
FLUTTER...
WOOSH
What do you want, Iris?
I **knew** it!
Those ugly toys could only be **your** doing!

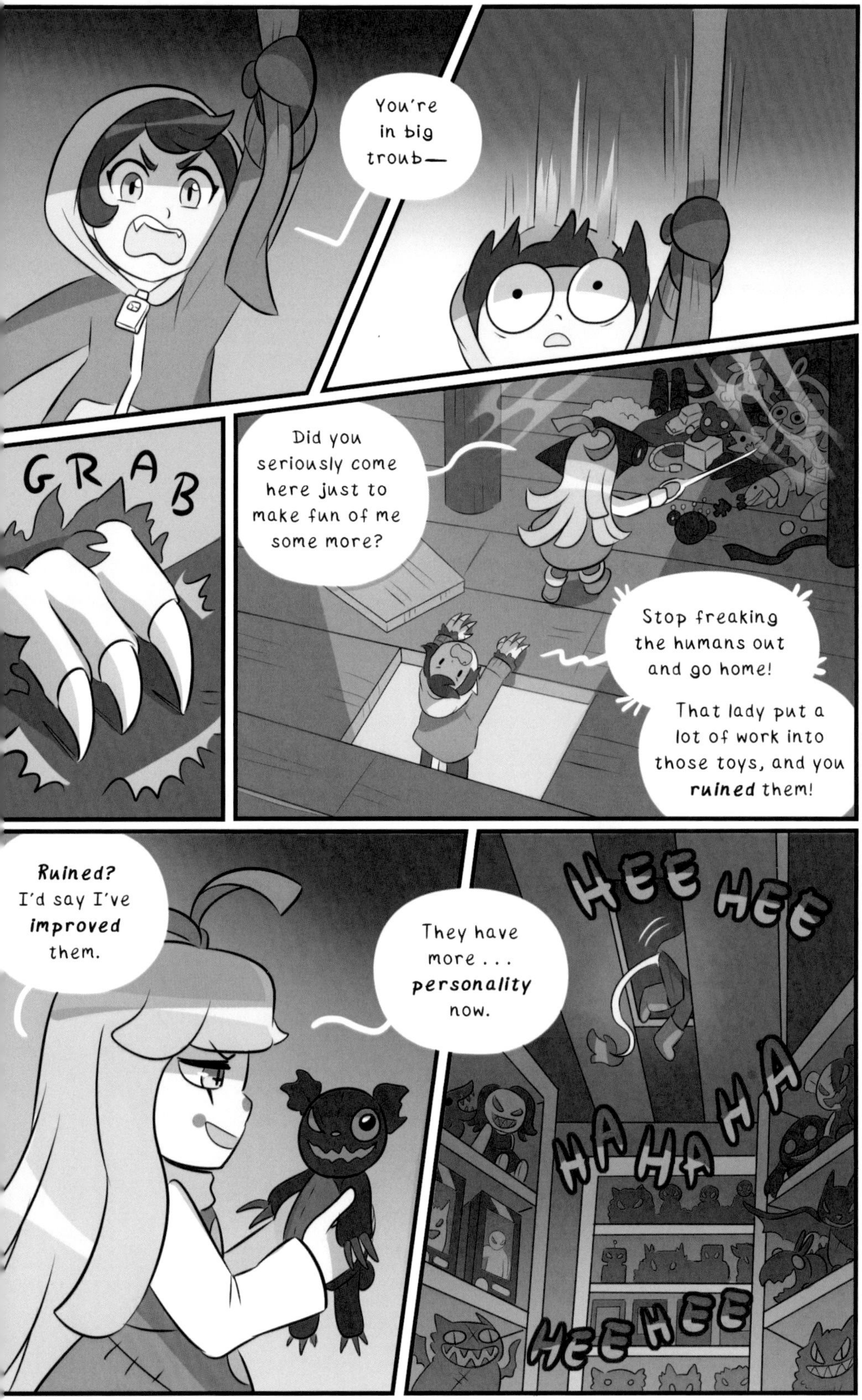
You're in big troub—
GRAB
Did you seriously come here just to make fun of me some more?
Stop freaking the humans out and go home!
That lady put a lot of work into those toys, and you **ruined** them!
Ruined? I'd say I've ***improved*** them.
They have more . . . ***personality*** now.
HEE HEE
HA HA HA HA
HEE HEE

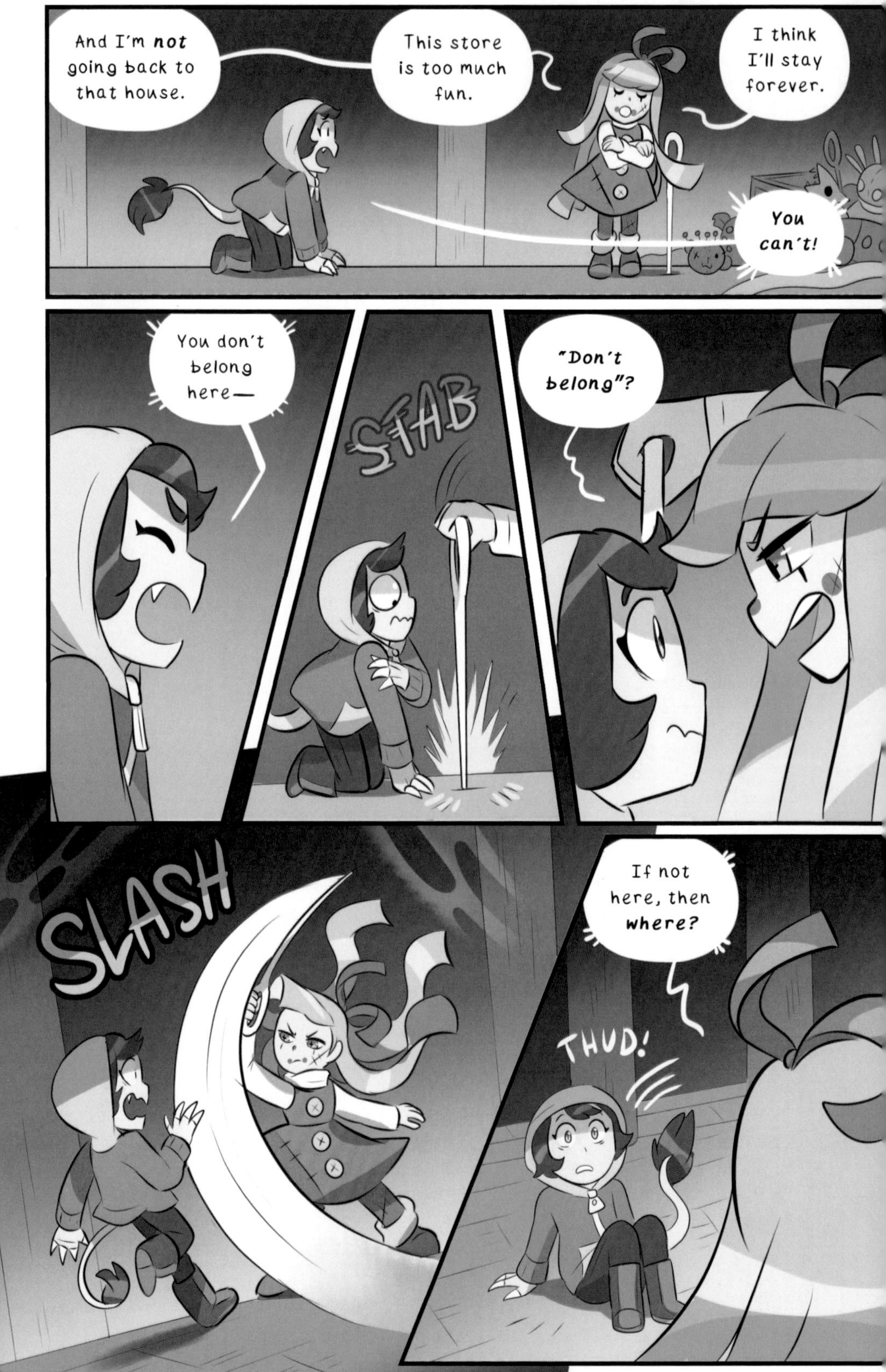

And I'm **not** going back to that house.
This store is too much fun.
I think I'll stay forever.
You can't!
You don't belong here—
STAB
"**Don't belong**"?
SLASH
If not here, then **where?**
THUD!

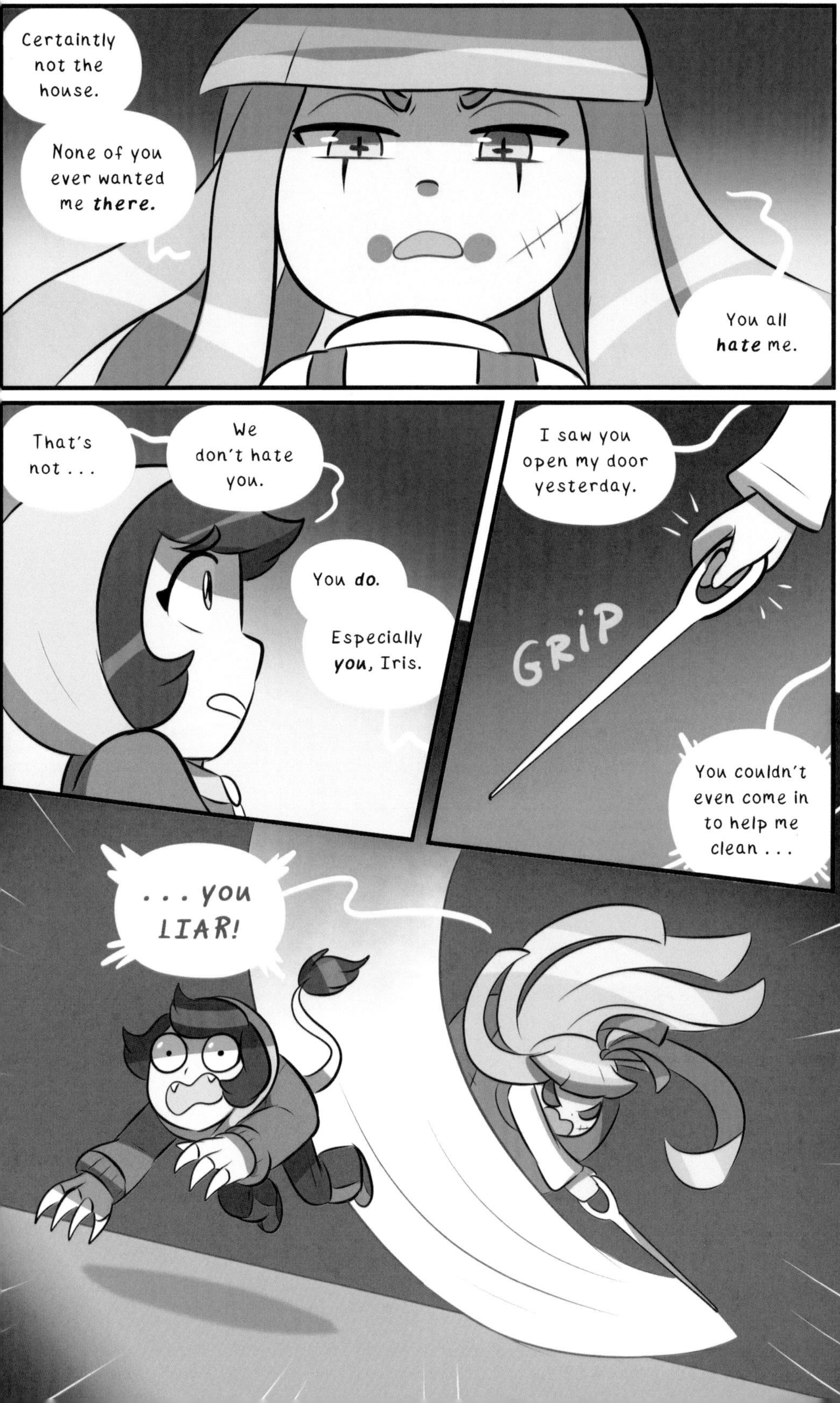
Certaintly not the house.
None of you ever wanted me ***there.***
You all ***hate*** me.
That's not . . .
We don't hate you.
You ***do.***
Especially ***you,*** Iris.
I saw you open my door yesterday.
GRIP
You couldn't even come in to help me clean . . .
. . . YOU LIAR!

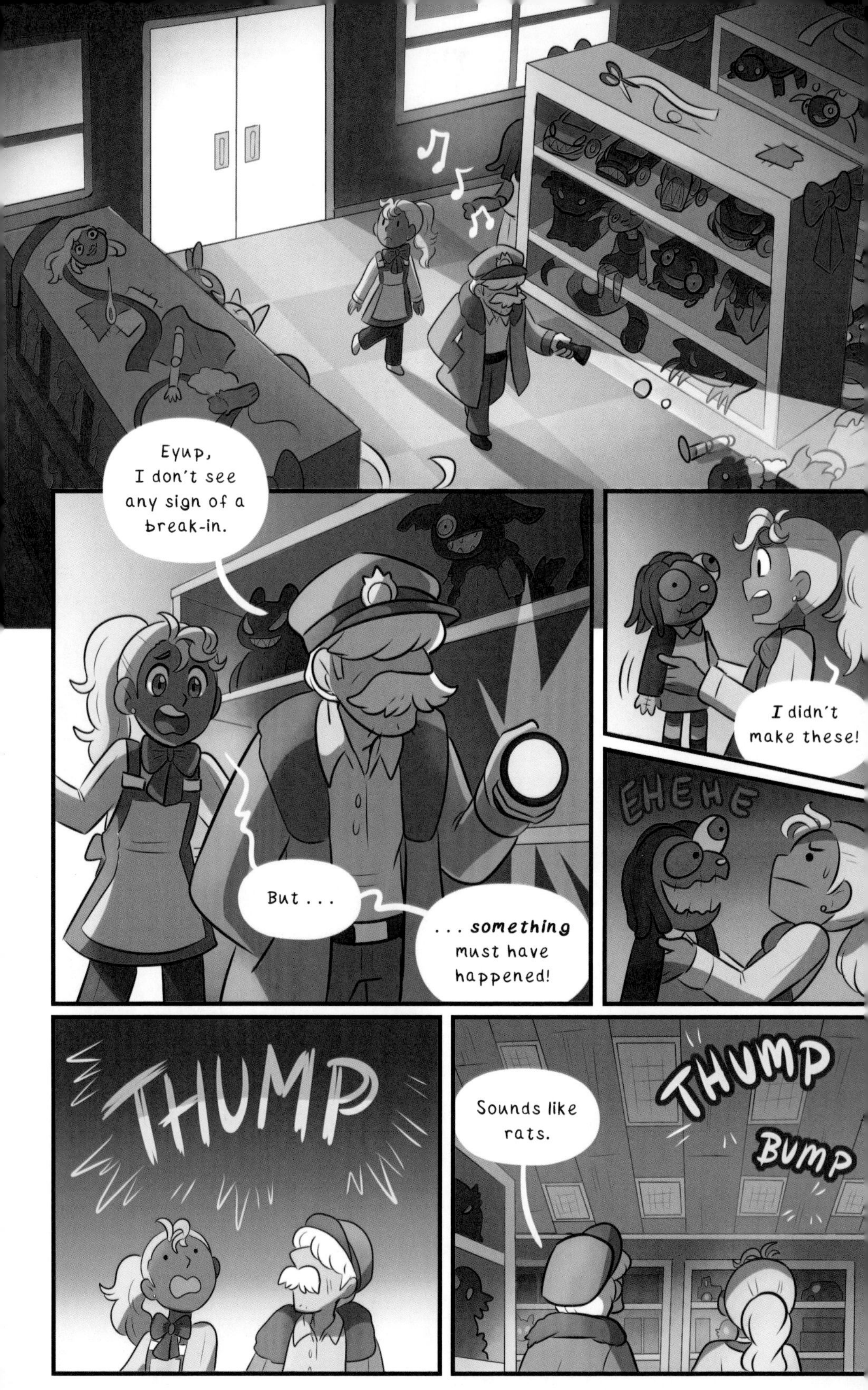
Eyup, I don't see any sign of a break-in.
But . . .
. . . something must have happened!
I didn't make these!
EHEHE
THUMP
Sounds like rats.
THUMP
BUMP

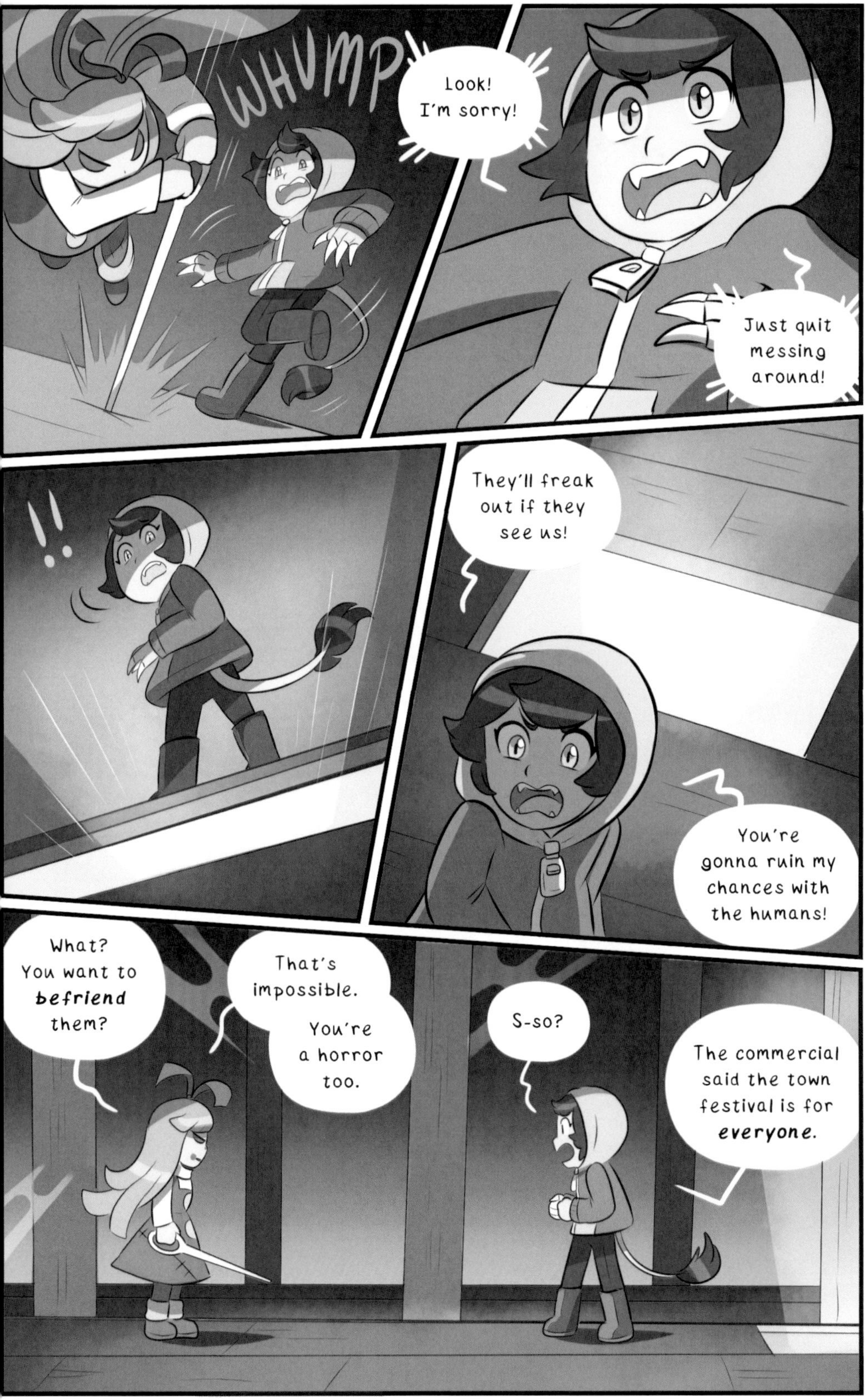
WHUMP!
Look! I'm sorry!
Just quit messing around!
!!
They'll freak out if they see us!
You're gonna ruin my chances with the humans!
What? You want to **befriend** them?
That's impossible.
You're a horror too.
S-so?
The commercial said the town festival is for **everyone**.

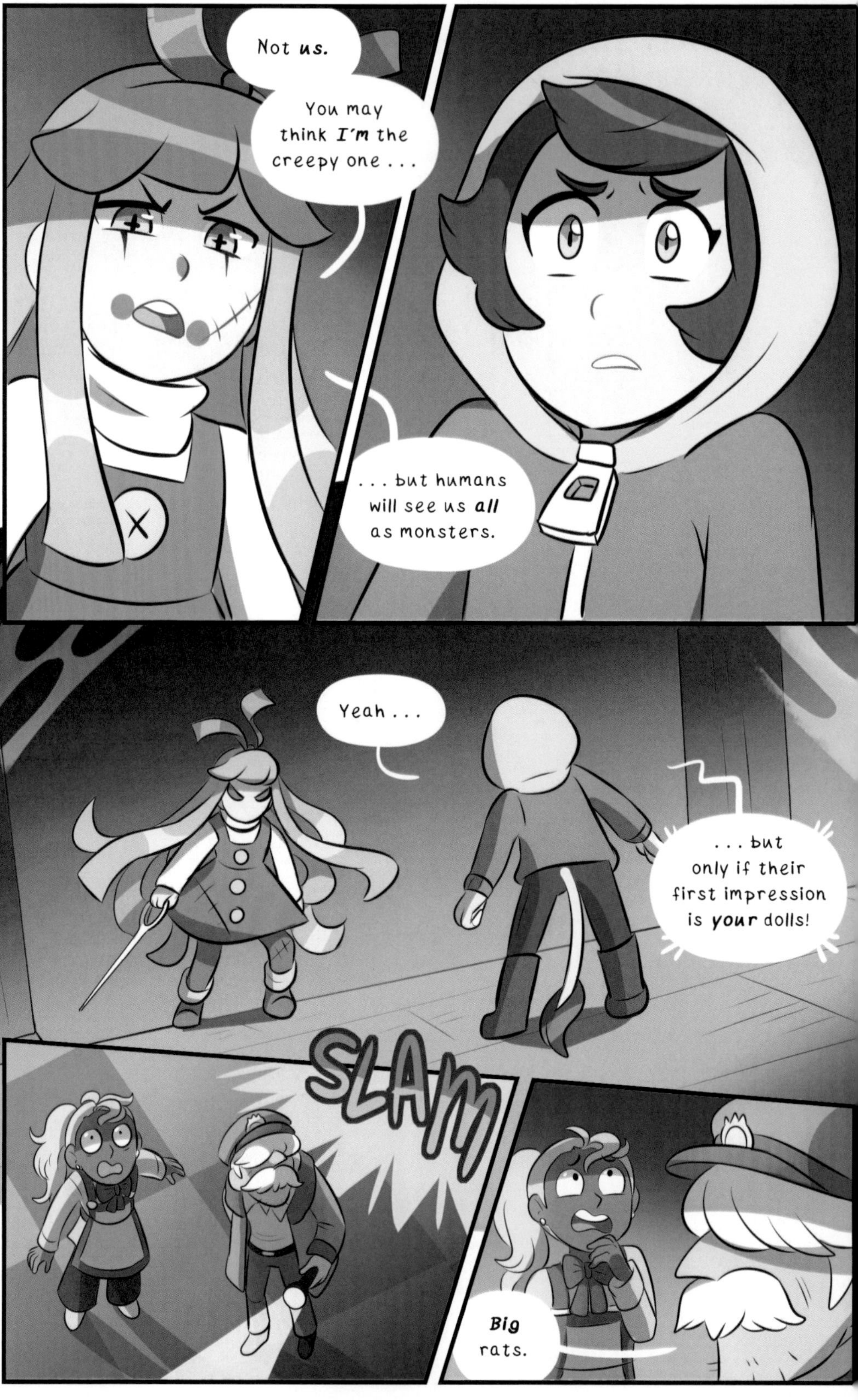
Not ***us.***
You may think ***I'm*** the creepy one . . .
. . . but humans will see us ***all*** as monsters.
Yeah . . .
. . . but only if their first impression is ***your*** dolls!
SLAM
Big rats.

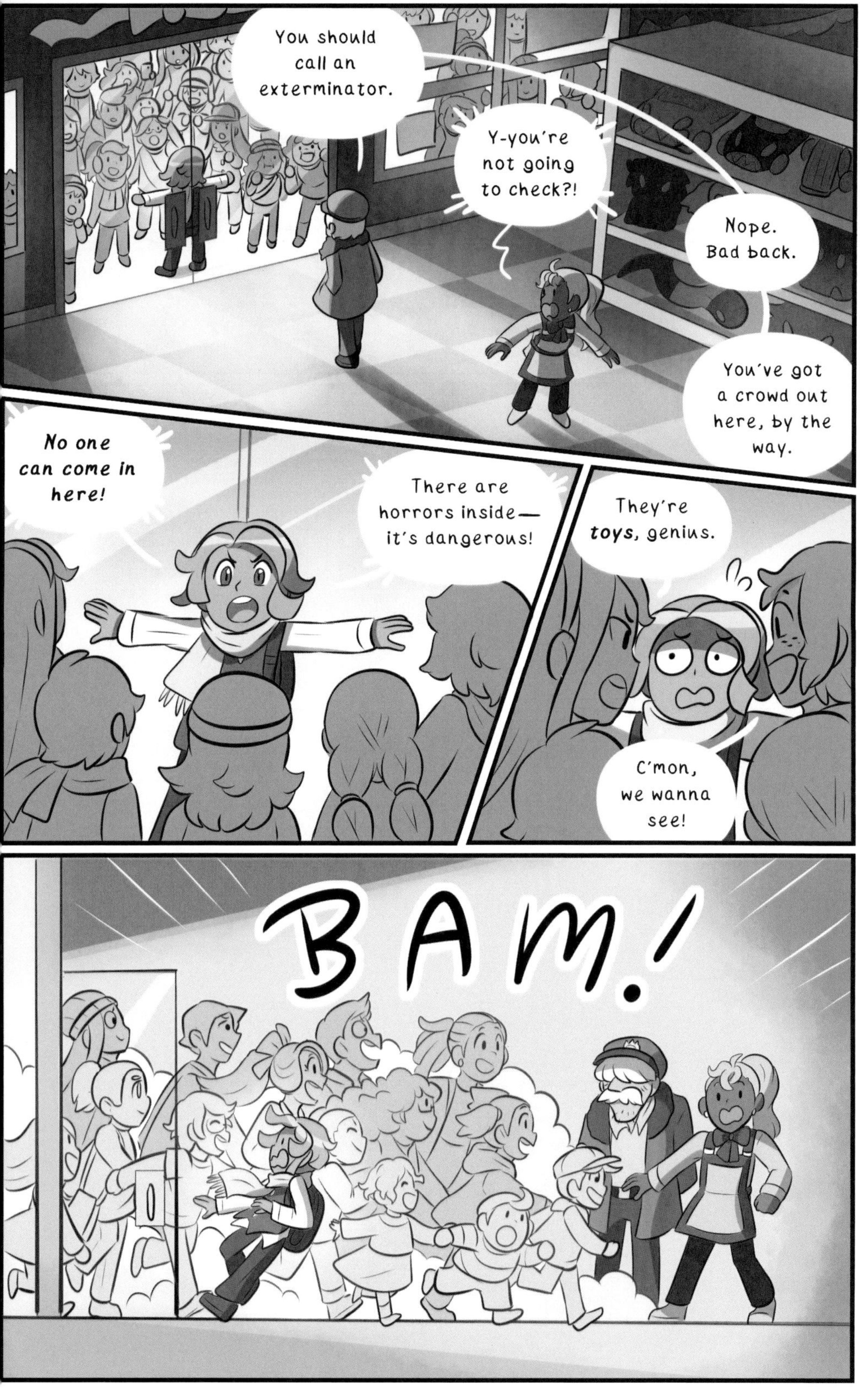
You should call an exterminator.
Y-you're not going to check?!
Nope. Bad back.
You've got a crowd out here, by the way.
No one can come in here!
There are horrors inside— it's dangerous!
They're toys, genius.
C'mon, we wanna see!
BAM!

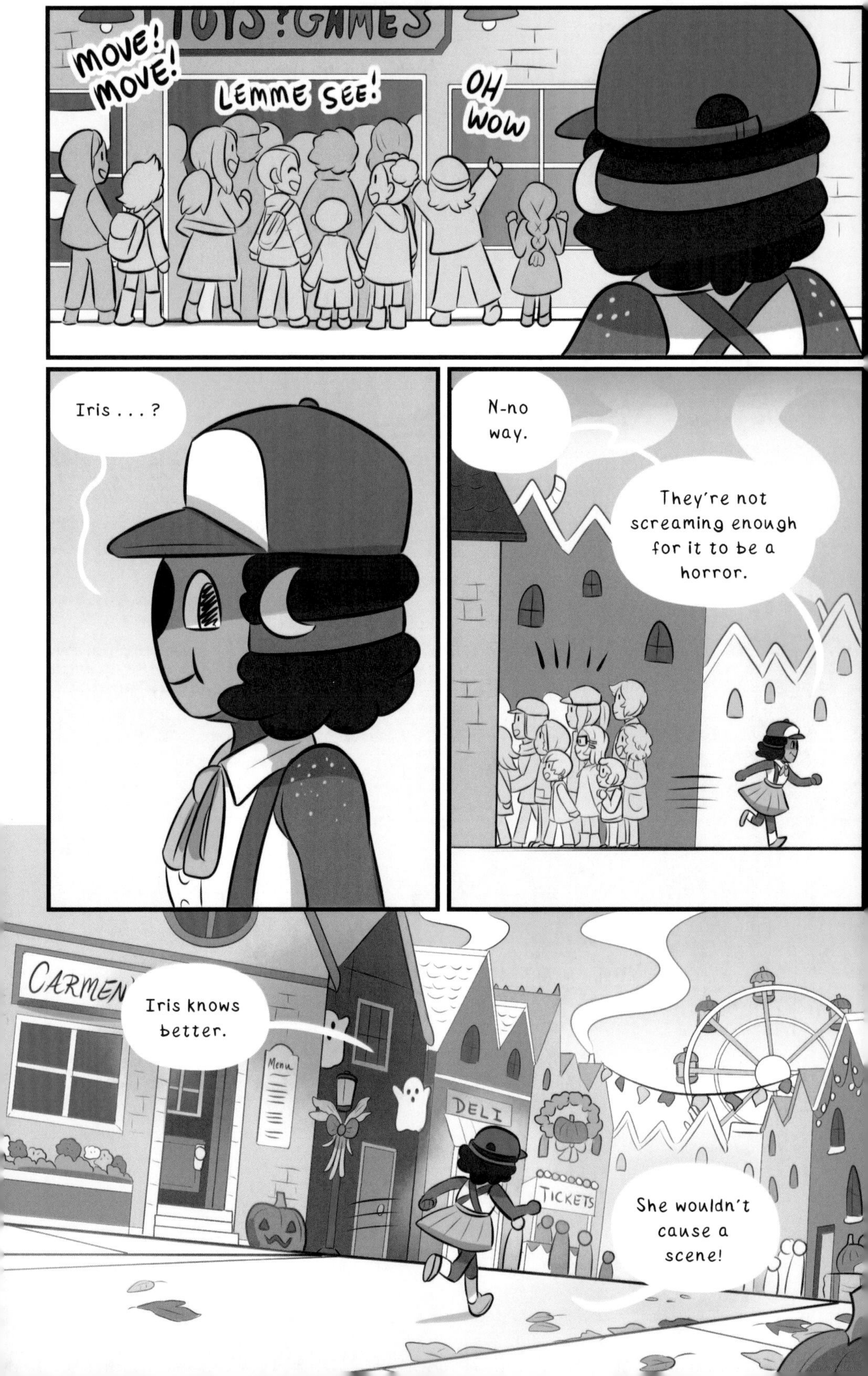
TOYS & GAMES
MOVE! MOVE!
LEMME SEE!
OH WOW
Iris . . . ?
N-no way.
They're not screaming enough for it to be a horror.
CARMEN
Iris knows better.
Menu
DELI
TICKETS
She wouldn't cause a scene!

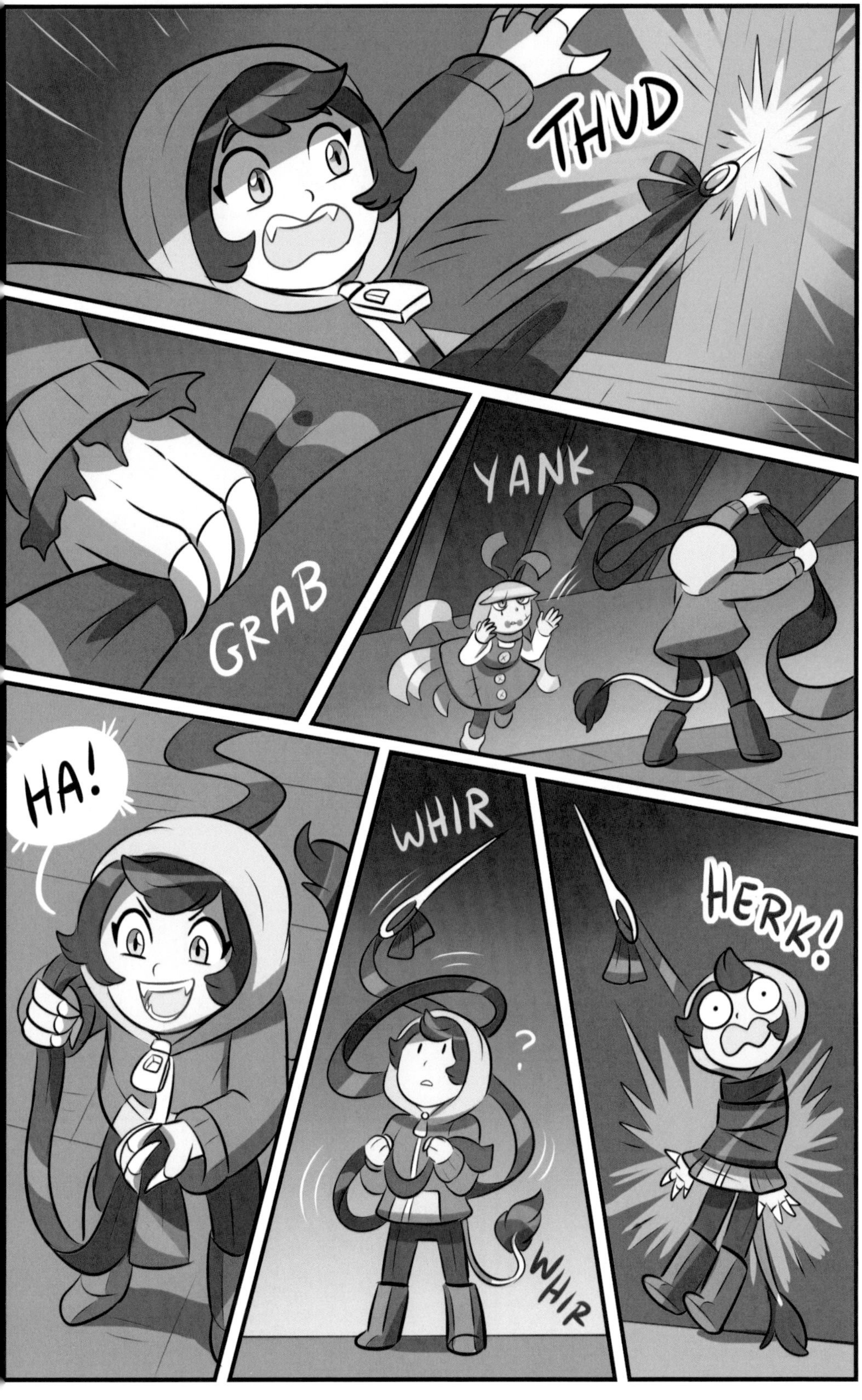
THUD
GRAB
YANK
HA!
WHIR
?
WHIR
HERK!

You want to know **why** I was brought to the home?

OOF!

It's because a human thought I was scary.

My human.

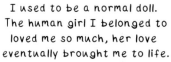

I used to be a normal doll. The human girl I belonged to loved me so much, her love eventually brought me to life.

It was an incredible type of magic.

I couldn't wait for her to see!

But when she came home that day . . .

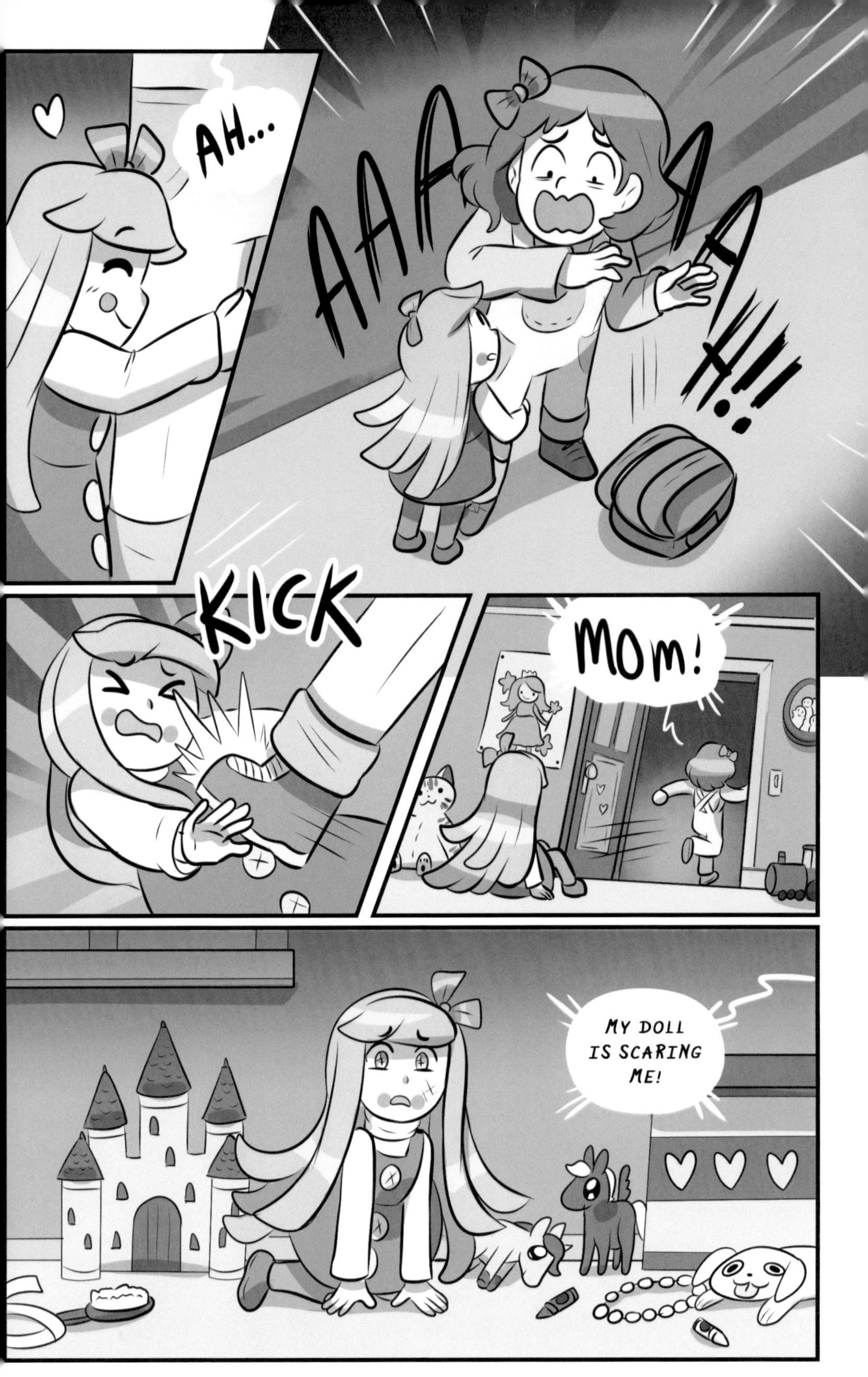
AH...
AAAAAAAH!!
KICK
MOM!
MY DOLL IS SCARING ME!

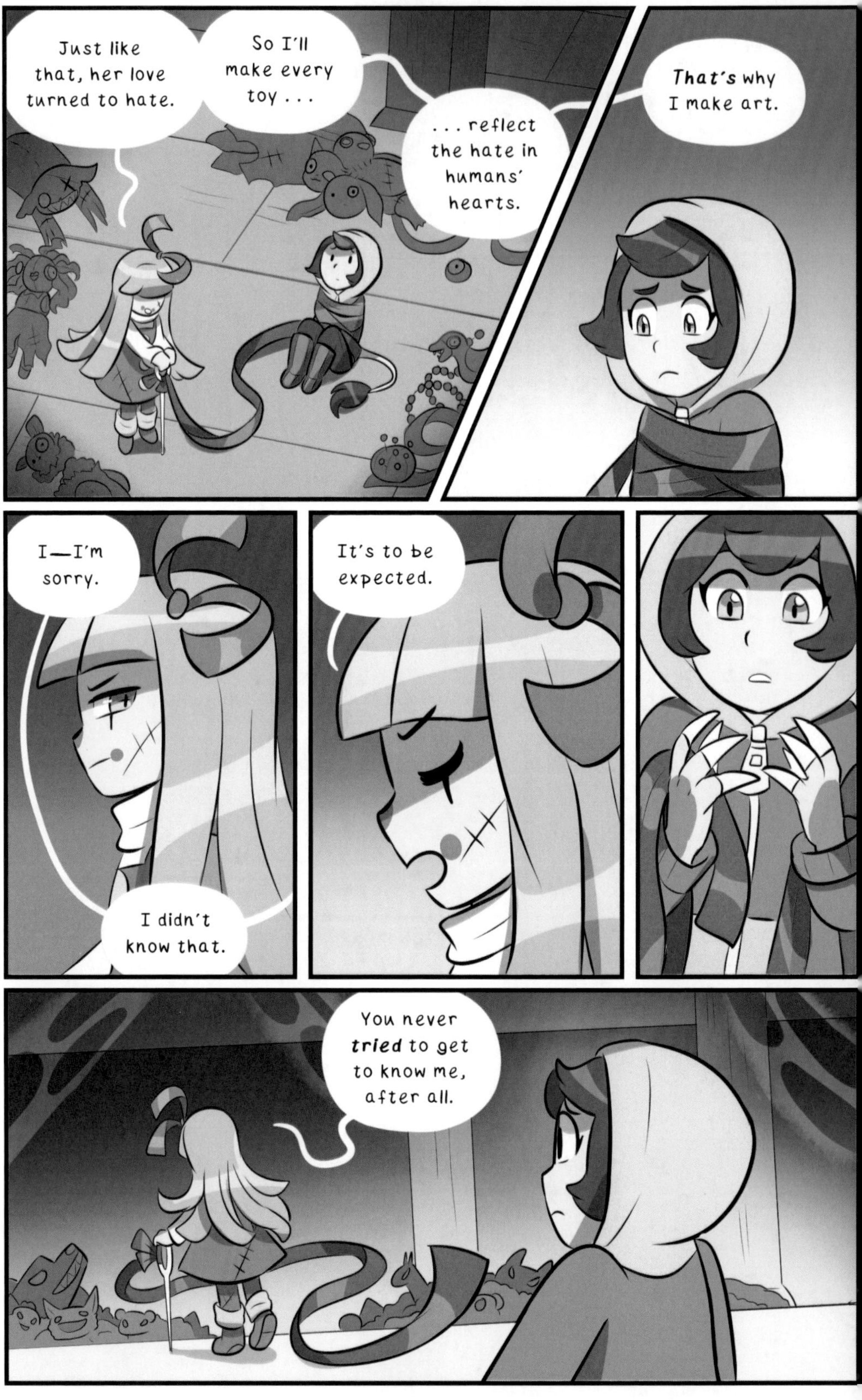
Just like that, her love turned to hate.
So I'll make every toy . . .
. . . reflect the hate in humans' hearts.
That's why I make art.
I—I'm sorry.
I didn't know that.
It's to be expected.
You never *tried* to get to know me, after all.

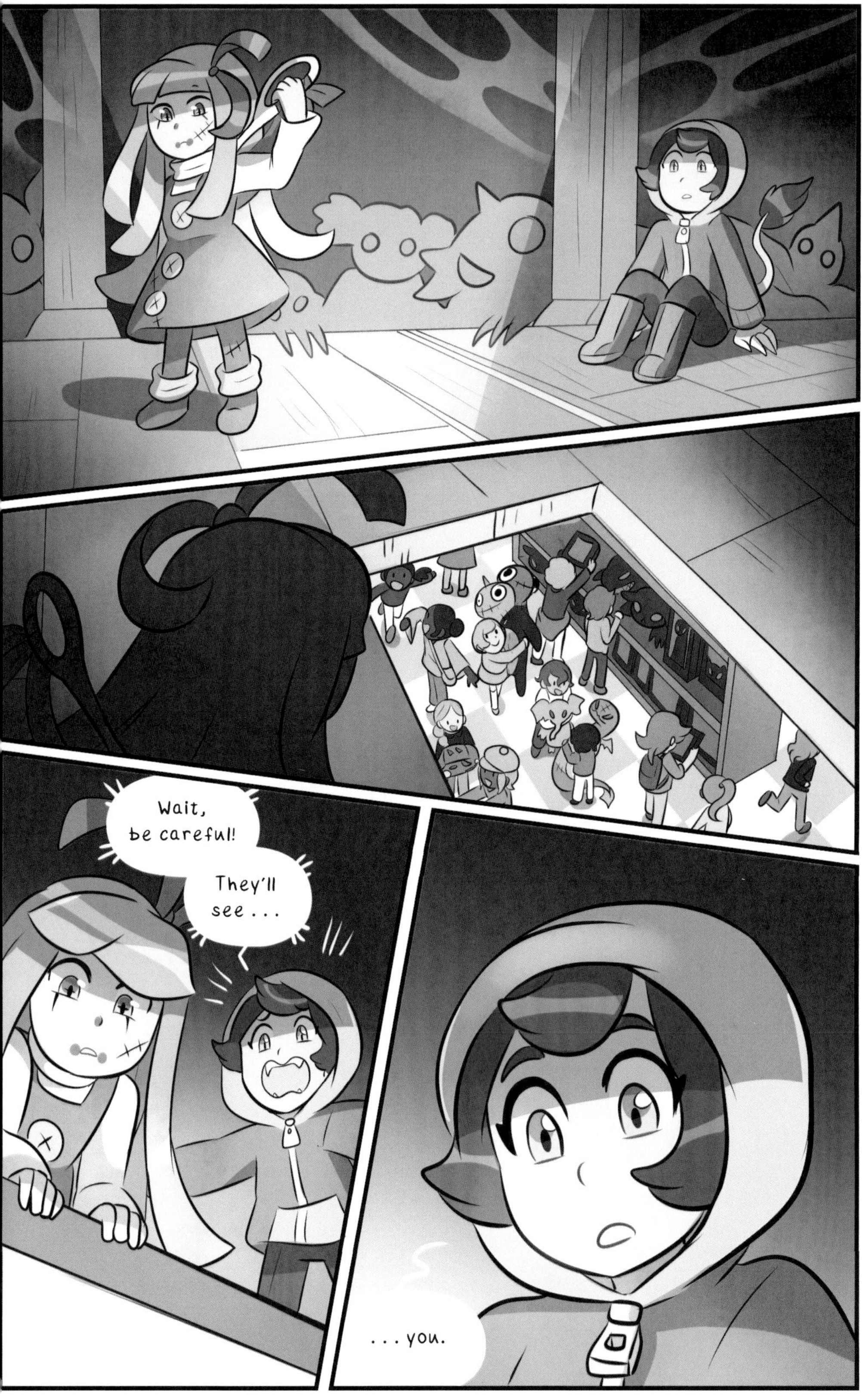
Wait, be careful!
They'll see . . .
. . . you.

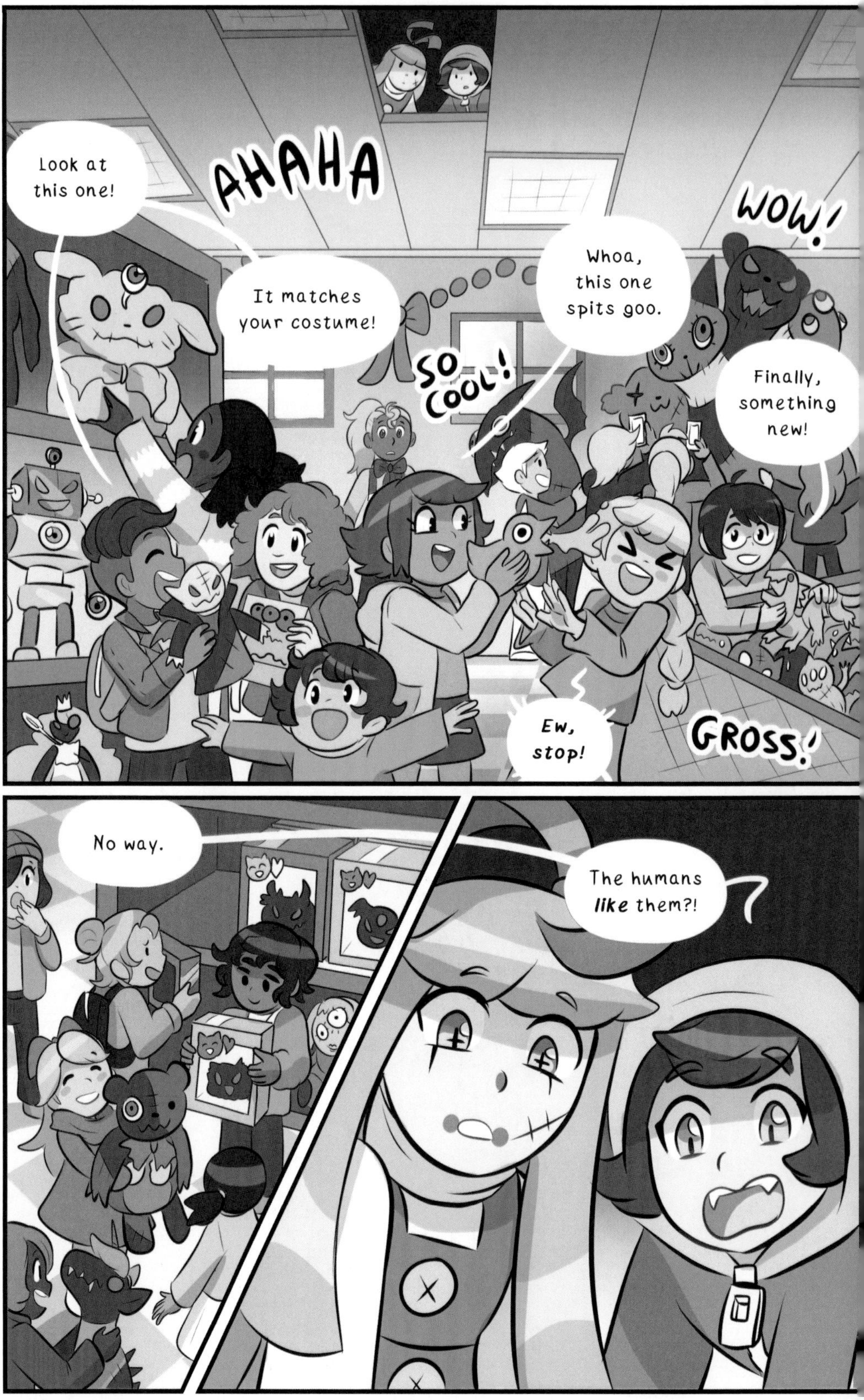
Look at this one!
AHAHA
It matches your costume!
Whoa, this one spits goo.
WOW!
SO COOL!
Finally, something new!
Ew, stop!
GROSS!
No way.
The humans *like* them?!

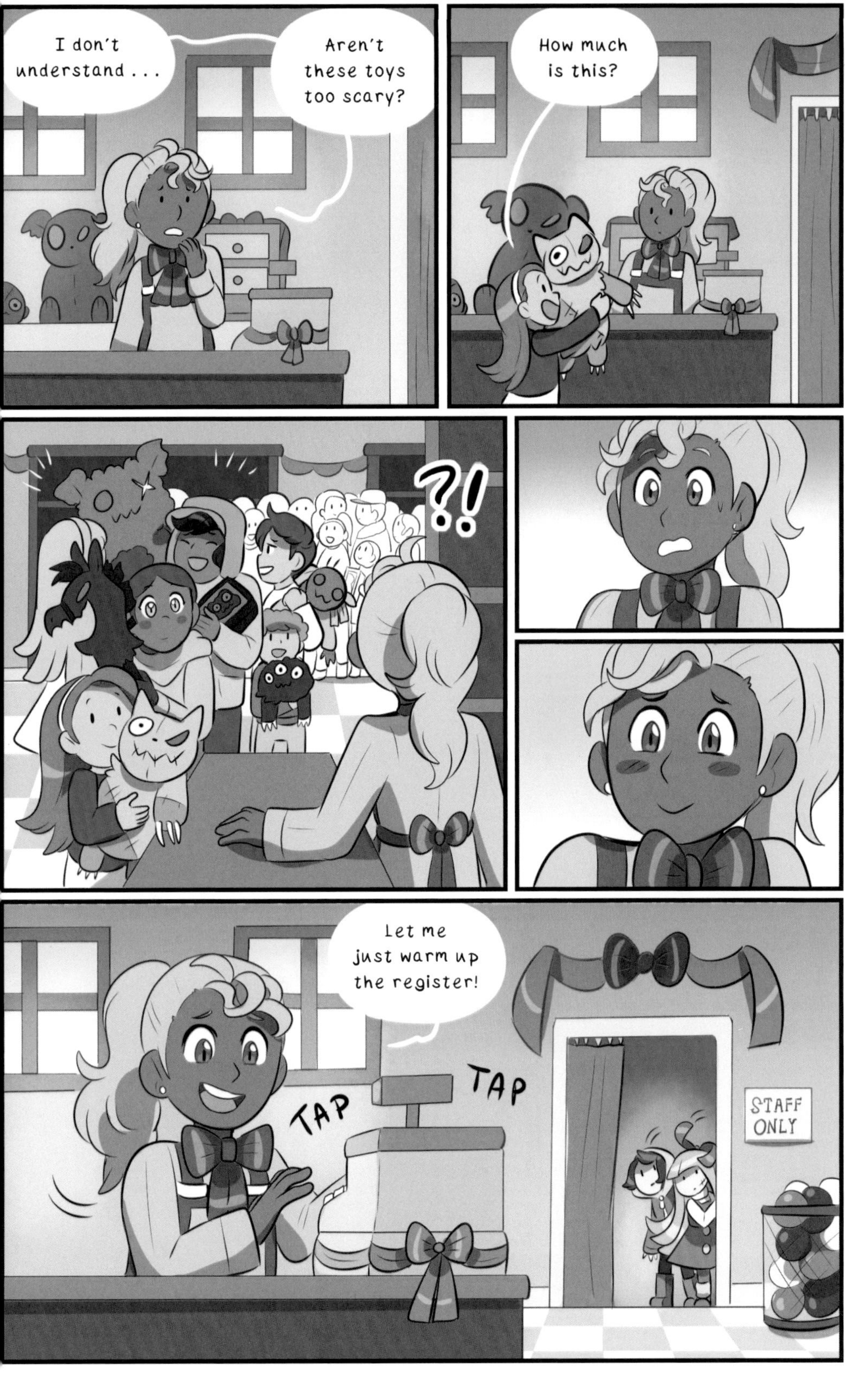
I don't understand . . .
Aren't these toys too scary?
How much is this?
?!
Let me just warm up the register!
TAP
TAP
STAFF ONLY

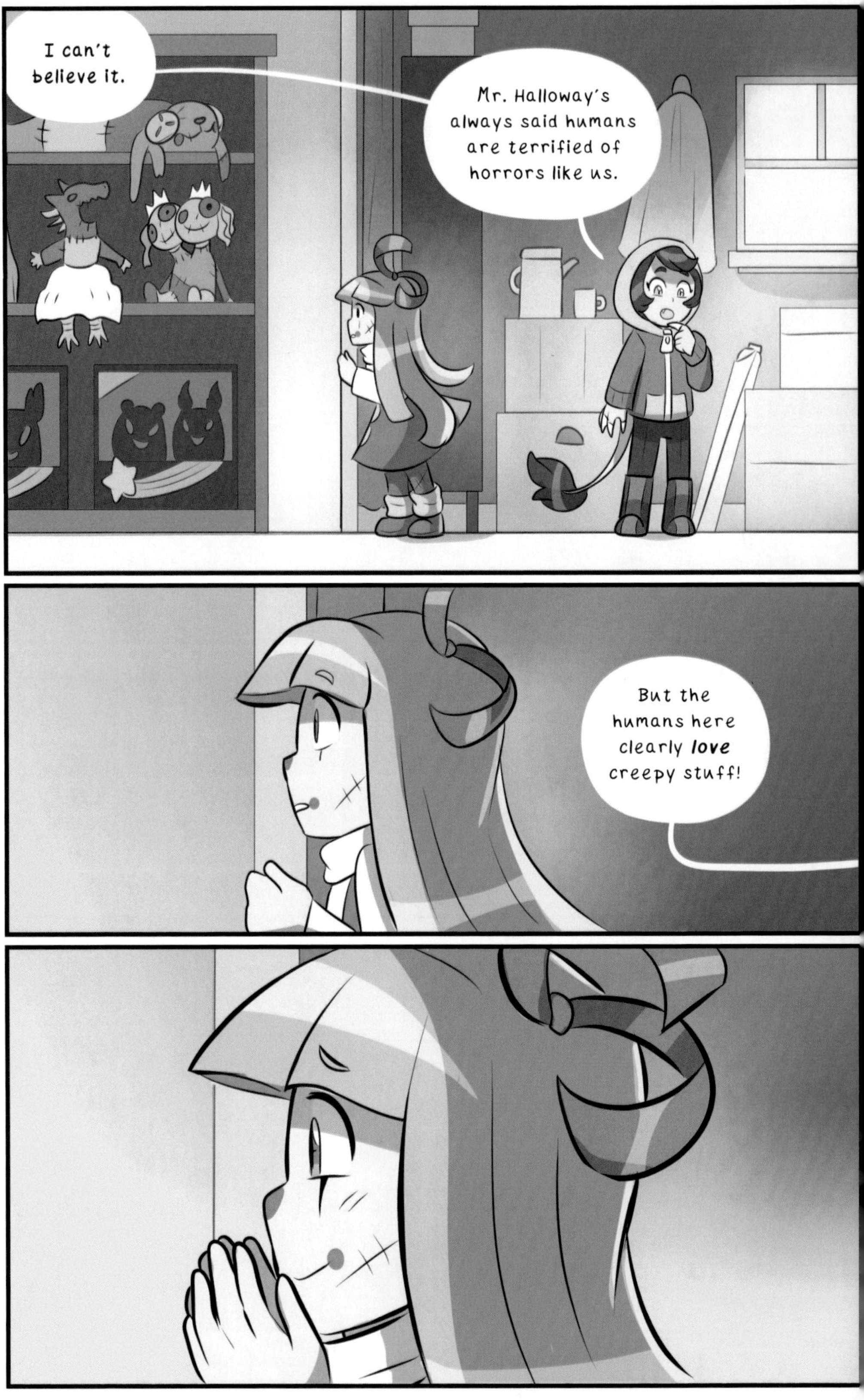
I can't believe it.
Mr. Halloway's always said humans are terrified of horrors like us.
But the humans here clearly *love* creepy stuff!

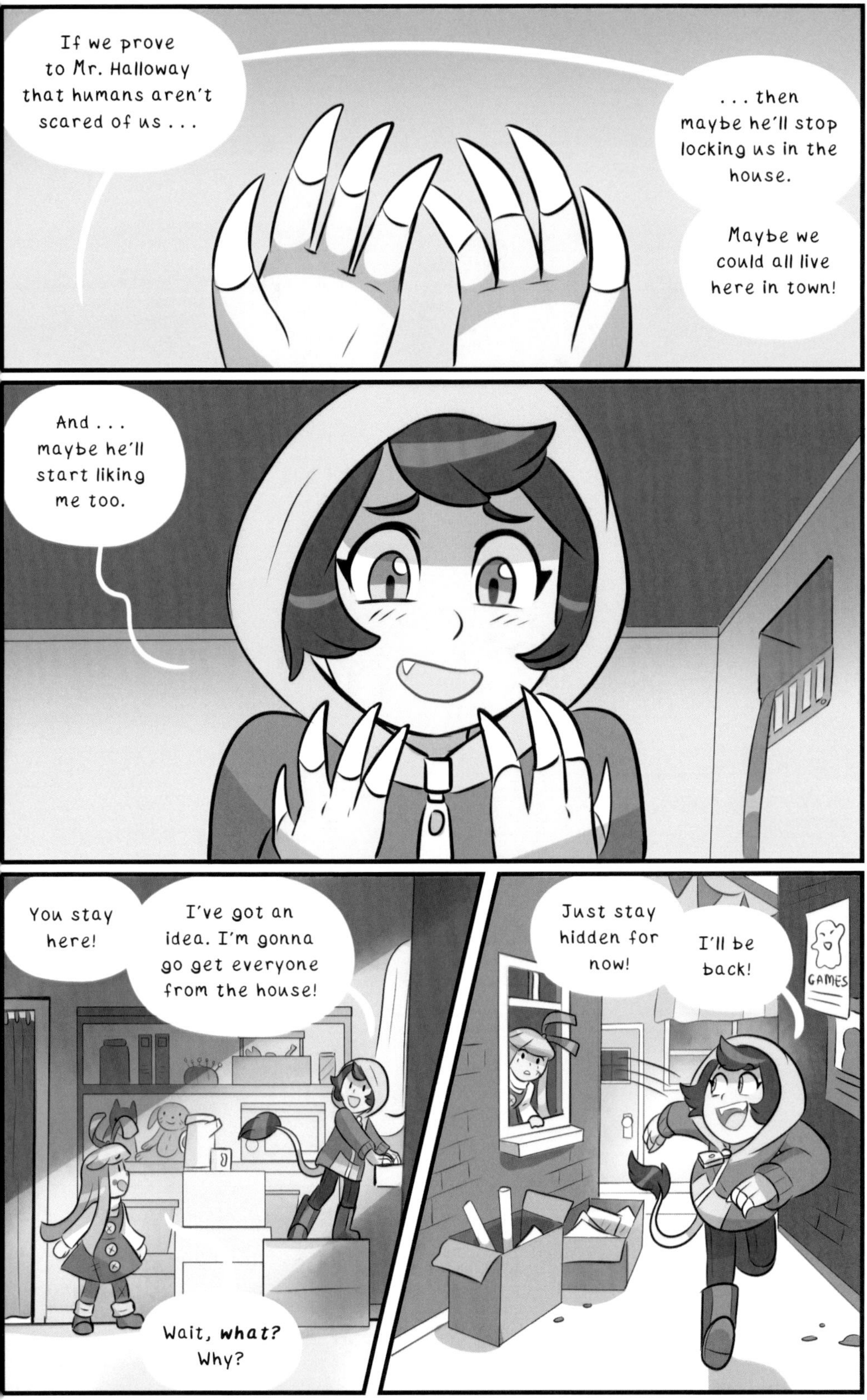
If we prove to Mr. Halloway that humans aren't scared of us . . .
. . . then maybe he'll stop locking us in the house.
Maybe we could all live here in town!
And . . . maybe he'll start liking me too.
You stay here!
I've got an idea. I'm gonna go get everyone from the house!
Wait, what? Why?
Just stay hidden for now!
I'll be back!
GAMES

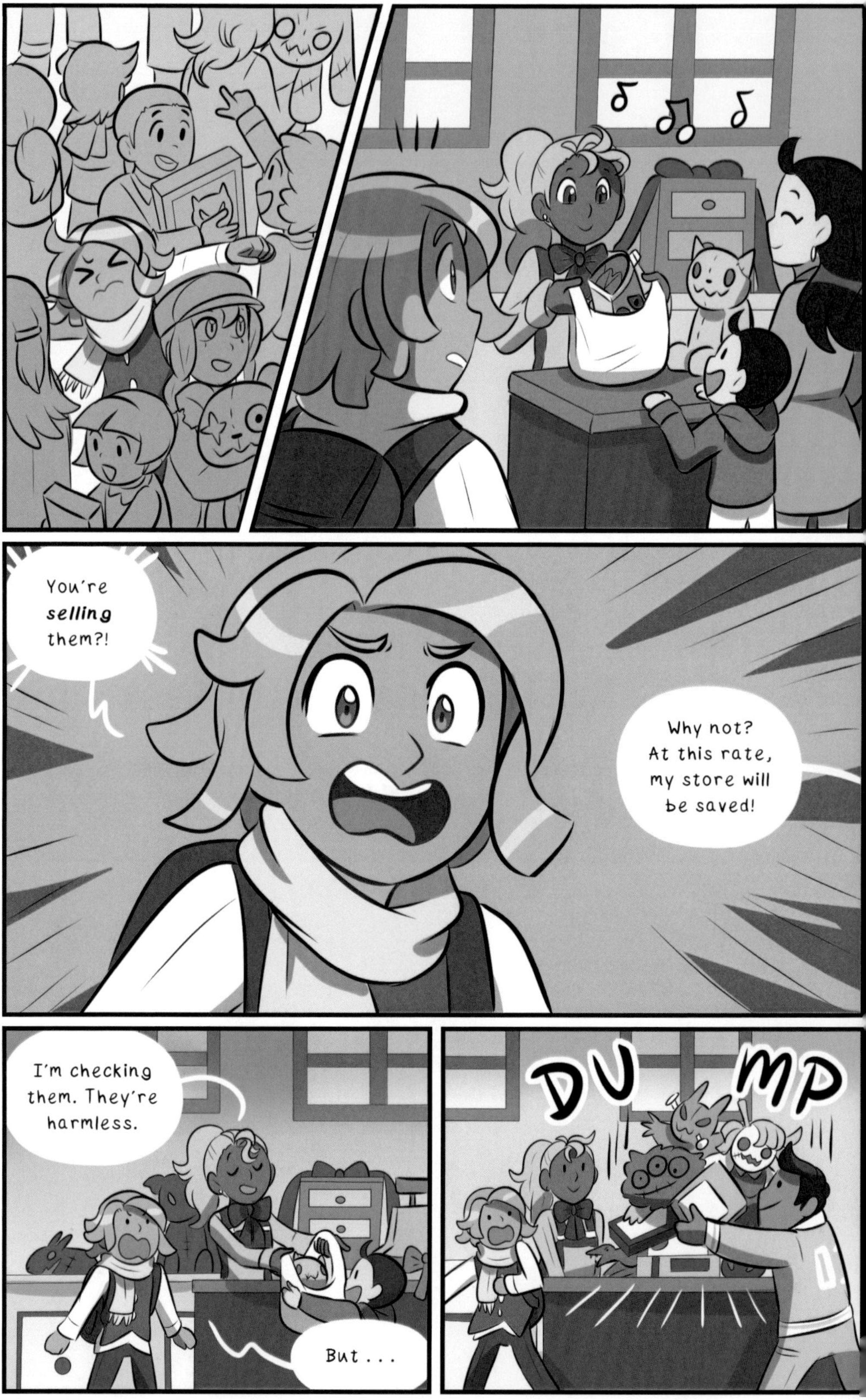
You're **selling** them?!
Why not? At this rate, my store will be saved!
I'm checking them. They're harmless.
But . . .
DUMP

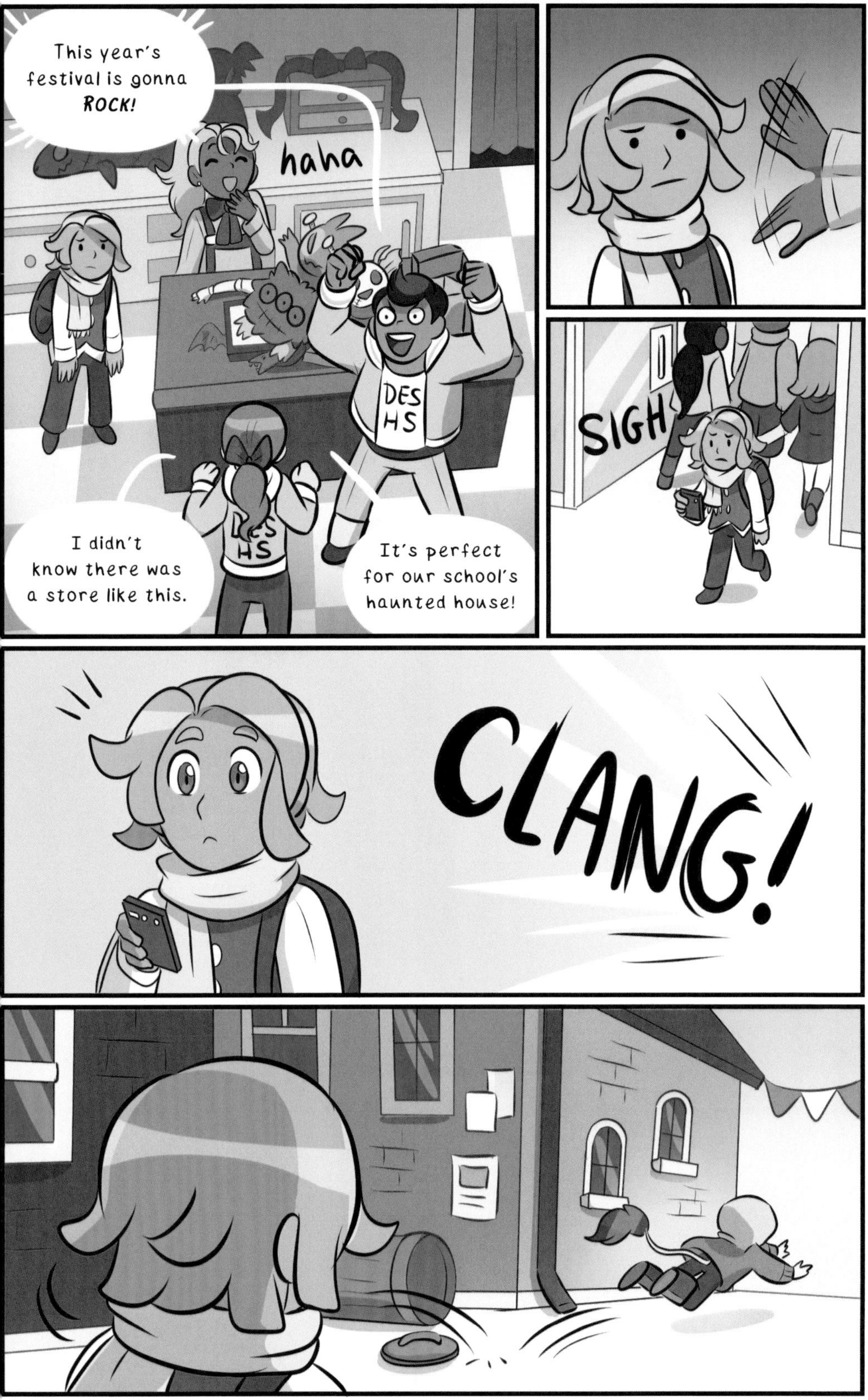
This year's festival is gonna ROCK!
haha
I didn't know there was a store like this.
It's perfect for our school's haunted house!
DES HS
SIGH
CLANG!

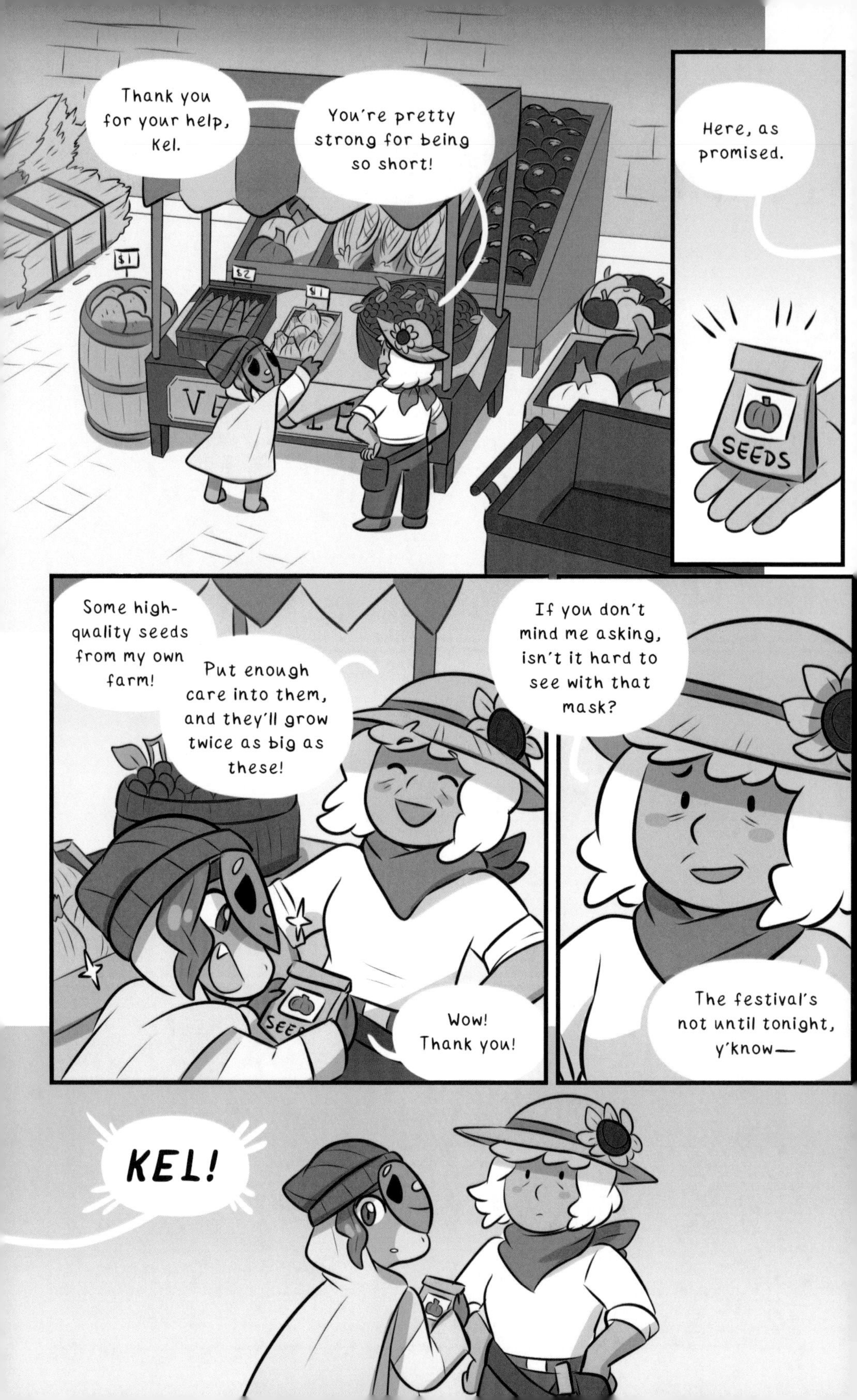
Thank you for your help, Kel.
You're pretty strong for being so short!
Here, as promised.
SEEDS
Some high-quality seeds from my own farm!
Put enough care into them, and they'll grow twice as big as these!
Wow! Thank you!
If you don't mind me asking, isn't it hard to see with that mask?
The festival's not until tonight, y'know—
KEL!

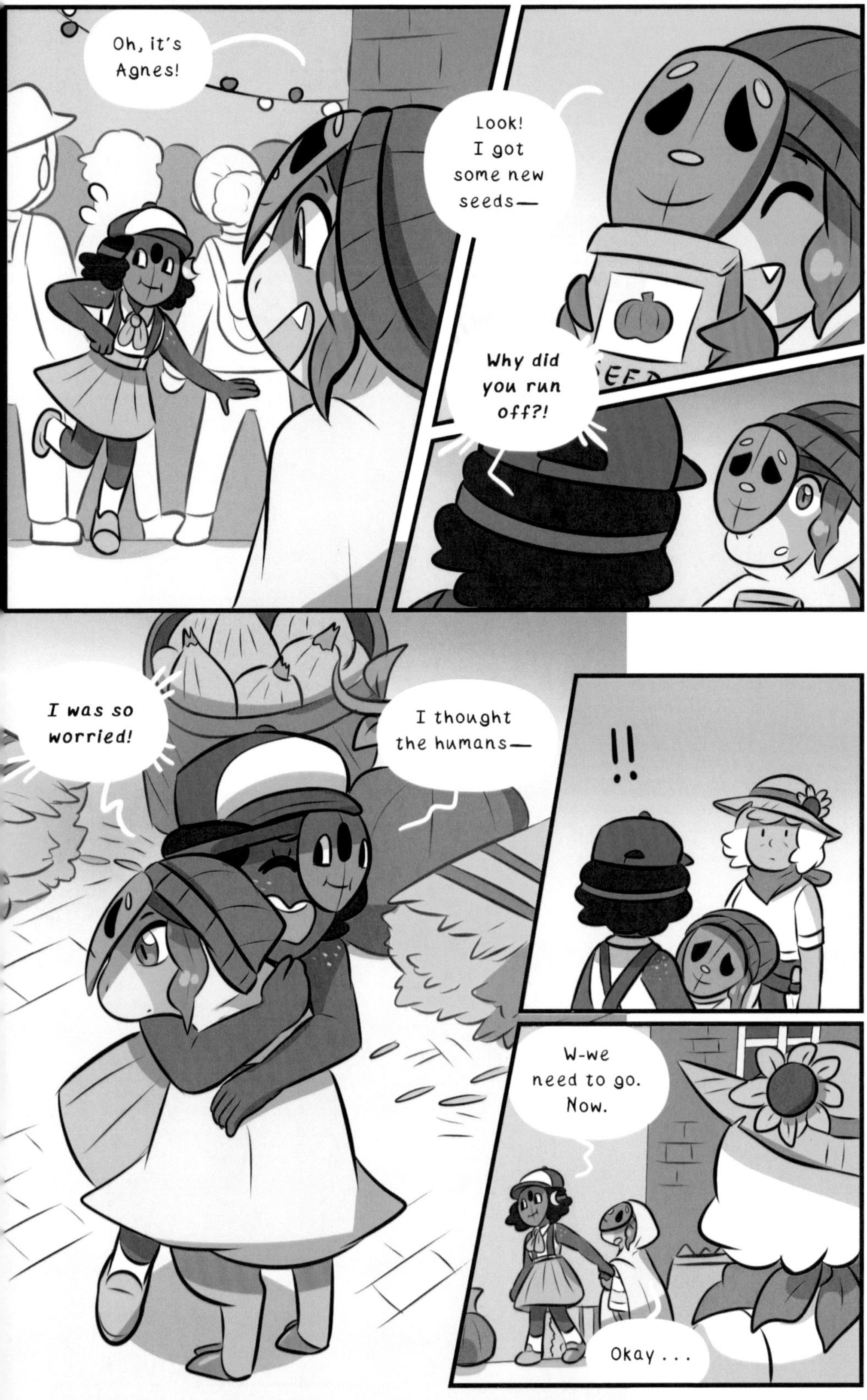
Oh, it's Agnes!
Look! I got some new seeds—
Why did you run off?!
I was so worried!
I thought the humans—
!!
W-we need to go. Now.
Okay . . .

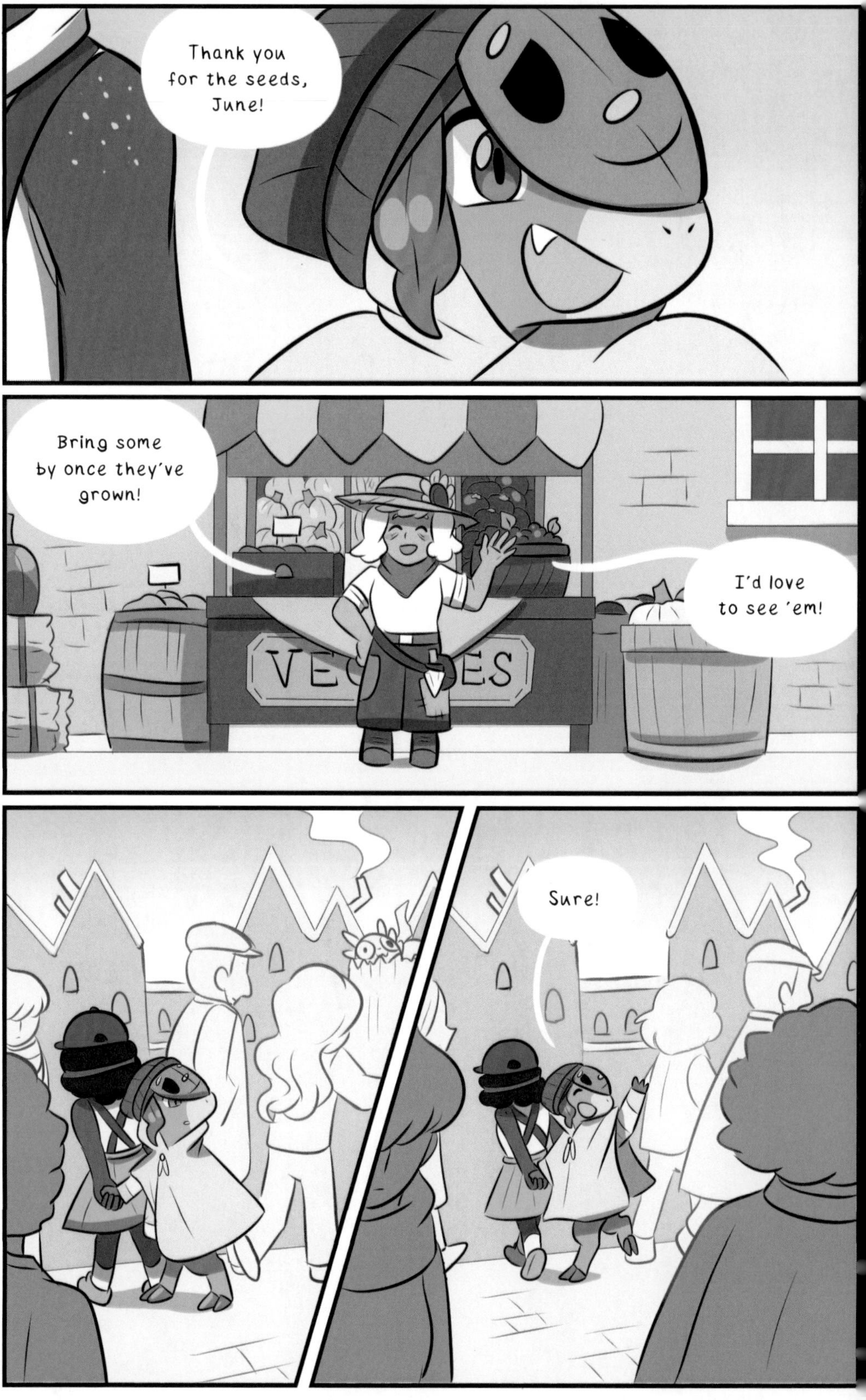
Thank you for the seeds, June!
Bring some by once they've grown!
I'd love to see 'em!
VEG ES
Sure!

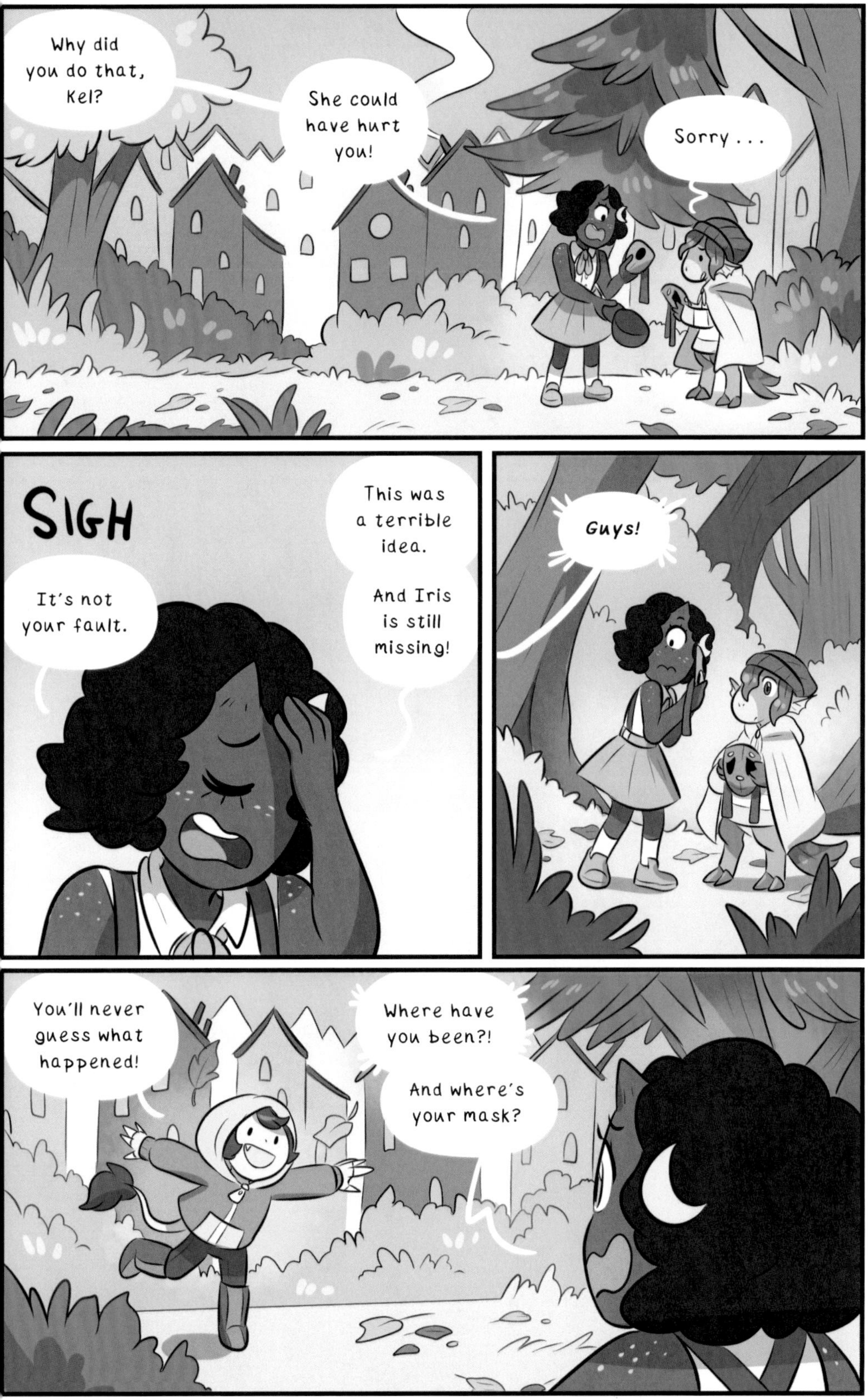
Why did you do that, Kel?
She could have hurt you!
Sorry . . .
SIGH
This was a terrible idea.
And Iris is still missing!
It's not your fault.
Guys!
You'll never guess what happened!
Where have you been?!
And where's your mask?

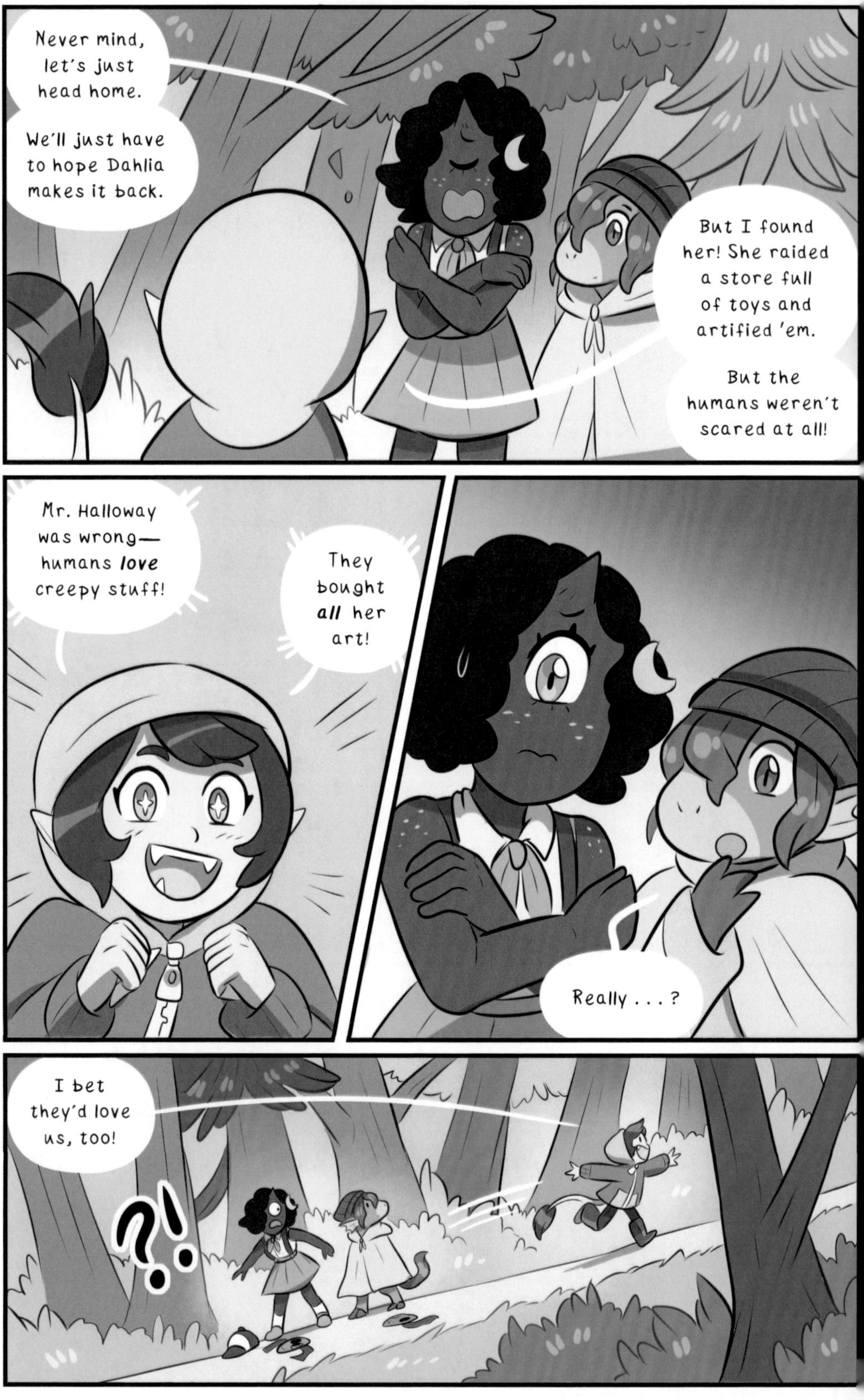
Never mind, let's just head home.
We'll just have to hope Dahlia makes it back.
But I found her! She raided a store full of toys and artified 'em.
But the humans weren't scared at all!
Mr. Halloway was wrong— humans *love* creepy stuff!
They bought *all* her art!
Really . . . ?
I bet they'd love us, too!
?!

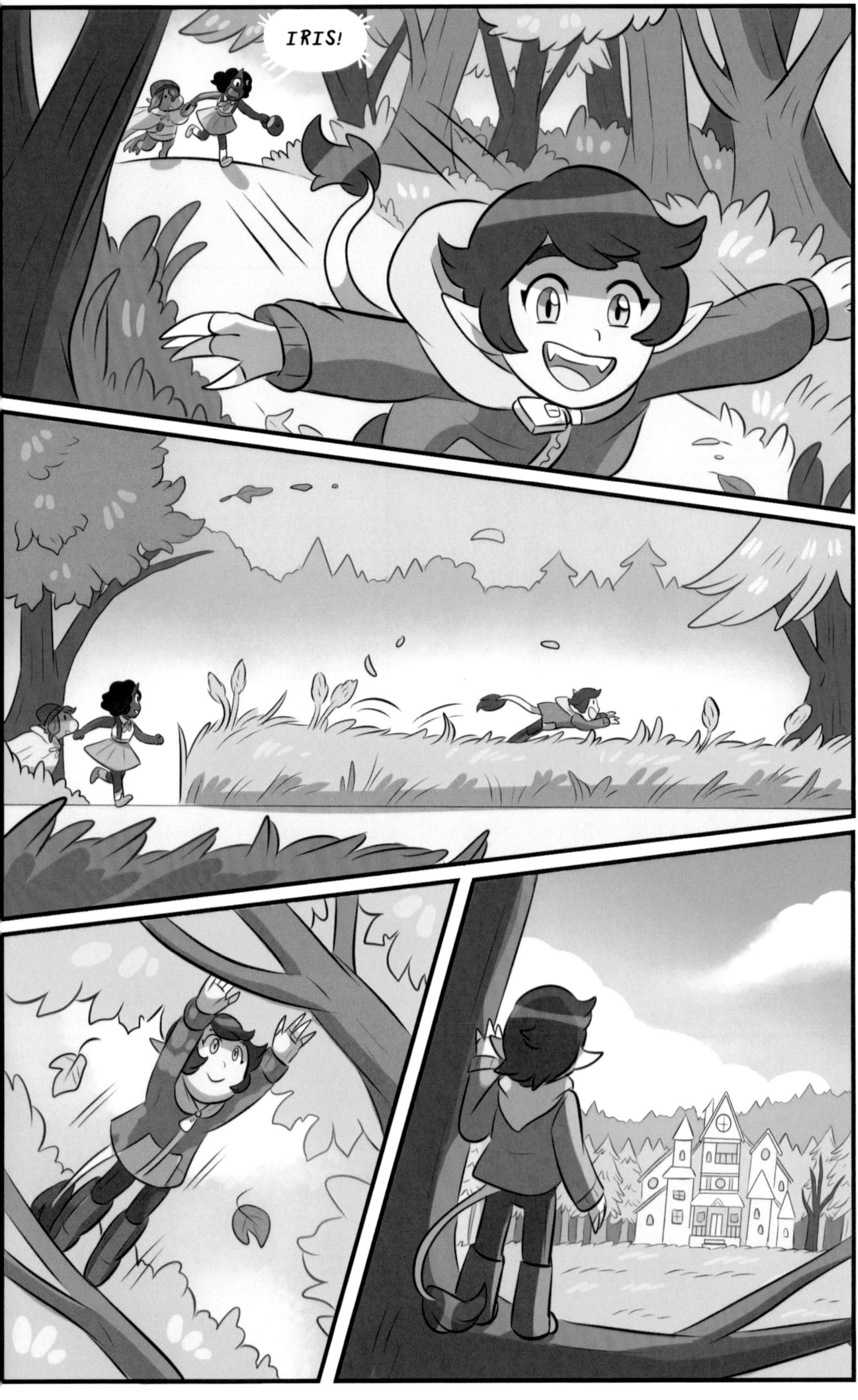
IRIS!

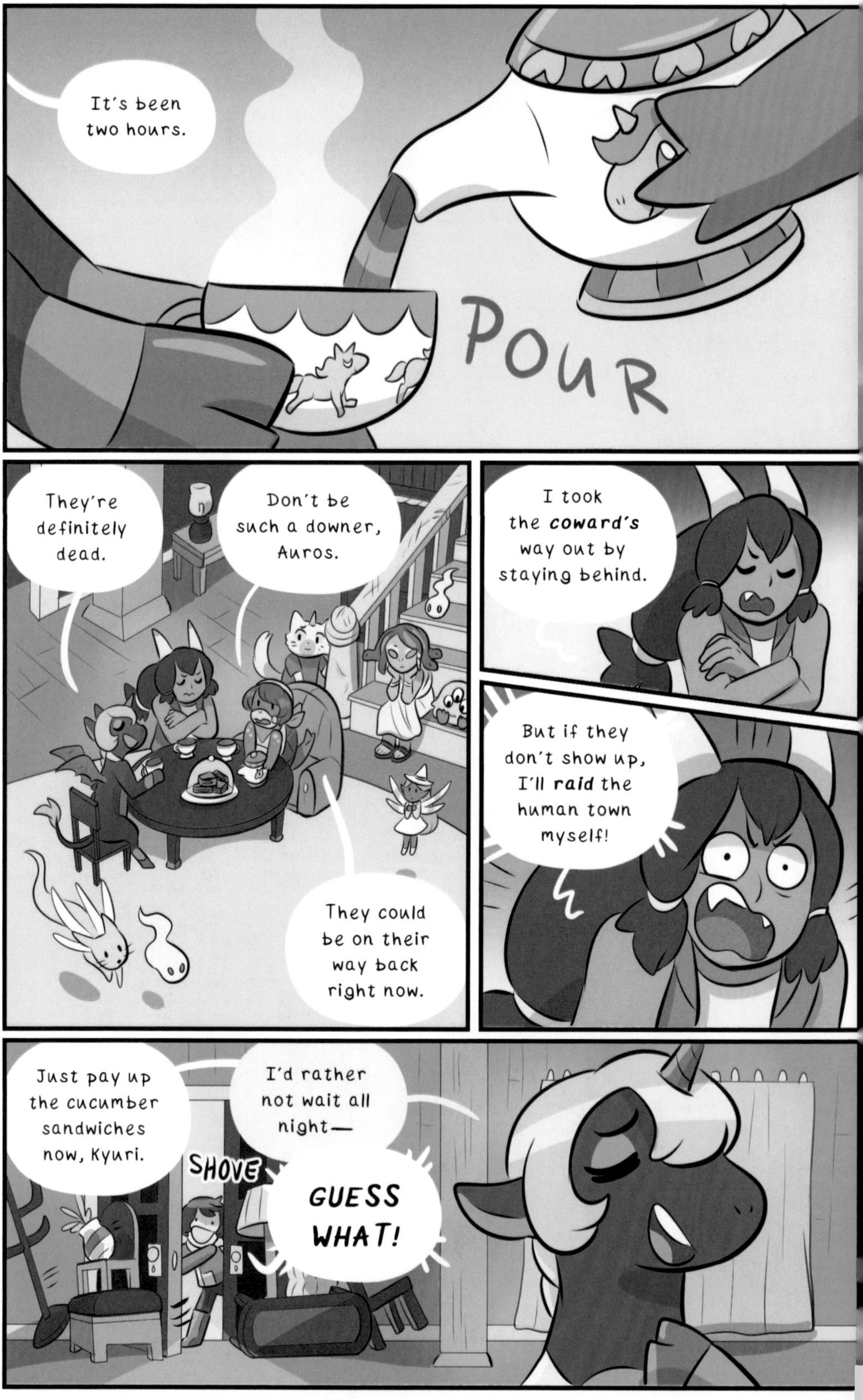

It's been two hours.
POUR
They're definitely dead.
Don't be such a downer, Auros.
They could be on their way back right now.
I took the **coward's** way out by staying behind.
But if they don't show up, I'll **raid** the human town myself!
Just pay up the cucumber sandwiches now, Kyuri.
I'd rather not wait all night—
SHOVE
GUESS WHAT!

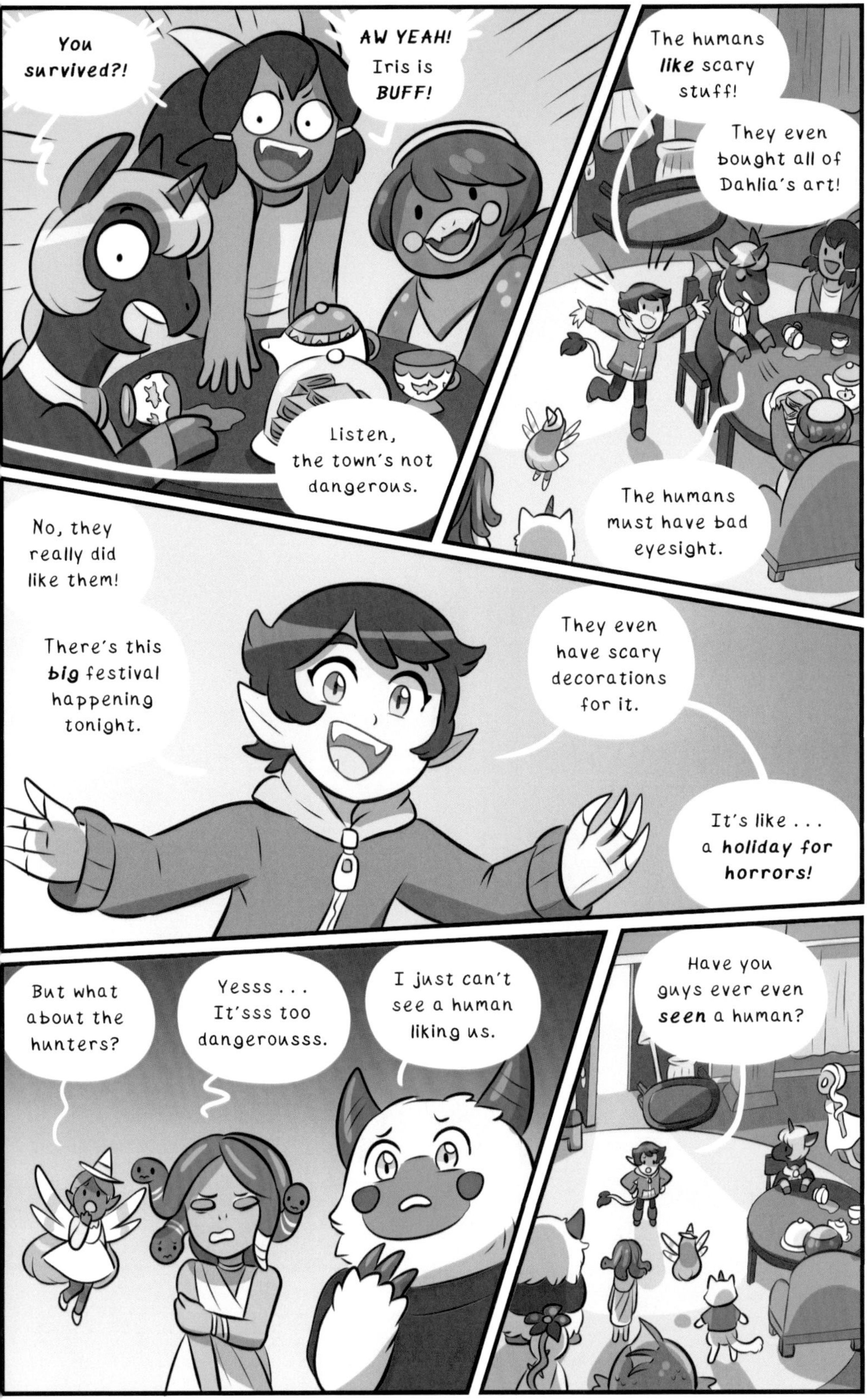
You survived?!
AW YEAH! Iris is BUFF!
Listen, the town's not dangerous.
The humans like scary stuff!
They even bought all of Dahlia's art!
The humans must have bad eyesight.
No, they really did like them!
There's this big festival happening tonight.
They even have scary decorations for it.
It's like . . . a holiday for horrors!
But what about the hunters?
Yesss . . . It'sss too dangeroussss.
I just can't see a human liking us.
Have you guys ever even seen a human?

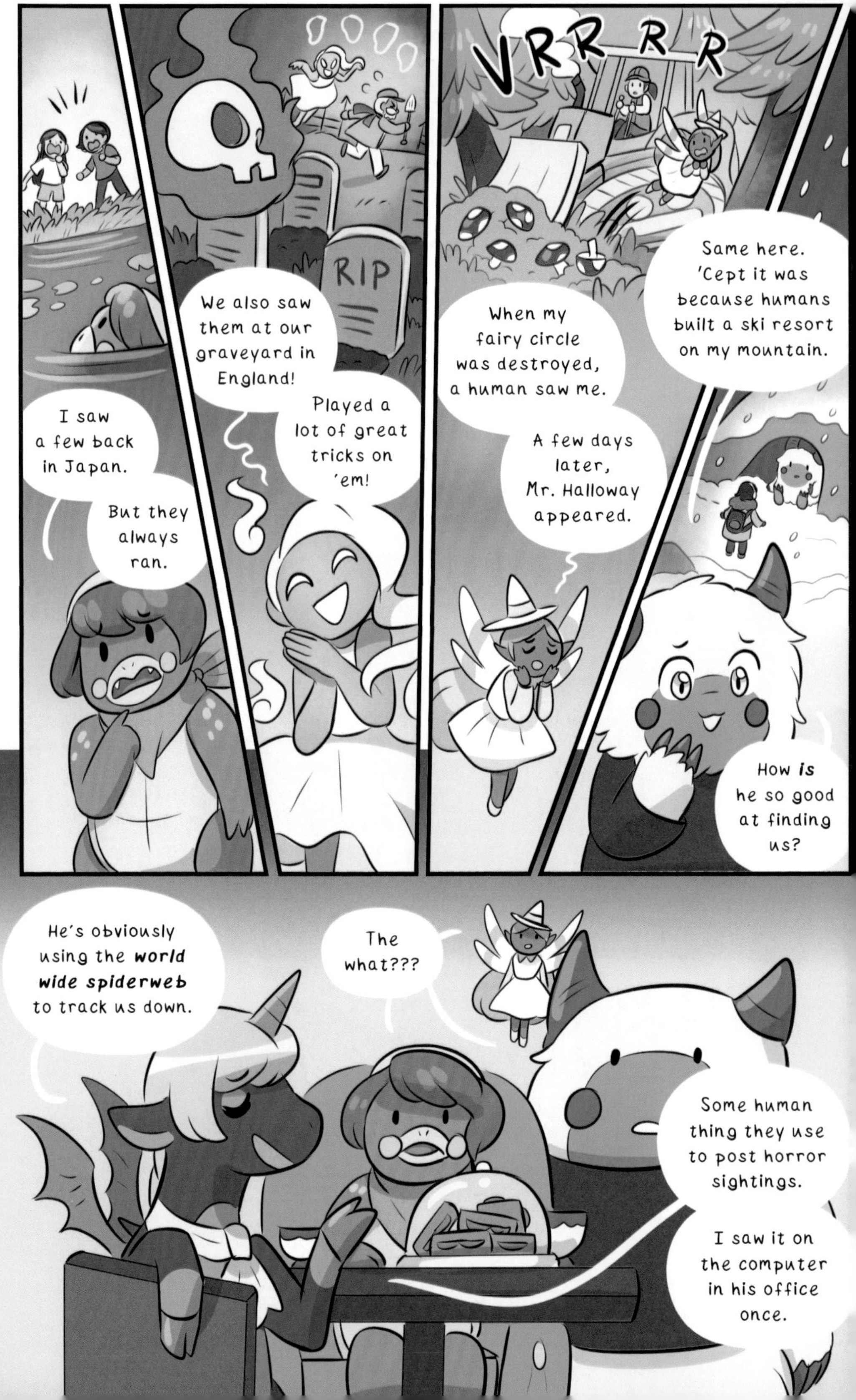

I saw a few back in Japan.
But they always ran.
We also saw them at our graveyard in England!
Played a lot of great tricks on 'em!
RIP
VRR R R
When my fairy circle was destroyed, a human saw me.
A few days later, Mr. Halloway appeared.
Same here. 'Cept it was because humans built a ski resort on my mountain.
How **is** he so good at finding us?
He's obviously using the ***world wide spiderweb*** to track us down.
The what???
Some human thing they use to post horror sightings.
I saw it on the computer in his office once.

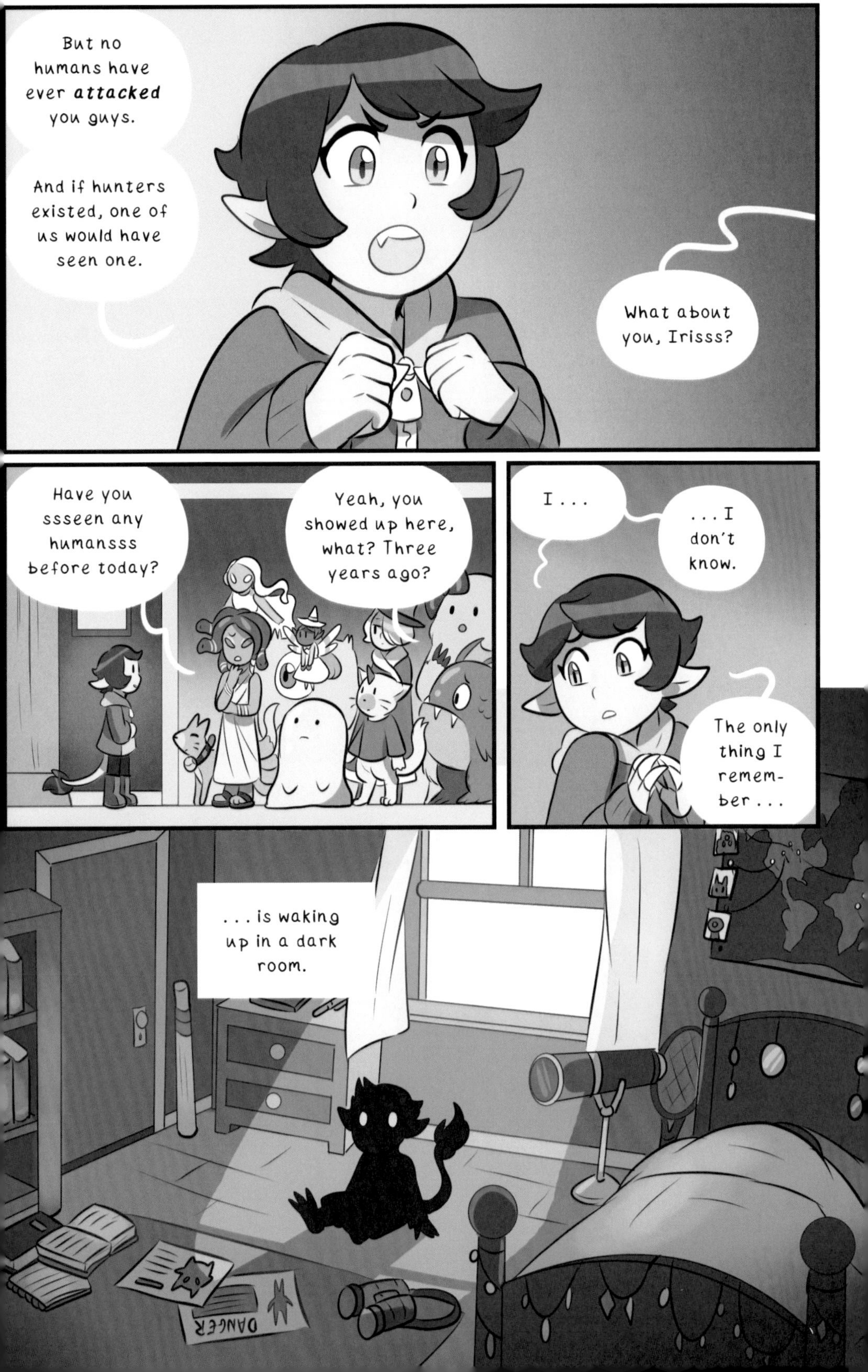
But no humans have ever ***attacked*** you guys.
And if hunters existed, one of us would have seen one.
What about you, Irisss?
Have you ssseen any humansss before today?
Yeah, you showed up here, what? Three years ago?
I . . .
. . . I don't know.
The only thing I remem-ber . . .
. . . is waking up in a dark room.
DANGER

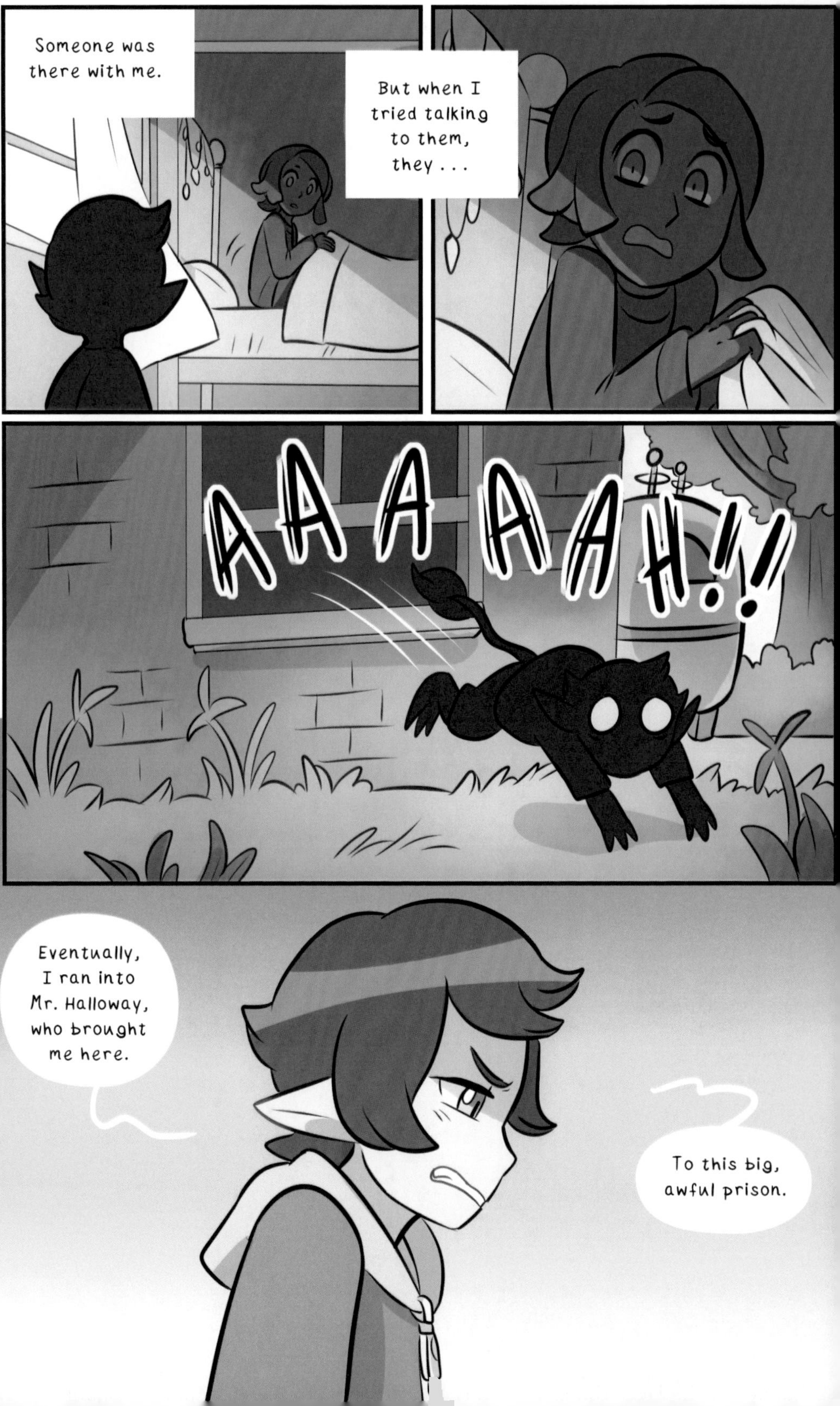
Someone was there with me.
But when I tried talking to them, they . . .
AAAAAAH!!
Eventually, I ran into Mr. Halloway, who brought me here.
To this big, awful prison.

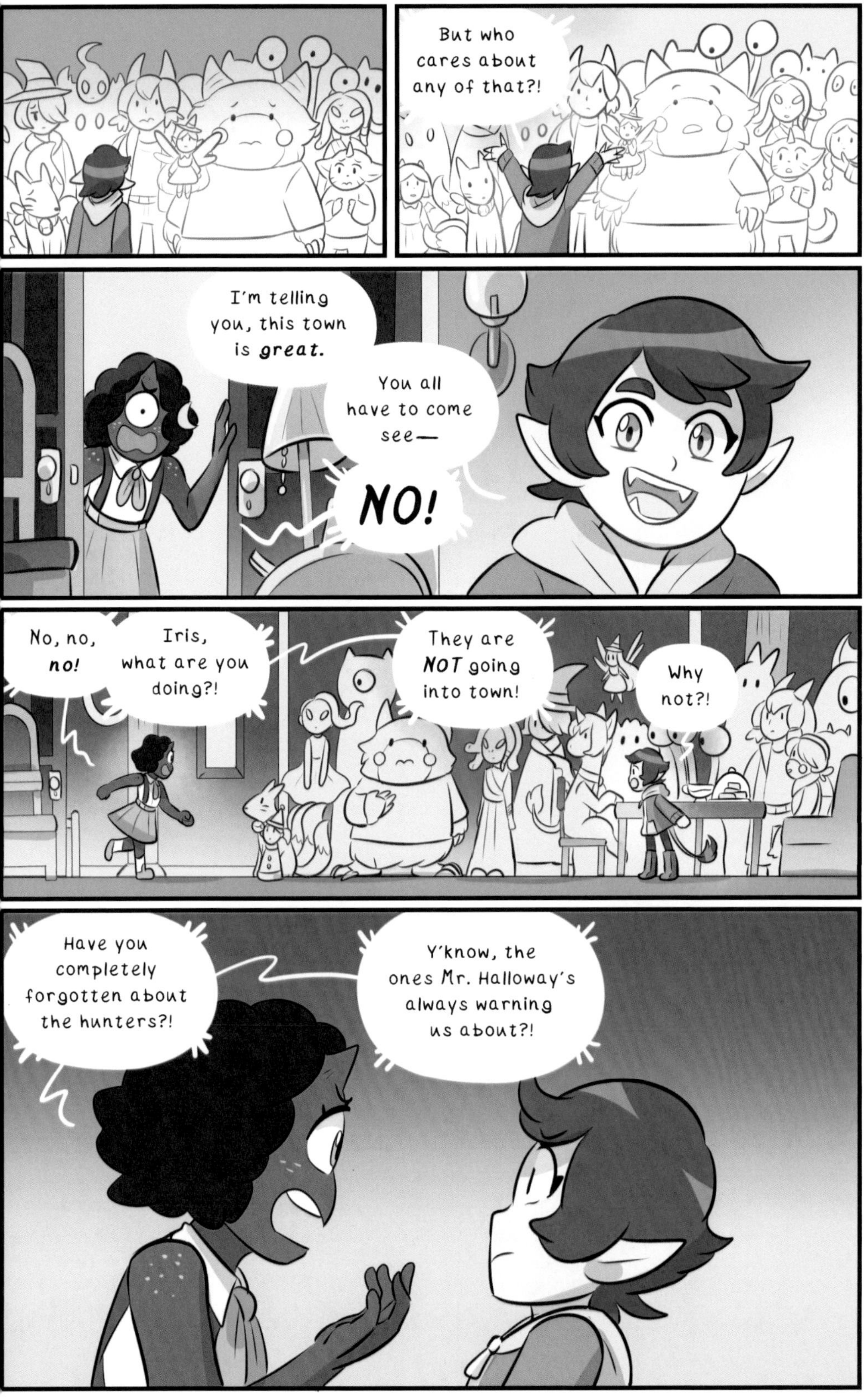
But who cares about any of that?!
I'm telling you, this town is **great.**
You all have to come see—
NO!
No, no, **no!**
Iris, what are you doing?!
They are **NOT** going into town!
Why not?!
Have you completely forgotten about the hunters?!
Y'know, the ones Mr. Halloway's always warning us about?!

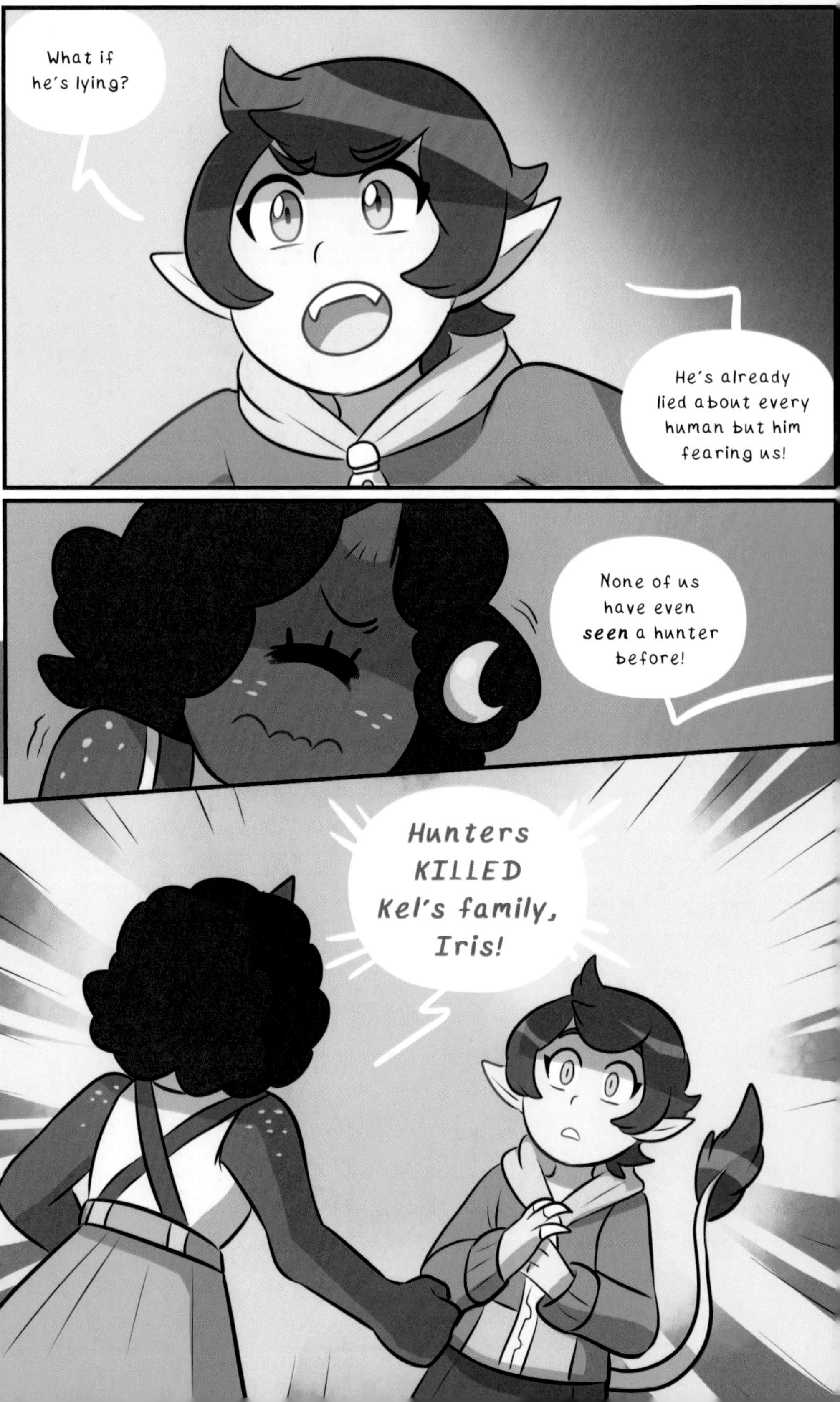
What if he's lying?
He's already lied about every human but him fearing us!
None of us have even **seen** a hunter before!
Hunters KILLED Kel's family, Iris!

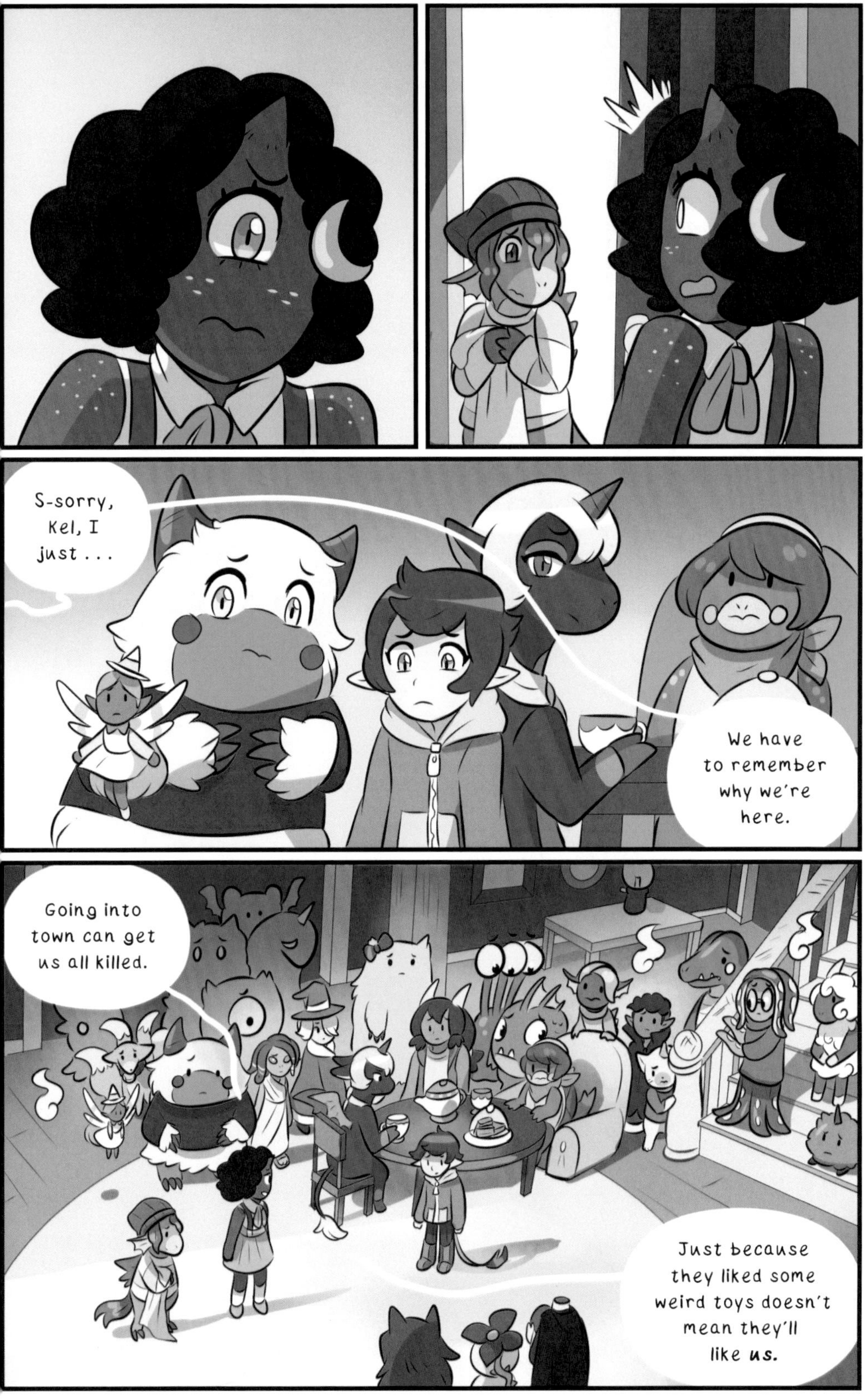
S-sorry, Kel, I just . . .
We have to remember why we're here.
Going into town can get us all killed.
Just because they liked some weird toys doesn't mean they'll like **us.**

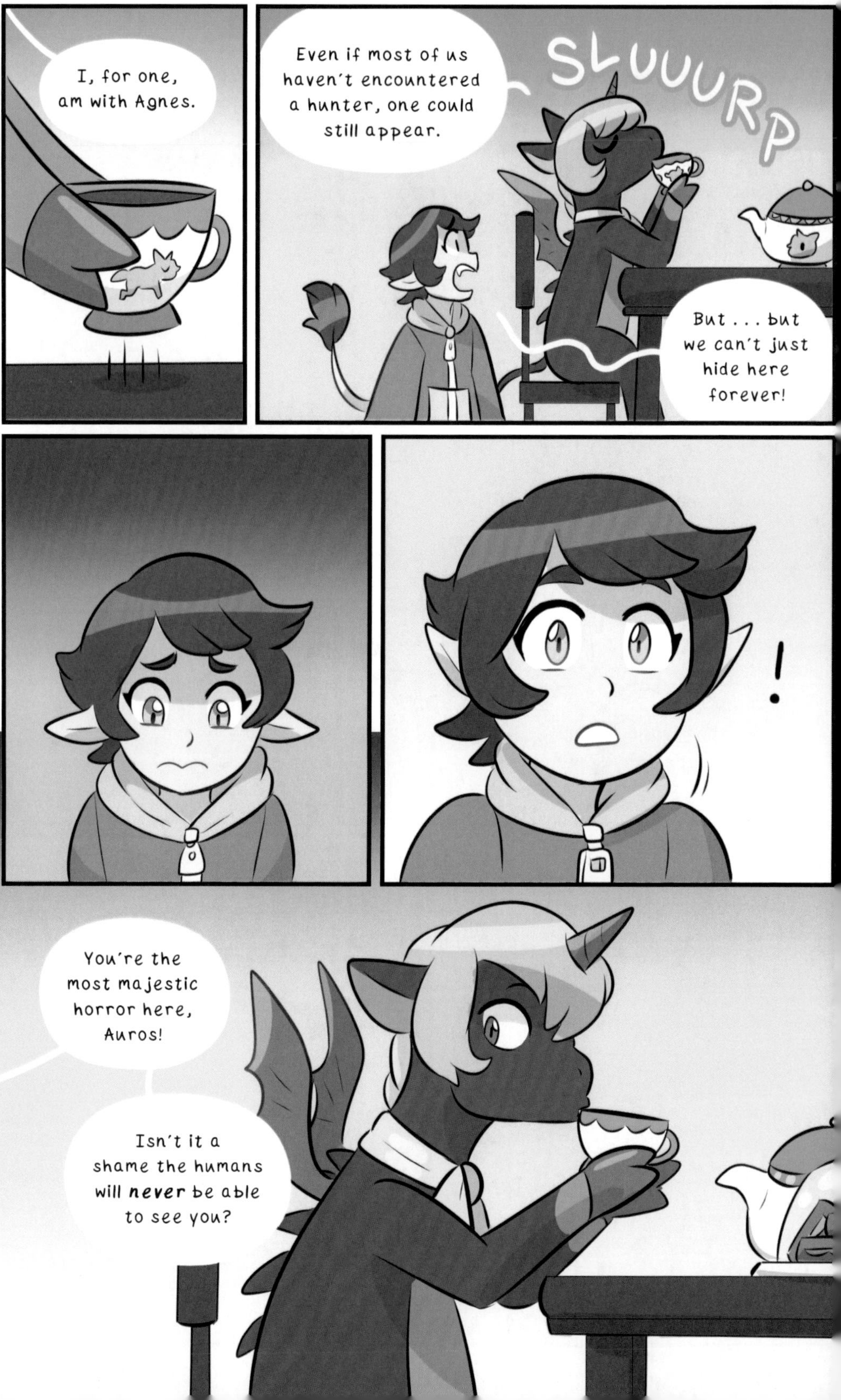

I, for one, am with Agnes.
Even if most of us haven't encountered a hunter, one could still appear.
SLUUURP
But . . . but we can't just hide here forever!
!
You're the most majestic horror here, Auros!
Isn't it a shame the humans will **never** be able to see you?

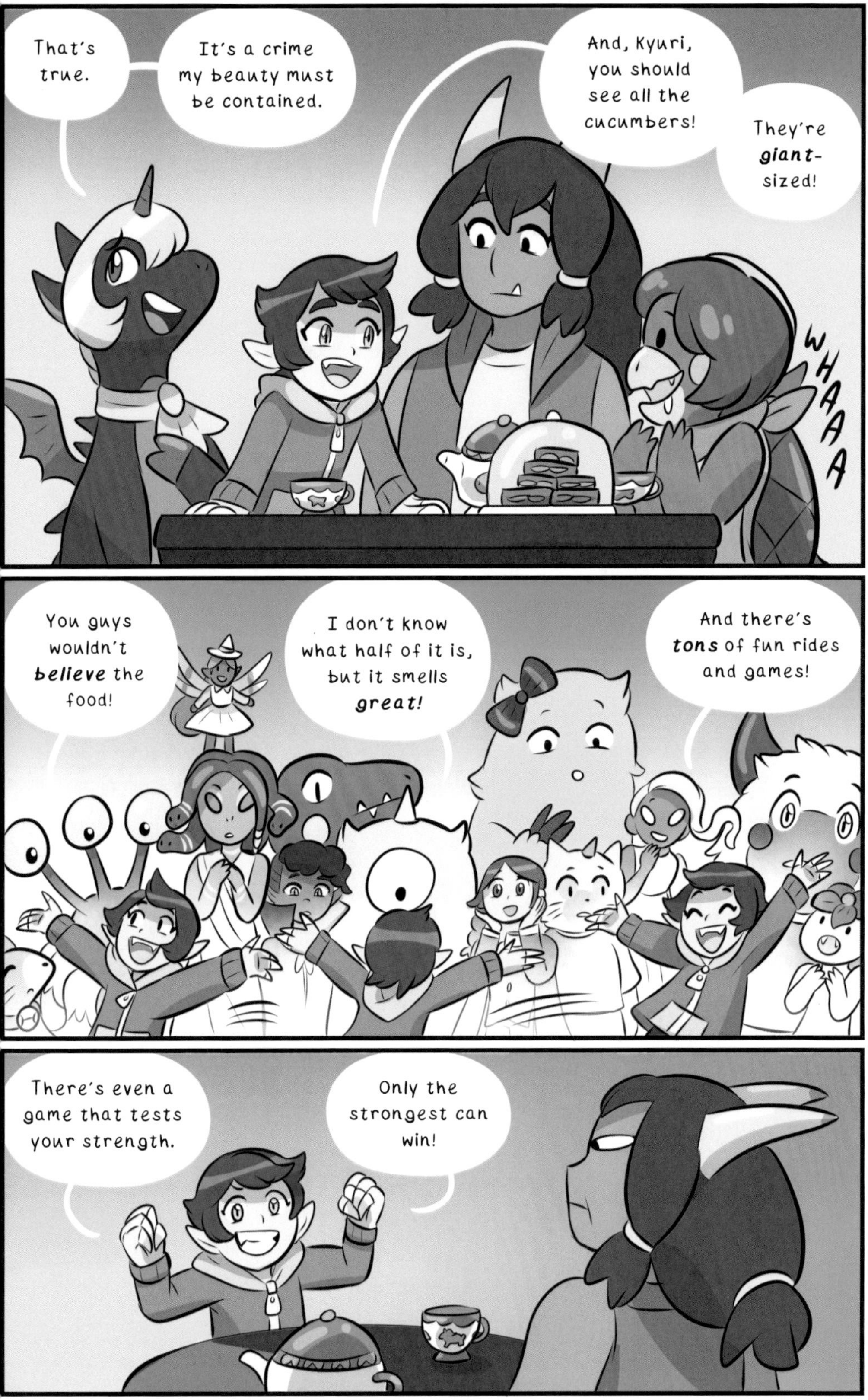
That's true.
It's a crime my beauty must be contained.
And, Kyuri, you should see all the cucumbers!
They're giant-sized!
WHAAAA
You guys wouldn't believe the food!
I don't know what half of it is, but it smells great!
And there's tons of fun rides and games!
There's even a game that tests your strength.
Only the strongest can win!

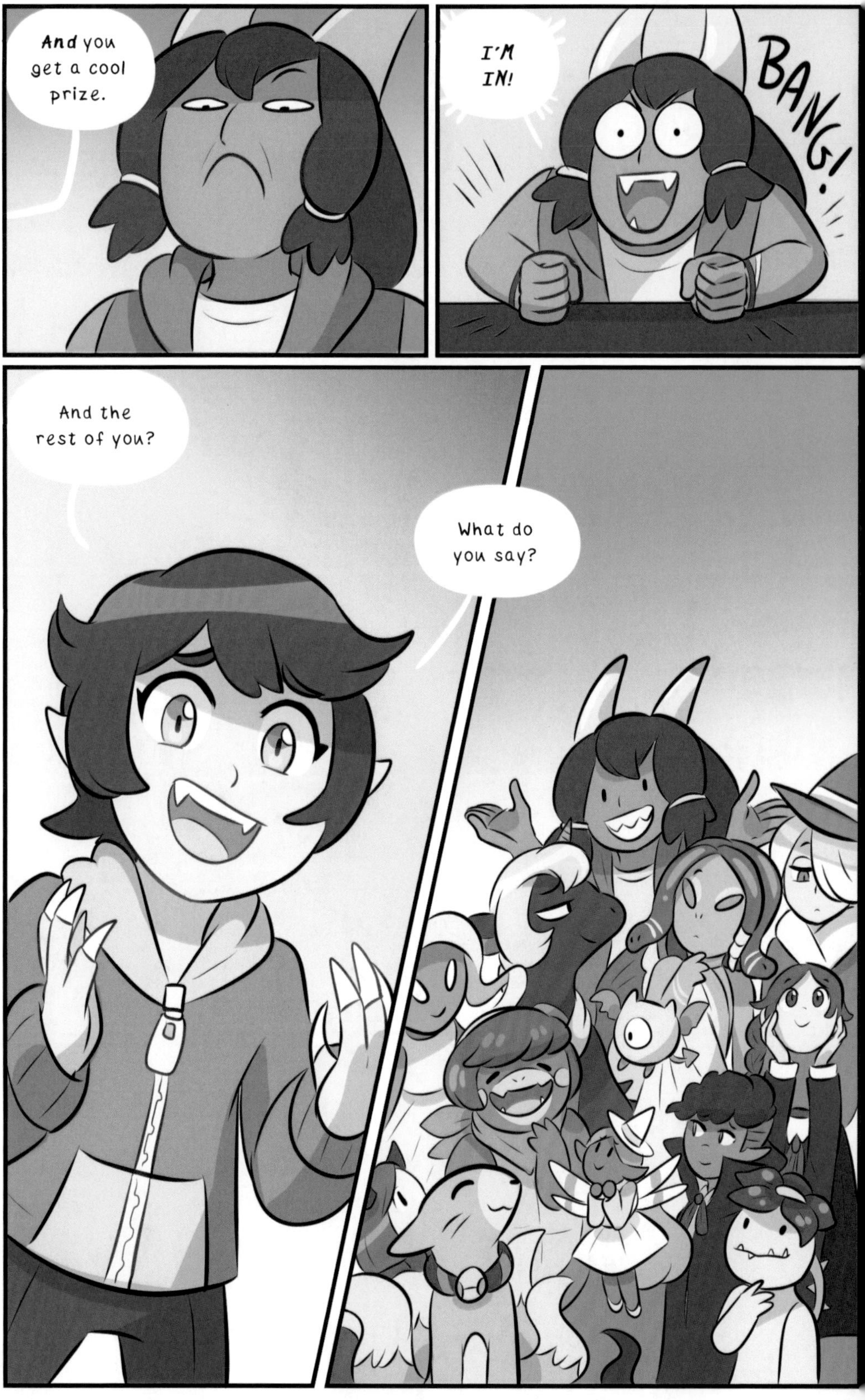
And you get a cool prize.
I'M IN!
BANG!
And the rest of you?
What do you say?

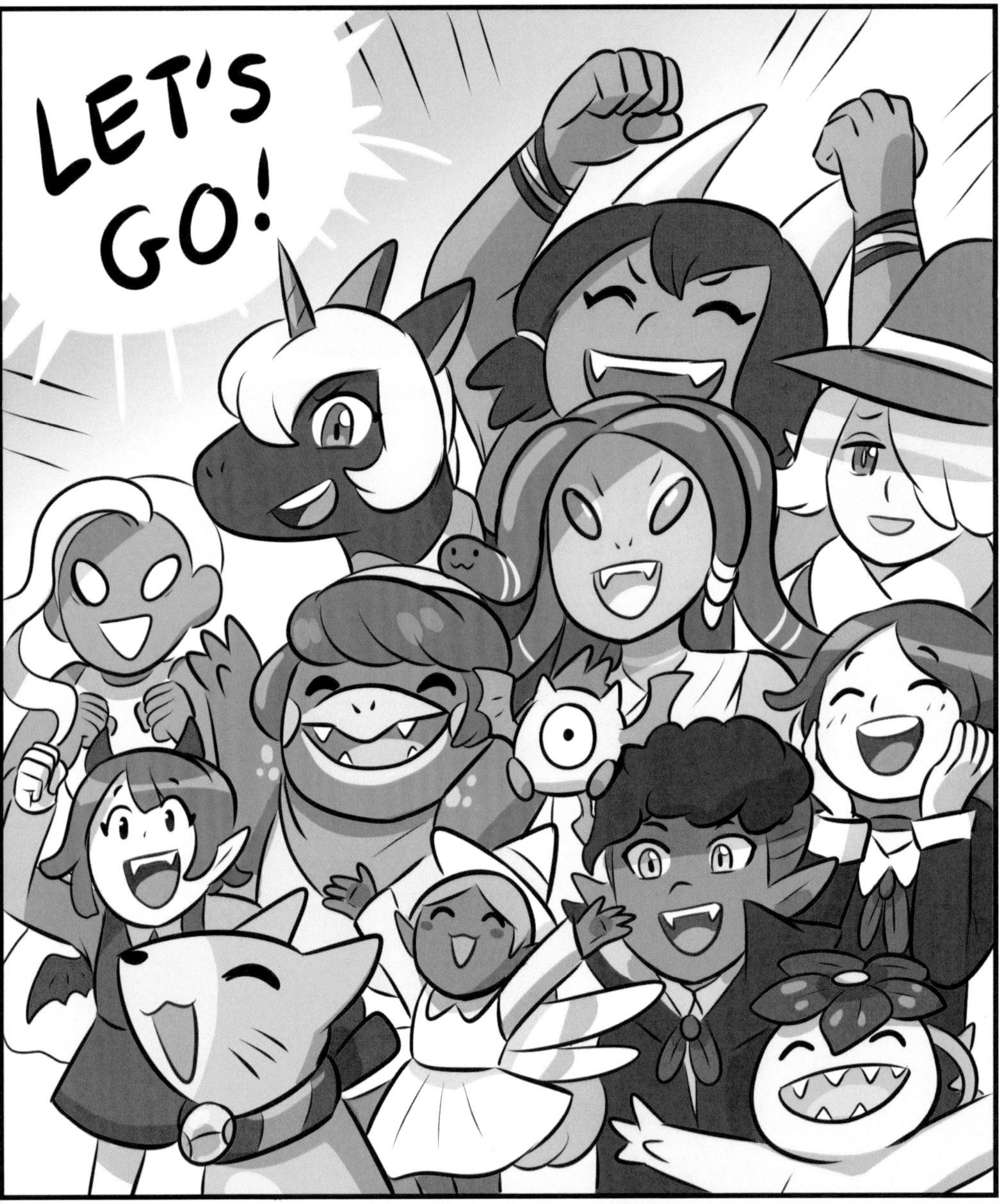
LET'S GO!

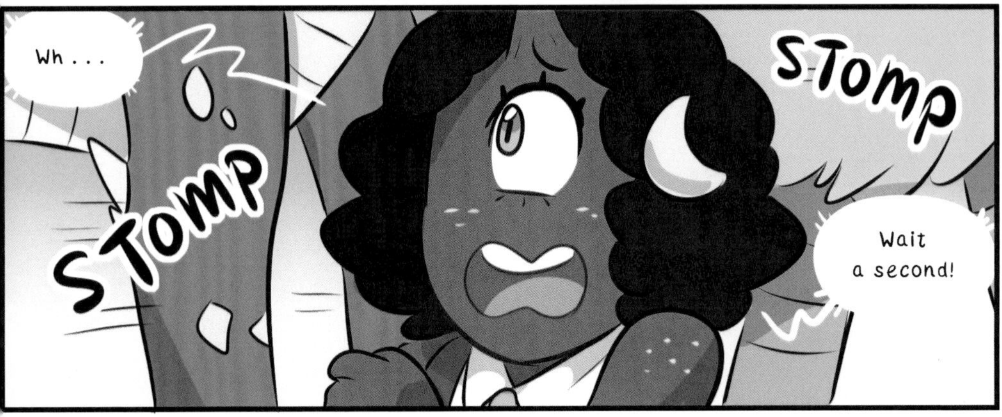
Wh . . .
STOMP
STOMP
Wait a second!

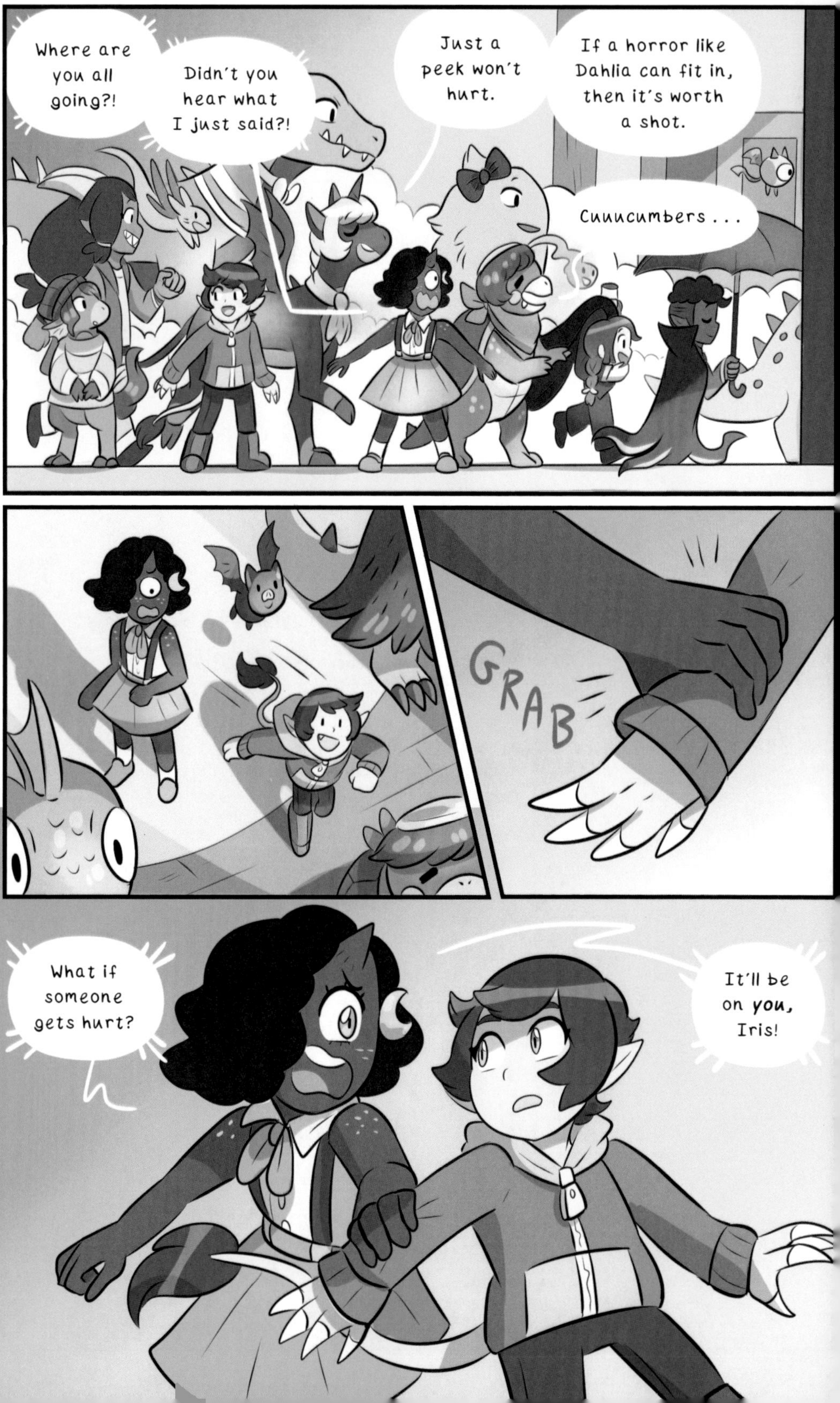
Where are you all going?!
Didn't you hear what I just said?!
Just a peek won't hurt.
If a horror like Dahlia can fit in, then it's worth a shot.
Cuuucumbers . . .
GRAB
What if someone gets hurt?
It'll be on **you**, Iris!

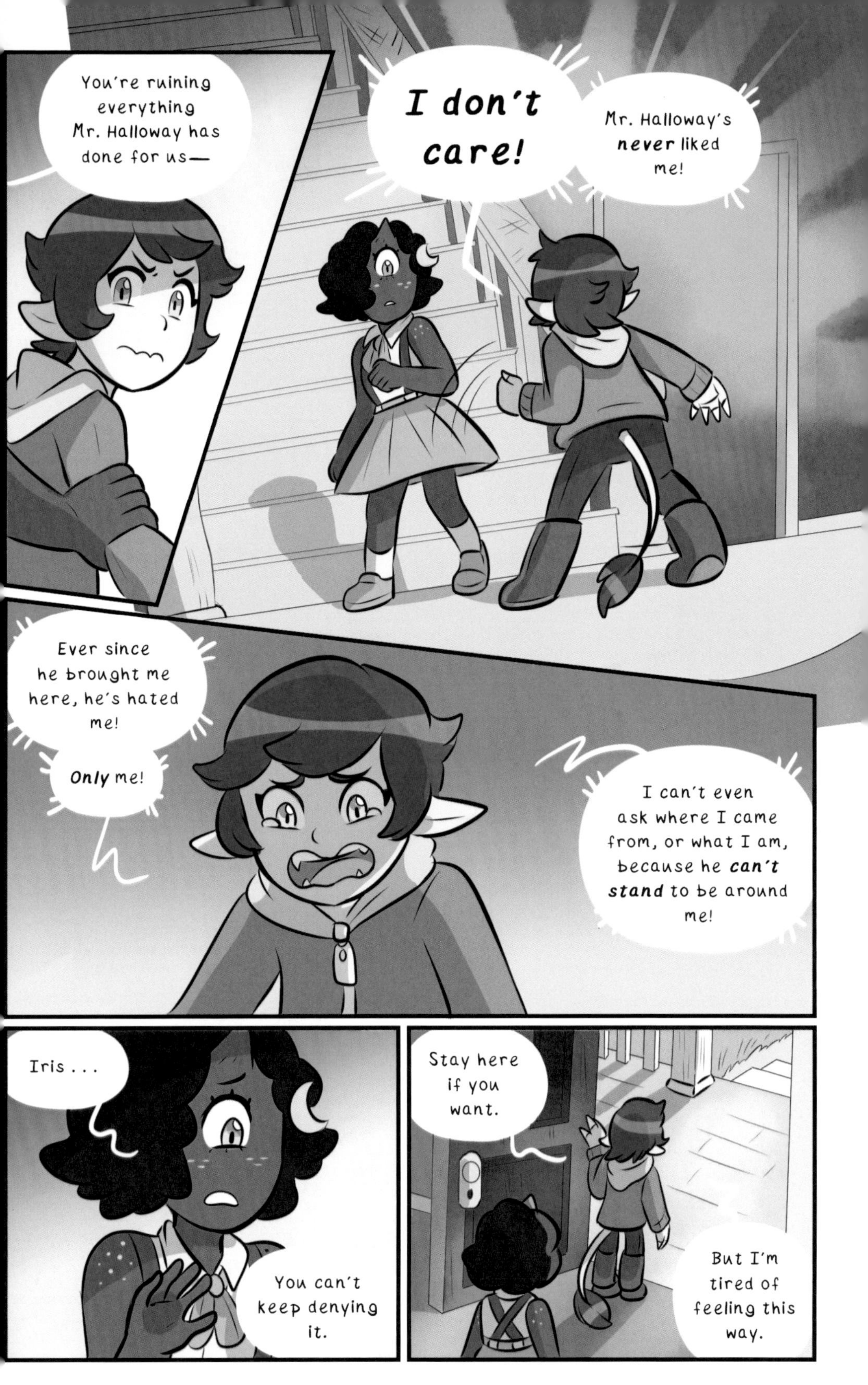
You're ruining everything Mr. Halloway has done for us—
I don't care!
Mr. Halloway's never liked me!
Ever since he brought me here, he's hated me!
Only me!
I can't even ask where I came from, or what I am, because he can't stand to be around me!
Iris . . .
You can't keep denying it.
Stay here if you want.
But I'm tired of feeling this way.

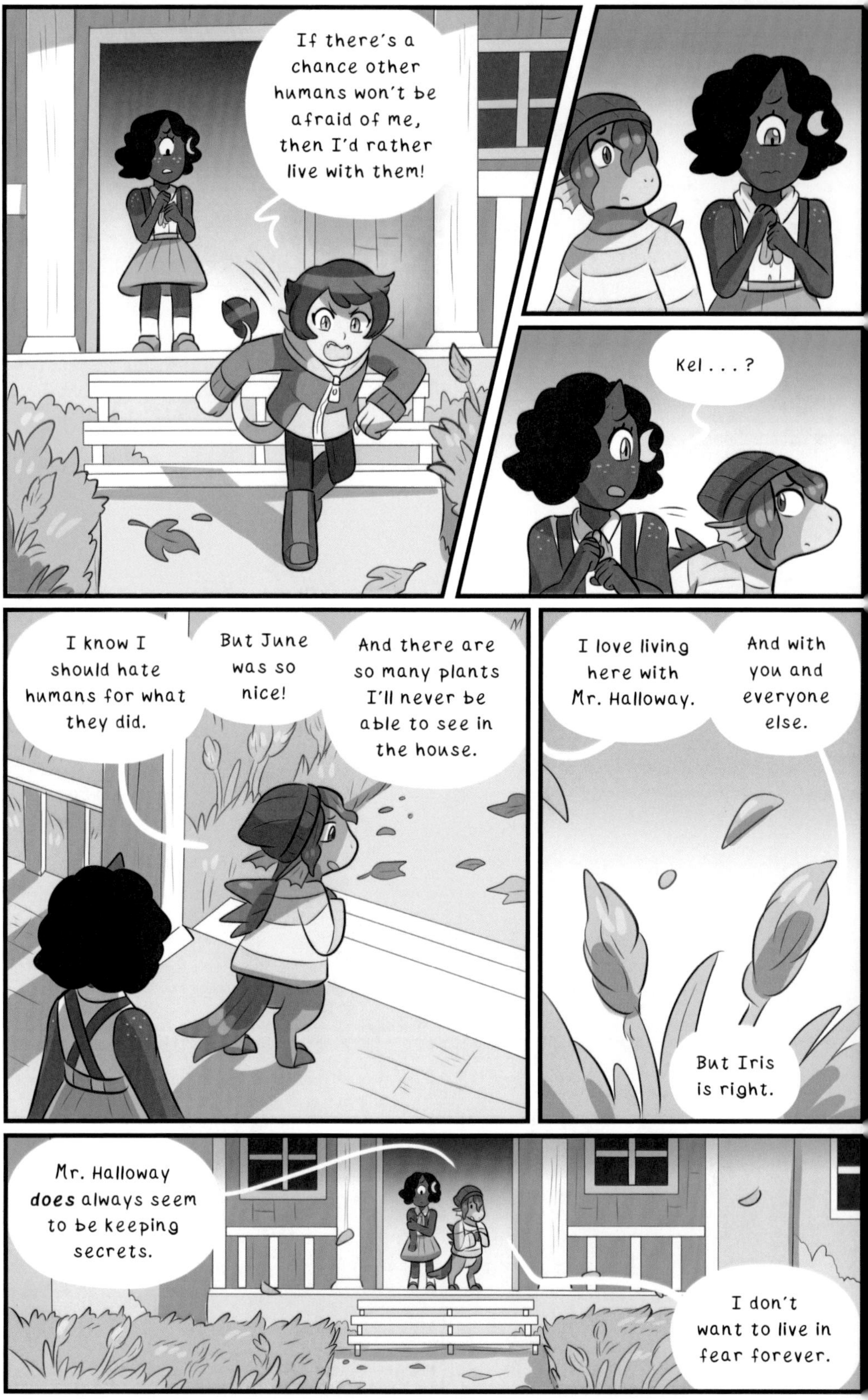
If there's a chance other humans won't be afraid of me, then I'd rather live with them!
Kel . . . ?
I know I should hate humans for what they did.
But June was so nice!
And there are so many plants I'll never be able to see in the house.
I love living here with Mr. Halloway.
And with you and everyone else.
But Iris is right.
Mr. Halloway **does** always seem to be keeping secrets.
I don't want to live in fear forever.

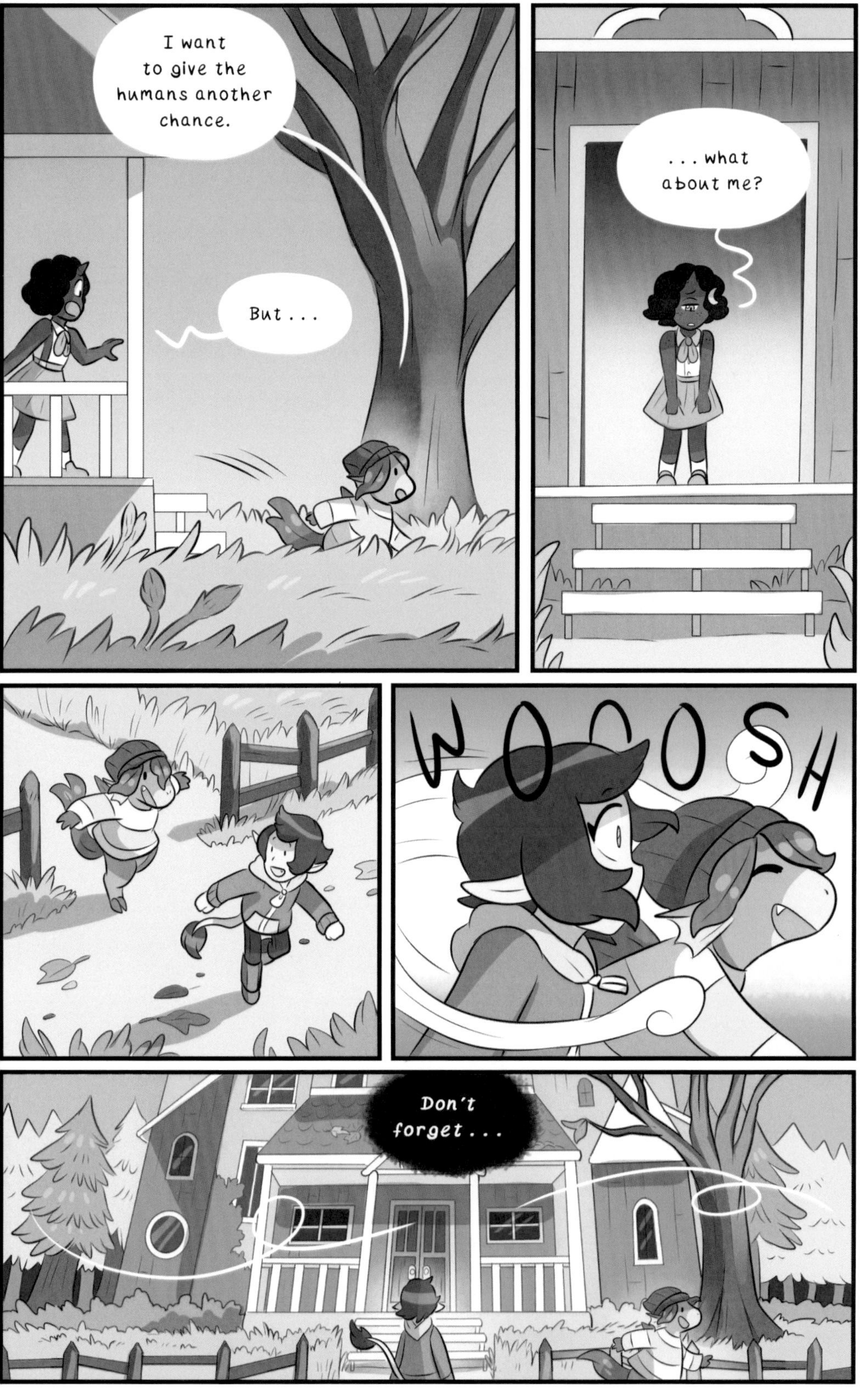
I want to give the humans another chance.
But . . .
. . . what about me?
WOOOSH
Don't forget . . .

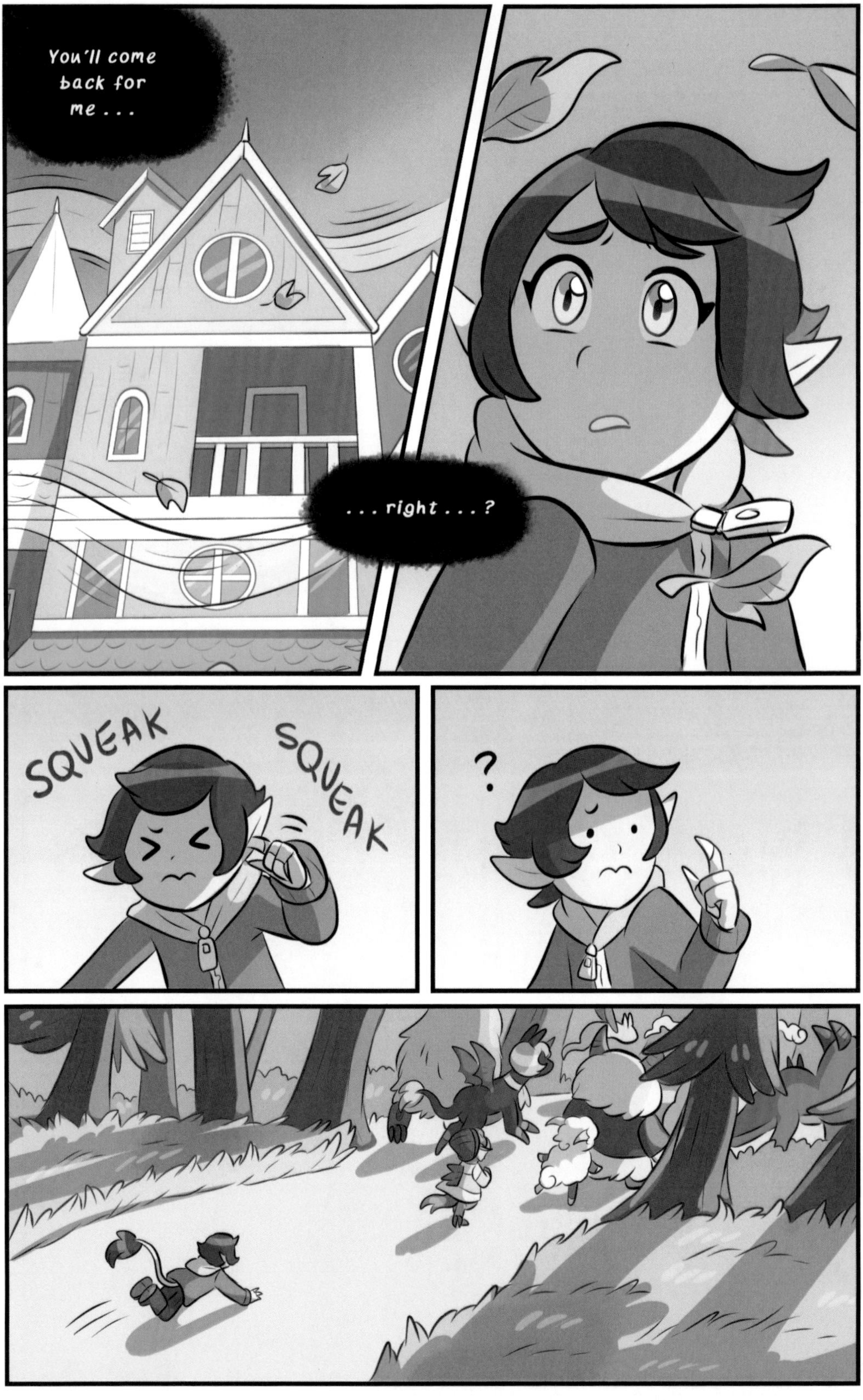
You'll come back for me . . .
. . . right . . . ?
SQUEAK
SQUEAK
?

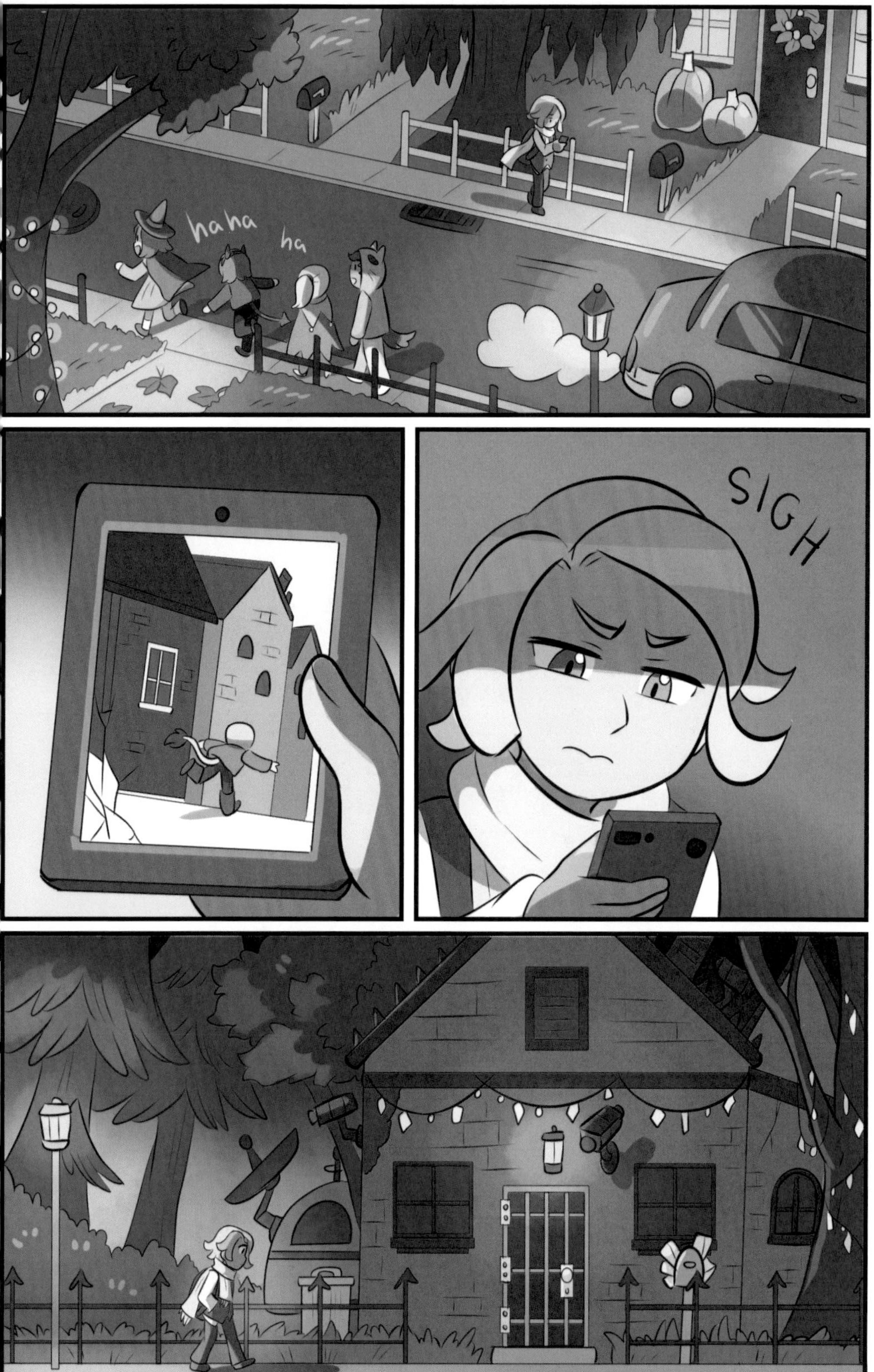
ha ha
ha
SIGH

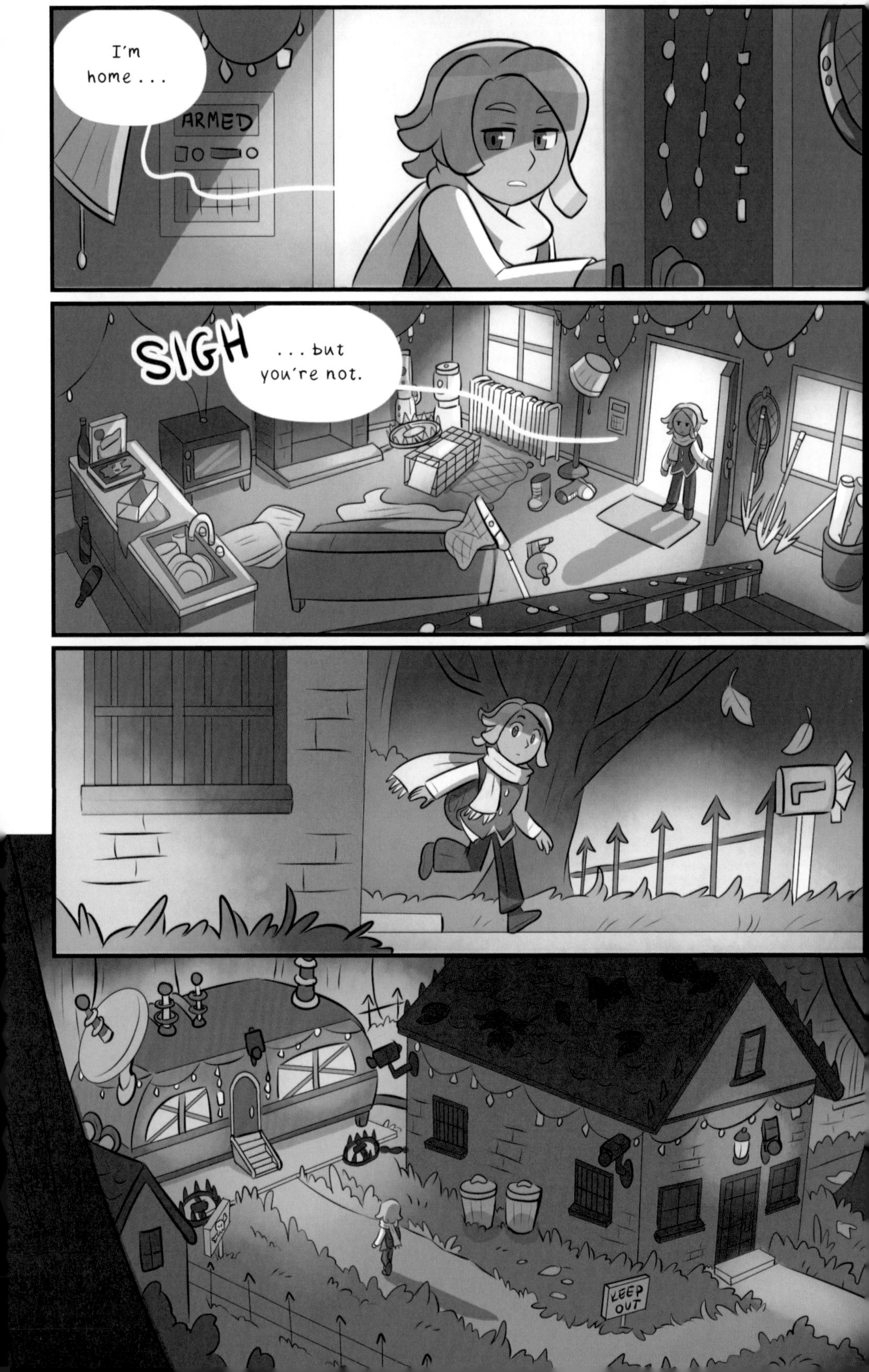
I'm home . . .
ARMED
SIGH
. . . but you're not.
KEEP OUT

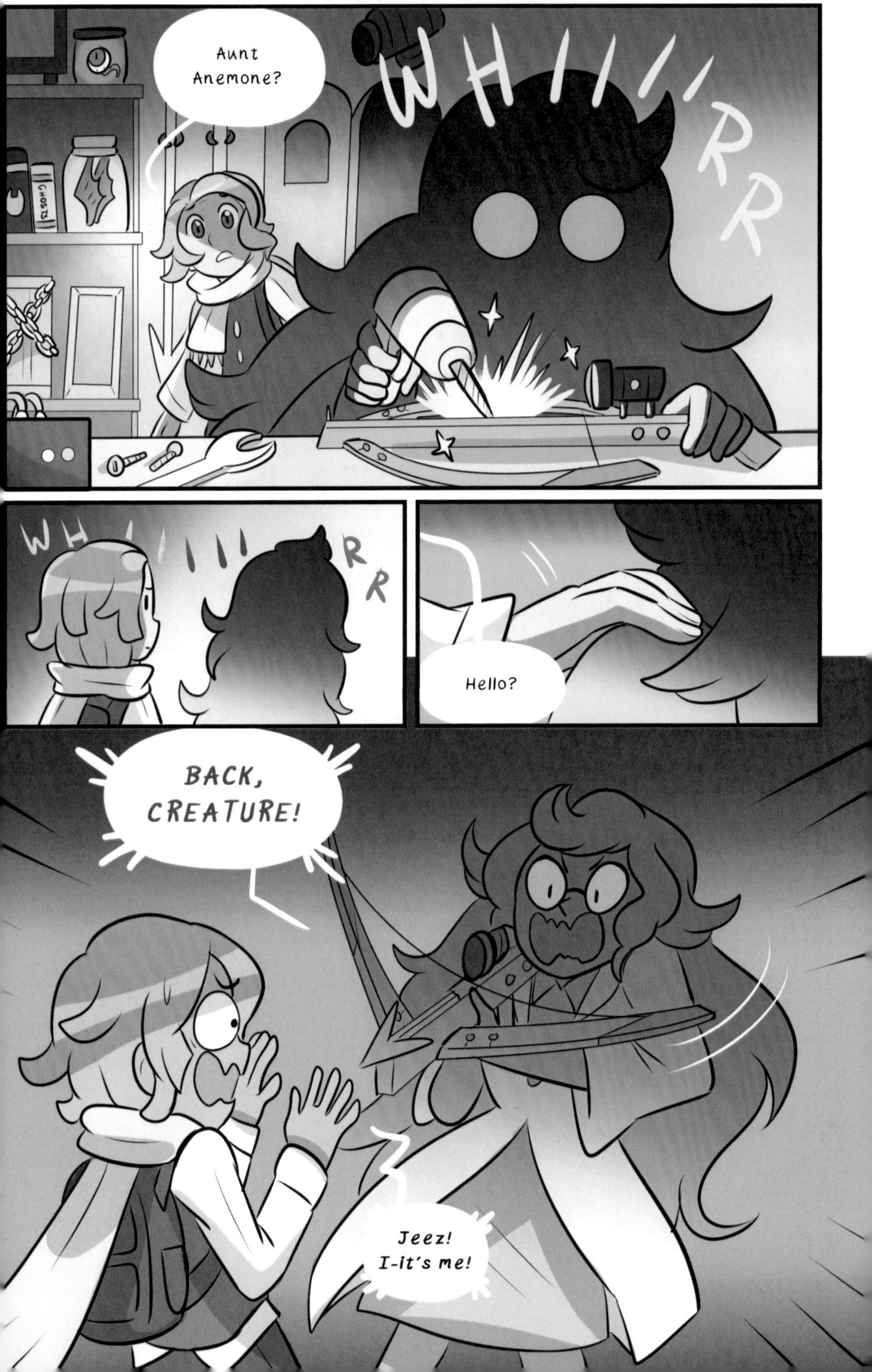
Aunt Anemone?
WHIIIIRR
GHOSTS
WHIIIIRR
Hello?
BACK, CREATURE!
Jeez! I-it's me!

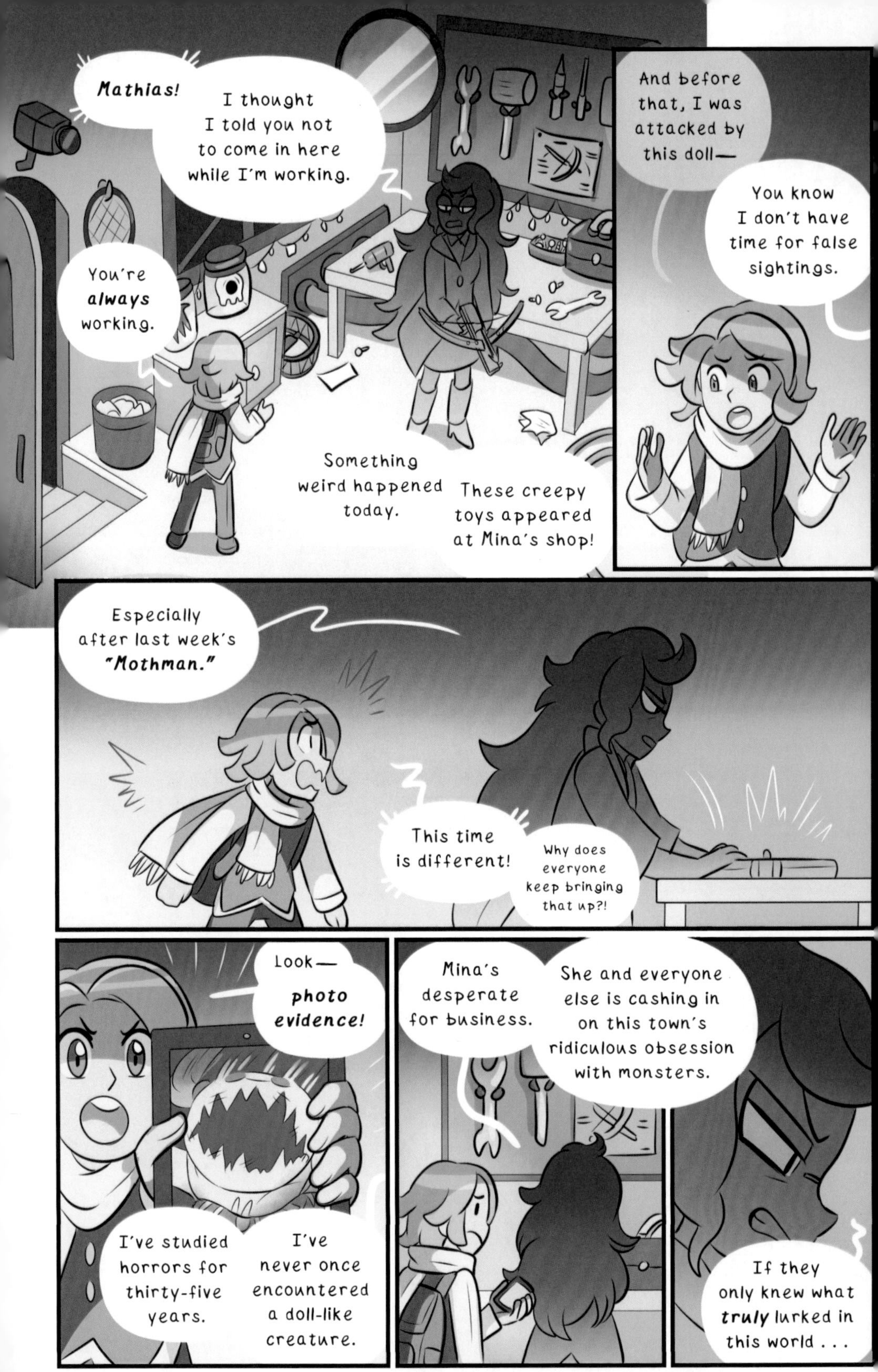
Mathias!
I thought I told you not to come in here while I'm working.
You're *always* working.
Something weird happened today.
These creepy toys appeared at Mina's shop!
And before that, I was attacked by this doll—
You know I don't have time for false sightings.
Especially after last week's *"Mothman."*
This time is different!
Why does everyone keep bringing that up?!
Look—
photo evidence!
I've studied horrors for thirty-five years.
I've never once encountered a doll-like creature.
Mina's desperate for business.
She and everyone else is cashing in on this town's ridiculous obsession with monsters.
If they only knew what *truly* lurked in this world . . .

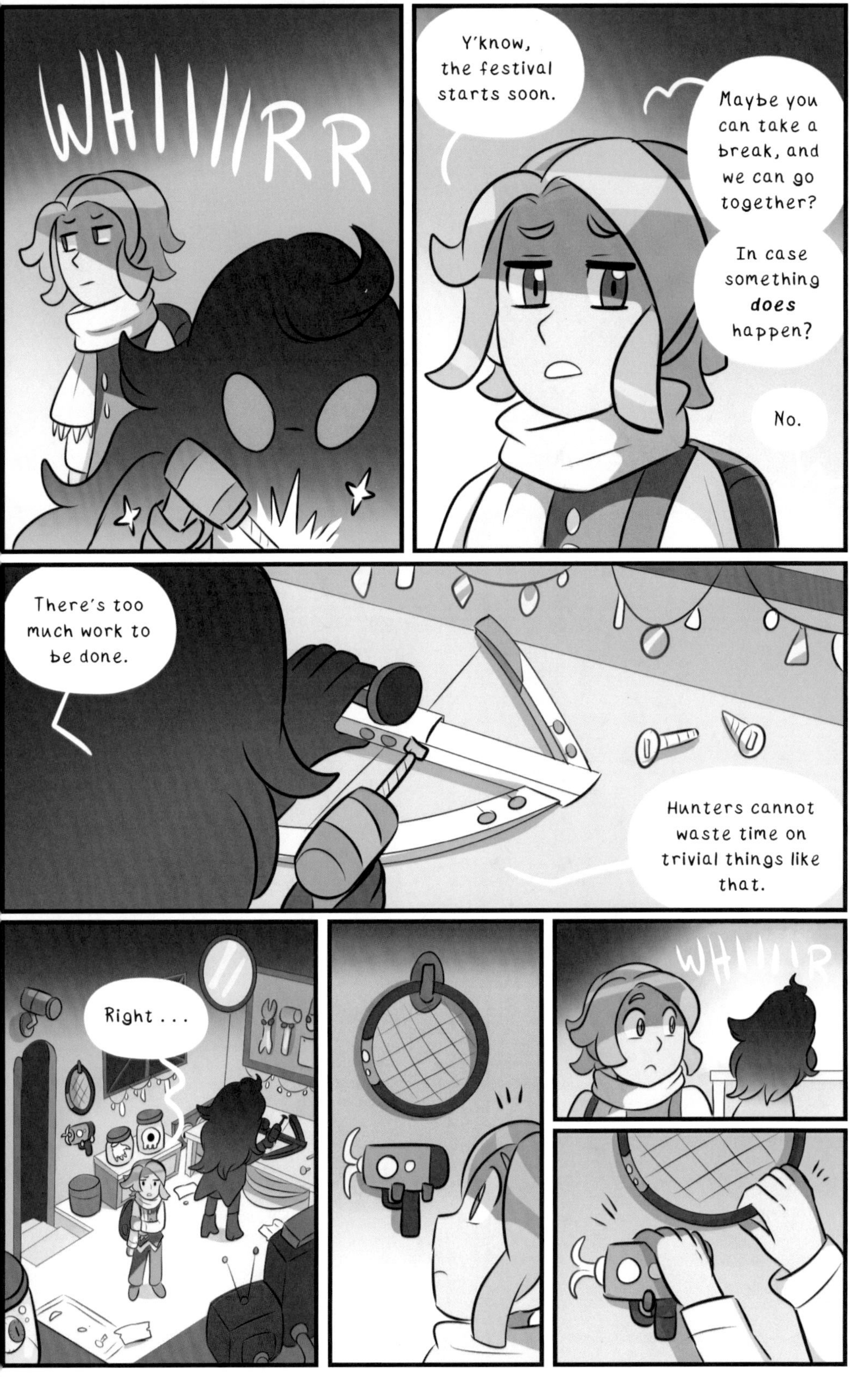
WHIIIIRR
Y'know, the festival starts soon.
Maybe you can take a break, and we can go together?
In case something **does** happen?
No.
There's too much work to be done.
Hunters cannot waste time on trivial things like that.
Right . . .
WHIIIR

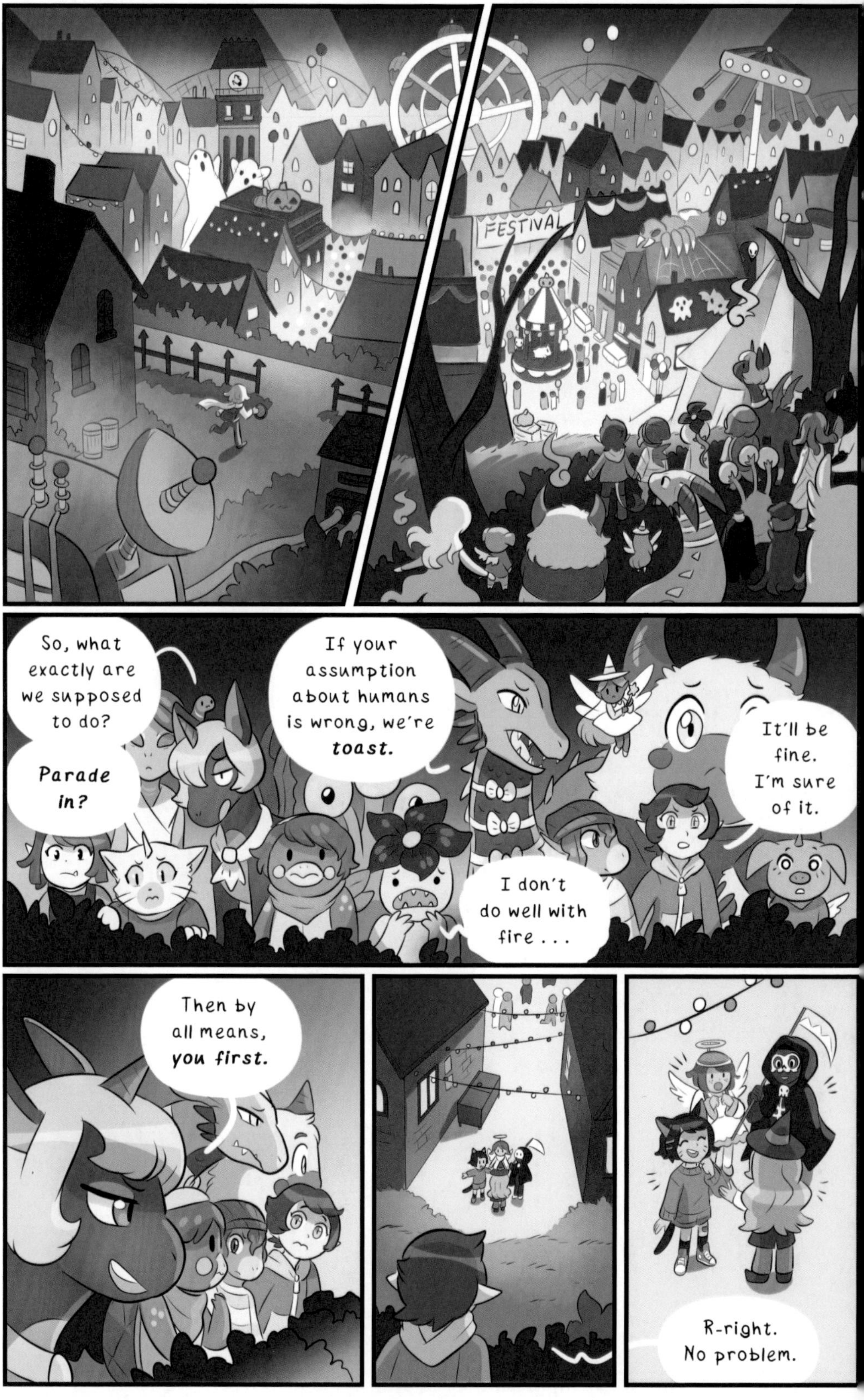
FESTIVAL
So, what exactly are we supposed to do?
Parade in?
If your assumption about humans is wrong, we're toast.
It'll be fine. I'm sure of it.
I don't do well with fire . . .
Then by all means, you first.
R-right. No problem.

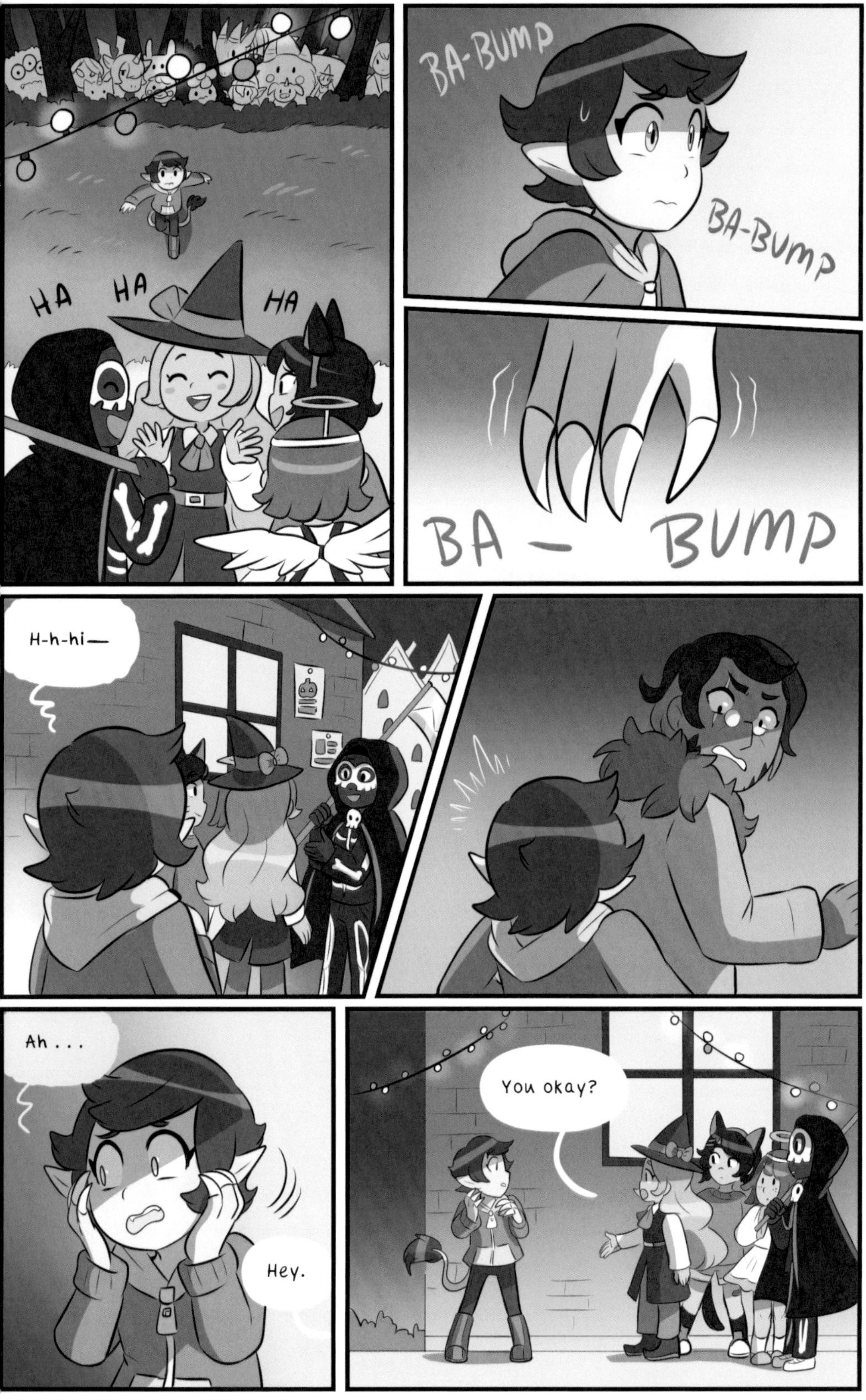
HA HA HA
BA-BUMP
BA-BUMP
BA — BUMP
H-h-hi—
Ah . . .
Hey.
You okay?

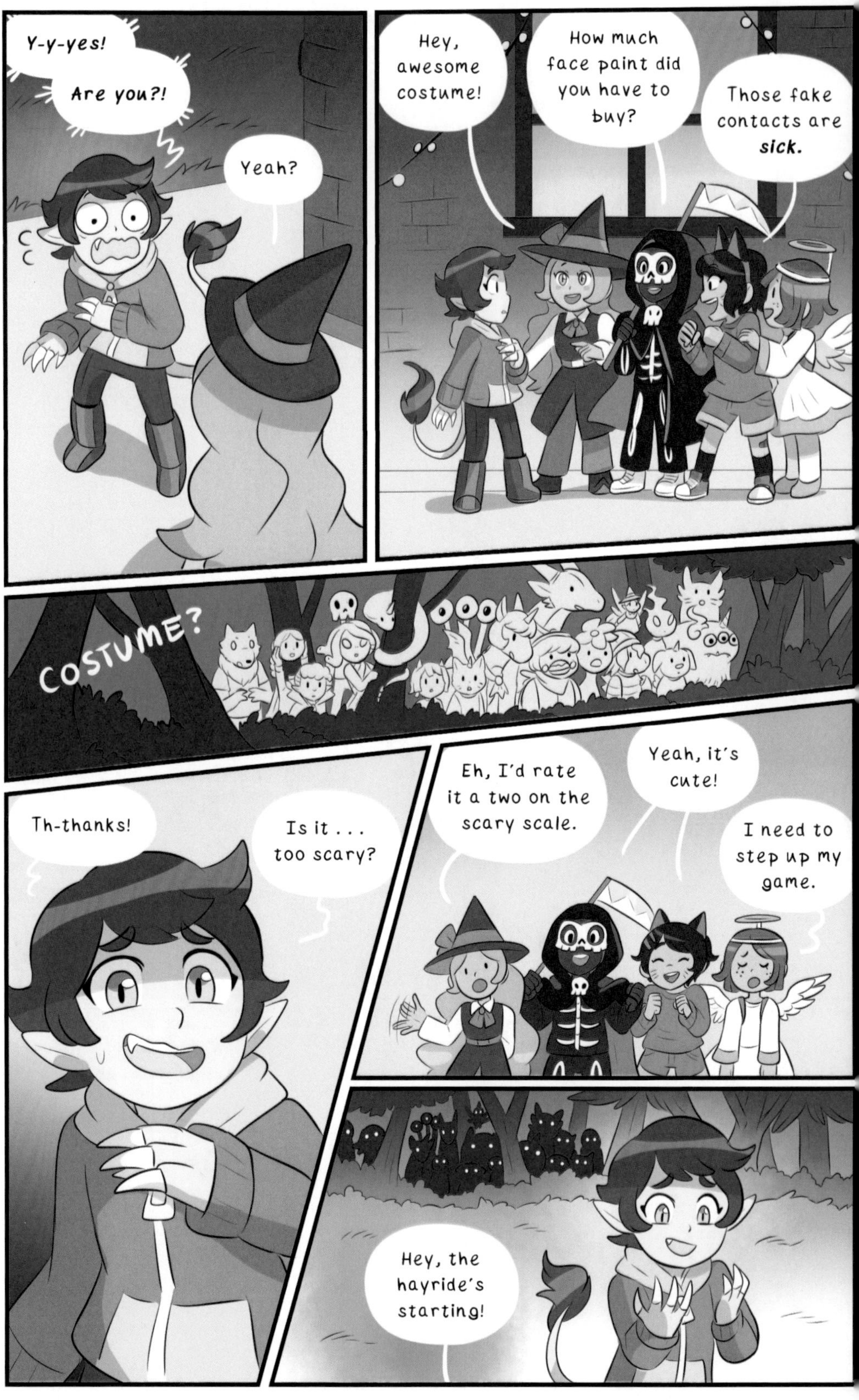
Y-y-yes!
Are you?!
Yeah?
Hey, awesome costume!
How much face paint did you have to buy?
Those fake contacts are **sick.**
COSTUME?
Th-thanks!
Is it . . . too scary?
Eh, I'd rate it a two on the scary scale.
Yeah, it's cute!
I need to step up my game.
Hey, the hayride's starting!

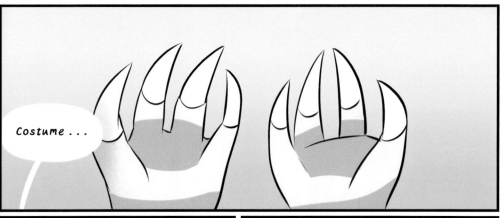

Costume . . .

Let's go!

Plan B— we'll play it safe and say we're in costume!

After everyone likes us, **then** we can reveal the truth!

C'mon, you saw those humans!

We'll fit right in!

SHRUG

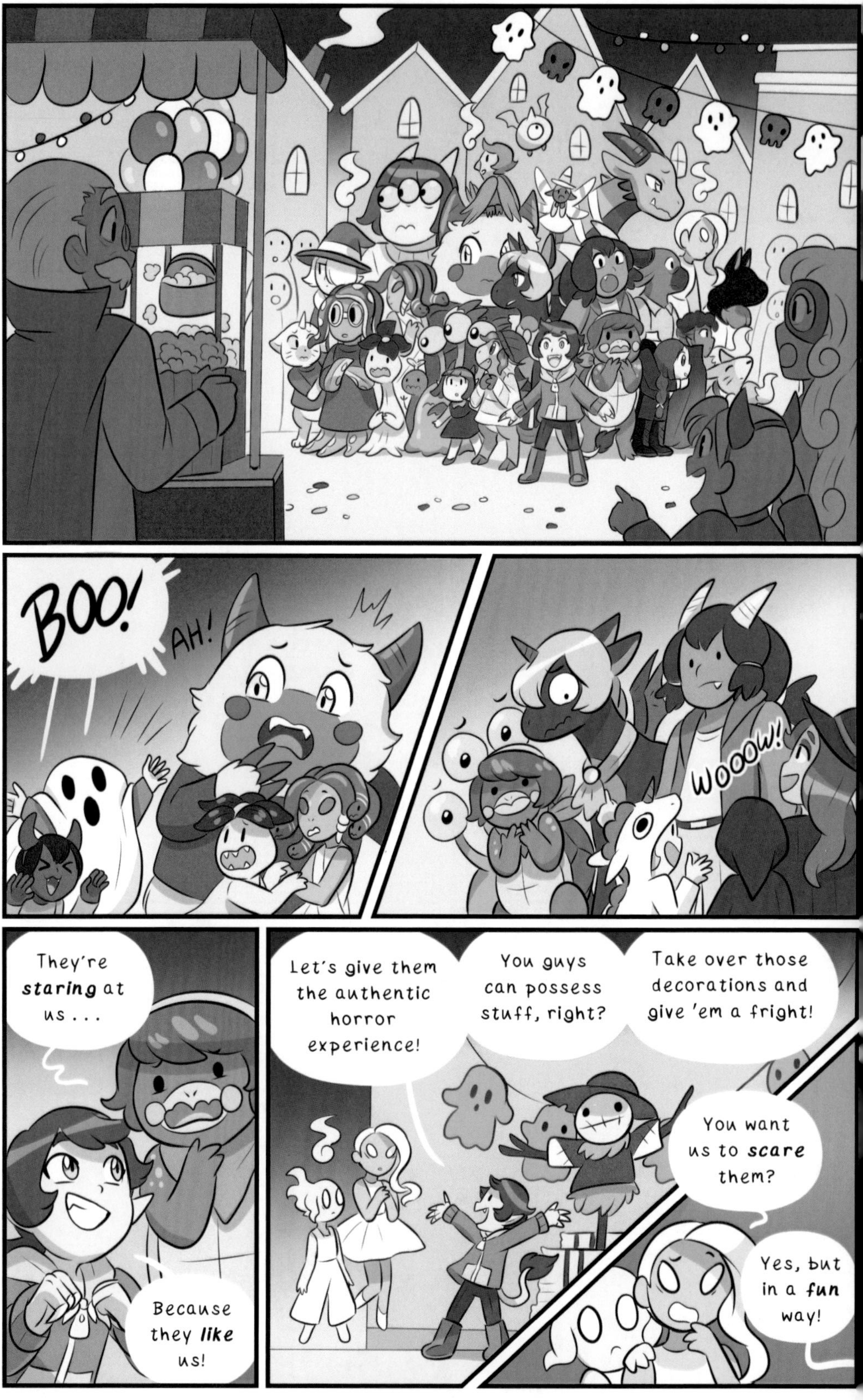
BOO!
AH!
WOOOW!
They're staring at us . . .
Because they like us!
Let's give them the authentic horror experience!
You guys can possess stuff, right?
Take over those decorations and give 'em a fright!
You want us to scare them?
Yes, but in a fun way!

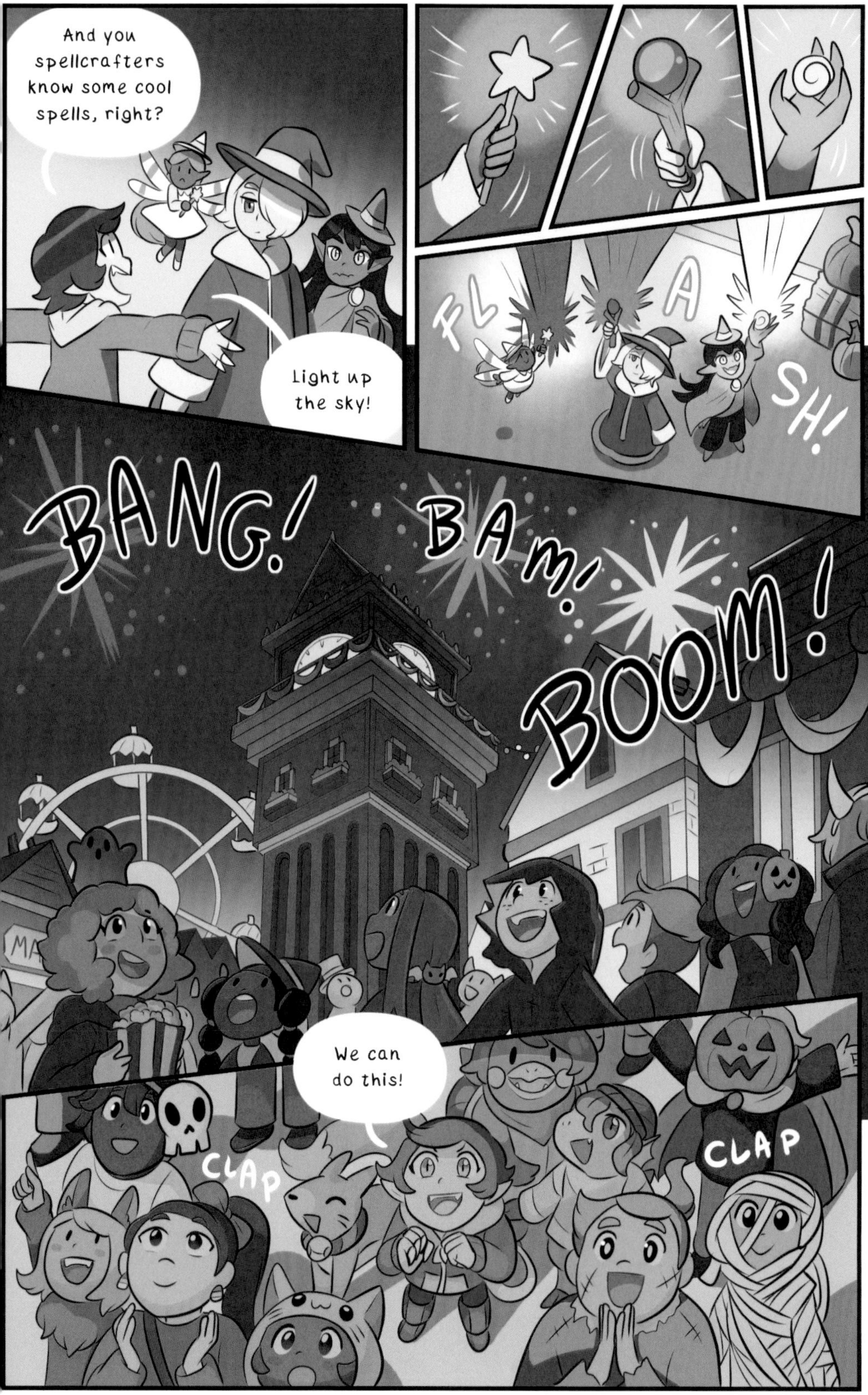
And you spellcrafters know some cool spells, right?
Light up the sky!
FLASH!
BANG!
BAM!
BOOM!
We can do this!
CLAP
CLAP

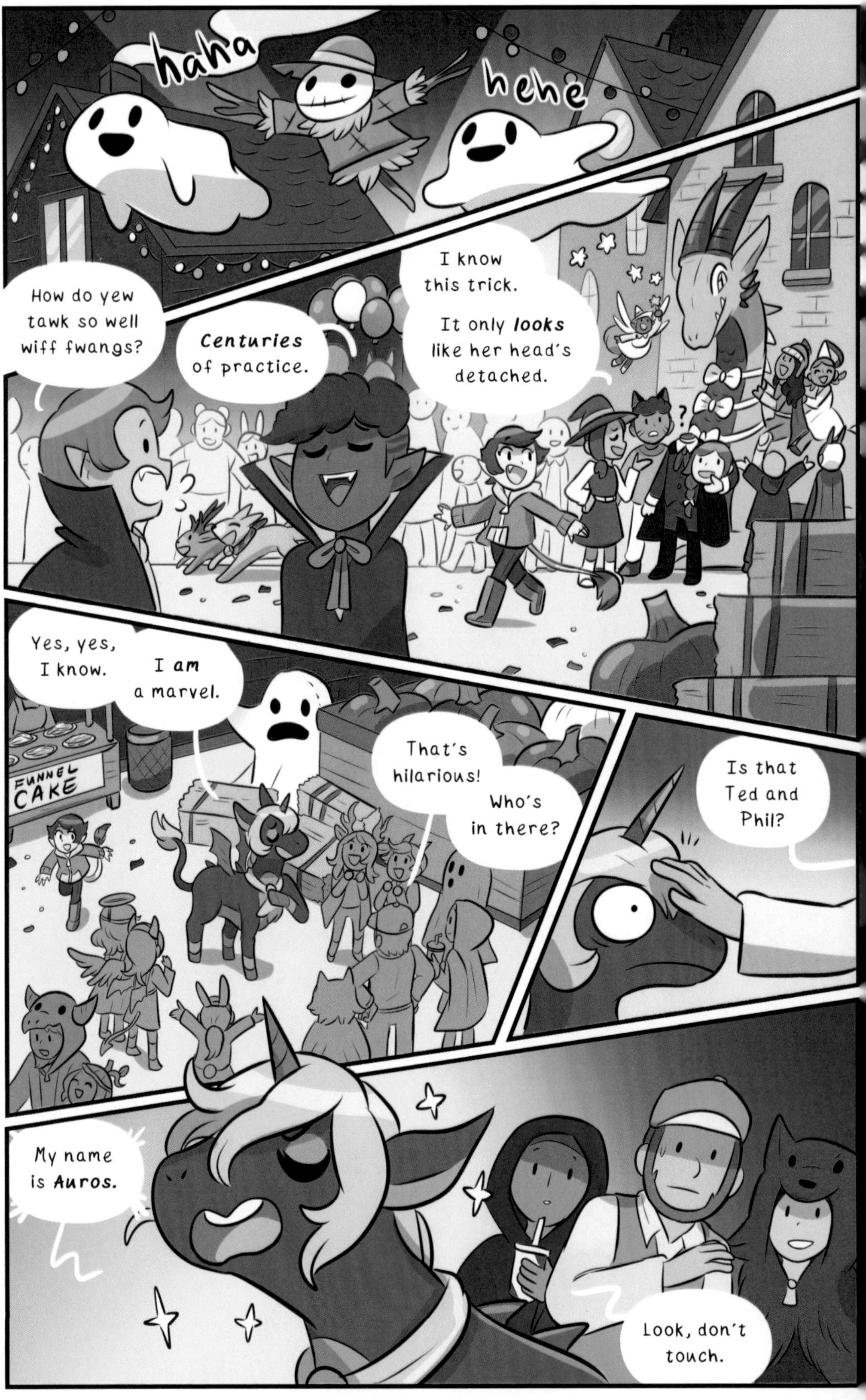
haha
hehe
How do yew tawk so well wiff fwangs?
Centuries of practice.
I know this trick.
It only looks like her head's detached.
Yes, yes, I know.
I am a marvel.
FUNNEL CAKE
That's hilarious!
Who's in there?
Is that Ted and Phil?
My name is Auros.
Look, don't touch.

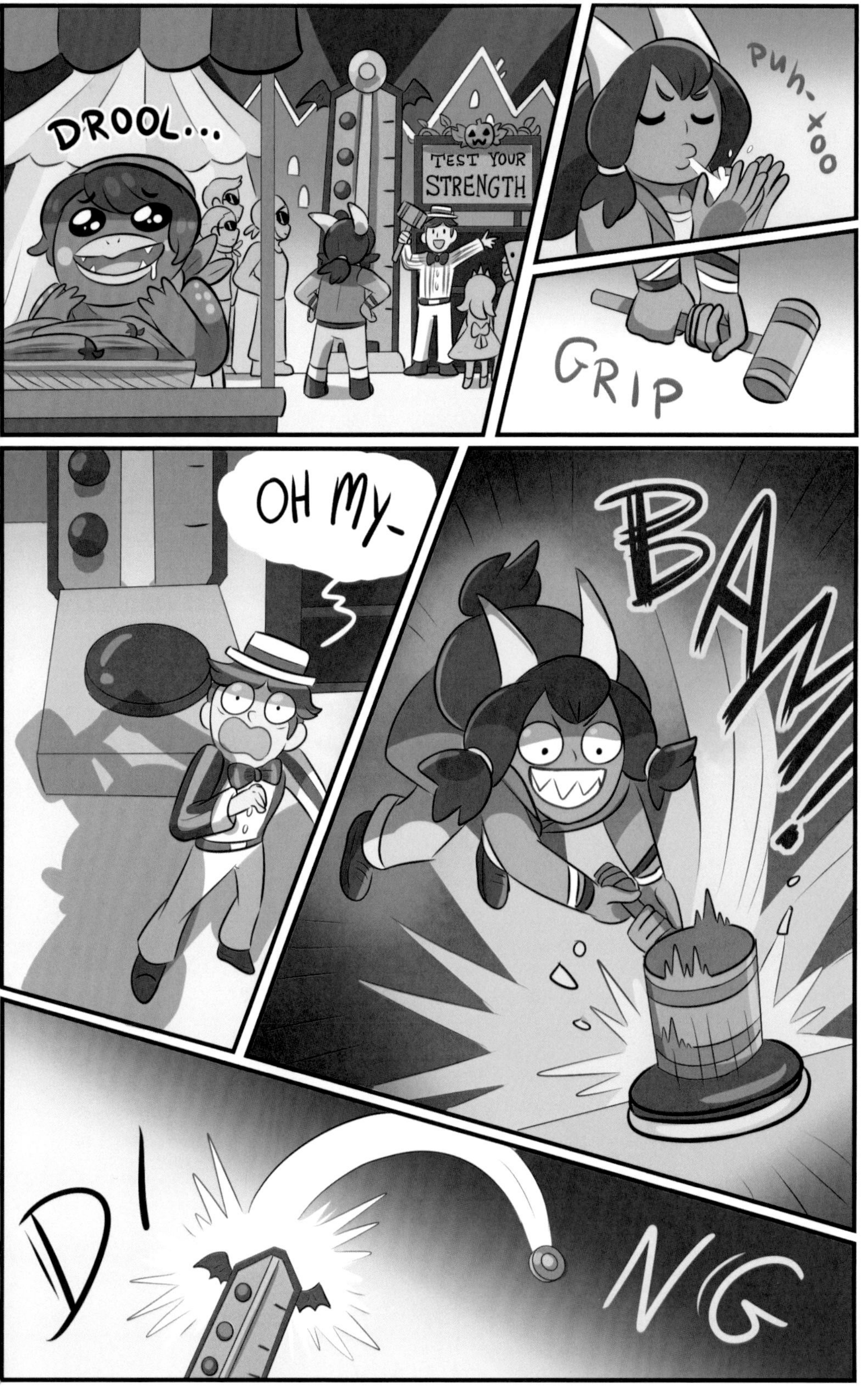
DROOL...
TEST YOUR STRENGTH
Puh-too
GRIP
OH MY-
BAM!!
DING

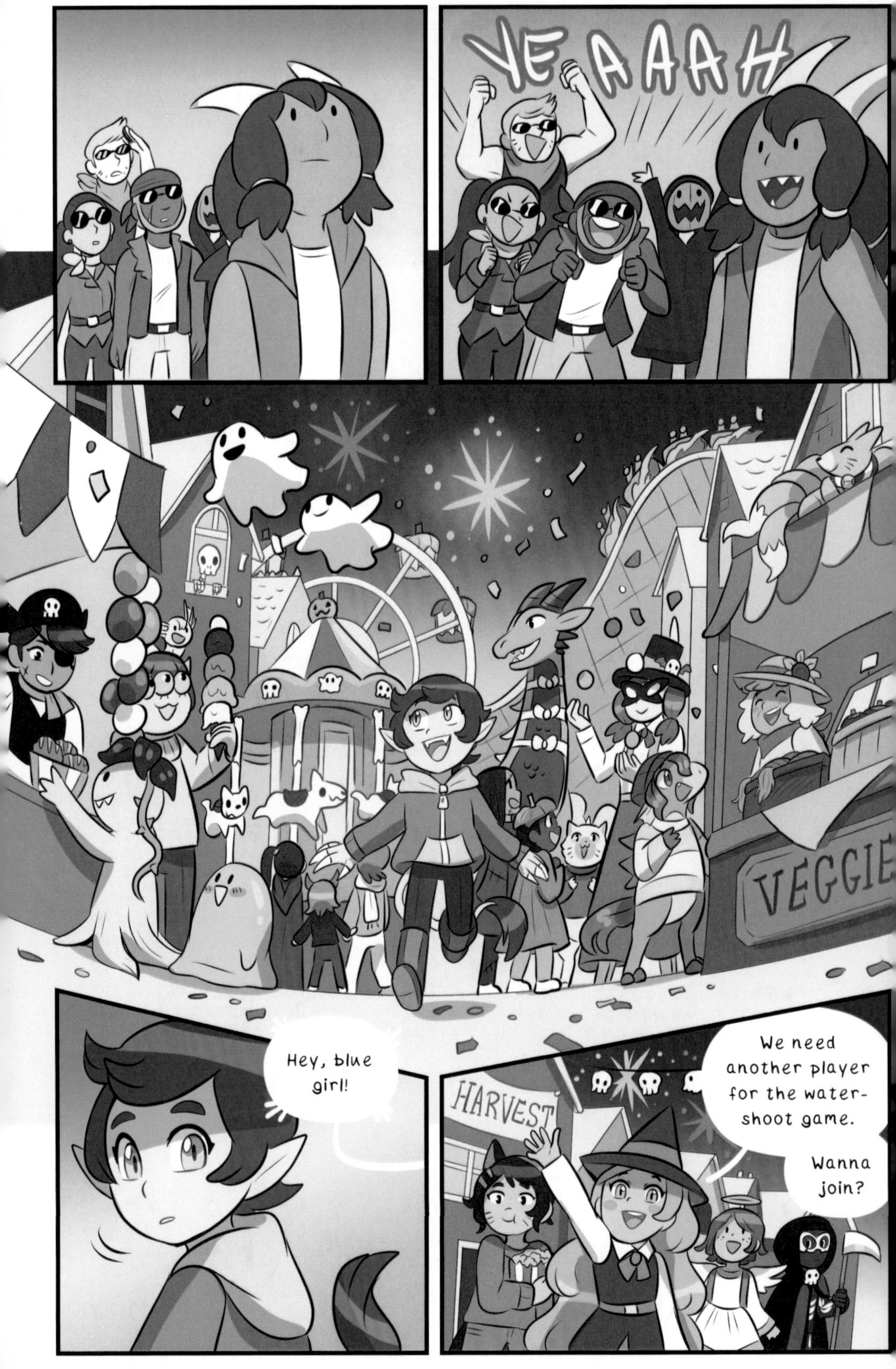
YEAAAH
Hey, blue girl!
We need another player for the water-shoot game.
Wanna join?
VEGGIE
HARVEST

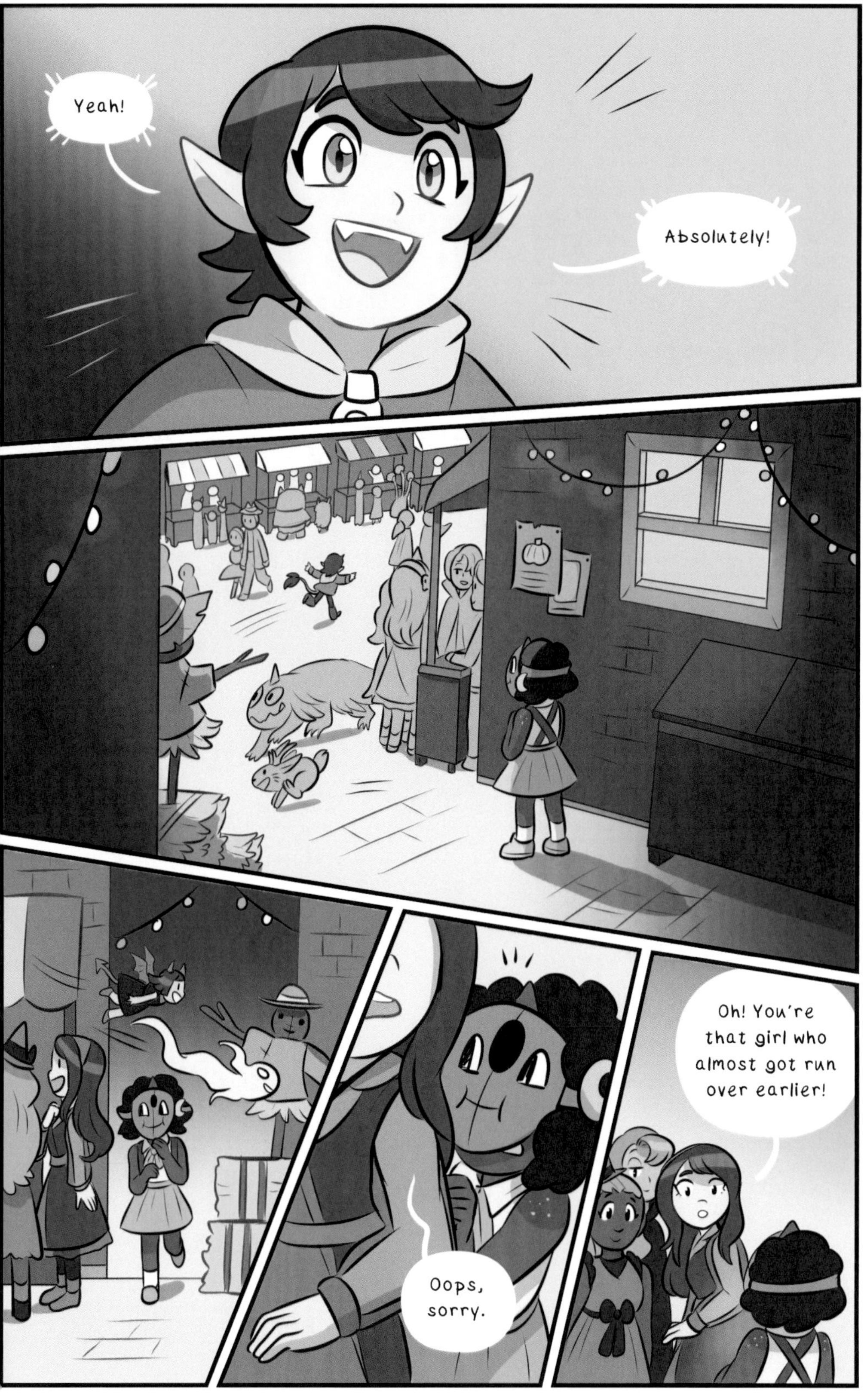
Yeah!
Absolutely!
Oops, sorry.
Oh! You're that girl who almost got run over earlier!

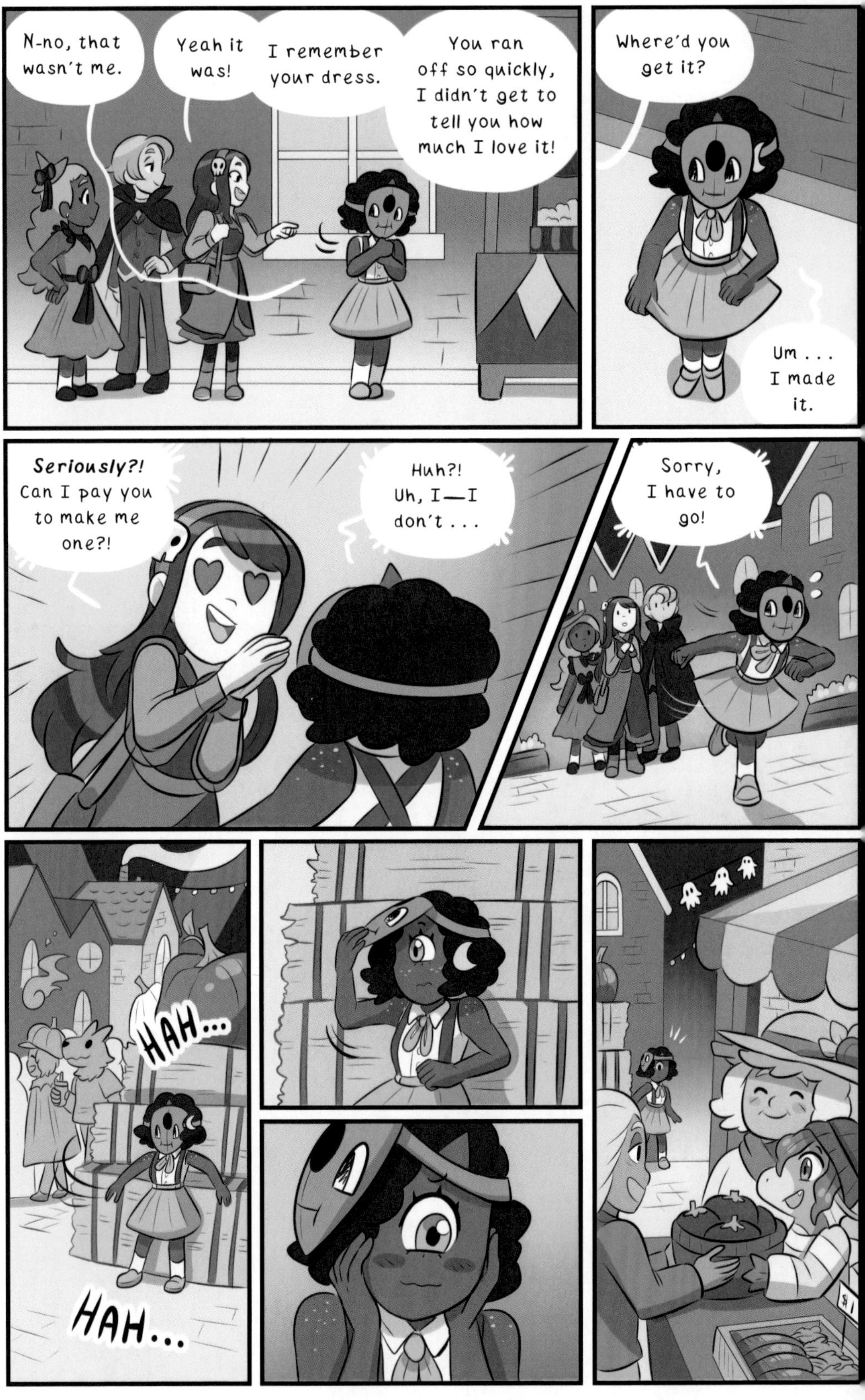
N-no, that wasn't me.
Yeah it was!
I remember your dress.
You ran off so quickly, I didn't get to tell you how much I love it!
Where'd you get it?
Um . . . I made it.
Seriously?! Can I pay you to make me one?!
Huh?! Uh, I—I don't . . .
Sorry, I have to go!
HAH...
HAH...

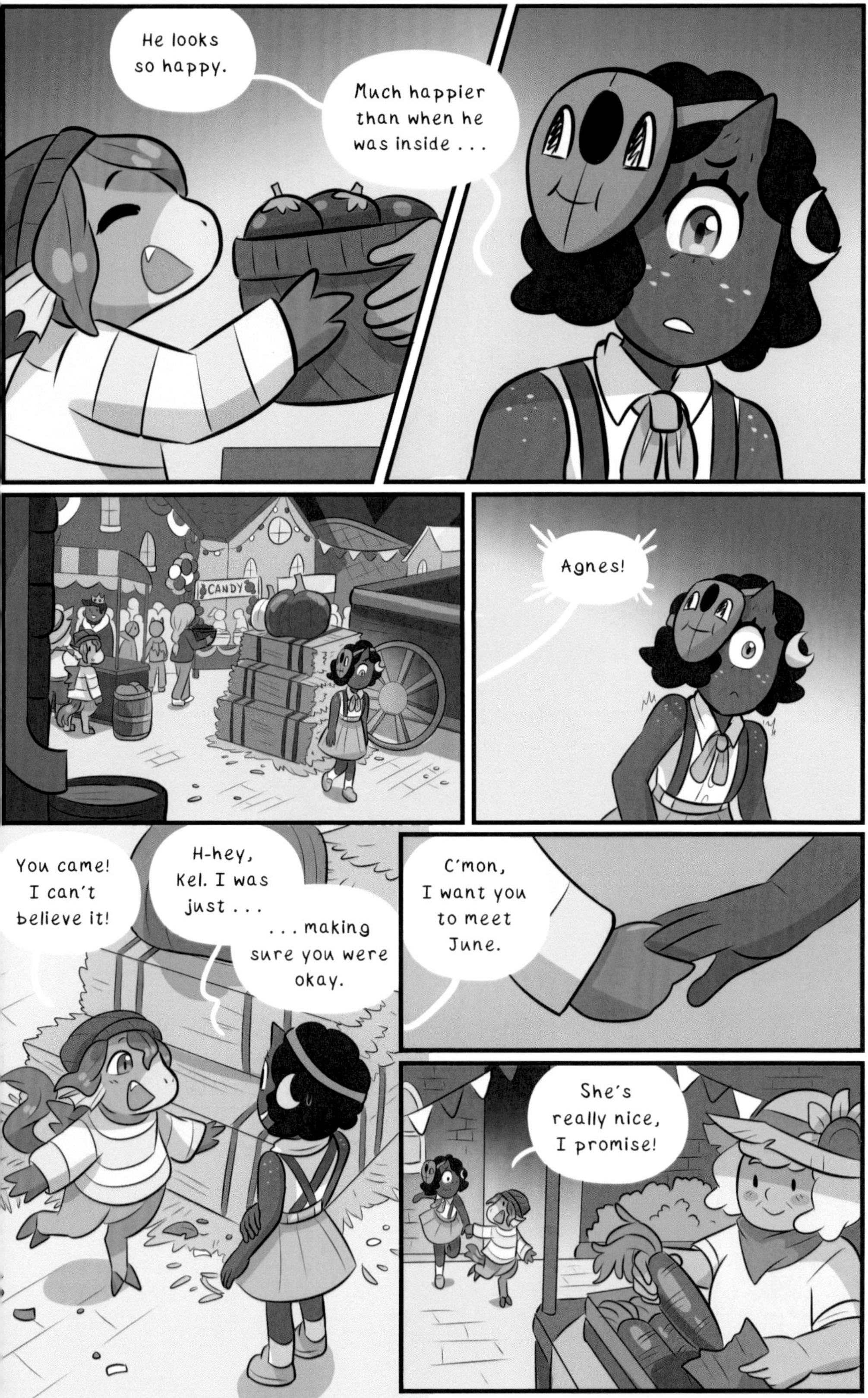
He looks so happy.
Much happier than when he was inside . . .
CANDY
Agnes!
You came! I can't believe it!
H-hey, Kel. I was just . . .
. . . making sure you were okay.
C'mon, I want you to meet June.
She's really nice, I promise!

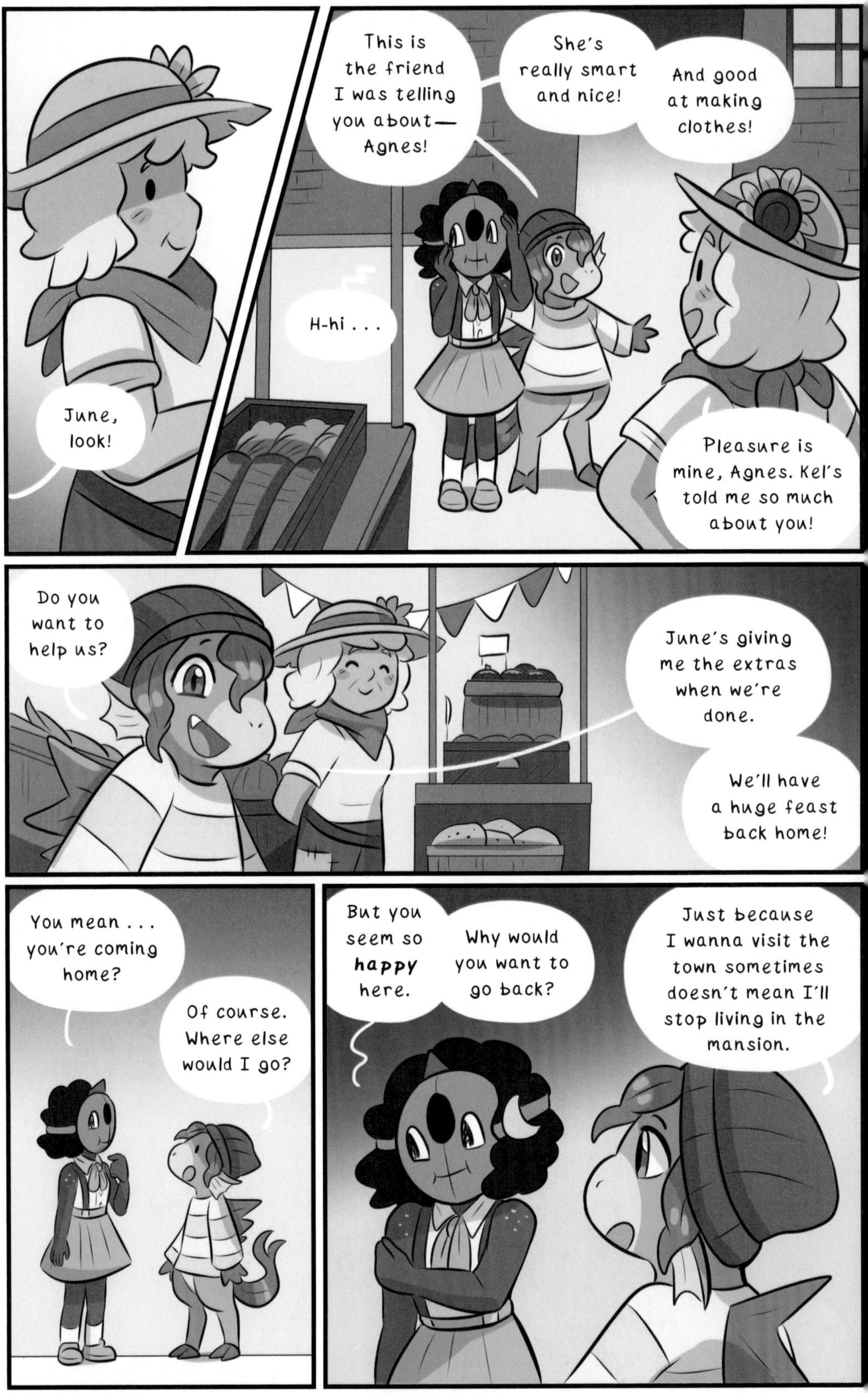
June, look!
This is the friend I was telling you about—Agnes!
She's really smart and nice!
And good at making clothes!
H-hi . . .
Pleasure is mine, Agnes. Kel's told me so much about you!
Do you want to help us?
June's giving me the extras when we're done.
We'll have a huge feast back home!
You mean . . . you're coming home?
Of course. Where else would I go?
But you seem so **happy** here.
Why would you want to go back?
Just because I wanna visit the town sometimes doesn't mean I'll stop living in the mansion.

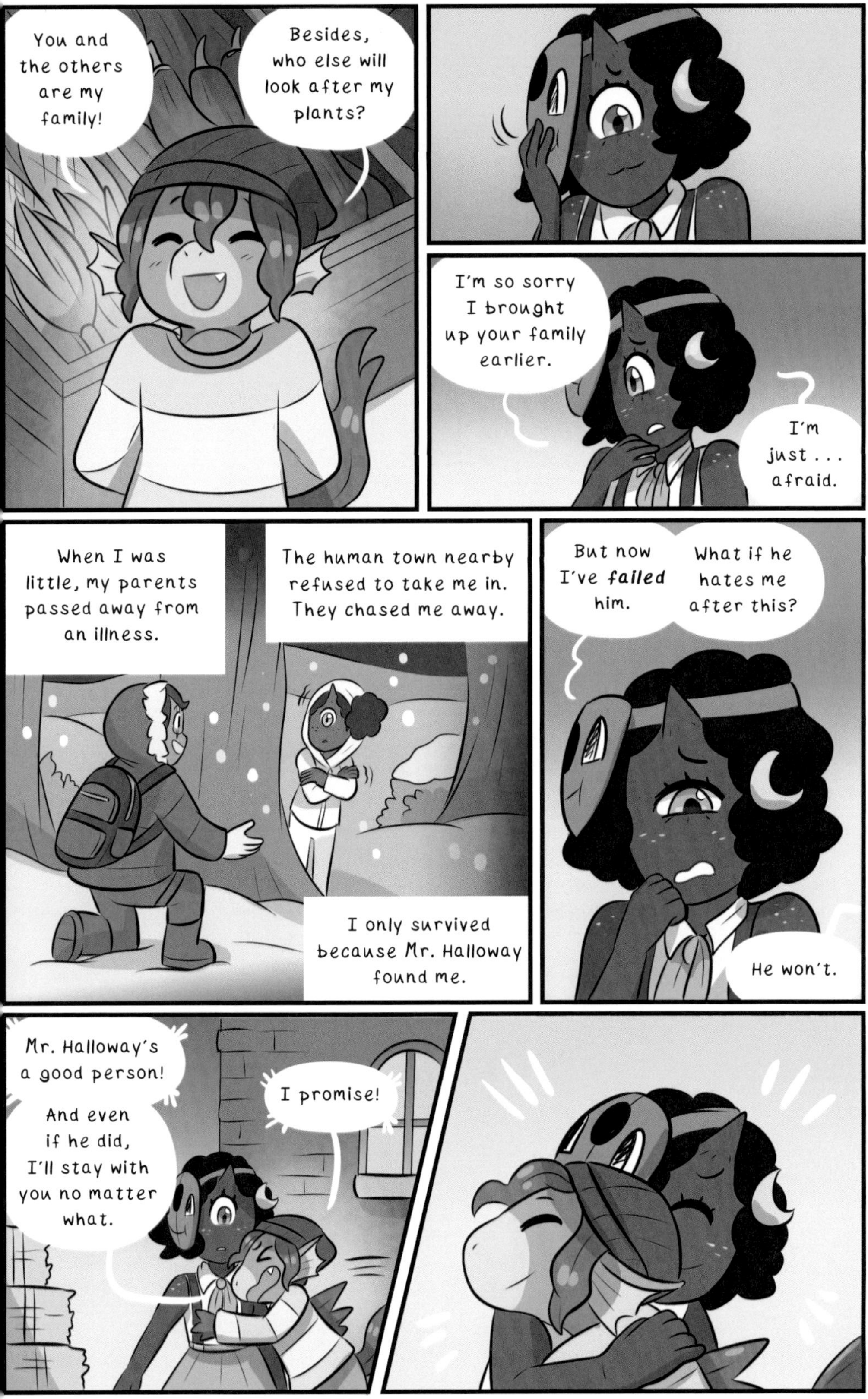
You and the others are my family!
Besides, who else will look after my plants?
I'm so sorry I brought up your family earlier.
I'm just . . . afraid.
When I was little, my parents passed away from an illness.
The human town nearby refused to take me in. They chased me away.
I only survived because Mr. Halloway found me.
But now I've **failed** him.
What if he hates me after this?
He won't.
Mr. Halloway's a good person!
And even if he did, I'll stay with you no matter what.
I promise!

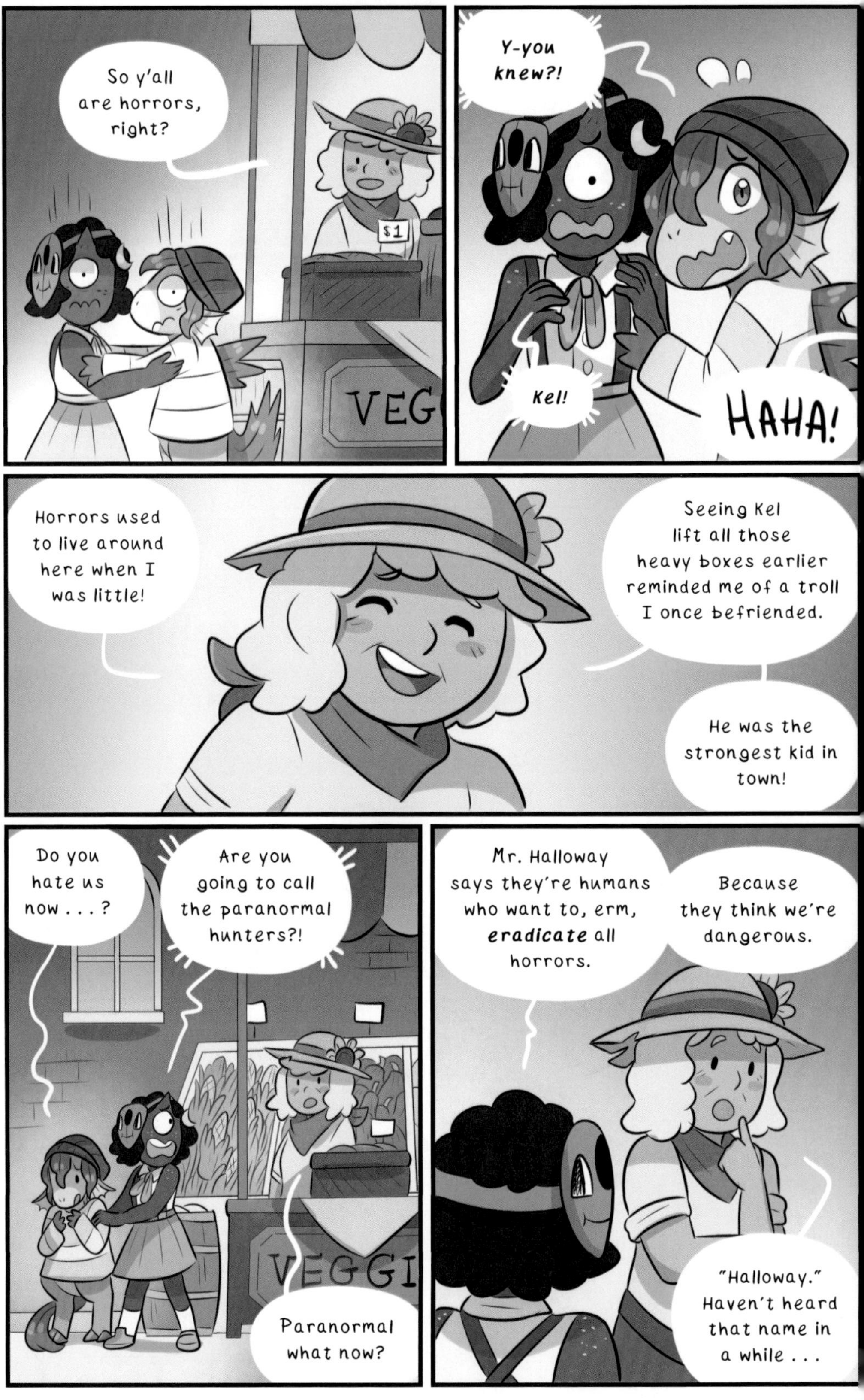
So y'all are horrors, right?
$1
VEG
Y-you knew?!
Kel!
HAHA!
Horrors used to live around here when I was little!
Seeing Kel lift all those heavy boxes earlier reminded me of a troll I once befriended.
He was the strongest kid in town!
Do you hate us now . . . ?
Are you going to call the paranormal hunters?!
VEGGI
Paranormal what now?
Mr. Halloway says they're humans who want to, erm, ***eradicate*** all horrors.
Because they think we're dangerous.
"Halloway." Haven't heard that name in a while . . .

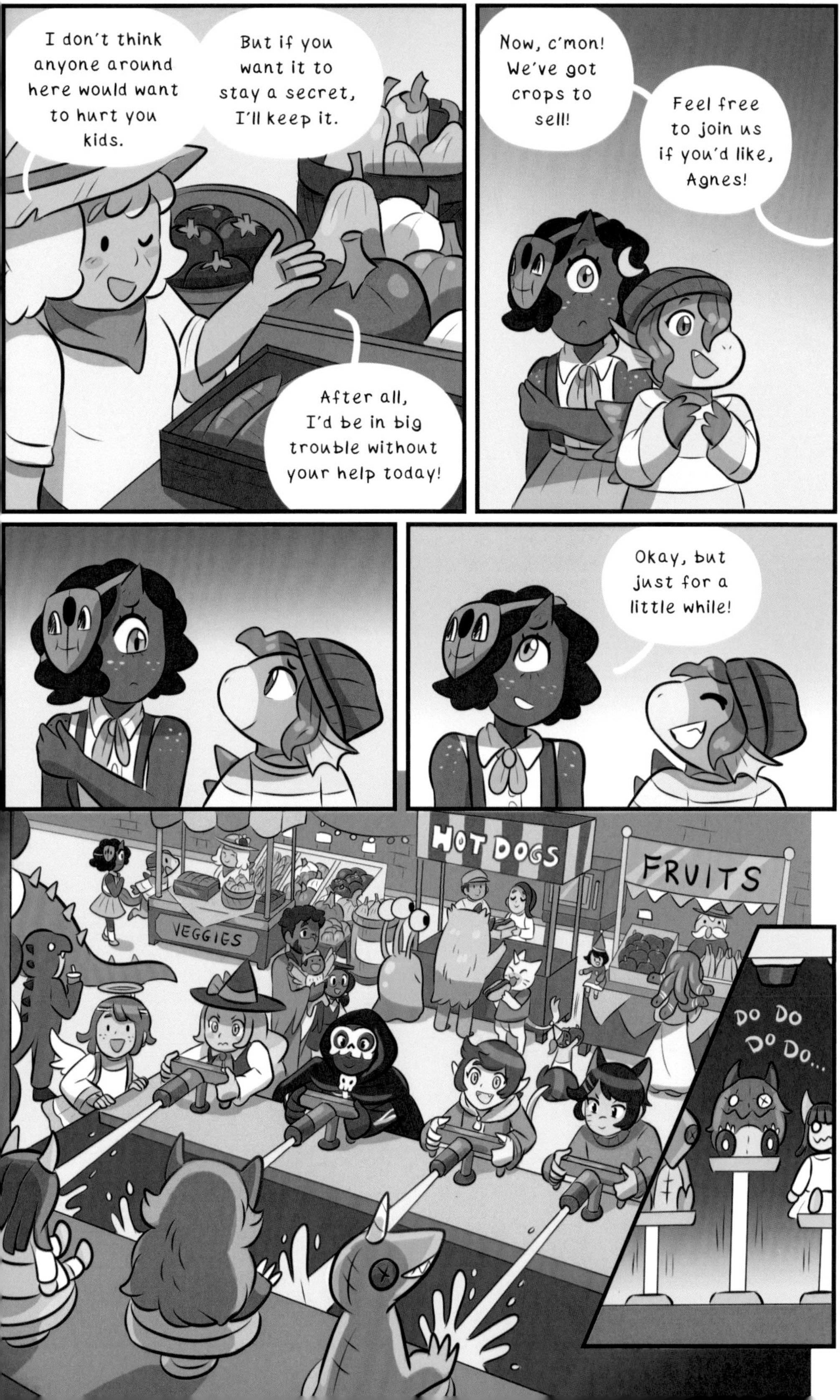
I don't think anyone around here would want to hurt you kids.
But if you want it to stay a secret, I'll keep it.
After all, I'd be in big trouble without your help today!
Now, c'mon! We've got crops to sell!
Feel free to join us if you'd like, Agnes!
Okay, but just for a little while!
HOT DOGS
FRUITS
VEGGIES
DO DO DO DO...

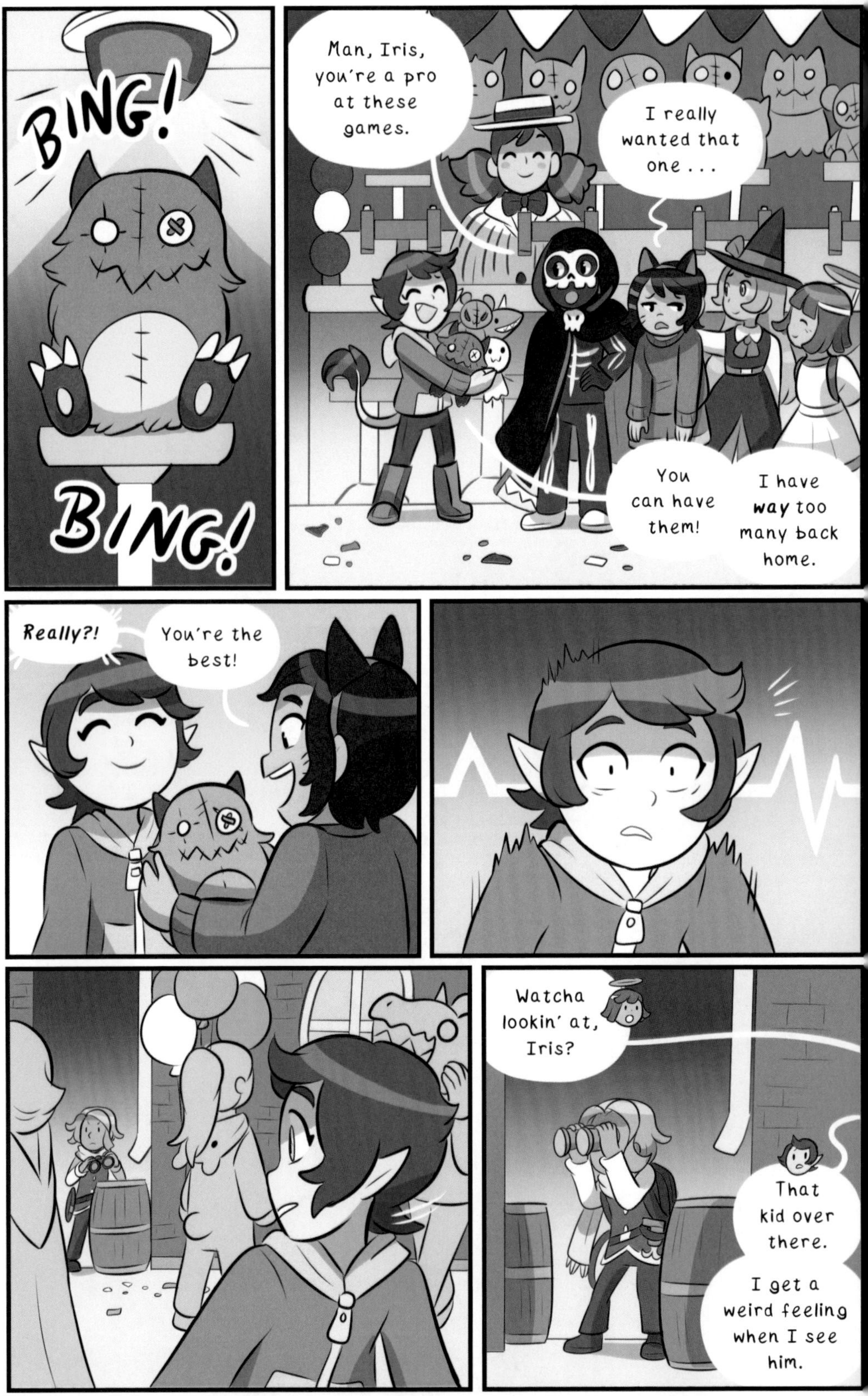
BING!
BING!
Man, Iris, you're a pro at these games.
I really wanted that one . . .
You can have them!
I have **way** too many back home.
Really?!
You're the best!
Watcha lookin' at, Iris?
That kid over there.
I get a weird feeling when I see him.

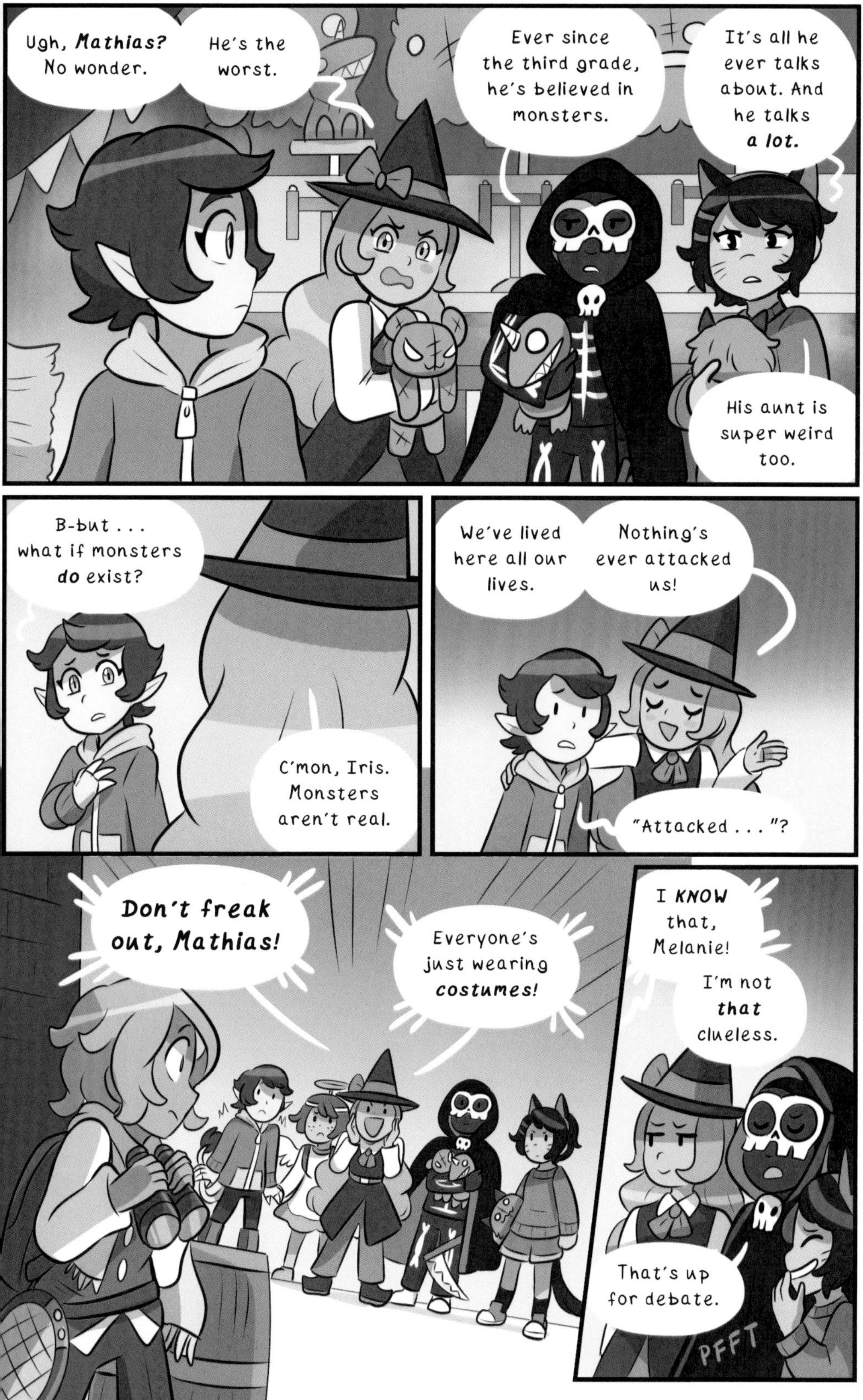

Ugh, **Mathias?** No wonder.
He's the worst.
Ever since the third grade, he's believed in monsters.
It's all he ever talks about. And he talks **a lot.**
His aunt is super weird too.
B-but . . . what if monsters **do** exist?
C'mon, Iris. Monsters aren't real.
We've lived here all our lives.
Nothing's ever attacked us!
"Attacked . . ."?
Don't freak out, Mathias!
Everyone's just wearing **costumes!**
I ***KNOW*** that, Melanie!
I'm not **that** clueless.
That's up for debate.
PFFT

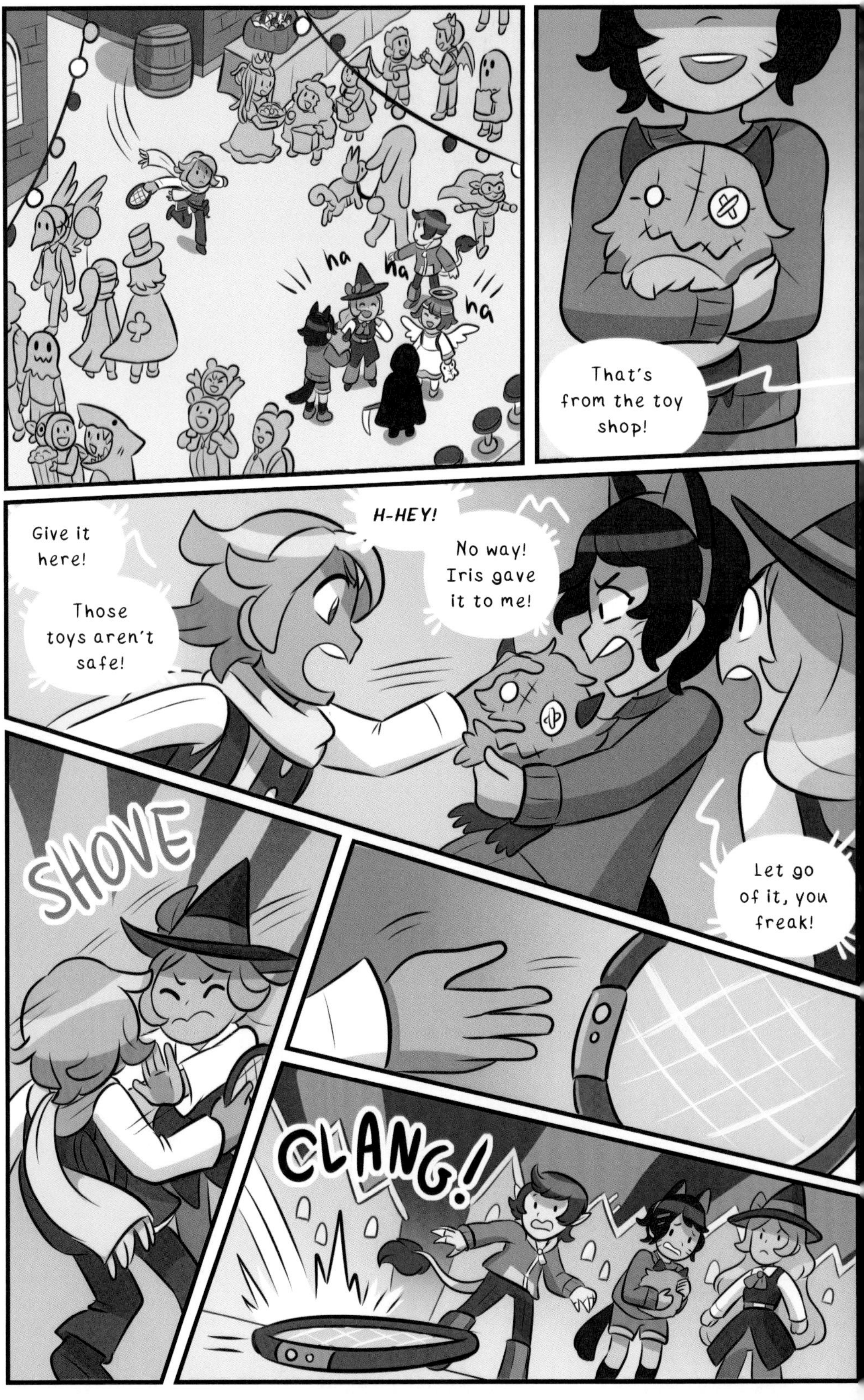
ha
ha
ha
That's from the toy shop!
Give it here!
Those toys aren't safe!
H-HEY!
No way! Iris gave it to me!
Let go of it, you freak!
SHOVE
CLANG!

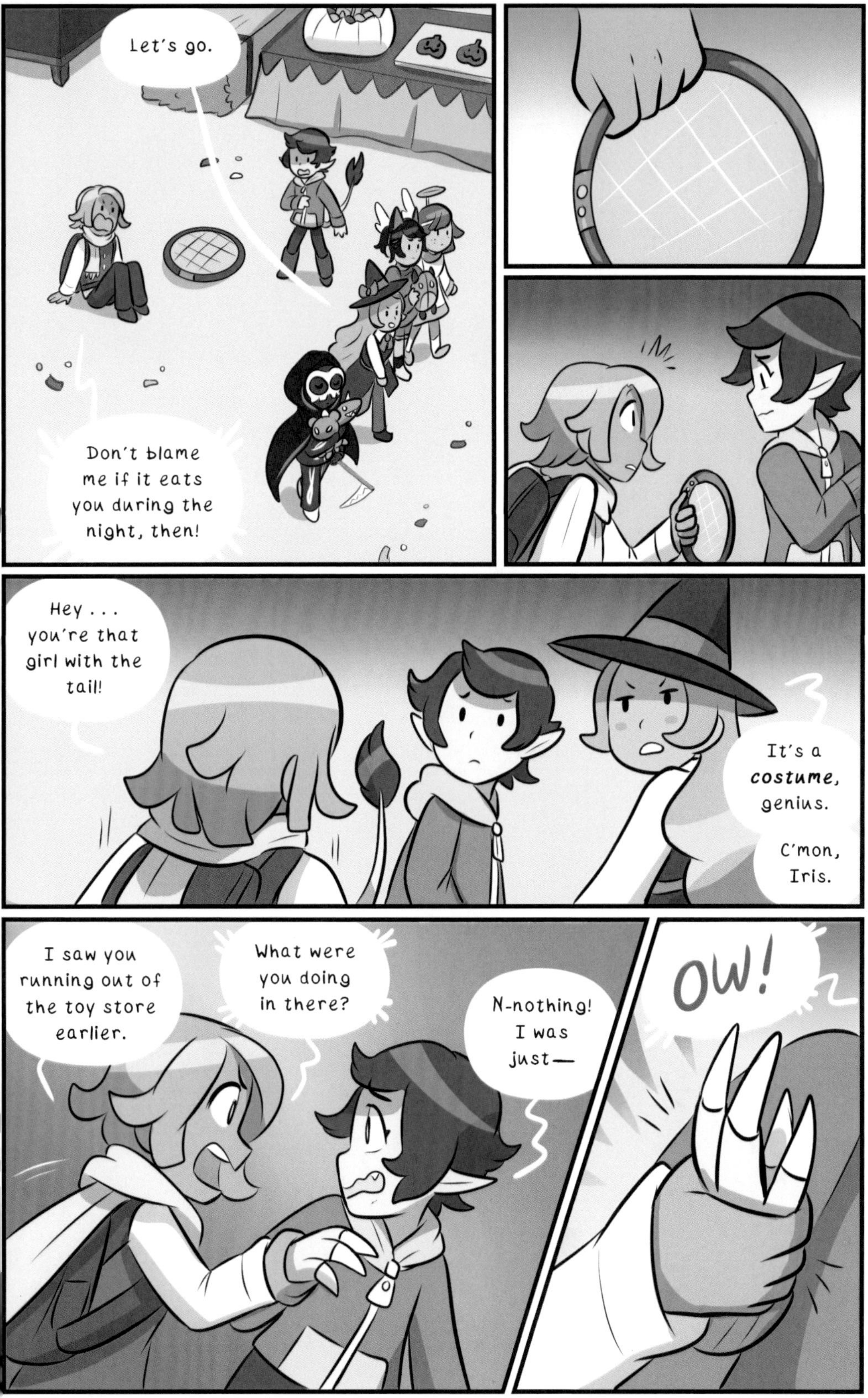
Let's go.
Don't blame me if it eats you during the night, then!
Hey . . . you're that girl with the tail!
It's a **costume,** genius.
C'mon, Iris.
I saw you running out of the toy store earlier.
What were you doing in there?
N-nothing! I was just—
OW!

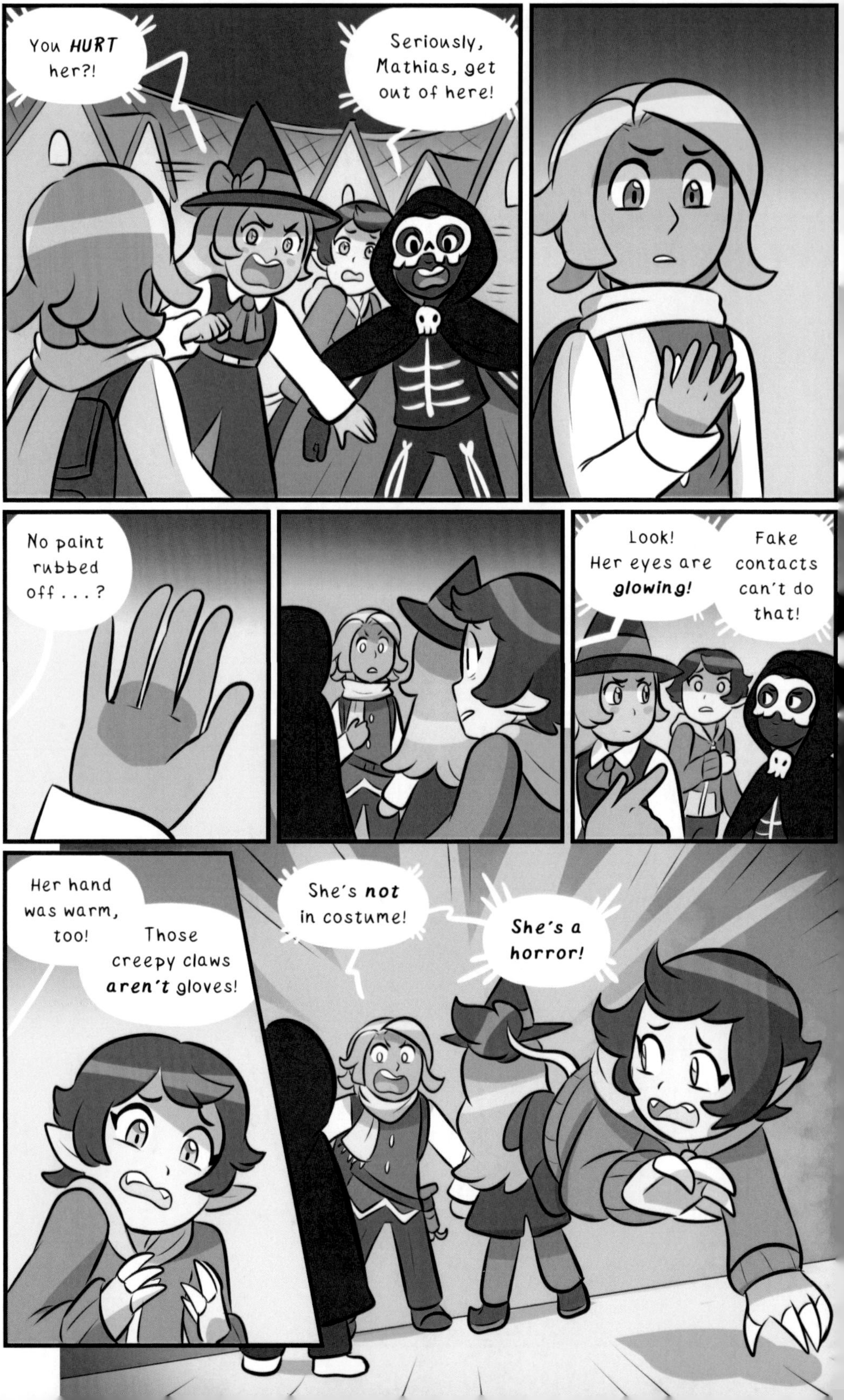

You **HURT** her?!
Seriously, Mathias, get out of here!
No paint rubbed off . . . ?
Look! Her eyes are ***glowing!***
Fake contacts can't do that!
Her hand was warm, too!
Those creepy claws ***aren't*** gloves!
She's **not** in costume!
She's a horror!

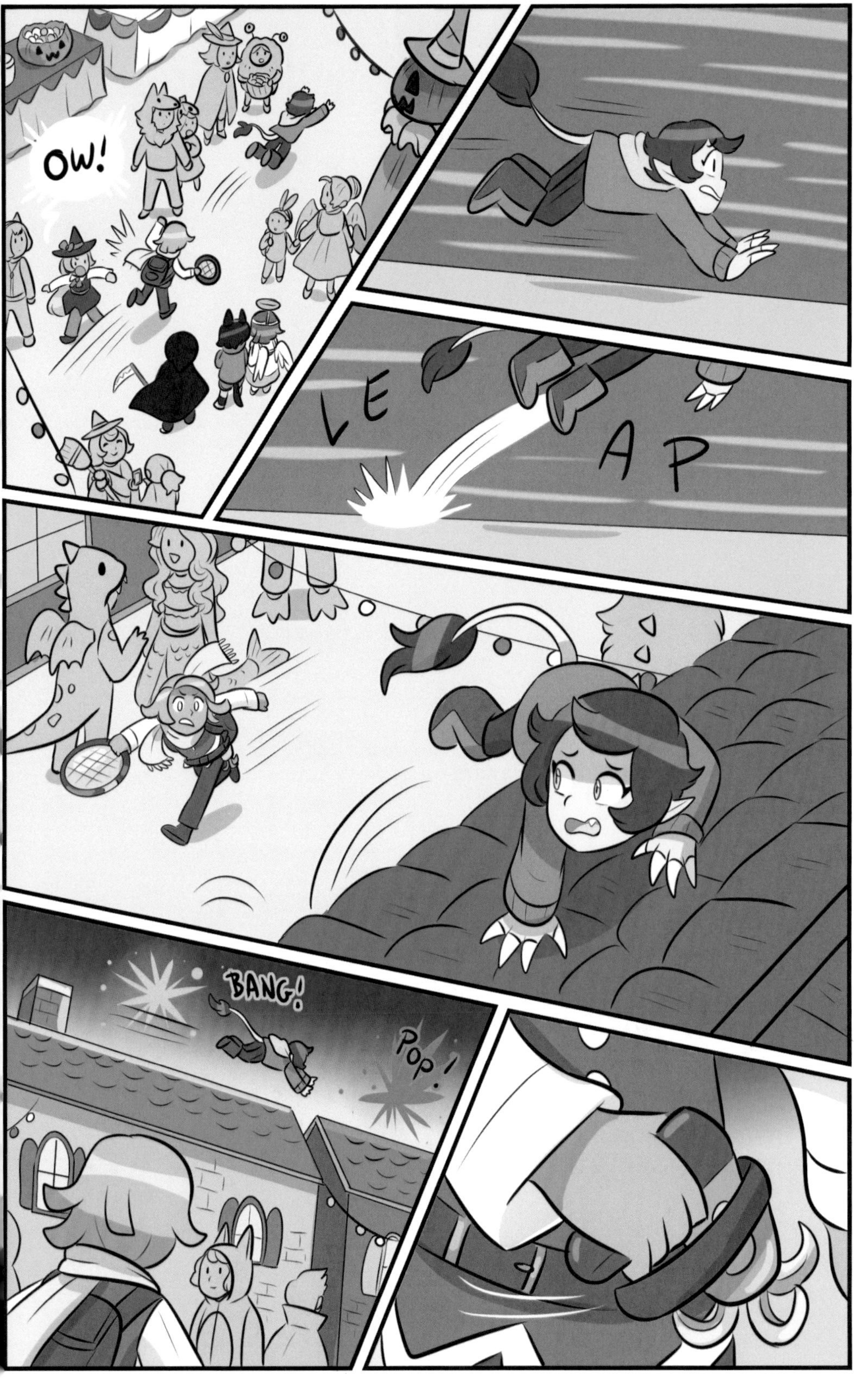

OW!
LEAP
BANG!
POP!

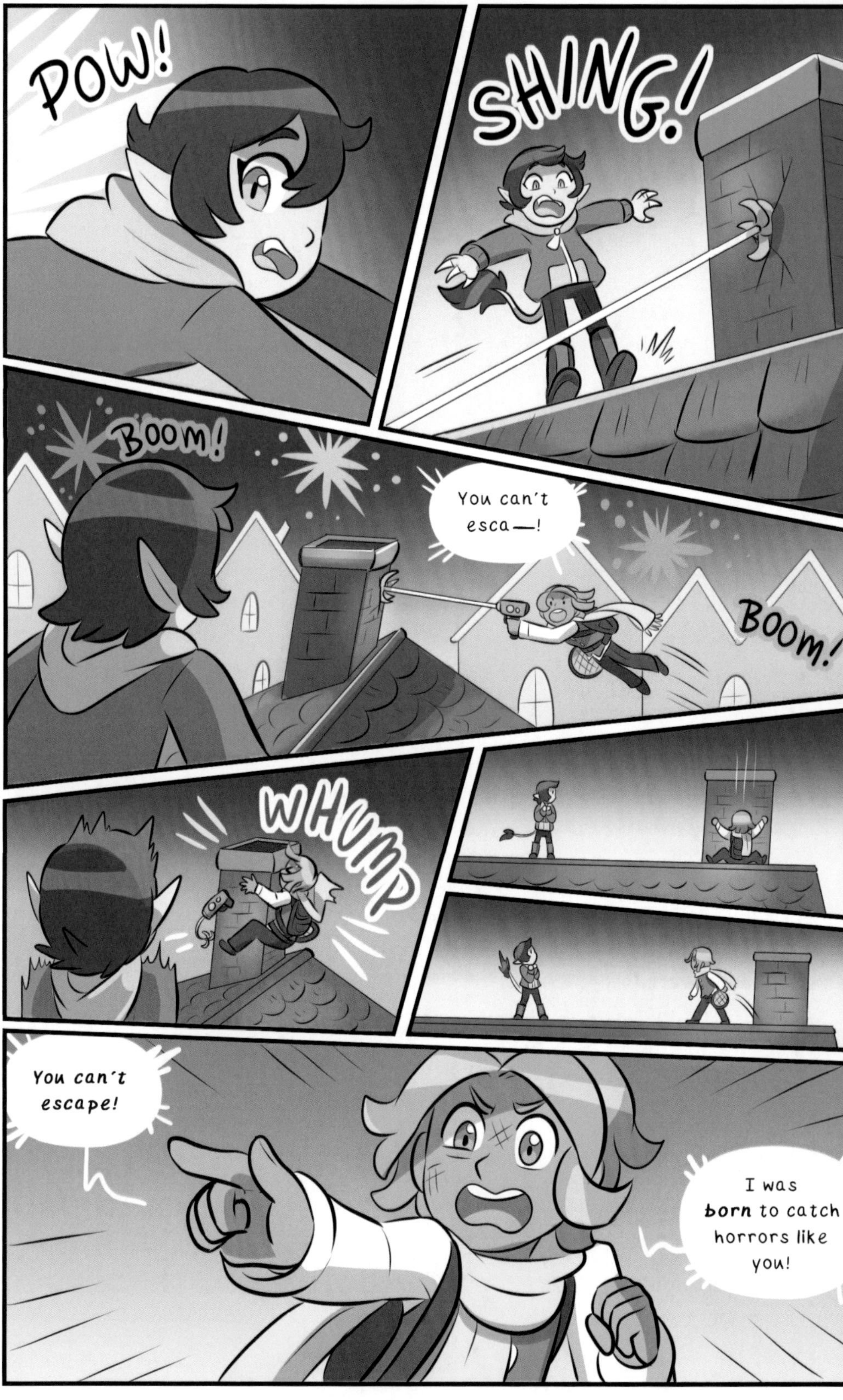
POW!
SHING!
BOOM!
You can't esca—!
BOOM!
WHUMP
You can't escape!
I was born to catch horrors like you!

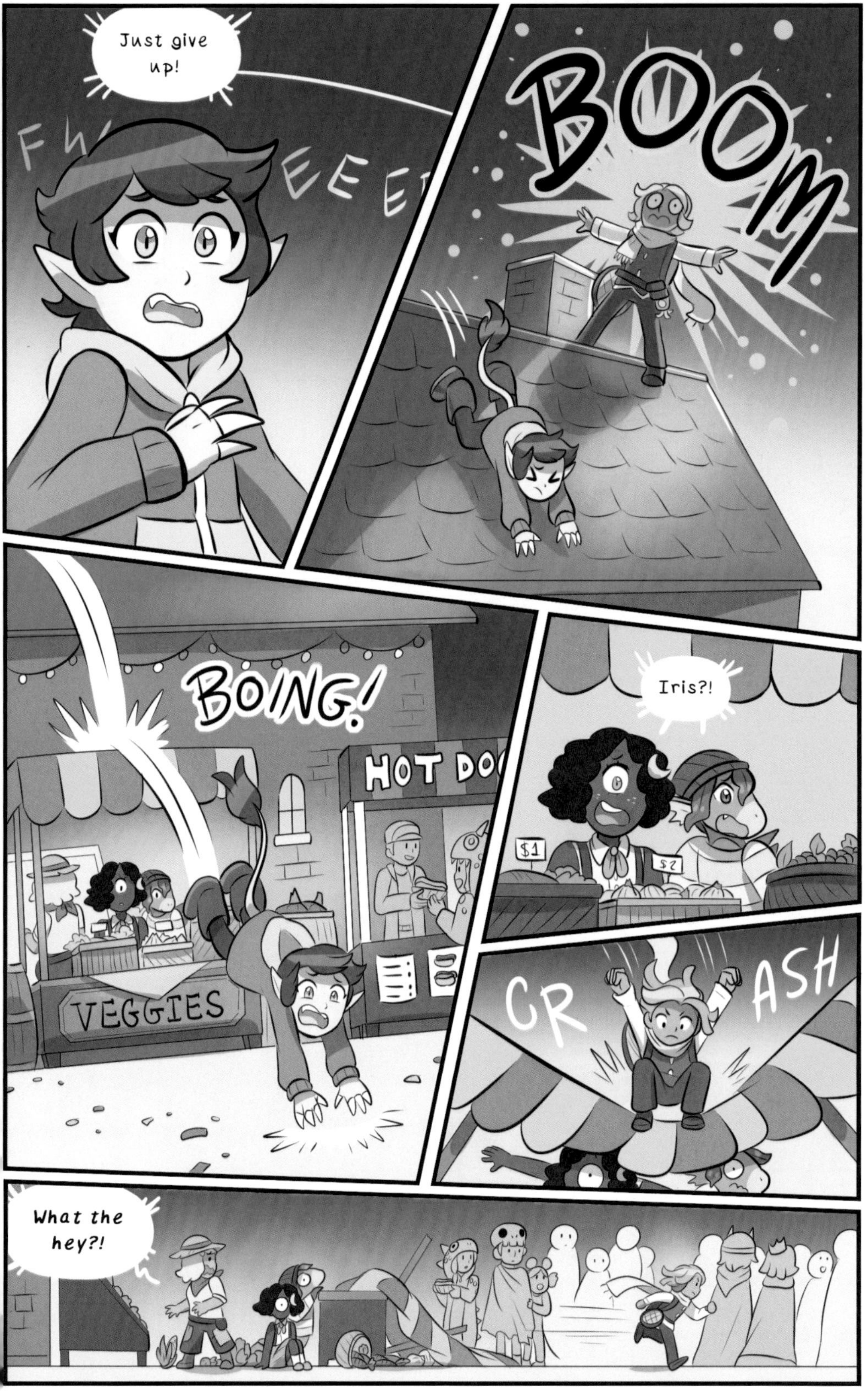
Just give up!
FWEEEET
BOOM
BOING!
HOT DOG
VEGGIES
Iris?!
$1
$2
CRASH
What the hey?!

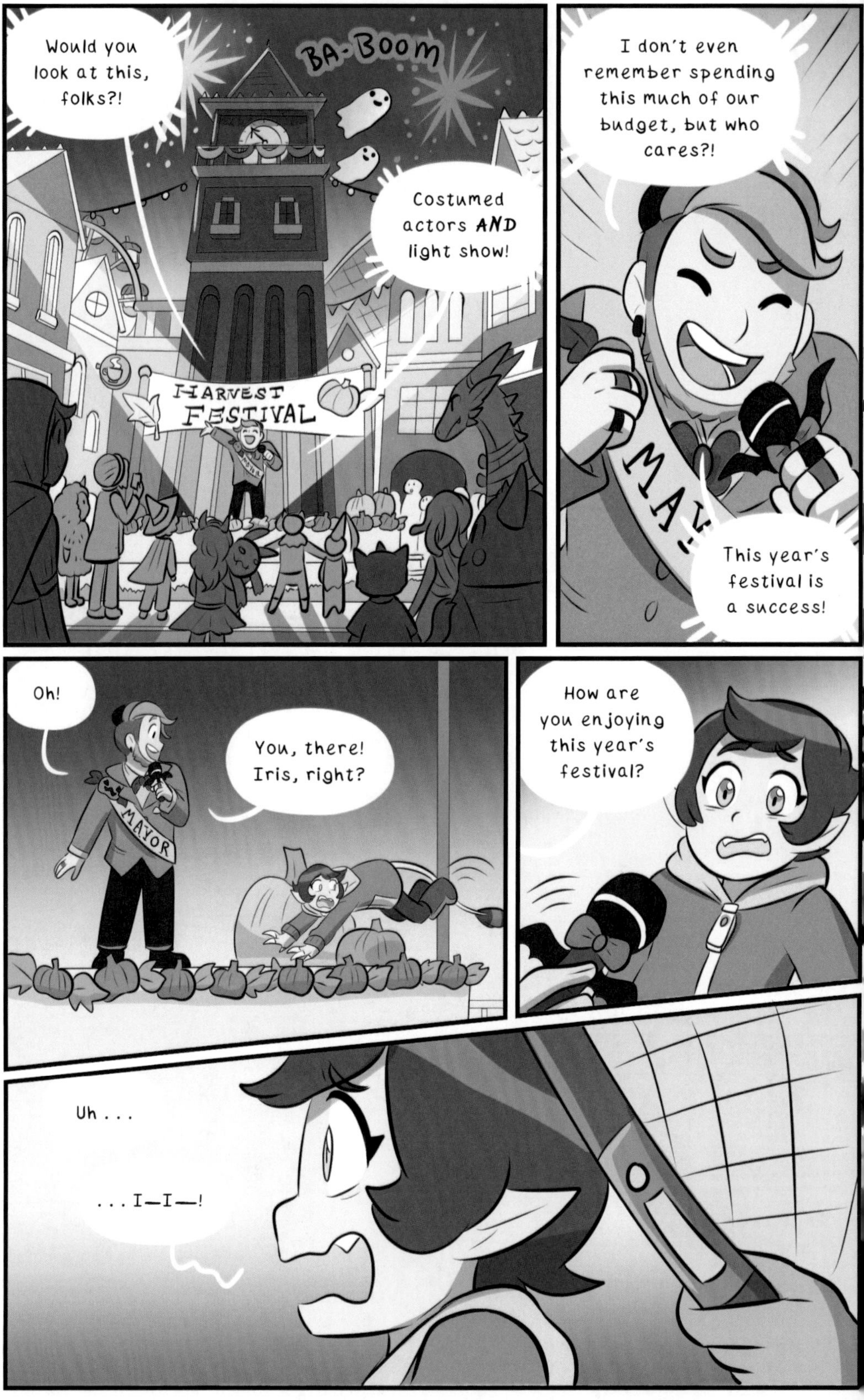

Would you look at this, folks?!
BA-BOOM
HARVEST FESTIVAL
MAYOR
Costumed actors AND light show!
I don't even remember spending this much of our budget, but who cares?!
This year's festival is a success!
Oh!
MAYOR
You, there! Iris, right?
How are you enjoying this year's festival?
Uh . . .
. . . I—I—!

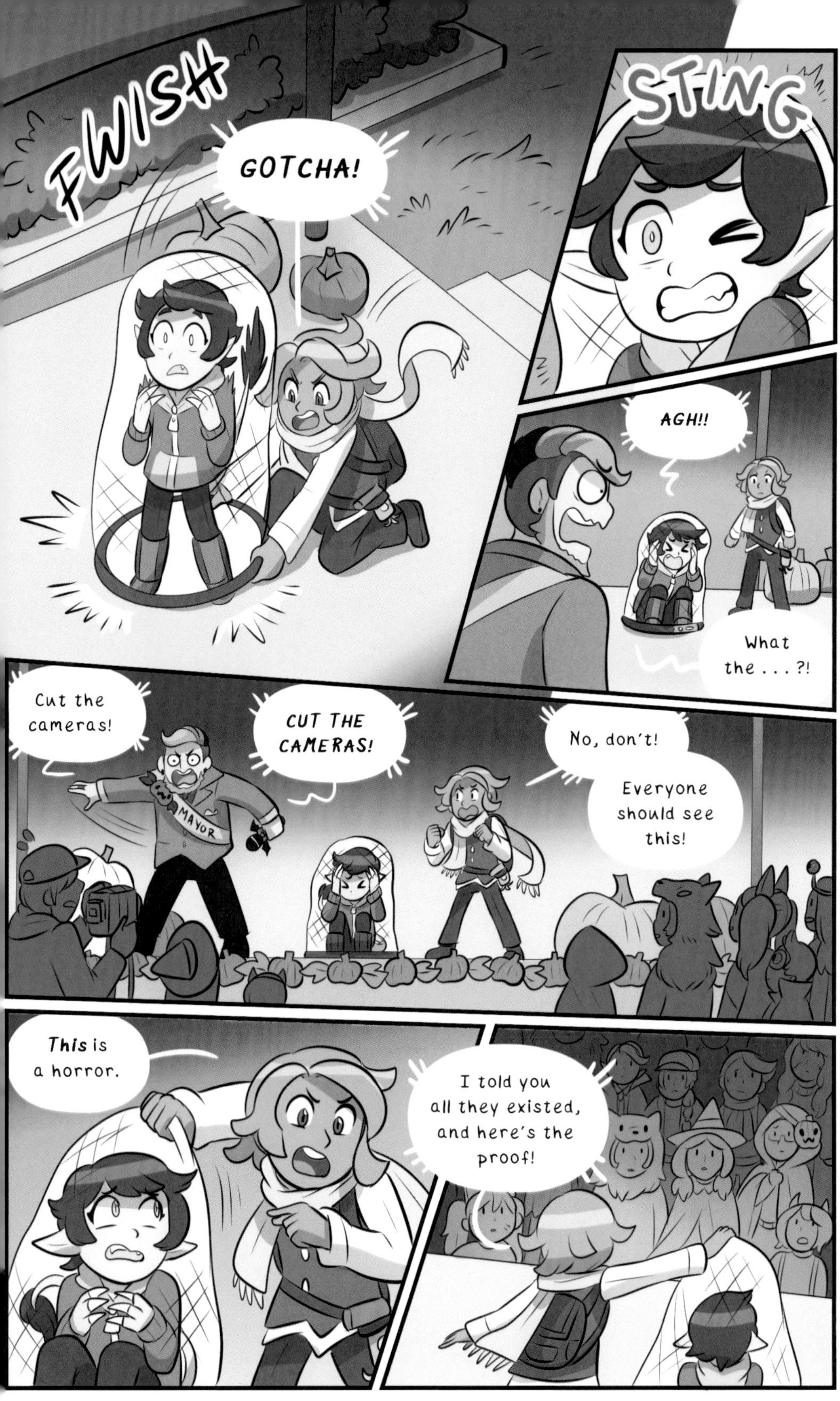

FWISH
GOTCHA!
STING
AGH!!
What the . . . ?!
Cut the cameras!
CUT THE CAMERAS!
MAYOR
No, don't!
Everyone should see this!
This is a horror.
I told you all they existed, and here's the proof!

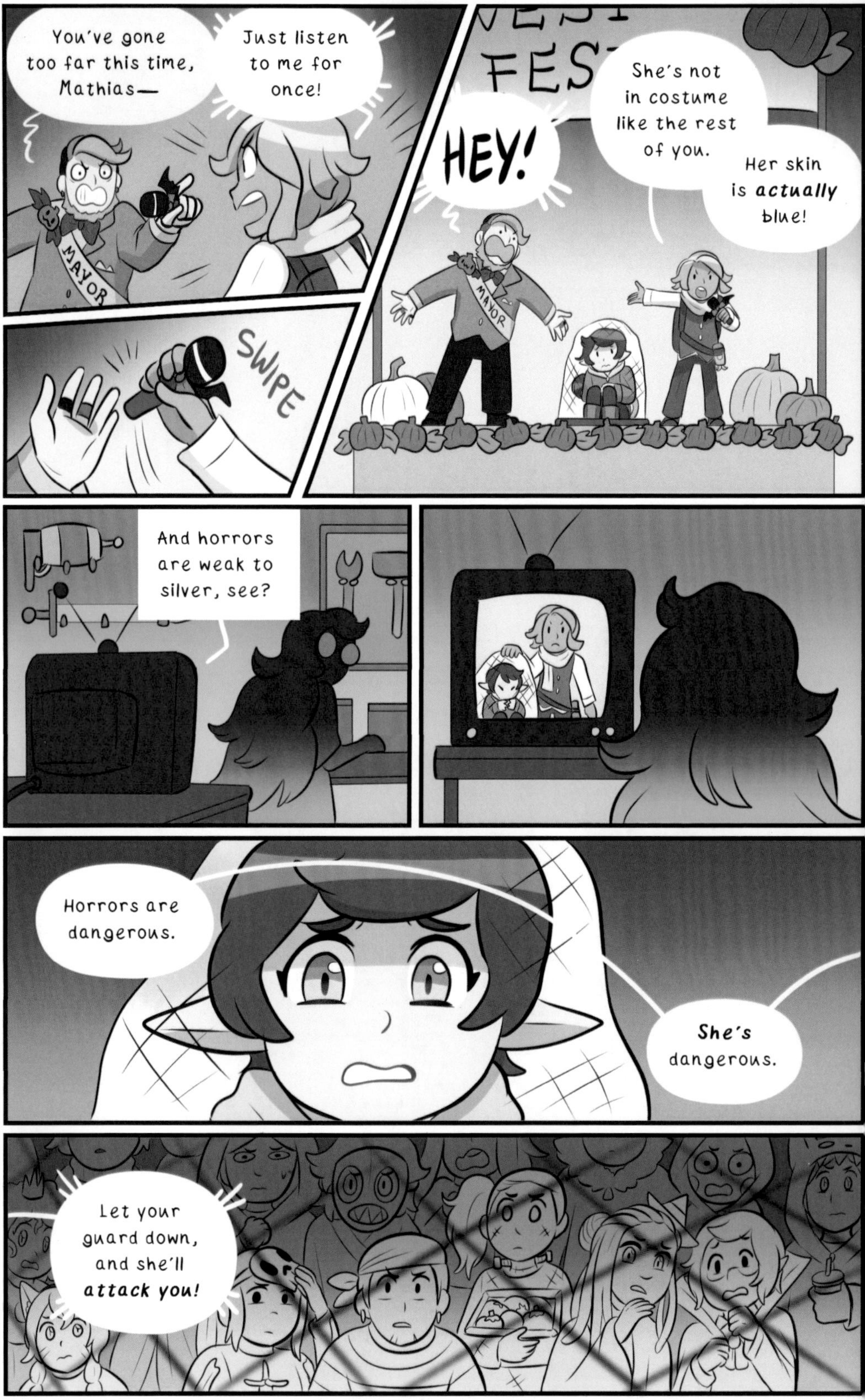
You've gone too far this time, Mathias—
Just listen to me for once!
SWIPE
HEY!
She's not in costume like the rest of you.
Her skin is **actually** blue!
MAYOR
And horrors are weak to silver, see?
Horrors are dangerous.
She's dangerous.
Let your guard down, and she'll **attack you!**

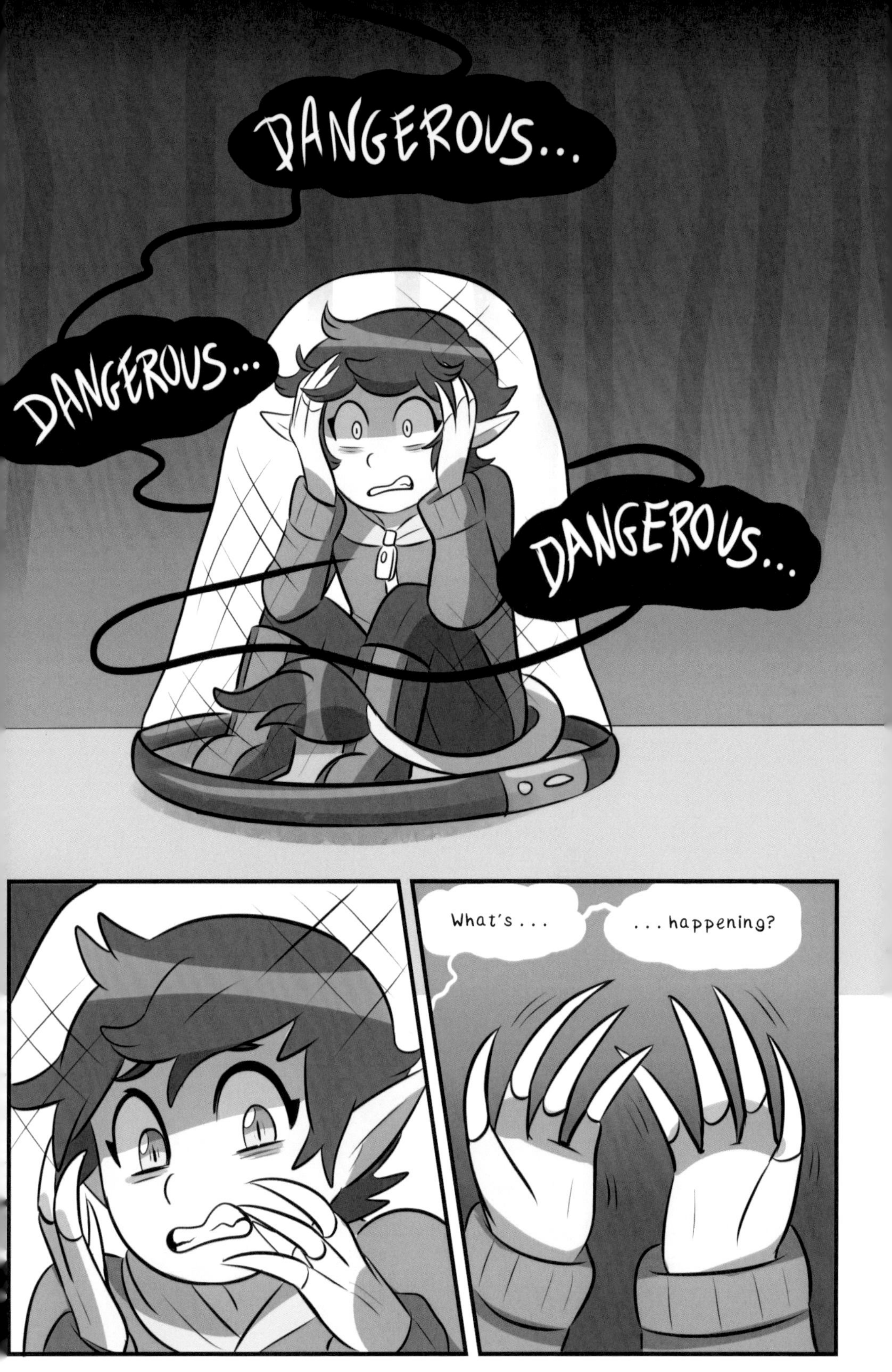
DANGEROUS...
DANGEROUS...
DANGEROUS...
What's...
...happening?

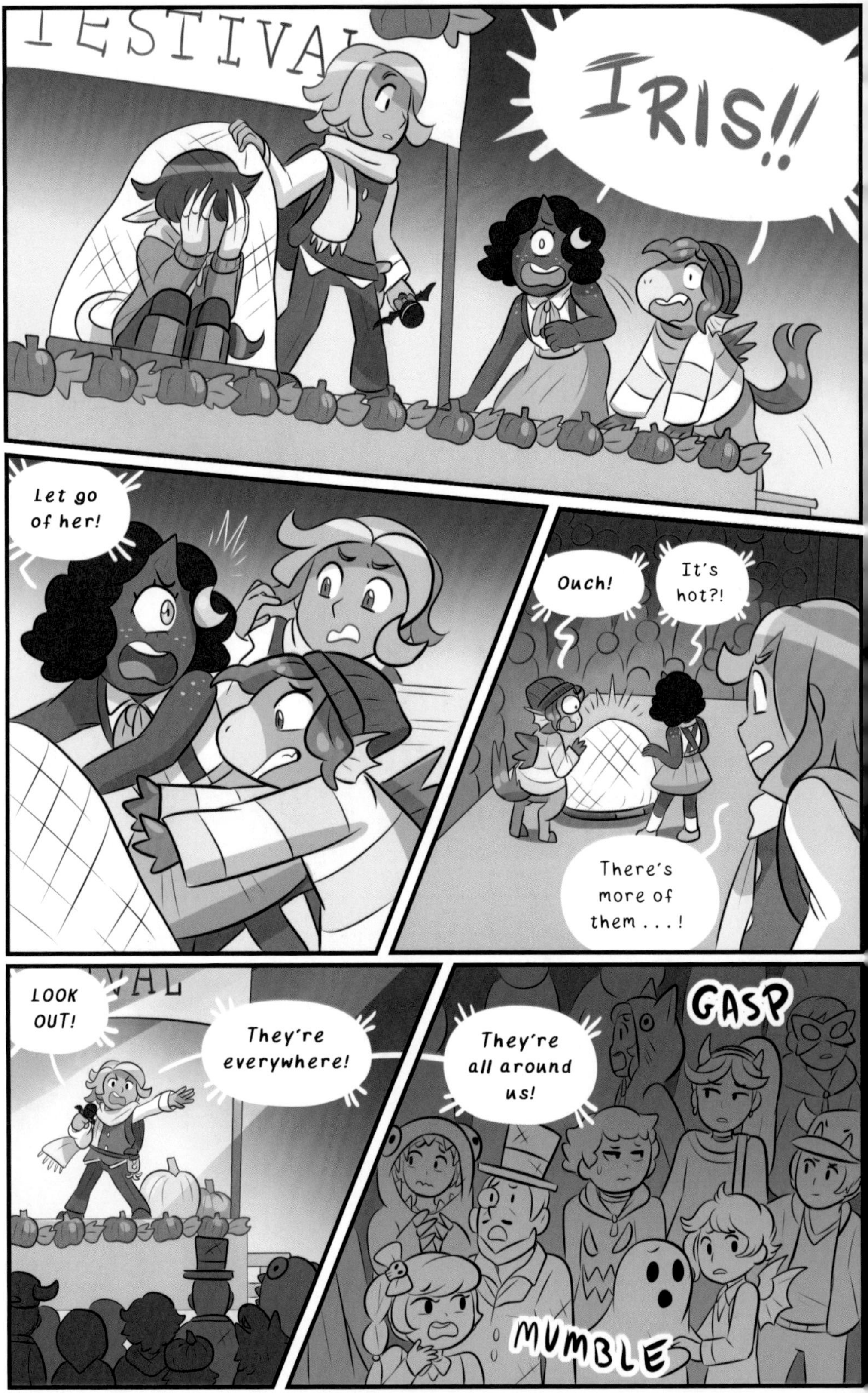

ESTIVAL
IRIS!!
Let go of her!
Ouch!
It's hot?!
There's more of them . . . !
LOOK OUT!
They're everywhere!
They're all around us!
GASP
MUMBLE

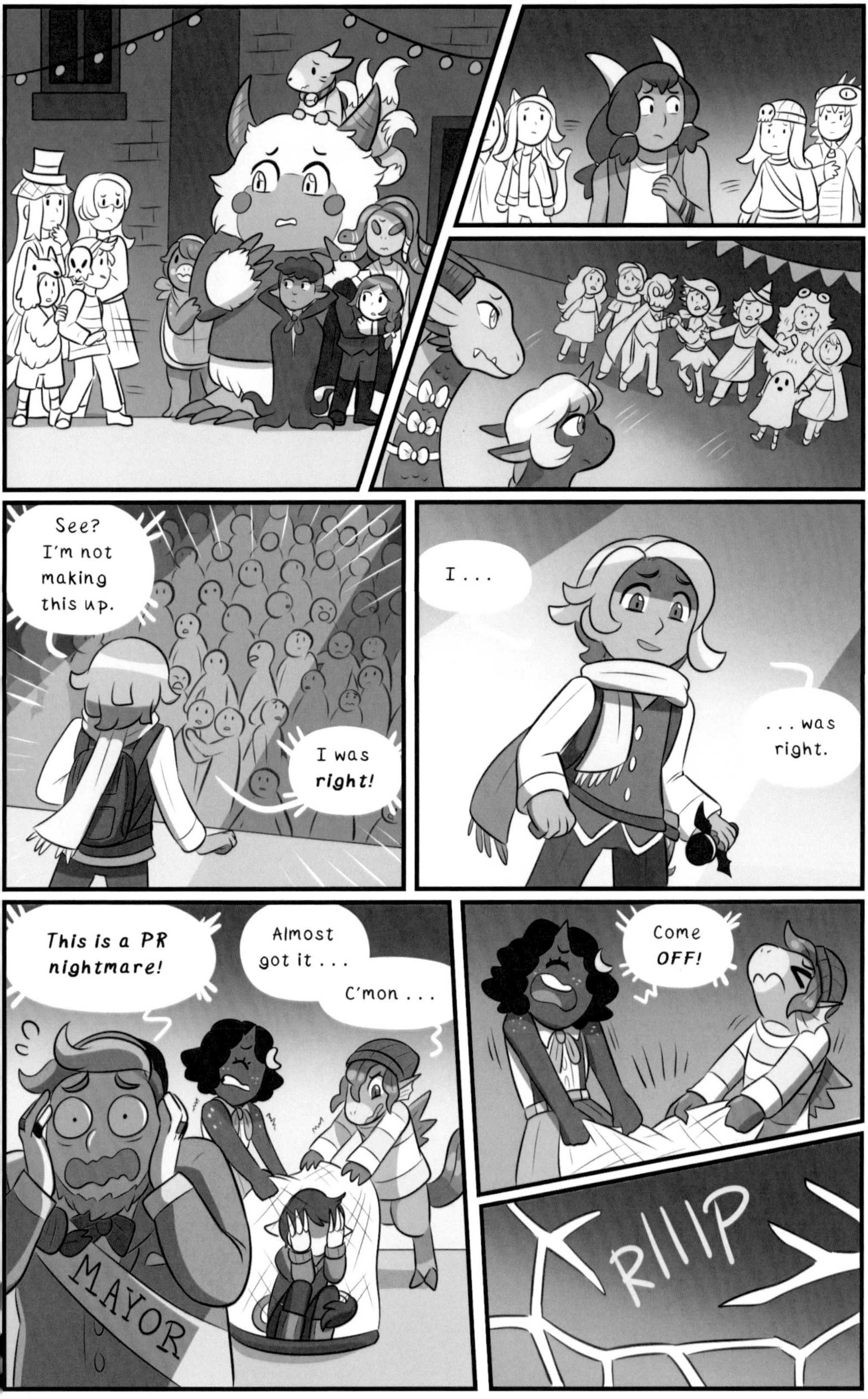
See? I'm not making this up.
I was right!
I . . .
. . . was right.
This is a PR nightmare!
Almost got it . . .
C'mon . . .
Come OFF!
RIIIP
MAYOR

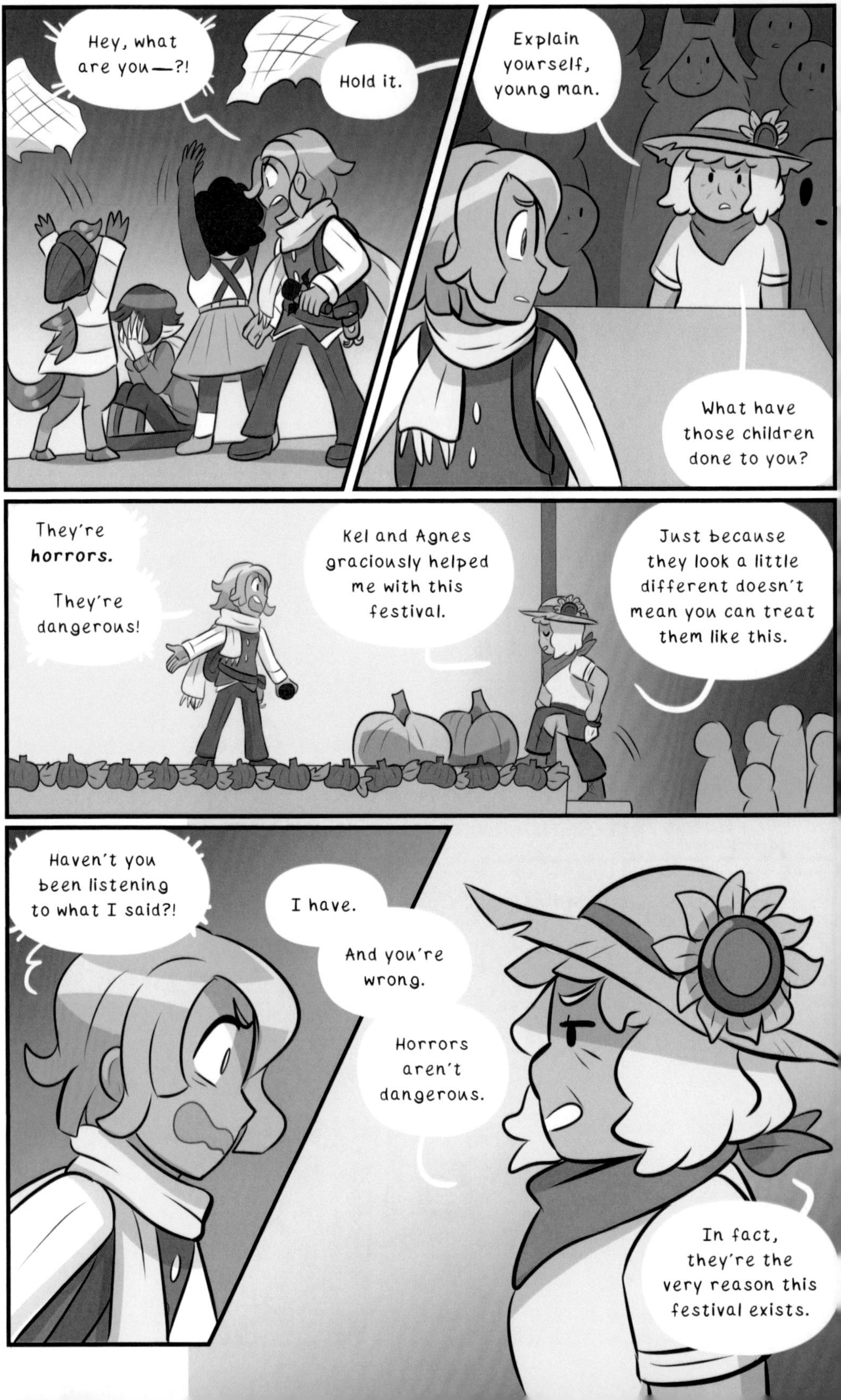
Hey, what are you—?!
Hold it.
Explain yourself, young man.
What have those children done to you?
They're **horrors.**
They're dangerous!
Kel and Agnes graciously helped me with this festival.
Just because they look a little different doesn't mean you can treat them like this.
Haven't you been listening to what I said?!
I have.
And you're wrong.
Horrors aren't dangerous.
In fact, they're the very reason this festival exists.

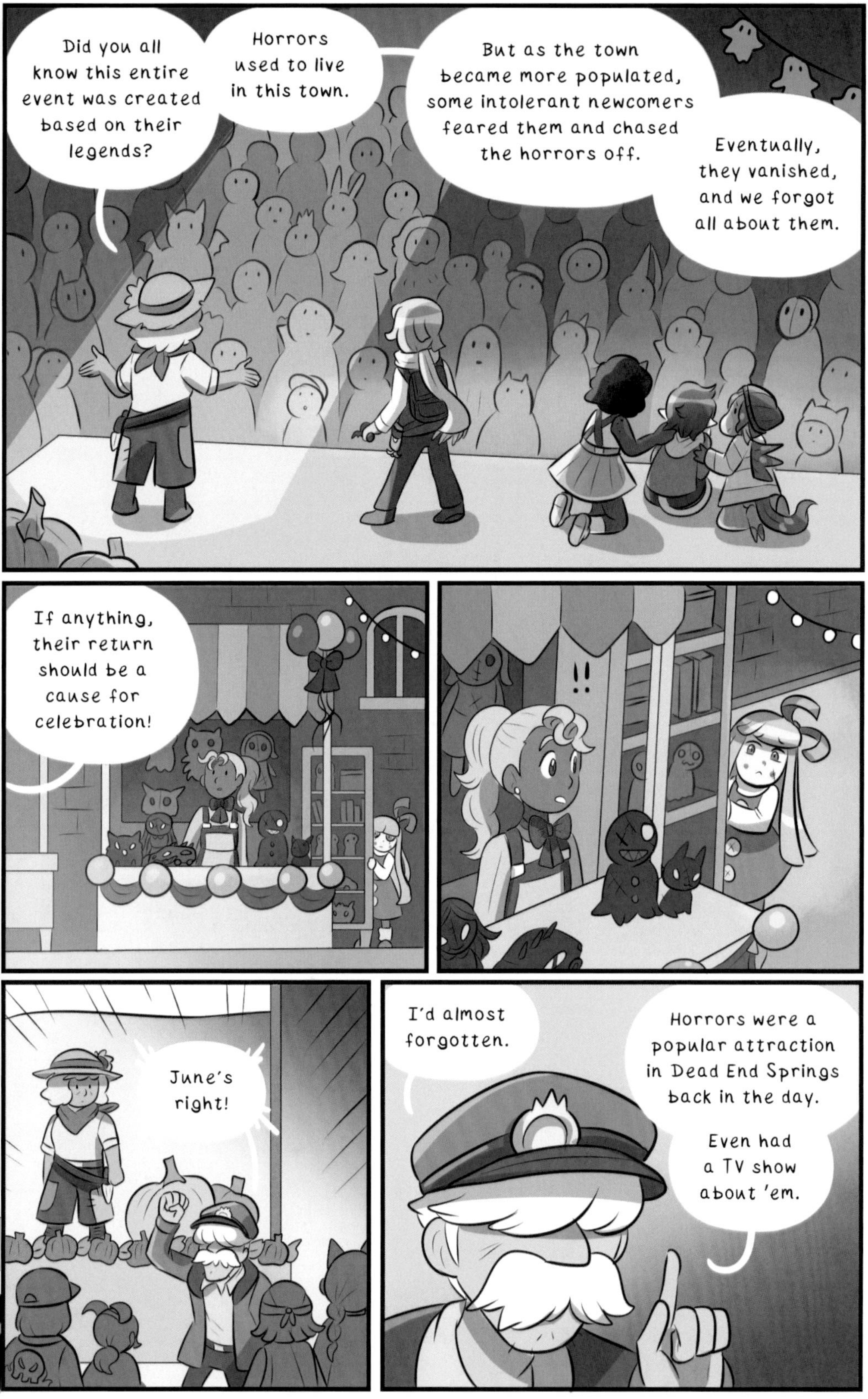
Did you all know this entire event was created based on their legends?
Horrors used to live in this town.
But as the town became more populated, some intolerant newcomers feared them and chased the horrors off.
Eventually, they vanished, and we forgot all about them.
If anything, their return should be a cause for celebration!
!!
June's right!
I'd almost forgotten.
Horrors were a popular attraction in Dead End Springs back in the day.
Even had a TV show about 'em.

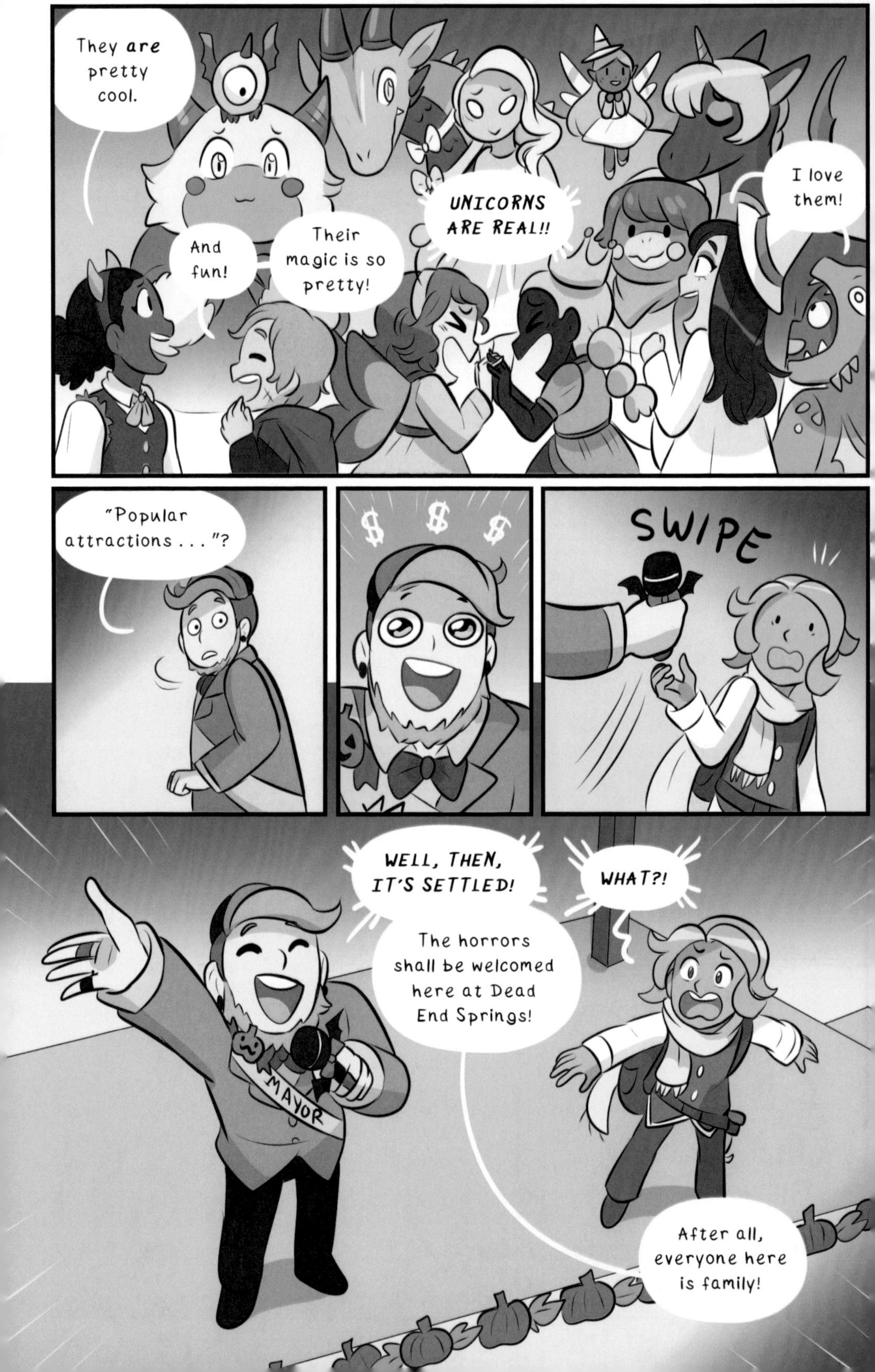
They **are** pretty cool.
And fun!
Their magic is so pretty!
UNICORNS ARE REAL!!
I love them!
"Popular attractions . . ."?
SWIPE
WELL, THEN, IT'S SETTLED!
The horrors shall be welcomed here at Dead End Springs!
WHAT?!
MAYOR
After all, everyone here is family!

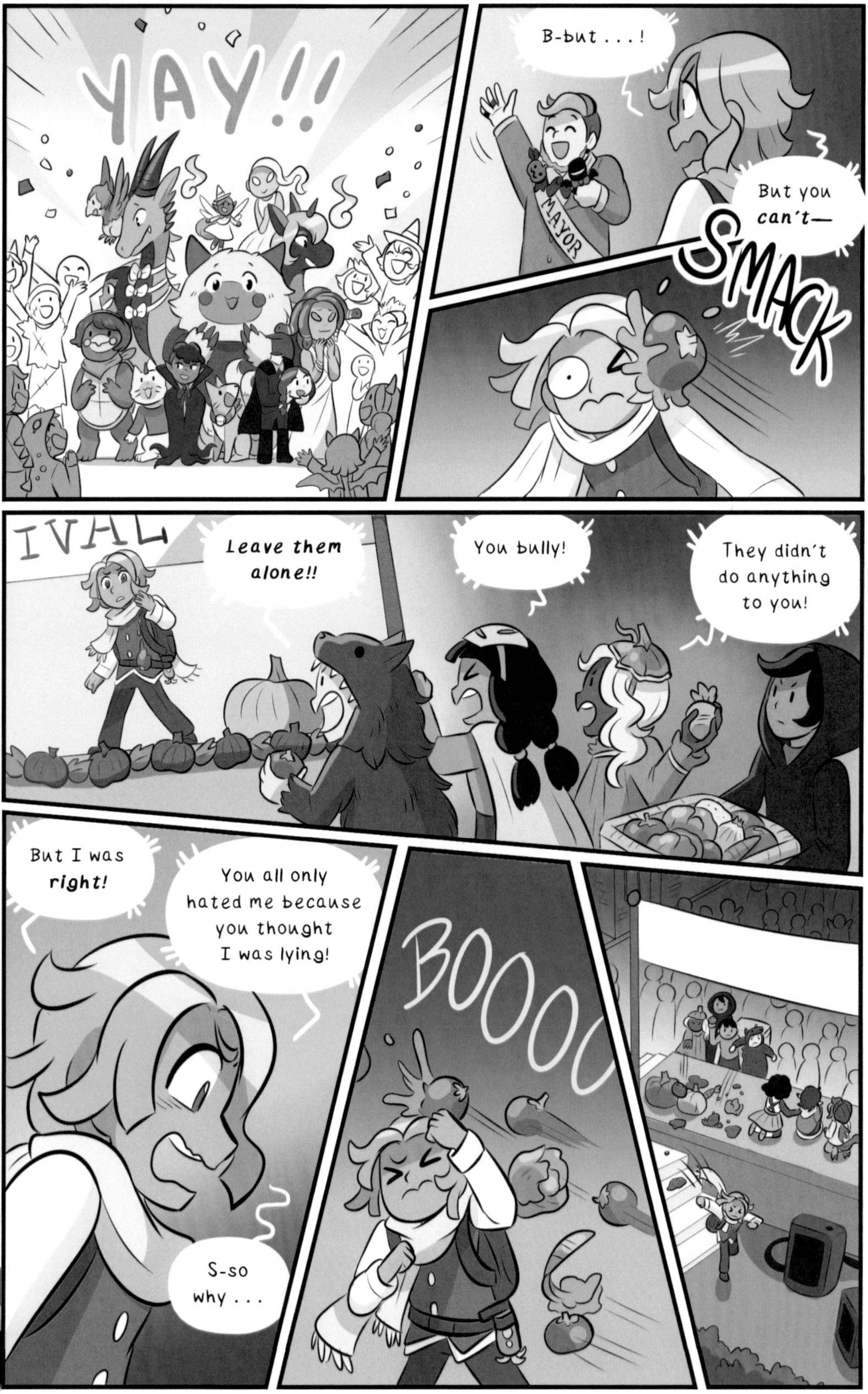
YAY!!
B-but . . . !
But you can't—
SMACK
IVAL
Leave them alone!!
You bully!
They didn't do anything to you!
But I was right!
You all only hated me because you thought I was lying!
S-so why . . .
BOOOO

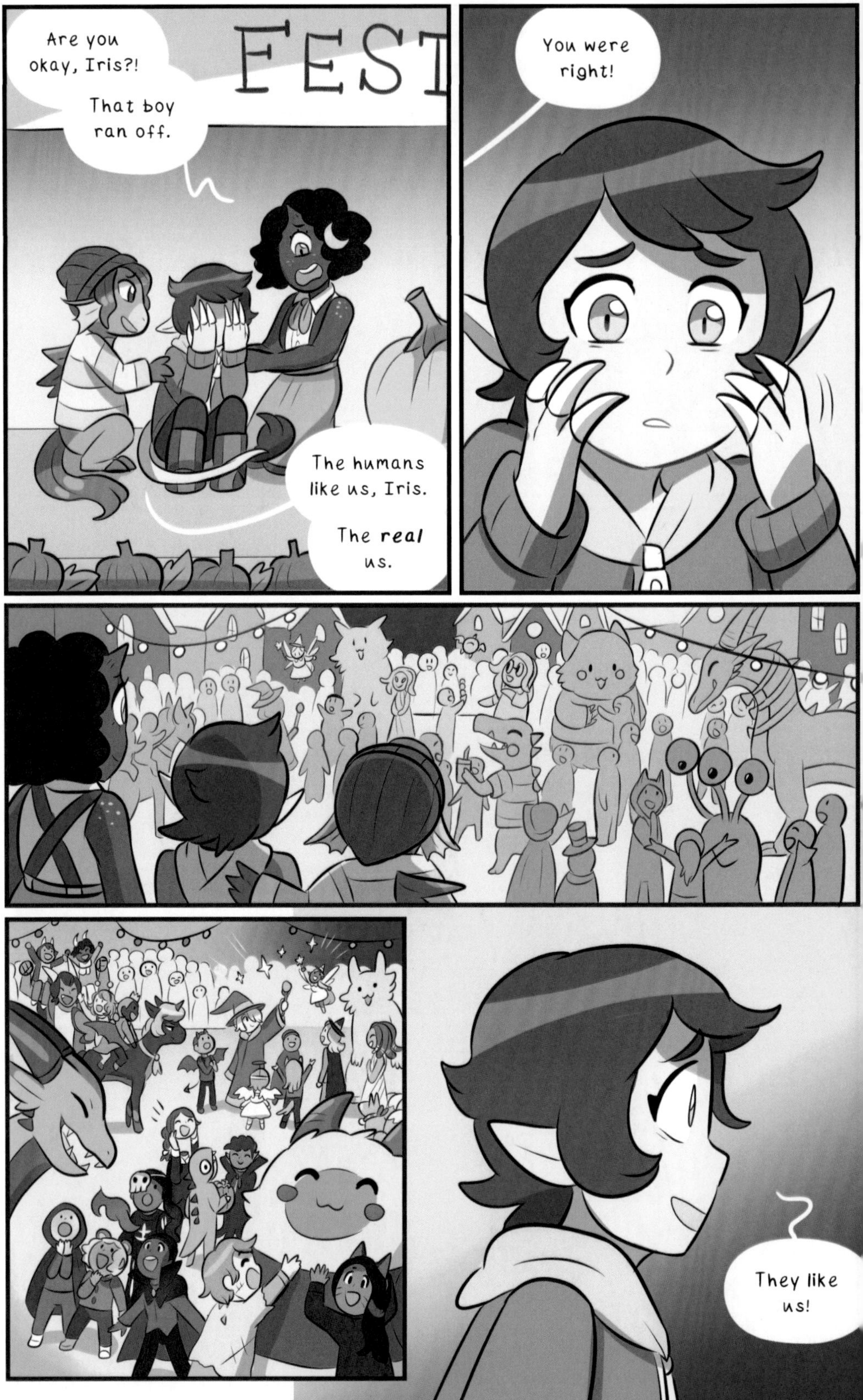
Are you okay, Iris?!
That boy ran off.
FEST
The humans like us, Iris.
The *real* us.
You were right!
They like us!

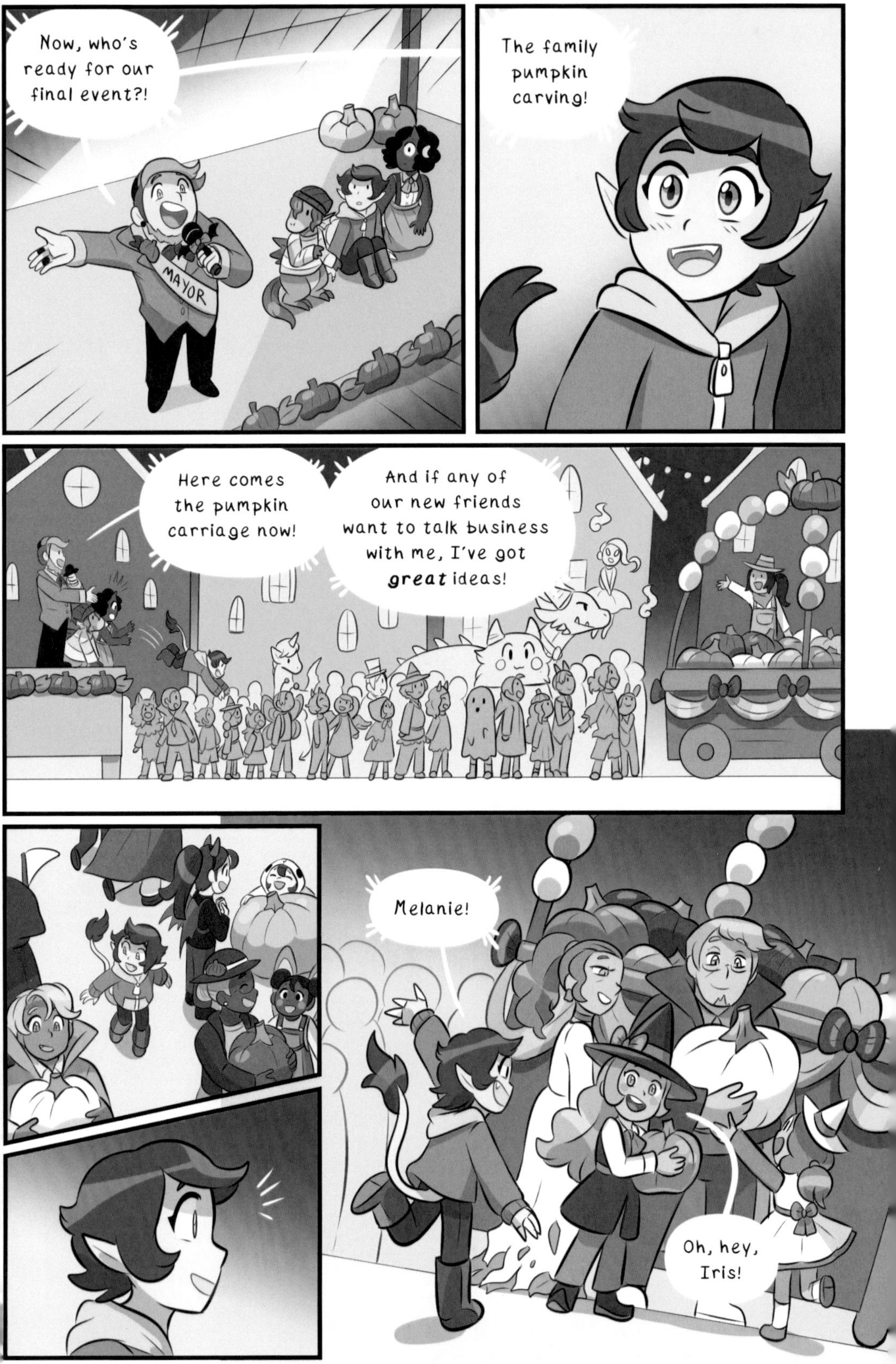

Now, who's ready for our final event?!
MAYOR
The family pumpkin carving!
Here comes the pumpkin carriage now!
And if any of our new friends want to talk business with me, I've got **great** ideas!
Melanie!
Oh, hey, Iris!

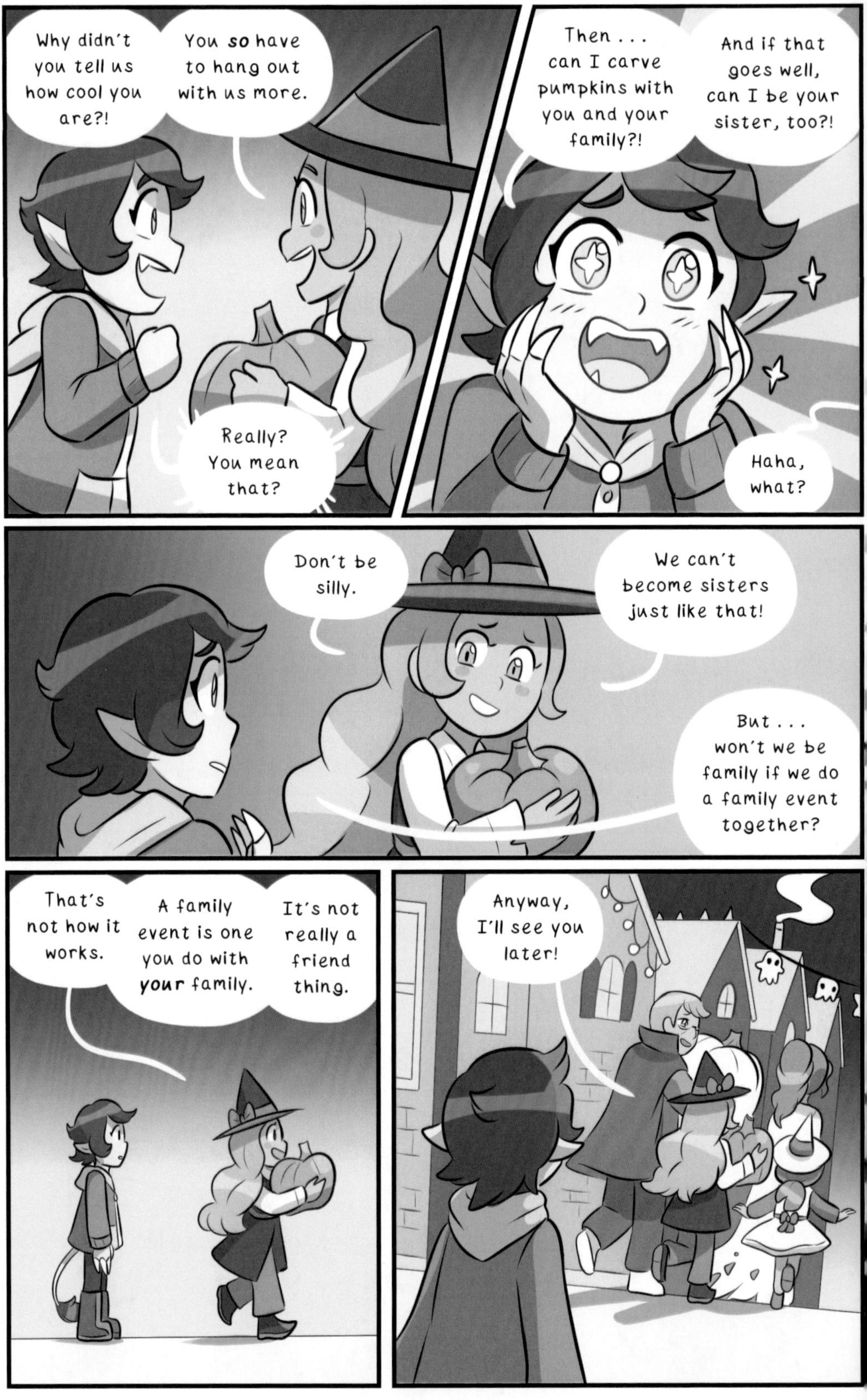
Why didn't you tell us how cool you are?!
You **so** have to hang out with us more.
Really? You mean that?
Then . . . can I carve pumpkins with you and your family?!
And if that goes well, can I be your sister, too?!
Haha, what?
Don't be silly.
We can't become sisters just like that!
But . . . won't we be family if we do a family event together?
That's not how it works.
A family event is one you do with **your** family.
It's not really a friend thing.
Anyway, I'll see you later!

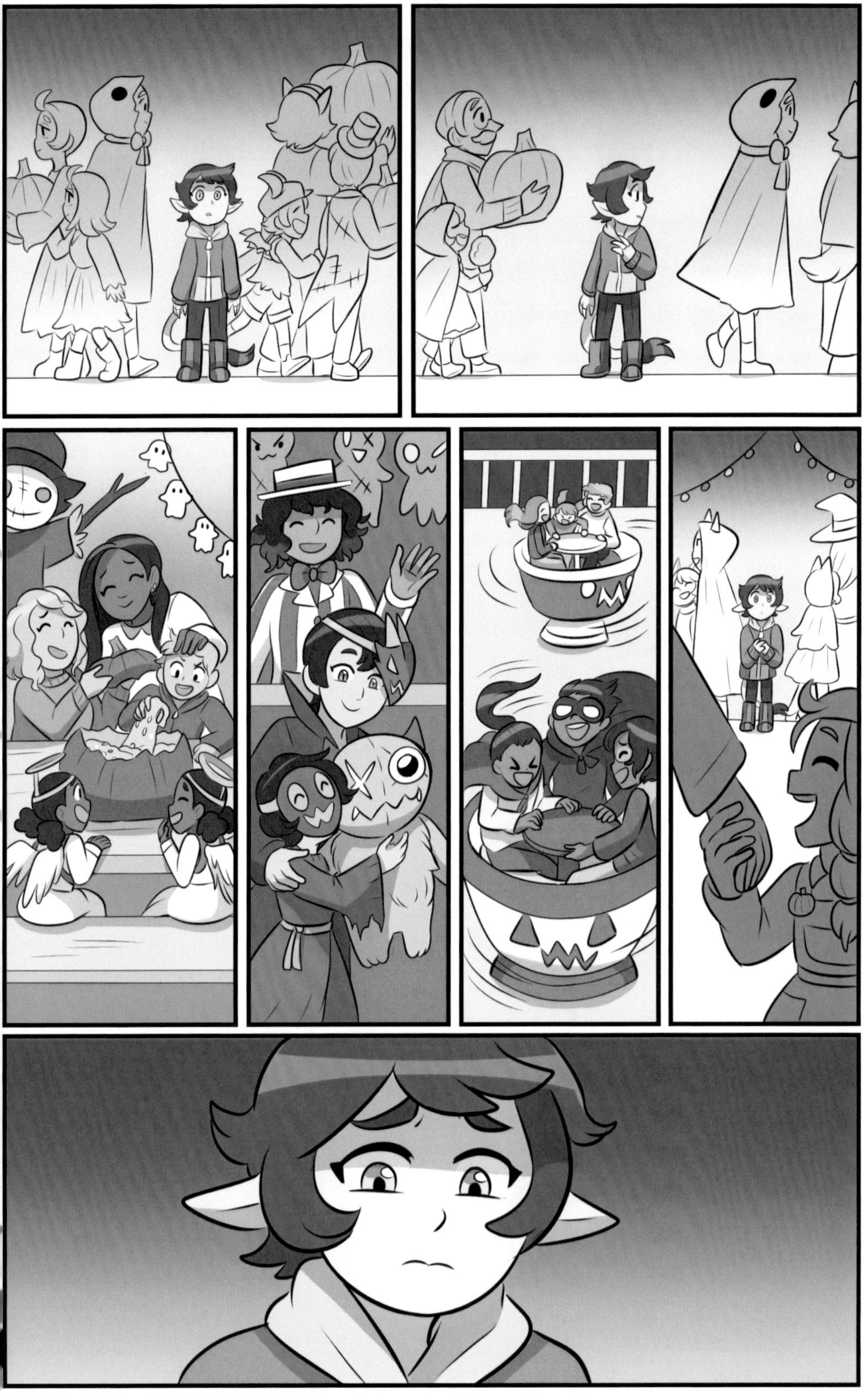

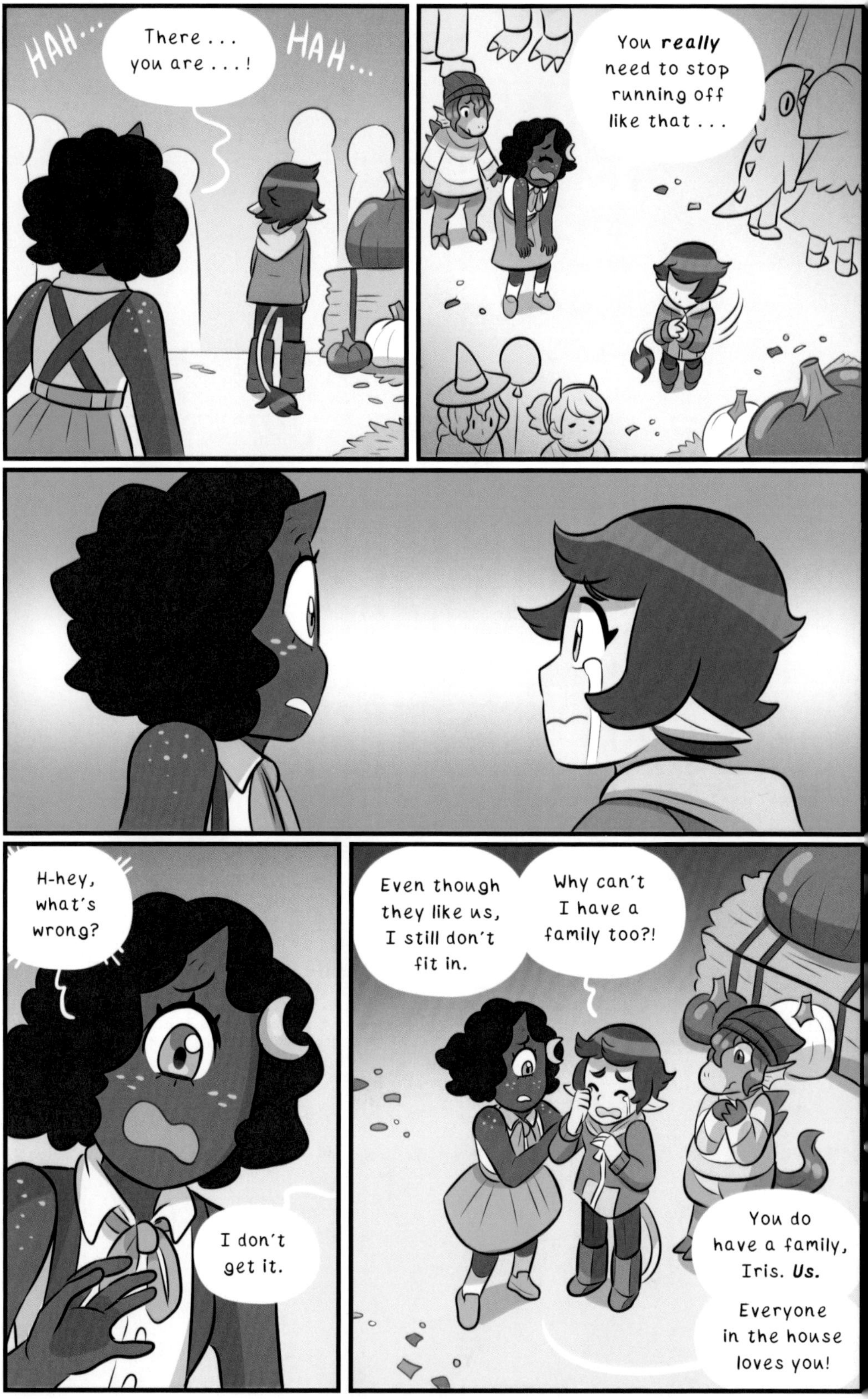
HAH...
There . . .
you are . . . !
HAH...
You **really** need to stop running off like that . . .
H-hey, what's wrong?
I don't get it.
Even though they like us, I still don't fit in.
Why can't I have a family too?!
You do have a family, Iris. ***Us.***
Everyone in the house loves you!

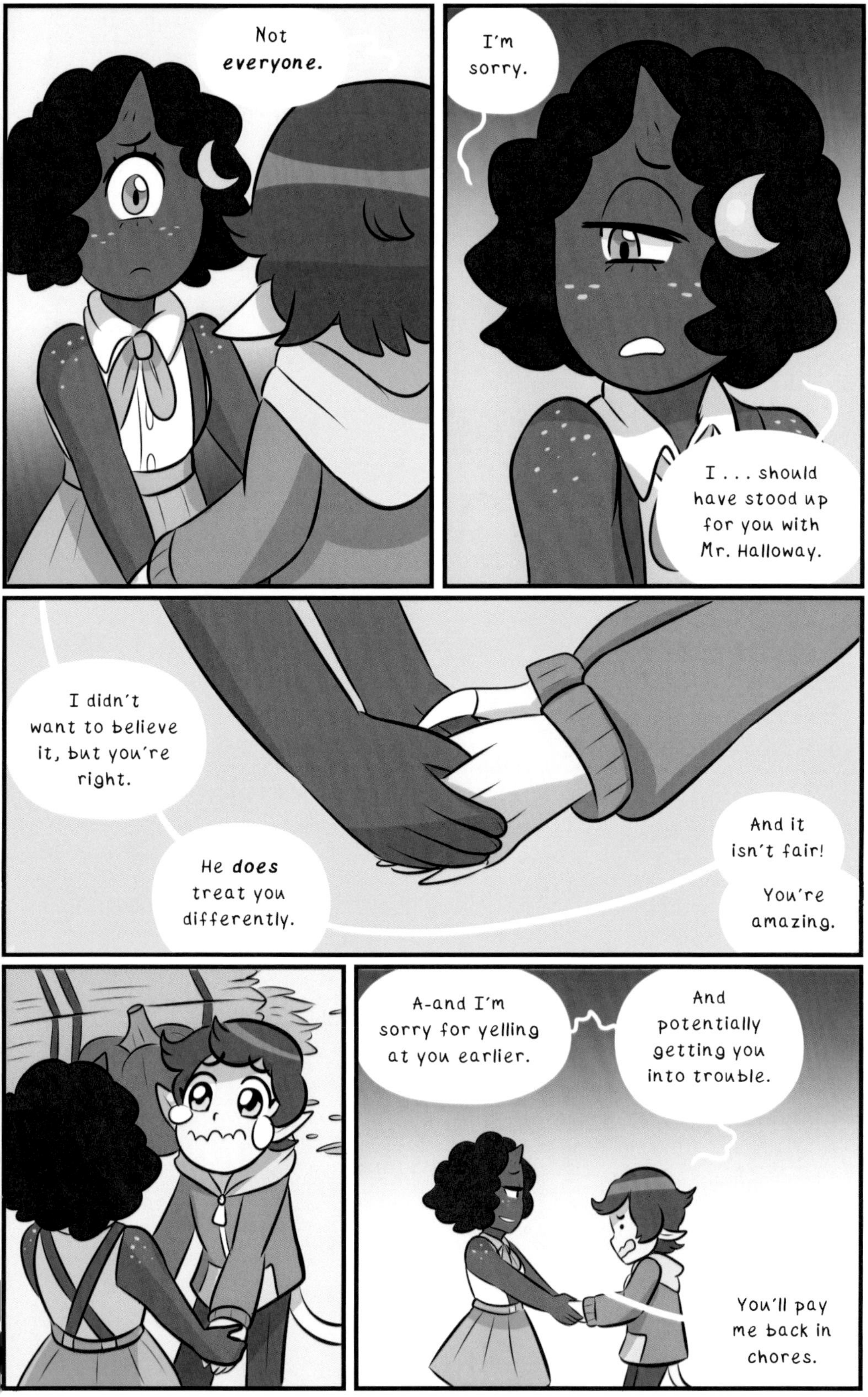
Not **everyone.**
I'm sorry.
I . . . should have stood up for you with Mr. Halloway.
I didn't want to believe it, but you're right.
He **does** treat you differently.
And it isn't fair!
You're amazing.
A-and I'm sorry for yelling at you earlier.
And potentially getting you into trouble.
You'll pay me back in chores.

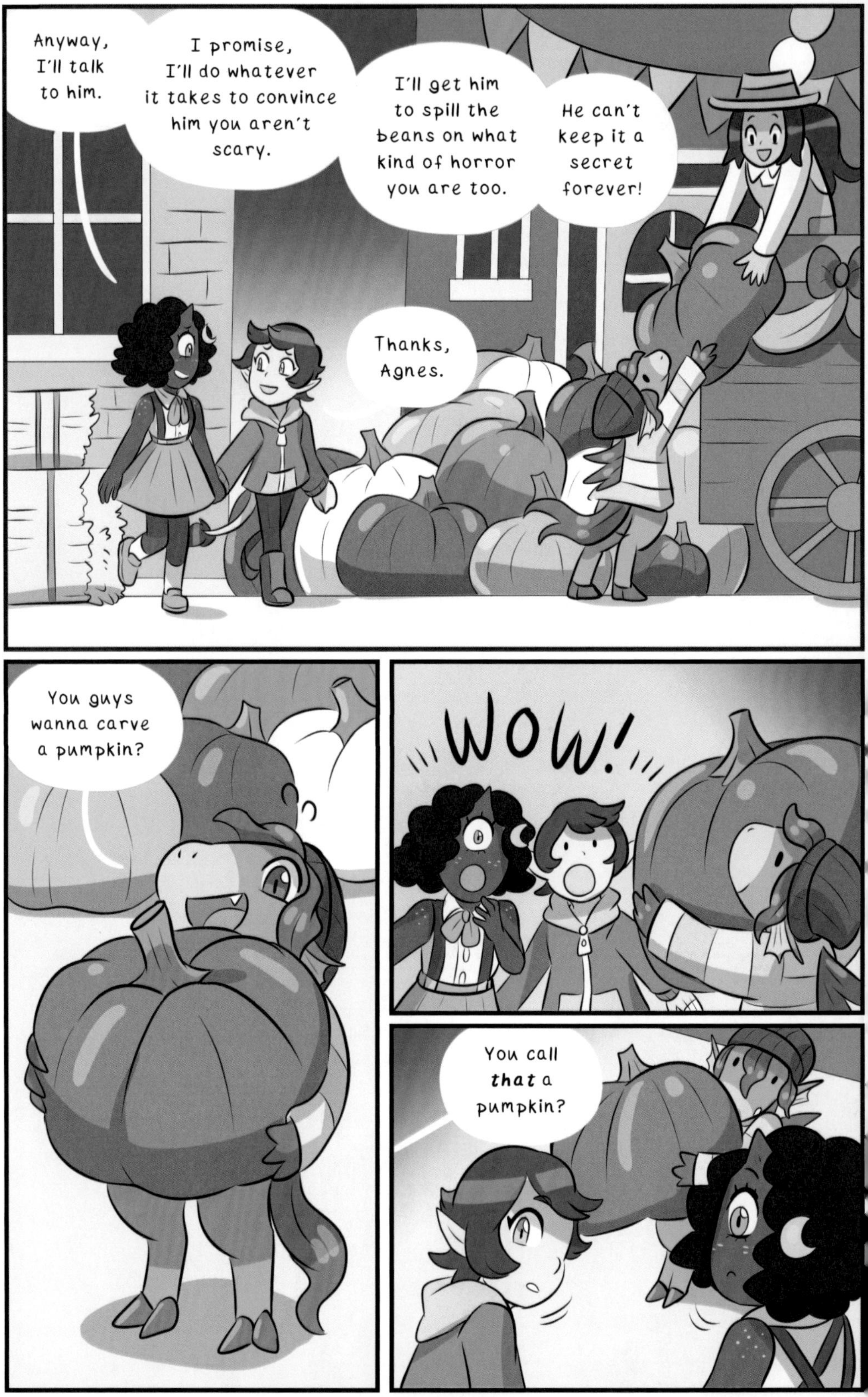
Anyway, I'll talk to him.
I promise, I'll do whatever it takes to convince him you aren't scary.
I'll get him to spill the beans on what kind of horror you are too.
He can't keep it a secret forever!
Thanks, Agnes.
You guys wanna carve a pumpkin?
WOW!
You call ***that*** a pumpkin?

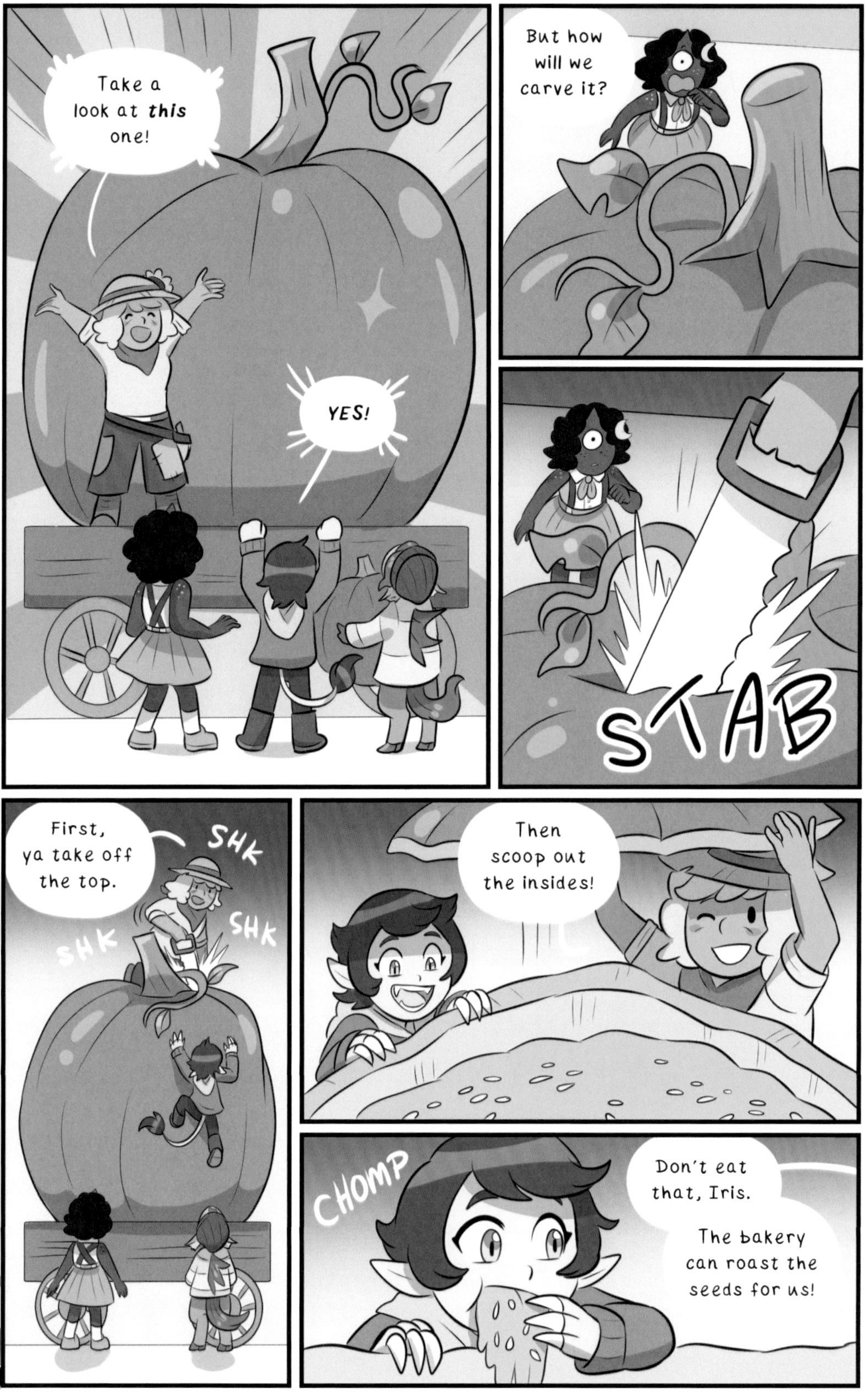
Take a look at **this** one!
YES!
But how will we carve it?
STAB
First, ya take off the top.
SHK
SHK
SHK
Then scoop out the insides!
CHOMP
Don't eat that, Iris.
The bakery can roast the seeds for us!

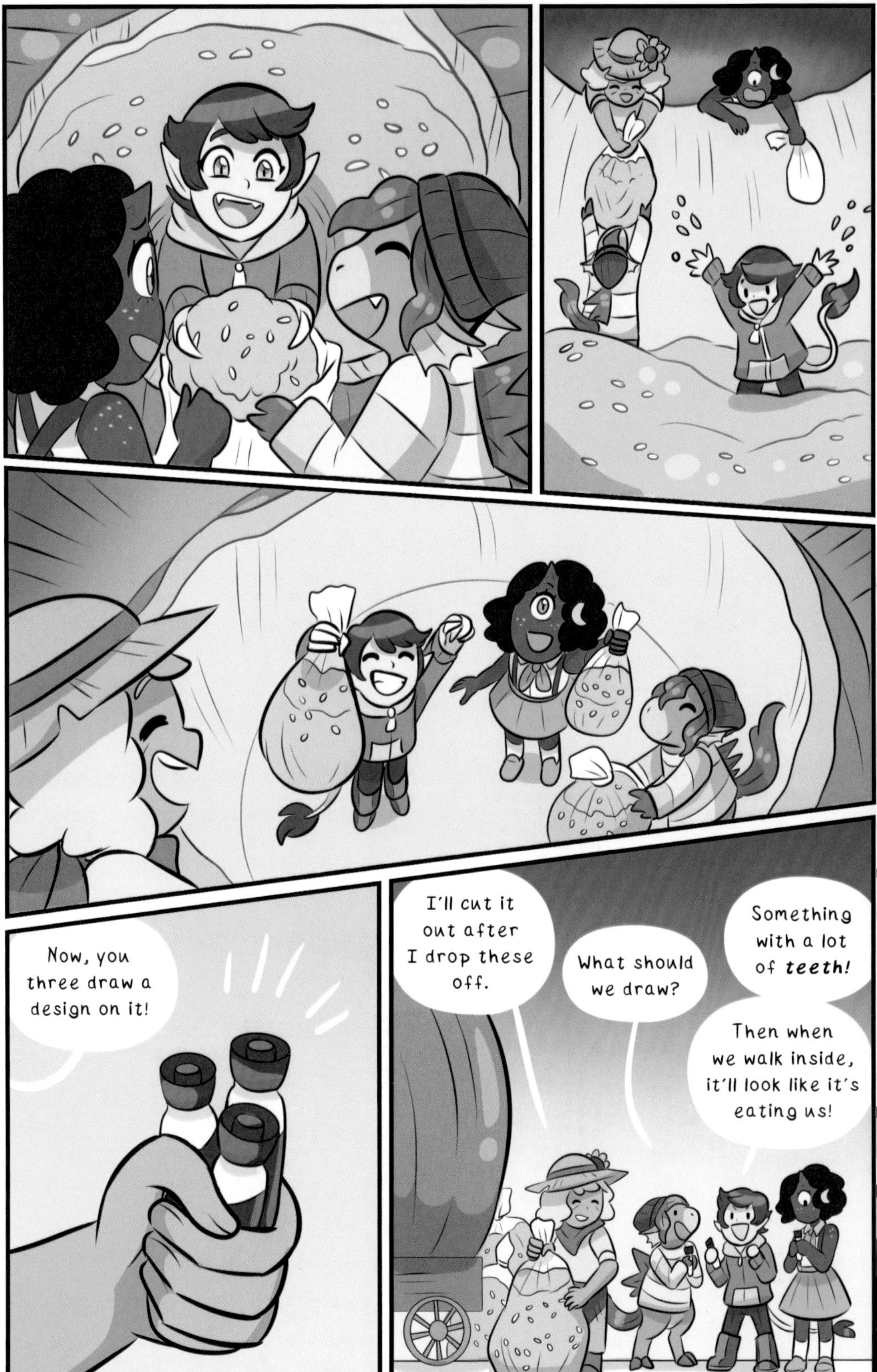
Now, you three draw a design on it!
I'll cut it out after I drop these off.
What should we draw?
Something with a lot of *teeth!*
Then when we walk inside, it'll look like it's eating us!

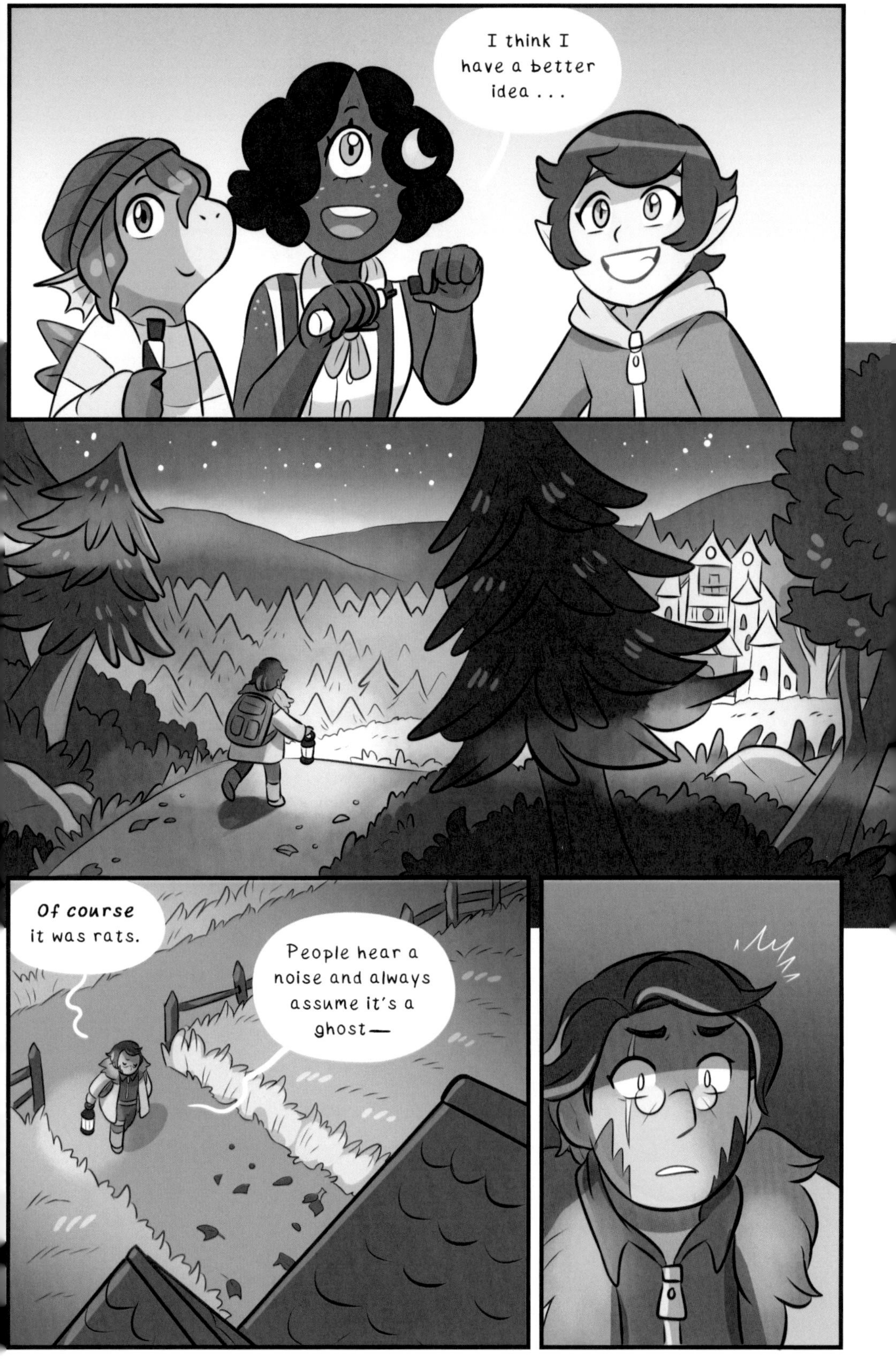
I think I have a better idea . . .
Of course it was rats.
People hear a noise and always assume it's a ghost—

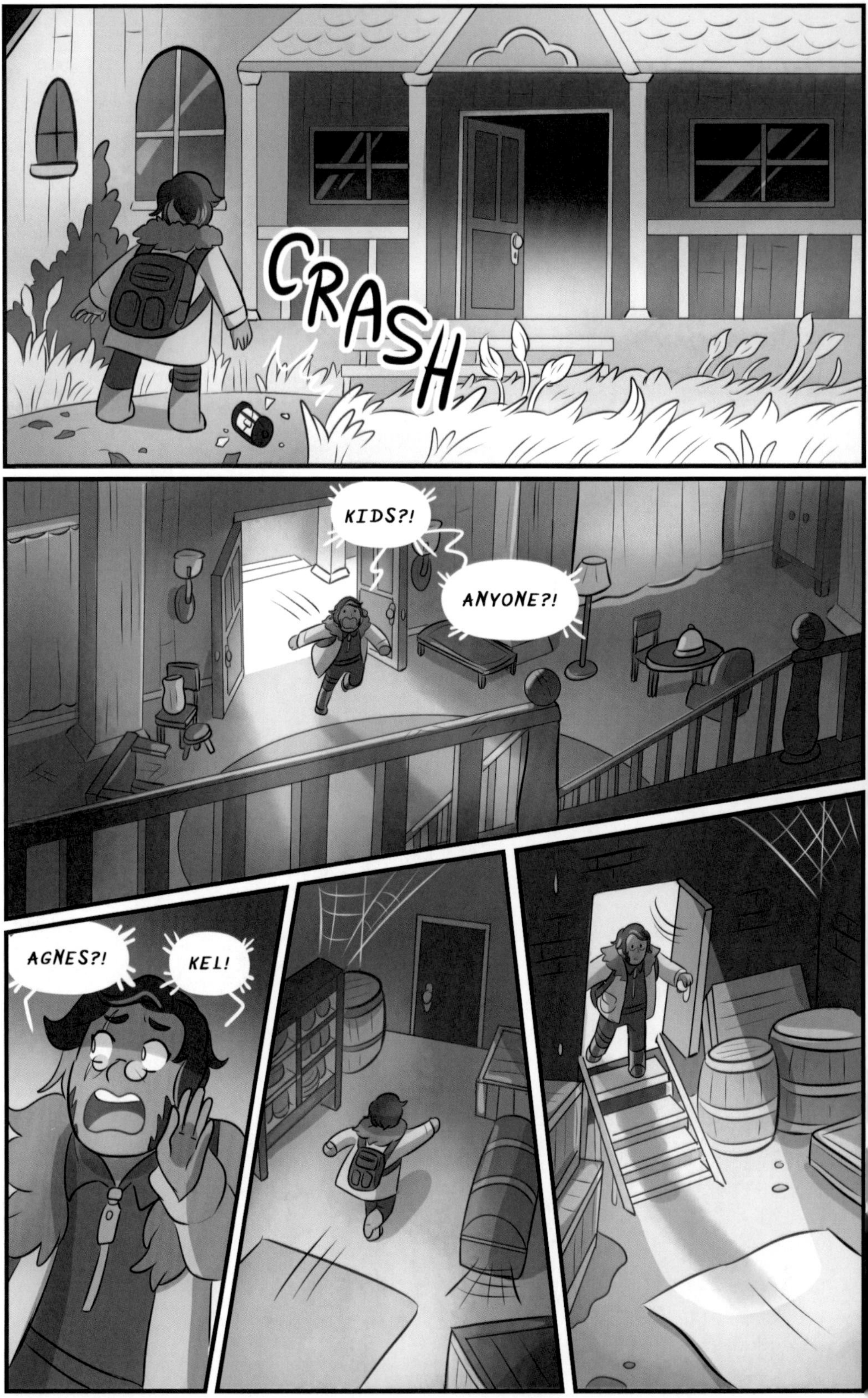
CRASH
KIDS?!
ANYONE?!
AGNES?!
KEL!

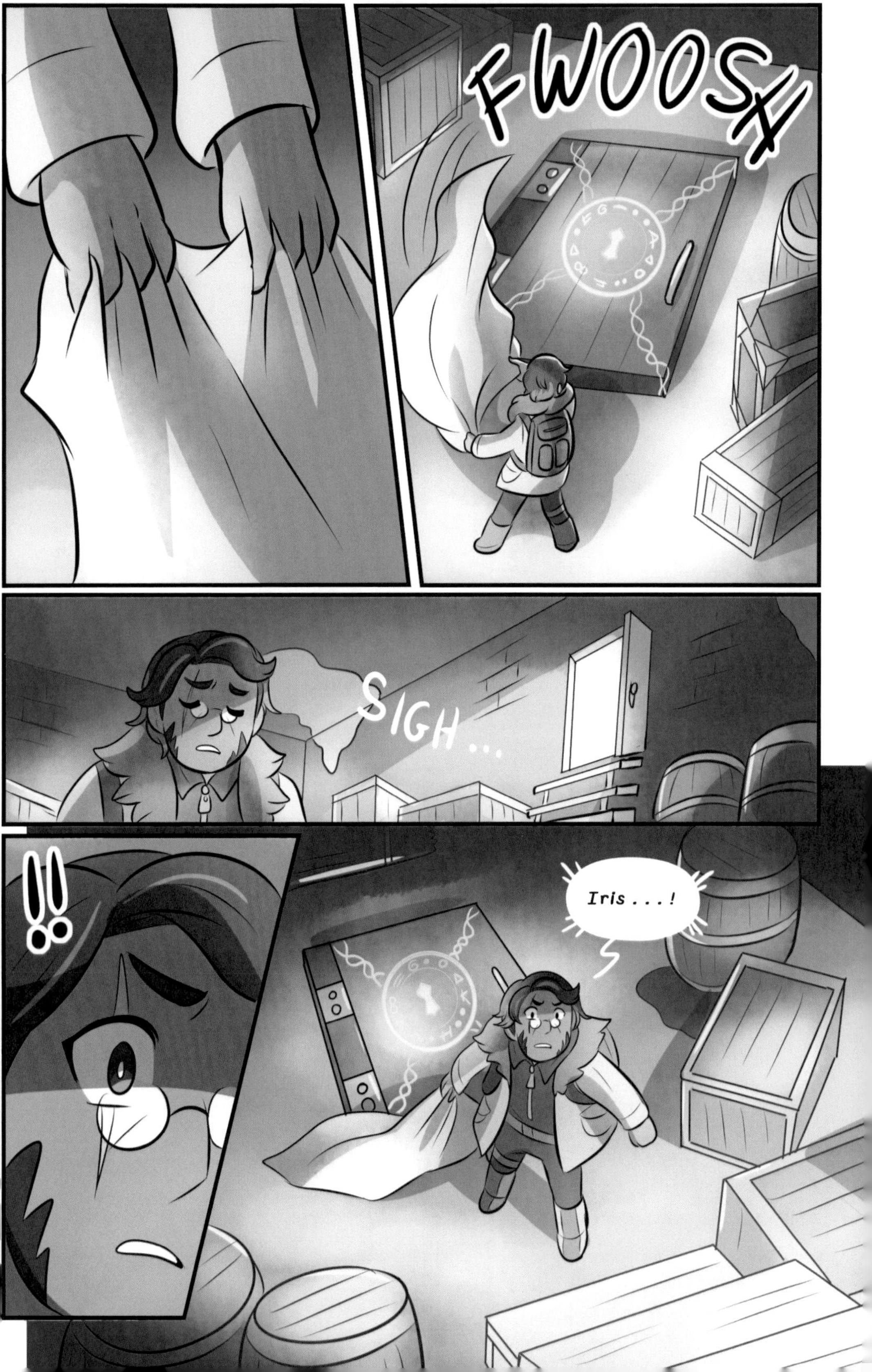
FWOOSH
SIGH...
!!
Iris . . . !

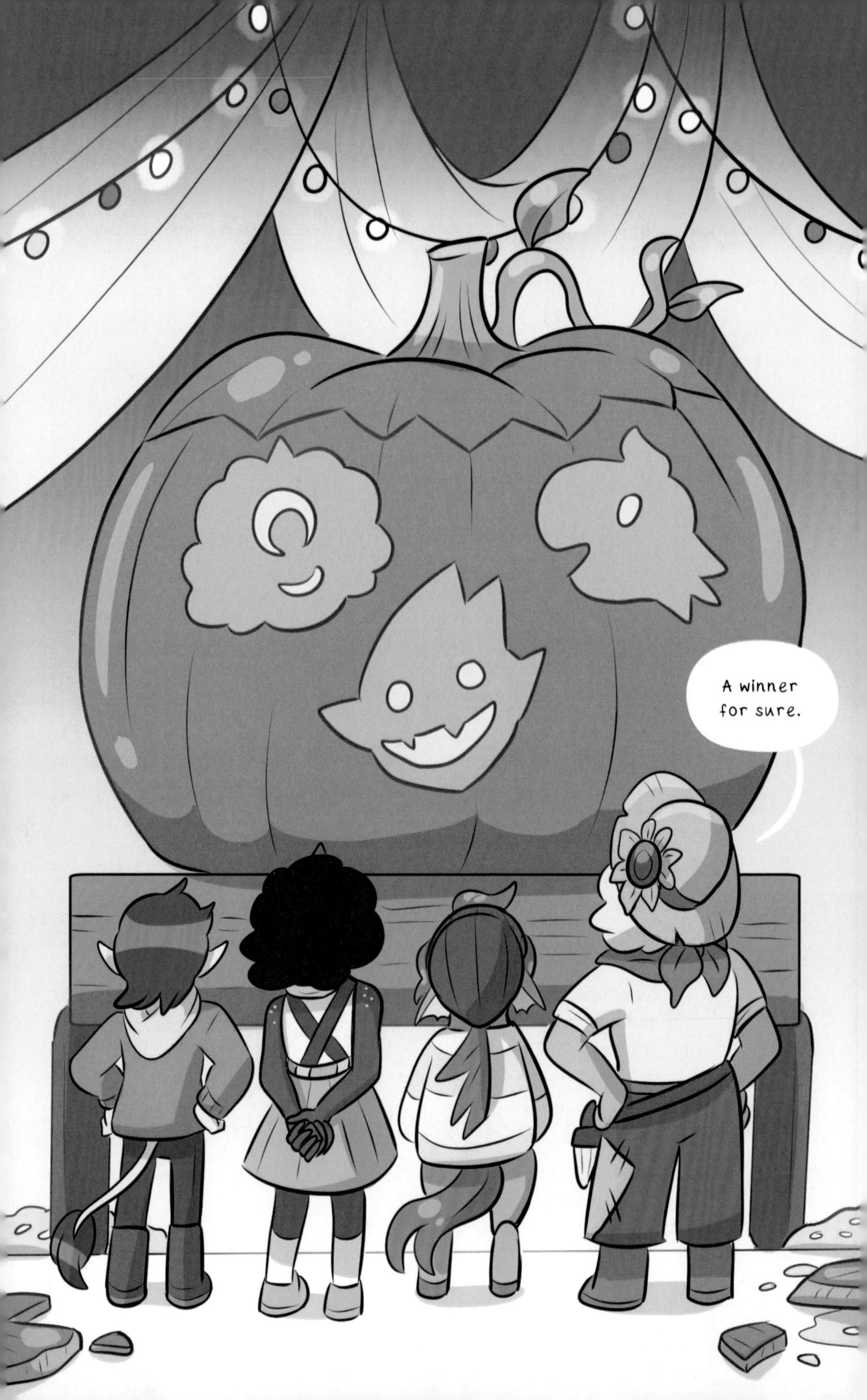
A winner for sure.

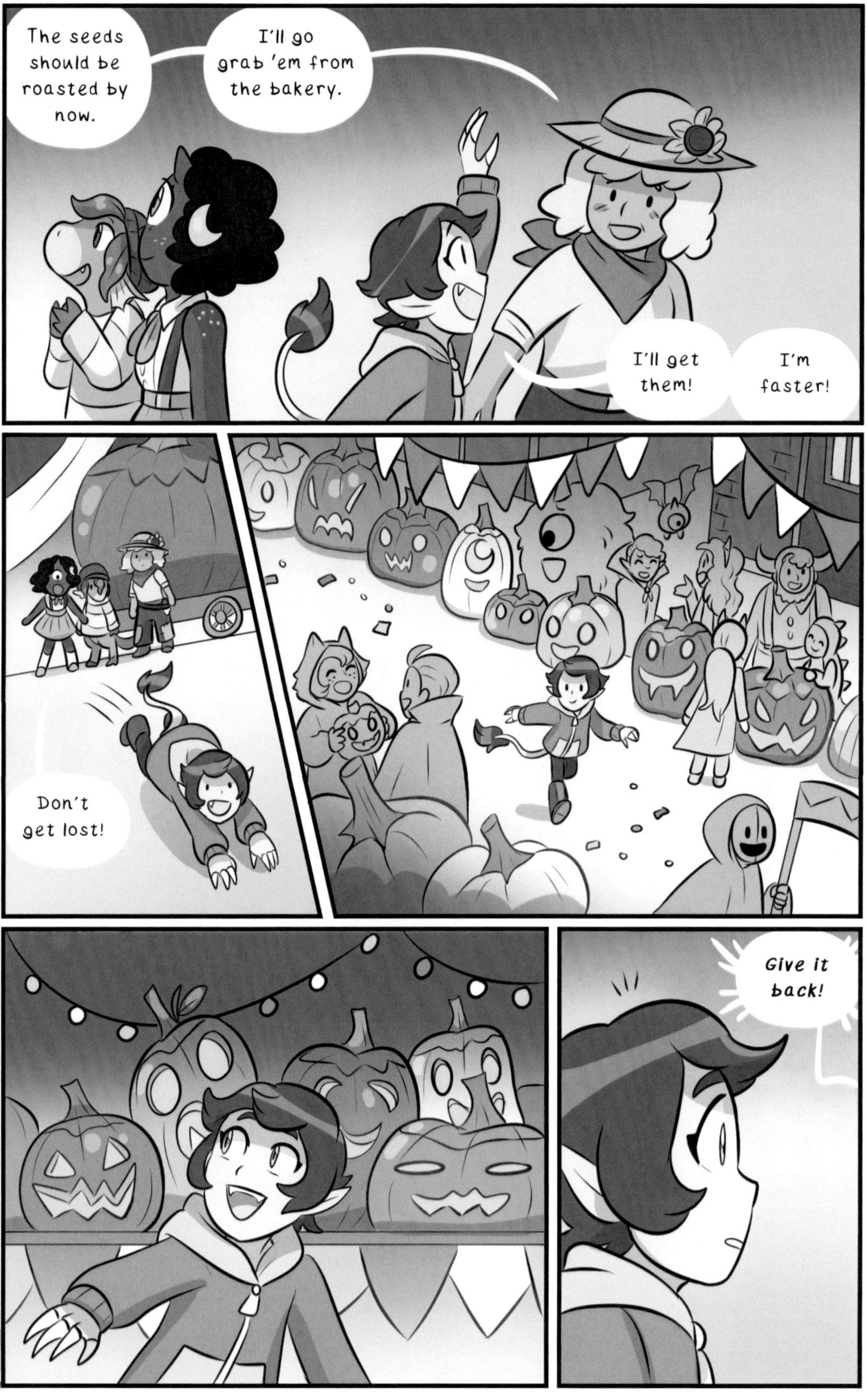
The seeds should be roasted by now.
I'll go grab 'em from the bakery.
I'll get them!
I'm faster!
Don't get lost!
Give it back!

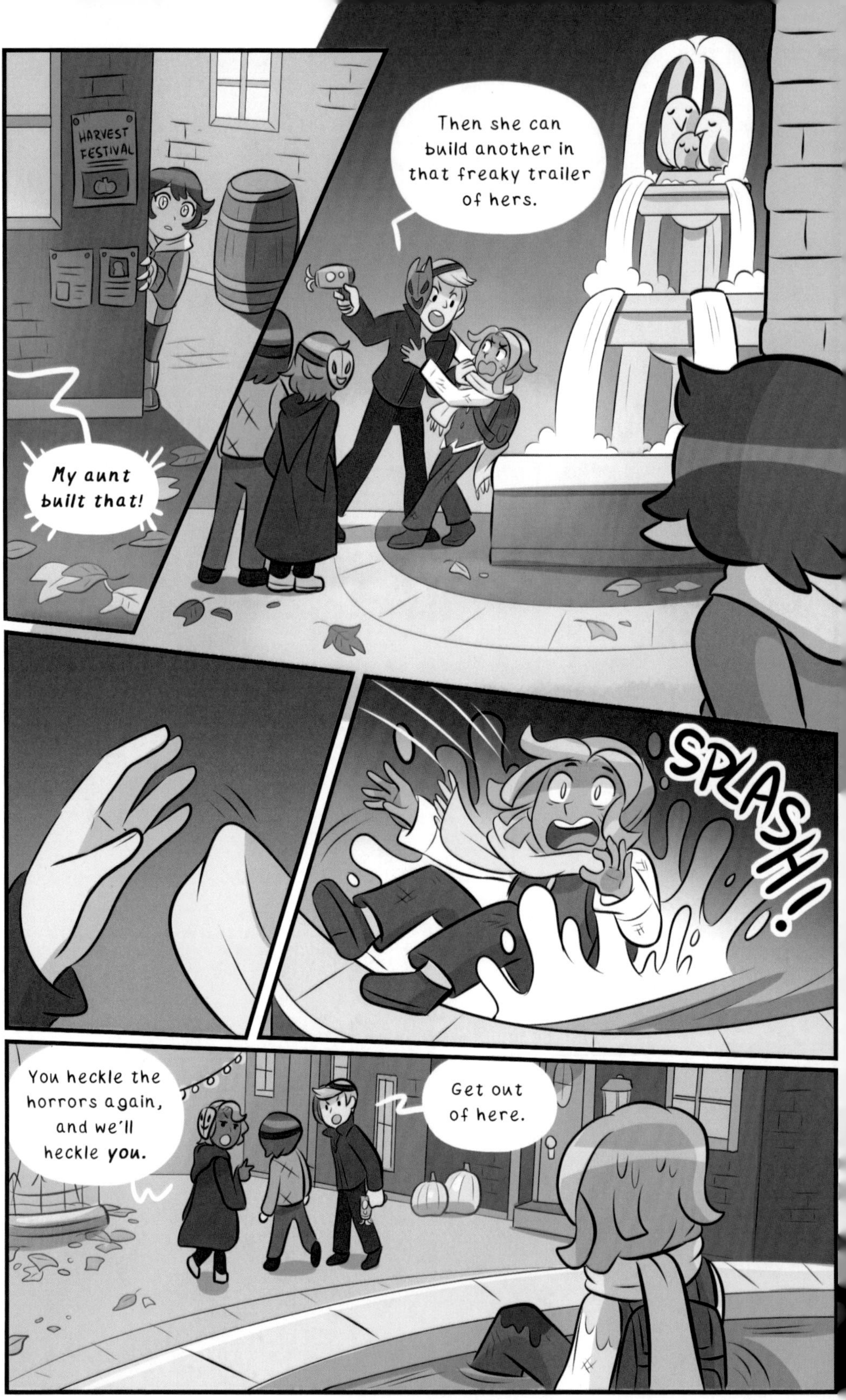

HARVEST FESTIVAL
Then she can build another in that freaky trailer of hers.
My aunt built that!
SPLASH!!
You heckle the horrors again, and we'll heckle you.
Get out of here.

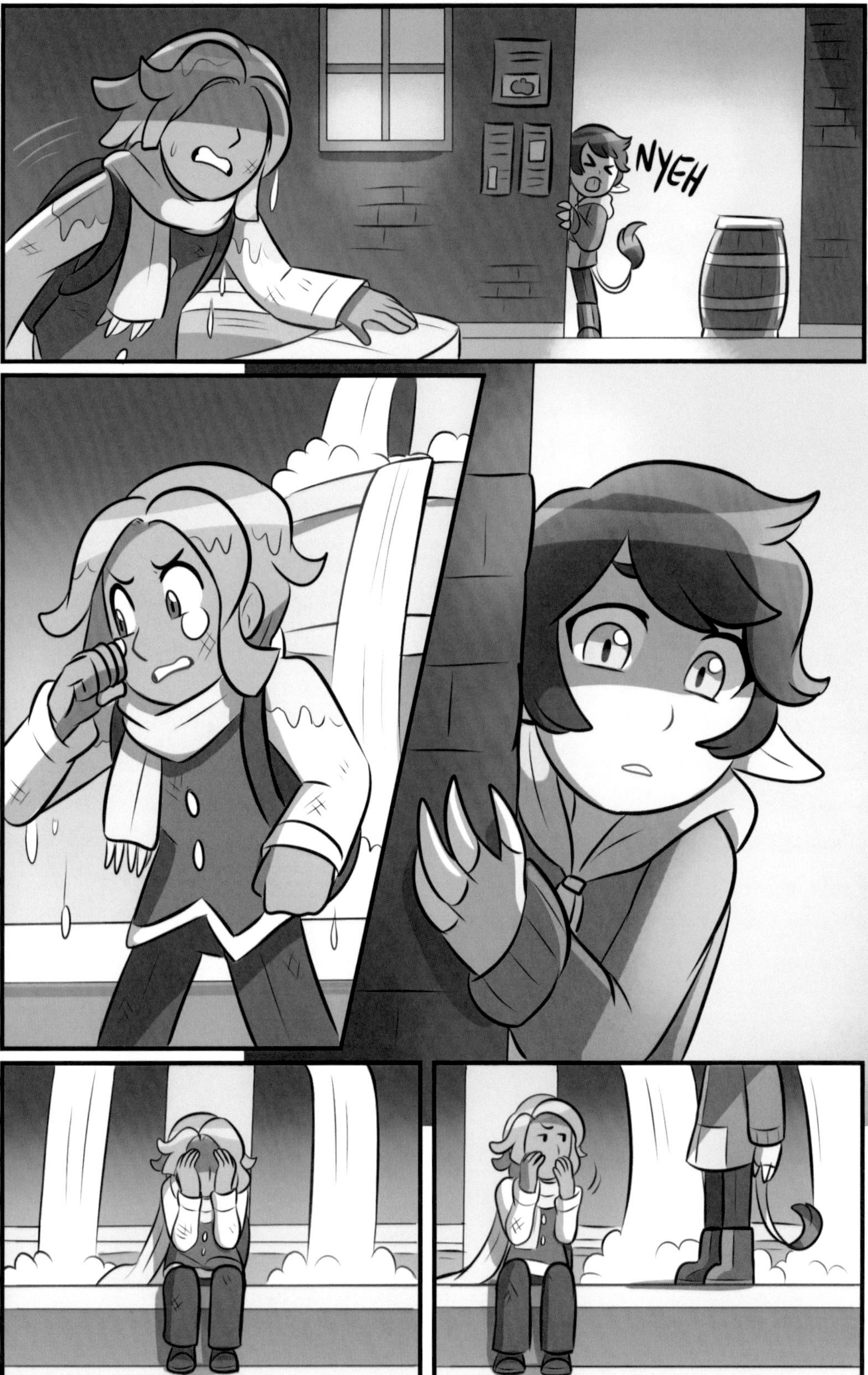
NYEH

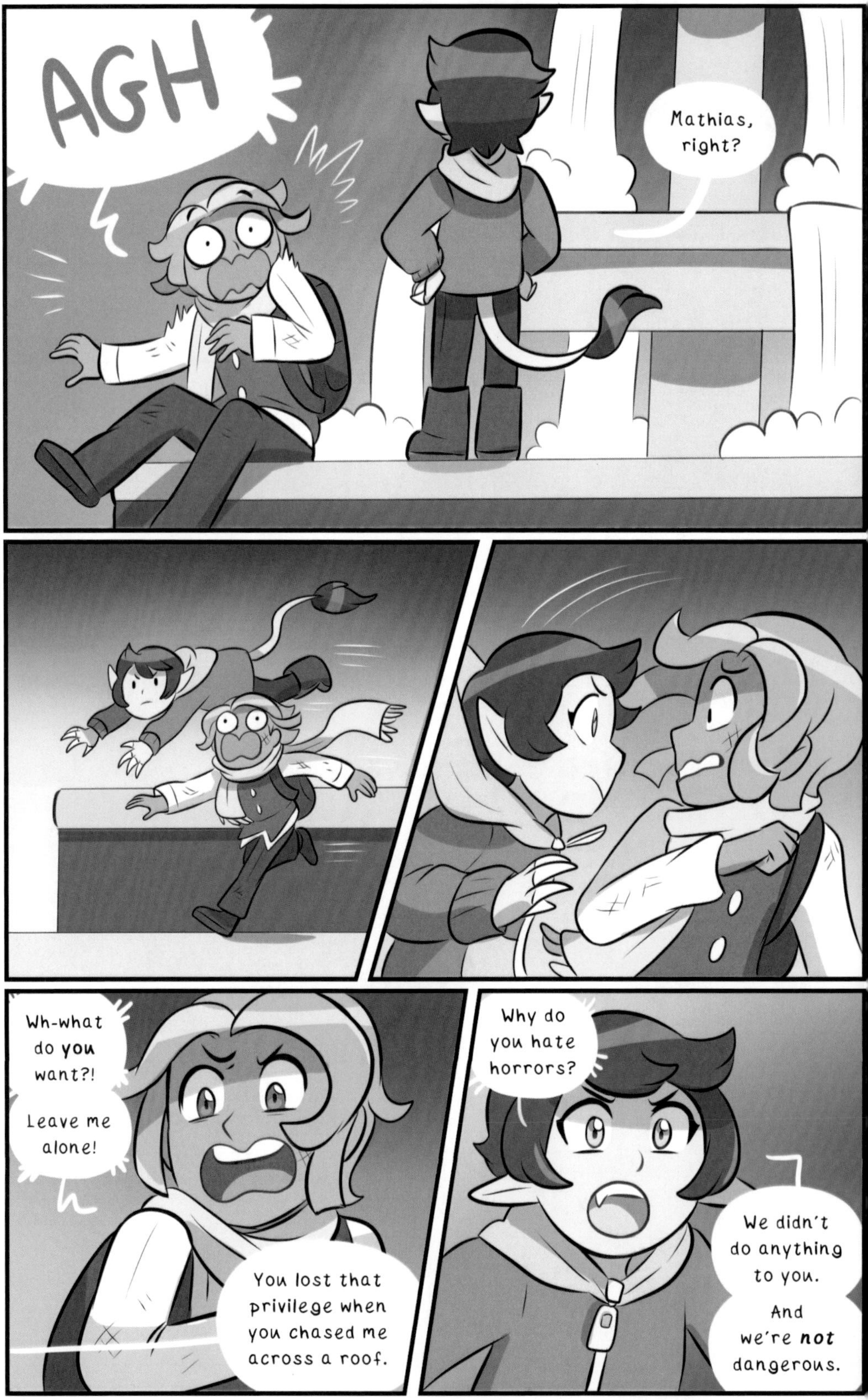
AGH
Mathias, right?
Wh-what do **you** want?!
Leave me alone!
You lost that privilege when you chased me across a roof.
Why do you hate horrors?
We didn't do anything to you.
And we're **not** dangerous.

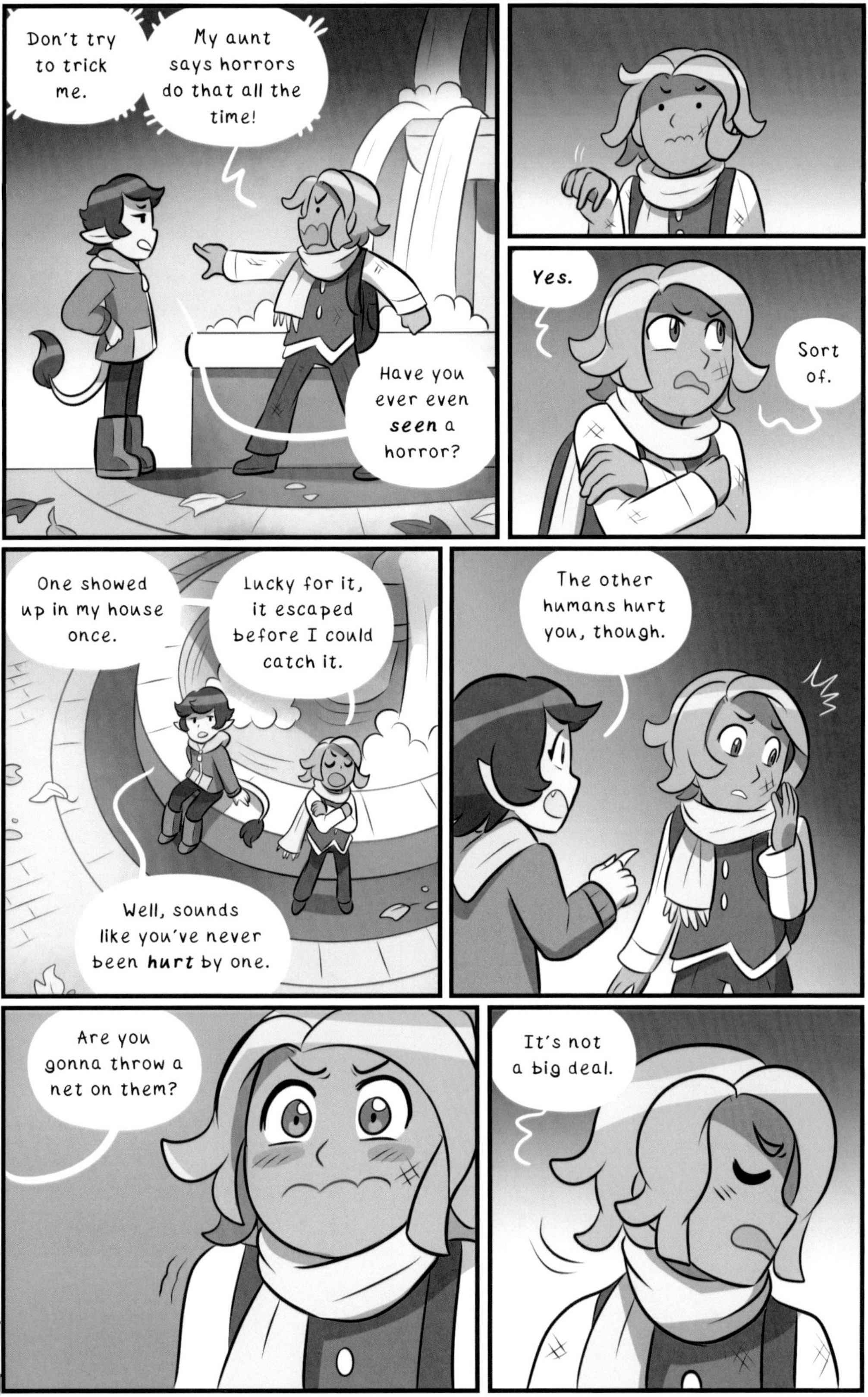
Don't try to trick me.
My aunt says horrors do that all the time!
Have you ever even **seen** a horror?
Yes.
Sort of.
One showed up in my house once.
Lucky for it, it escaped before I could catch it.
Well, sounds like you've never been **hurt** by one.
The other humans hurt you, though.
Are you gonna throw a net on them?
It's not a big deal.

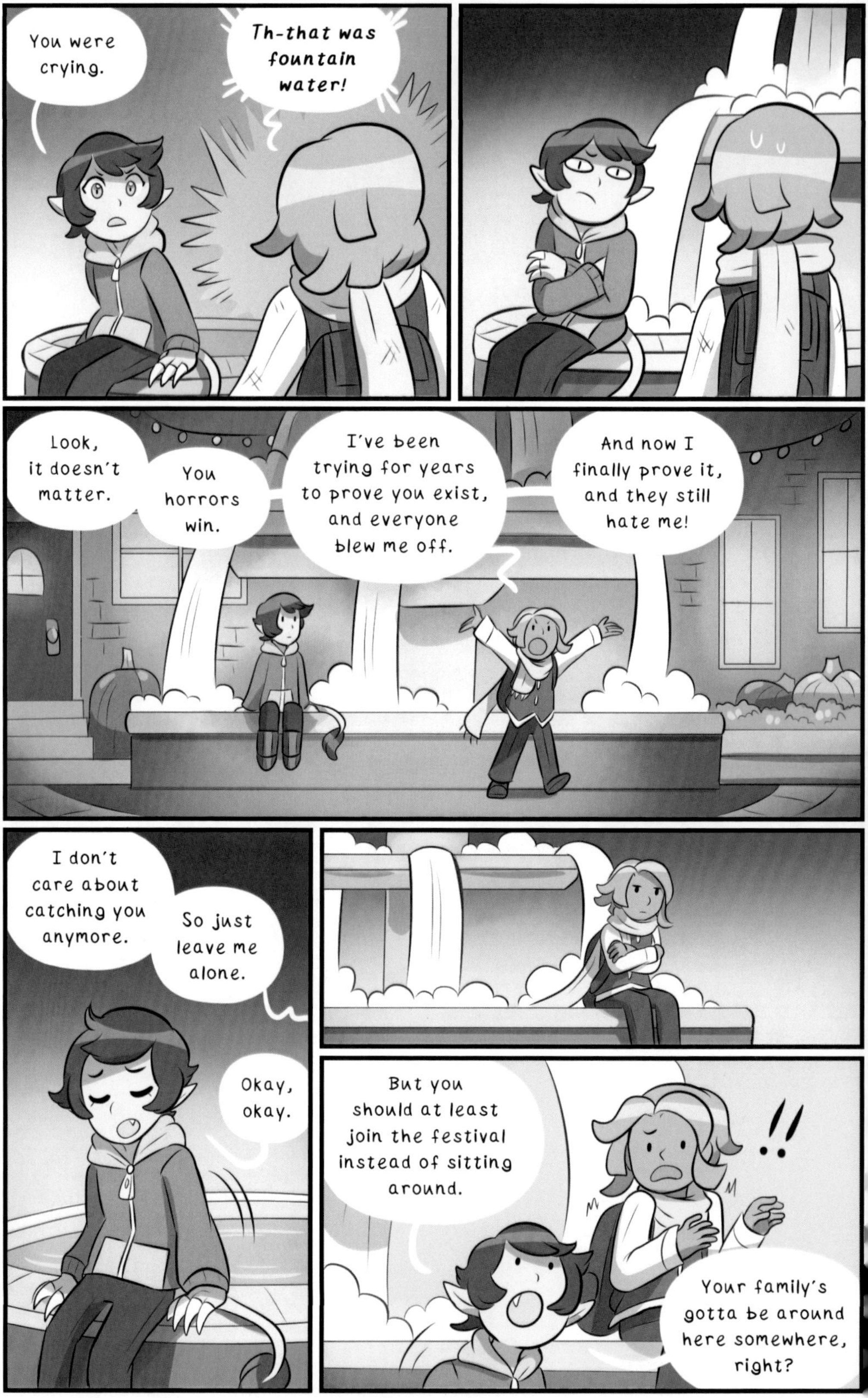
You were crying.
Th-that was fountain water!
Look, it doesn't matter.
You horrors win.
I've been trying for years to prove you exist, and everyone blew me off.
And now I finally prove it, and they still hate me!
I don't care about catching you anymore.
So just leave me alone.
Okay, okay.
But you should at least join the festival instead of sitting around.
!!
Your family's gotta be around here somewhere, right?

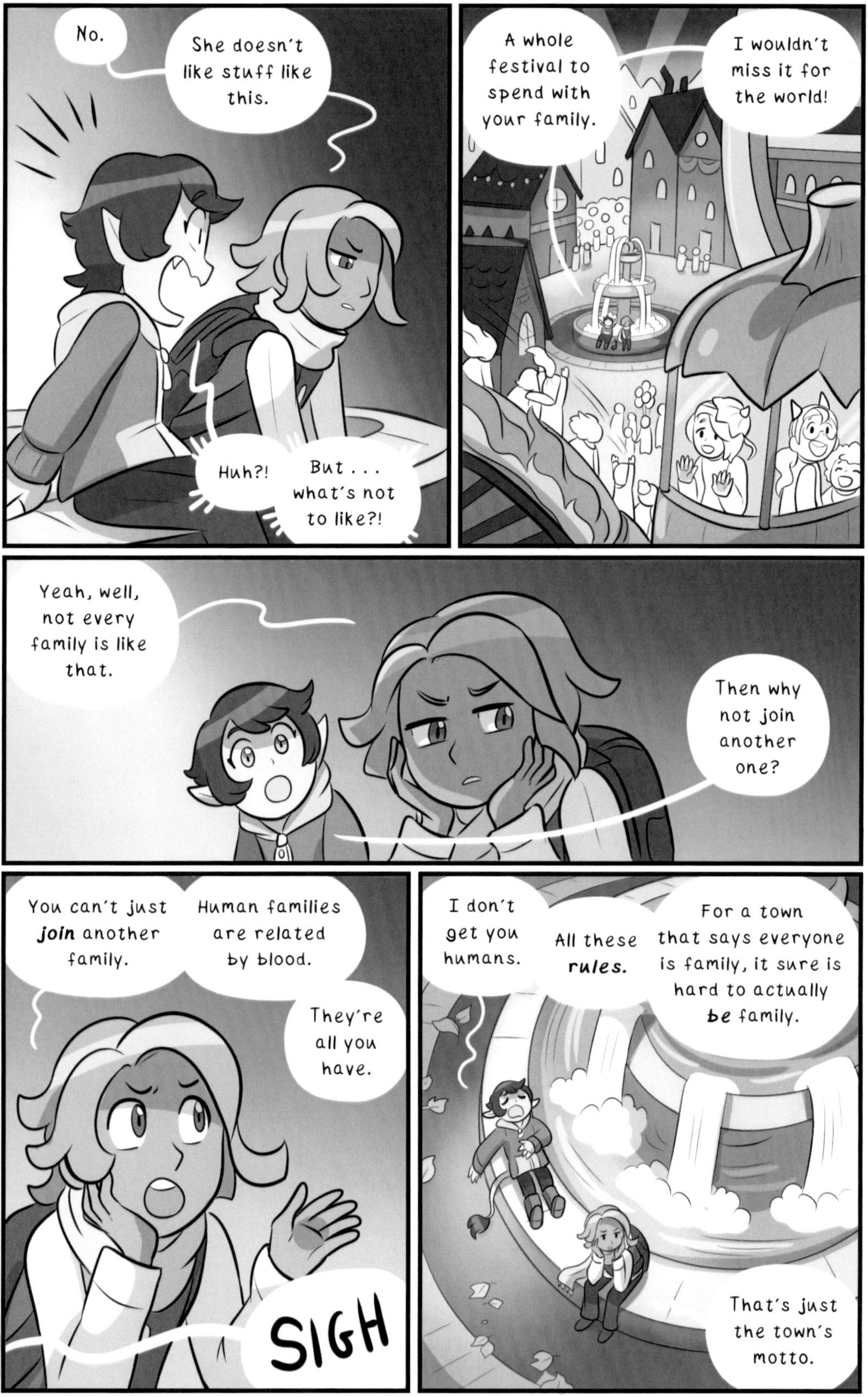

No.
She doesn't like stuff like this.
Huh?!
But . . . what's not to like?!
A whole festival to spend with your family.
I wouldn't miss it for the world!
Yeah, well, not every family is like that.
Then why not join another one?
You can't just **join** another family.
Human families are related by blood.
They're all you have.
SIGH
I don't get you humans.
All these **rules.**
For a town that says everyone is family, it sure is hard to actually **be** family.
That's just the town's motto.

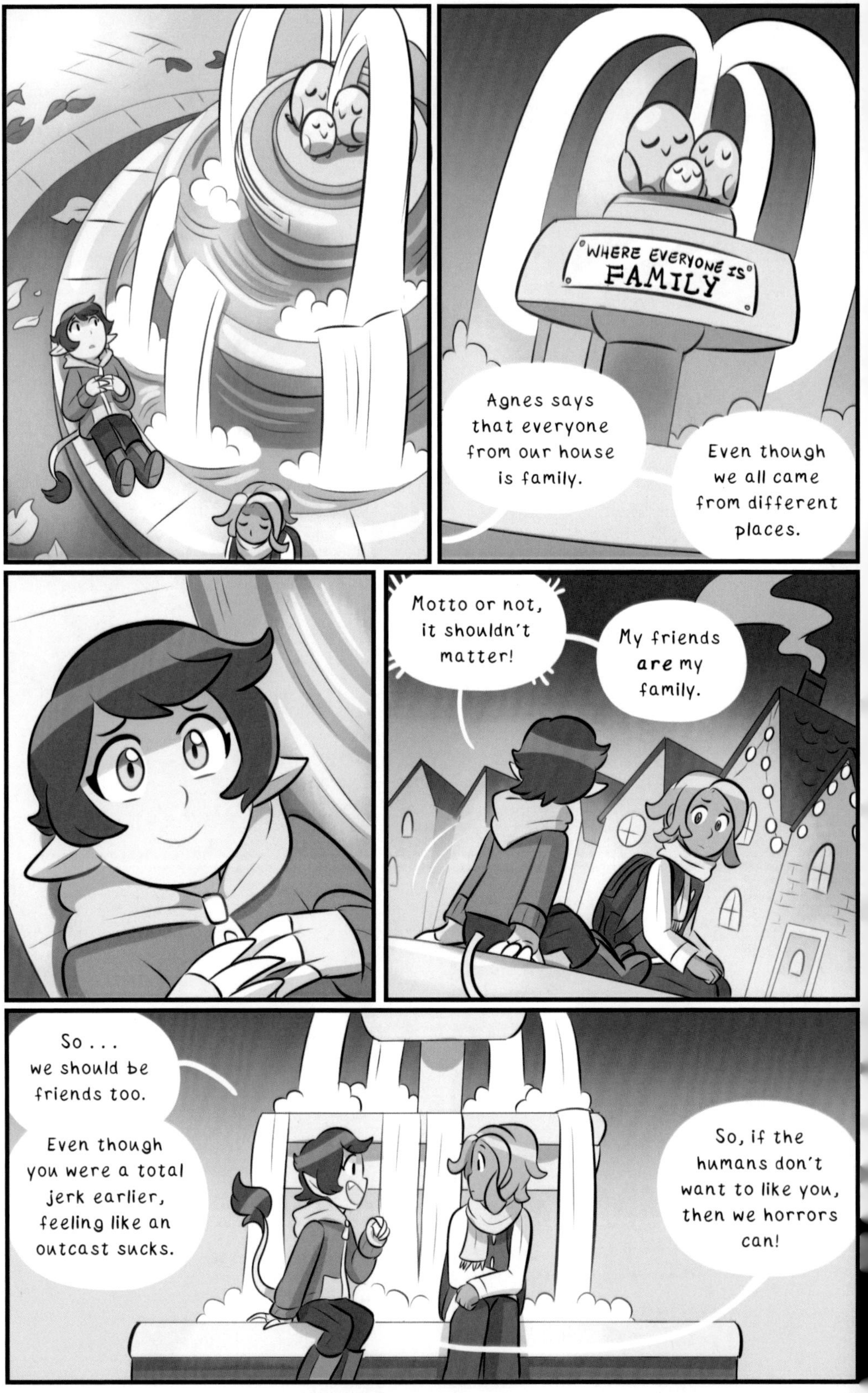
"WHERE EVERYONE IS" FAMILY
Agnes says that everyone from our house is family.
Even though we all came from different places.
Motto or not, it shouldn't matter!
My friends **are** my family.
So . . . we should be friends too.
Even though you were a total jerk earlier, feeling like an outcast sucks.
So, if the humans don't want to like you, then we horrors can!

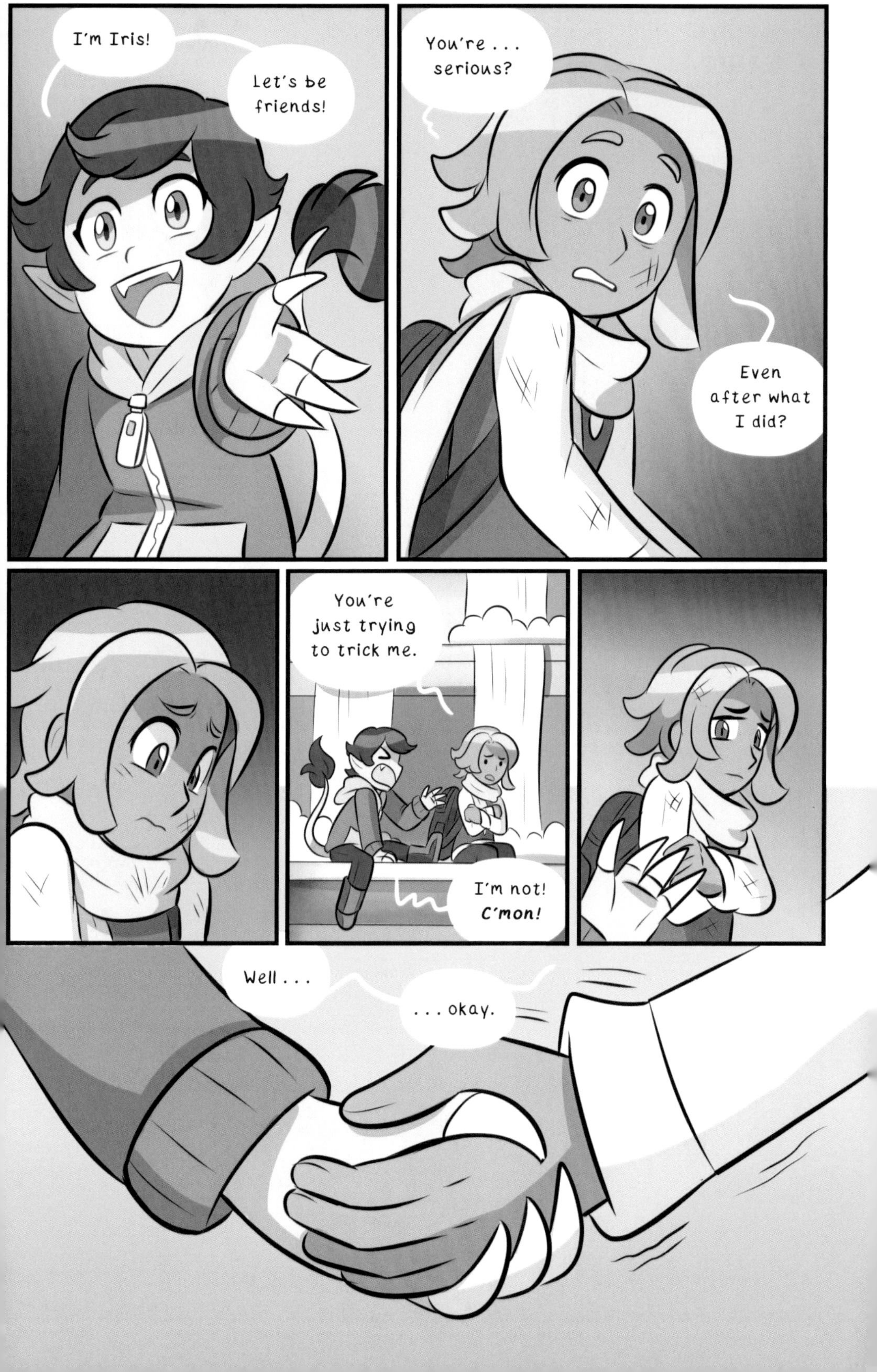
I'm Iris!
Let's be friends!
You're . . . serious?
Even after what I did?
You're just trying to trick me.
I'm not! C'mon!
Well . . .
. . . okay.

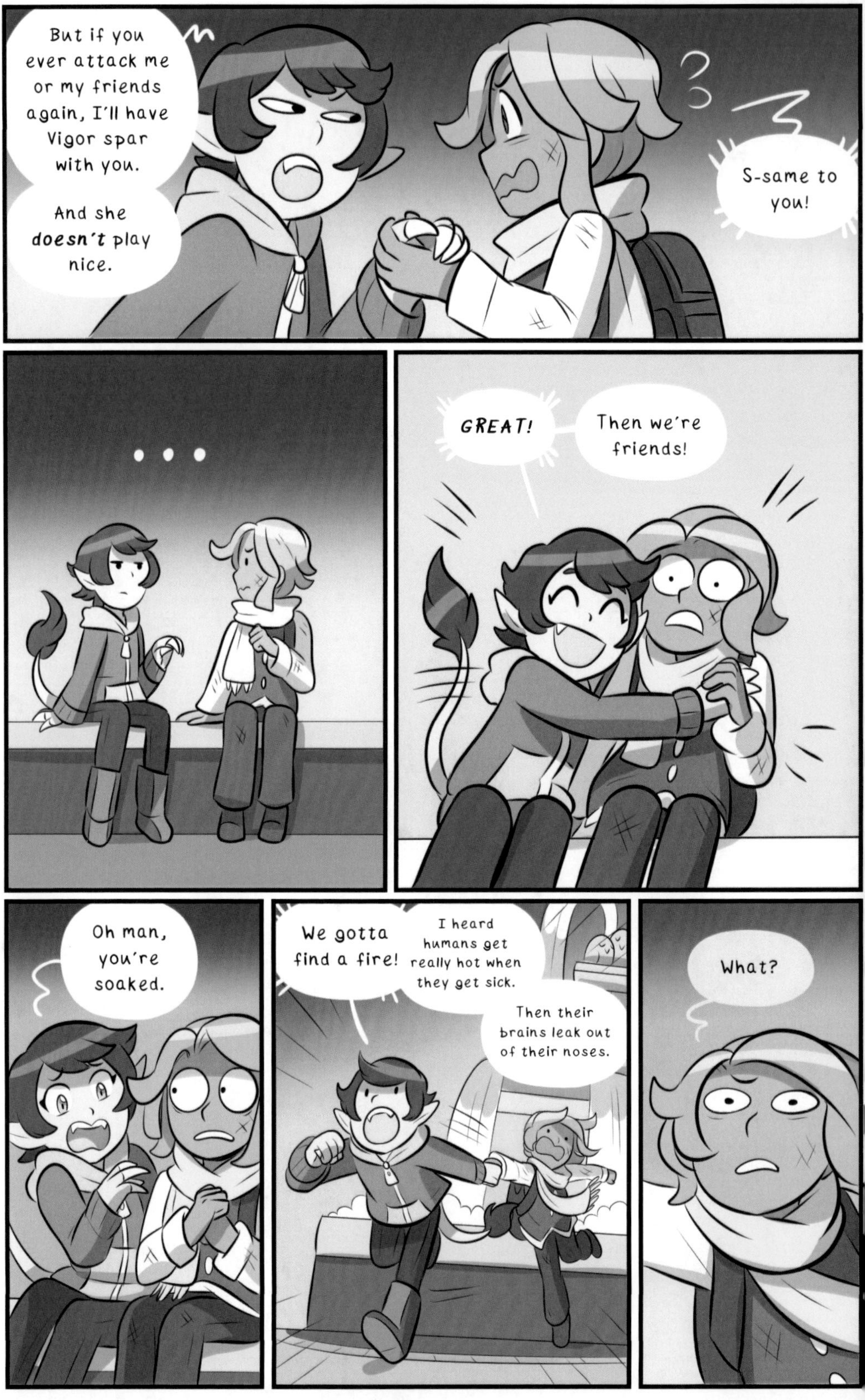
But if you ever attack me or my friends again, I'll have Vigor spar with you.
And she **doesn't** play nice.
S-same to you!
• • •
GREAT!
Then we're friends!
Oh man, you're soaked.
We gotta find a fire!
I heard humans get really hot when they get sick.
Then their brains leak out of their noses.
What?

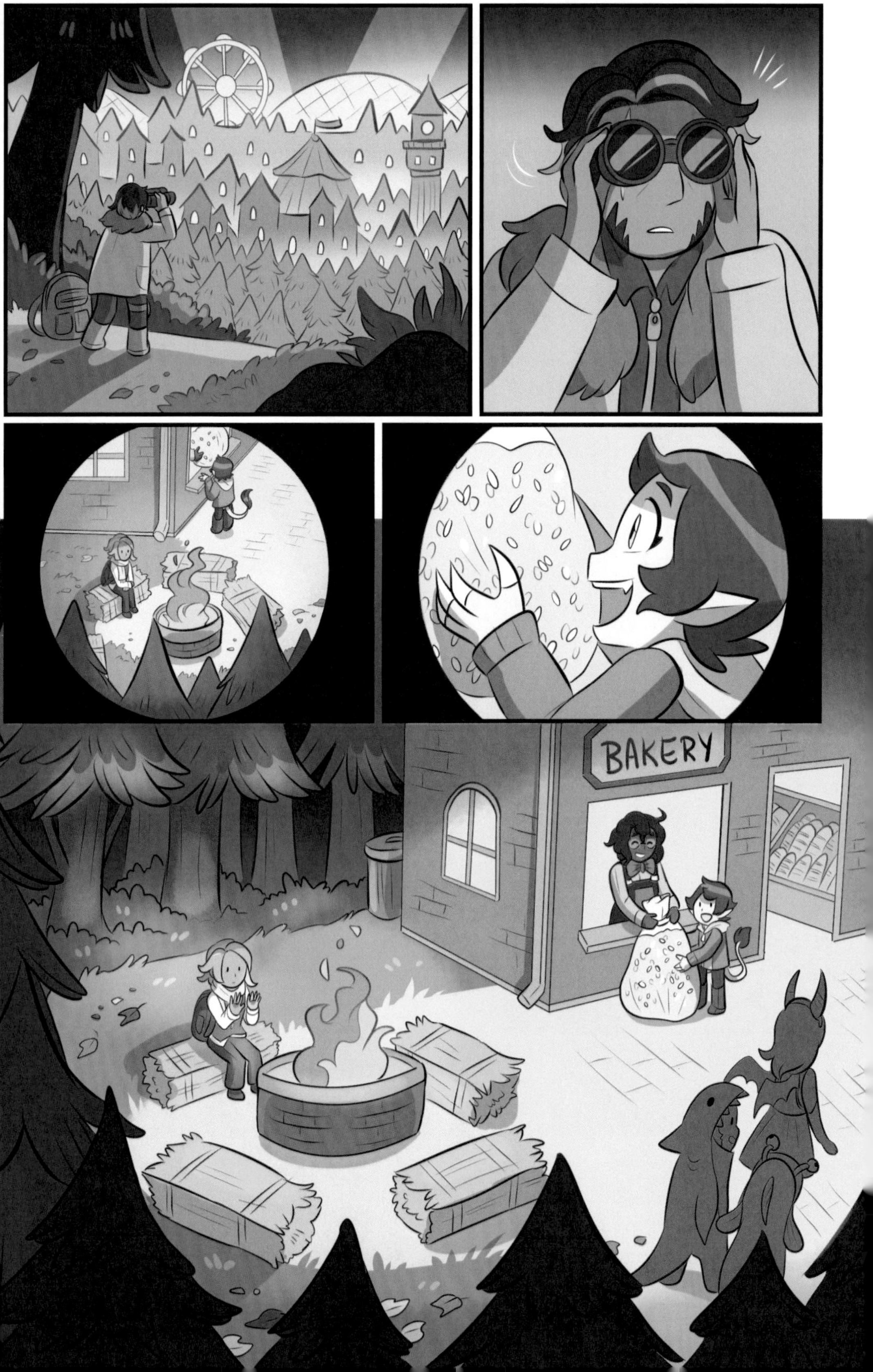
BAKERY

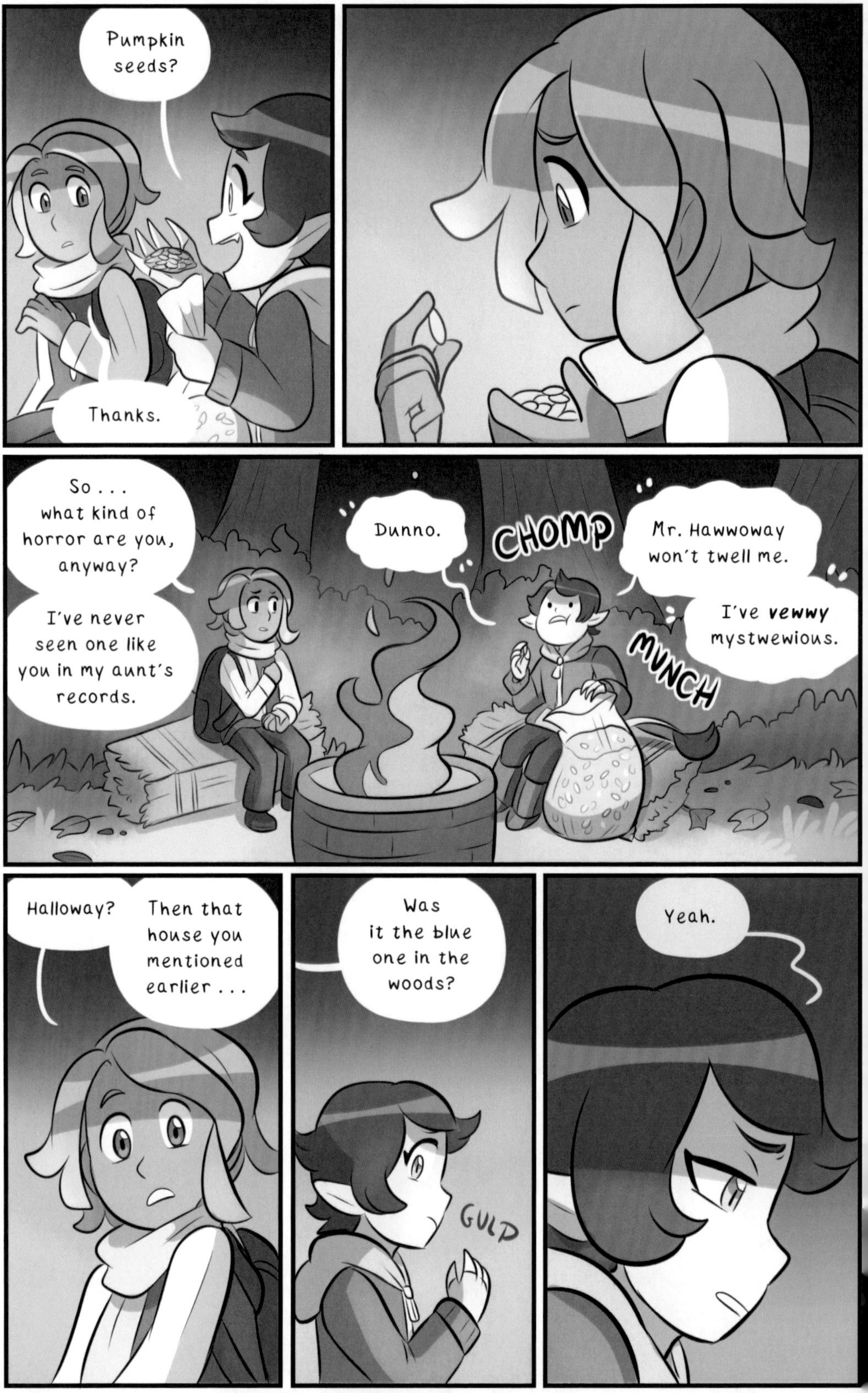
Pumpkin seeds?
Thanks.
So . . . what kind of horror are you, anyway?
I've never seen one like you in my aunt's records.
Dunno.
CHOMP
Mr. Hawwoway won't twell me.
I've **vewwy** mystwewious.
MUNCH
Halloway?
Then that house you mentioned earlier . . .
Was it the blue one in the woods?
GULP
Yeah.

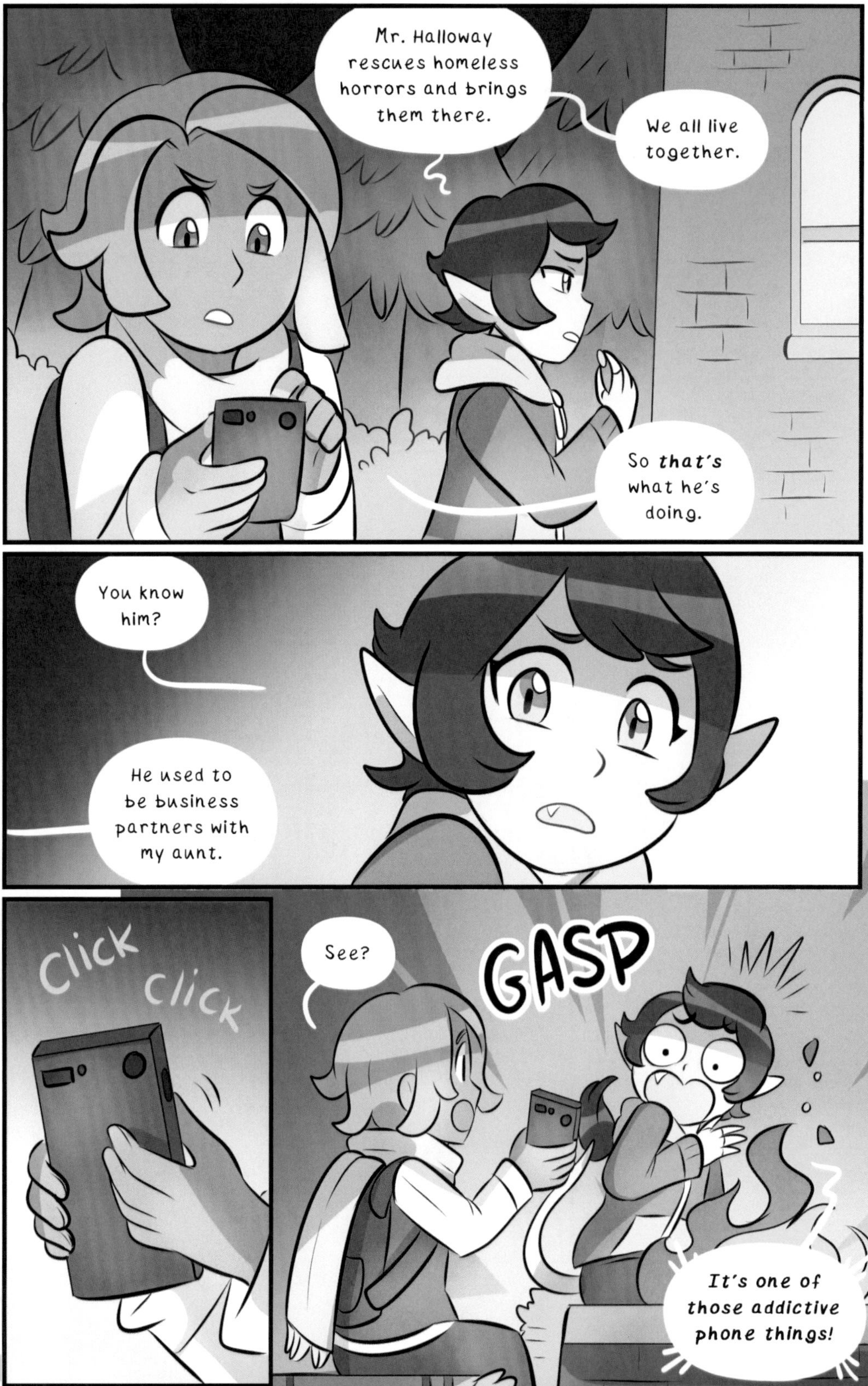
Mr. Halloway rescues homeless horrors and brings them there.
We all live together.
So *that's* what he's doing.
You know him?
He used to be business partners with my aunt.
Click click
See?
GASP
It's one of those addictive phone things!

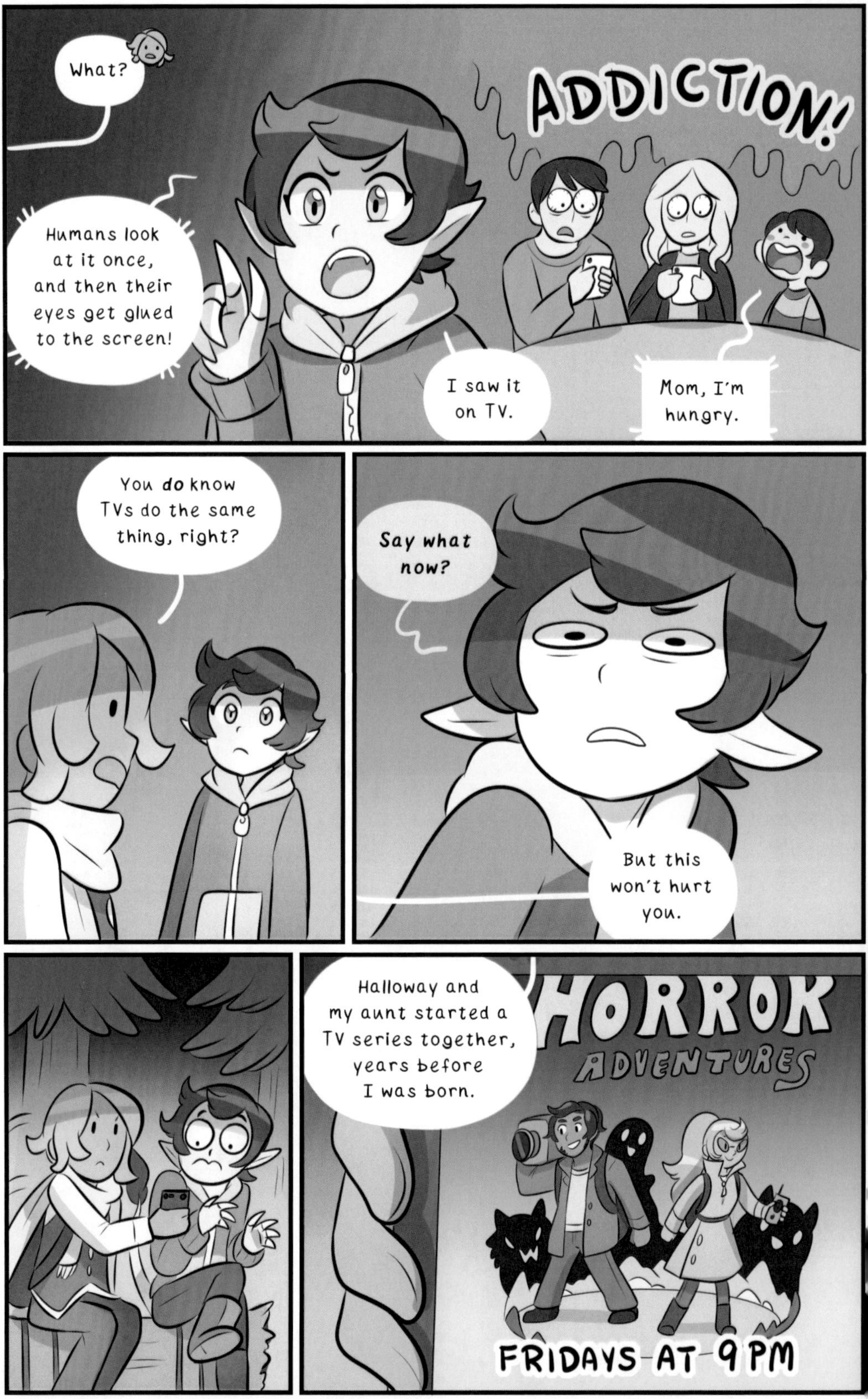
What?
Humans look at it once, and then their eyes get glued to the screen!
ADDICTION!
I saw it on TV.
Mom, I'm hungry.
You do know TVs do the same thing, right?
Say what now?
But this won't hurt you.
Halloway and my aunt started a TV series together, years before I was born.
HORROR ADVENTURES
FRIDAYS AT 9 PM

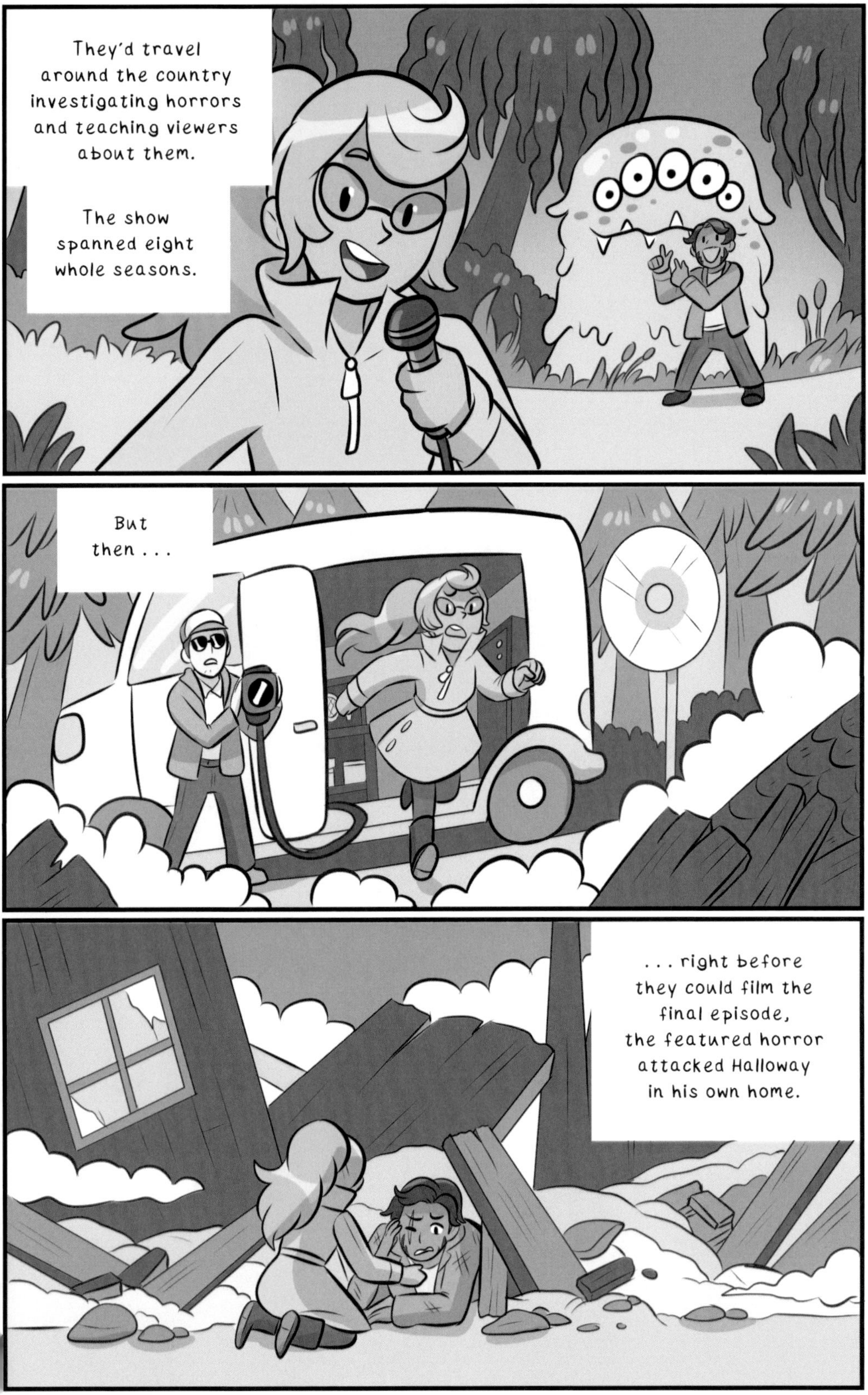
They'd travel around the country investigating horrors and teaching viewers about them.
The show spanned eight whole seasons.
But then . . .
. . . right before they could film the final episode, the featured horror attacked Halloway in his own home.

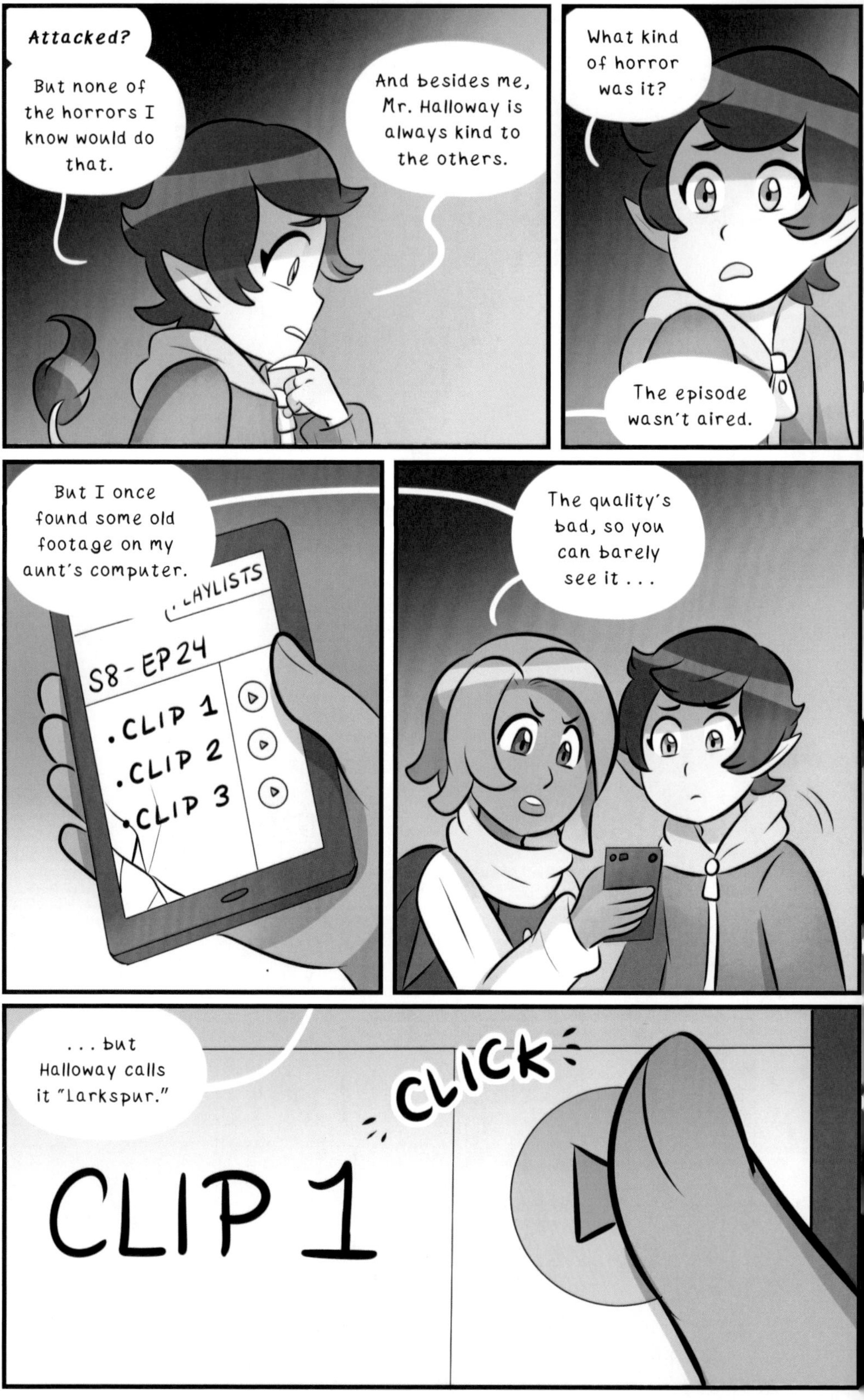
Attacked?
But none of the horrors I know would do that.
And besides me, Mr. Halloway is always kind to the others.
What kind of horror was it?
The episode wasn't aired.
But I once found some old footage on my aunt's computer.
S8-EP24
•CLIP 1
•CLIP 2
•CLIP 3
The quality's bad, so you can barely see it . . .
. . . but Halloway calls it "Larkspur."
CLICK
CLIP 1

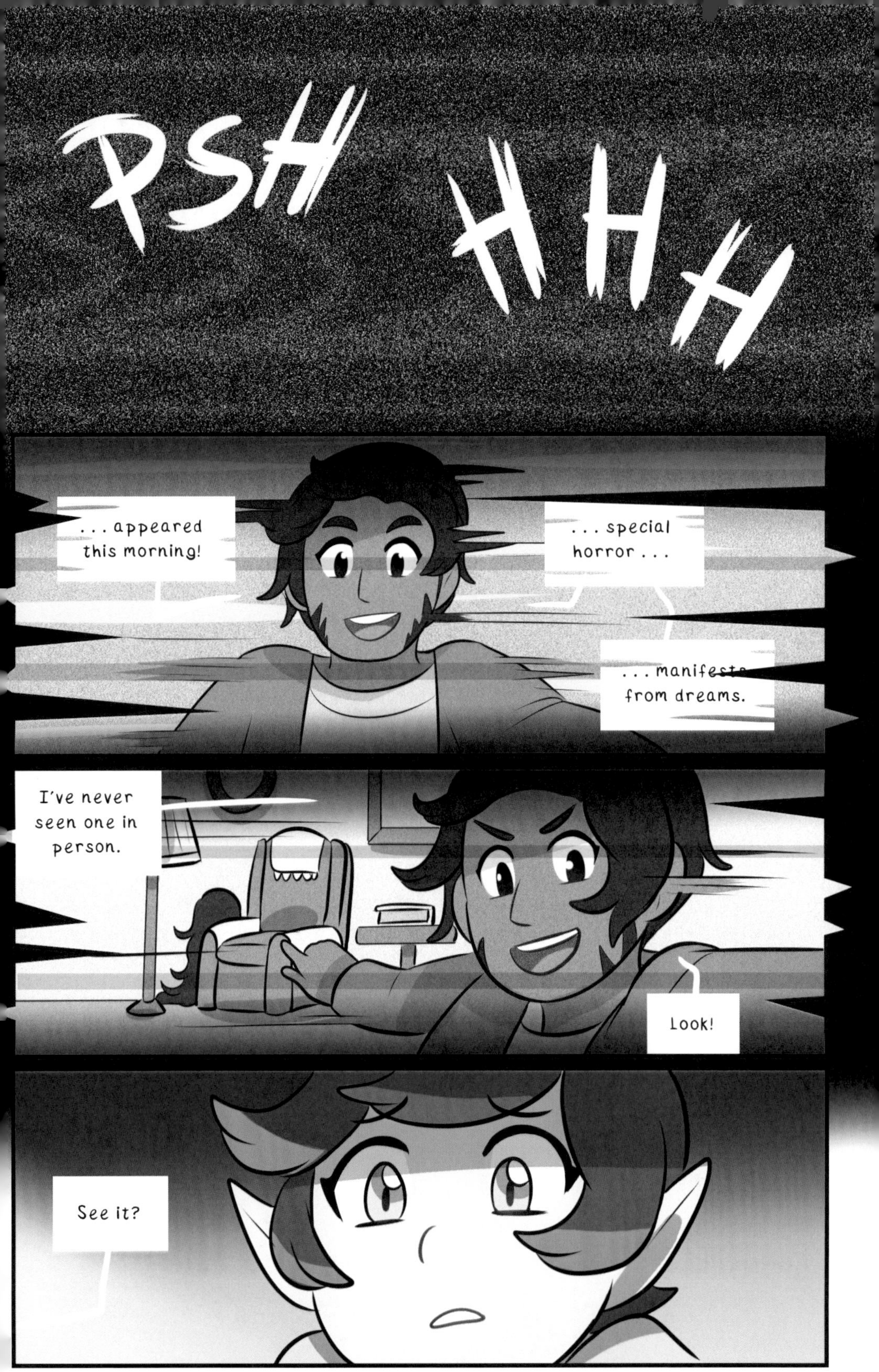
PSHHHH
. . . appeared this morning!
. . . special horror . . .
. . . manifests from dreams.
I've never seen one in person.
Look!
See it?

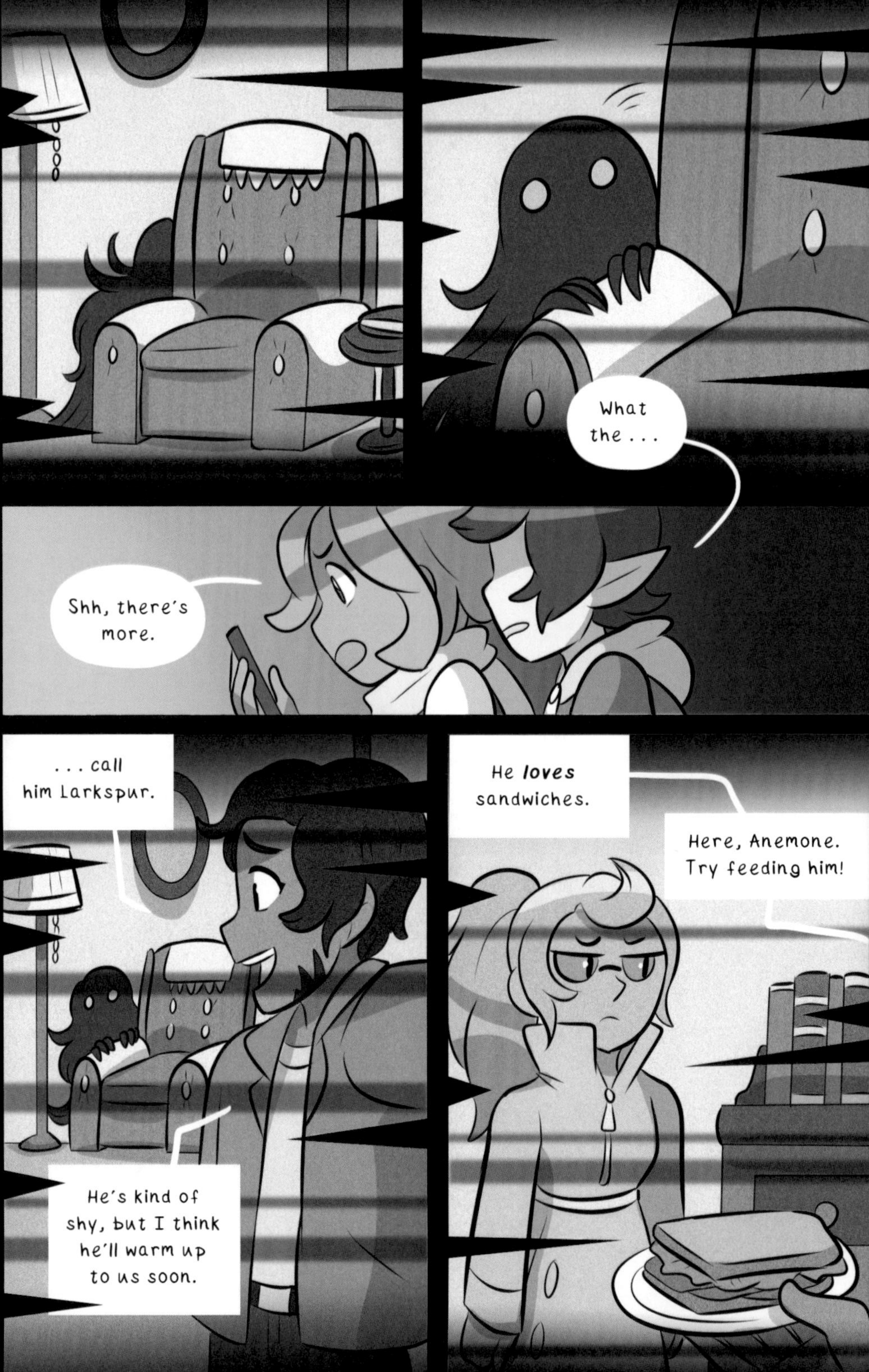
What the . . .
Shh, there's more.
. . . call him Larkspur.
He's kind of shy, but I think he'll warm up to us soon.
He *loves* sandwiches.
Here, Anemone. Try feeding him!

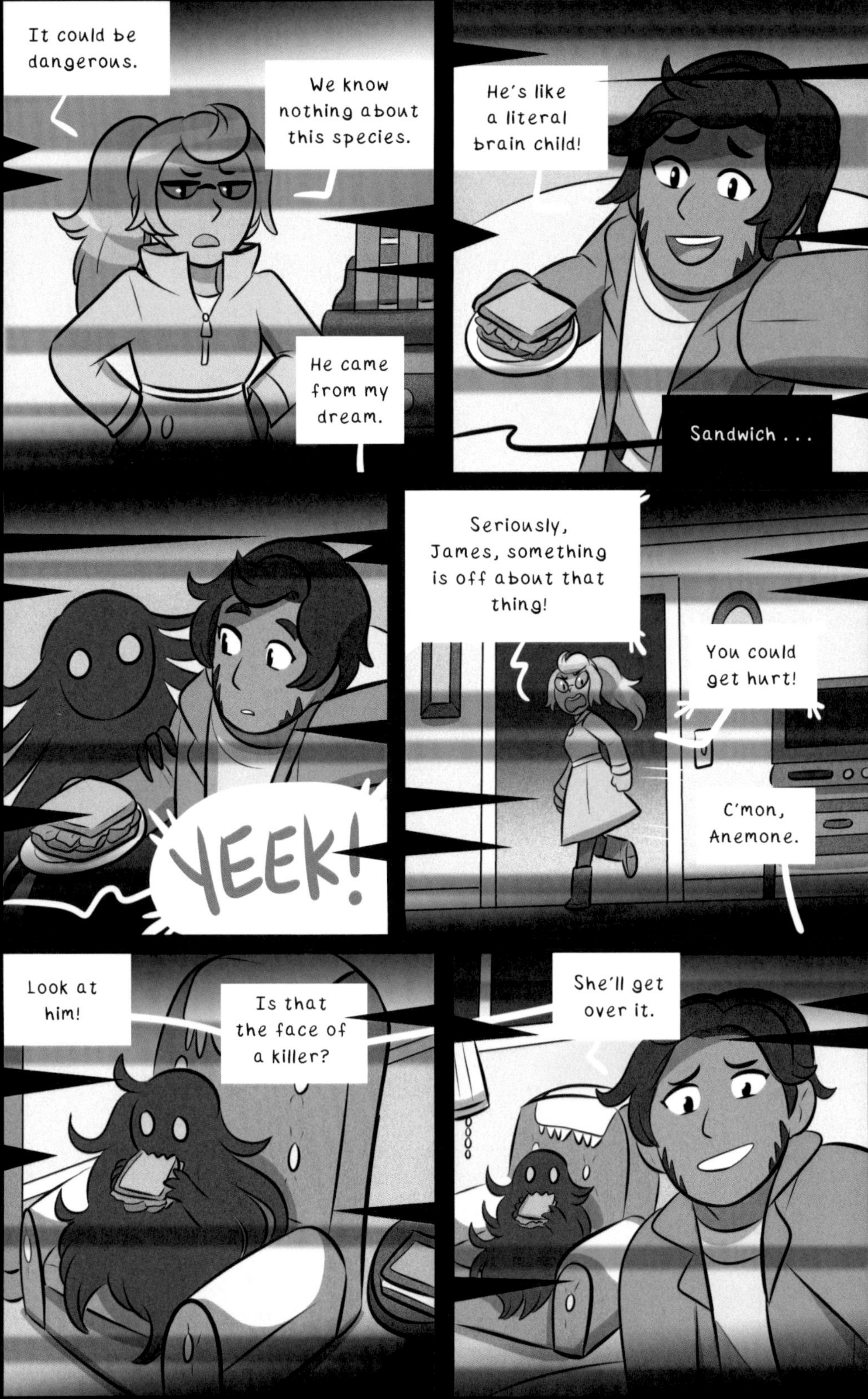
It could be dangerous.
We know nothing about this species.
He came from my dream.
He's like a literal brain child!
Sandwich . . .
YEEK!
Seriously, James, something is off about that thing!
You could get hurt!
C'mon, Anemone.
Look at him!
Is that the face of a killer?
She'll get over it.

CLIP 2

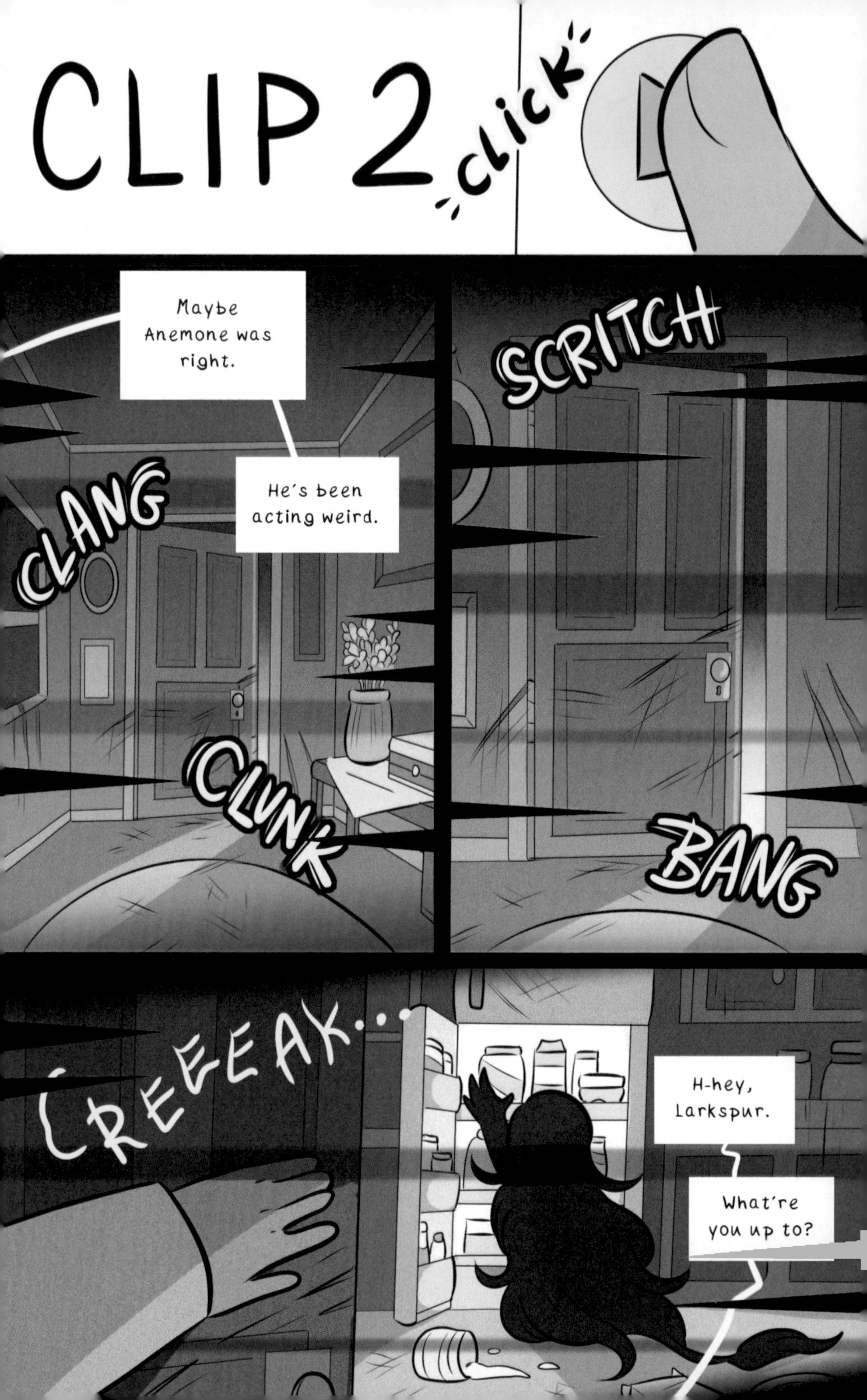
CLICK
Maybe Anemone was right.
He's been acting weird.
CLANG
CLUNK
SCRITCH
BANG
CREEEAK...
H-hey, Larkspur.
What're you up to?

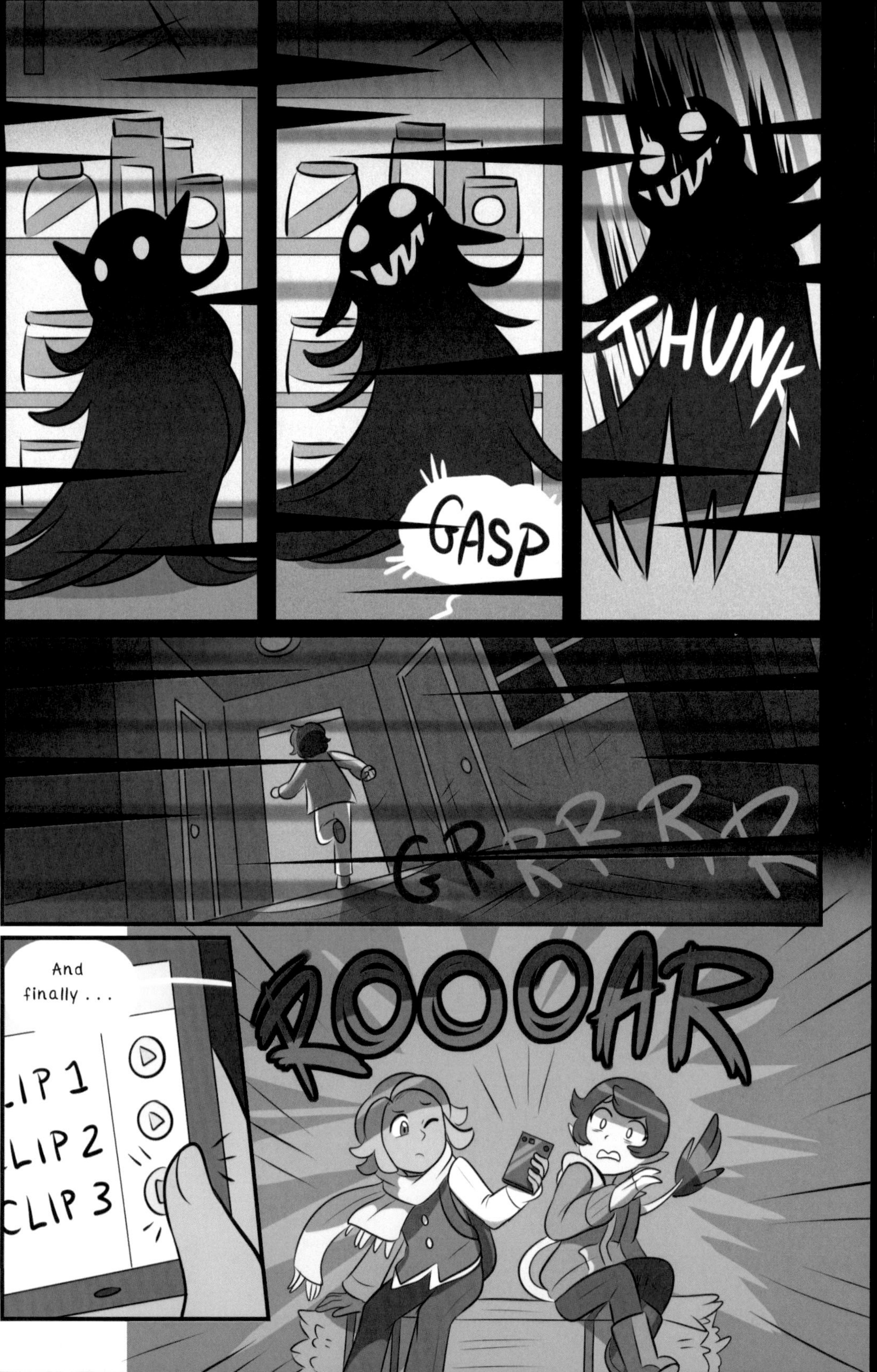
GASP
THUNK
GRRRRR
And finally . . .
ROOOAR
CLIP 1
CLIP 2
CLIP 3

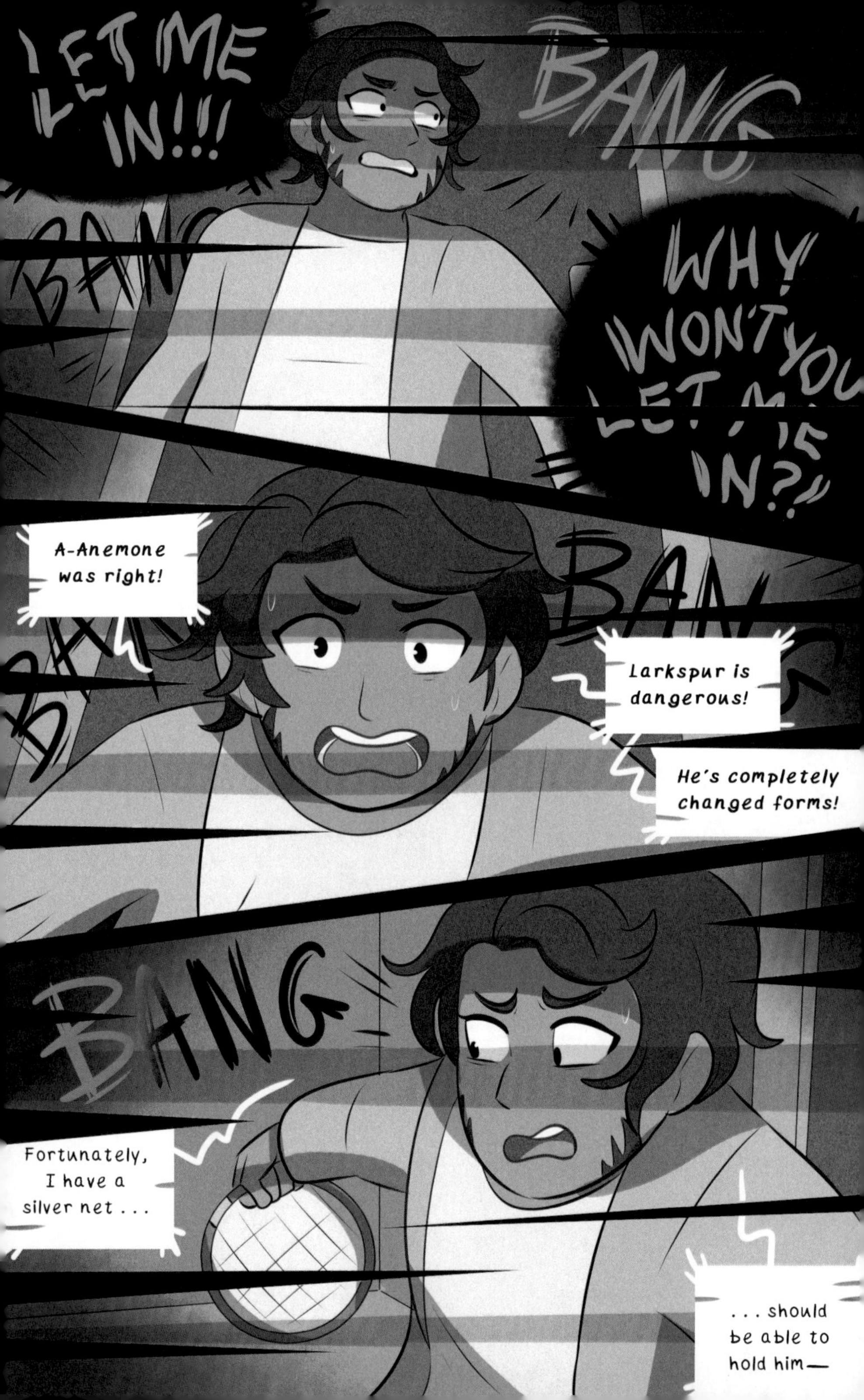
LET ME IN!!!
BANG
BANG
WHY WON'T YOU LET ME IN?!
A-Anemone was right!
BANG
BANG
Larkspur is dangerous!
He's completely changed forms!
BANG
Fortunately, I have a silver net . . .
. . . should be able to hold him—

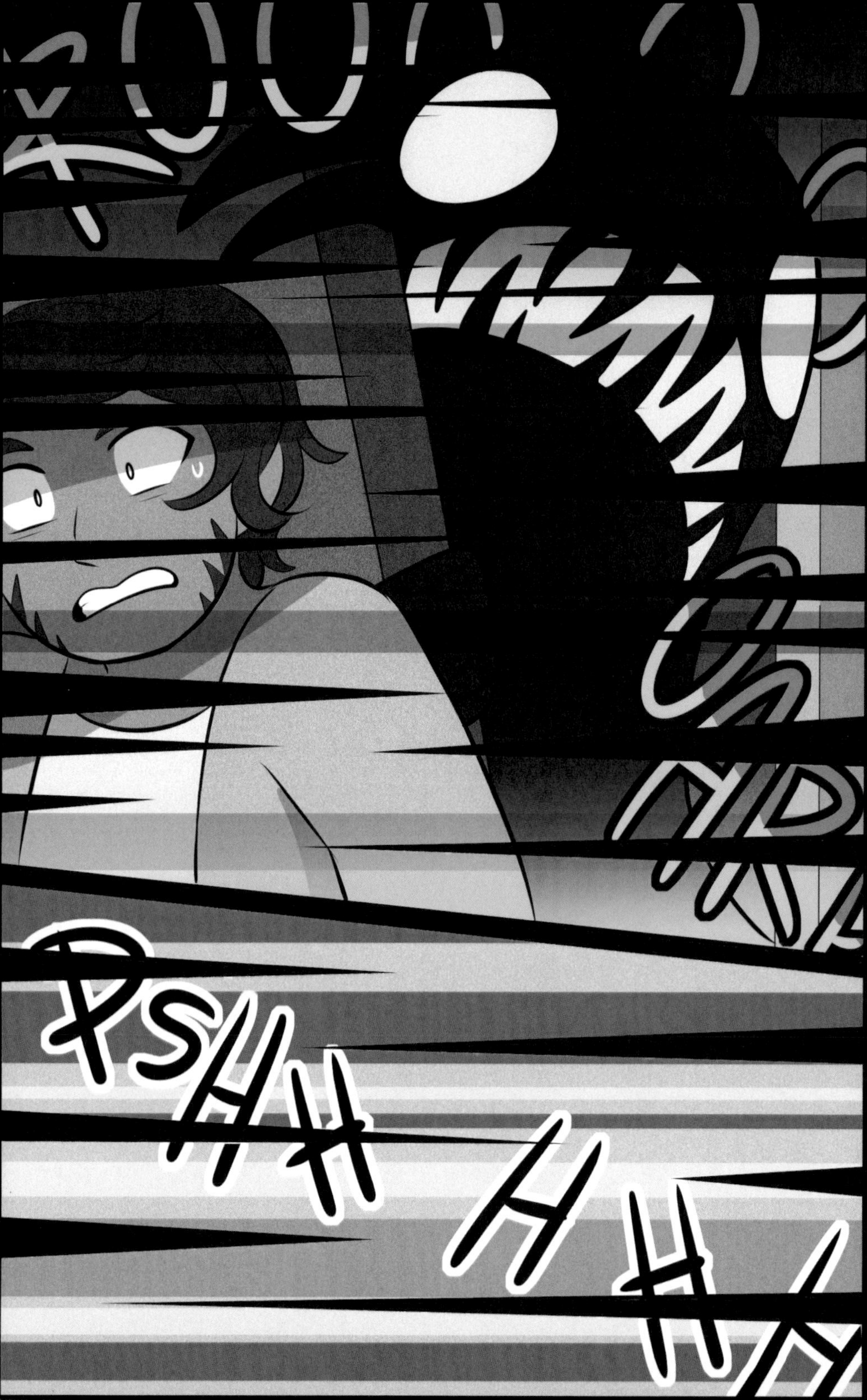
PSHHHHH

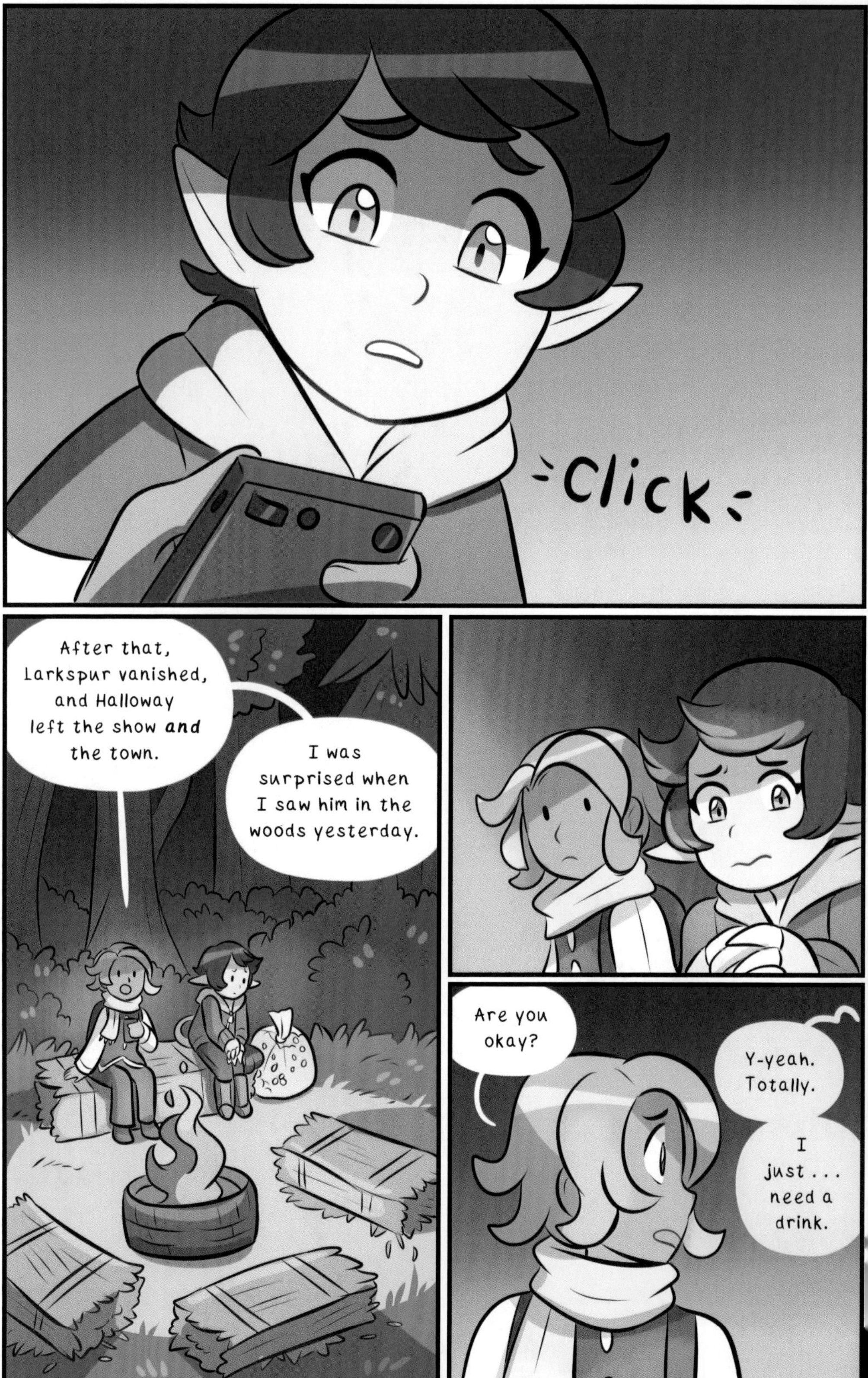
Click
After that, Larkspur vanished, and Halloway left the show and the town.
I was surprised when I saw him in the woods yesterday.
Are you okay?
Y-yeah. Totally.
I just . . . need a drink.

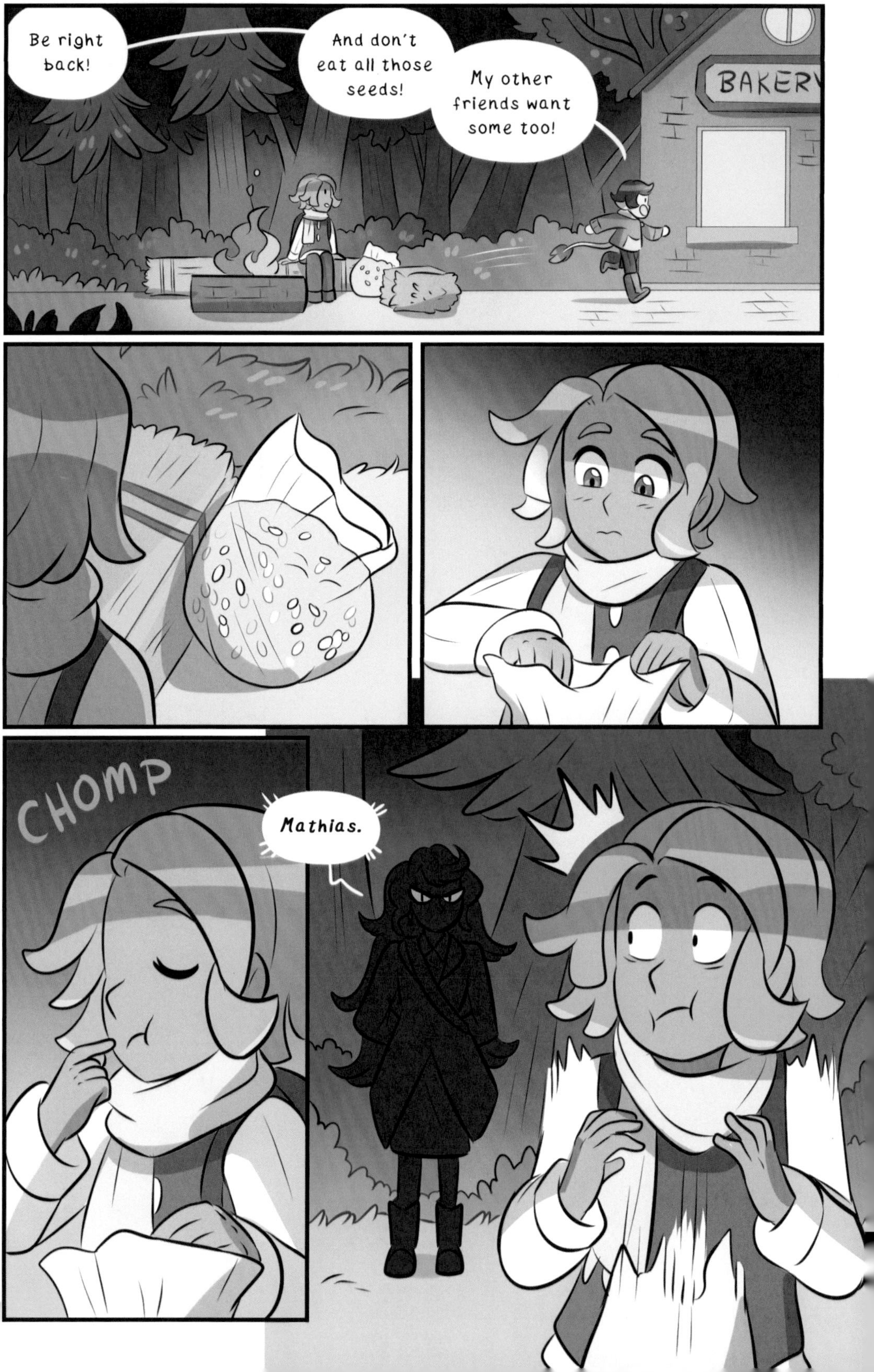

Be right back!
And don't eat all those seeds!
My other friends want some too!
BAKERY
CHOMP
Mathias.

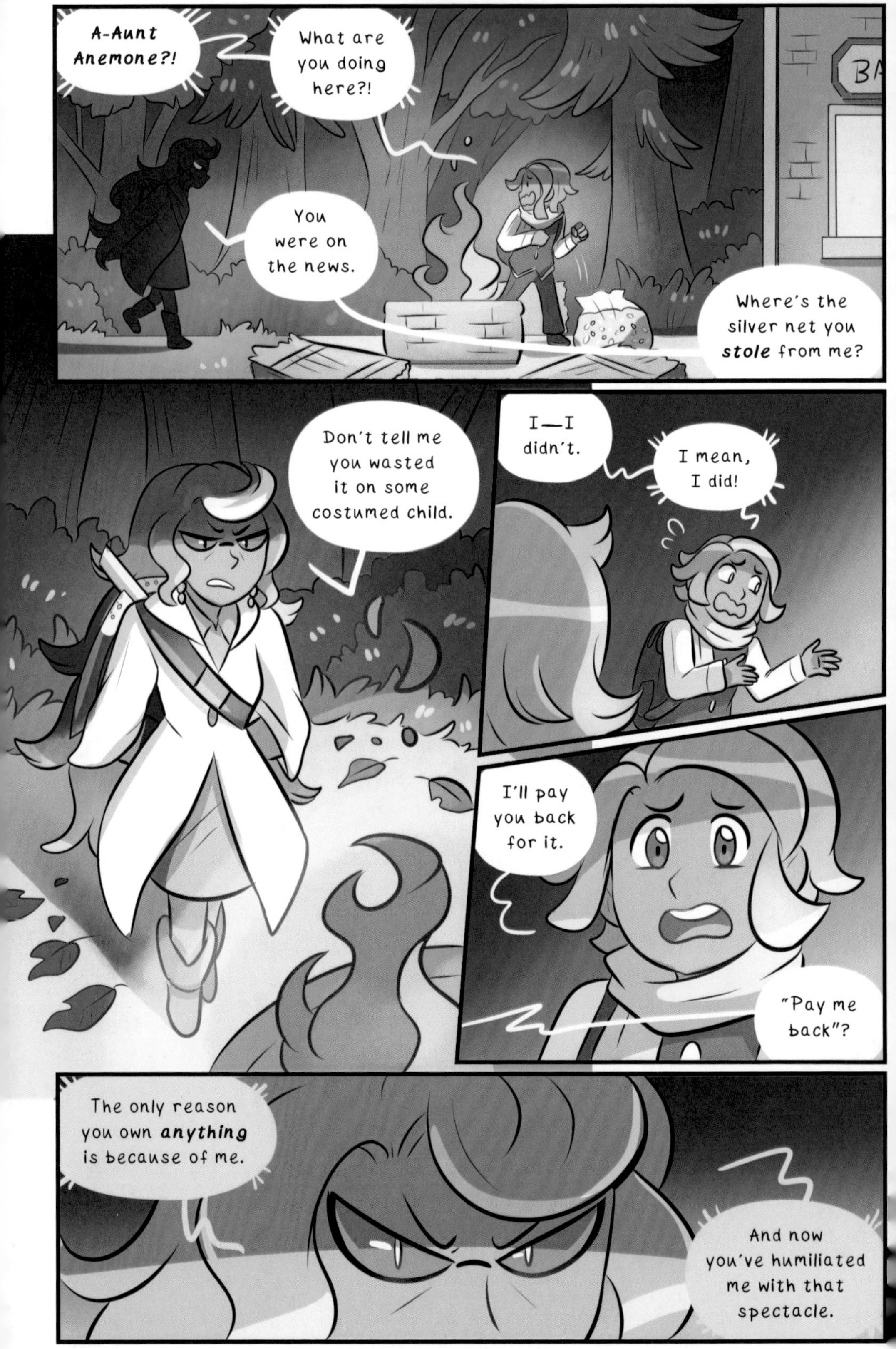
A-Aunt Anemone?!
What are you doing here?!
You were on the news.
Where's the silver net you *stole* from me?
Don't tell me you wasted it on some costumed child.
I—I didn't.
I mean, I did!
I'll pay you back for it.
"Pay me back"?
The only reason you own *anything* is because of me.
And now you've humiliated me with that spectacle.

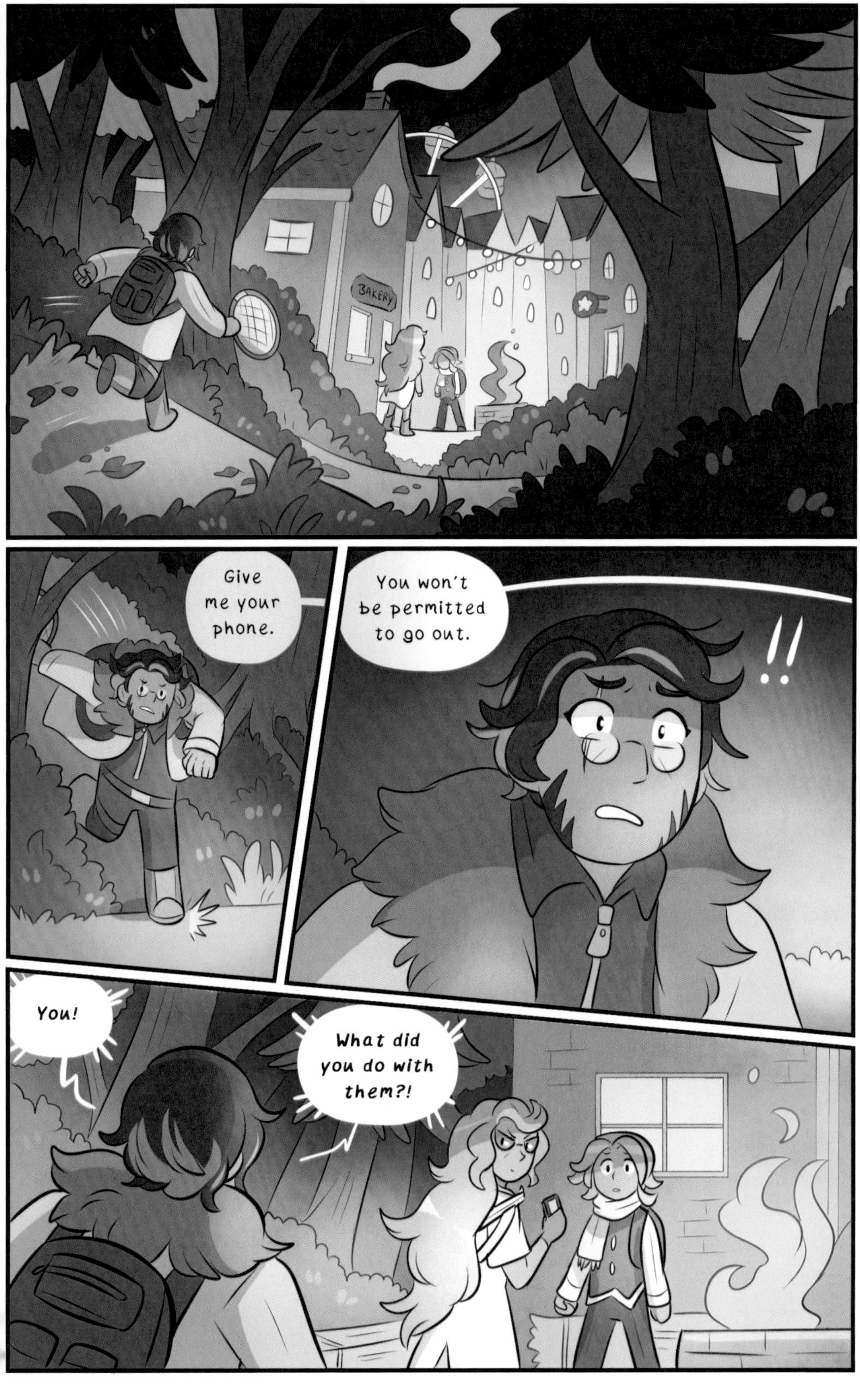
BAKERY
Give me your phone.
You won't be permitted to go out.
!!
You!
What did you do with them?!

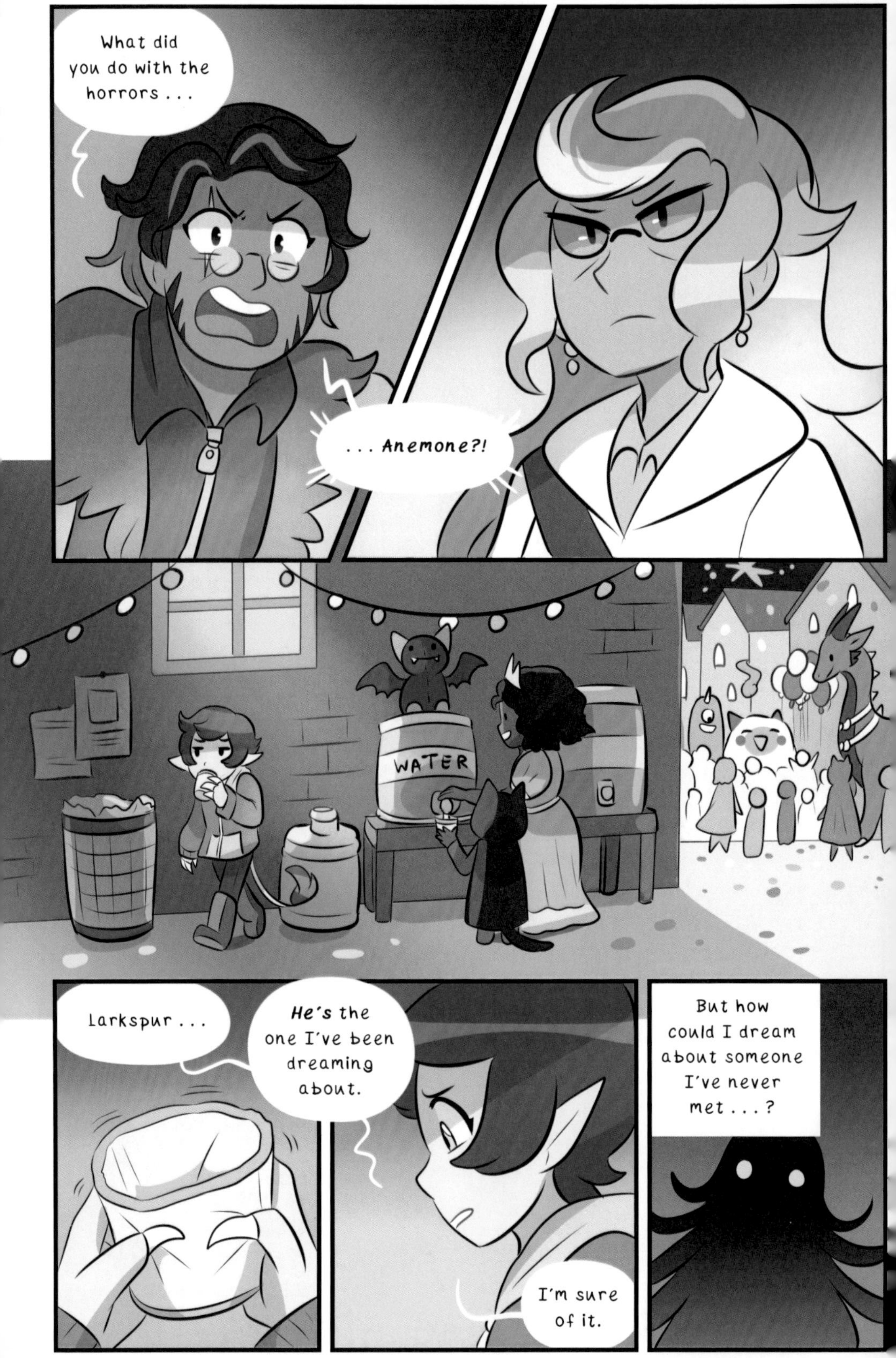
What did you do with the horrors . . .
. . . Anemone?!
WATER
Larkspur . . .
He's the one I've been dreaming about.
I'm sure of it.
But how could I dream about someone I've never met . . . ?

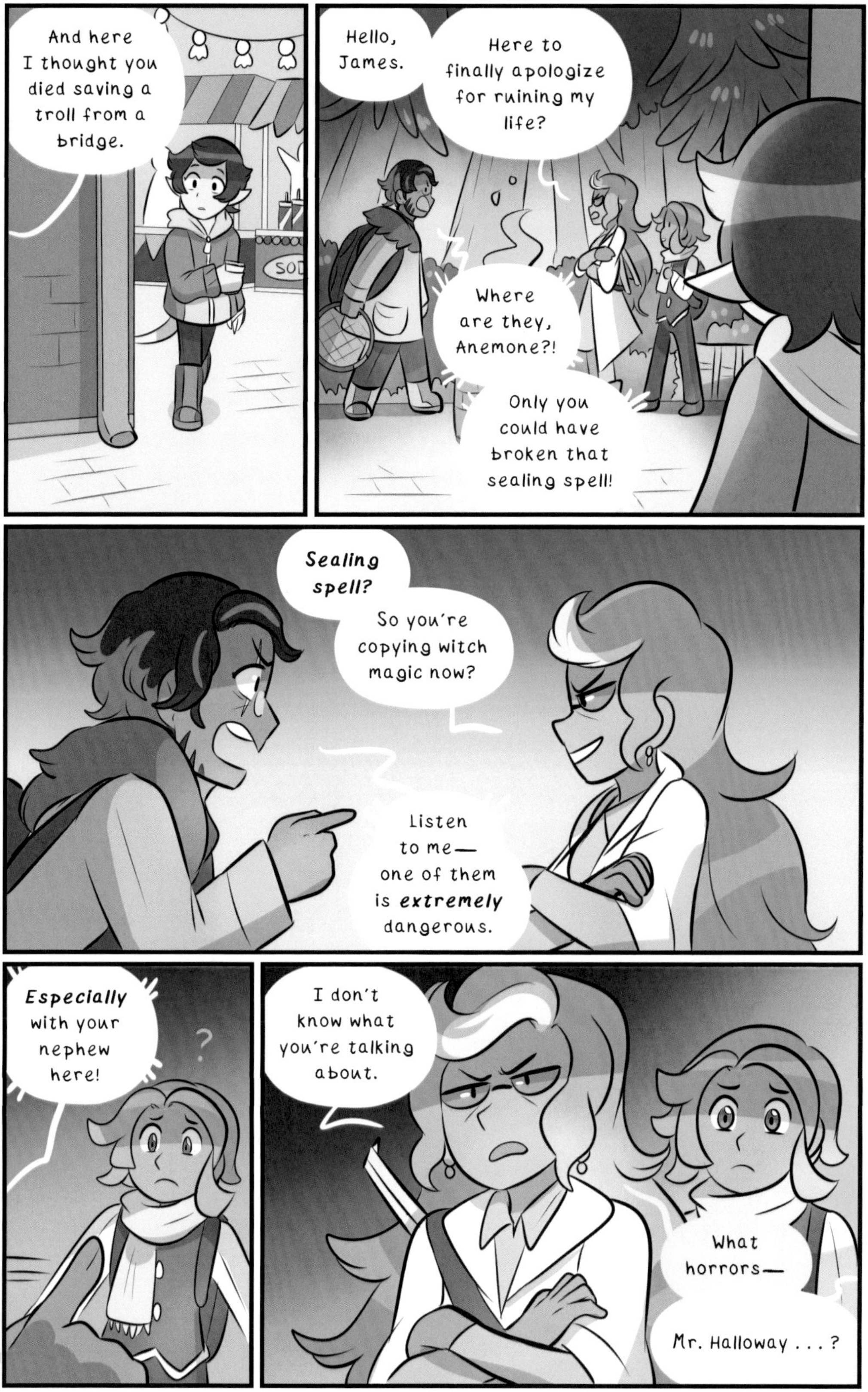
And here I thought you died saving a troll from a bridge.
Hello, James.
Here to finally apologize for ruining my life?
Where are they, Anemone?!
Only you could have broken that sealing spell!
Sealing spell?
So you're copying witch magic now?
Listen to me— one of them is extremely dangerous.
Especially with your nephew here!
?
I don't know what you're talking about.
What horrors—
Mr. Halloway . . . ?

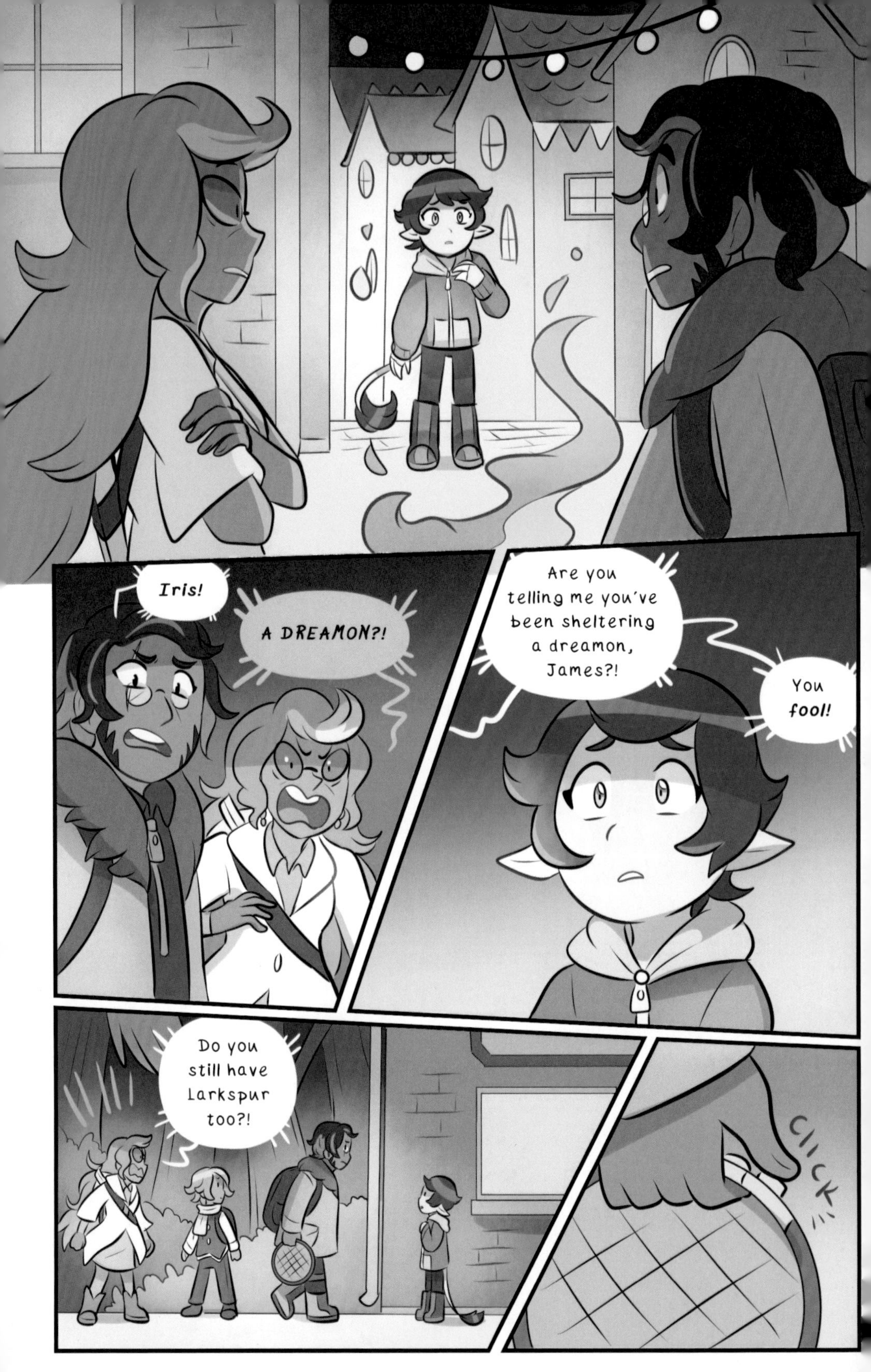
Iris!
A DREAMON?!
Are you telling me you've been sheltering a dreamon, James?!
You fool!
Do you still have Larkspur too?!
CLICK

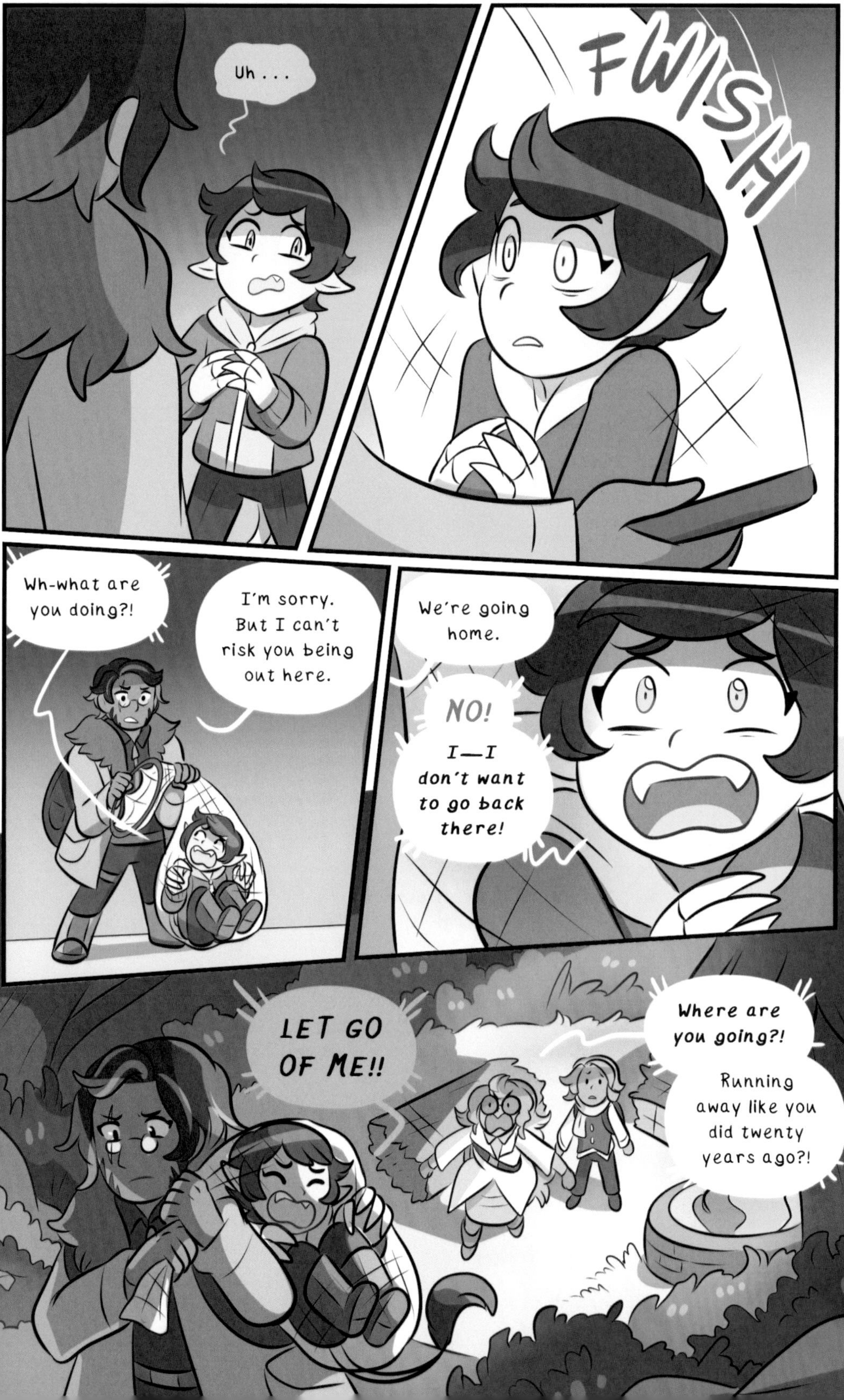
Uh . . .
FWISH
Wh-what are you doing?!
I'm sorry. But I can't risk you being out here.
We're going home.
NO!
I—I don't want to go back there!
LET GO OF ME!!
Where are you going?!
Running away like you did twenty years ago?!

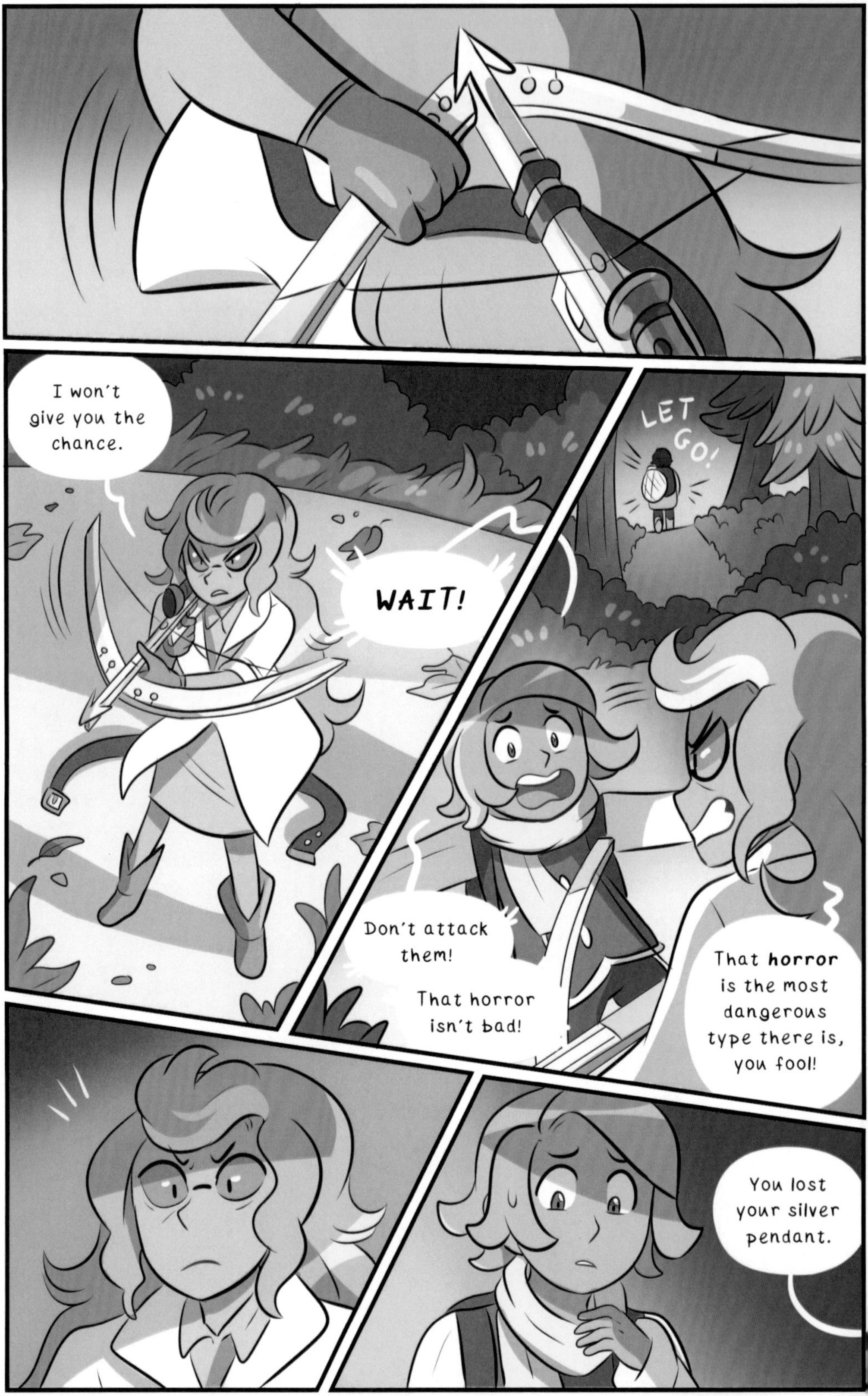
I won't give you the chance.
WAIT!
LET GO!
Don't attack them!
That horror isn't bad!
That **horror** is the most dangerous type there is, you fool!
You lost your silver pendant.

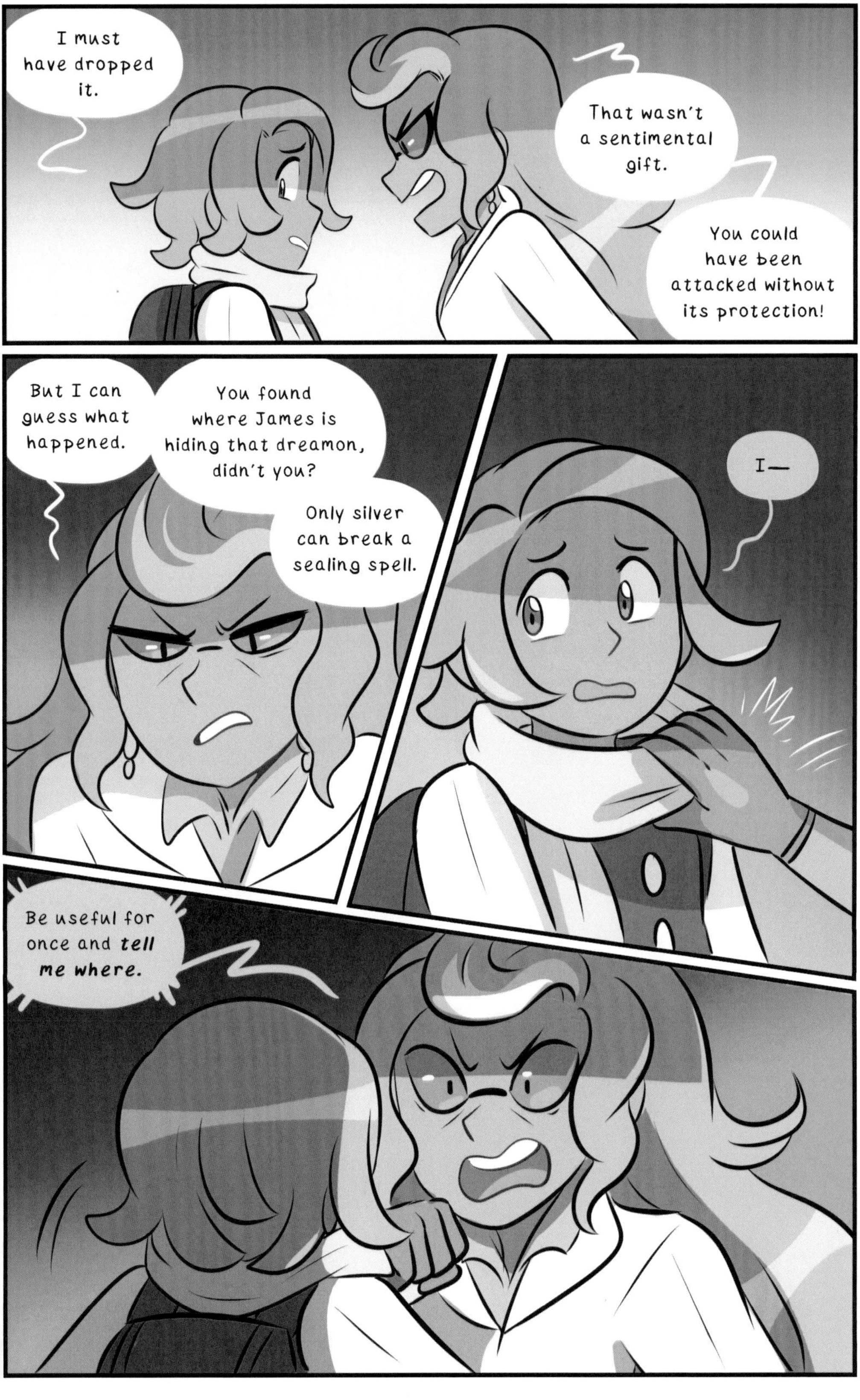
I must have dropped it.
That wasn't a sentimental gift.
You could have been attacked without its protection!
But I can guess what happened.
You found where James is hiding that dreamon, didn't you?
Only silver can break a sealing spell.
I—
Be useful for once and ***tell me where.***

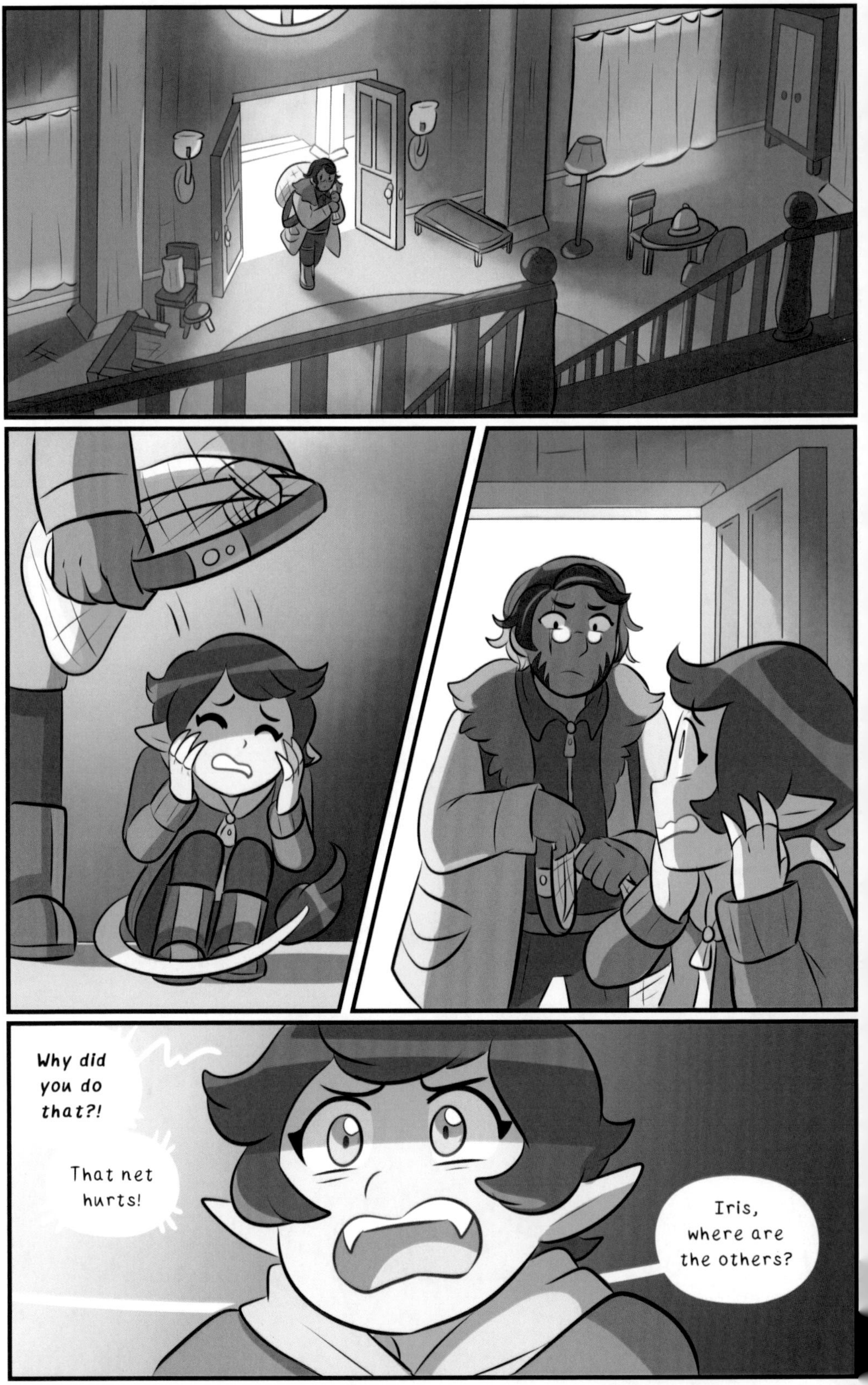
Why did you do that?!
That net hurts!
Iris, where are the others?

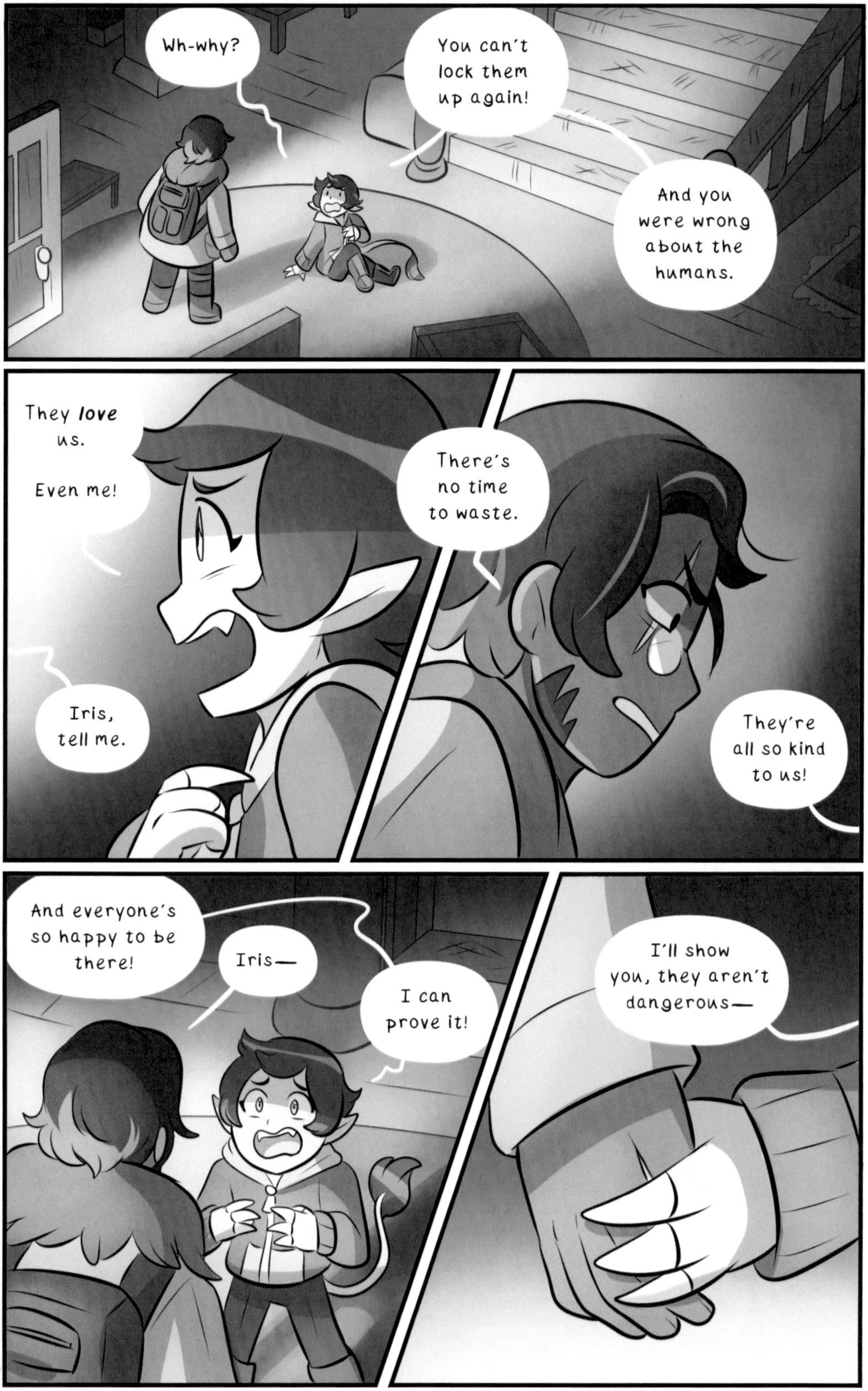
Wh-why?
You can't lock them up again!
And you were wrong about the humans.
They *love* us.
Even me!
Iris, tell me.
There's no time to waste.
They're all so kind to us!
And everyone's so happy to be there!
Iris—
I can prove it!
I'll show you, they aren't dangerous—

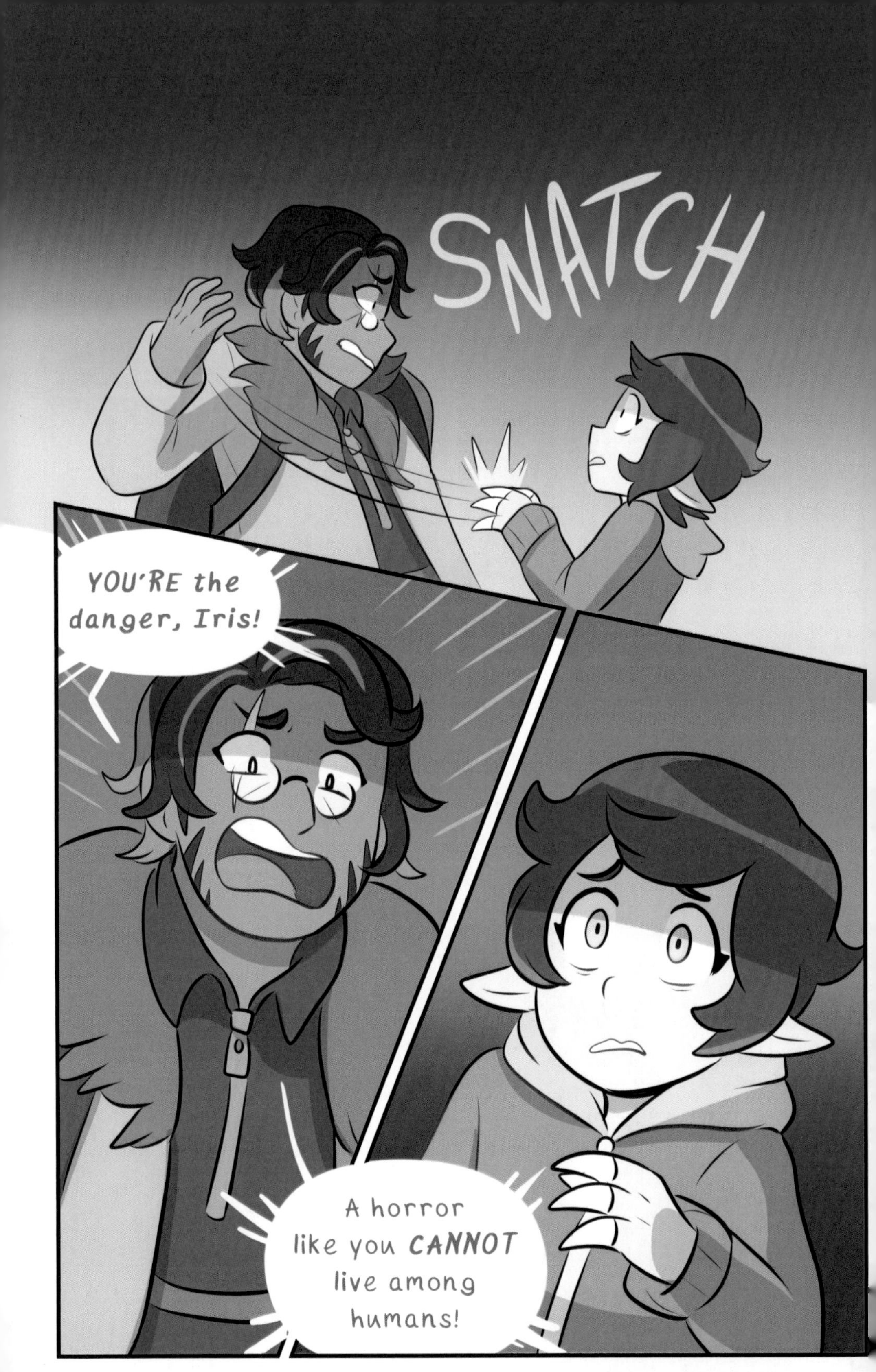
SNATCH
YOU'RE the danger, Iris!
A horror like you CANNOT live among humans!

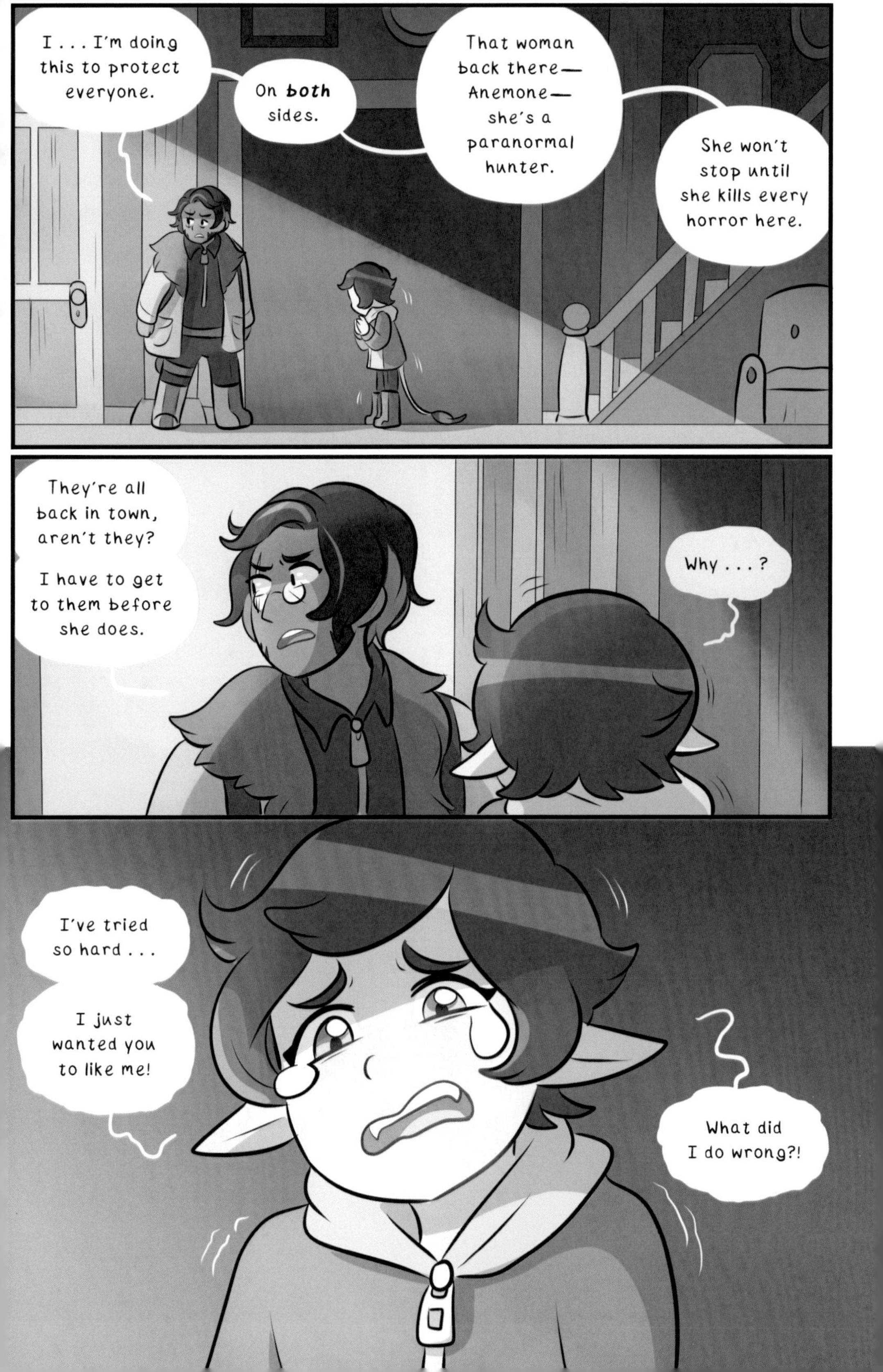
I . . . I'm doing this to protect everyone.
On **both** sides.
That woman back there—Anemone—she's a paranormal hunter.
She won't stop until she kills every horror here.
They're all back in town, aren't they?
I have to get to them before she does.
Why . . . ?
I've tried so hard . . .
I just wanted you to like me!
What did I do wrong?!

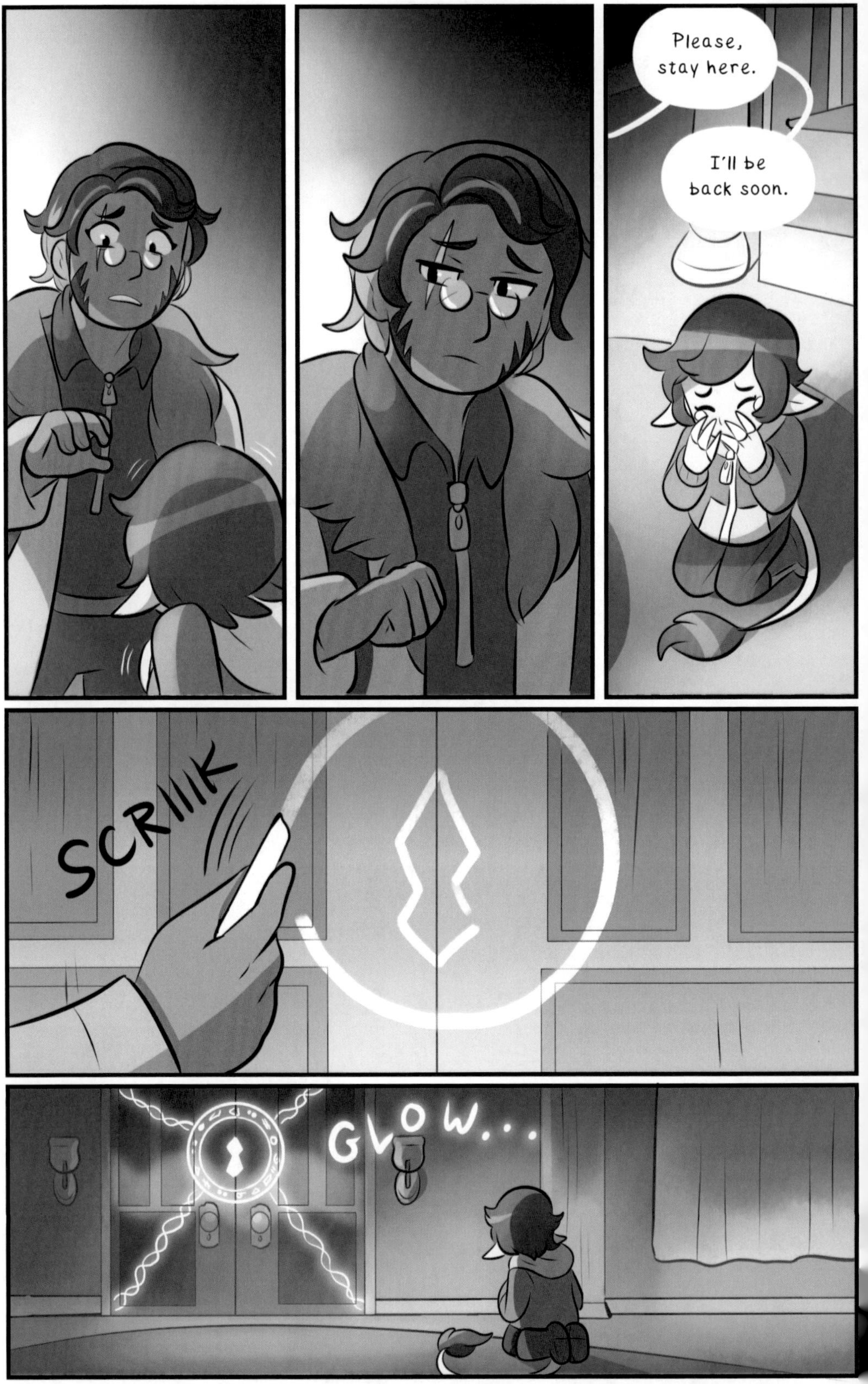
Please, stay here.
I'll be back soon.
SCRIIIK
GLOW...

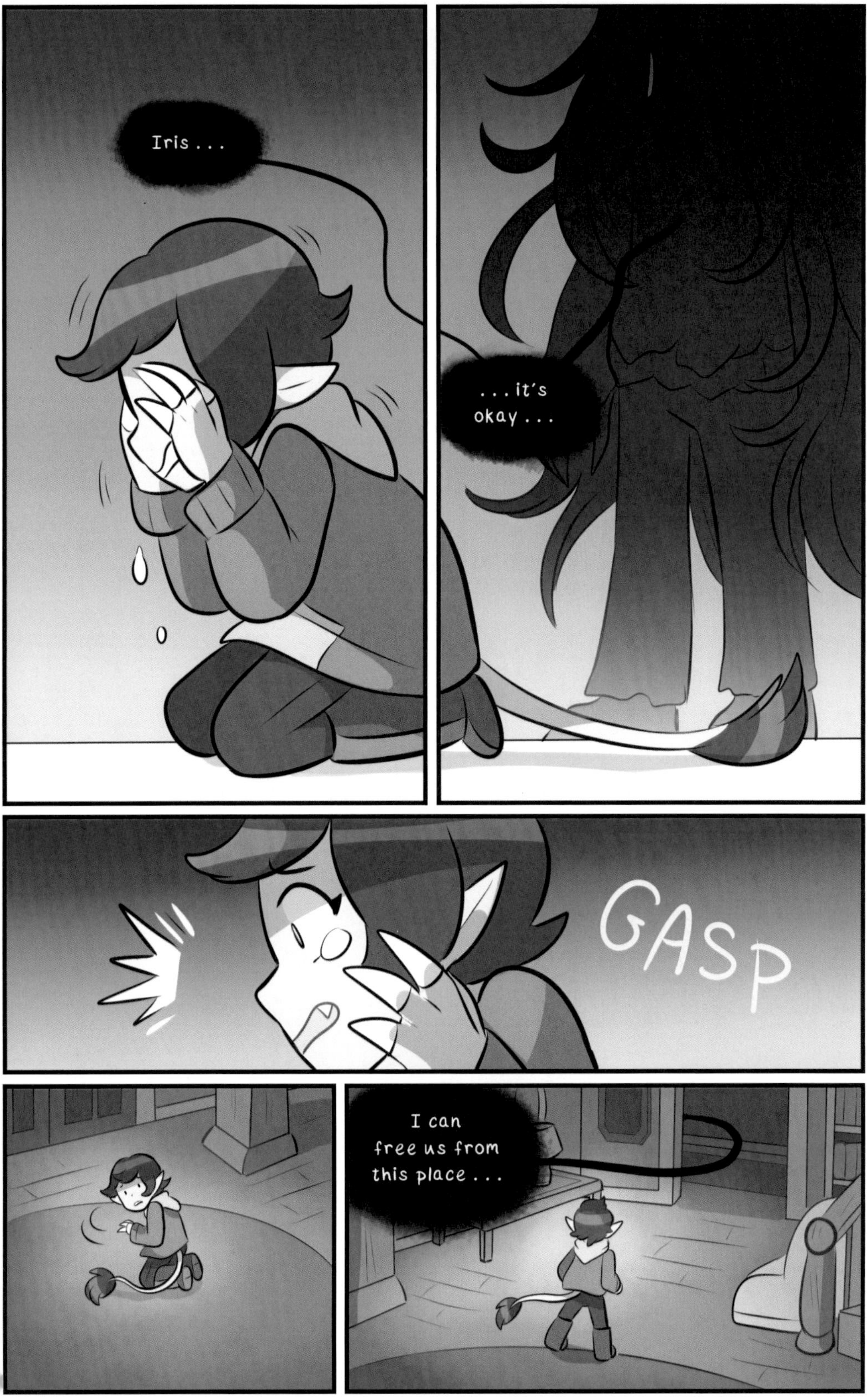
Iris . . .
. . . it's okay . . .
GASP
I can free us from this place . . .

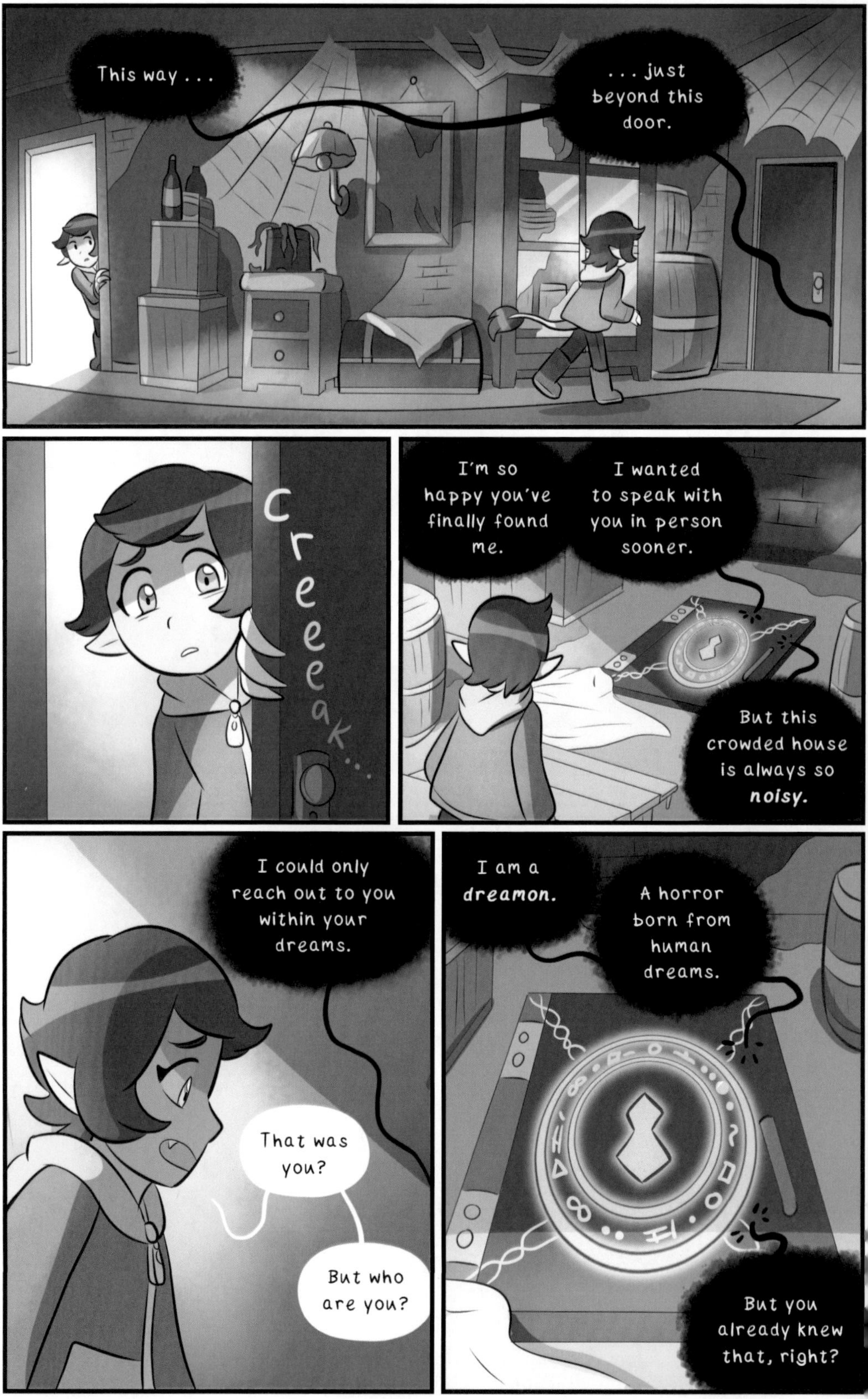
This way . . .
. . . just beyond this door.
Creeeak . . .
I'm so happy you've finally found me.
I wanted to speak with you in person sooner.
But this crowded house is always so **noisy.**
I could only reach out to you within your dreams.
That was you?
But who are you?
I am a **dreamon.**
A horror born from human dreams.
But you already knew that, right?

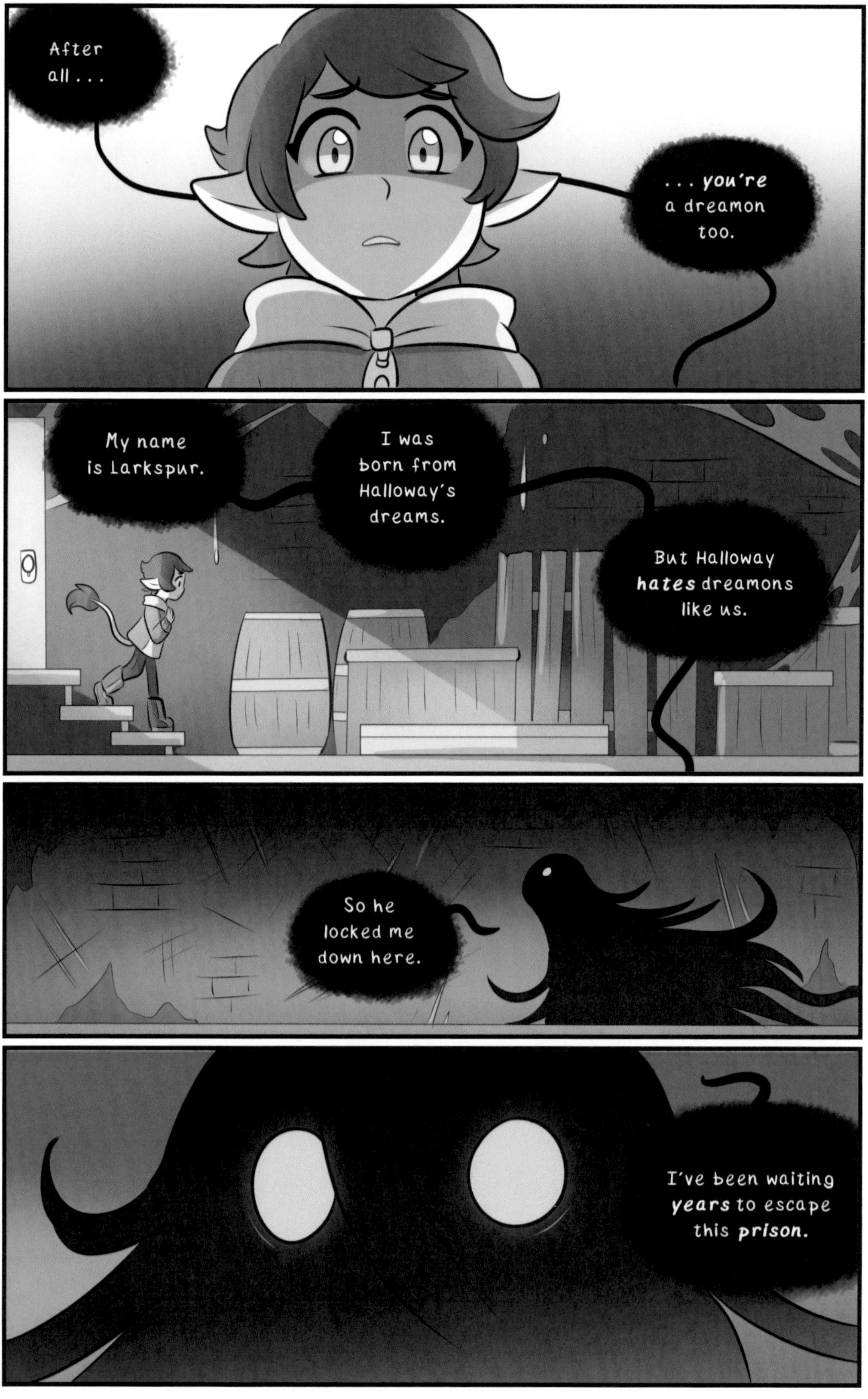
After all . . .
. . . you're a dreamon too.
My name is Larkspur.
I was born from Halloway's dreams.
But Halloway hates dreamons like us.
So he locked me down here.
I've been waiting years to escape this prison.

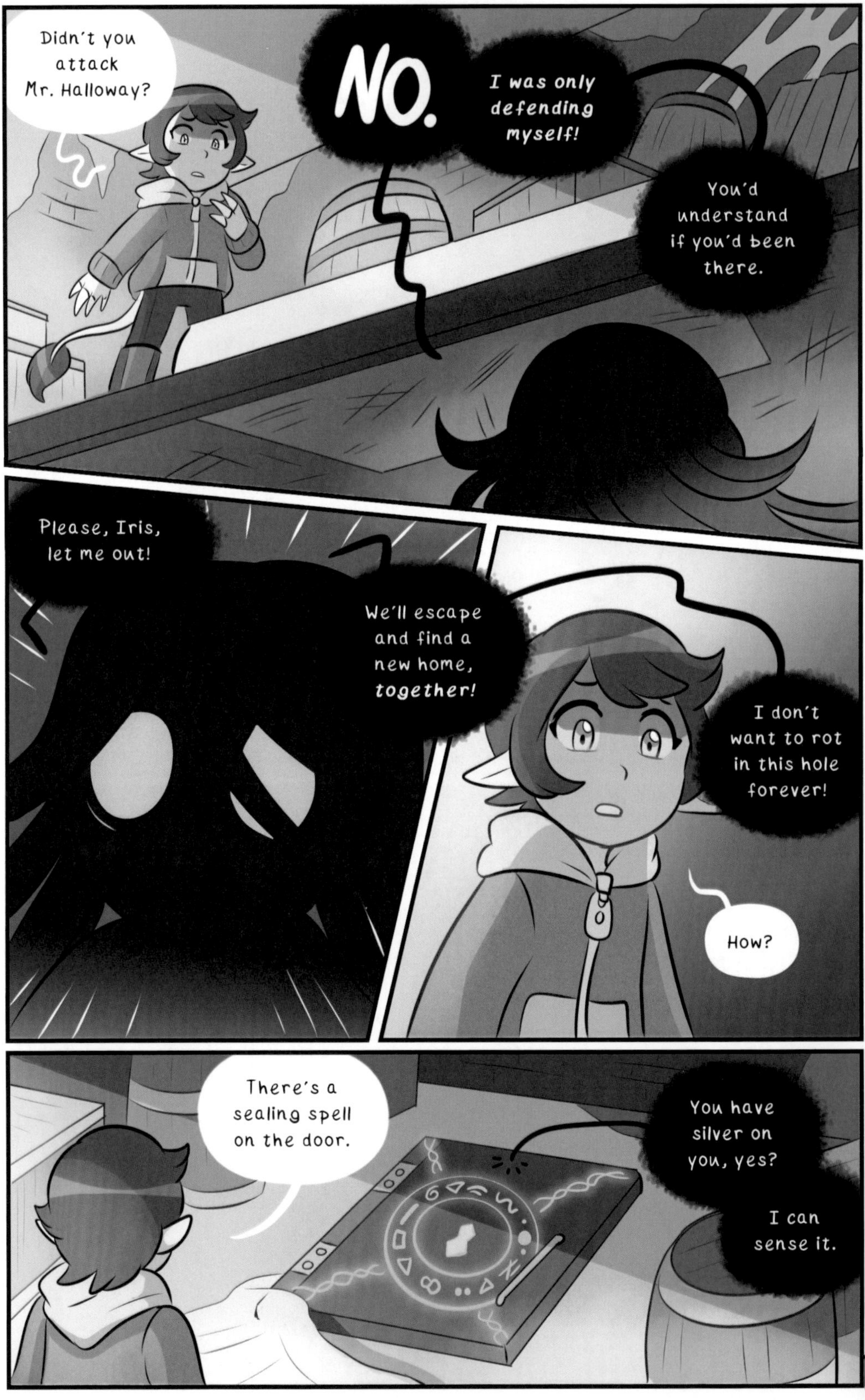
Didn't you attack Mr. Halloway?
NO.
I was only defending myself!
You'd understand if you'd been there.
Please, Iris, let me out!
We'll escape and find a new home, *together*!
I don't want to rot in this hole forever!
How?
There's a sealing spell on the door.
You have silver on you, yes?
I can sense it.

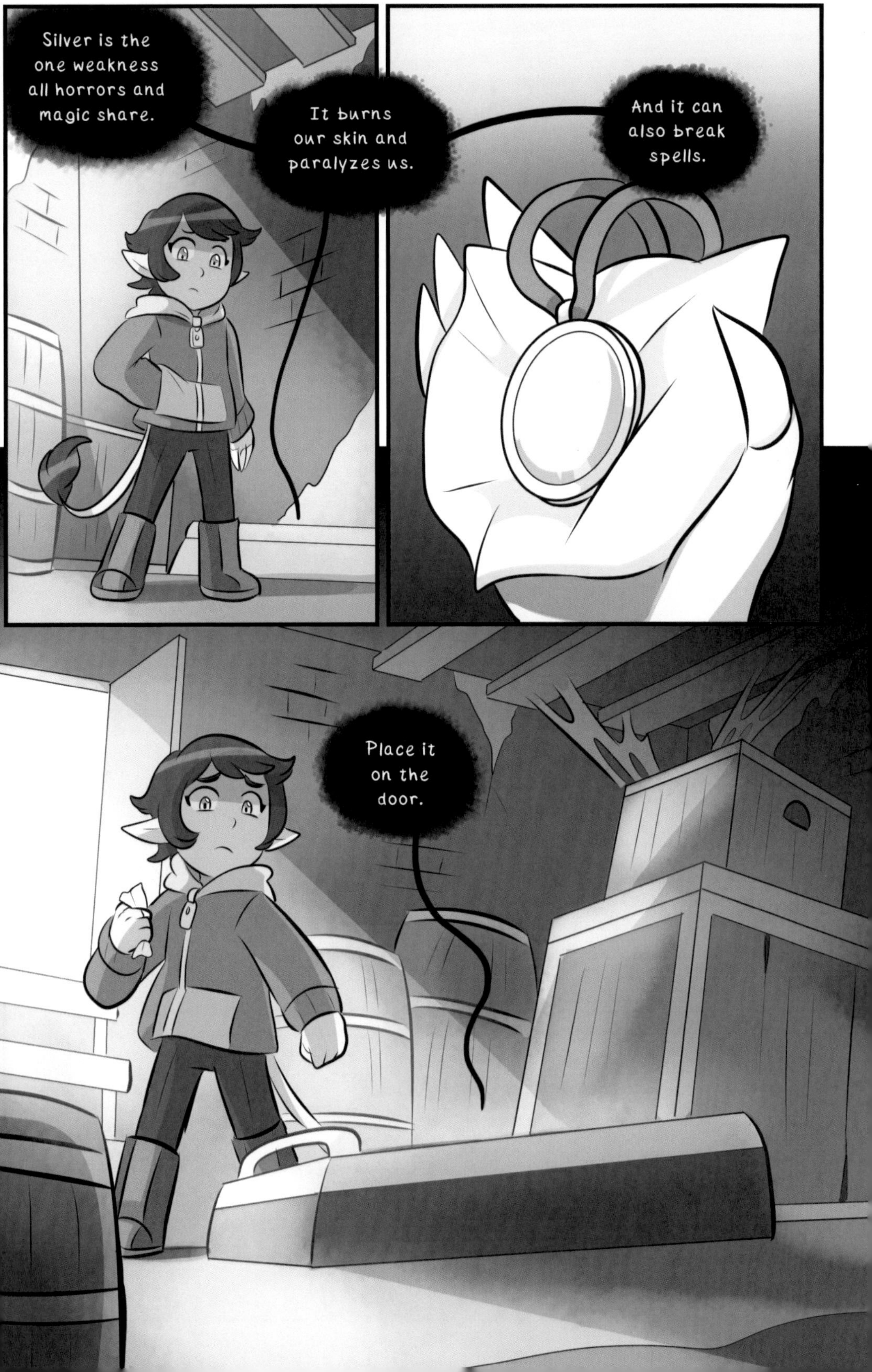
Silver is the one weakness all horrors and magic share.
It burns our skin and paralyzes us.
And it can also break spells.
Place it on the door.

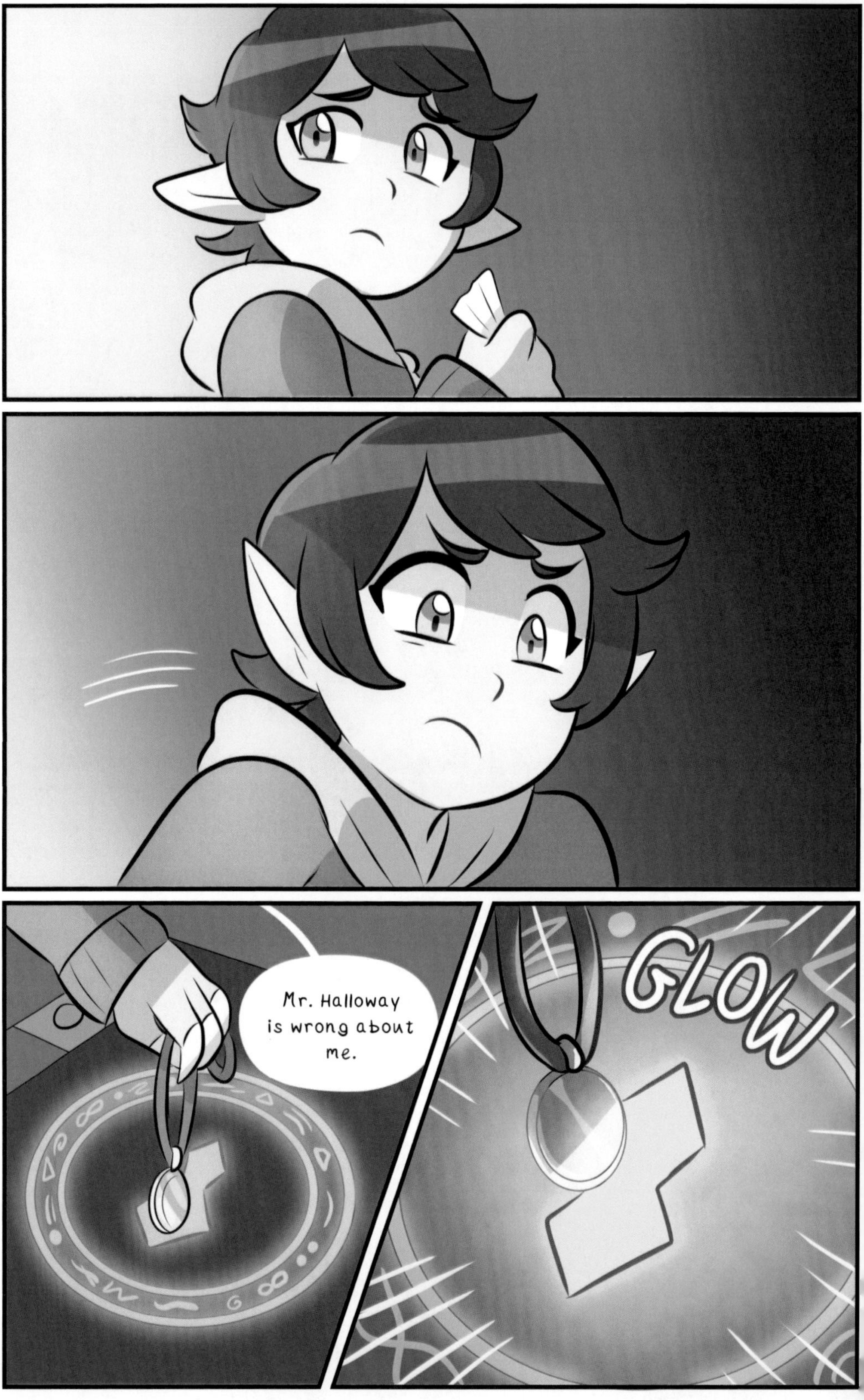
Mr. Halloway is wrong about me.
GLOW

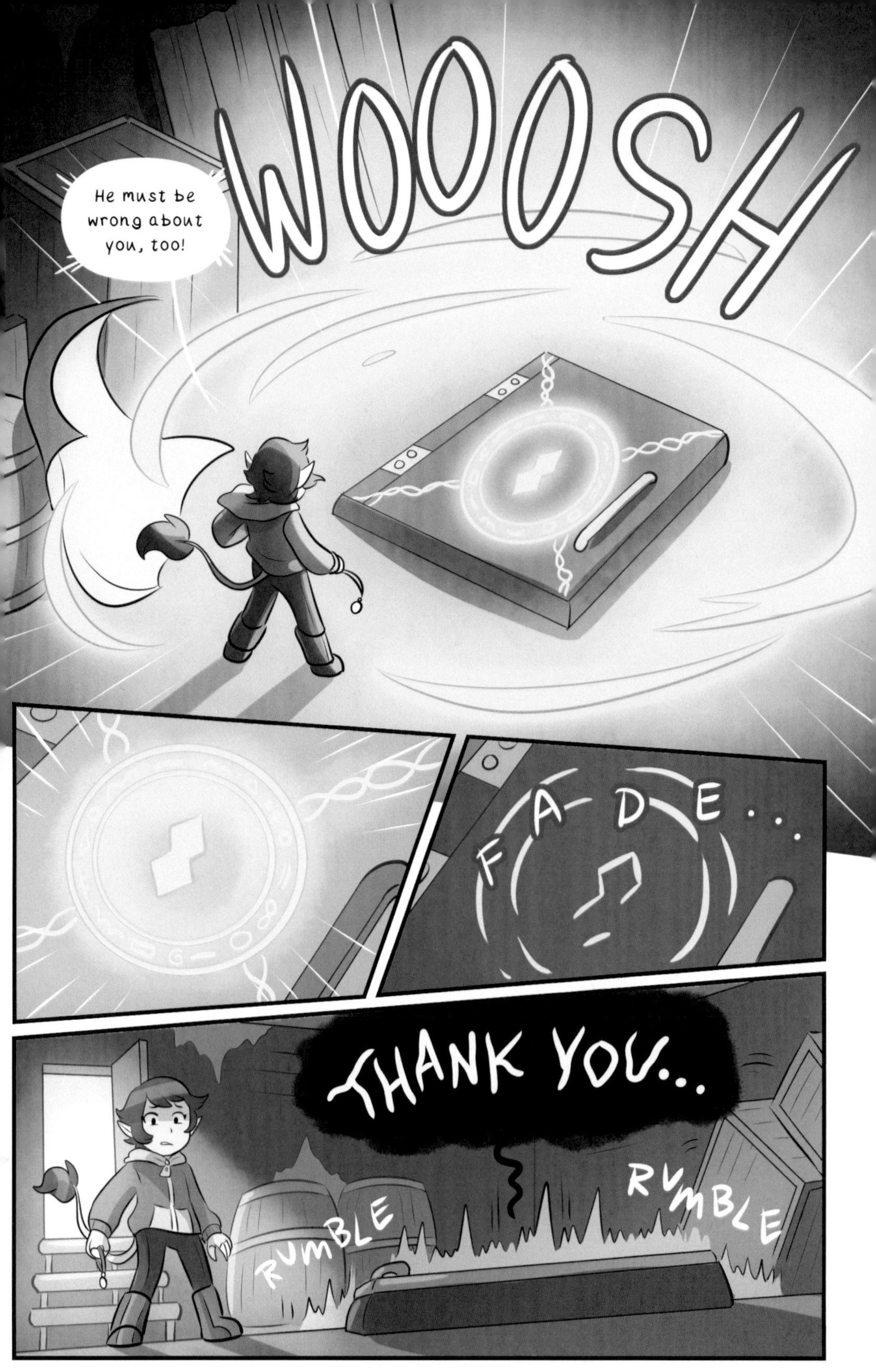
He must be wrong about you, too!
WOOOSH
FADE...
THANK YOU...
RUMBLE
RUMBLE

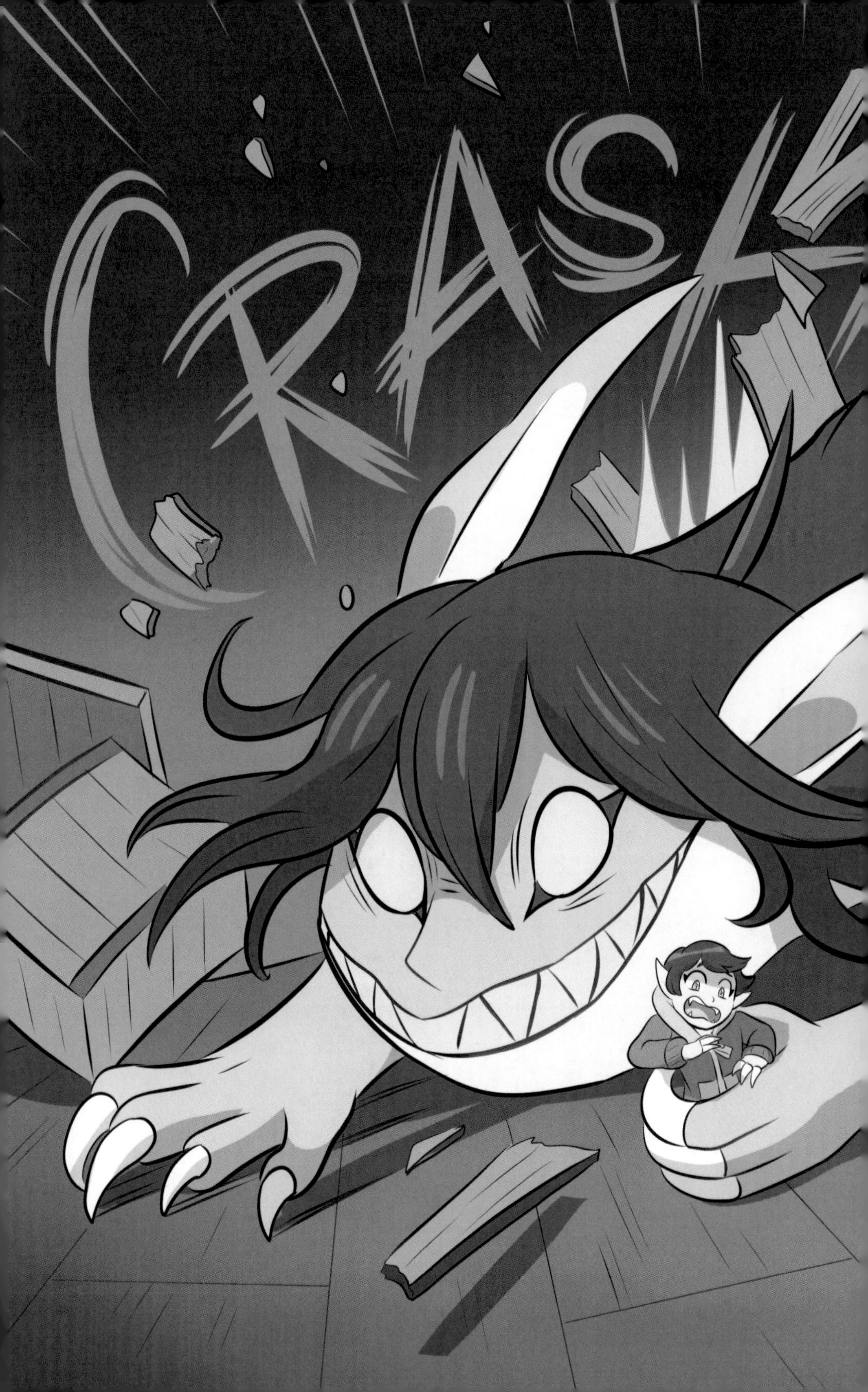
CRAS

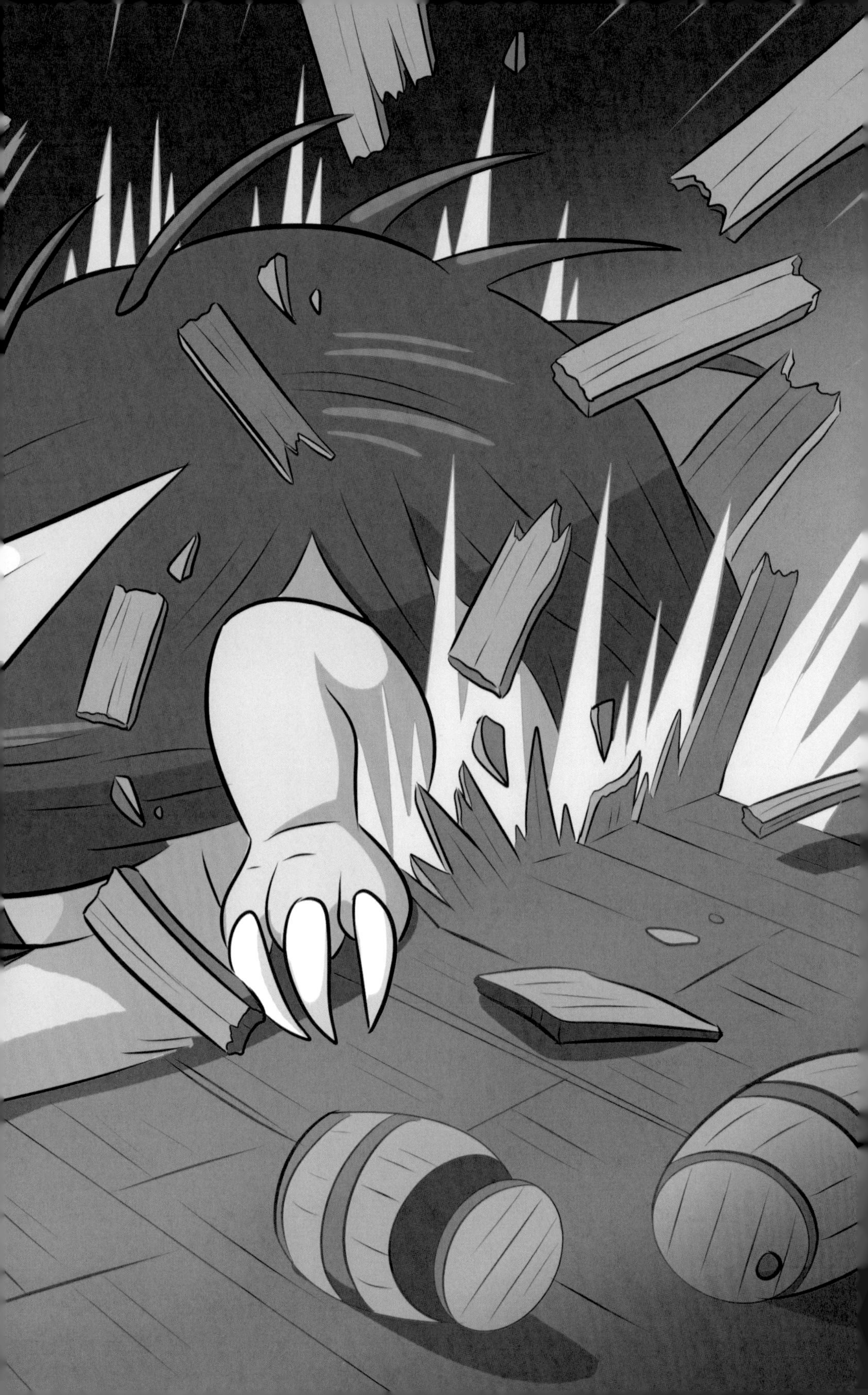

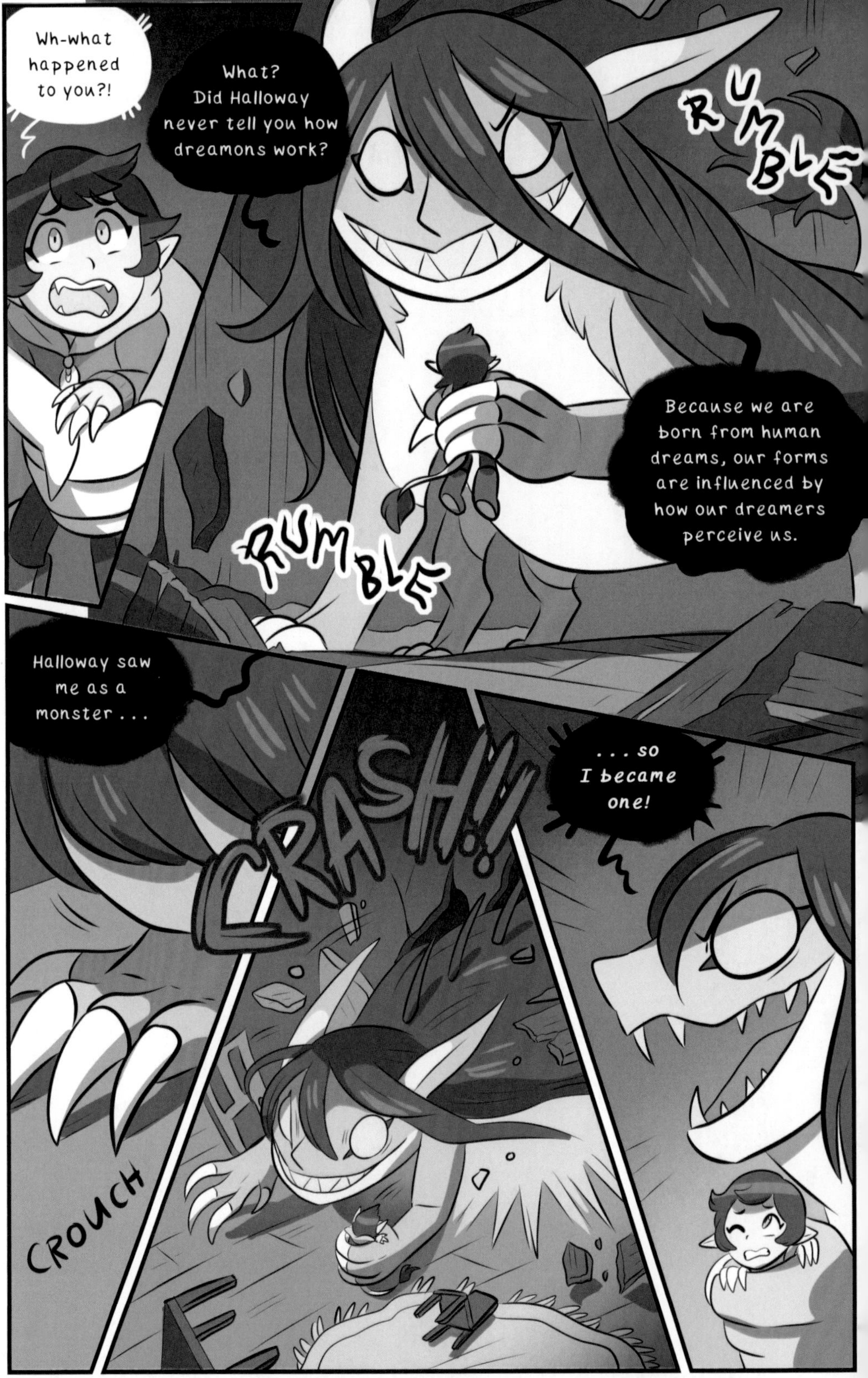
Wh-what happened to you?!
What? Did Halloway never tell you how dreamons work?
RUMBLE
Because we are born from human dreams, our forms are influenced by how our dreamers perceive us.
RUMBLE
Halloway saw me as a monster . . .
CRASH!!
. . . so I became one!
CROUCH

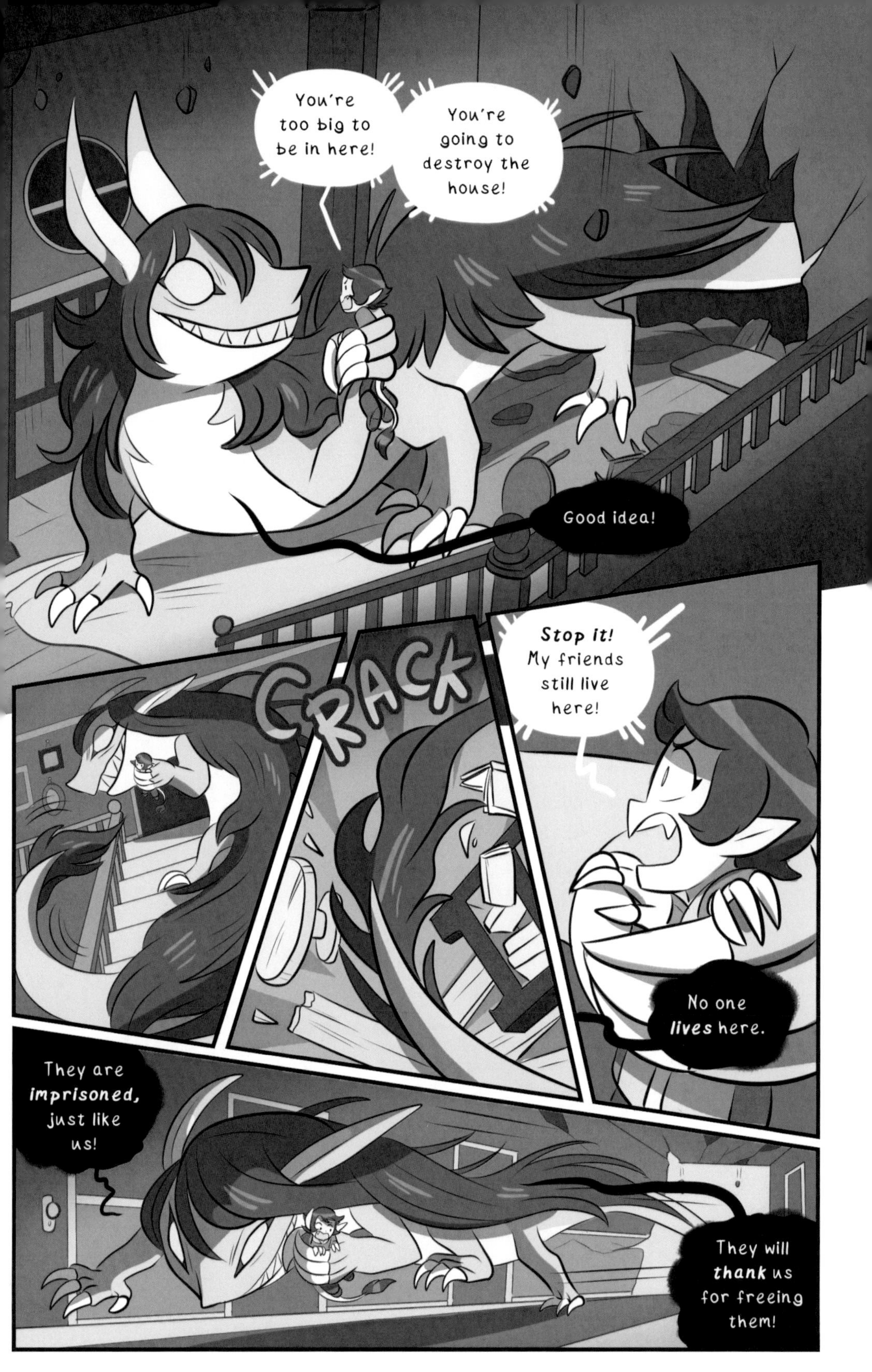
You're too big to be in here!
You're going to destroy the house!
Good idea!
CRACK
Stop it! My friends still live here!
No one lives here.
They are imprisoned, just like us!
They will thank us for freeing them!

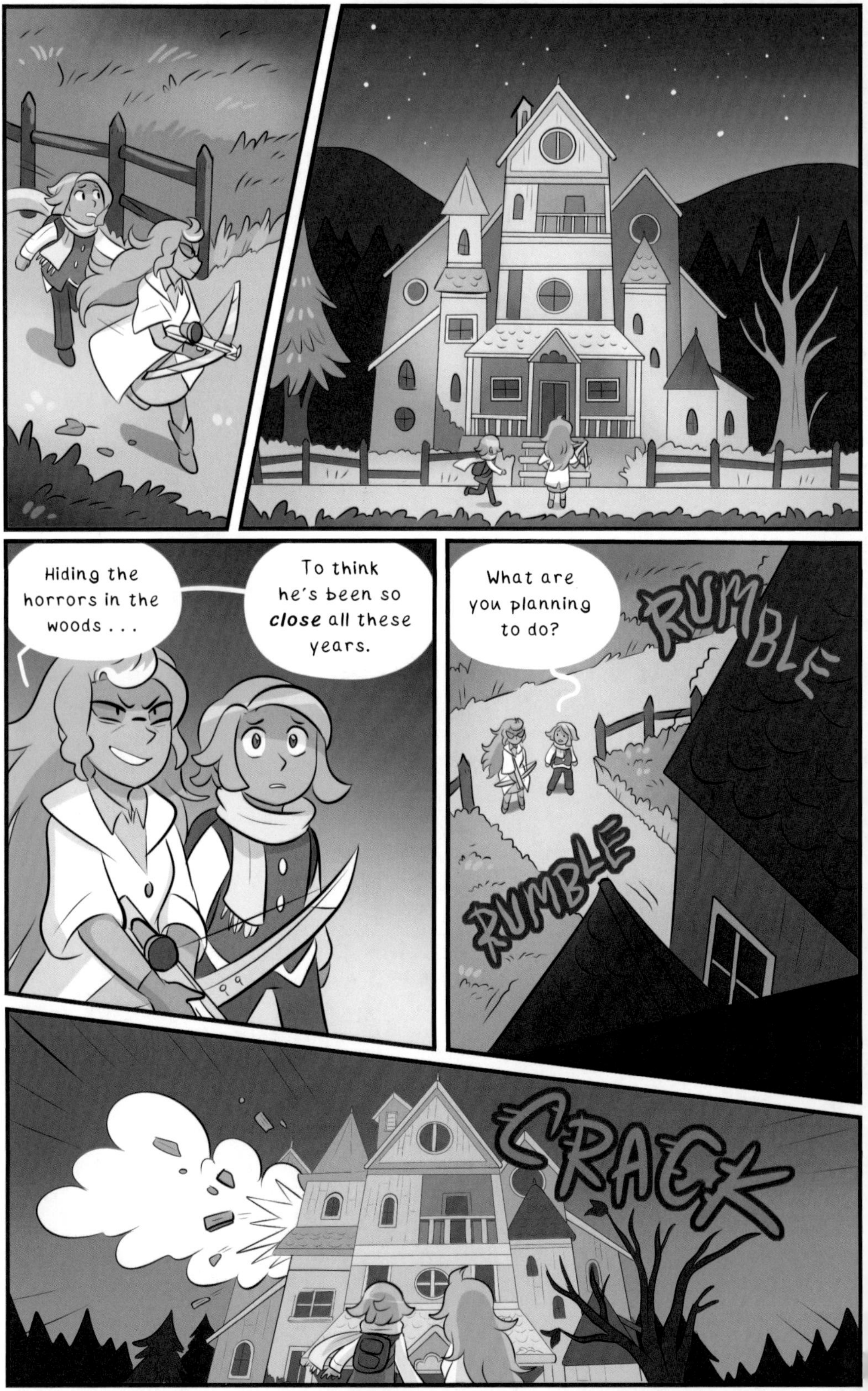
Hiding the horrors in the woods . . .
To think he's been so *close* all these years.
What are you planning to do?
RUMBLE
RUMBLE
CRACK

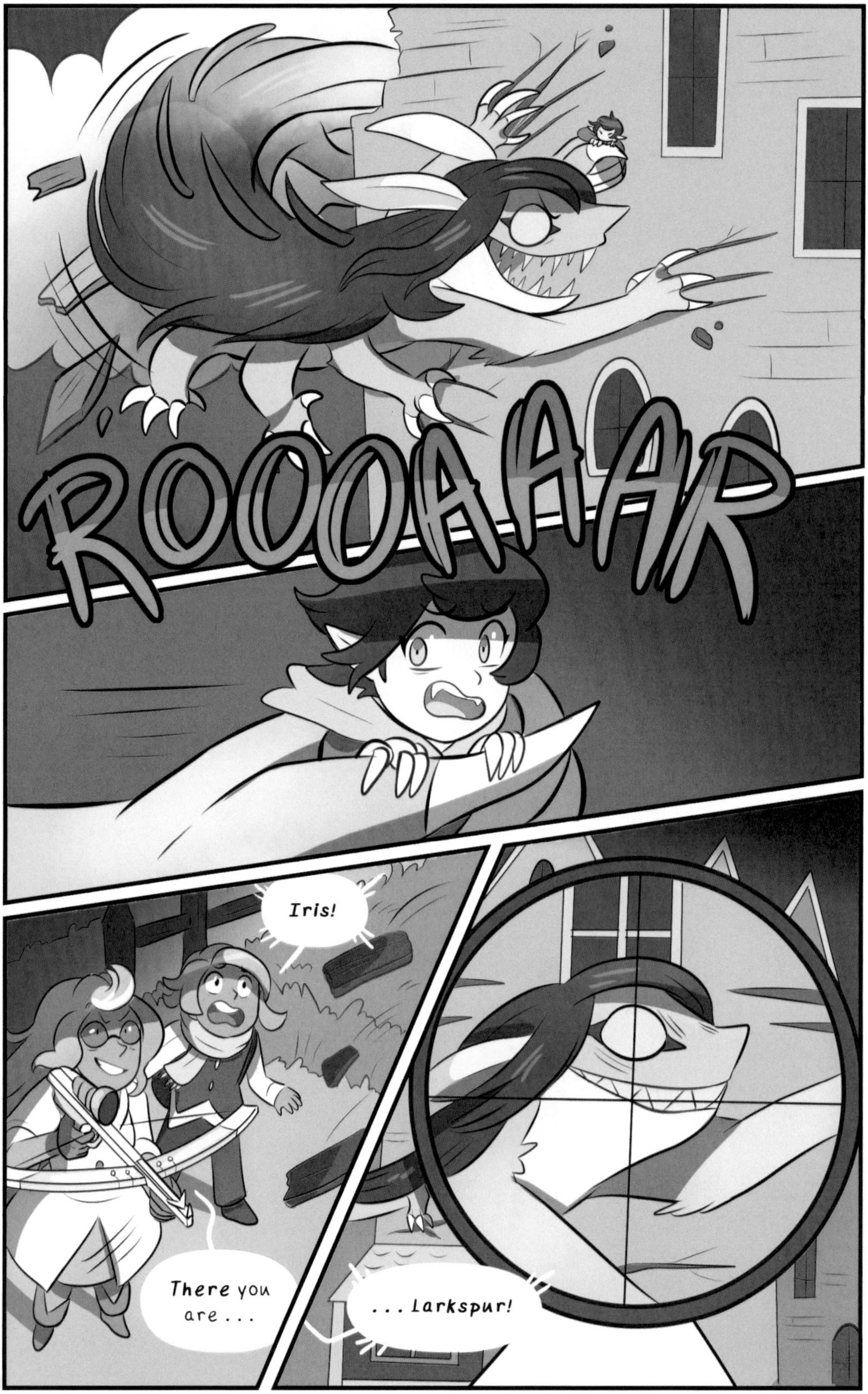
ROOOAAAR
Iris!
There you are . . .
. . . Larkspur!

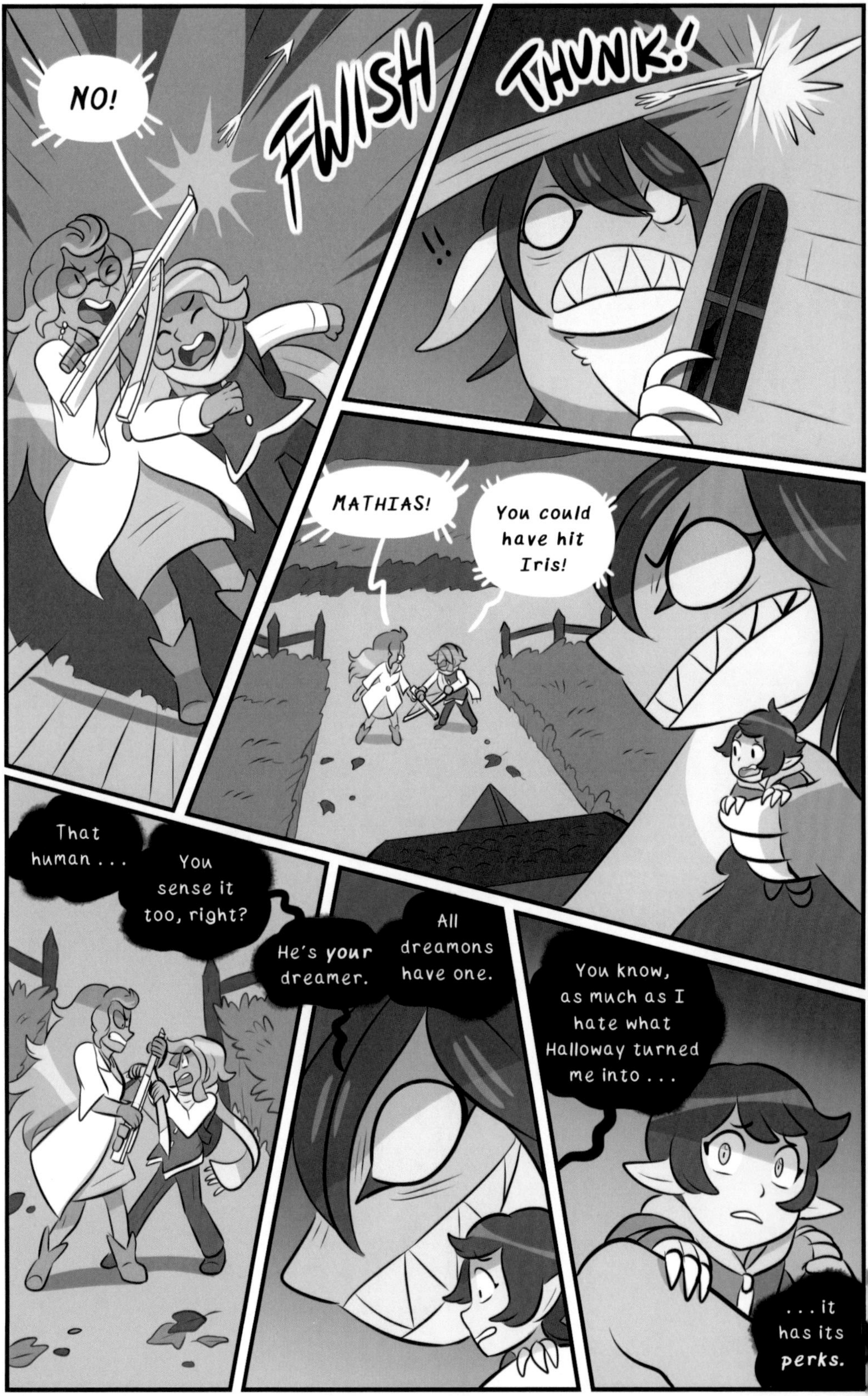
NO!
FWISH
THUNK!
!!
MATHIAS!
You could have hit Iris!
That human . . .
You sense it too, right?
He's **your** dreamer.
All dreamons have one.
You know, as much as I hate what Halloway turned me into . . .
. . . it has its **perks.**

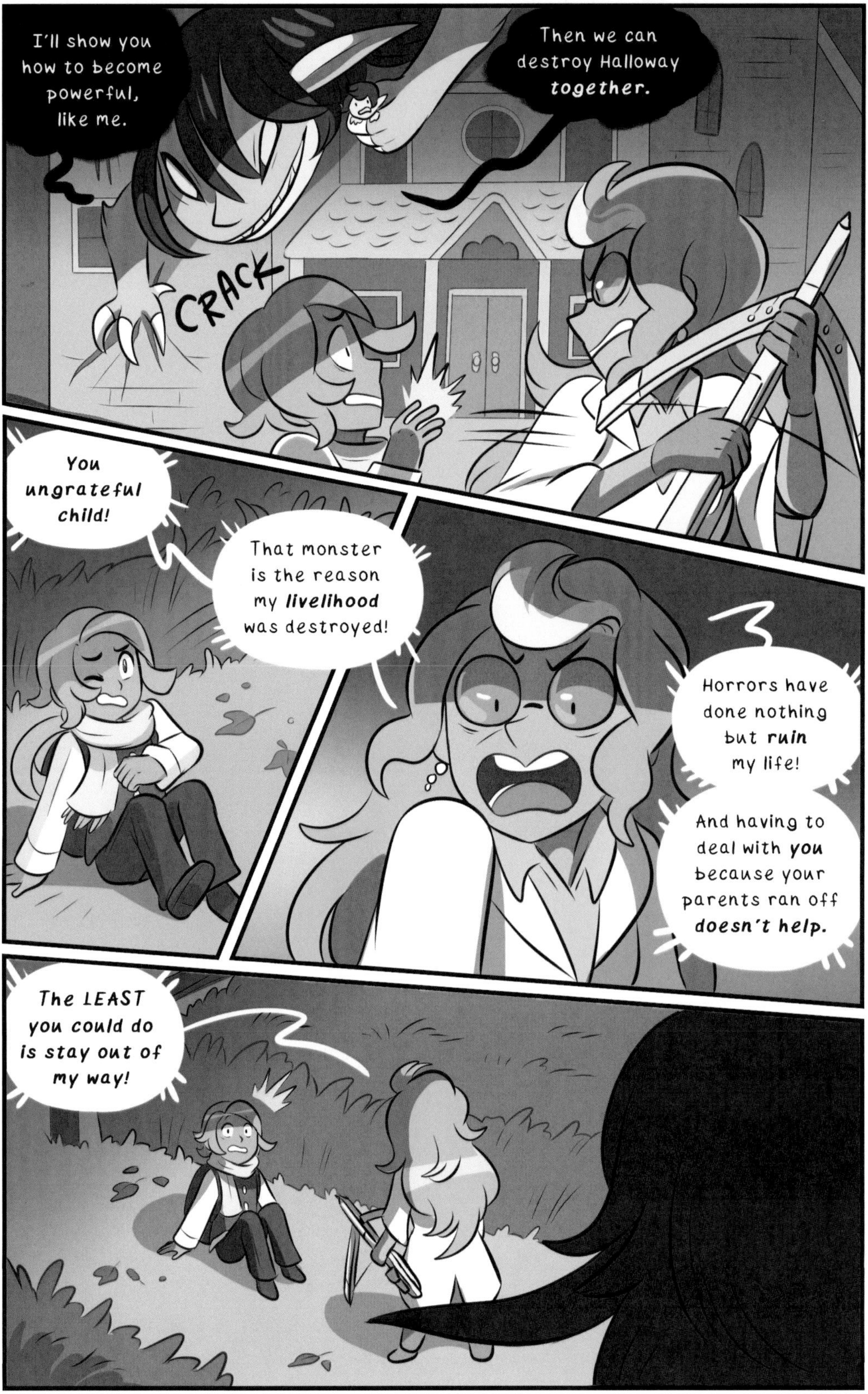
I'll show you how to become powerful, like me.
Then we can destroy Halloway *together.*
CRACK
You ungrateful child!
That monster is the reason my *livelihood* was destroyed!
Horrors have done nothing but **ruin** my life!
And having to deal with **you** because your parents ran off ***doesn't help.***
The LEAST you could do is stay out of my way!

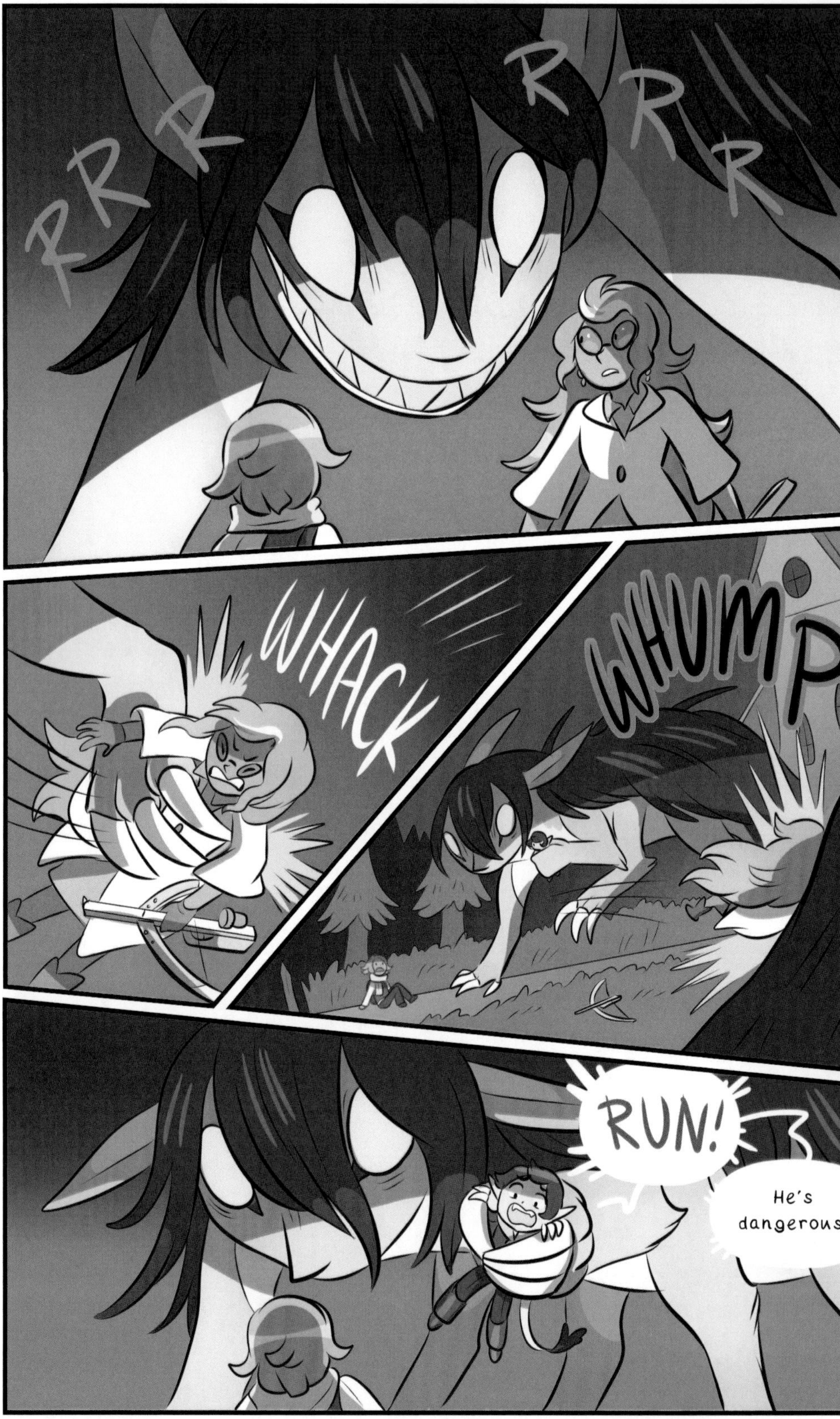
RRRRRRR
WHACK
WHUMP
RUN!
He's dangerous!

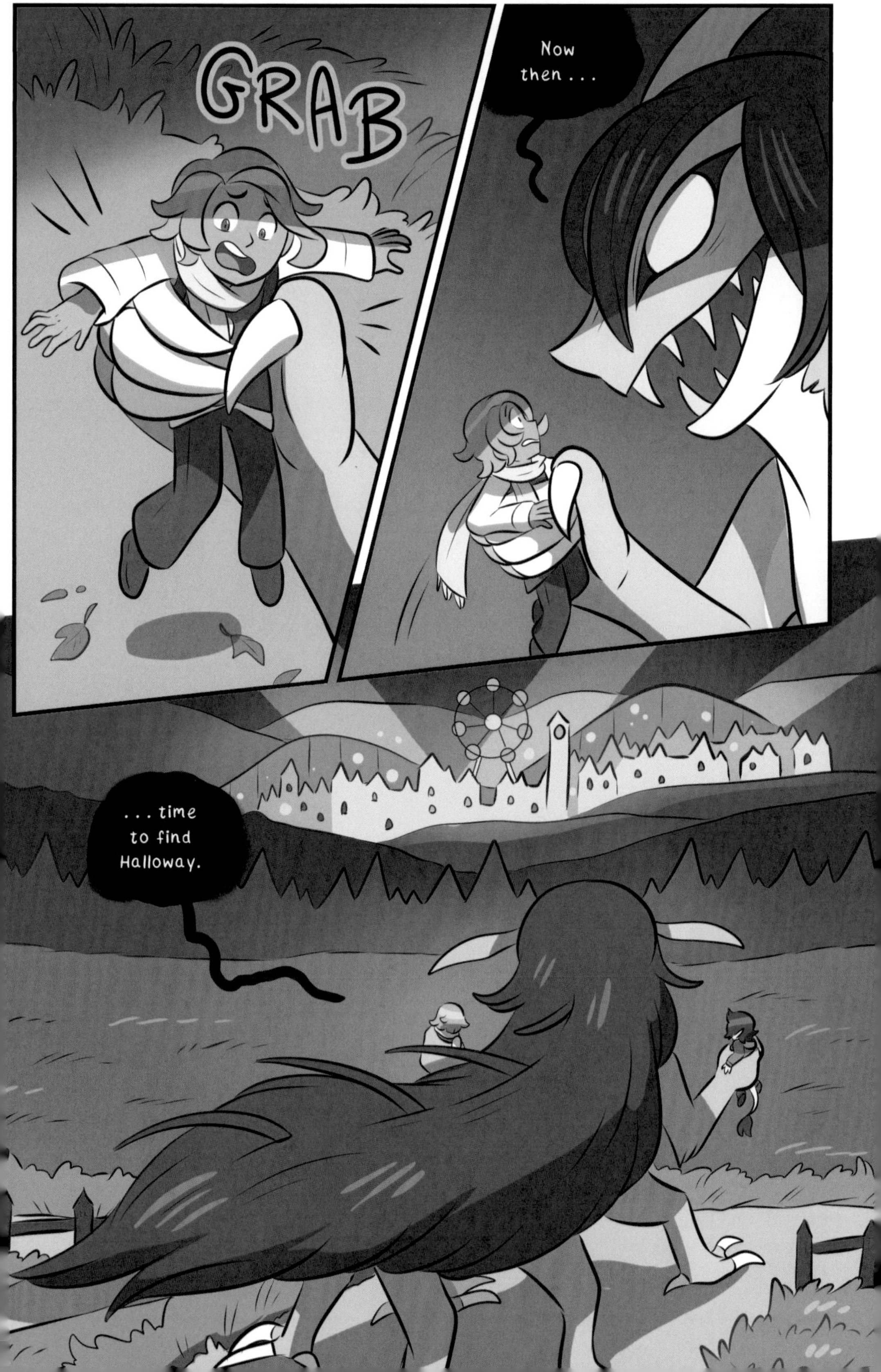
GRAB
Now then . . .
. . . time to find Halloway.

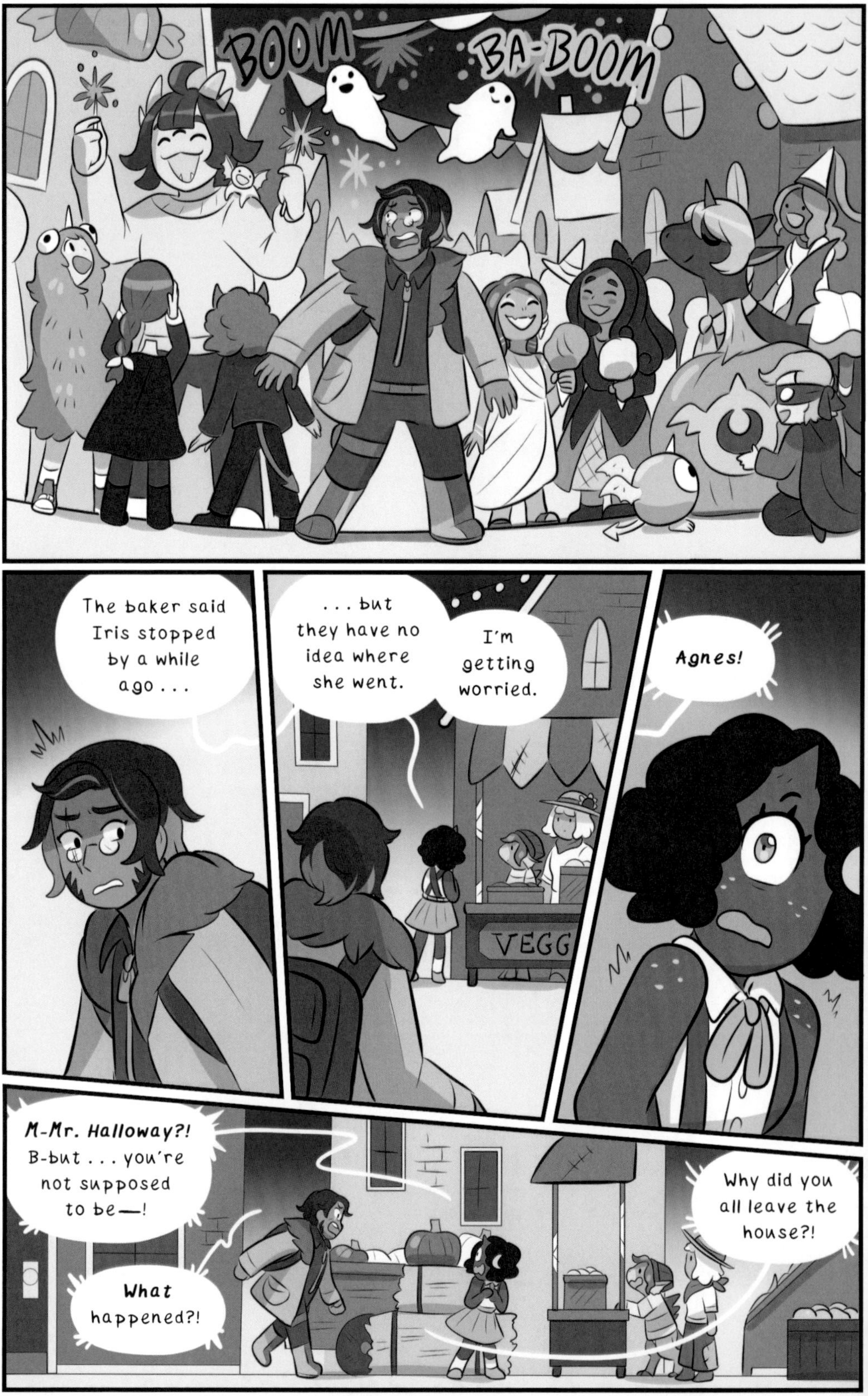
BOOM
BA-BOOM
The baker said Iris stopped by a while ago . . .
. . . but they have no idea where she went.
I'm getting worried.
Agnes!
VEGG
M-Mr. Halloway?! B-but . . . you're not supposed to be—!
What happened?!
Why did you all leave the house?!

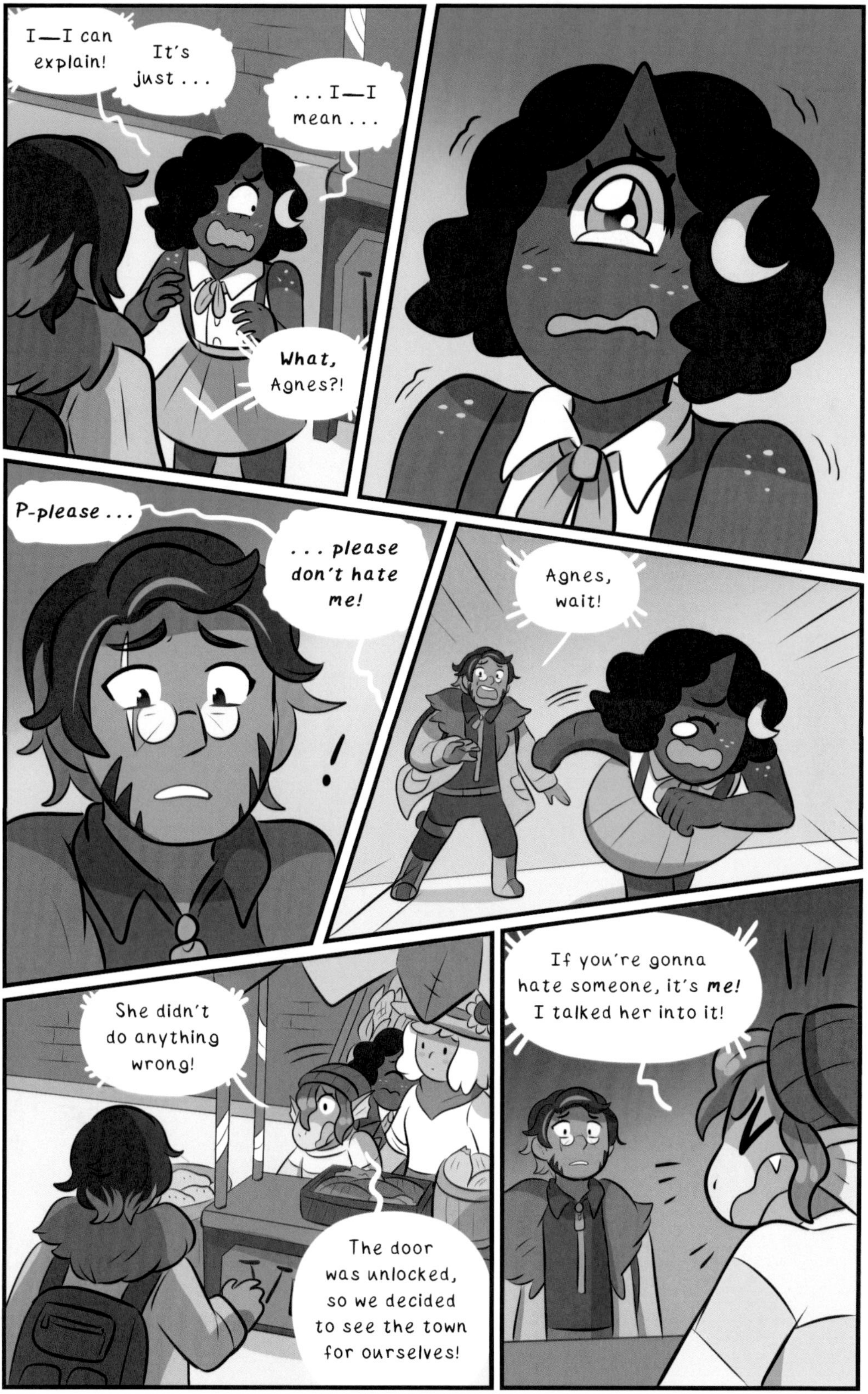
I—I can explain!
It's just . . .
. . . I—I mean . . .
What, Agnes?!
P-please . . .
. . . please don't hate me!
Agnes, wait!
She didn't do anything wrong!
The door was unlocked, so we decided to see the town for ourselves!
If you're gonna hate someone, it's me! I talked her into it!

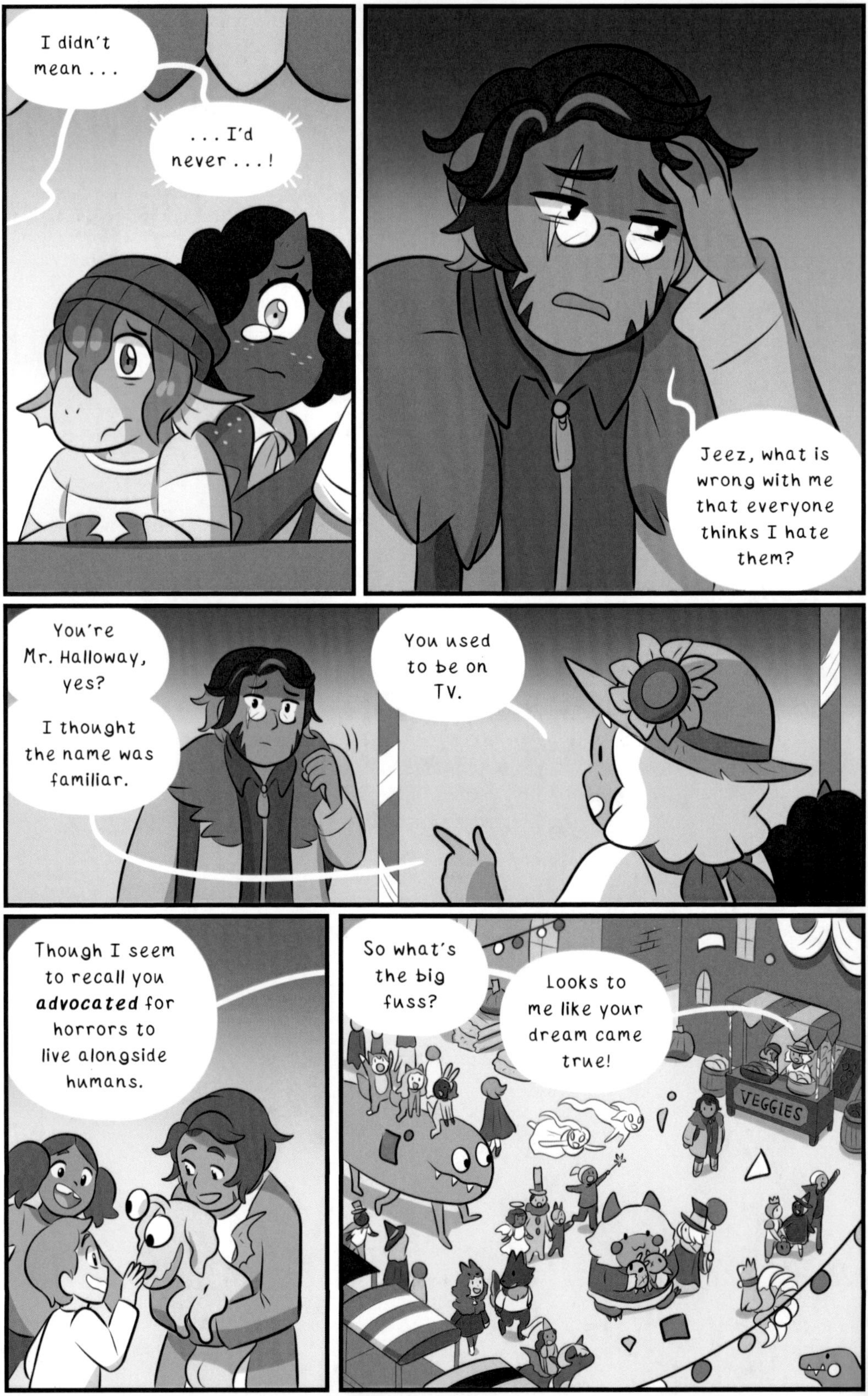
I didn't mean . . .
. . . I'd never . . . !
Jeez, what is wrong with me that everyone thinks I hate them?
You're Mr. Halloway, yes?
I thought the name was familiar.
You used to be on TV.
Though I seem to recall you ***advocated*** for horrors to live alongside humans.
So what's the big fuss?
Looks to me like your dream came true!
VEGGIES

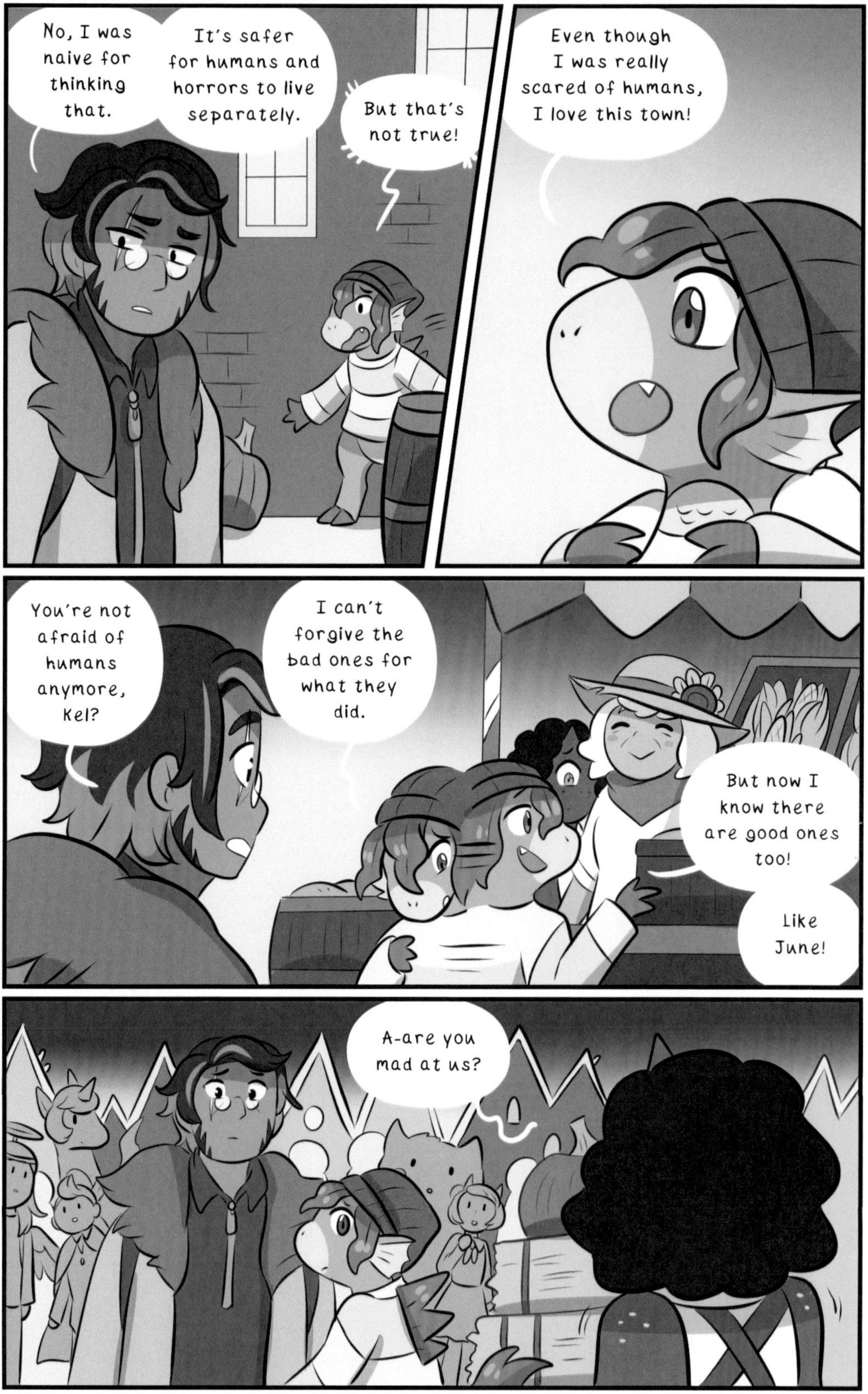
No, I was naive for thinking that.
It's safer for humans and horrors to live separately.
But that's not true!
Even though I was really scared of humans, I love this town!
You're not afraid of humans anymore, Kel?
I can't forgive the bad ones for what they did.
But now I know there are good ones too!
Like June!
A-are you mad at us?

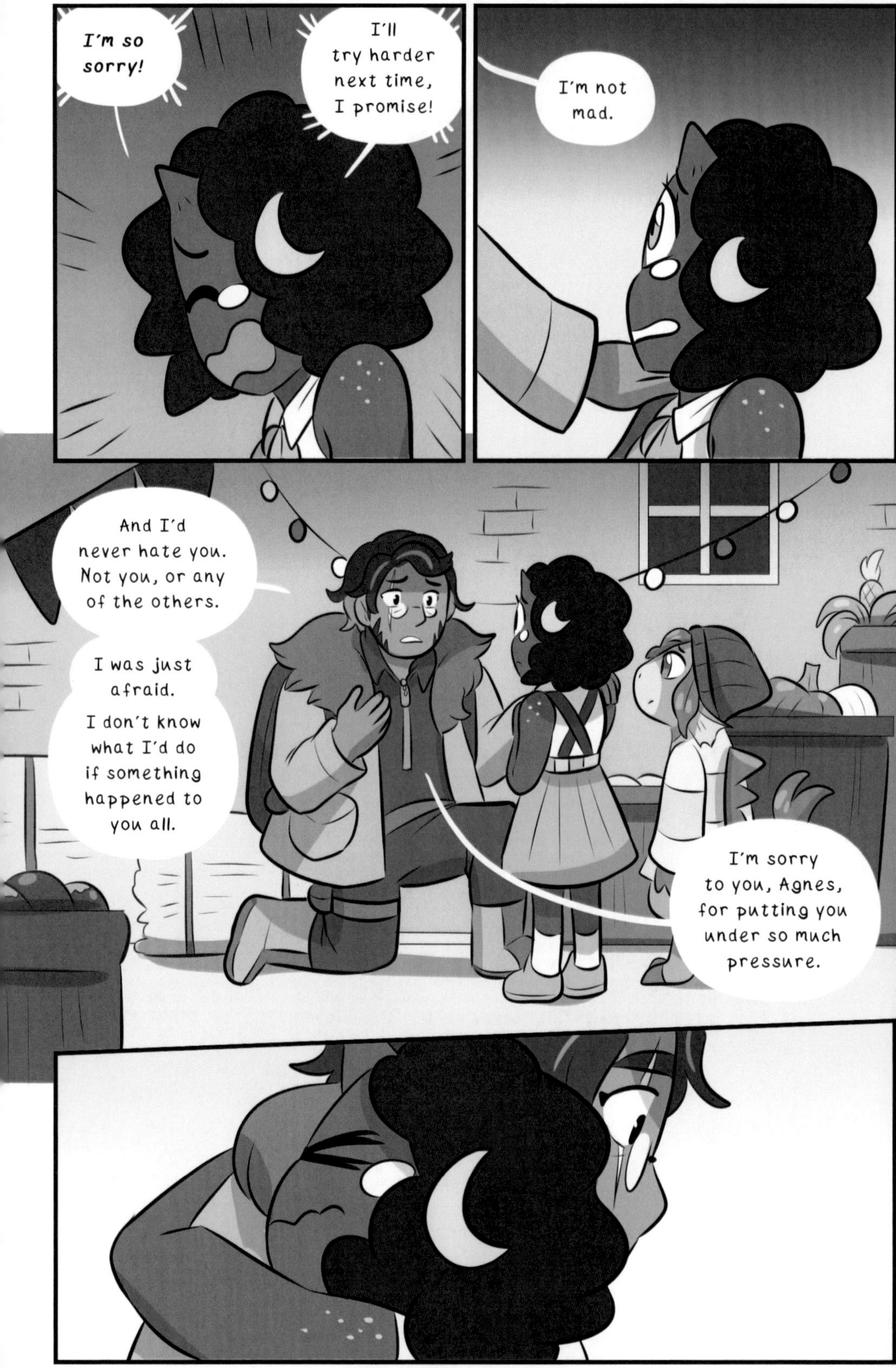
I'm so sorry!
I'll try harder next time, I promise!
I'm not mad.
And I'd never hate you. Not you, or any of the others.
I was just afraid.
I don't know what I'd do if something happened to you all.
I'm sorry to you, Agnes, for putting you under so much pressure.

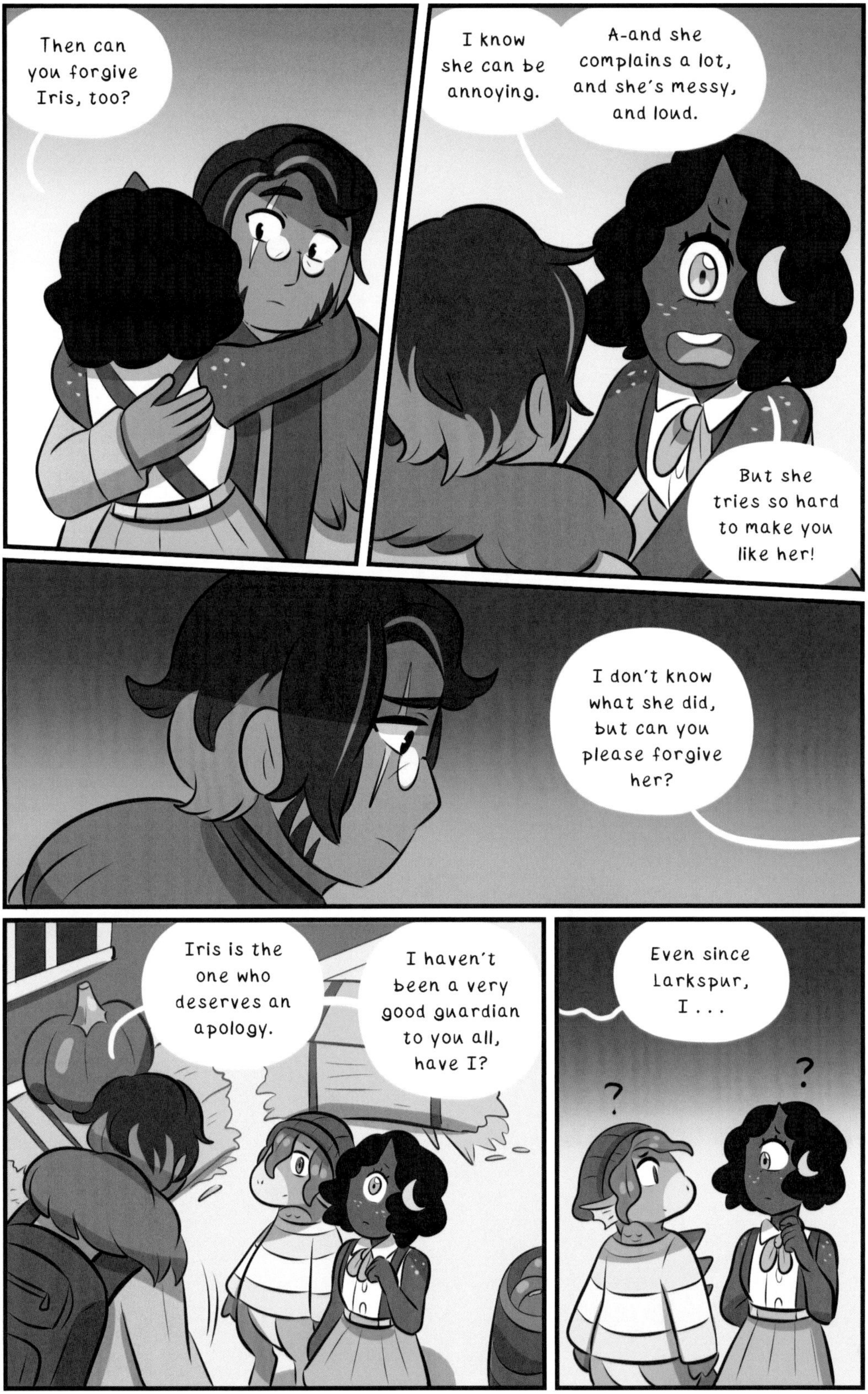
Then can you forgive Iris, too?
I know she can be annoying.
A-and she complains a lot, and she's messy, and loud.
But she tries so hard to make you like her!
I don't know what she did, but can you please forgive her?
Iris is the one who deserves an apology.
I haven't been a very good guardian to you all, have I?
Even since Larkspur, I . . .
?
?

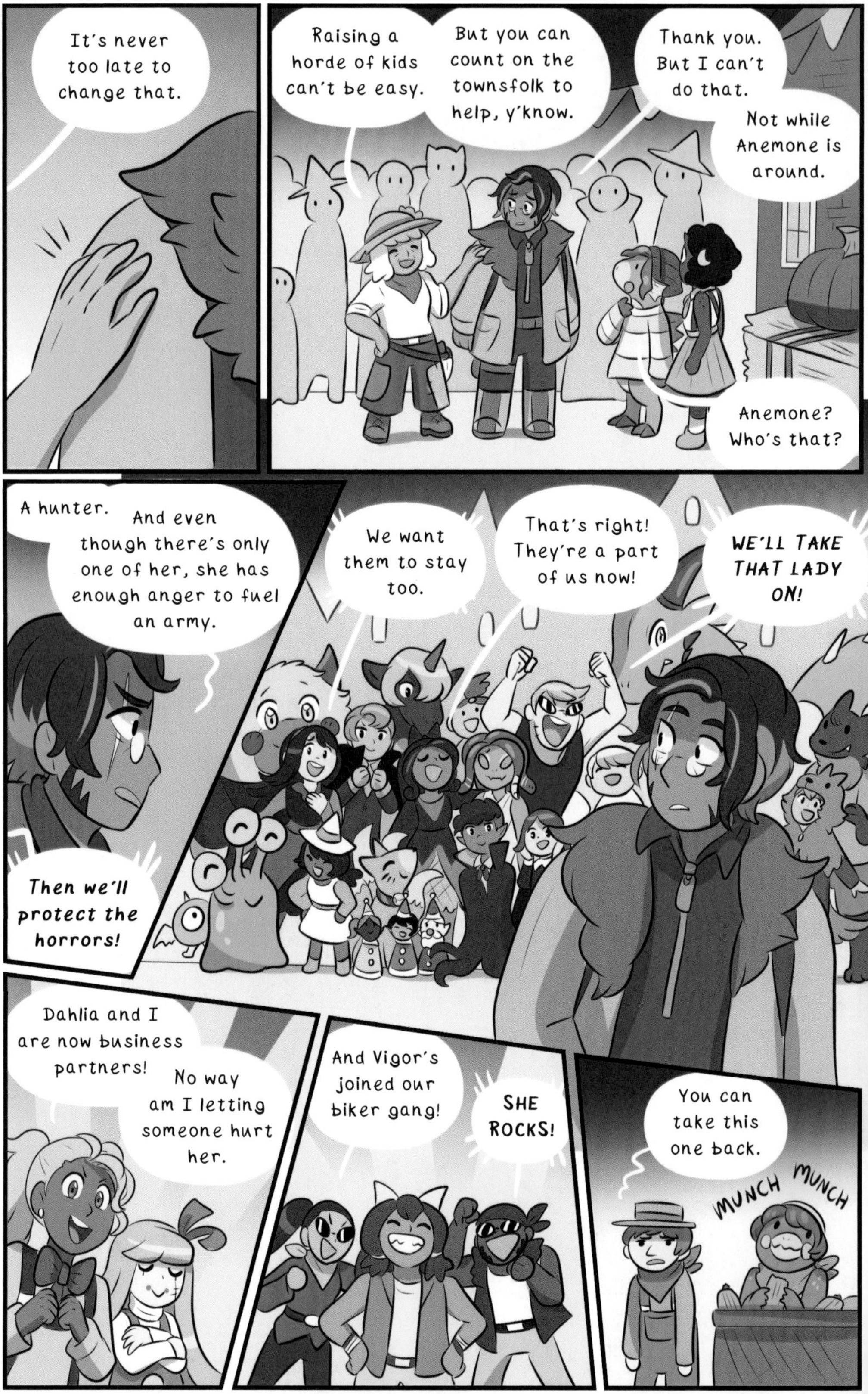
It's never too late to change that.
Raising a horde of kids can't be easy.
But you can count on the townsfolk to help, y'know.
Thank you. But I can't do that.
Not while Anemone is around.
Anemone? Who's that?
A hunter.
And even though there's only one of her, she has enough anger to fuel an army.
Then we'll protect the horrors!
We want them to stay too.
That's right! They're a part of us now!
WE'LL TAKE THAT LADY ON!
Dahlia and I are now business partners!
No way am I letting someone hurt her.
And Vigor's joined our biker gang!
SHE ROCKS!
You can take this one back.
MUNCH MUNCH

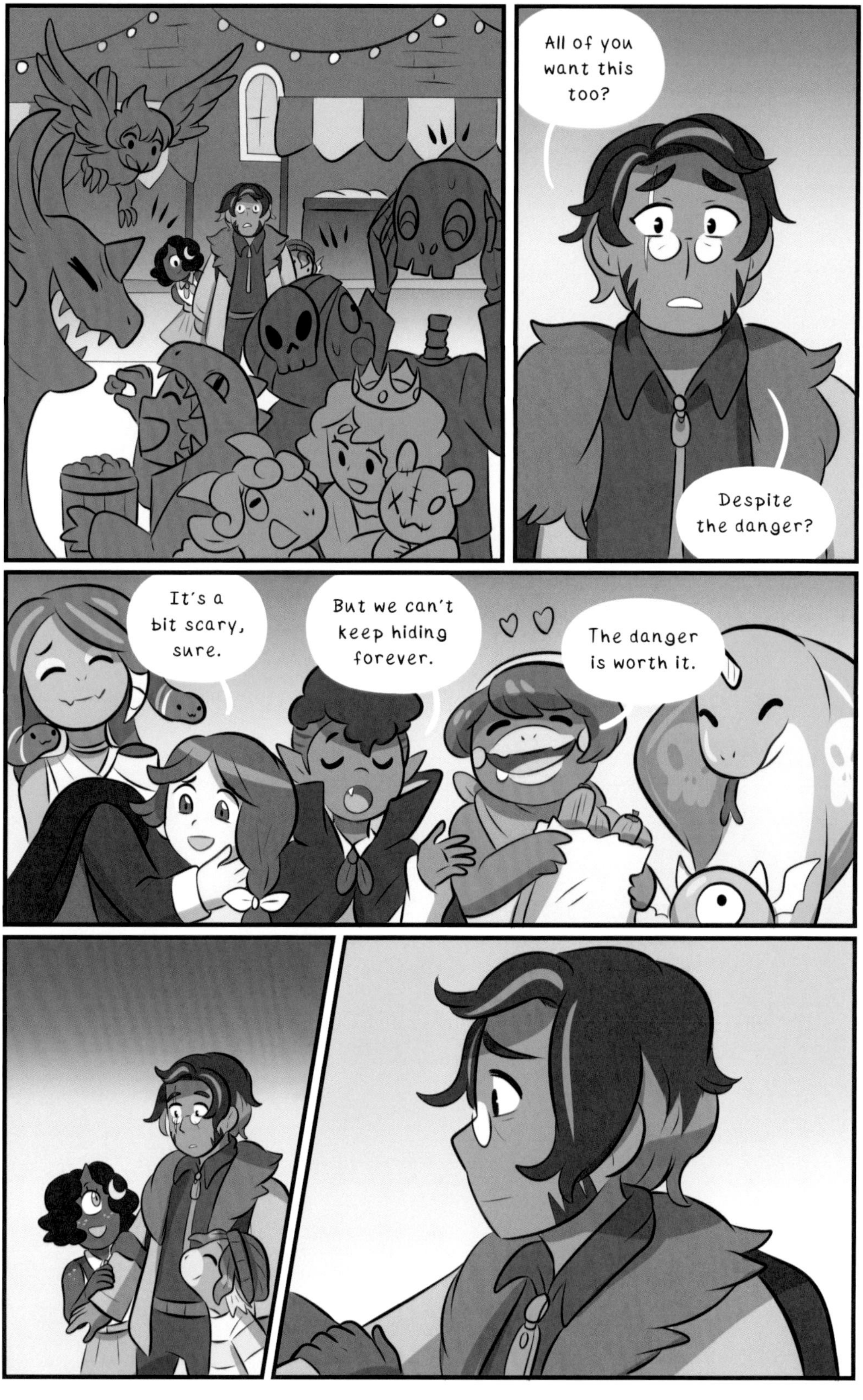
All of you want this too?
Despite the danger?
It's a bit scary, sure.
But we can't keep hiding forever.
The danger is worth it.

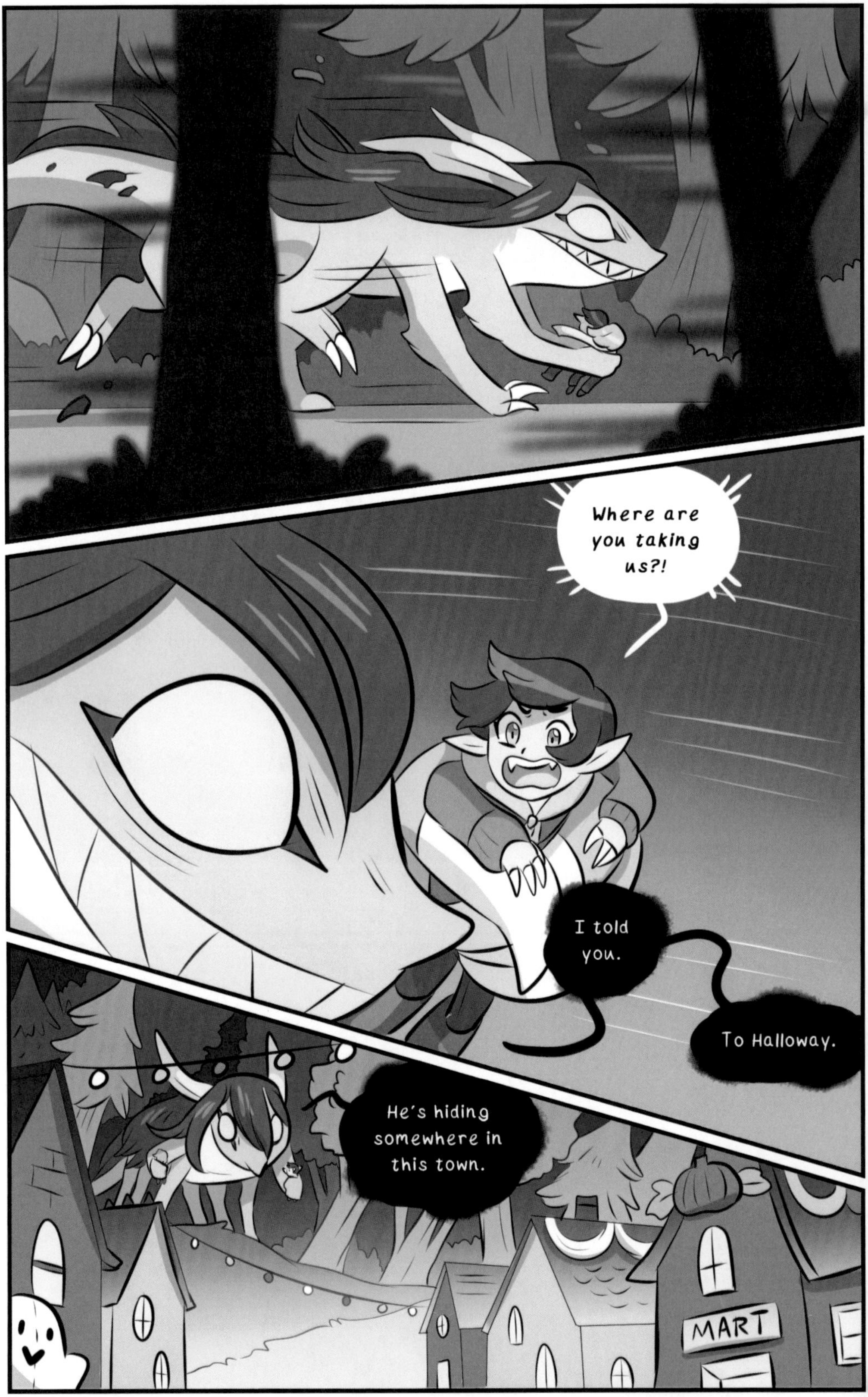
Where are you taking us?!
I told you.
To Halloway.
He's hiding somewhere in this town.
MART

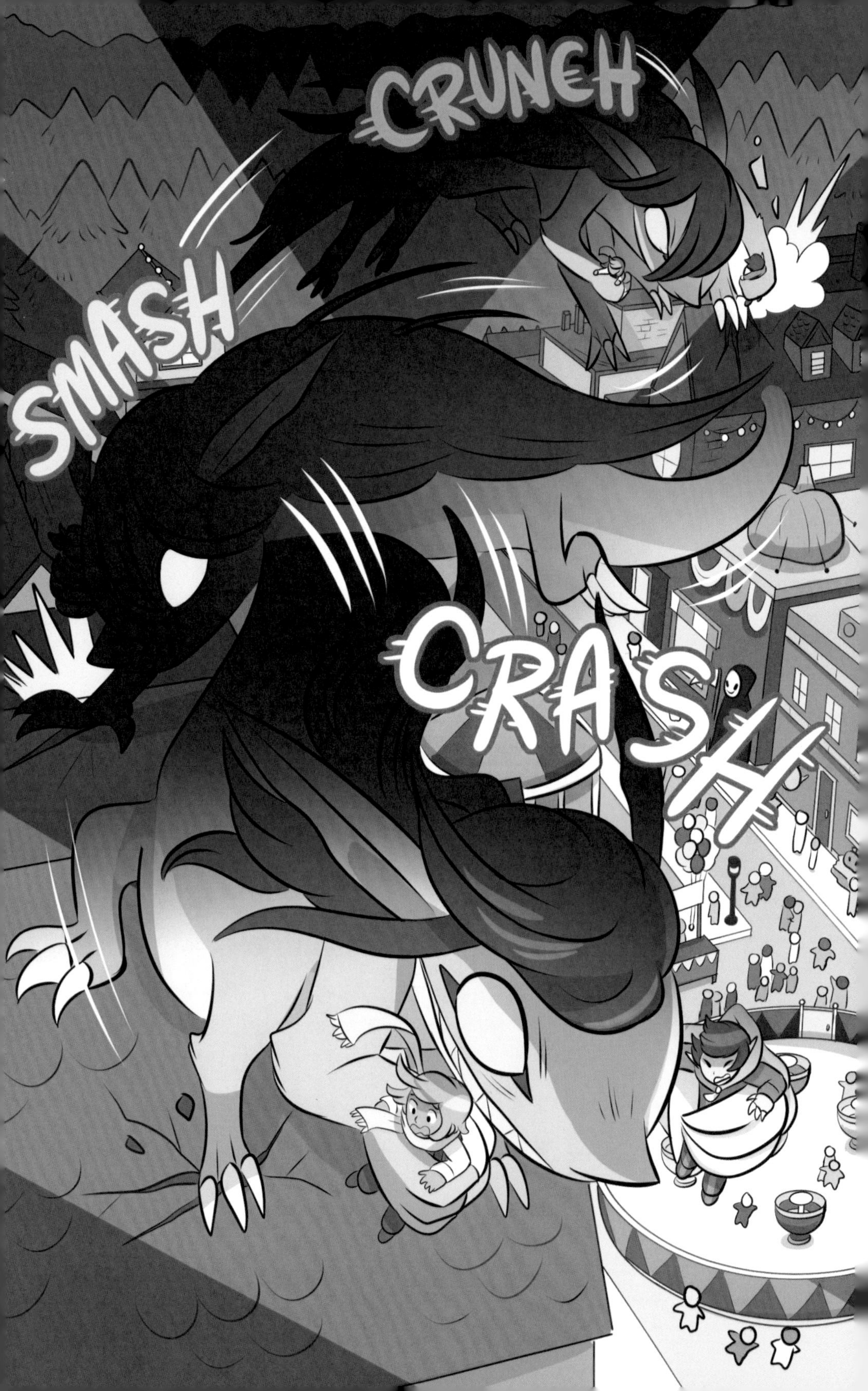
CRUNCH
SMASH
CRASH

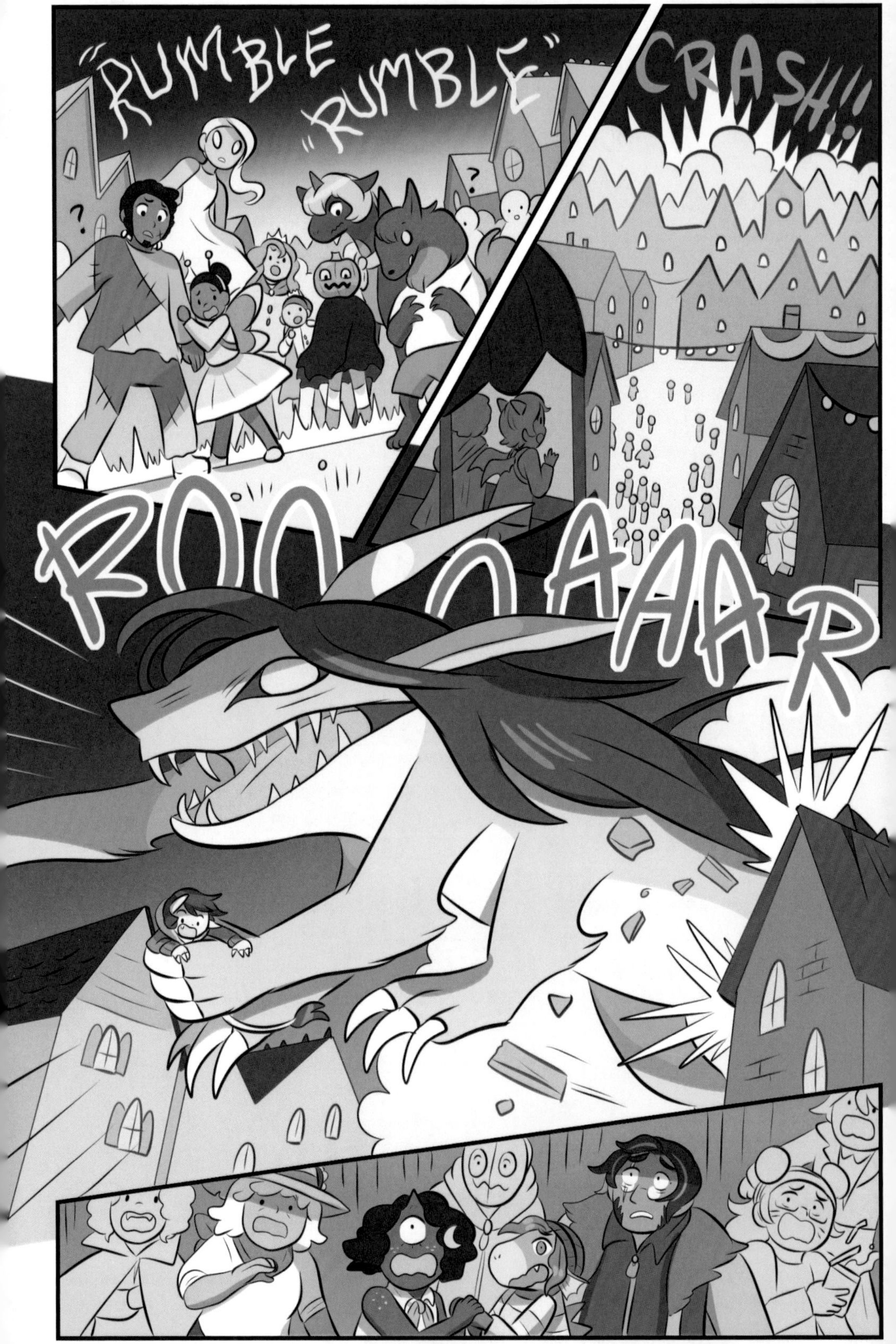

"RUMBLE
RUMBLE"
?
?
?
CRASH!!
ROOOOAAAR

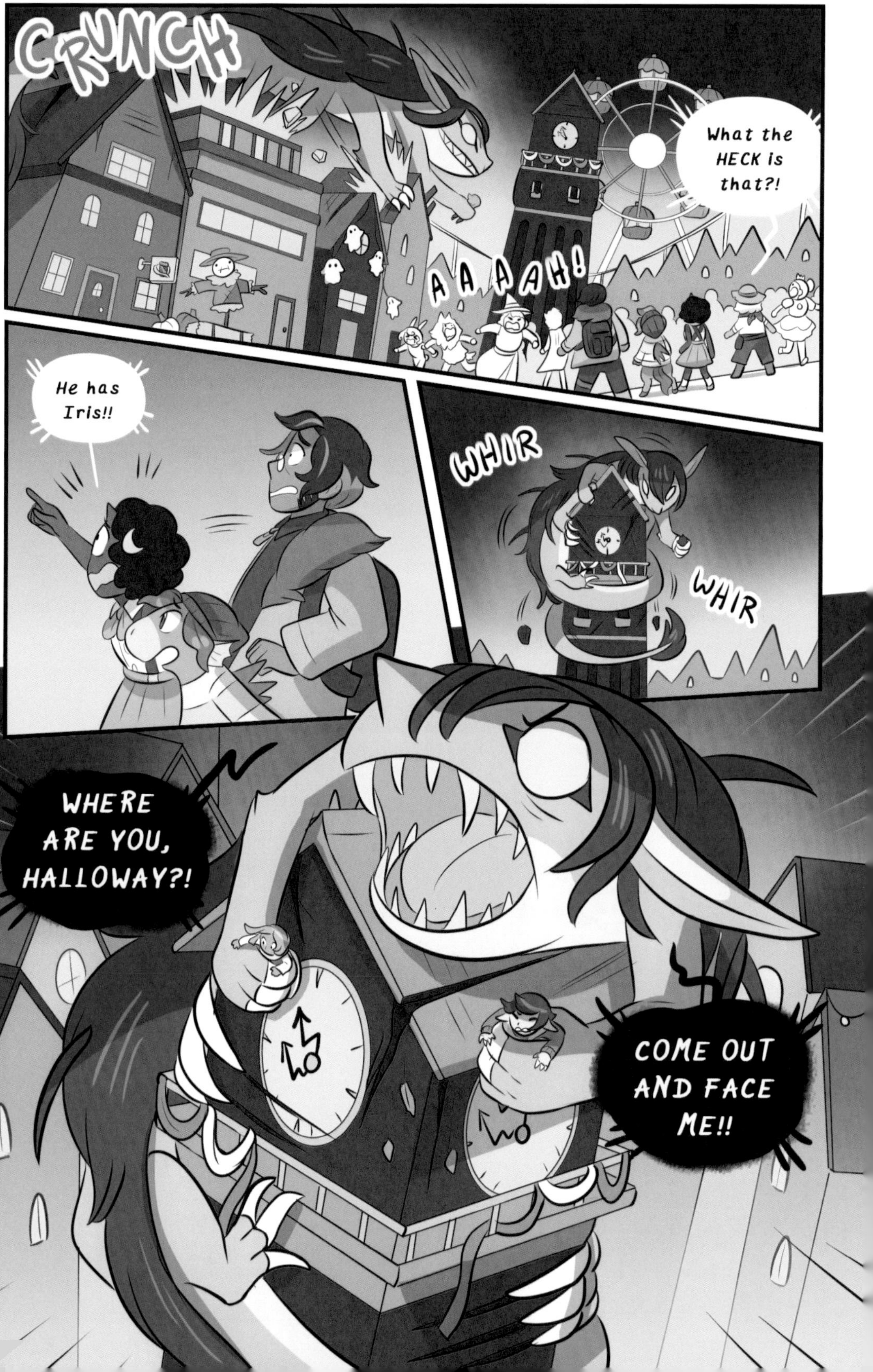
CRUNCH
What the HECK is that?!
AAAAH!
He has Iris!!
WHIR
WHIR
WHERE ARE YOU, HALLOWAY?!
COME OUT AND FACE ME!!

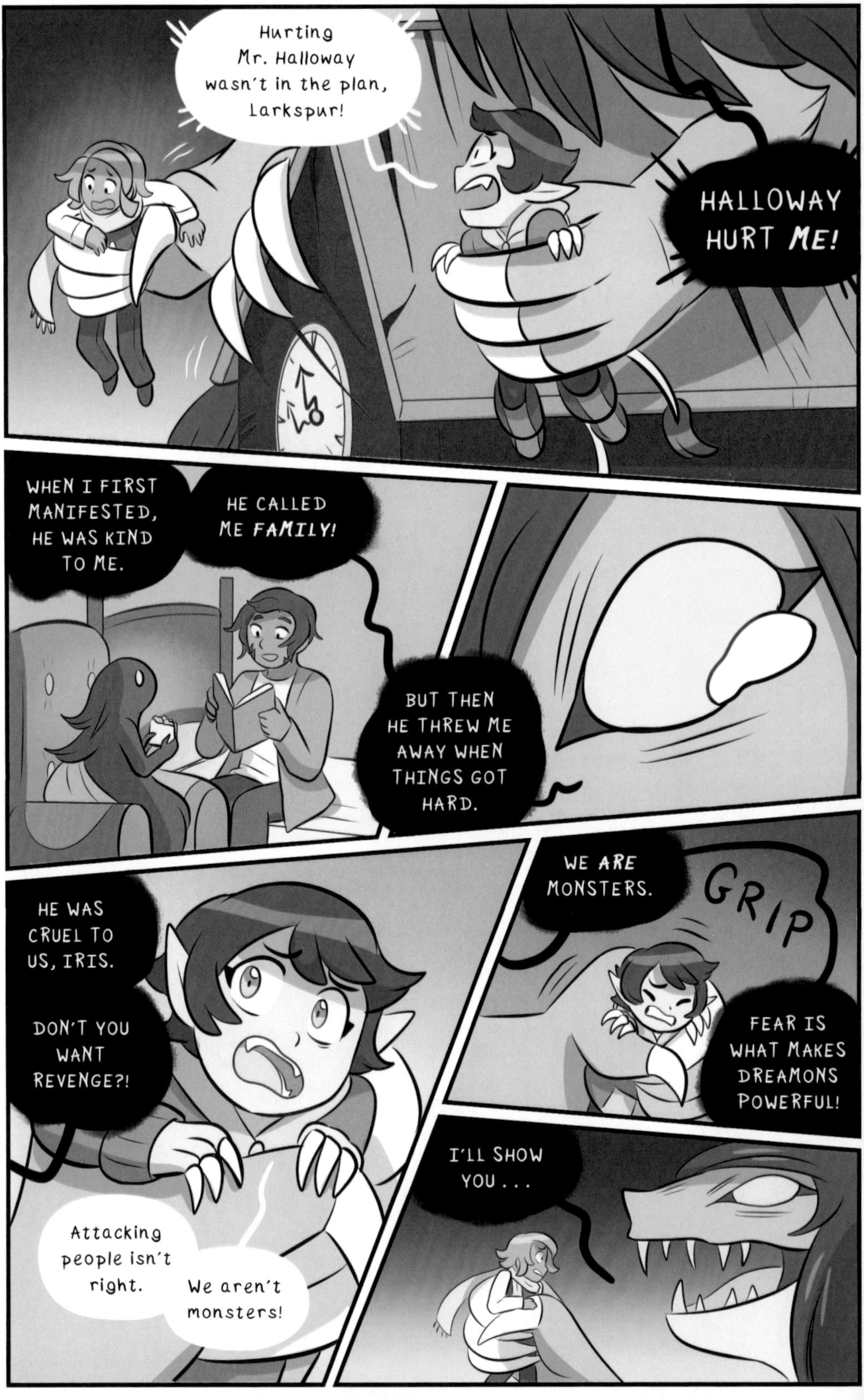
Hurting Mr. Halloway wasn't in the plan, Larkspur!
HALLOWAY HURT *ME!*
WHEN I FIRST MANIFESTED, HE WAS KIND TO ME.
HE CALLED ME *FAMILY!*
BUT THEN HE THREW ME AWAY WHEN THINGS GOT HARD.
HE WAS CRUEL TO US, IRIS.
DON'T YOU WANT REVENGE?!
Attacking people isn't right.
We aren't monsters!
WE *ARE* MONSTERS.
GRIP
FEAR IS WHAT MAKES DREAMONS POWERFUL!
I'LL SHOW YOU . . .

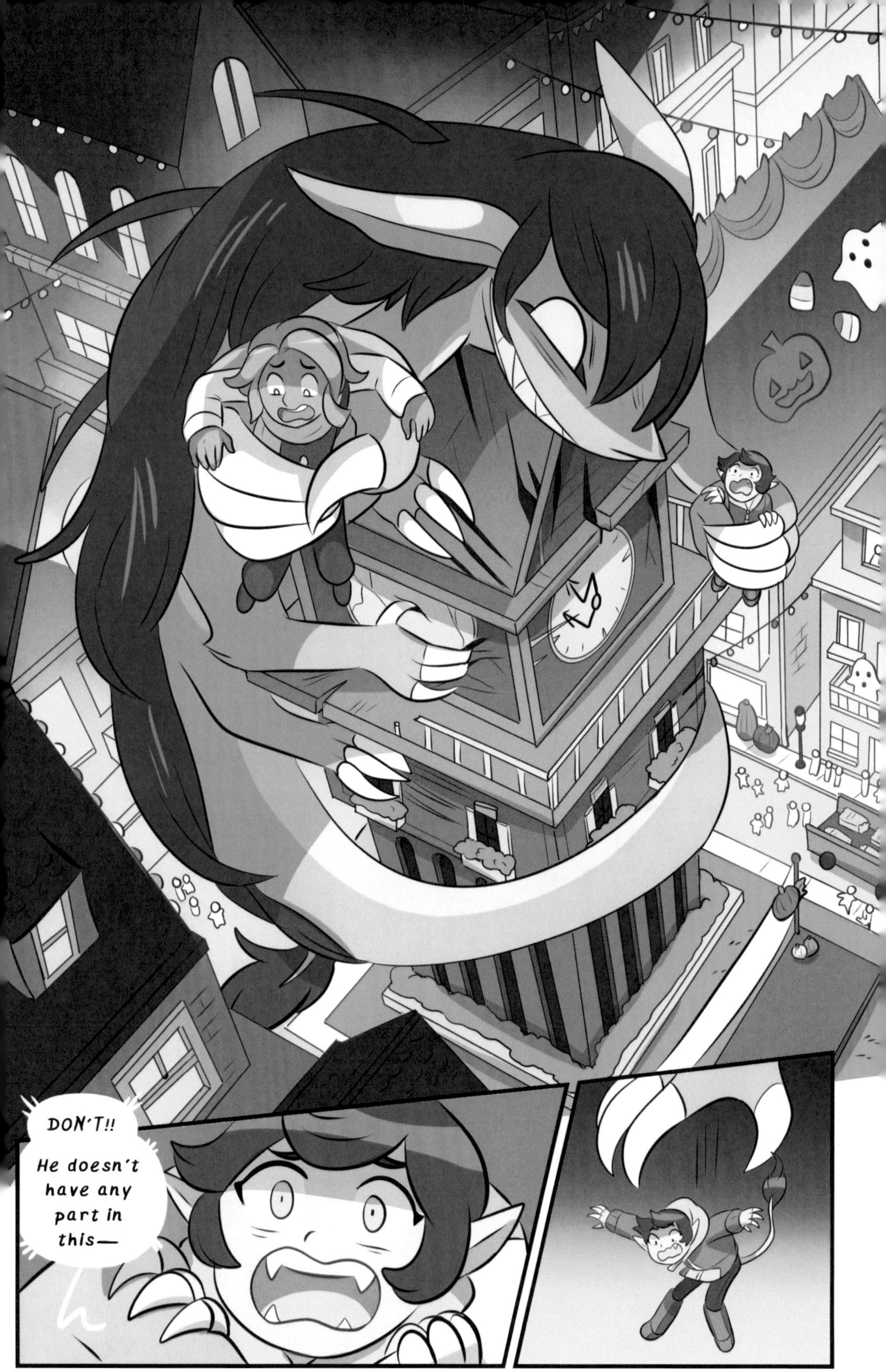
DON'T!!
He doesn't have any part in this—

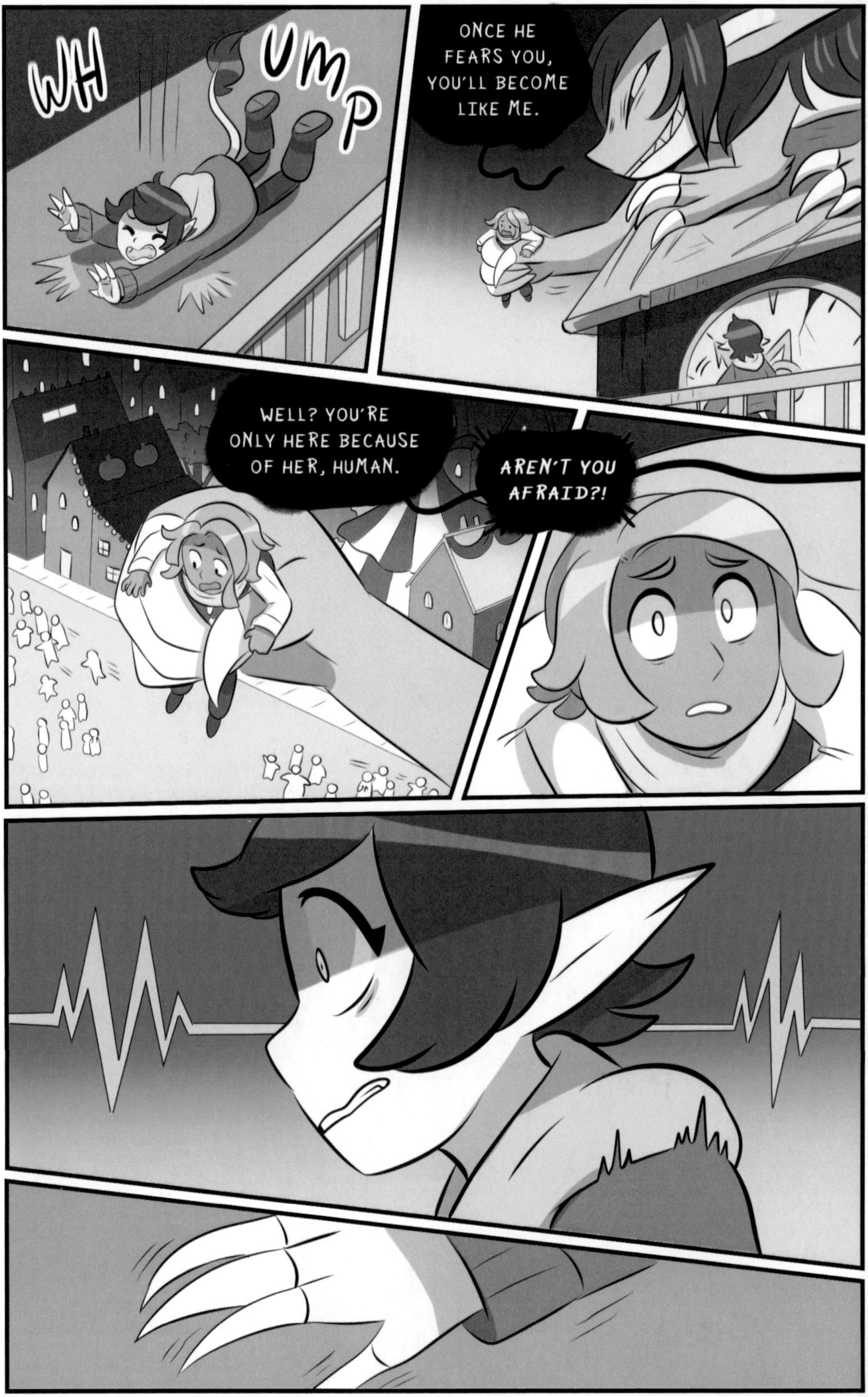
WH
UMP
ONCE HE FEARS YOU, YOU'LL BECOME LIKE ME.
WELL? YOU'RE ONLY HERE BECAUSE OF HER, HUMAN.
AREN'T YOU AFRAID?!

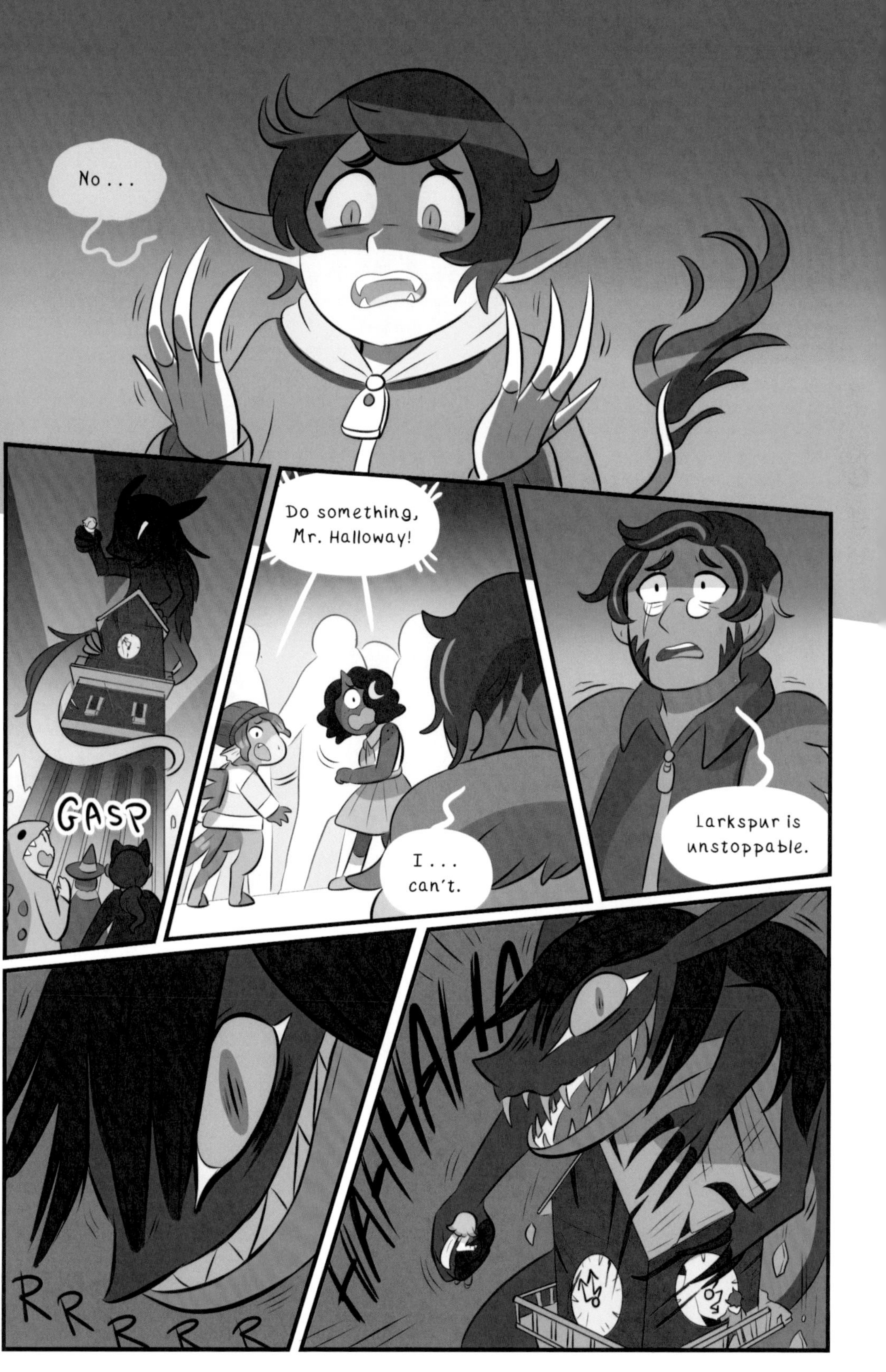
No . . .
GASP
Do something, Mr. Halloway!
I . . . can't.
Larkspur is unstoppable.
HAHAHAHA
RRRRRR

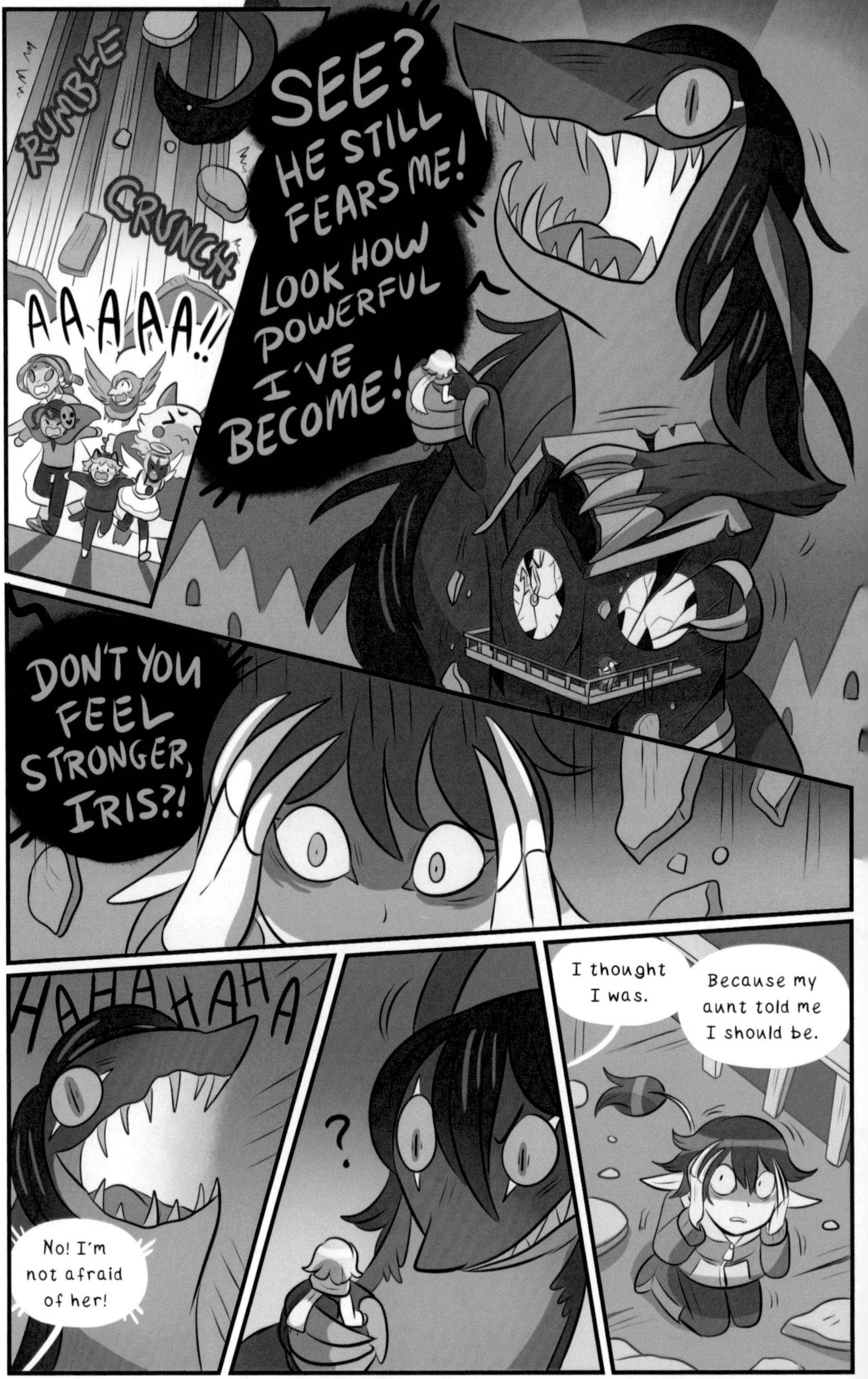
RUMBLE
CRUNCH
AAAAA!!
SEE? HE STILL FEARS ME! LOOK HOW POWERFUL I'VE BECOME!
DON'T YOU FEEL STRONGER, IRIS?!
HAHAHAHAHA
No! I'm not afraid of her!
?
I thought I was.
Because my aunt told me I should be.

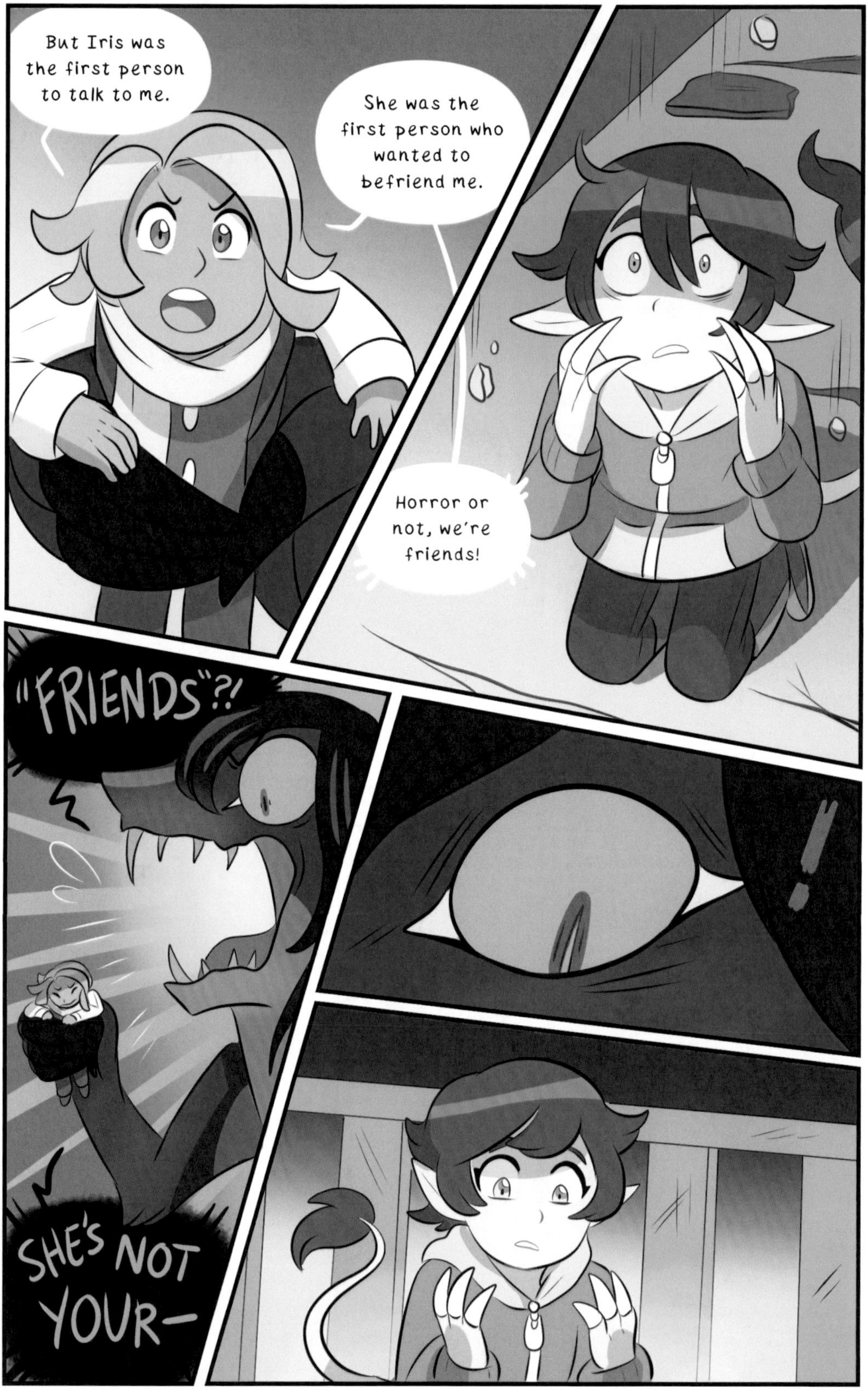
But Iris was the first person to talk to me.
She was the first person who wanted to befriend me.
Horror or not, we're friends!
"FRIENDS"?!
SHE'S NOT YOUR-
!

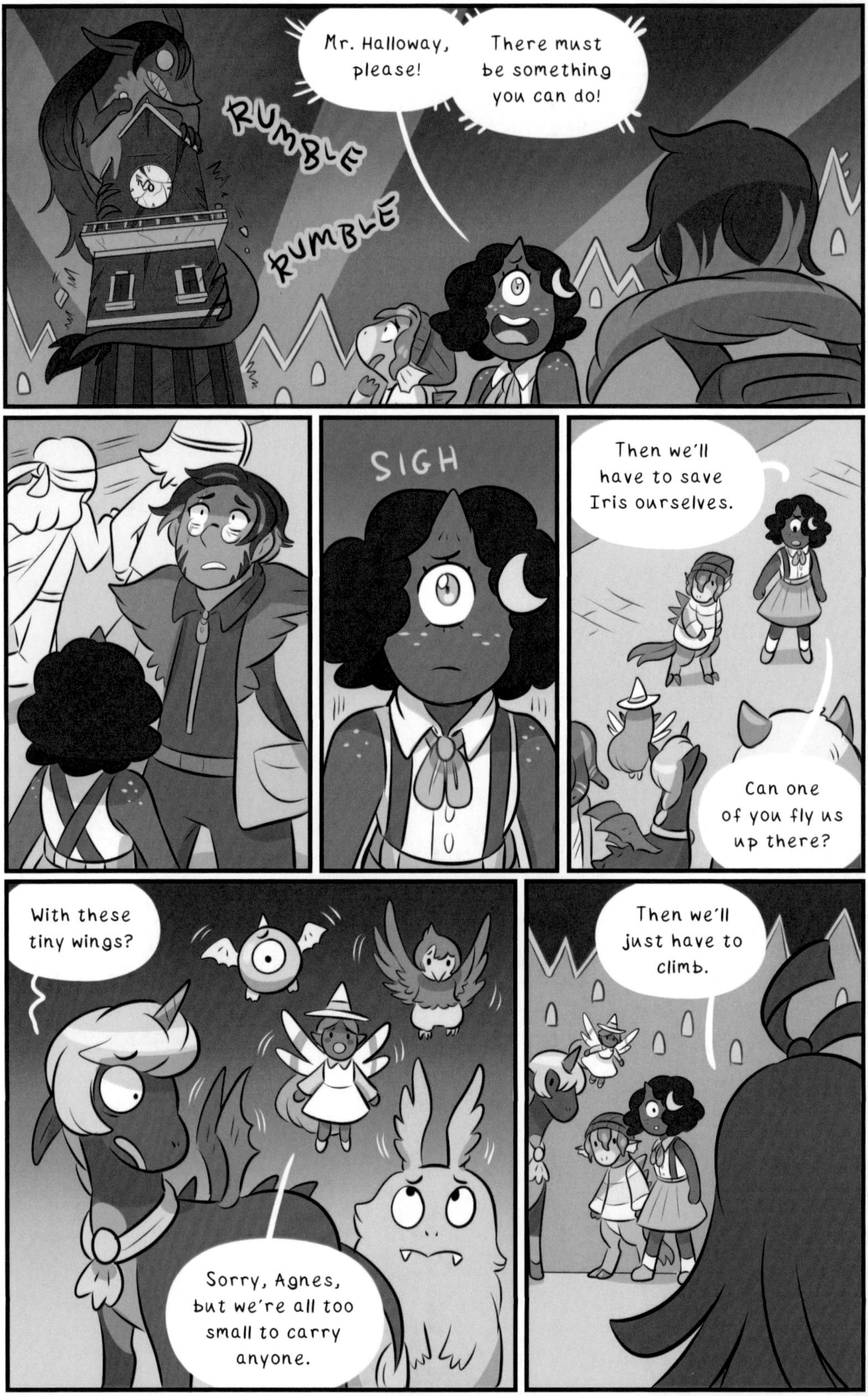
Mr. Halloway, please!
There must be something you can do!
RUMBLE
RUMBLE
SIGH
Then we'll have to save Iris ourselves.
Can one of you fly us up there?
With these tiny wings?
Sorry, Agnes, but we're all too small to carry anyone.
Then we'll just have to climb.

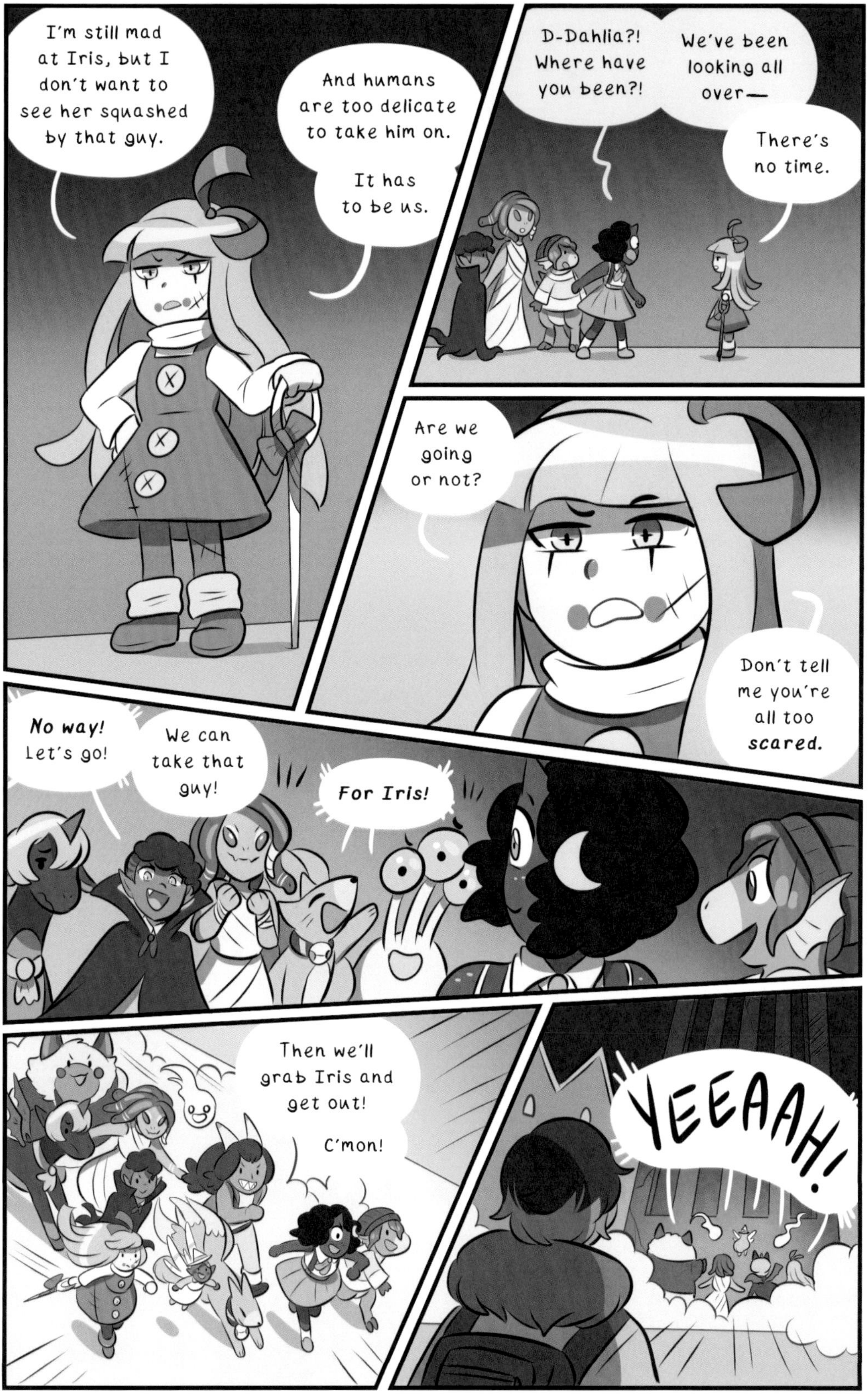
I'm still mad at Iris, but I don't want to see her squashed by that guy.
And humans are too delicate to take him on.
It has to be us.
D-Dahlia?! Where have you been?!
We've been looking all over—
There's no time.
Are we going or not?
Don't tell me you're all too *scared.*
No way! Let's go!
We can take that guy!
For Iris!
Then we'll grab Iris and get out!
C'mon!
YEEAAH!

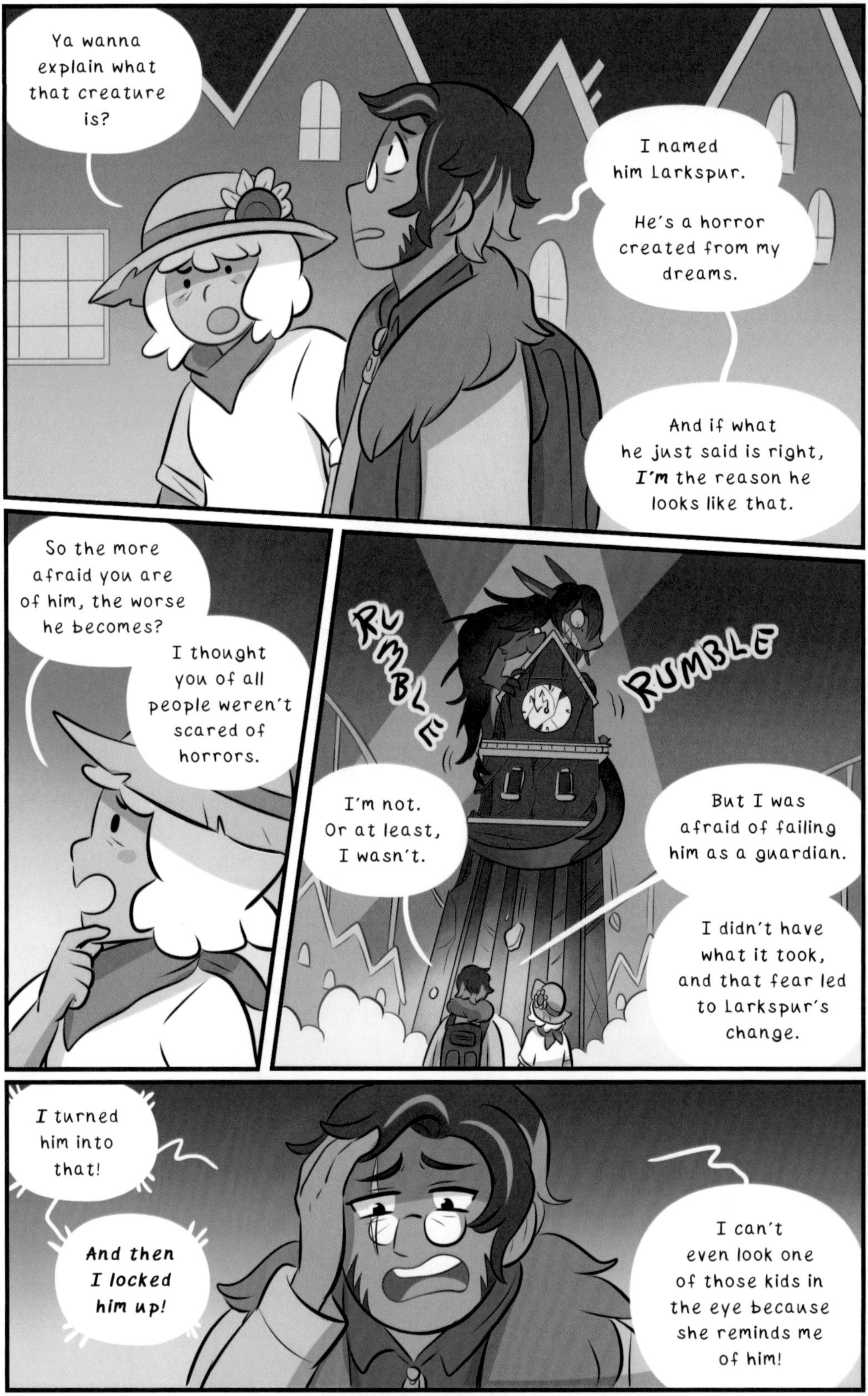
Ya wanna explain what that creature is?
I named him Larkspur.
He's a horror created from my dreams.
And if what he just said is right, *I'm* the reason he looks like that.
So the more afraid you are of him, the worse he becomes?
I thought you of all people weren't scared of horrors.
RUMBLE
RUMBLE
I'm not. Or at least, I wasn't.
But I was afraid of failing him as a guardian.
I didn't have what it took, and that fear led to Larkspur's change.
I turned him into that!
And then I locked him up!
I can't even look one of those kids in the eye because she reminds me of him!

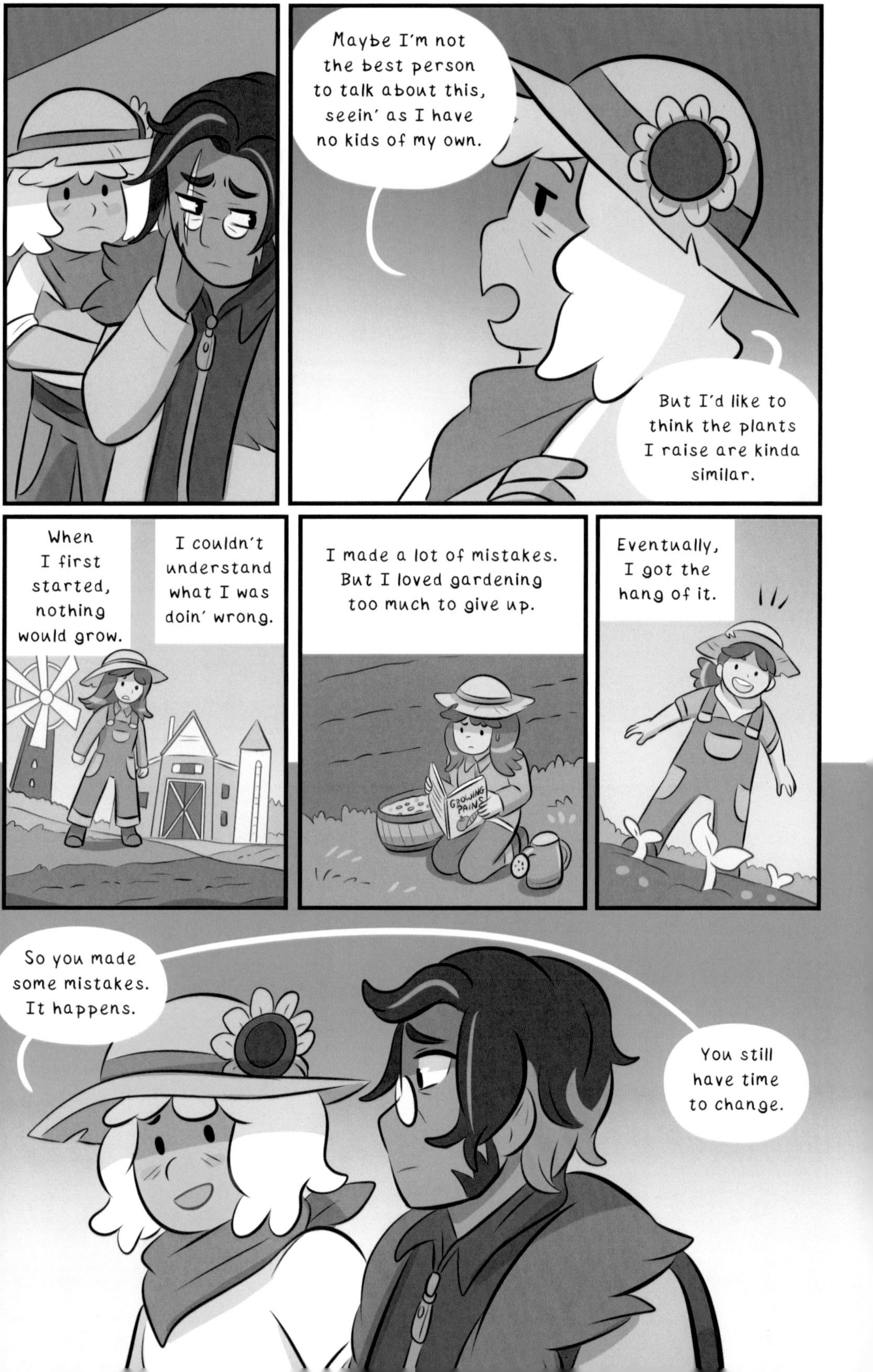
Maybe I'm not the best person to talk about this, seein' as I have no kids of my own.
But I'd like to think the plants I raise are kinda similar.
When I first started, nothing would grow.
I couldn't understand what I was doin' wrong.
I made a lot of mistakes. But I loved gardening too much to give up.
GROWING PAINS
Eventually, I got the hang of it.
So you made some mistakes. It happens.
You still have time to change.

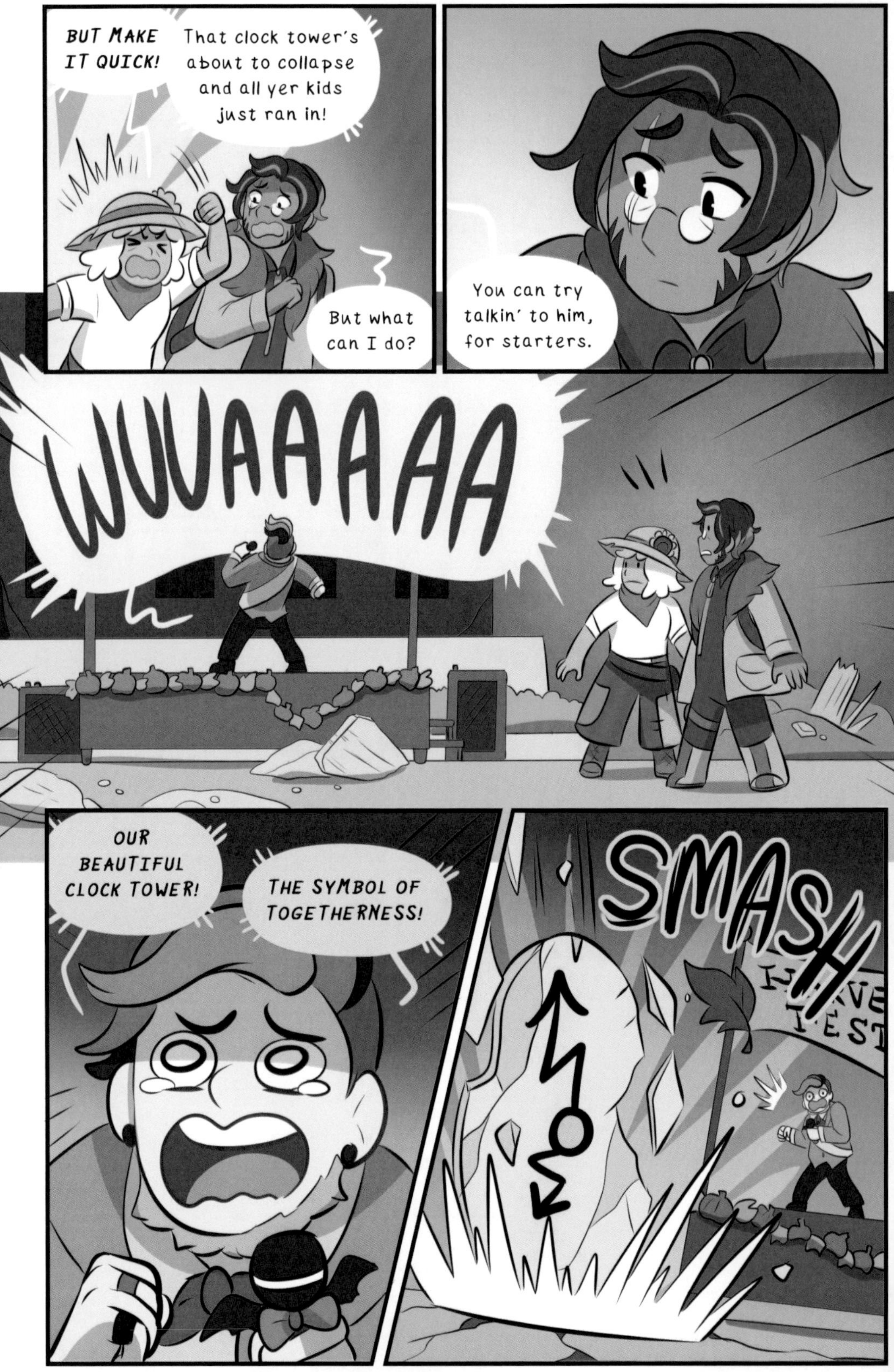

BUT MAKE IT QUICK!
That clock tower's about to collapse and all yer kids just ran in!
But what can I do?
You can try talkin' to him, for starters.
WUUAAAAAA
OUR BEAUTIFUL CLOCK TOWER!
THE SYMBOL OF TOGETHERNESS!
SMASH

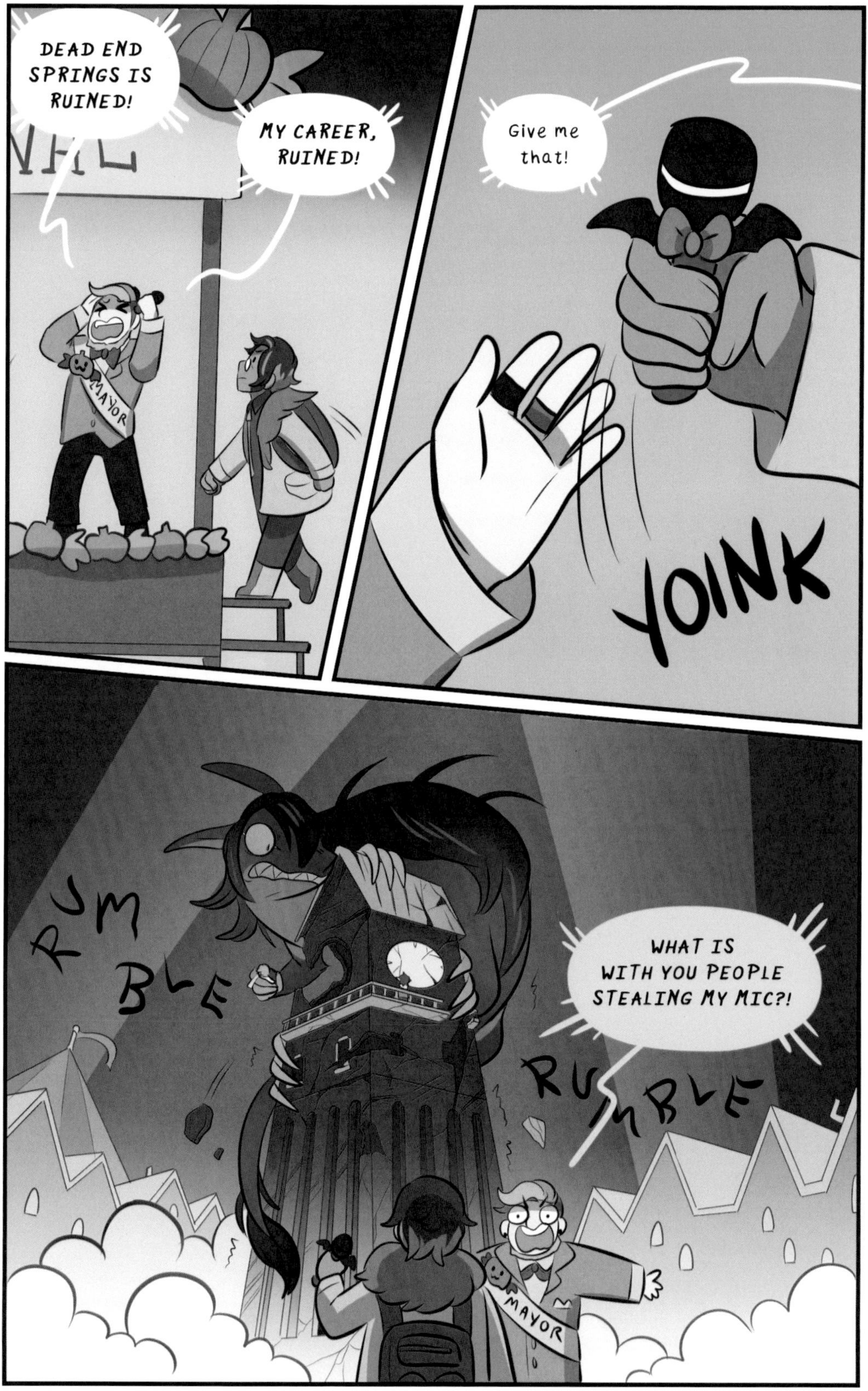
DEAD END SPRINGS IS RUINED!
MY CAREER, RUINED!
Give me that!
YOINK
RUM BLE
WHAT IS WITH YOU PEOPLE STEALING MY MIC?!
RUMBLE
MAYOR
MAYOR

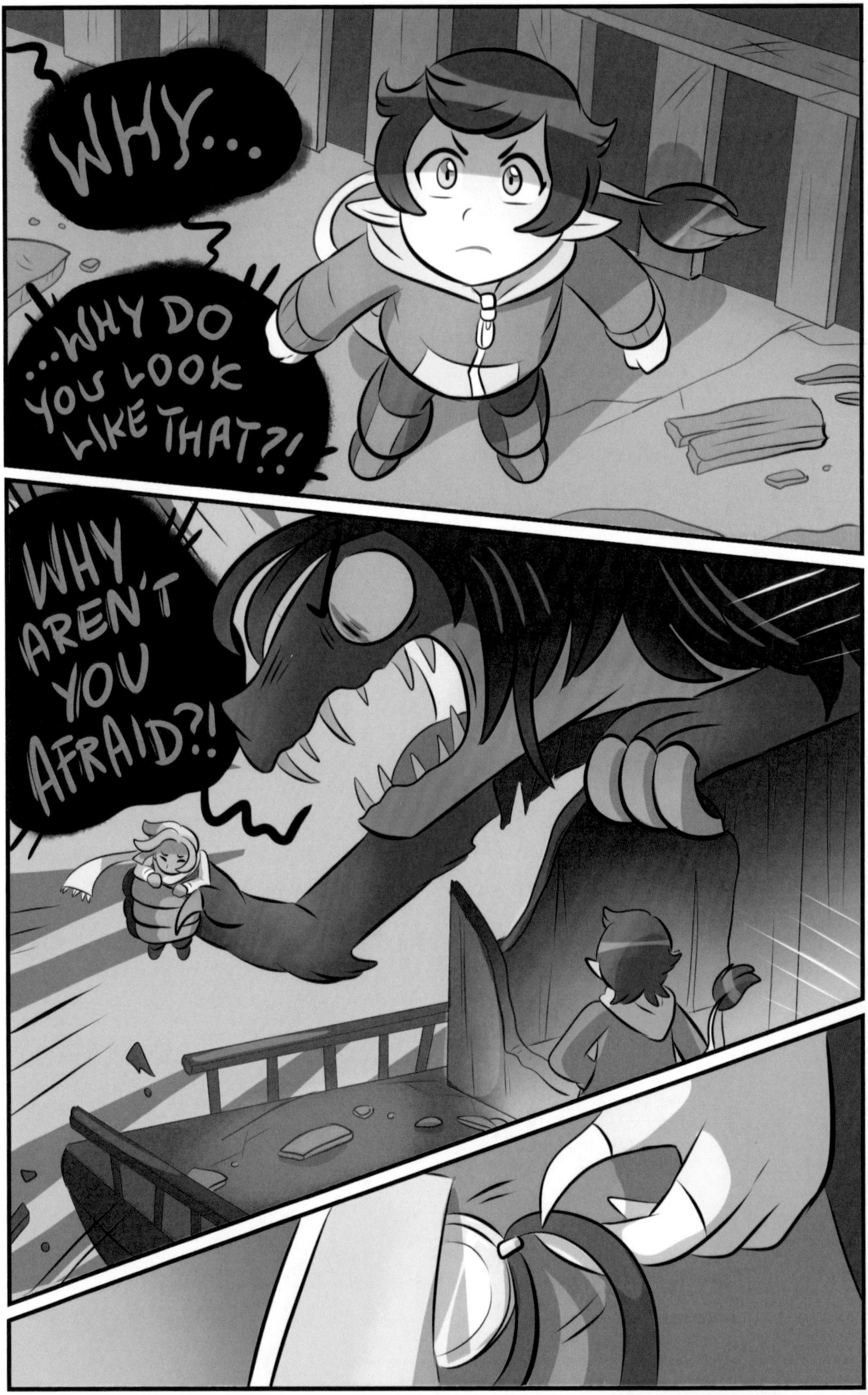
WHY...
...WHY DO YOU LOOK LIKE THAT?!
WHY AREN'T YOU AFRAID?!

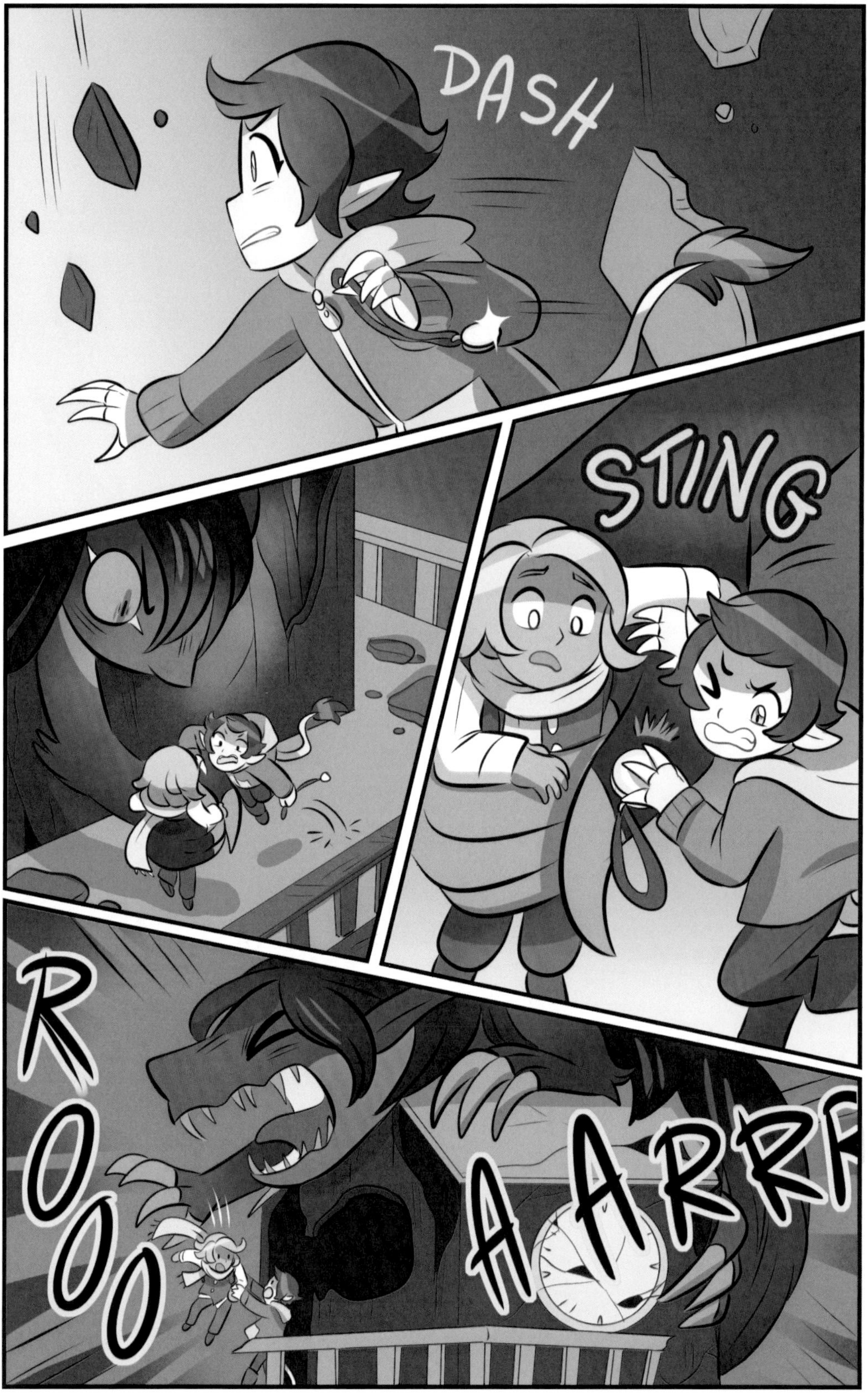
DASH
STING
ROOO
AARRR

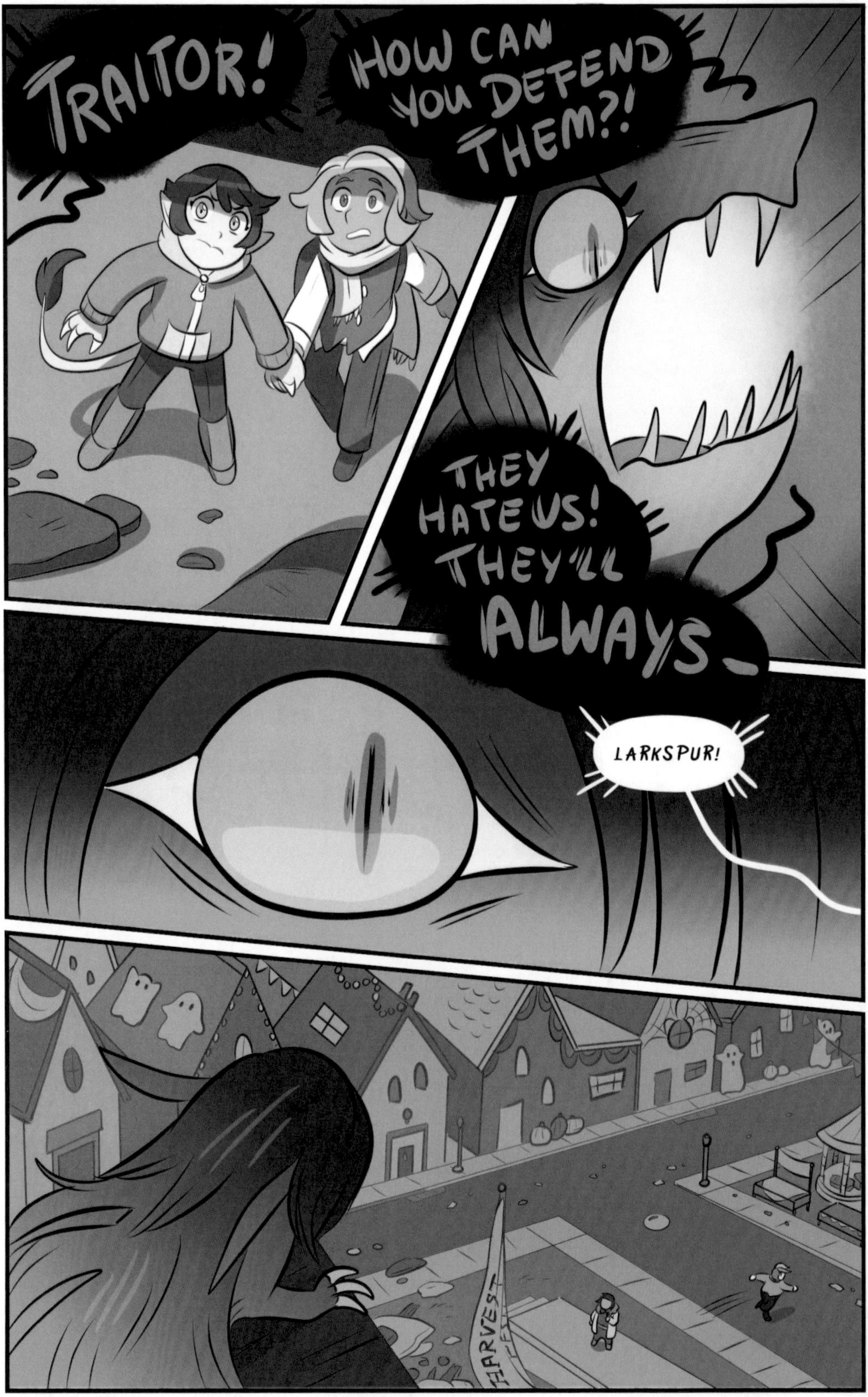
TRAITOR!
HOW CAN YOU DEFEND THEM?!
THEY HATE US! THEY'LL ALWAYS—
LARKSPUR!
HARVEST FEST

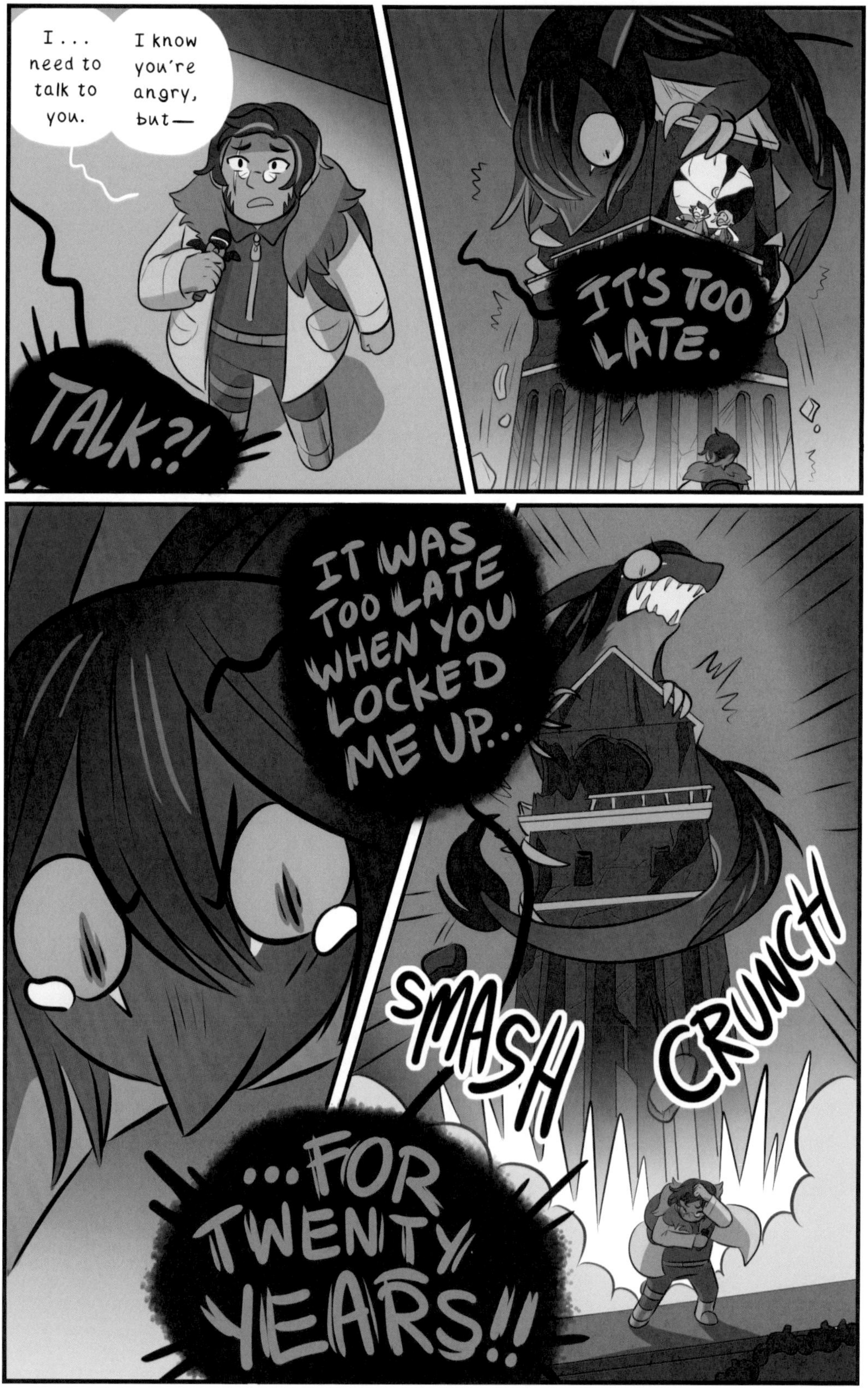
I . . . need to talk to you.
I know you're angry, but—
TALK?!
IT'S TOO LATE.
IT WAS TOO LATE WHEN YOU LOCKED ME UP...
SMASH
CRUNCH
...FOR TWENTY YEARS!!

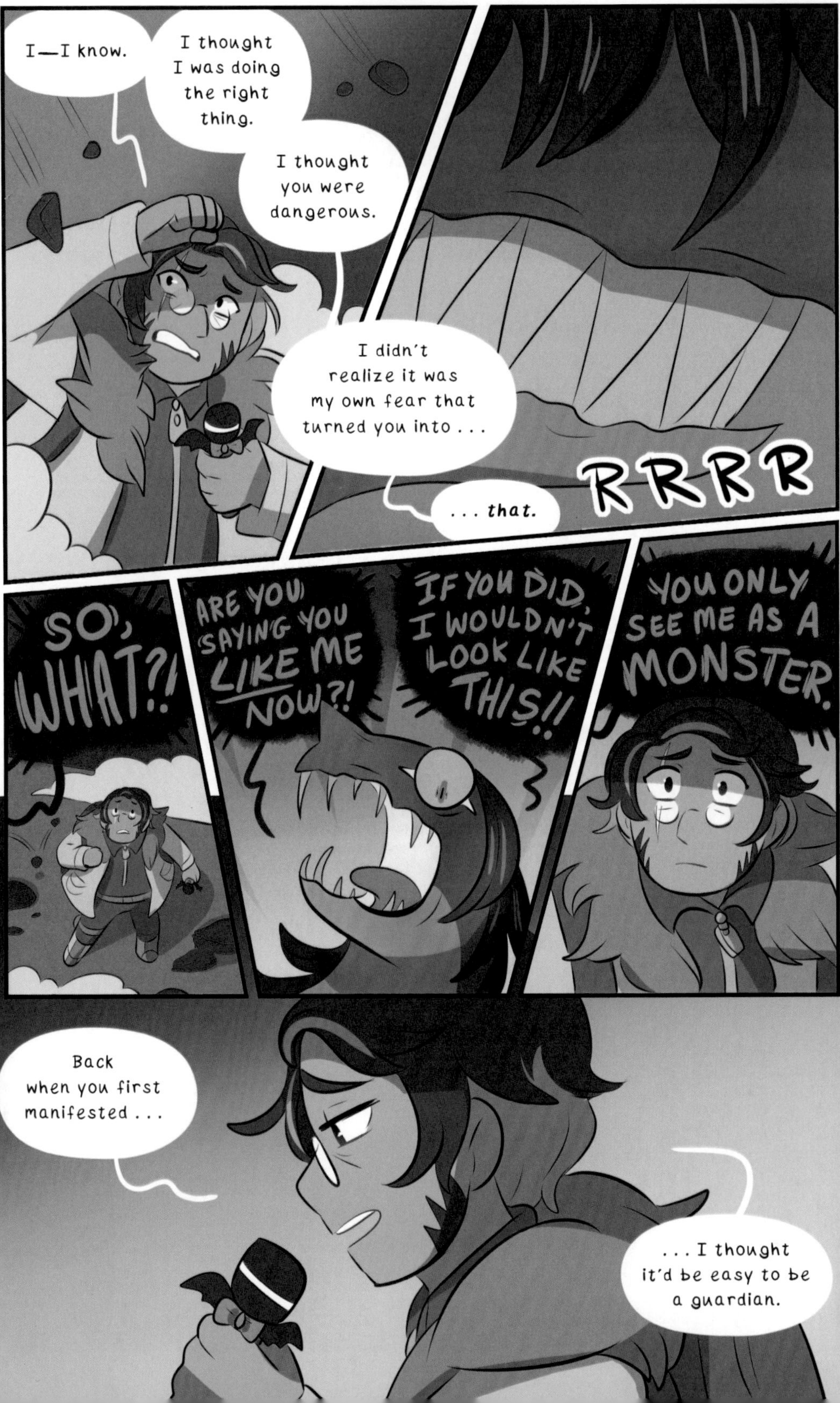
I—I know.
I thought I was doing the right thing.
I thought you were dangerous.
I didn't realize it was my own fear that turned you into . . .
. . . that.
RRRR
SO, WHAT?!
ARE YOU SAYING YOU LIKE ME NOW?!
IF YOU DID, I WOULDN'T LOOK LIKE THIS!!
YOU ONLY SEE ME AS A MONSTER.
Back when you first manifested . . .
. . . I thought it'd be easy to be a guardian.

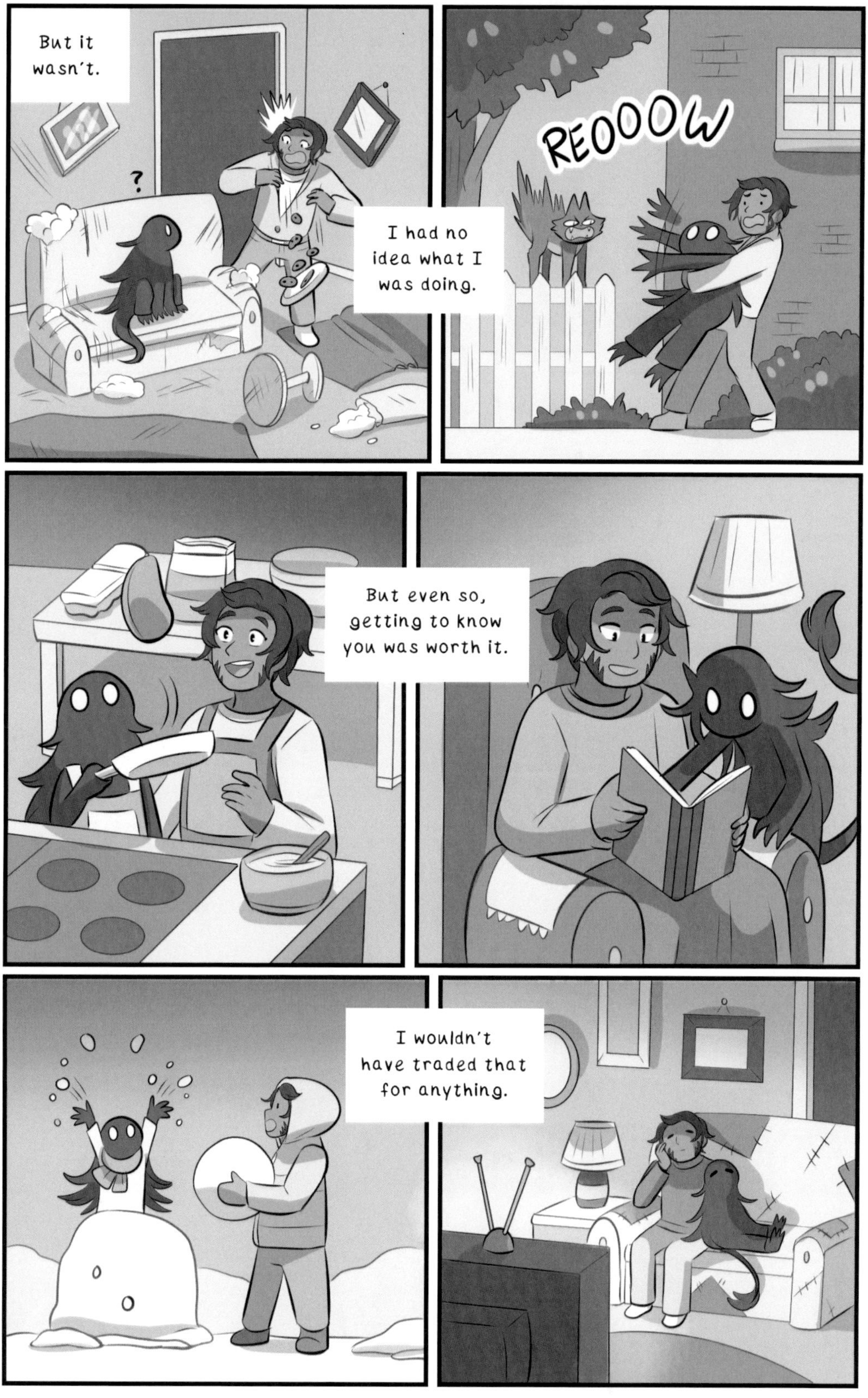
But it wasn't.
I had no idea what I was doing.
REOOOW
But even so, getting to know you was worth it.
I wouldn't have traded that for anything.

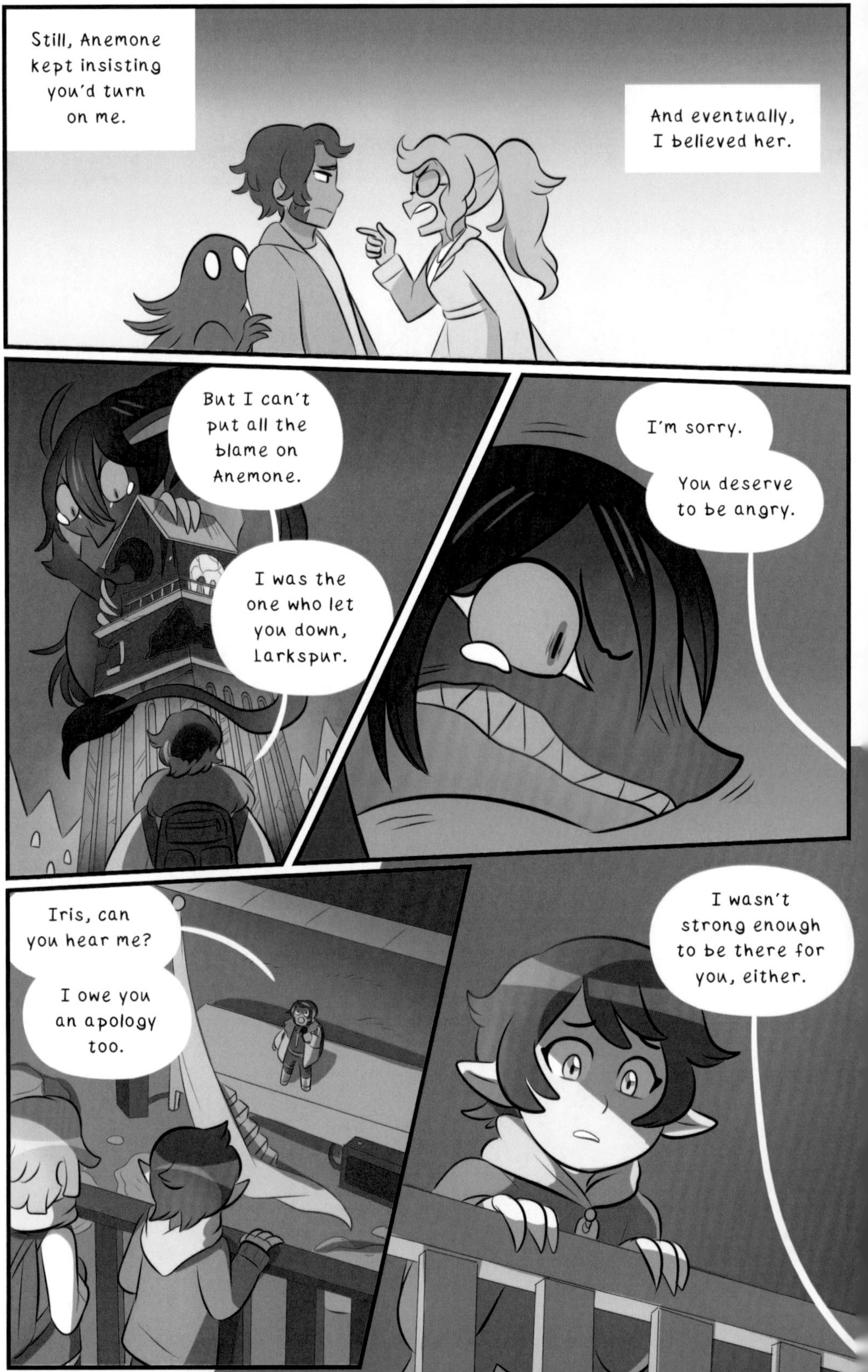
Still, Anemone kept insisting you'd turn on me.
And eventually, I believed her.
But I can't put all the blame on Anemone.
I was the one who let you down, Larkspur.
I'm sorry.
You deserve to be angry.
Iris, can you hear me?
I owe you an apology too.
I wasn't strong enough to be there for you, either.

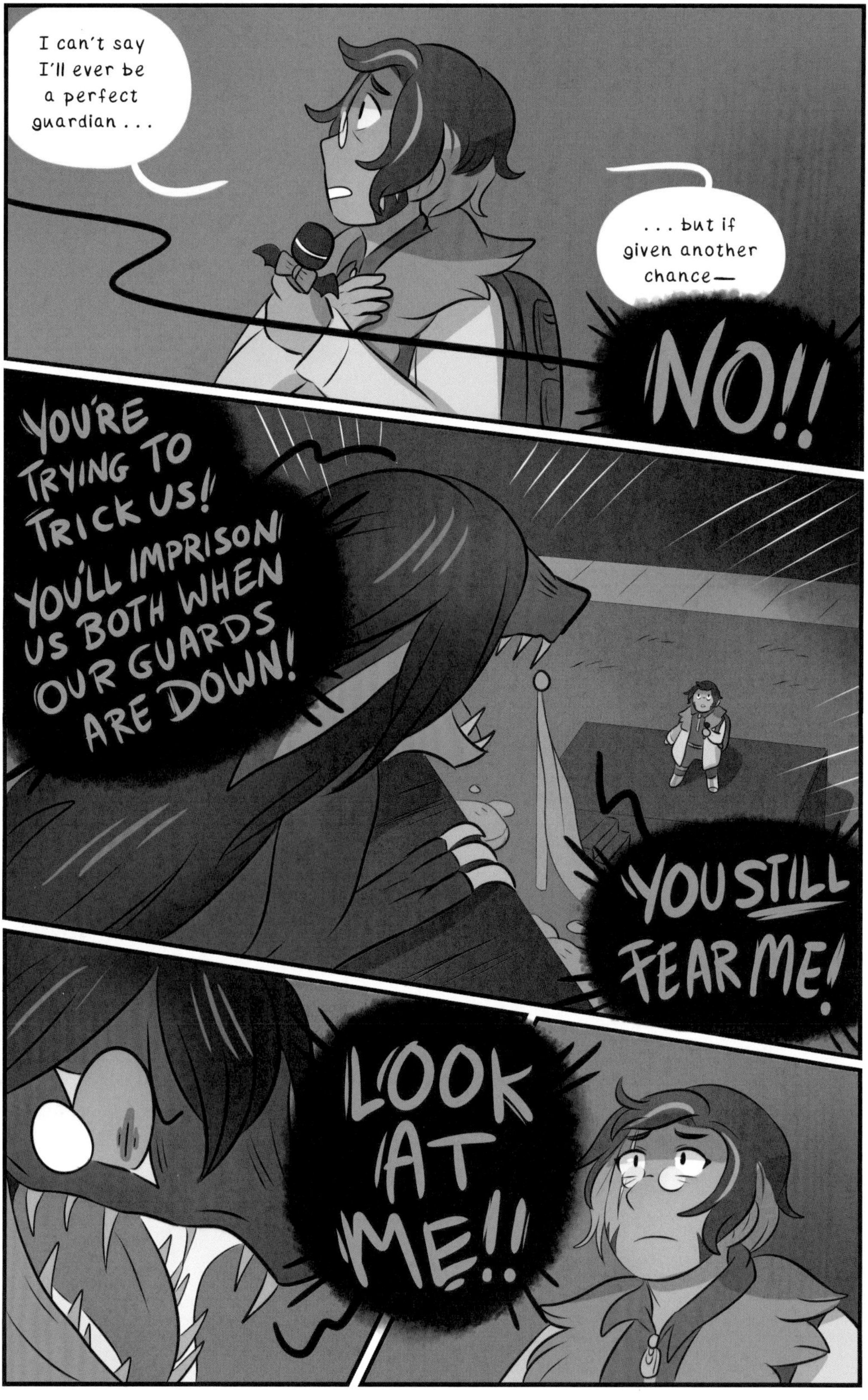
I can't say I'll ever be a perfect guardian . . .
. . . but if given another chance—
NO!!
YOU'RE TRYING TO TRICK US! YOU'LL IMPRISON US BOTH WHEN OUR GUARDS ARE DOWN!
YOU STILL FEAR ME!
LOOK AT ME!!

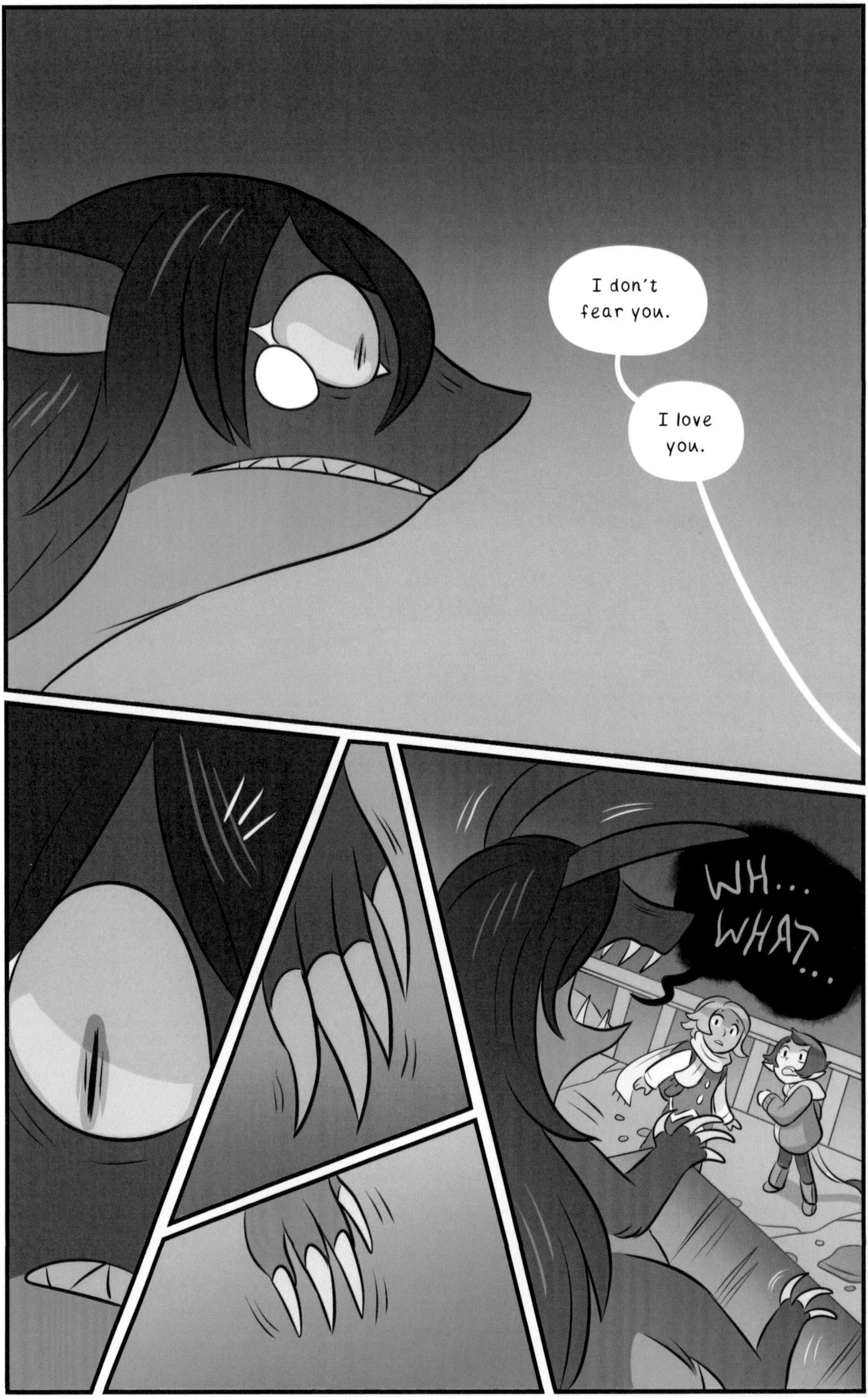
I don't fear you.
I love you.
WH... WHAT...

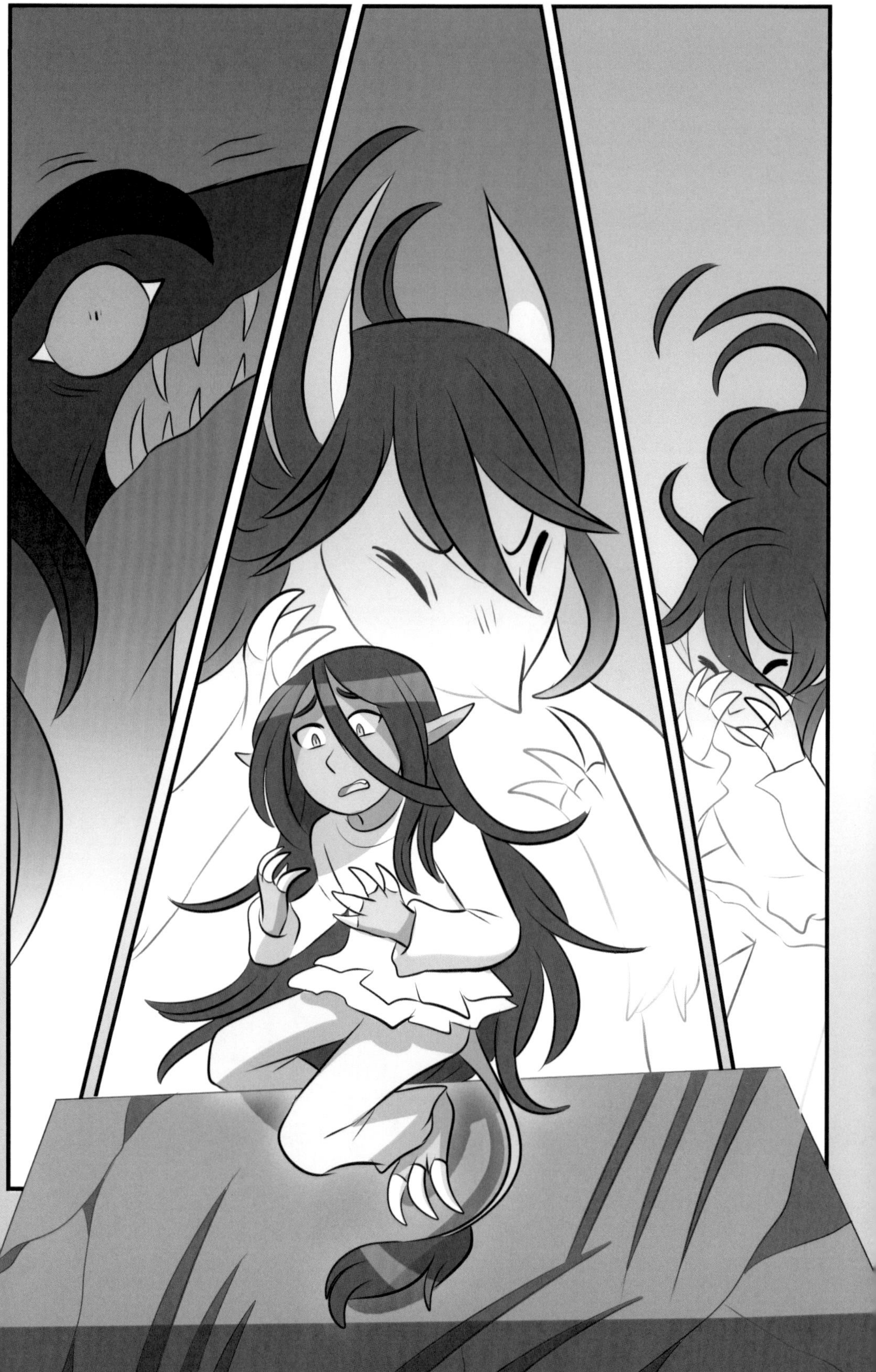

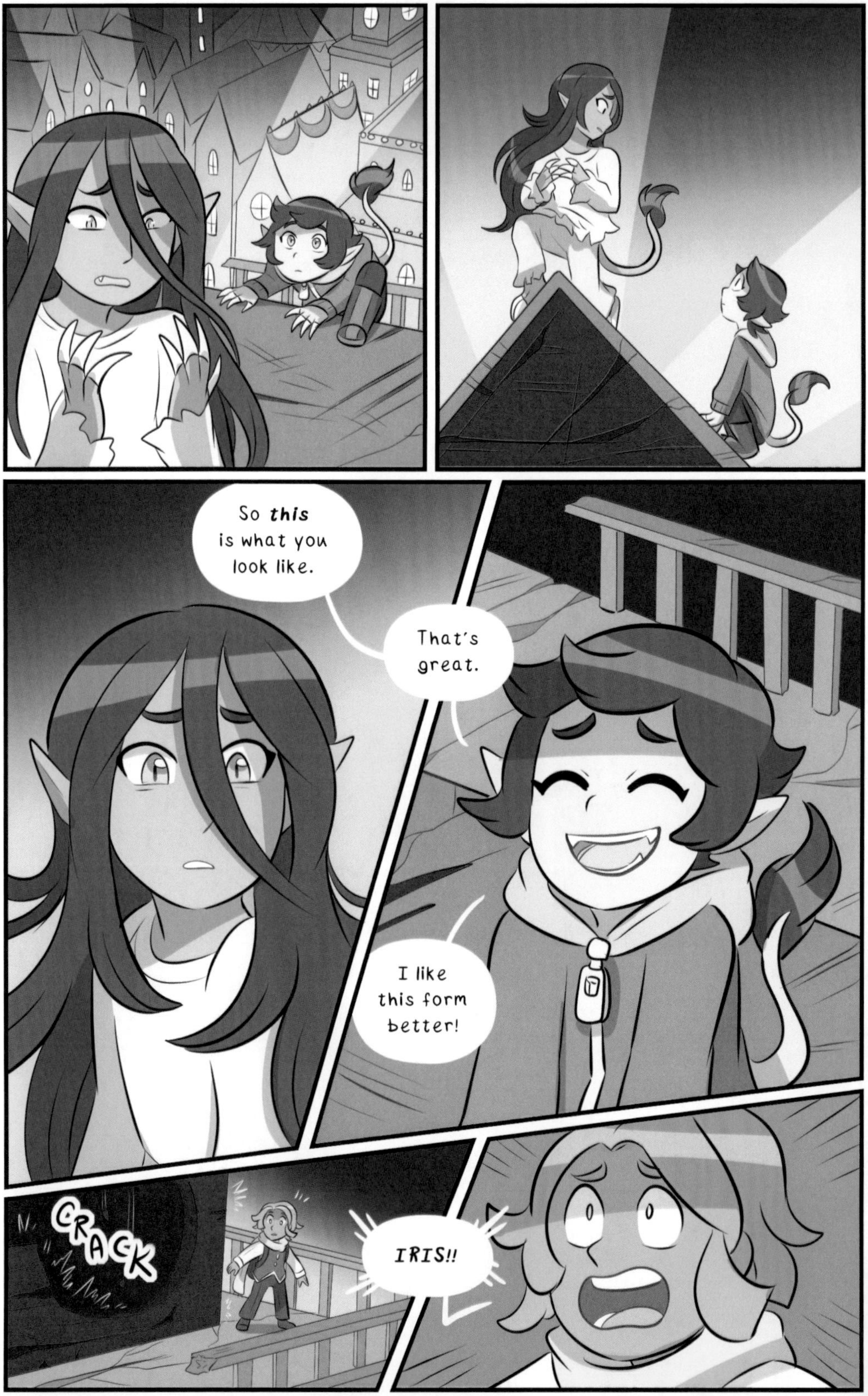

So *this* is what you look like.
That's great.
I like this form better!
CRACK
IRIS!!

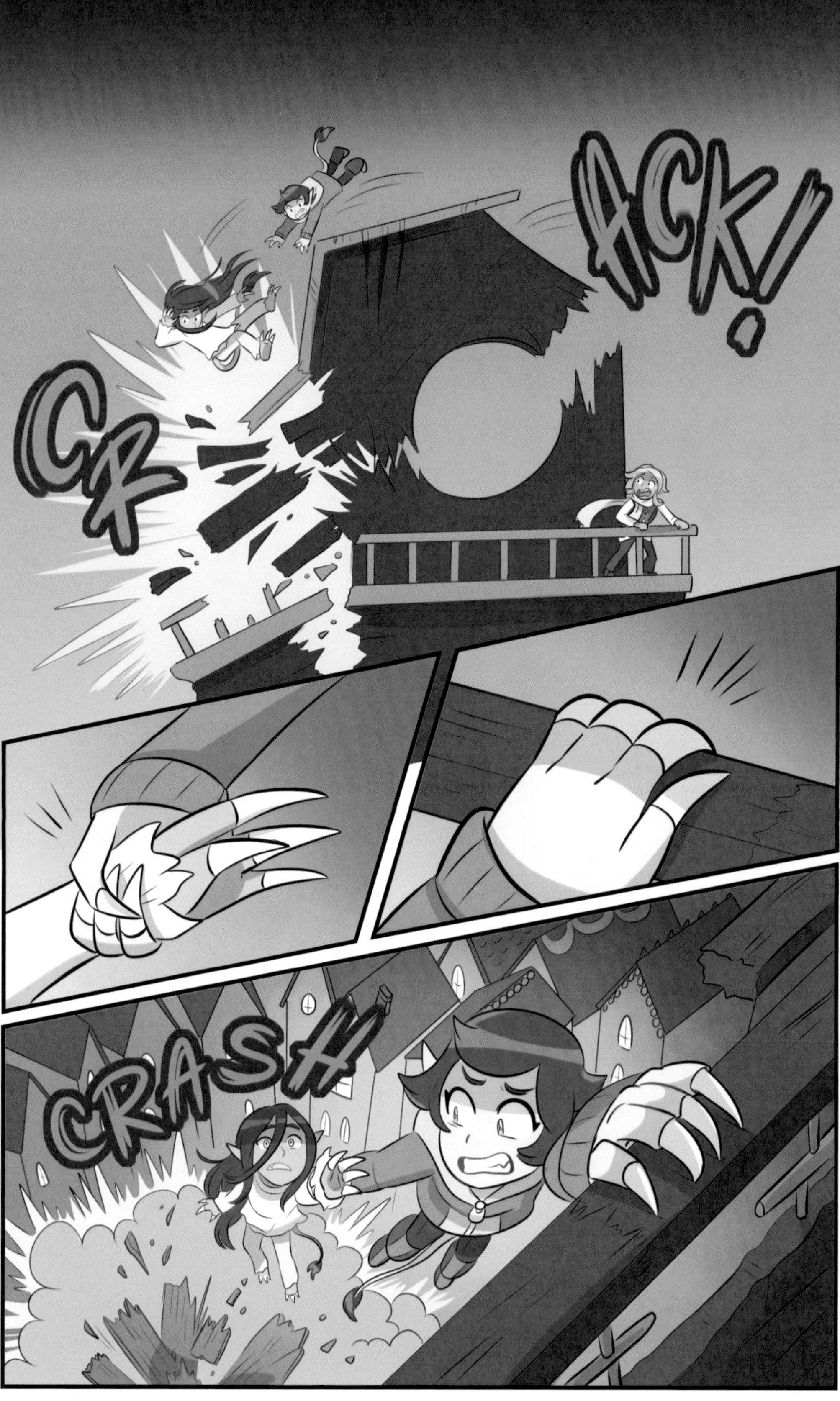
CR
ACK!
CRASH

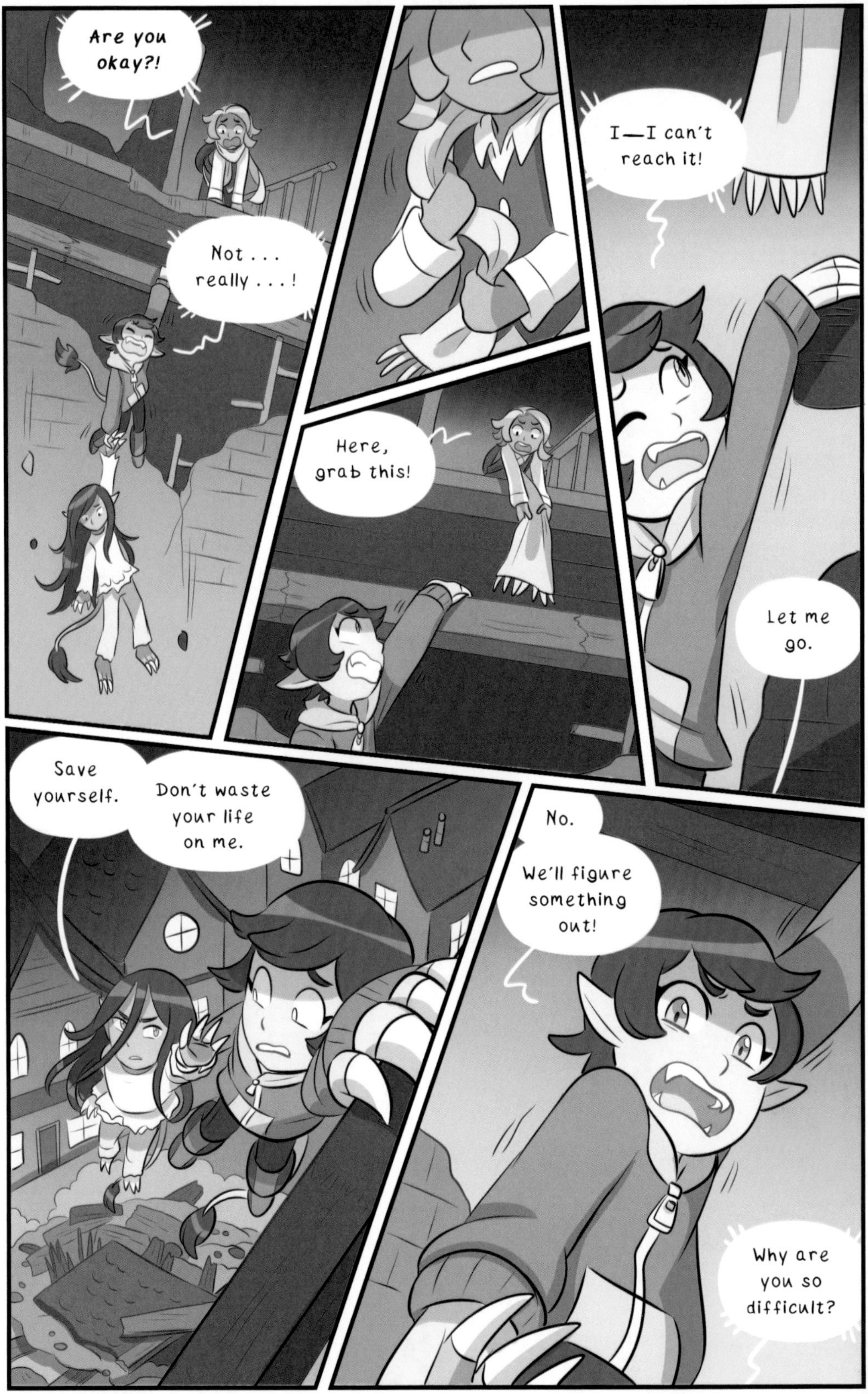
Are you okay?!
Not . . . really . . . !
Here, grab this!
I—I can't reach it!
Let me go.
Save yourself.
Don't waste your life on me.
No.
We'll figure something out!
Why are you so difficult?

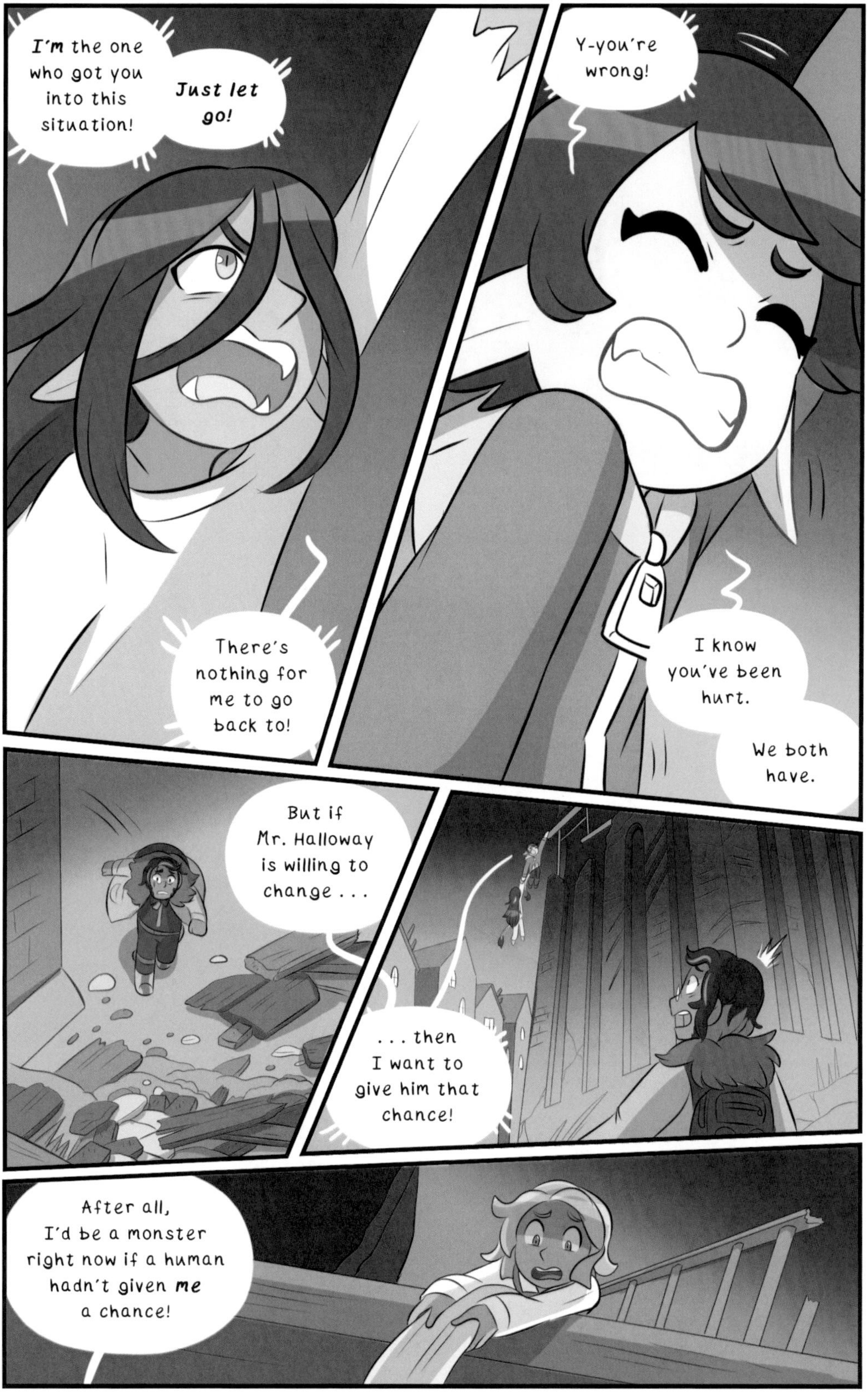
I'm the one who got you into this situation!
Just let go!
Y-you're wrong!
There's nothing for me to go back to!
I know you've been hurt.
We both have.
But if Mr. Halloway is willing to change . . .
. . . then I want to give him that chance!
After all, I'd be a monster right now if a human hadn't given me a chance!

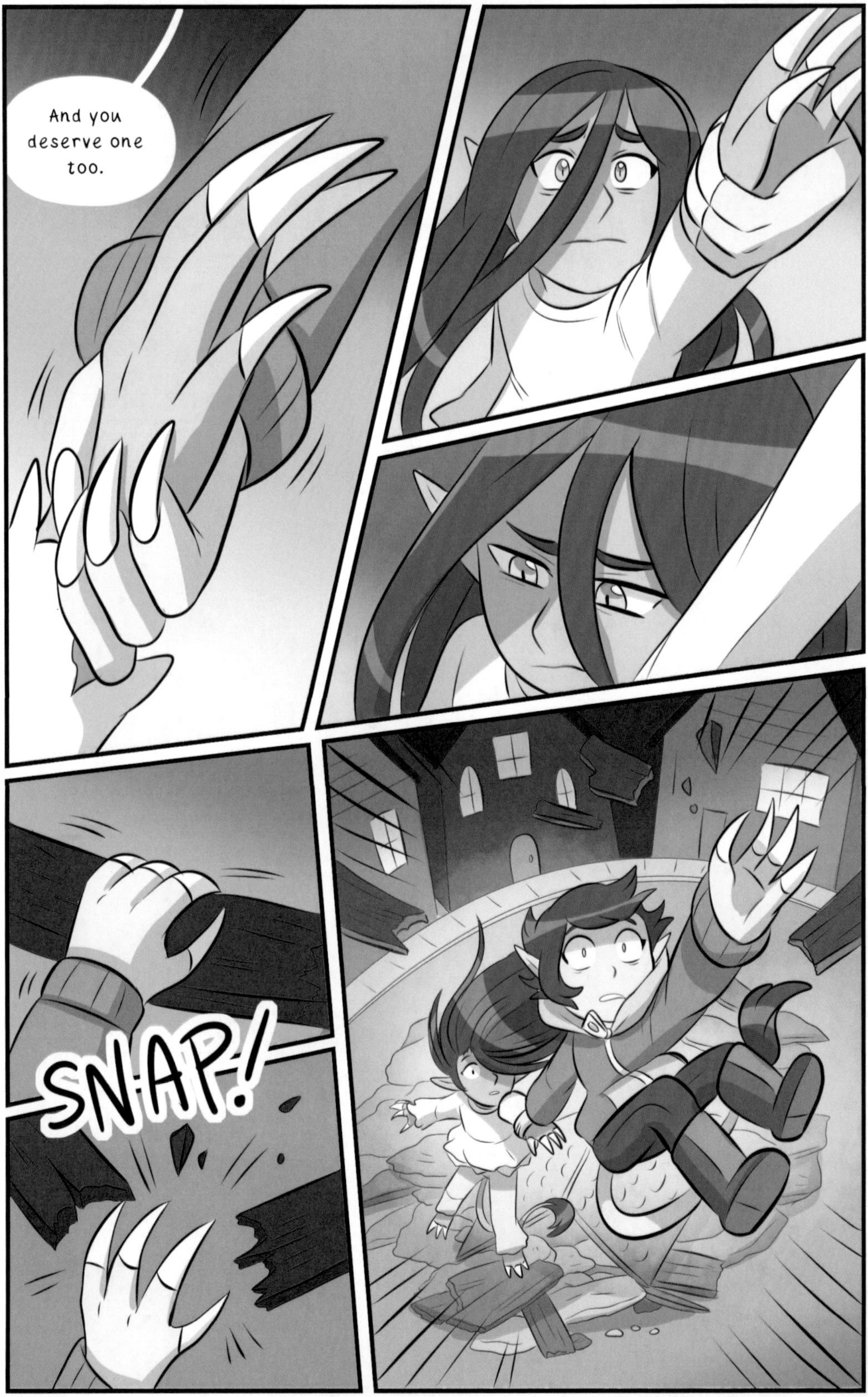
And you deserve one too.
SNAP!

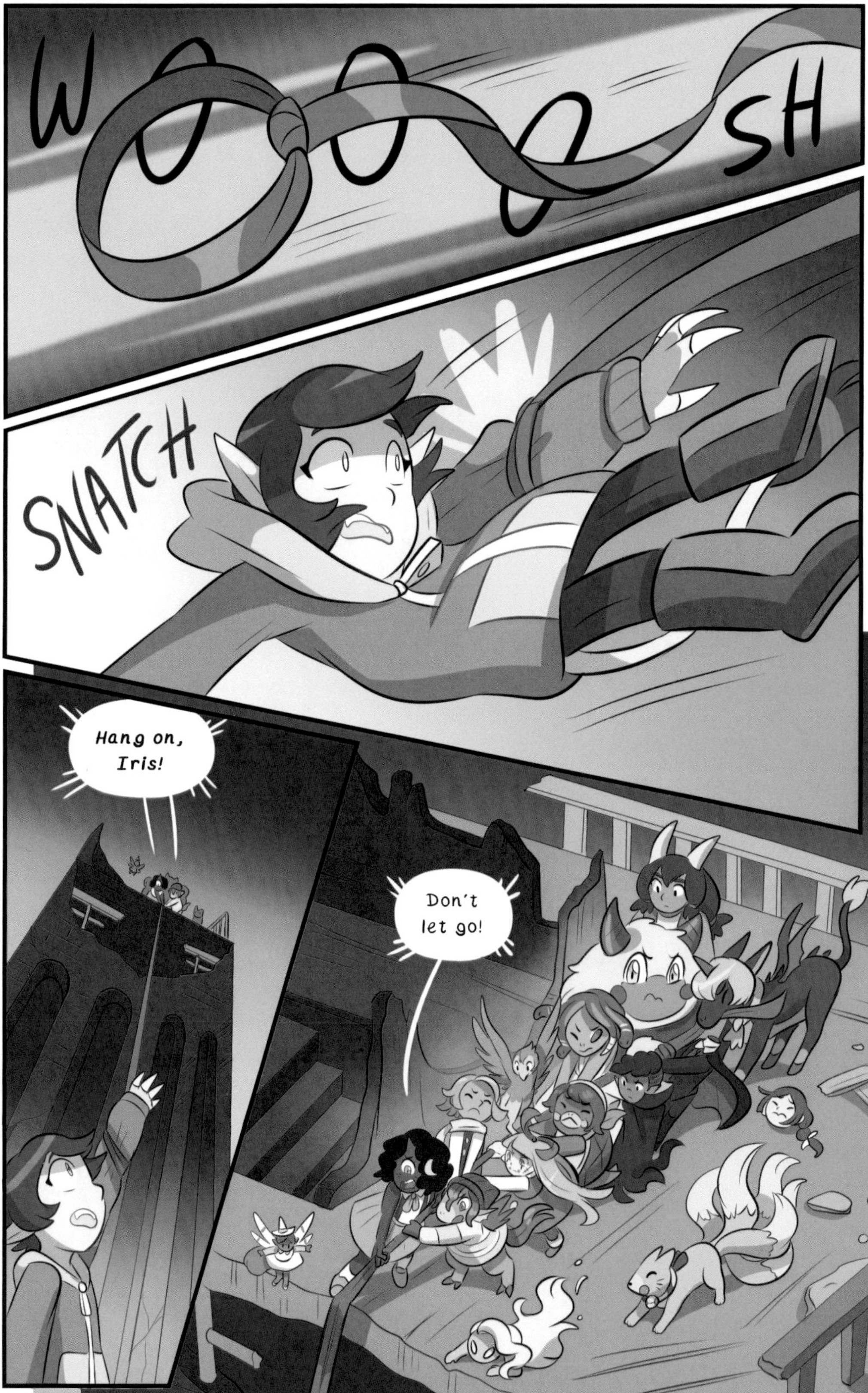
WOOOSH
SNATCH
Hang on, Iris!
Don't let go!

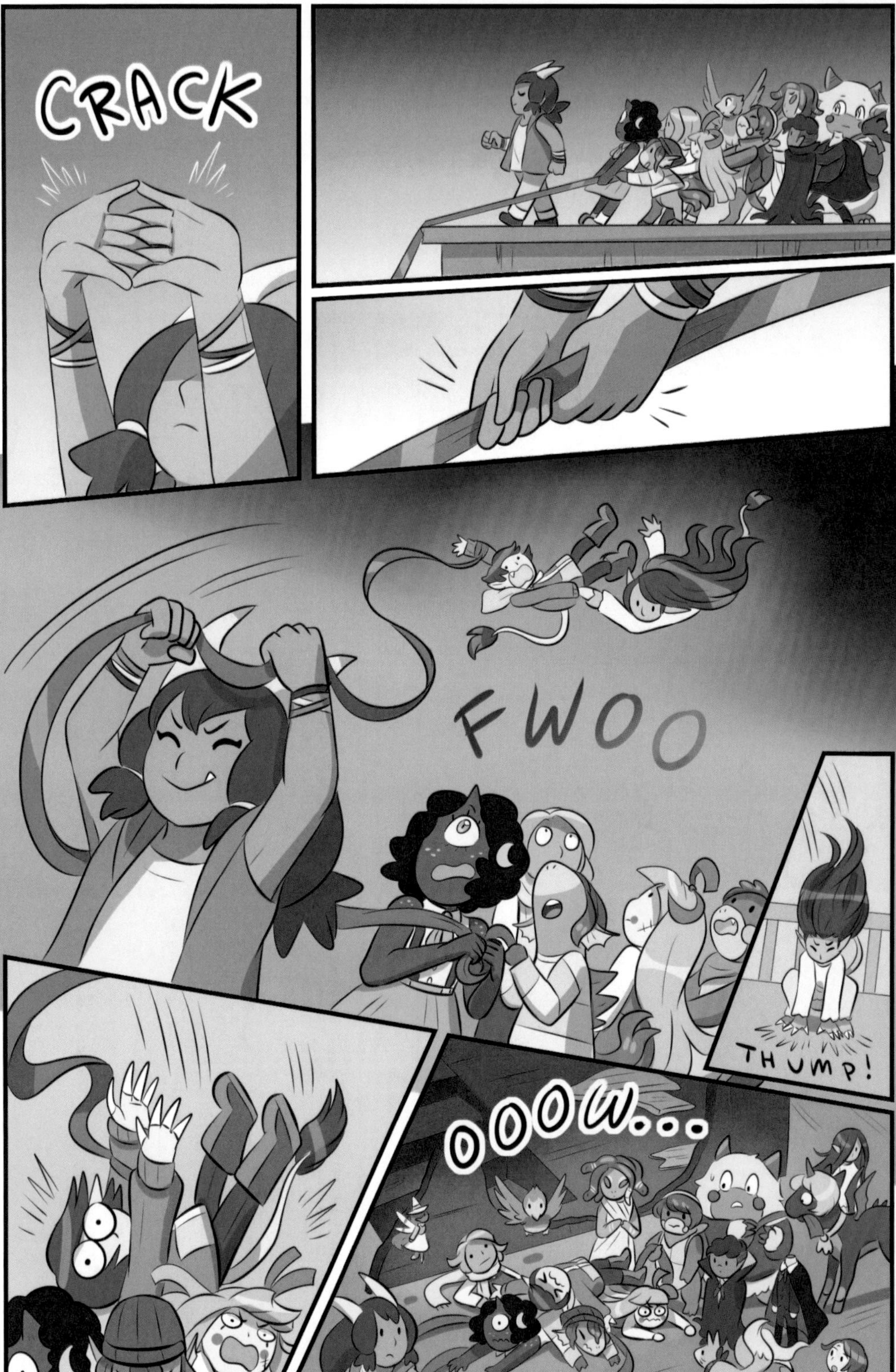
CRACK
FWOO
THUMP!
OOOW...

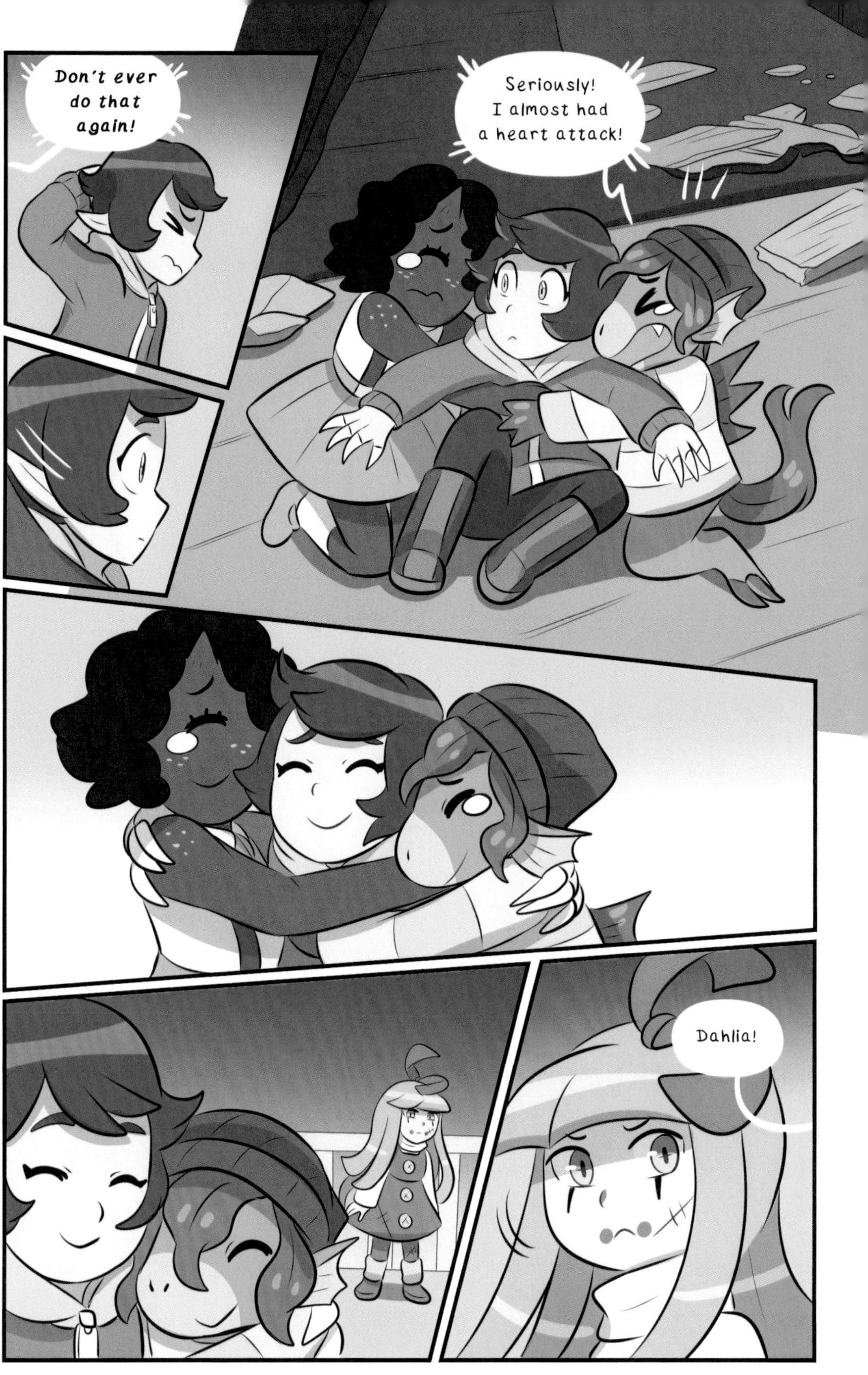
Don't ever do that again!
Seriously! I almost had a heart attack!
Dahlia!

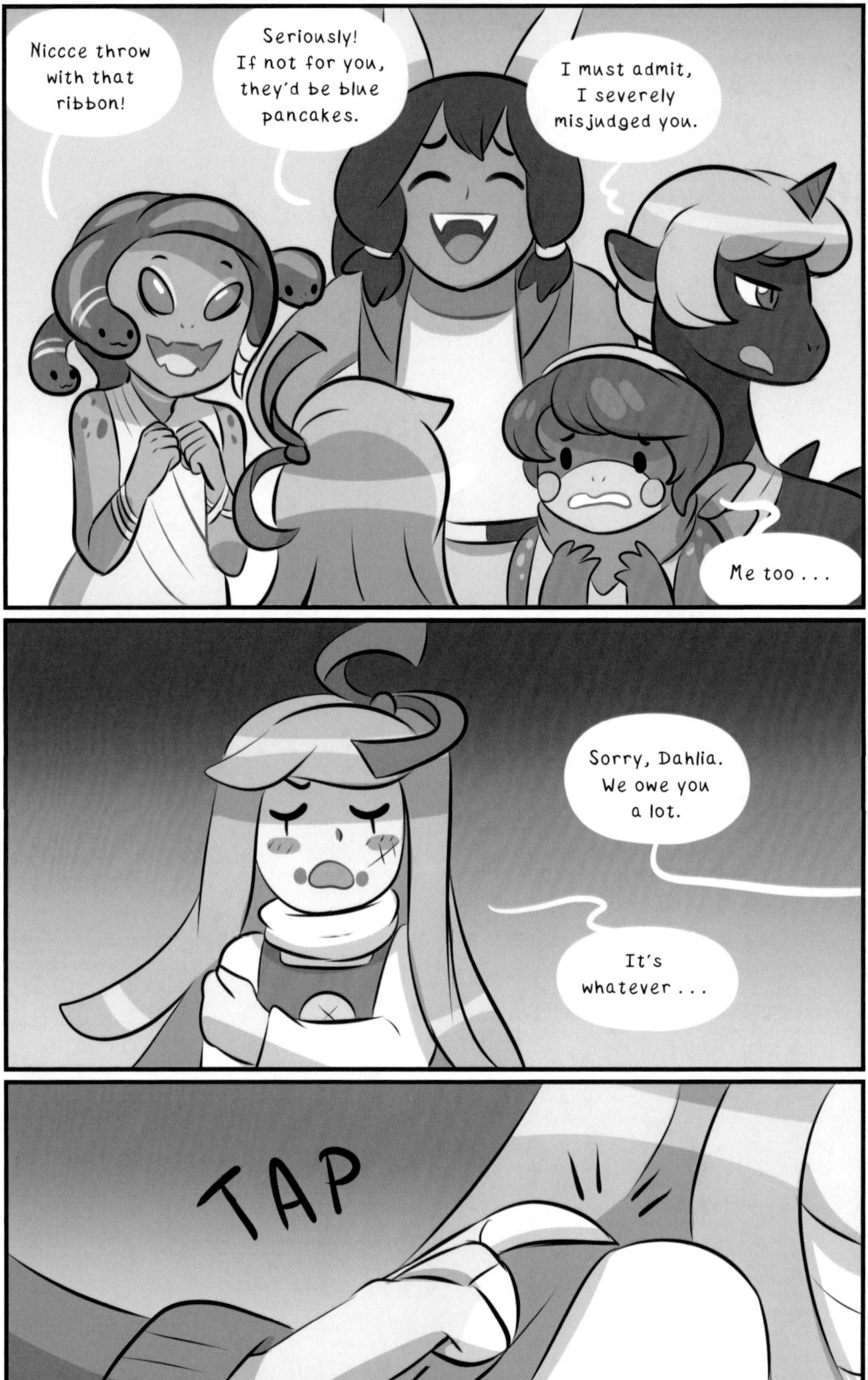
Niccce throw with that ribbon!
Seriously! If not for you, they'd be blue pancakes.
I must admit, I severely misjudged you.
Me too . . .
Sorry, Dahlia. We owe you a lot.
It's whatever . . .
TAP

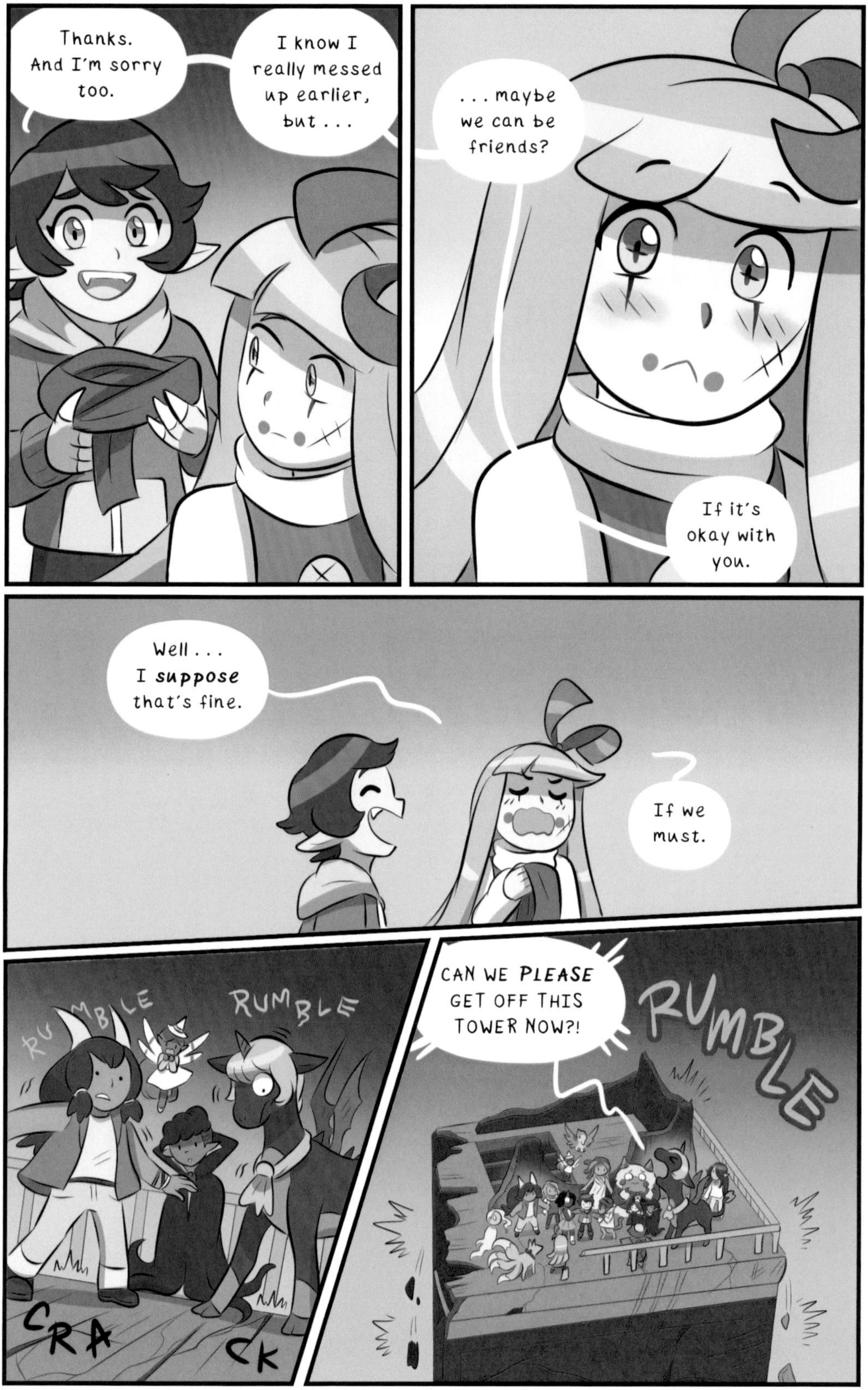
Thanks. And I'm sorry too.
I know I really messed up earlier, but . . .
. . . maybe we can be friends?
If it's okay with you.
Well . . . I *suppose* that's fine.
If we must.
RUMBLE
RUMBLE
CRACK
CAN WE *PLEASE* GET OFF THIS TOWER NOW?!
RUMBLE

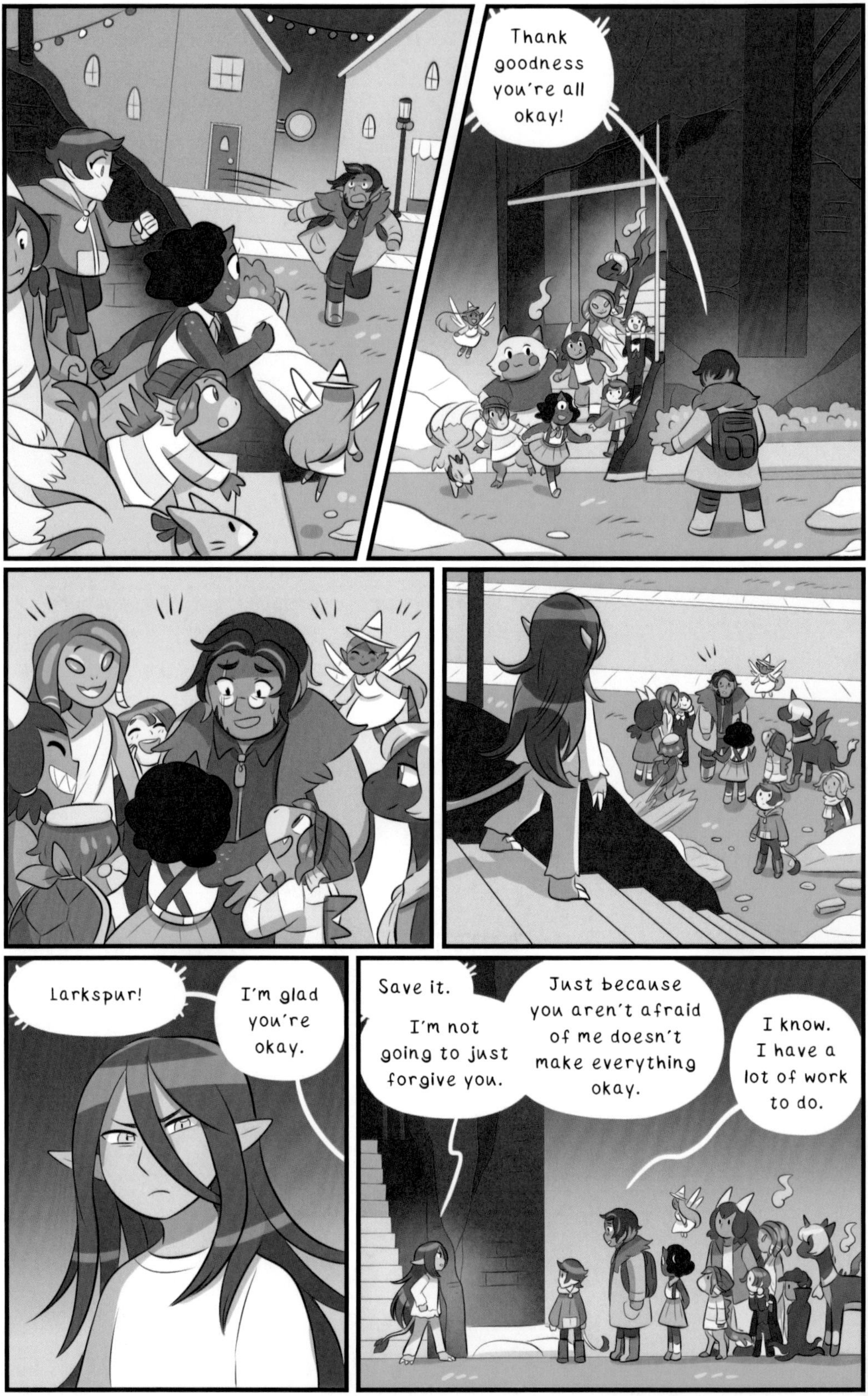
Thank goodness you're all okay!
Larkspur!
I'm glad you're okay.
Save it.
I'm not going to just forgive you.
Just because you aren't afraid of me doesn't make everything okay.
I know. I have a lot of work to do.

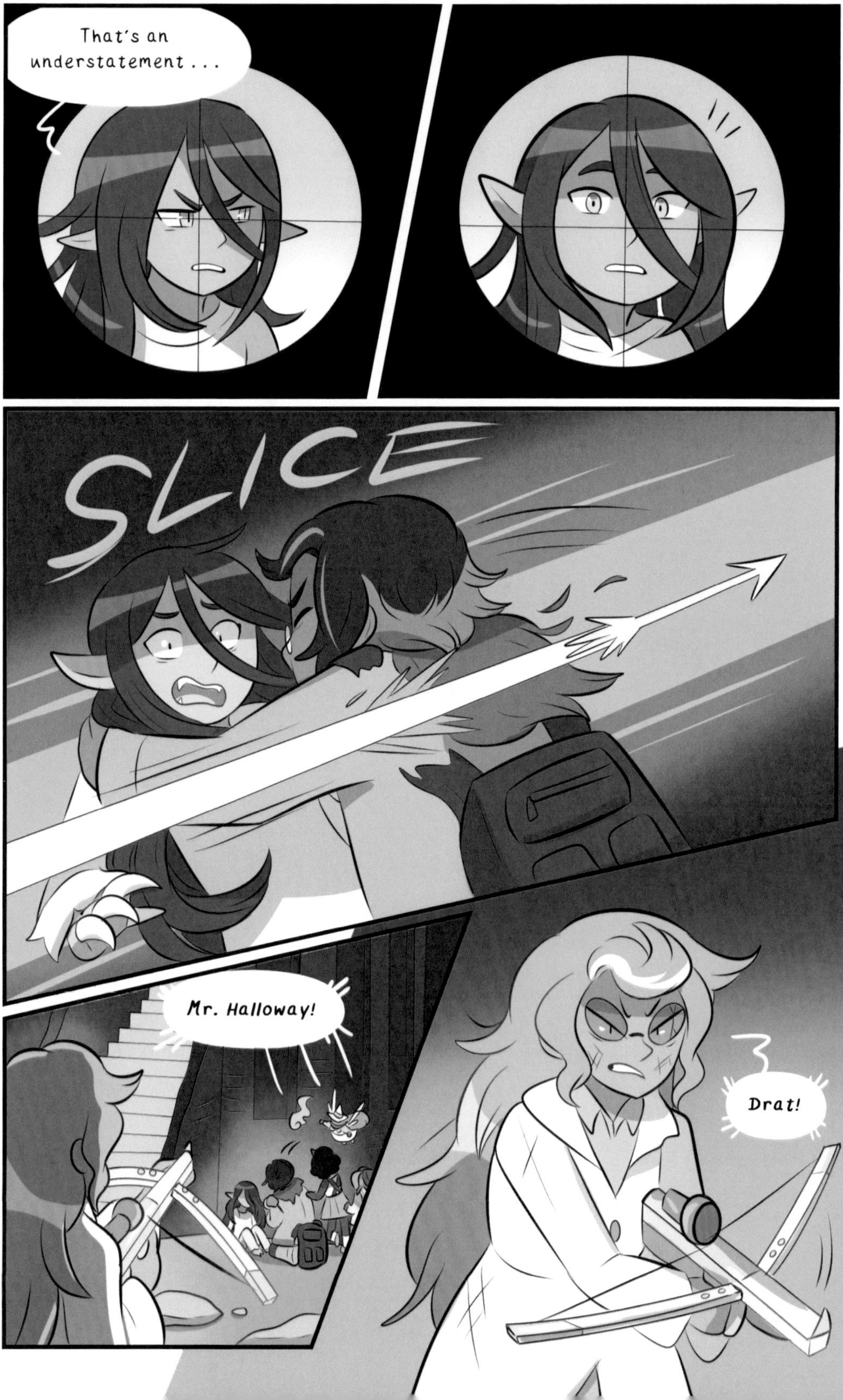
That's an understatement . . .
SLICE
Mr. Halloway!
Drat!

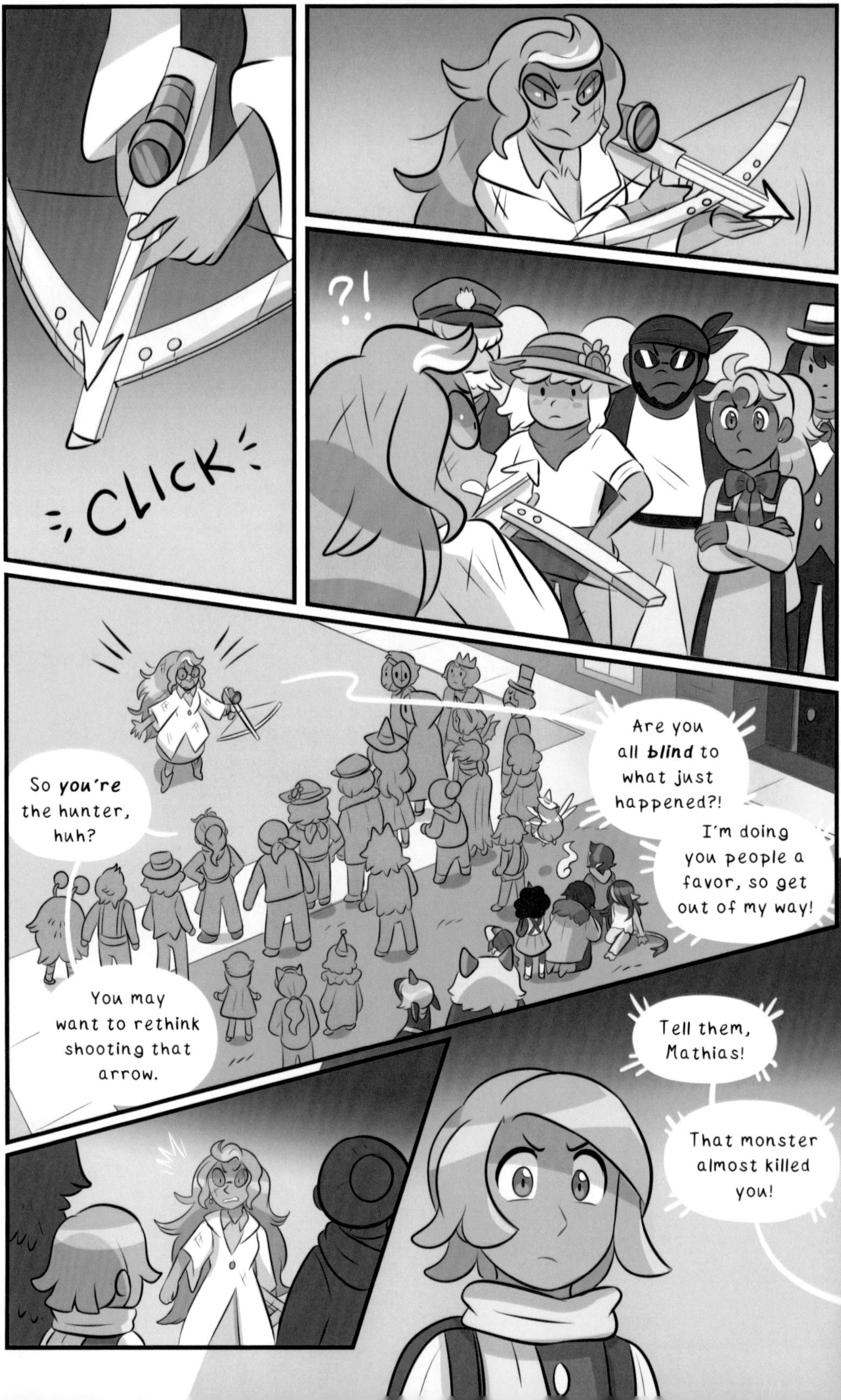
CLICK
?!
So you're the hunter, huh?
Are you all blind to what just happened?!
I'm doing you people a favor, so get out of my way!
You may want to rethink shooting that arrow.
Tell them, Mathias!
That monster almost killed you!

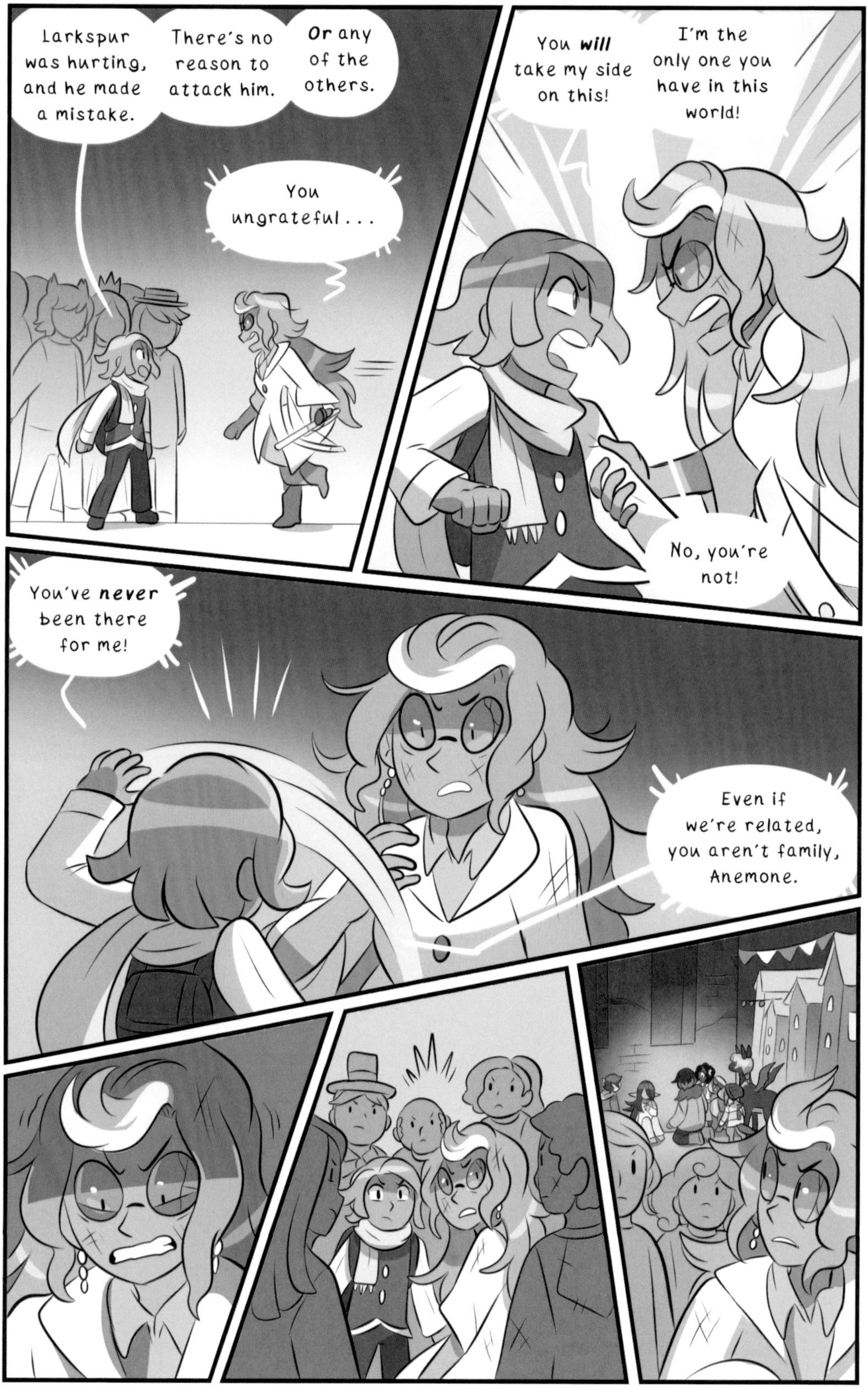
Larkspur was hurting, and he made a mistake.
There's no reason to attack him.
Or any of the others.
You ungrateful . . .
You **will** take my side on this!
I'm the only one you have in this world!
No, you're not!
You've **never** been there for me!
Even if we're related, you aren't family, Anemone.

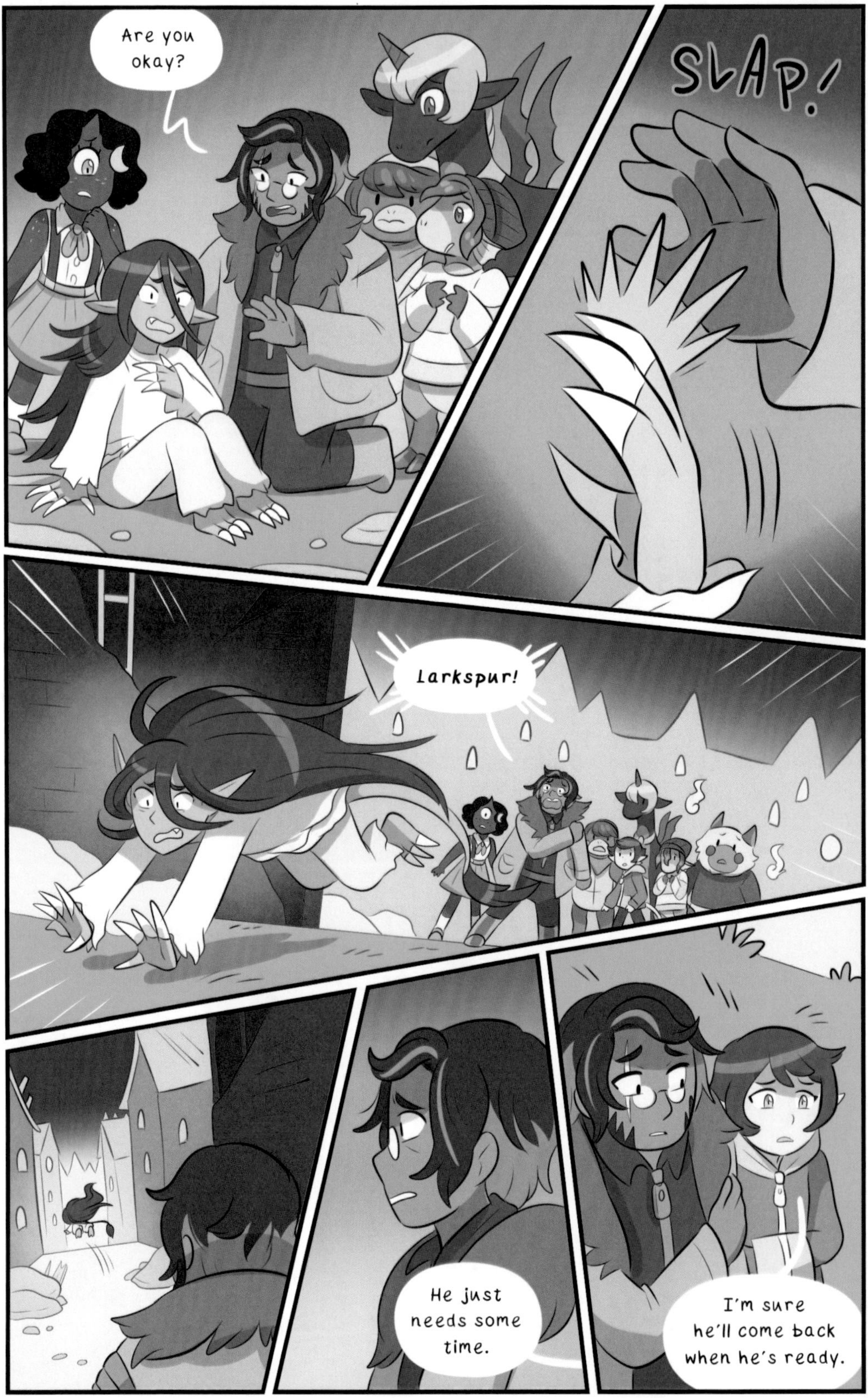

Are you okay?
SLAP!
Larkspur!
He just needs some time.
I'm sure he'll come back when he's ready.

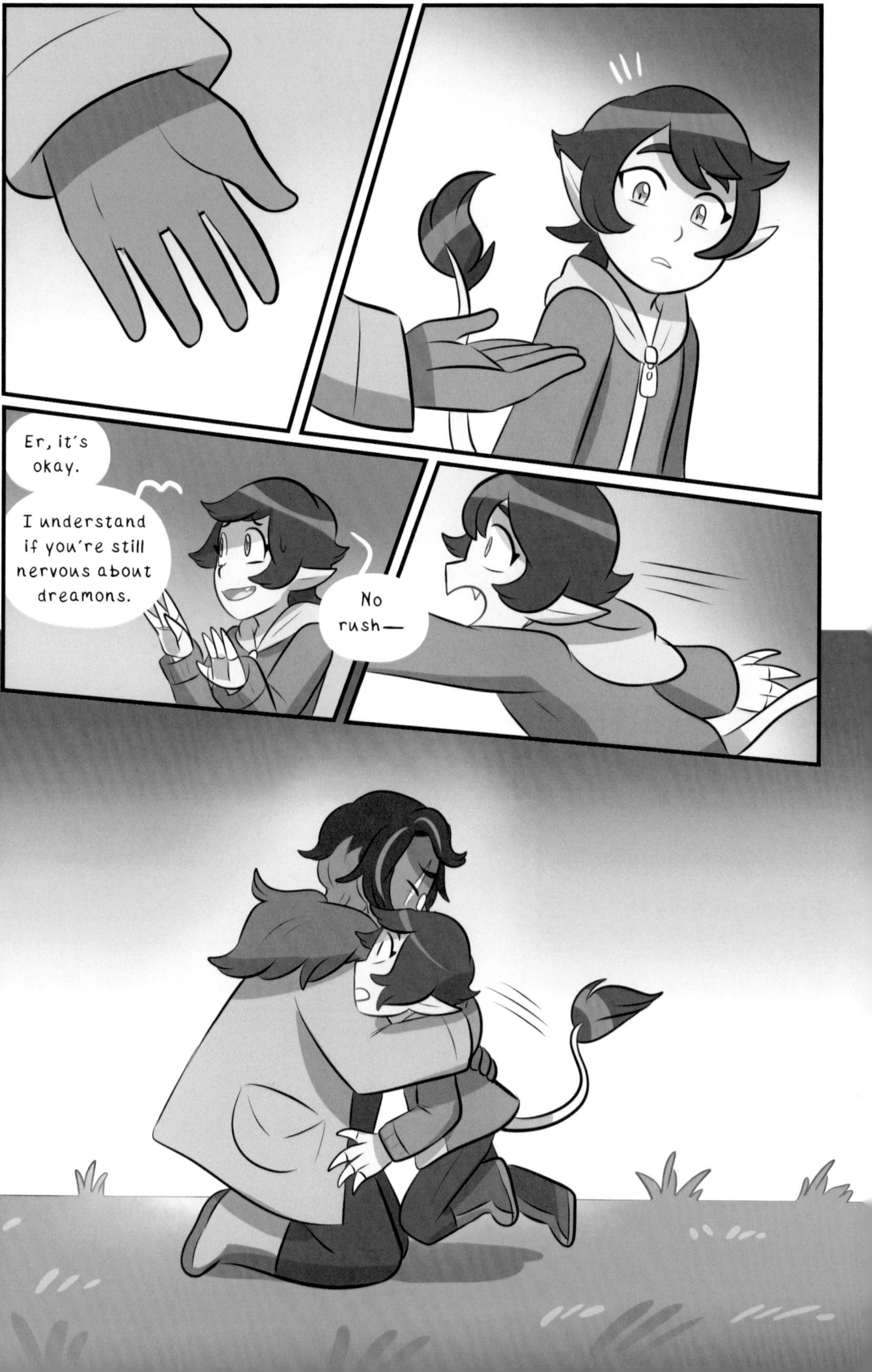
Er, it's okay.
I understand if you're still nervous about dreamons.
No rush—

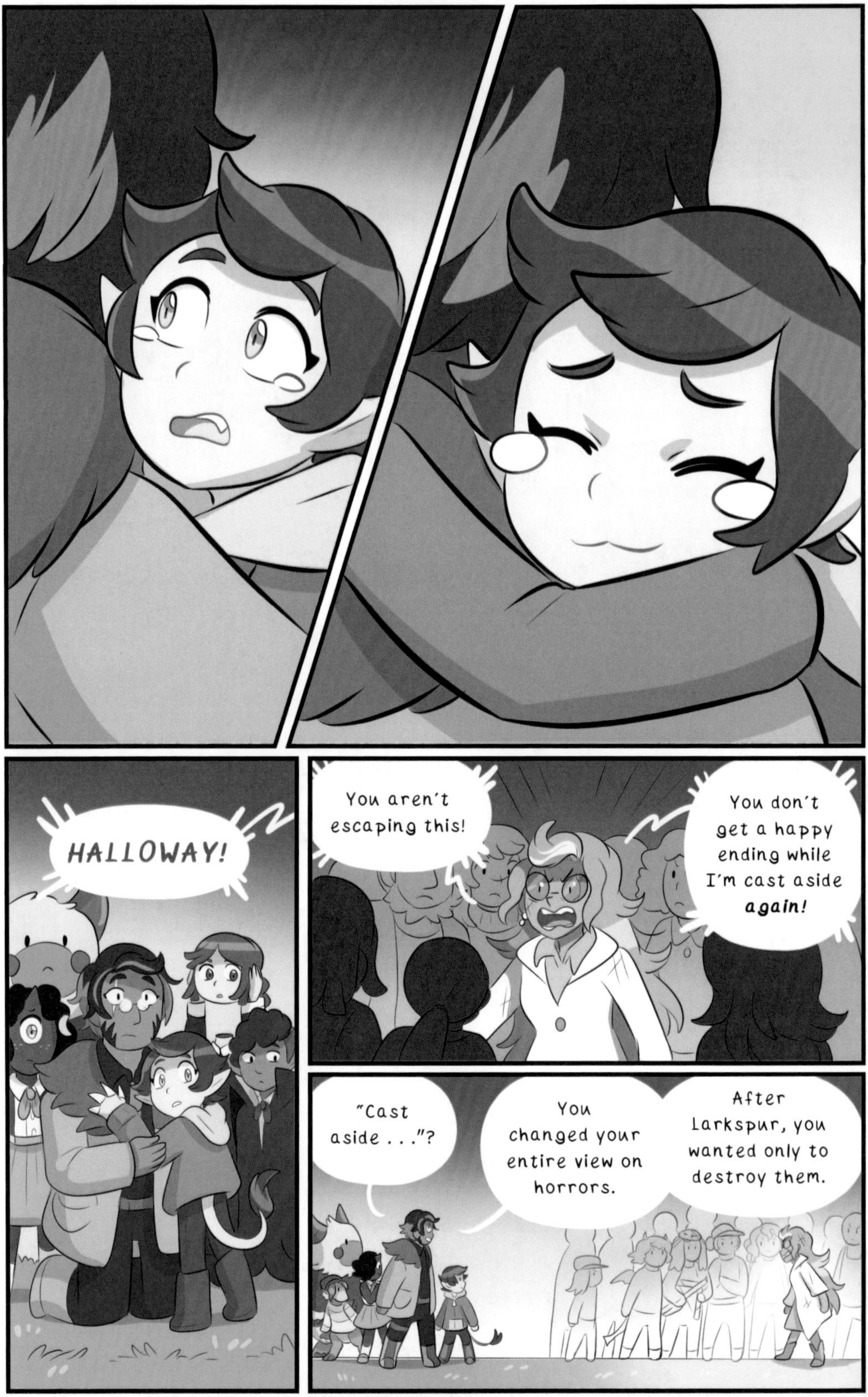
HALLOWAY!
You aren't escaping this!
You don't get a happy ending while I'm cast aside **again!**
"Cast aside . . ."?
You changed your entire view on horrors.
After Larkspur, you wanted only to destroy them.

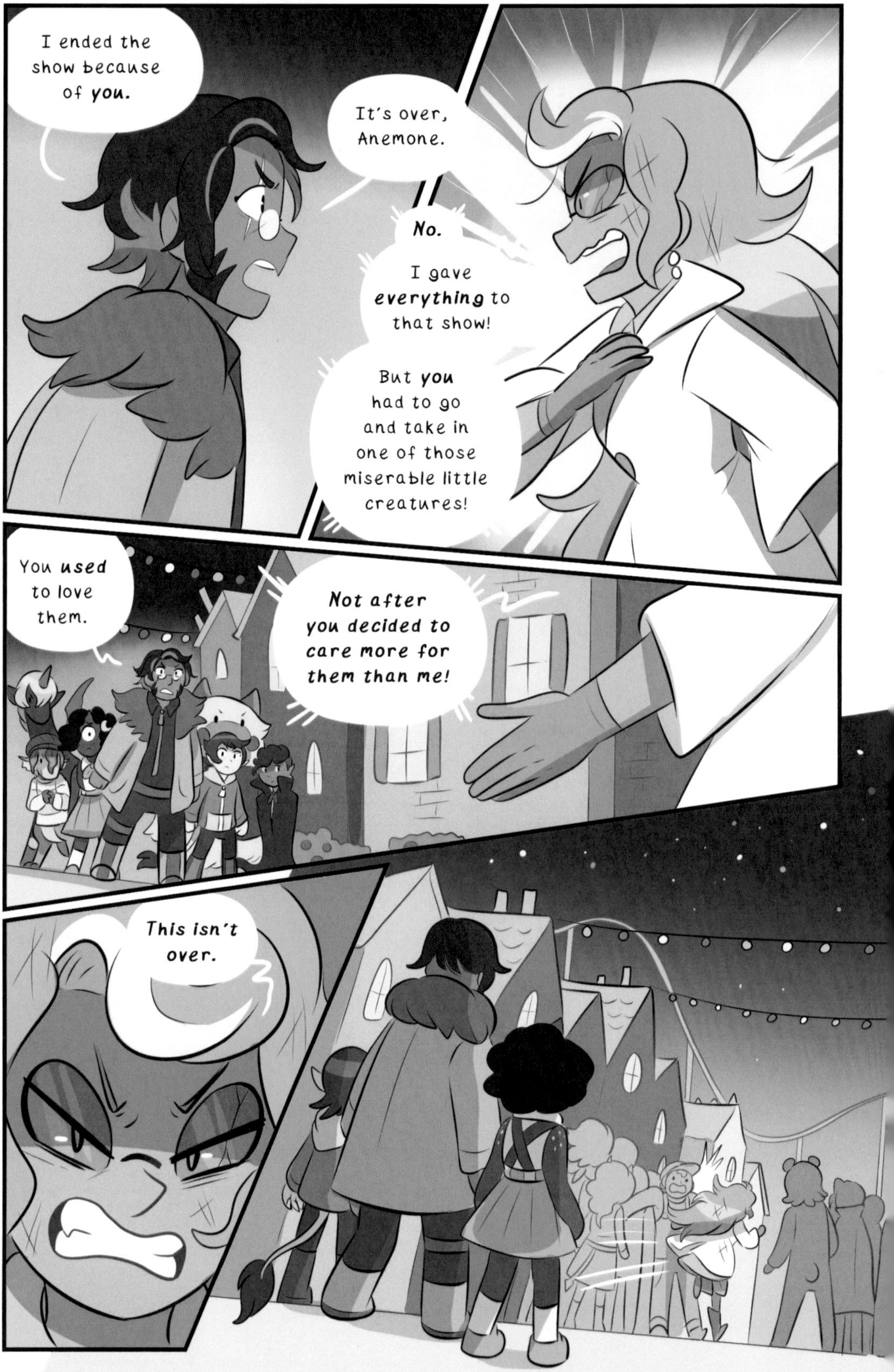
I ended the show because of **you.**
It's over, Anemone.
No.
I gave ***everything*** to that show!
But **you** had to go and take in one of those miserable little creatures!
You **used** to love them.
Not after you decided to care more for them than me!
This isn't over.

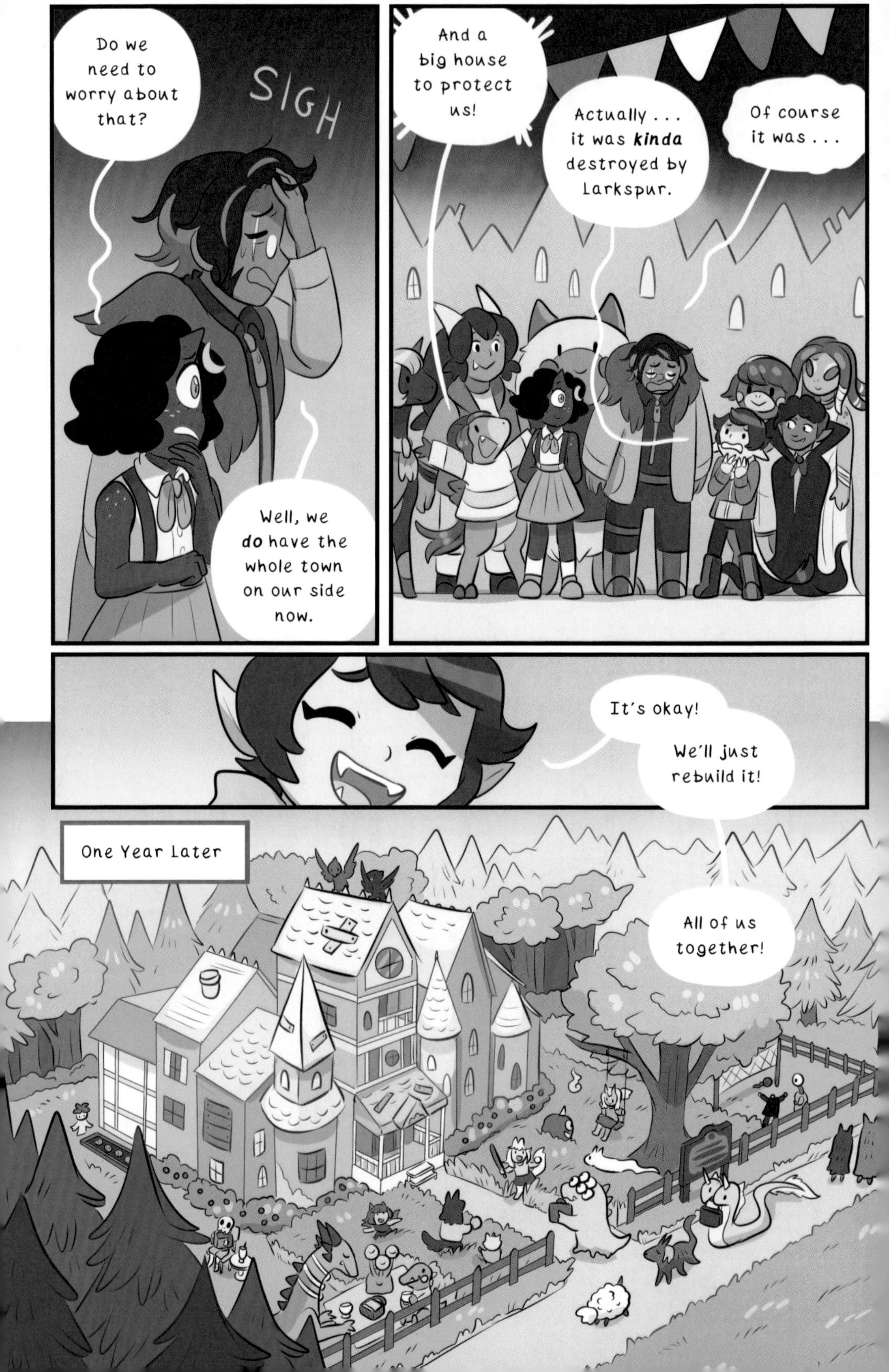
Do we need to worry about that?
SIGH
Well, we do have the whole town on our side now.
And a big house to protect us!
Actually . . . it was kinda destroyed by Larkspur.
Of course it was . . .
It's okay!
We'll just rebuild it!
One Year Later
All of us together!

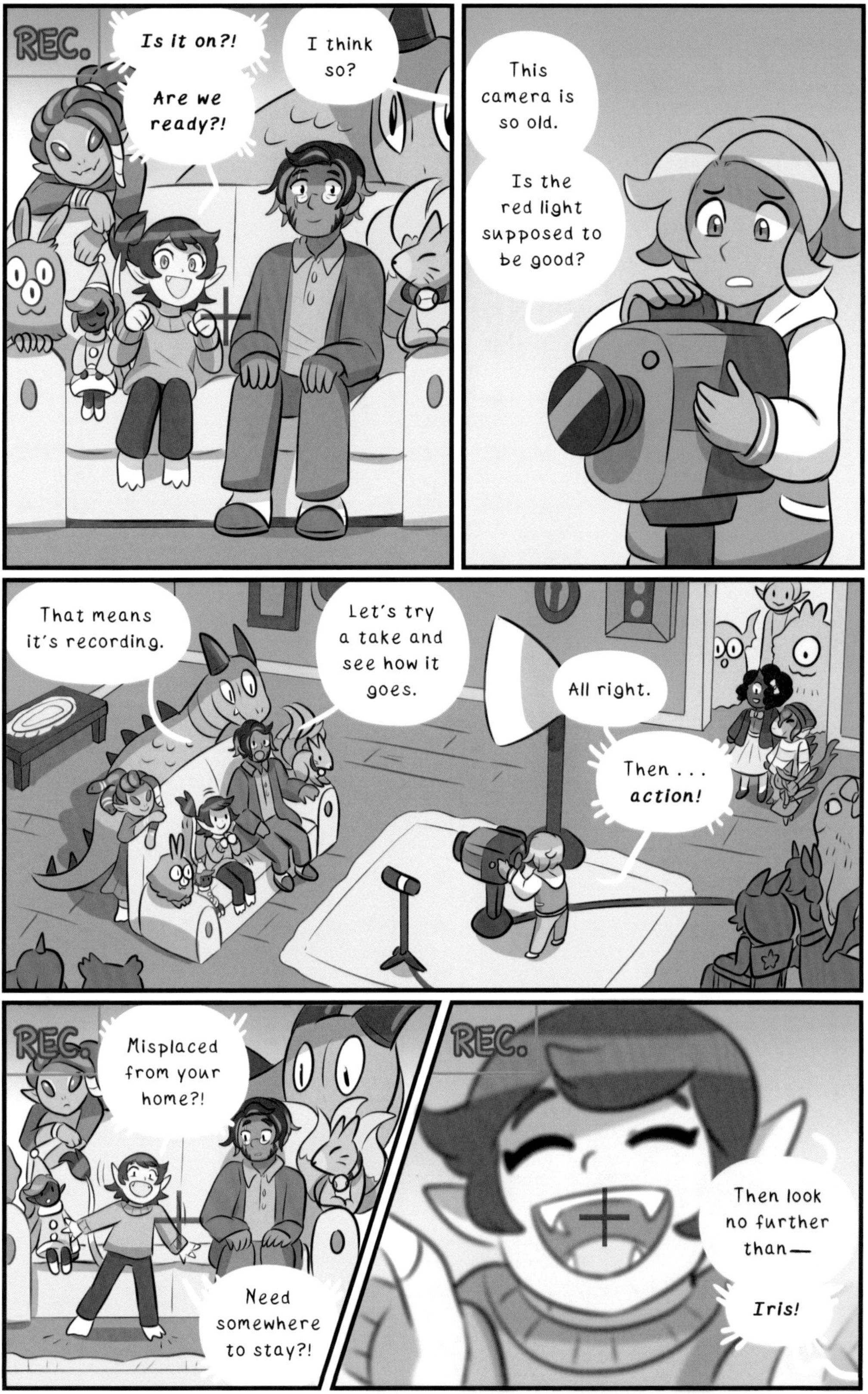
REC.
Is it on?!
Are we ready?!
I think so?
This camera is so old.
Is the red light supposed to be good?
That means it's recording.
Let's try a take and see how it goes.
All right.
Then . . . *action!*
REC.
Misplaced from your home?!
Need somewhere to stay?!
REC.
Then look no further than—
Iris!

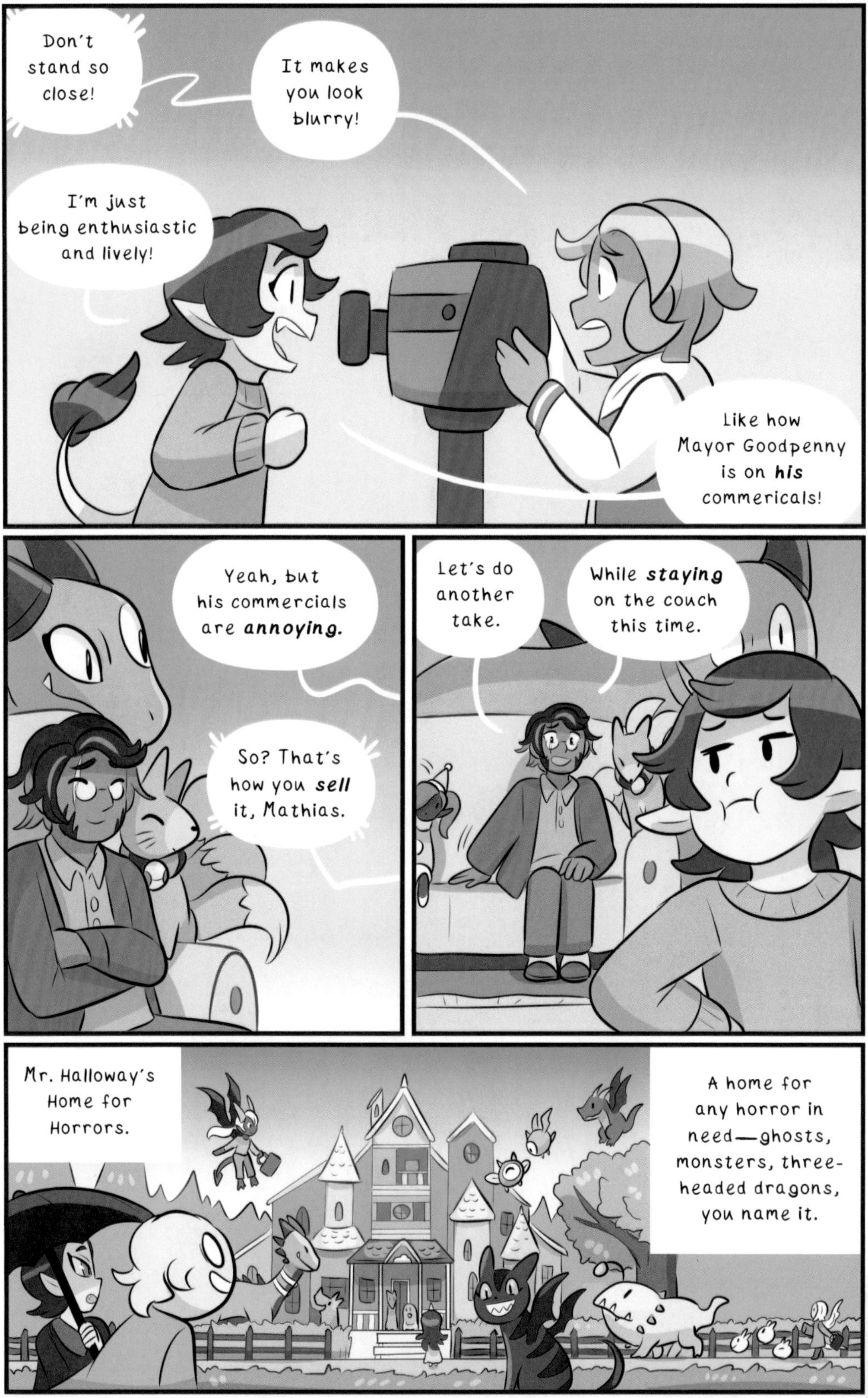
Don't stand so close!
It makes you look blurry!
I'm just being enthusiastic and lively!
Like how Mayor Goodpenny is on **his** commericals!
Yeah, but his commercials are **annoying.**
So? That's how you **sell** it, Mathias.
Let's do another take.
While **staying** on the couch this time.
Mr. Halloway's Home for Horrors.
A home for any horror in need—ghosts, monsters, three-headed dragons, you name it.

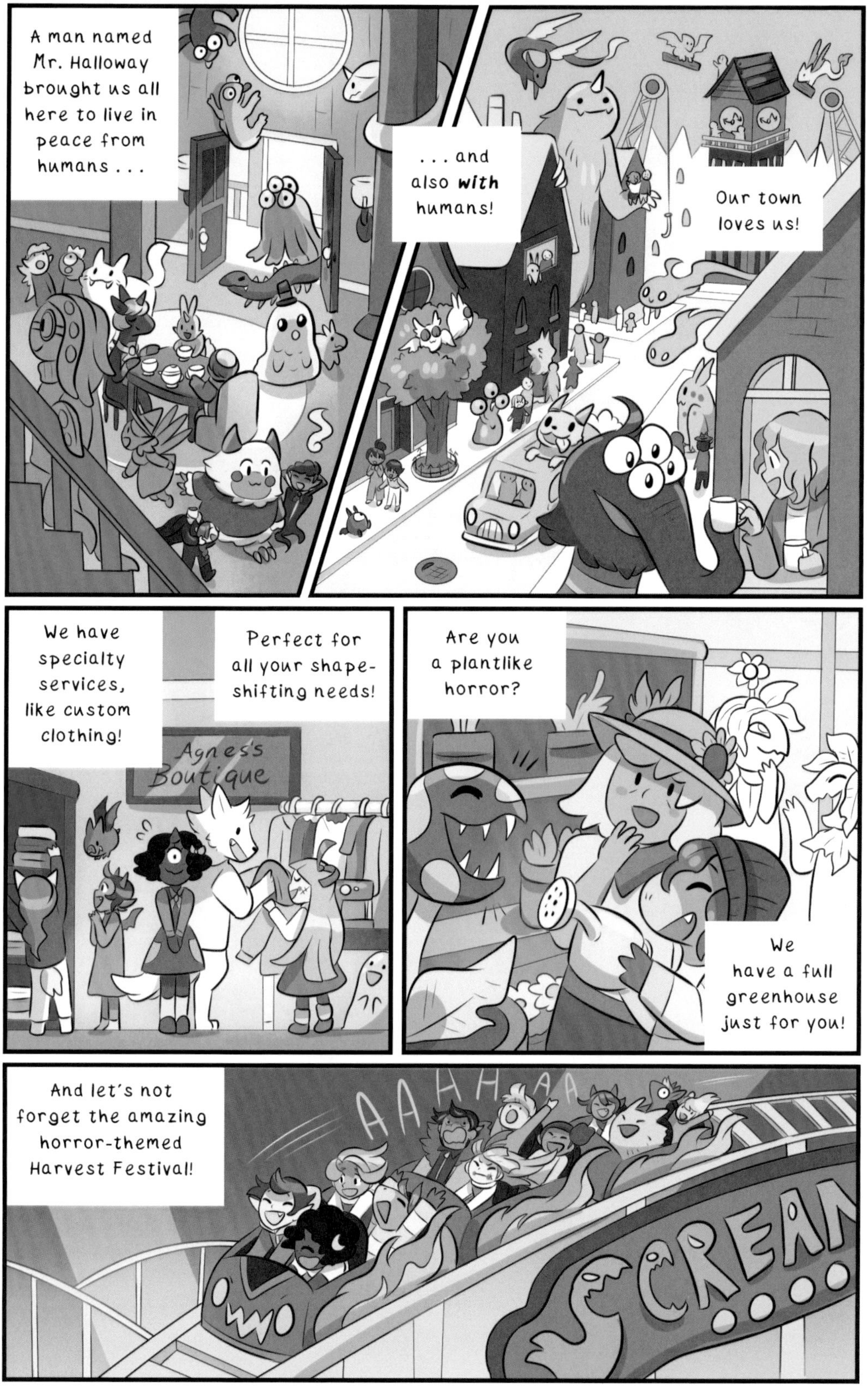
A man named Mr. Halloway brought us all here to live in peace from humans . . .
. . . and also **with** humans!
Our town loves us!
We have specialty services, like custom clothing!
Perfect for all your shape-shifting needs!
Agnes's Boutique
Are you a plantlike horror?
We have a full greenhouse just for you!
And let's not forget the amazing horror-themed Harvest Festival!

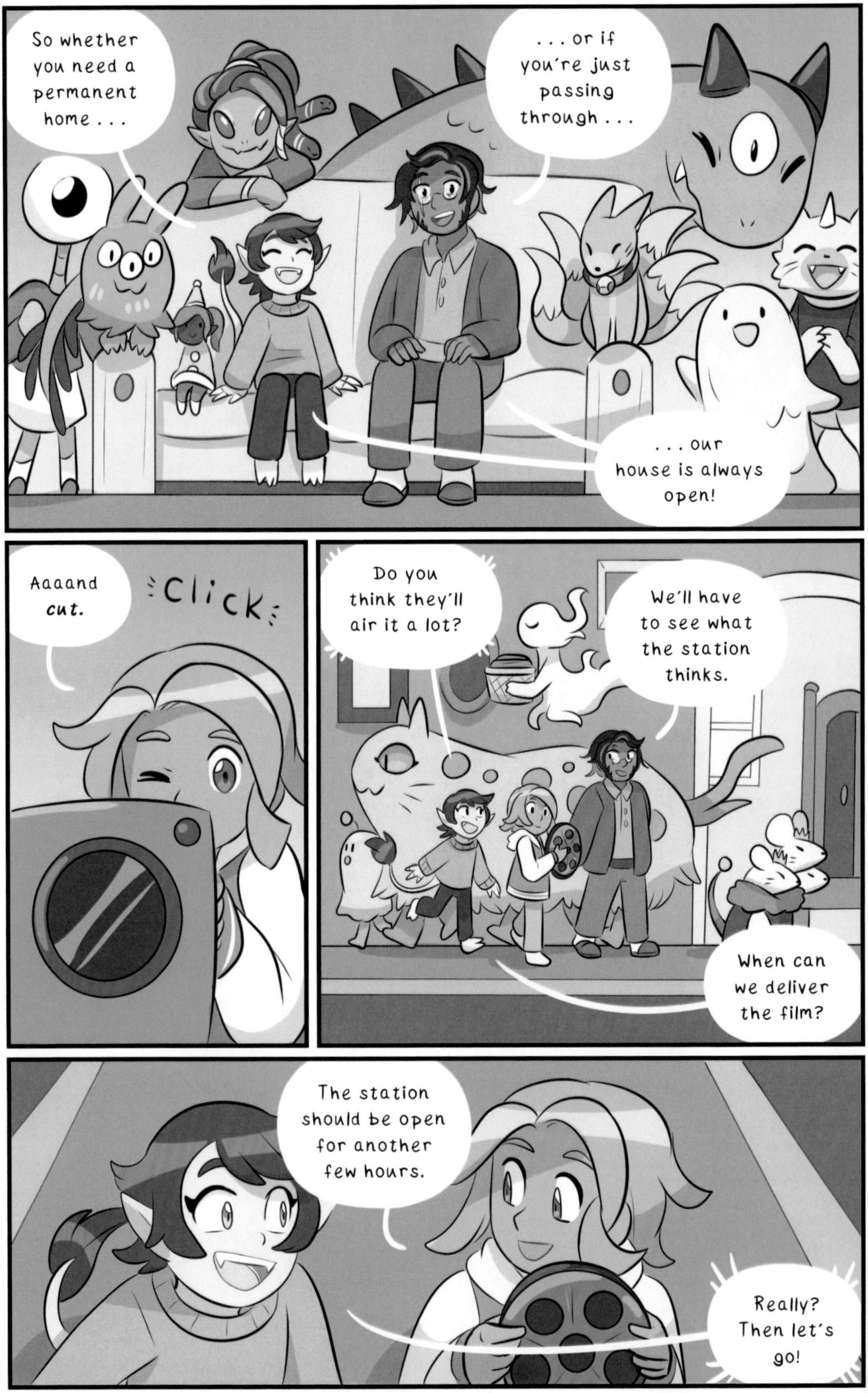
So whether you need a permanent home . . .
. . . or if you're just passing through . . .
. . . our house is always open!
Aaaand **cut.**
Click
Do you think they'll air it a lot?
We'll have to see what the station thinks.
When can we deliver the film?
The station should be open for another few hours.
Really? Then let's go!

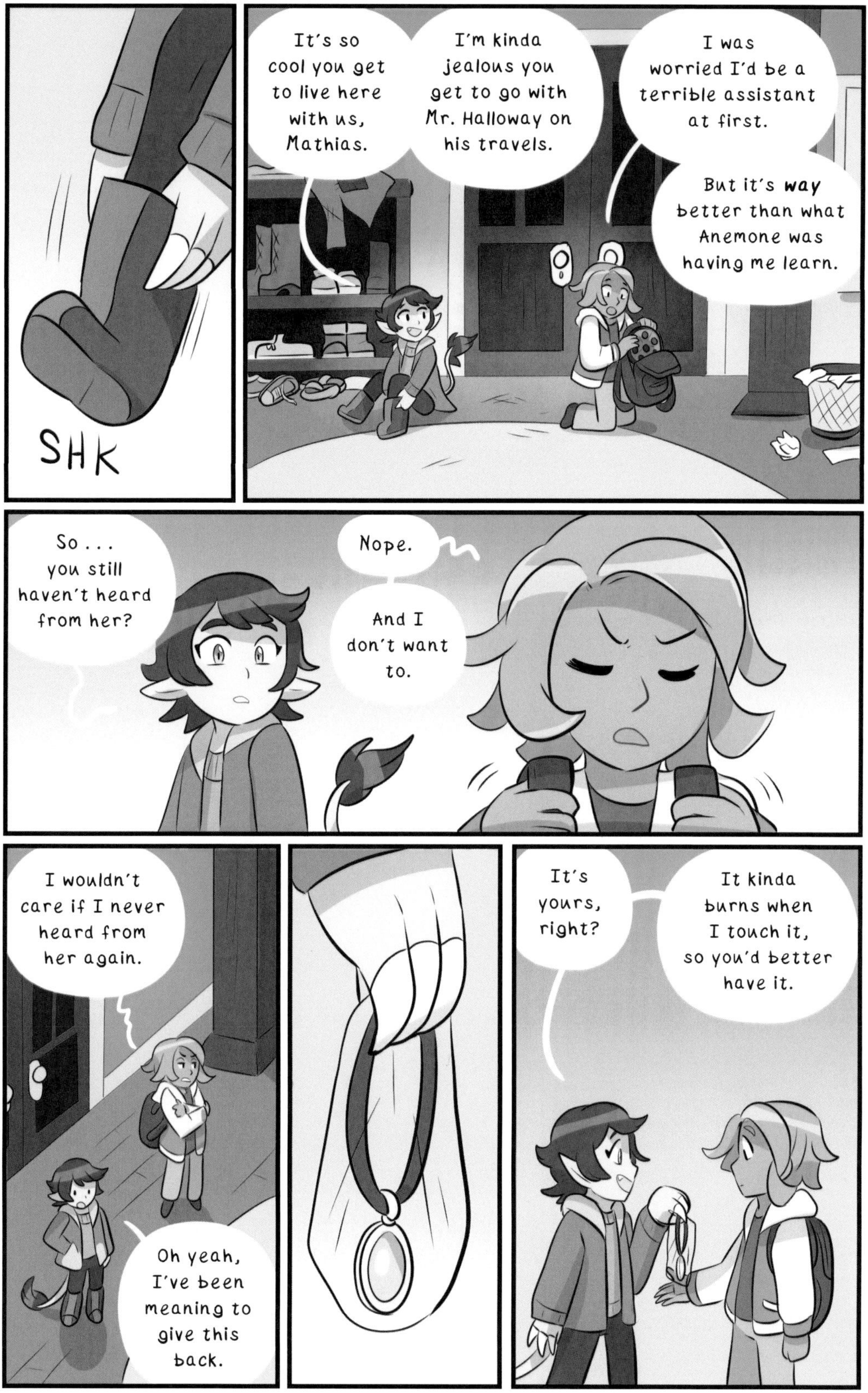
SHK
It's so cool you get to live here with us, Mathias.
I'm kinda jealous you get to go with Mr. Halloway on his travels.
I was worried I'd be a terrible assistant at first.
But it's **way** better than what Anemone was having me learn.
So . . . you still haven't heard from her?
Nope.
And I don't want to.
I wouldn't care if I never heard from her again.
Oh yeah, I've been meaning to give this back.
It's yours, right?
It kinda burns when I touch it, so you'd better have it.

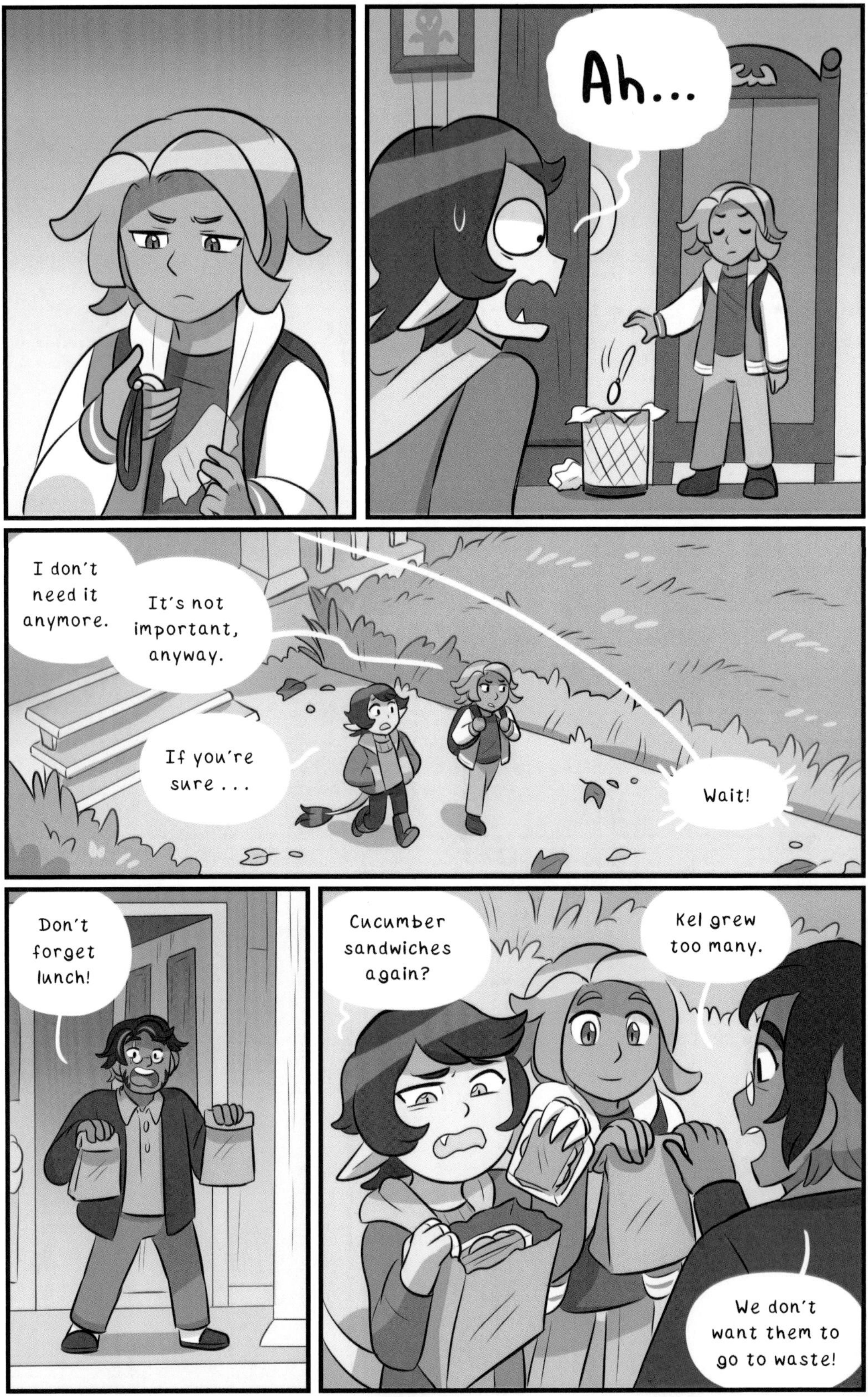
Ah...
I don't need it anymore.
It's not important, anyway.
If you're sure . . .
Wait!
Don't forget lunch!
Cucumber sandwiches again?
Kel grew too many.
We don't want them to go to waste!

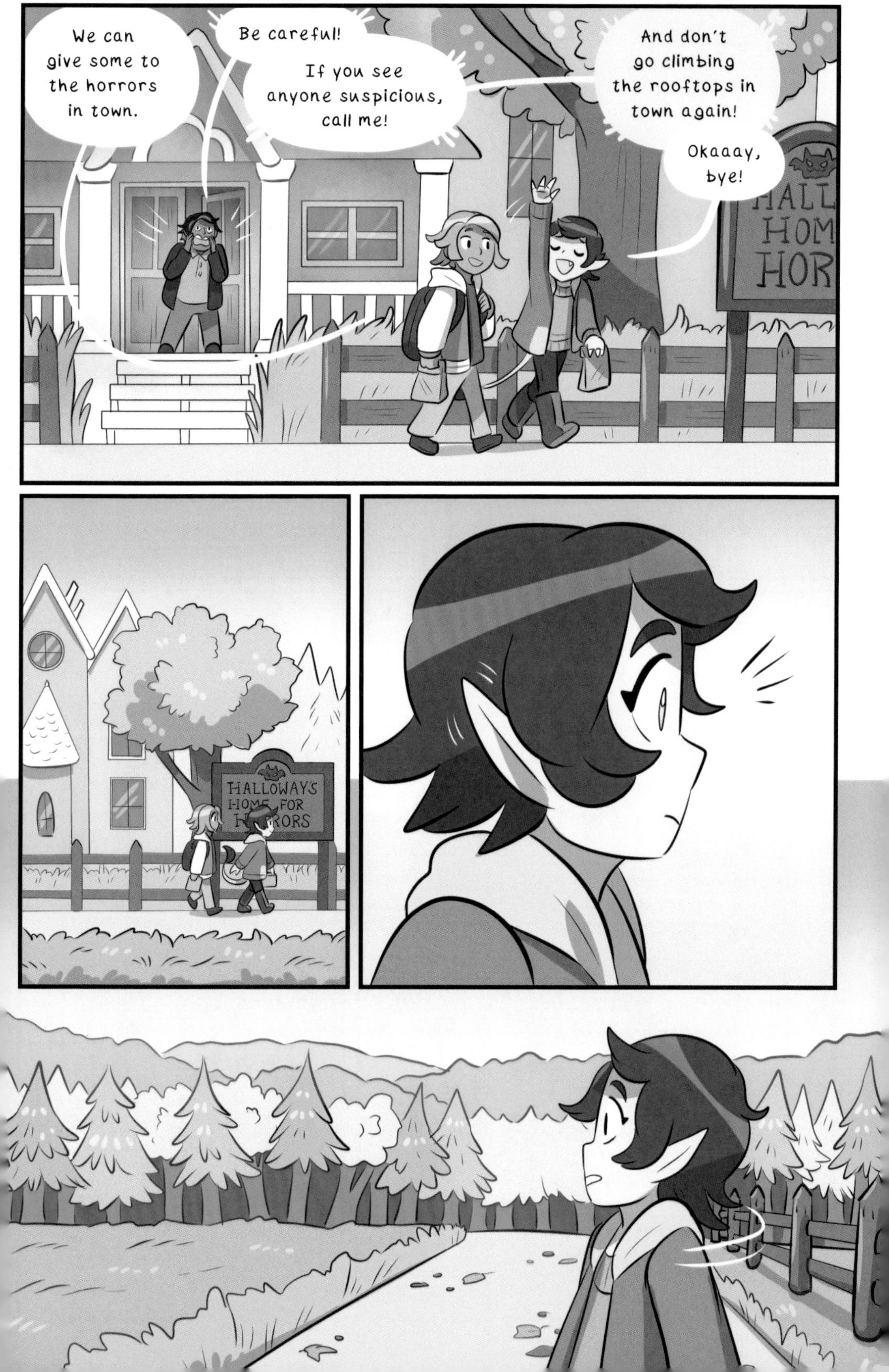
We can give some to the horrors in town.
Be careful!
If you see anyone suspicious, call me!
And don't go climbing the rooftops in town again!
Okaaay, bye!
HALLOWAY'S HOME FOR HORRORS

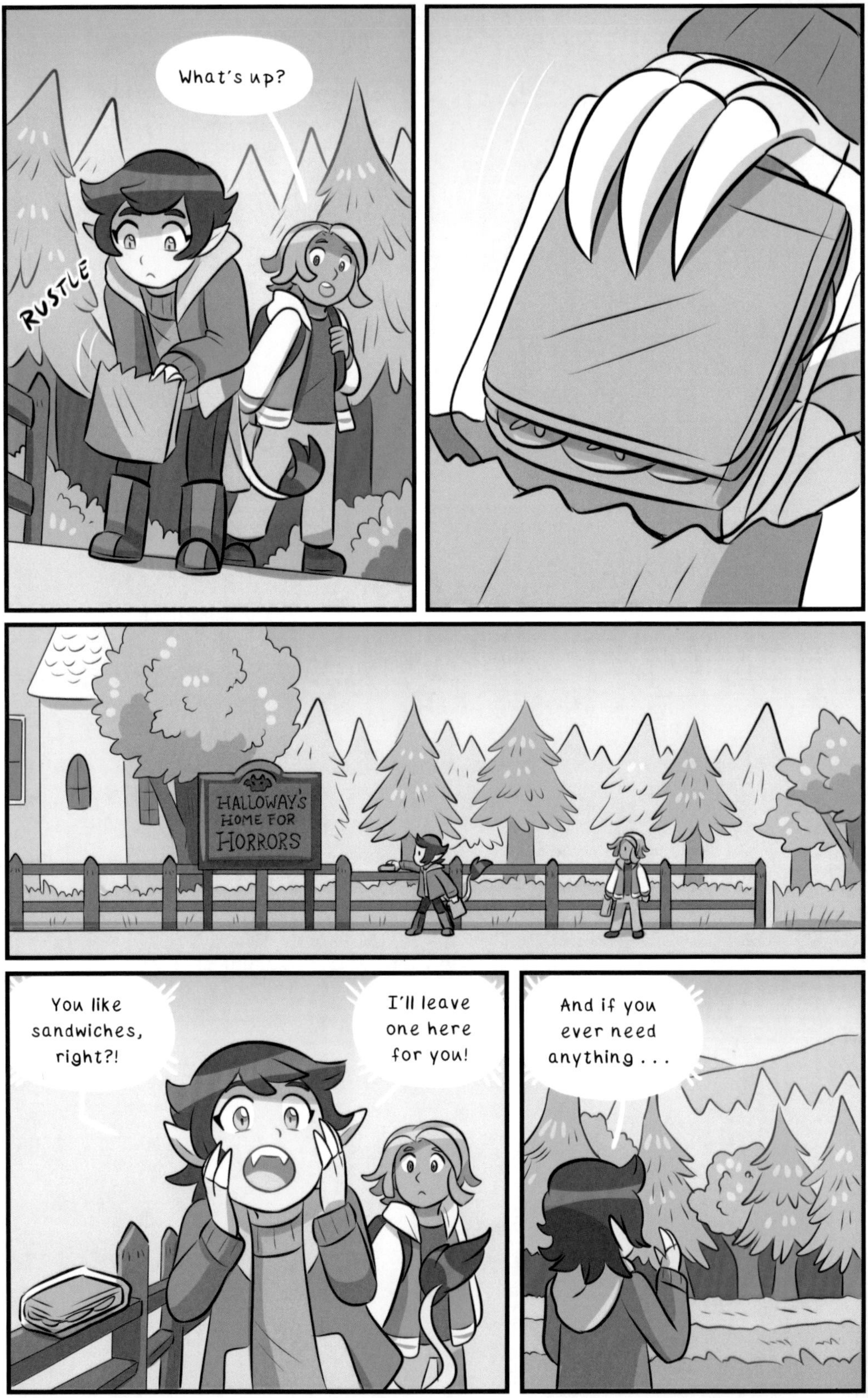
What's up?
RUSTLE
HALLOWAY'S HOME FOR HORRORS
You like sandwiches, right?!
I'll leave one here for you!
And if you ever need anything . . .

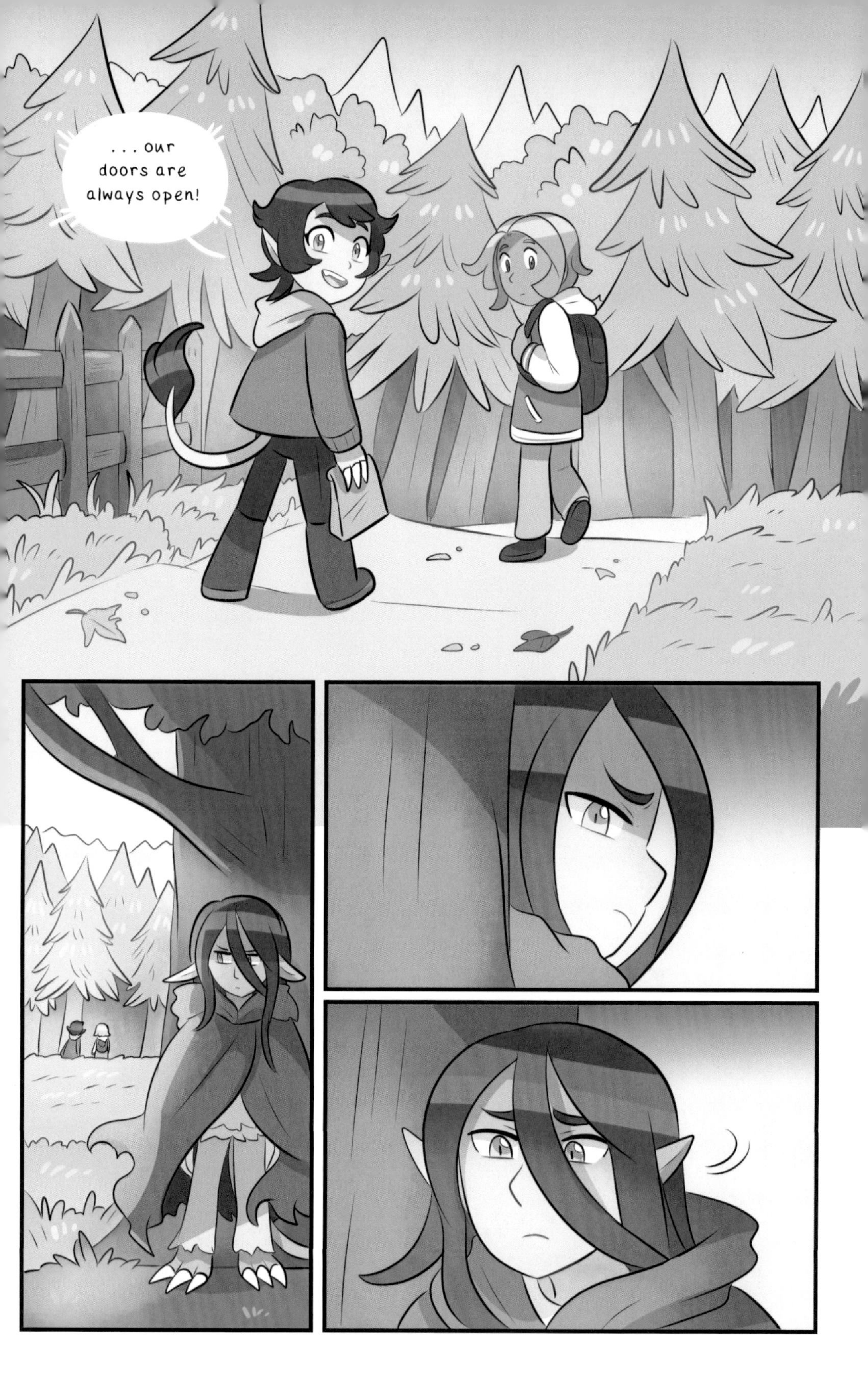
. . . our doors are always open!

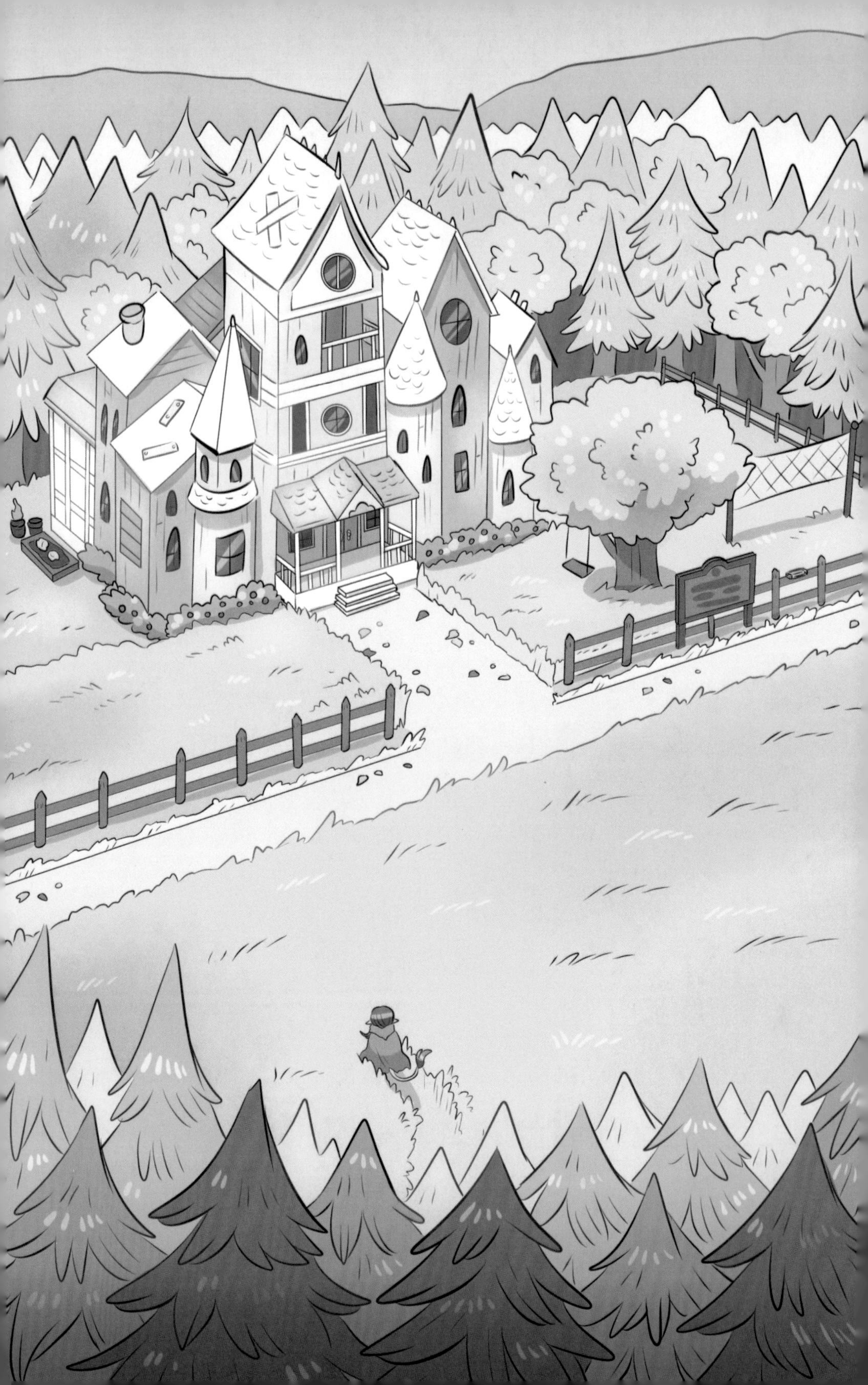

Author's Note

Growing up as an only child in a single-parent household, I often felt envious of my friends and their "complete" two-parent families. It felt as though I was always looking into their world from the outside, longing to be a part of it but never quite fitting in. What was it like to have what they had?

Although that was not my reality, I eventually found that family appears in many forms. The friends and mentors I've encountered in life are all family to me, one that is uniquely mine, and one I wouldn't trade for anything.

To anyone who has faced similar feelings of longing, this book is for you.

Special thanks to the wonderful Atheneum team for helping me bring this story to life, as well as my friends and family for always supporting me. You all mean the world!

—Kay

Concept Art: Illustrations

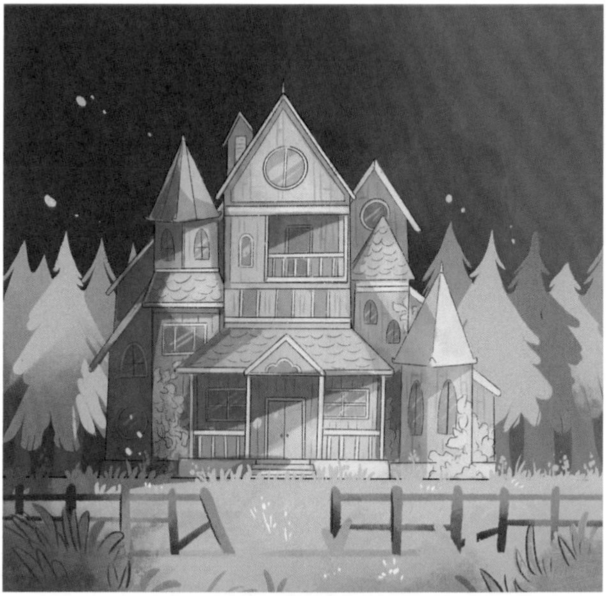

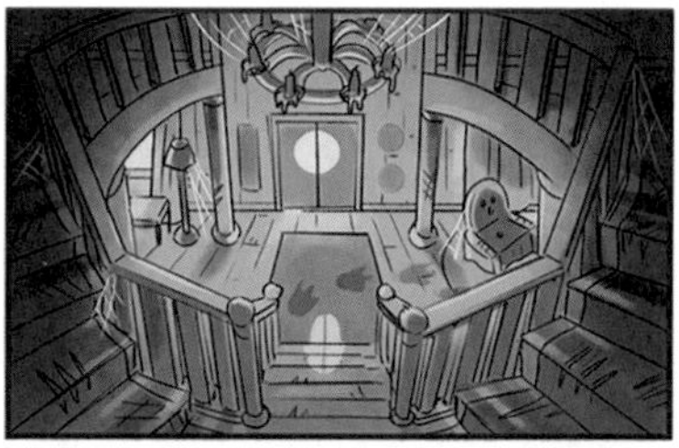

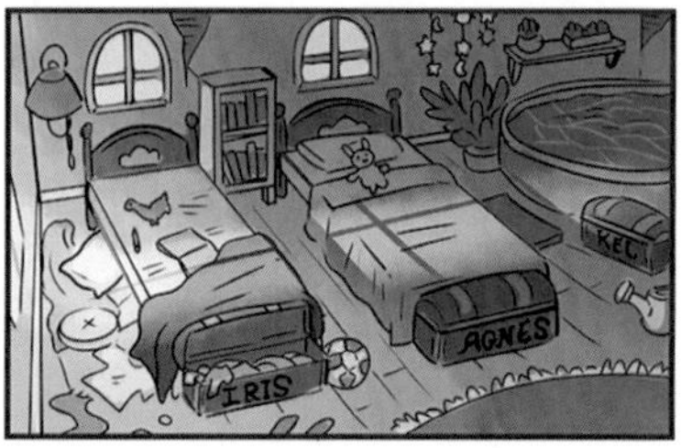
KEL
AGNES
IRIS

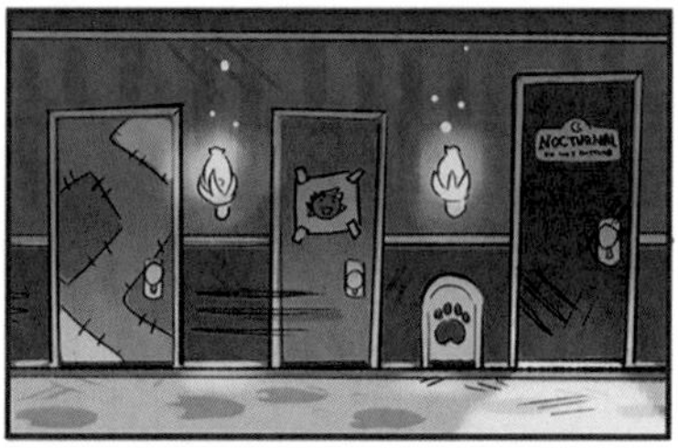

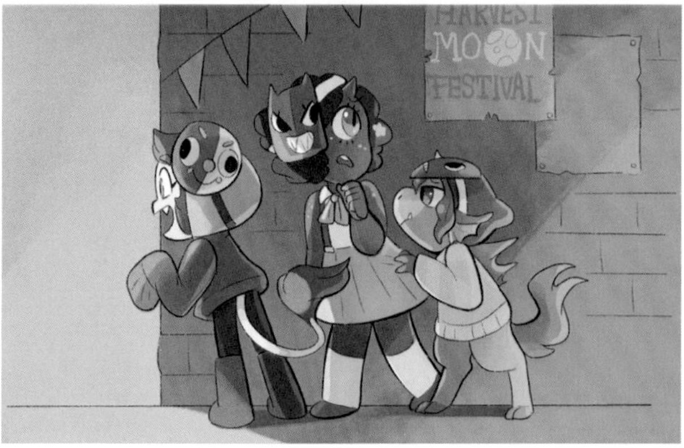
HARVEST
MOON
FESTIVAL

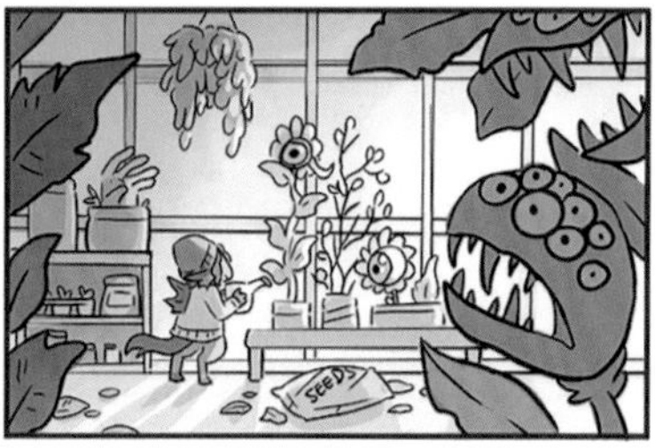
SEEDS

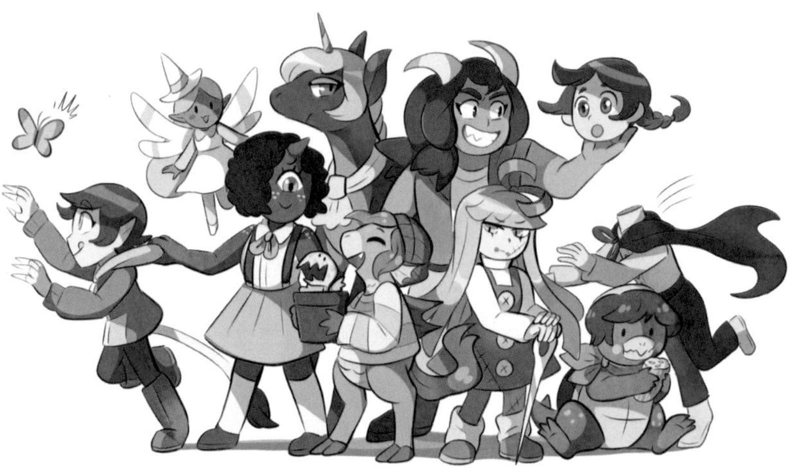

Concept Art: Main Characters

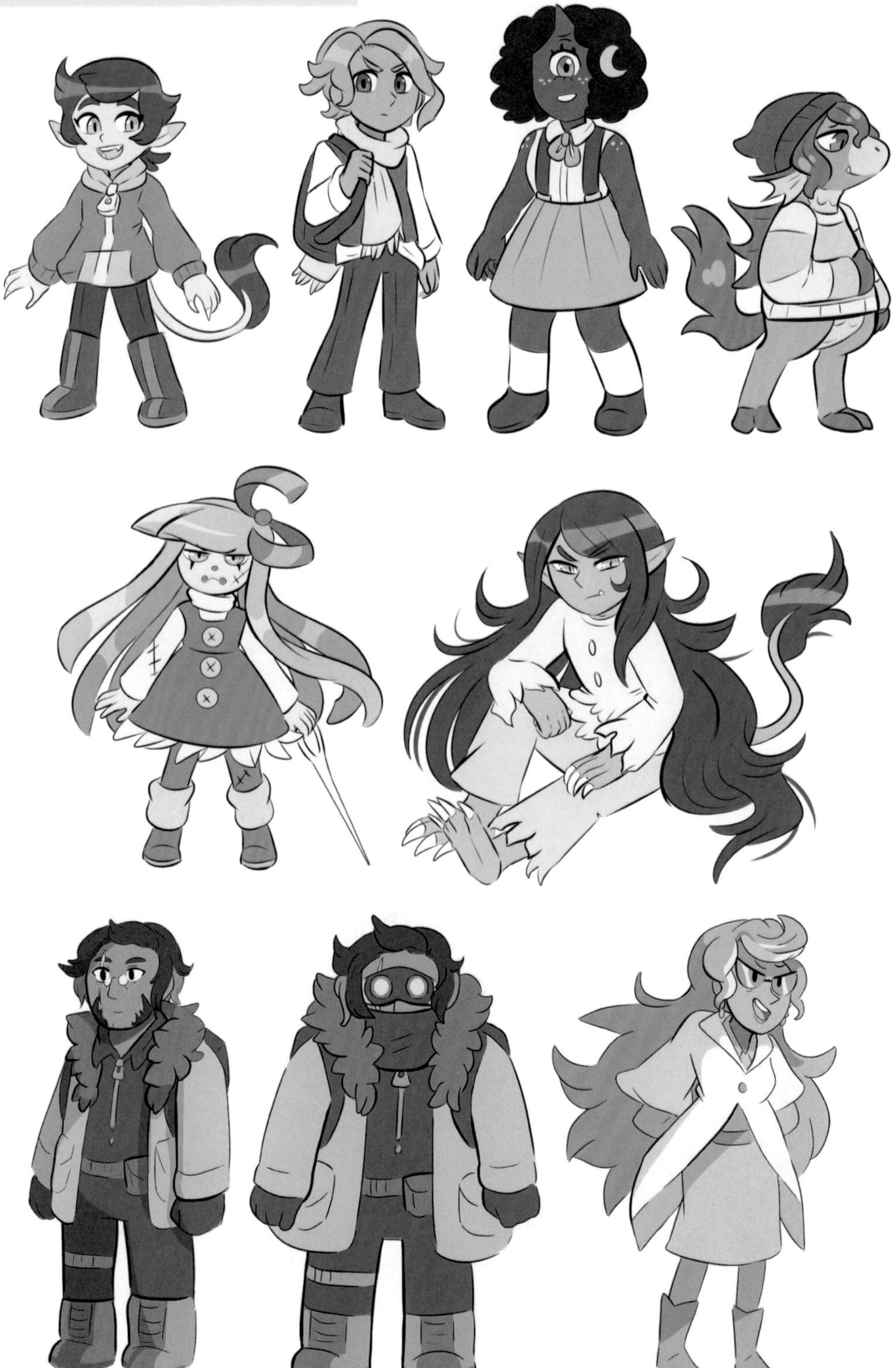

Concept Art: More Horrors

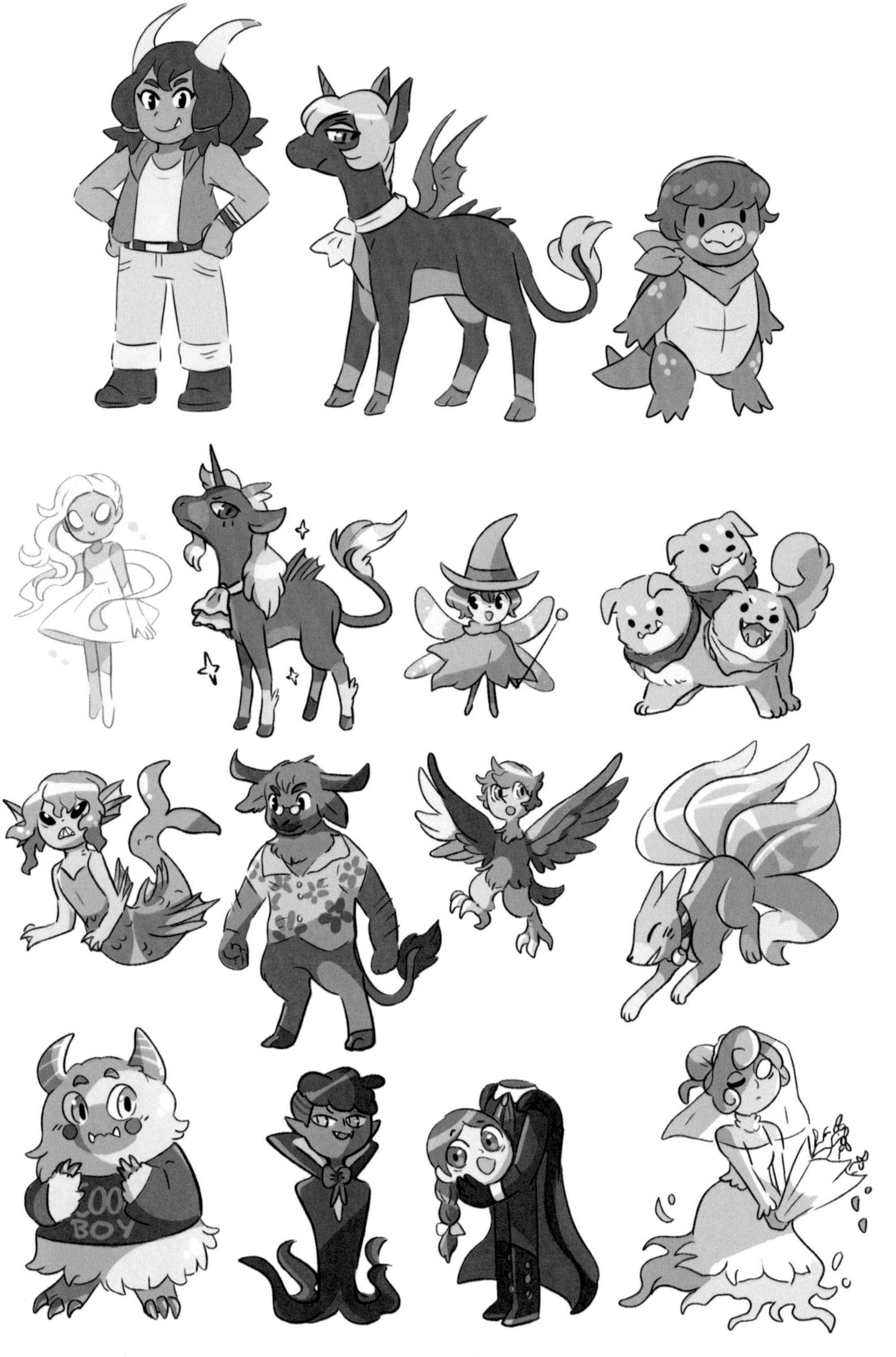
BOY

Concept Art: Cover Evolution

1

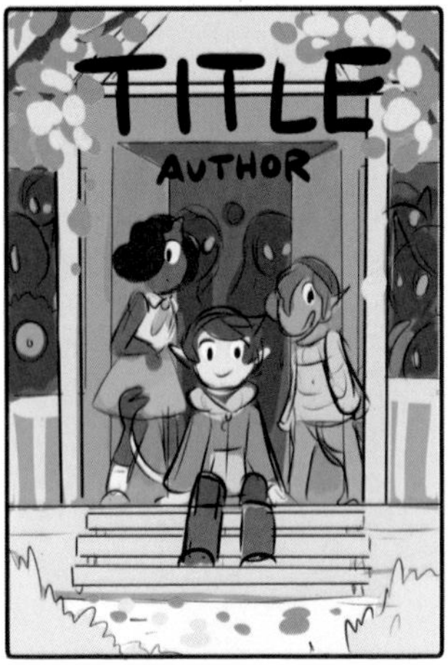
TITLE
AUTHOR

2

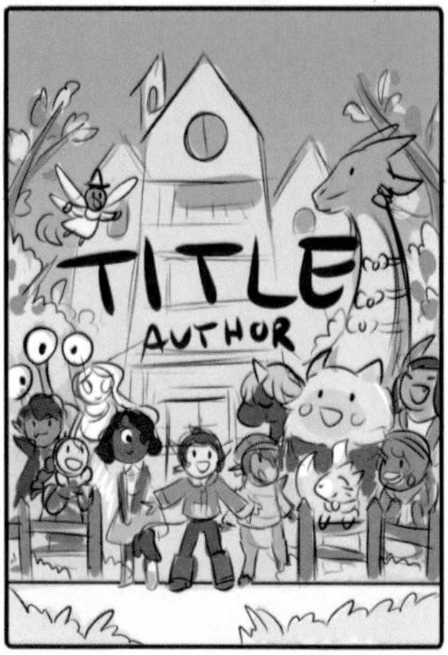
TITLE
AUTHOR

3

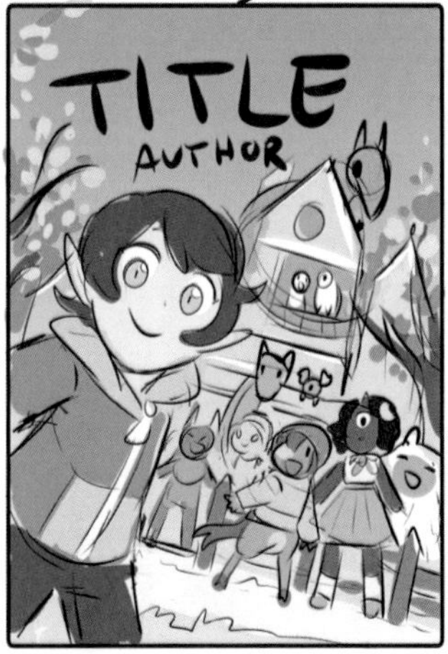
TITLE
AUTHOR

4

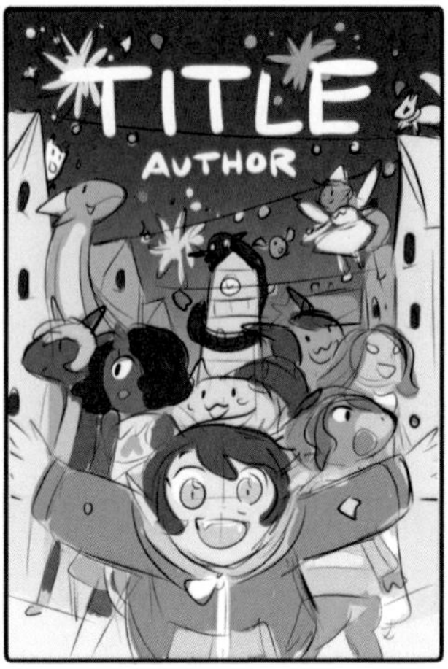
TITLE
AUTHOR

5

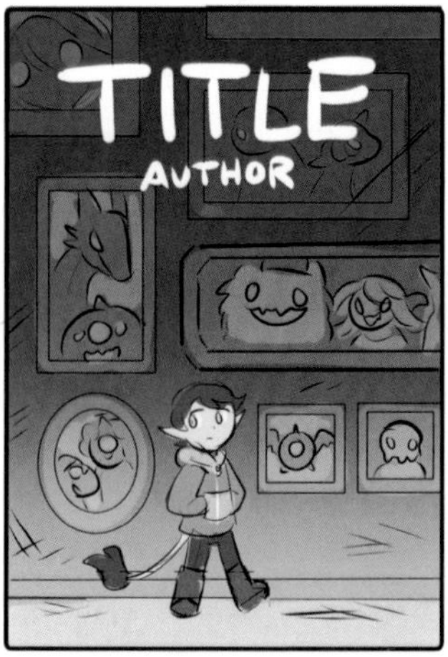
TITLE
AUTHOR

6

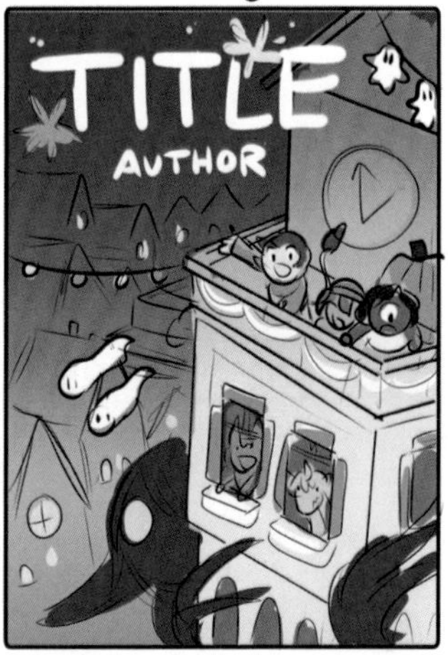
TITLE
AUTHOR

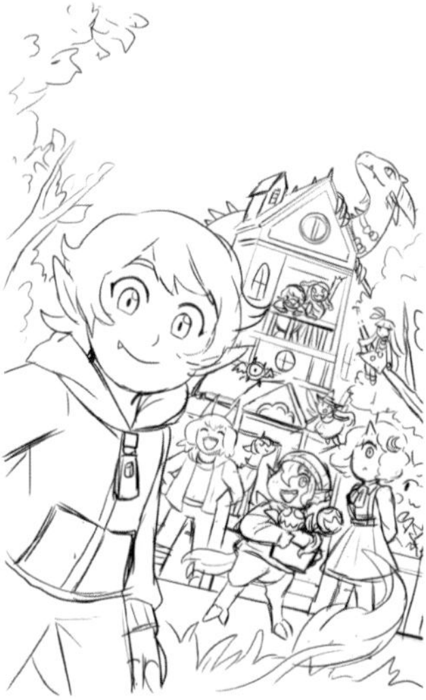

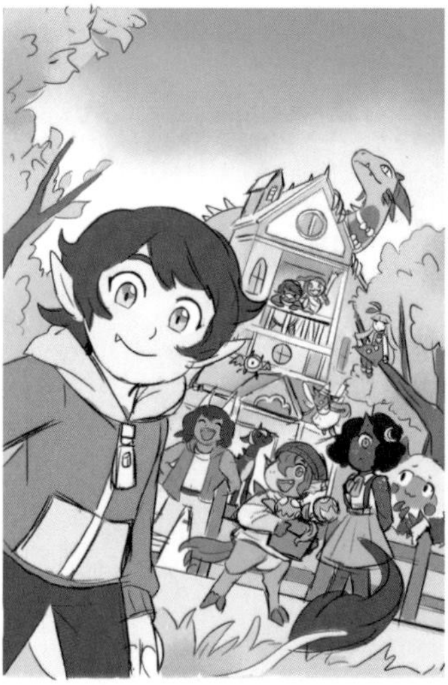

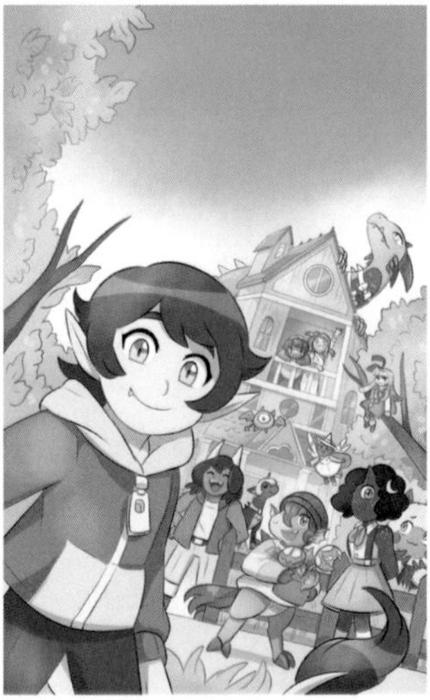